He who finds his life
will lose it,
and he who loses his life . . .

—MATTHEW 10:39

SEVEN OX SEVEN

A STORY OF SOME WAYS IN THE WEST

To: J.B.   8/8/09
Your dad was a great
help to me at Barnes + Noble.

SEVEN OX SEVEN

A STORY OF SOME WAYS IN THE WEST

Part One ESCONDIDO BOUND

all the best,

P. A. [signature]

P. A. RITZER

SEVEN OX PRESS
AURORA, COLORADO

SEVEN OX PRESS

Athanasius, LLC
P.O. Box 472467
Aurora, Colorado 80047-2467
sevenoxpress.com
Seven Ox Press is an imprint of Athanasius, LLC. Athanasius is a registered trademark.

For information about purchasing books in quantity
for promotion, fundraising, etc., please contact Seven Ox Press, above,
or call (toll free) 888-433-6094 or (fax) 720-207-9397.

This novel is a work of fiction. The characters, events,
and places depicted in it are fictional or are used fictionally.

Endpapers: (Front) Buffalo at Fort Robinson, Nebraska © 2006 by P. A. Ritzer
(Back) Longhorns at Fort Robinson, Nebraska © 2006 by P. A. Ritzer

Book Design by F + P Graphic Design, Inc.

PRINTED IN THE UNITED STATES OF AMERICA

1. Fiction / Historical 2. Fiction / Westerns

Library of Congress Control Number: 2005904702

ISBN-13: 978-1-933363-01-1
ISBN-10: 1-933363-01-0

Dedicated to

the

SH *of J and M*

and to

Hiep

CONTENTS

PREFACE

THIS STORY WAS BORN in the almost casual suggestion of my brother-in-law Brian Meyer, of Montana Blue and the Big Sky Cowboys, that we make a Western movie. I considered that a movie would require a soundtrack, and a soundtrack could require Montana Blue. Entertaining no illusions about the odds against a screenplay being made into a movie, I made up my mind that I would never have a chance at beating those odds, as some had done, without first writing one. Thus, I set to work. It was 1992.

Some time after I had finished the manuscript, I bought a book to help me format the work into a screenplay, and after an initial attempt, I decided that for all that it would take for me to do so, I might as well write the book. Here, before me, lay the challenge I had wished for and feared ever since I was a boy who used to pray, "Lord, let me write, and write well, and bring people to You through my writing." As a boy I had imagined writing a book, but never without a pang of anxiety that such a task was too overwhelming for me to start, let alone finish. Overwhelmed or not, I realized that I was still young and single enough to fail, but old enough that if I did not do it now, I might never do it. It was time to jump in, and I found a receptive ocean in research.

The Wisconsin State Historical Society Library provided unique access to that ocean of research, and I took advantage of it. In that first period of research and writing in Wisconsin, certain historical figures and places rose up out of my reading as central to my story: Henry Ossian Flipper, Charles Goodnight, Wyatt Earp, Bat Masterson, Palo Duro Canyon, Dodge City, San Antonio, El Paso. Though some of these people and places would later drift to the edges of my story, I realized, in early 1995, that to these places I must go.

By August I had my papers, books, and other belongings packed, cataloged, and stored; my modest savings pulled together (about twenty percent of it sacrificed for the purchase of a Macintosh powerbook); my 1988 Dodge Aries (with over 100,000 miles on it) packed with what I thought I would need. After a brief stop at my sister's in St. Paul, Minnesota, where I brought in every item from my car, weighed it on her bathroom scale, itemized all of it, and cut out a substantial portion, I headed west.

Into and across the Great Plains I ventured in that August of 1995, trying to make some sense of what I was doing, allergies itching and watering my nose and eyes, as the heat and glare of a torrid summer pressed themselves upon and into the Aries, while attempts at air-conditioning were met with the screams of a chafing belt running over an immovable pulley. Nighttime brought some relief in a three-person dome tent at places like: Lake Shetek State Park, Minnesota; Bruce Park, Creighton, Nebraska; Branched Oak Lake State Recreation Area, Nebraska; Perry State Park, Kansas; Covered Wagon RV Camping, Abilene, Kansas; Afton Lake Park, Wichita, Kansas; Gunsmoke Campground, Dodge City, Kansas.

Places and events punctuated the trek and informed my mind: Murray County Fair in Slayton, Minnesota; the Exel Inn in Sioux Falls, South Dakota, which I had helped construct sixteen years before, earning money for my freshman year of college; Ashfall Fossil Beds State Historical Park, Nebraska; a providential incident outside Lincoln, Nebraska, in which I pulled off the road to look at my map and watched as a hay bale fell off an approaching truck at the spot where my car would have been had I not pulled off; Homestead National Monument, Beatrice, Nebraska; Pony Express Historical Marker; Blue Rapids, Kansas, the site of a baseball game between the Chicago White Sox and New York Giants in 1913, in which Jim Thorpe played; Marysville, Kansas, with the Original Pony Express Home Station, No. 1; St. Mary's, Kansas, the site of the Jesuit Mission to the Potawatomi Indians, St. Mary's Academy and College and Seminary, and the first cathedral between the Missouri River and the Rocky Mountains; a great insect hatch at Perry State Park, Kansas, that encouraged me to put up my tent in record time and dive inside to escape the plague, but not before discovering, with the ranger, a truly

impressive specimen of the mighty dobsonfly; the Treasure of the Czars
exhibit in Topeka, Kansas, which impressed me with, among other
things, its depiction of the nature of the relationship between church
and state in Russia before Peter the Great; the Kansas State Historical
Society; the Wild Bill Hickok Rodeo in Abilene, Kansas, the first professional rodeo I had ever seen, set in an idyllic evening cooled to sev-
enty-some degrees by a wafting breeze, which fanned the stands where
I sat thoroughly at home among families of middle America, taking
my cue on what made for a good or bad performance from the quiet-
mannered grandfather in the cowboy hat sitting in front of me; the
Cowtown Museum, Wichita, Kansas; Dodge City, Kansas with Old
Dodge City and the Kansas Heritage Center; a praying mantis stalk-
ing and striking a cicada in my campground outside of Dodge; Fort
Larned National Historical Site, Larned, Kansas; the awe-inspiring
German and German-Russian Catholic churches, long served by
Capuchin-Franciscan Friars, in Liebenthal, Pfeifer, and Victoria,
Kansas, where St. Fidelis was dubbed the Cathedral of the Plains by
William Jennings Bryan. It was within this sanctuary that, after lighting candles and praying, while making my way to the exit, I stepped
into a beam of sunlight that had filtered through the stained glass and
immediately felt light and warmth flush through me in an affirmation
that sustained me through inevitable questioning about this project
over the next several months and years.

After a rejuvenating stay with good friends in Denver, where I
attended Mass in the fourth cathedral since leaving Minnesota, I set
out for Texas for the first time in my life.

Texas. The great state of Texas, so much so, one senses, that only
by superior constraint does it condescend from its earlier nationhood
to fit that classification, and then, never without the adjective. It is that
big. I've seen it. I've seen the land, traveling from one place to another
to research and write my story, and in my work as a field tech, driving
one thousand miles every Monday and Tuesday to trap and count boll
weevils for the benefit of the native production of cotton. I've seen its
treeless prairies, its rugged escarpments, draws, and canyons. I've seen
its red dirt and felt the sting of it in my eyes and seen it climb skyward
to color dust devils in their dance across the parched land and through
the arid heat. I've seen its skies, because one sky's not big enough for

Texas: blue blue skies; then with some white of clouds, massing to blue and gray; then purple, pink, yellow, black, red, orange, all at once; then suddenly a sunburst through all that mess of cloud color, and more color, organized this time, in a full rainbow off to the side. I've seen its prehistory, learned of its rocks, seabeds, animals, people. I've seen its history, old enough to be nearly as big as any other on the continent. I've seen its people; I've met them: cowboys, farmers, ranchers, townsfolk. I've met their spirit.

I speak of west Texas, now. It's the Texas the world knows, has read and written about, and watched on the big and little screens. I've seen parts of the rest of it, too, but west Texas is big enough; leave it to Texas to have even more.

I went into Texas a stranger to it, and left, a friend. I lived four big, full years there, even, at times, when its vastness, solitude, and quiet emptied me out, empty enough to need filling by its Creator, my Creator, who seeks to super-fill us all. He gave me good friends there; a wife, a marriage, a family there; and He allowed and, I hope, inspired me to write this story there, a big story, as anything less out of Texas just wouldn't seem right.

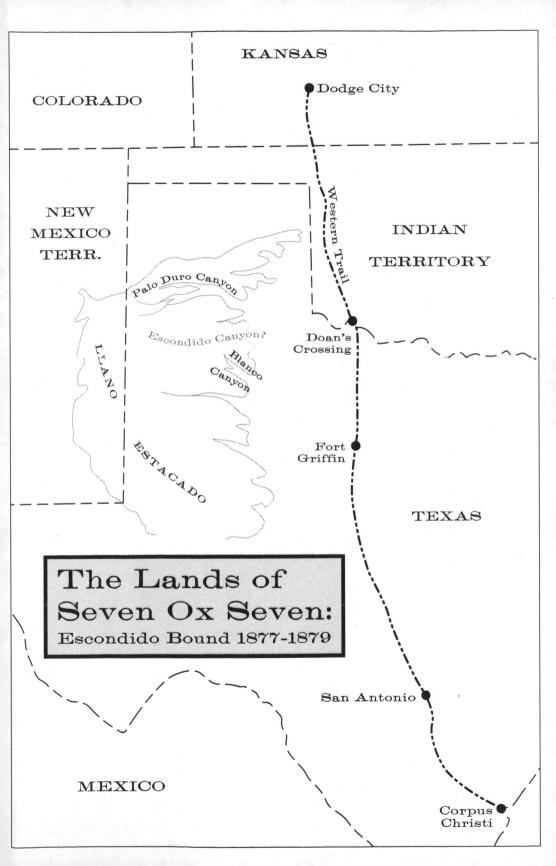

KANSAS

COLORADO

Dodge City

NEW
MEXICO
TERR.

INDIAN

TERRITORY

Palo Duro Canyon

Western Trail

Escondido Canyon?

Blanco
Canyon

LLANO

Doan's
Crossing

ESTACADO

Fort
Griffin

TEXAS

The Lands of
Seven Ox Seven:
Escondido Bound 1877-1879

San Antonio

MEXICO

Corpus
Christi

Chapter One

MEETINGS IN DODGE CITY

From the end spring new beginnings.
—PLINY THE ELDER

A WIDE OPEN GATE WAS DODGE CITY, KANSAS. Through that gate passed the beeves of the prairie. The original beeves, the formidable American bison called *buffalo*, passed through in pieces, having been killed, skinned, and sometimes butchered, according to the demand of the time, based on the needs, tastes, and fancies of people far from the prairie. The Atchison, Topeka and Santa Fe Railroad, newly arrived at the end of summer 1872, greatly facilitated the supply for that demand and, thus also, its prerequisite, profligate slaughter. In a few short years, the annual shipment of the pieces of hundreds of thousands of buffalo dwindled to the pieces of tens of thousands of buffalo, mostly bones, and thereafter was negligible, and then no more.

But close not that wide gate. The beeves of the prairie take a new form, less formidable, though formidable enough. These are the beeves of the long horn, originally introduced to the Americas by the Spanish, centuries before, grown innumerable on the Texas plains during the absence of men called away to a momentous civil conflict to determine the integrity of a nation, a people. The settlement of the great conflict freed the men to return to the plains, where they gathered the long-horns and sent them north, then east, nourishment for a country only beginning its long convalescence after a long fever, which had finally spiked and only recently broken.

Thus, the longhorns went east, and civilization came west, though by the term *civilization* is not meant so much a state achieved, as a process continuing. One dictionary lists these definitions for the word *civilize*: "to bring out of a savage state; to introduce order and civic organization among; to refine and enlighten; to elevate in social life." A strong case can be made for a civilizing process in Dodge of this period, along the order of the first two definitions, though the methods used in the process may argue against the latter two definitions in the eyes of some purists.

On the western edge of this peculiar civilizing wave rode the title "cowtown," or "cattletown," according to preference. This title and its corresponding reputation rode west through Kansas with the railroad. It rode just ahead of developed agricultural settlements and their quarantine lines against Texas fever or splenic fever, a deadly bovine disease caused by a tick carried by Texas cattle, to which they were immune but more domesticated livestock were not. The tick's complicity being then unknown, all blame fell at the feet of the cattle. Hence, the quarantine line was established to keep Texas cattle away from the domesticated livestock. Consequently, as agricultural settlement moved westward, so did the quarantine line. As the quarantine line moved westward, so did the cowtowns. The cowtowns (Abilene, Ellsworth, Wichita, Caldwell, Dodge, and others) all served as gates to the cattle tramping in and rolling out. And just as at one point each was opened, so at one point each was closed. The gate opened longest was Dodge.

With the cattle came the men—cattlemen, buyers, drovers, and cowboys (herders, cowhands, cowpokes, cowpunchers, trailhands)—to whom Dodge proved a wide gate indeed. To the cowboys, in particular, Dodge offered its own broad way, which contrasted sharply to the strait way that had brought them there. From the deprivation of the trail—deprivation of food, drink, shelter, sleep, comfort, cleanliness, and feminine companionship—Dodge offered abundant relief in fine foods, strong drinks, clean rooms with clean beds, baths and shaves, available women, and convenient gambling.

By July 1877, Dodge had already witnessed a great influx of cattle and men. This influx brought its share of challenges, not the least of which was law enforcement. In one incident, the famous William Barclay (Bartholomew) "Bat" Masterson had been jailed for "affectionately" interfering in the arrest of one Robert Gilmore. Masterson, a former policeman himself, fought Marshal Larry Deger, Policeman Joe Mason, and "half a dozen Texas men," as the Dodge City *Times* of June 9, 1877, described the incident, until the marshal could "draw his gun and beat Bat over the head until the blood flew," after which Masterson was finally wrestled to the calaboose. Later that year, Masterson would defeat Deger in the election for the sheriff of Ford County and make a name for himself by tracking and capturing train robbers, among other things. Lately returned to Dodge was another celebrated lawman, who had served as a powerful assistant marshal the previous season, Wyatt Earp, a man who Masterson would later claim was "destitute of fear," with "unshakable courage." Of Earp's return, the Dodge City *Times*, July 7, 1877, reported:

> Wyatt Earp, who was on our city police force last summer, is in town again. We hope he will accept a position on the force once more. He had a quiet way of taking the most desperate characters into custody which invariably gave one the impression that the city was able to enforce her mandates and preserve her dignity. It wasn't considered policy to draw a gun on Wyatt unless you got the drop and meant to burn powder without any preliminary talk.

The need for such lawmen was but a single feature of the complex character of Dodge City, Kansas, in July 1877. The aptly named Front Street was the face of Dodge City, and both sides of that face need be considered to render an accurate account of the character of Dodge. The street lay sixty to ninety yards wide and was referred to as "the Plaza." Down the middle of the Plaza ran the tracks of the Atchison, Topeka and Santa Fe. It is somehow fitting that, of the two, the northern side of the face received the greater share of sunlight, because, though the northern side may not have been the last bastion of purity, the deeds wrought on the southern side were more often of the kind to avoid exposure to the light of day.

The "Deadline" separated north and south at the railroad tracks. Law enforcement turned a blind eye to the happenings on the south side of town, save for serious gunplay or murder. North of the Deadline, on the other hand, the law, including the forbiddance of weapons, was enforced, if not always perfectly or to the satisfaction of the town's residents.

Into this Dodge of early July 1877 rode one more cowboy. He rode a large bay, which, despite its slow gait, held its head up and stepped high, its muscles taut, betraying an affinity for less restrictive service. The man held a more relaxed posture than did his mount, though not without a hint of the same strength and readiness. He was tall and lean, though well proportioned. He had a well-cut face with blue eyes under dark brows. He wore a dark beard of a few weeks' growth, and light brown hair stuck out from under his weathered, broad-brimmed hat. The intense overhead light of the early afternoon sun bleached out much of the color that remained in his faded clothing: the hat; a light-colored, collarless shirt; a red bandanna; and pants and boots that had originally been very dark in color. Still, the sun could not bleach out the dirty, dust-covered, and sweat-stained character of these articles.

The cowboy rode north on Bridge Street under this bleaching light, which did not seem to shine down from above so much as to saturate the very air in its intensity, along with its companion heat, which rendered one's clothing hot to the touch and gave one the feeling that any object, including oneself, could readily burst into flames at the slightest provocation. North from the Arkansas River he rode, within this atmosphere of light and heat, and of fine yellow dust, in which thicker clouds of dust twisted around him, stirred by wagons, horses, cattle, and the incessant prairie wind. Incessant, though not invariable in its intensity, the wind rose and fell, drawing forth sound from the very air itself and from objects in its path, like the board-and-batten outbuilding past which the cowboy now rode, which creaked and shuddered against the press of a capricious gust. These inconstant sounds punctuated the backdrop of the sounds of the city. Within the matrix of the whir and chirp of cicadas could be heard the low and bawl of cattle, and the rumble of their driven herds; the snorts and calls of horses, mules, and oxen, and the clopping of their hooves on the dusty ways; add to it all the clatter of buggies and wagons, and the various sounds of industry.

These sounds of industry pointed to the chief sound maker, in fact, the producer, arranger, and conductor of much of the sound now heard, contributing both by call and movement: man, both male and female, man in buggies and wagons, on horses and on foot. These the cowboy passed as he rode north toward Front Street, though he did not pass them in great numbers, because the south side of town was just beginning to come to life again after the revelry of the previous evening, night, and early morning (which had got rather late).

Arriving finally at the Plaza, the cowboy rode out into it. He stopped before reaching the railroad tracks and pulled off to his right. He leaned forward, resting his forearms on the horn of his saddle, and looked across the Plaza. Despite his relaxed posture and a casual slightly amused expression on his face, the cowboy's eyes betrayed a certain intensity as they drank in all that fell within their purview.

Wagons, buggies, horses, and mules were parked, in some places two or three deep, along the north side of Front Street, across the Plaza. Charles Rath and Co. (general merchandise), directly across from where the cowboy had stopped, and Hadder and Draper Mercantile Company appeared to be doing good volumes of business, though the various other stores, shops, saloons, restaurants, and hotels also saw their share of the denizens, long-term and temporary, of Dodge. These included the ubiquitous Texas cowhand as well as cowmen, drovers, buyers and sellers, bullwhackers and muleskinners, and citizenry of every description. So it was that men, women, and children came and went from the various establishments as others rested in chairs and on benches placed along the wooden sidewalks in the shade of wooden awnings.

After an unhurried general survey of Front Street, the cowboy turned his attention to a more specific survey of its saloons, his parched throat and lips demanding no less. He ran his eyes by the Alamo, the Long Branch, Hoover's, the Lone Star, the Saratoga, the Alhambra, Beatty and Kelly's, the Old House, the Occident, the Dodge House. These were all reputable saloons. Still, most offered gambling, and the better ones—like the Alamo, Long Branch, Beatty and Kelly's, Old House, Occident, and the Dodge House—offered billiard tables. The Saratoga, Hoover's, and the Occident had reputations for being strictly run. The Saratoga was known for its music, Hoover's for its disallowance of gambling, the Occident for its fine wines and spirits, and both of the latter two for their premium cigars.

These qualities appealed to the cowboy, who could imagine being bathed, shaved, and changed into a new outfit of clothes, and enjoying the goods, services, and atmospheres of any of the establishments mentioned. But the cowboy was not bathed, shaved, or changed, and yet he was thirsty. His was that deep thirst that had been born and nourished during months on the trail; a thirst that had been repressed throughout those sixteen to twenty-four-hour days of constant work, deprivation, and hardship; a thirst that now required a commensurate quenching, as he had completed his service to his trail outfit, which had just turned over its herd, and he was ready for an immediate start to the quenching—an immediate start that required no more in volume or duration than it did in refinement. But something else would be required, for there was a restlessness that had been born and nourished with the thirst, a restlessness born of loneliness, a loneliness for feminine companionship. And in light of that restlessness, he turned in his saddle to look back over his right shoulder to where his eyes fell upon the Lady Gay.

The Lady Gay was a dancehall that had been opened in April of that year by Dodge residents Ben Springer and Jim Masterson, brother to Bat. It was a long, narrow false-front building, like many of the saloons of Dodge. The cowboy looked it over, looked back at the establishments to the north across the Plaza, looked down for a moment, and then turned his horse and headed for the Lady Gay.

Arriving at the Lady Gay, the cowboy dismounted and wrapped the reins of his horse around the rail out front, where two other horses were tied. He stepped onto the sidewalk and entered the dancehall through its wide open doors.

As his eyes adjusted to removal from the bright sunlight, he took in the dancehall. A hall indeed, the room ran sixty feet deep, or better, and about twenty-five feet wide. Just inside the room to his right stood an ample bar, masterfully grained by the artist's brush. An immense mirror covered the wall behind the bar, adding width to the room. Windows, three on the left and one on the right, beyond the bar, and an open door, beyond that window, let light into the room, as well as dust, which drifted endlessly and visibly through the beams of light and into obscurity in shadow. The walls were brightly papered down to a chair rail about four feet from the floor, below which car siding covered the walls. Stained and polished wainscot covered the ceiling. The plank floors bore the stains and scars of drink, tobacco, lighted smokes, spurs, knives, and even a gunshot or two. Tables and chairs were distributed throughout the room, except in the last fifteen feet or so, which was reserved for dancing alone. Across the back of the room, a platform, decorated in bunting, rose up about two feet above the dance floor. Here the orchestra played or the occasional entertainer performed. But there was no orchestra to be heard yet, at this early hour of the afternoon. The establishment had just opened its doors again, after having closed them some time after four o'clock that morning. Mr. Charley Lawson's orchestra would not be arriving for at least a couple of hours. Business, at this time, was slow.

Though the room was not crowded, men sat at some of the tables playing games of chance: monte, faro, keno, hazard, poker, and others. Four or five women, scattered about the room, listened to lonely cow-hands and other men, and encouraged them to lift their spirits by drinking and gambling, as long as their money lasted. The sounds of active cards and chips mingled with gambling talk and calls and conversation.

The cowboy stepped up to the bar and spoke to the balding, bespectacled barkeeper. "I'd trouble you for a mug of your beer."

"Comin' right up," the barkeeper responded, as he turned and drew a draught from a tap. That done, he turned back to the cowboy and slid a heady mug of beer across the bar. The cowboy sipped off the top of the remarkably cold beer (due to ice shipped in from the Colorado mountains) as he slipped the barkeeper two bits. The barkeeper made change, and as he pushed the coins across the top of the bar, he asked the cowboy, "Where you up from?"

"Corpus Christi," the cowboy replied while pocketing his change.

"You don't sound like a Texan," noted the barkeeper, who did sound like one. This was no surprise because every Dodge City establishment went out of its way to hire Texans, and to do anything else to make the Texas cowboys feel at home. The cowboy knew what kind of accent the barkeeper expected. In that accent, *I* would sound like "Ah," *well* like "wayell," *dog* like "dowg," *there* almost like "thar," and *snake* almost like "snike." It was an accent the cowboy appreciated and still enjoyed, even after a few years in Texas, but one that had only slightly colored his own speech over time, as he would not affect it. Still, with the great influx of immigrants from various countries into Texas through Galveston, as well as immigrants from other states, it was not so easy to claim a single accent as Texan. Nevertheless, the cowboy knew what the barkeeper meant. He meant that the cowboy sounded like a Yankee, though he could not place him.

"Well, sir, I've been one lately," replied the cowboy.

"Been around a bit, have you?"

"That I have, and today I feel it."

"Well, enjoy that beer," the barkeeper said with apparent sincerity.

"That I will. Thank you kindly."

The cowboy stepped back from the bar and took another sip off the top of his beer, surveying the hall as he did so. He spied a seat by the window, at the far end of the bar, and moved smoothly toward the chair and into it.

This seat placed the cowboy's back to the wall, which suited him, between the end of the bar (on his left) and the window (on his right). He tipped the back of his chair against the wall and drank from his beer, as one who knew how to savor the finer things of life, like a cold Milwaukee beer on a hot Dodge City afternoon. As he drank, his gaze fell upon two members of the small, but slowly growing, early-afternoon patronage of the hall. They sat in his line of vision at a square table about six feet in front of him, a little off to his right. These were two seasoned cowhands, who had already drunk their share of whiskey and beer.

The two cowhands sat across from each other—one with his back to the bar, the other with his back to the dance floor—giving the cowboy a clear view of them from the side. The man with his back to the bar was a grizzled, stoop-shouldered, middle-aged man with a broad frame. The man with his back to the dance floor was a lean, extended specimen of about the same age, grizzled as well, angular, with long, pointed features, accentuated by the way he leaned over the table in a manner that made the cowboy think of a buzzard.

From these two, the cowboy shifted his gaze to his left, to the end of the bar. Though no one stood next to him, a young man was standing around the corner of the bar, at its end, facing the wall against which the cowboy was leaning. This gave the cowboy a clear view of the front of the fellow from about the chest up. The broad-shouldered, stocky young man, in his mid-twenties or so, leaned squarely onto the bar, resting his weight on both elbows. Securely under the influence of at least one manifestation of alcoholic spirits, the man was speaking sincerely and alternately to his drink and to a redheaded woman of about his same age, in a dark, high-collared, puffy-sleeved gingham dress, seated on a stool to his right. The man drank and talked, the woman listened—not an uncommon sight in such establishments.

When the cowboy next shifted his gaze to have it fall upon the woman, it settled gently there and rested, drinking in the pleasant warmth of the soft, rounded, slightly ruddy peaches-and-cream face, from which shone eyes of green. Delicate red, not quite auburn, curls here and there graced her forehead and elsewhere hung loose from the tresses pulled up on the back of her head. Full red lips framed straight white teeth, through which her words gaily flowed toward the man on her left, as her facial expressions betrayed a real affection for her companion, whom she could not have known very long.

When the cowboy was able to pull his eyes from this agreeable picture, they followed the direction of the woman's speech back to the face of the stocky young man on her left. This face, too, struck the cowboy as agreeable, in its own way, from what he could glimpse of it when the man's head was not drooping over his drink. Out of direct sunlight, as the man was, when he looked up toward the bright light from the window, his large light-blue eyes all but glowed out from under the broad forehead and dark brow of his tanned face. He wore a black beard, which was short and sparse, and black hair stuck out from under his hat. Judging by the condition of that hat, and of the shirt that covered his square, muscular torso, it appeared that he, too, was not long off the trail.

The cowboy could not help but overhear their conversation.

"Miss Molly," the man at the bar said to his drink, "it's just not right for men to talk to you the way they do. It's just not right."

"And why isn't it right, Luke?" Miss Molly asked respectfully, while allowing some of her amusement to peek through as she leaned closer to the man.

"Because you're a lady, and that's no way to treat a lady."

The cowboy against the wall smiled lightly at the innocent decency this comment and its delivery conveyed, as well as at its incongruity with the immediate surroundings. He could not help but think, as he smiled, that the accent in which the comment was delivered would meet with the barkeeper's approval.

The comment and delivery had their effect on Miss Molly. Laying her hand upon Luke's arm, she spoke out from under her long, full eyelashes. "And just how should a man treat a lady?"

Suddenly a mug banged down upon the square table in front of the cowboy, and his attention was immediately drawn to that table, though the sound went unnoticed by the couple at the bar. The noise had come from one of the two seasoned cowhands seated there, the stoop-shouldered one with his back to the bar. That man now sat slumped over his beer mug, the handle of which was firmly fixed in his grasp, the former contents of which now darkened the table around it. Brooding loud enough for the cowboy to hear, he slurred, "Whatta ya mean, she's touchin' 'im? I've had my fill of that Stuart. He saw me dancin' with her. She still touchin' 'im?"

As the cowboy watched and heard these words slog forward over the man's tongue and lips and out of his face, that face strongly impressed upon him its evidence of hard living, in lines, pocks, and the colors of brown, red, and gray.

The man's companion, as worn and weathered as the first, though not as drunk, responded, "She sure is, Jack. Yessir, she sure is." Judging by the negative effect this information had on Jack, the second man should not have enjoyed delivering it as much as he obviously did.

Jack responded, "I'm gonna set it right, Charlie. I'm gonna set it right." And he swung his head back and forth low over his mug, like a buffalo clearing snow to get at the browse beneath.

Upon hearing these words, and even before, Charlie's face took on the expression of a happy fox upon finding unwary prey. But he was not looking at the man across from him. He appeared to be looking over that man's shoulder, beyond him. The cowboy against the wall followed Charlie's line of vision to see it fall upon Luke and Molly at the end of the bar. As he looked back and forth between the couple at the bar and the two cowhands at the table, he heard Charlie say, "I'll get us a couple more, Jack."

The cowboy watched Charlie rise from his seat at the table and make his way shakily to the bar, beyond the couple. He looked back at Jack and noted the Colt .45 in the holster at his hip. Then his attention was drawn back to the bar.

"I can hardly wait to get back to my Elizabeth and the kids," Luke at the bar was saying. "I've been thinkin' about 'em every day and missin' 'em as you cannot imagine."

"Your Elizabeth must be a special woman," Molly said with a hint of wistfulness, as she withdrew her hand from his arm.

"Oh, that she is. There is no finer woman. The first thing I did when I got to town was to go yonder to Fringer's and check at the post office," he said, pointing out the door and across the Plaza at Fringer's drug store, "and there was this pack of letters from her just waitin' for me." Luke held up a packet of letters several inches high, bound together with string.

"And what did she have to say?"

At this question, Luke's eyebrows tensed, and he hung his head as his right hand that held the letters fell to the bar. He stared at the letters in his hand for a moment and then said, "Well, see, there's the trouble, Miss Molly. I can't read, so I don't know what she wrote." He turned his head and looked up at Molly, who drew back slightly, a little overtaken by the intense sincerity communicated by his wide-open eyes, as they caught the light from the door. Luke continued, "Elizabeth knows I can't, but she writes, regardless. Says she needs to talk to me whether I'm there or not, and if I can't find anybody to read 'em to me, then she'll read 'em to me when I get home."

Luke's face dropped clumsily away from Molly and turned its intense sincerity back to the letters in his hand. At these he stared. And Molly stared at him, at the drunken, homesick cowboy who could not read his letters from his beloved wife. She smiled lightly and started to reach out toward him with her left hand, but immediately checked herself and drew back her hand, contenting herself to stare at him out over her light smile. Finally, she said, with a voice made slightly timid by the possibility of rejection, "Would you like me to read your letters to you?"

Luke bobbed his head slightly, upon hearing her question, though he continued to stare at the letters in his hand. The cowboy in the chair against the wall had leaned forward, just a little bit, when Molly had voiced the question he had anticipated. No longer conscious of his unavoidable eavesdropping, he watched and listened for a reply.

"Hmh," Luke articulated, as he turned his head to look at Molly. "Can you read?" he asked, looking into her face.

"I certainly can," she replied, glad to see his face again.

Luke looked back down at his letters, the contents of which were only an affirmation away. After staring at them for a moment, he straightened up enough to look around at his surroundings, which did not appear to put him at ease. As Luke looked around, the cowboy in the chair against the wall became suddenly aware of his eavesdropping and quickly returned his attention to his beer.

His survey of the room complete, Luke leaned down over his letters again, staring at them.

"I need not read them if you would rather I didn't," Molly assured him, with a self-consciousness that had suddenly arisen with Luke's perusal of the room.

Luke thought for a moment, as his face still hung over the letters, and with a short nervous chuckle said, "Well, I don't know." He thought for a moment more and then hesitantly said, "I imagine it would be all right." Then with more conviction, he said, turning toward Molly as he did so, "I think Elizabeth would approve of a kind woman like yourself readin' her letters."

Obviously moved by his kindness and his good opinion of her, Molly said, "I would consider it an honor."

The cowboy against the wall, whose attention had not long been diverted to his beer, then watched as Luke fumbled with the packet in front of him. Finally, Molly assisted him and untied the packet.

"Mr. Fringer said they stacked 'em in the order they received 'em, so it makes sense to start with the bottom one," Luke reasoned aloud.

Molly pulled the bottom letter from the packet, opened it, and, after a moment, began to read:

April 12, 1877

My dearest Luke,

You have only just left this very day, and already my heart yearns for you. I dread to think that tonight, and for nights on end, I will not hear your tread on the porch and see your kind, handsome face when that door opens. I do believe that this child of ours, who plays within my body, shares this same sentiment, because, though I have not mentioned it, as it would seem a mother's fancy, on more than one occasion, he did seem to stir upon your approach, much as did that blessed child, John, in the womb of another Elizabeth, at the approach of the mother of our Lord, those many centuries past.

It may well be that the sacred bond that unites a mother to her unborn child fosters communication beyond the normal kind we know of in spoken word. If this be true, then there would be no question or wonder at the notion that this child would stir in joy at the approach of one who brings such joy of love to his mother.

Oh, and I do believe he is a he, as only she who carries him could know . . .

Molly paused, every hint of her earlier amusement now gone and replaced by a palpable wistfulness. Staring at the letter, she said, "This is a beautiful letter."

The cowboy at the wall silently agreed.

"That's my Elizabeth," Luke said, sobering a bit and looking down at his work-worn hands. "Don't know what she ever saw in me, though; she's so pretty and smart and educated, and I can't even read. All the fellows were after her hand."

"But you won it," Molly said, her eyes still on the letter, though her mind seemed to be focused somewhere else.

"Ma'am?" Luke said, turning to look at her.

Molly looked up from the letter to Luke and appeared to bring her mind back from the places to which it had wandered. "You won her hand, Luke," she said. "Elizabeth knows what she sees in you, and it runs through this letter." She paused, then added, "Maybe you should listen a little better."

Luke looked at her with a quizzical expression.

"Well, she's an honest woman, isn't she?"

"As honest as they come."

"Then believe what she says and writes about you," Molly insisted, leaning closer to Luke and laying a hand on his arm. "Your Elizabeth is obviously a fine woman, Luke, but it is obvious to me, and not only from this letter, that you are a very fine man. I know about fine men; I lost one."

Back at the square table, the developments at the end of the bar did not go unnoticed. Charlie had returned with two more beers and had settled back in. Molly's hand on Luke's arm provided just the spice that he needed to season his commentary. "She's touchin' 'im again, Jack. He needs a lesson, Jack. You teach 'im a lesson. I'll back you up with old Colonel Colt, here," Charlie said as he patted the gun in his holster.

"I don't need no backin' up," Jack slurred. "He still sparkin' her?"

"He surely is. You shouldn't even look, Jack. It'll make your blood boil; it surely will."

Jack was primed for action, and he acted. He stood up, as suddenly as he could in his condition, pushing his chair back as he did so. Turning around to his right, to face in the opposite direction, he yelled, "Stuart, get your hands off my woman."

At the sound of his last name, Luke jerked his head back, and he turned his head around to the left. When he saw Jack standing there, he straightened up from the bar and turned his body slowly toward

Jack, as if not sure that he had heard what he had and that it had been addressed to him. Obviously puzzled, as he stood facing Jack, Luke said, "I've not got my hands on any woman."

"Stay away from my woman."

"What are you talkin' about, Jack? Who's your woman?"

"That woman you been sparkin's my woman."

"I've not been sparkin' any woman."

Charlie, not about to let the truth ruin his fun, chimed in, "It's not so, Jack. He's been sparkin' her all right."

Jack clumsily began to pull his gun from its holster, as he snarled at Luke, "I oughtta kill you."

That was all he managed to get out. The cowboy from the chair against the wall, who had been watching the whole thing, was suddenly there at Jack's side, and in a few quick movements, he pushed Jack's gun hand down, removing the gun as he did so, and struck a sharp, angled blow with the bottom of his hand to Jack's neck. Jack turned toward him, stunned. The cowboy then lifted both his arms up over Jack's head and brought down his forearms quickly and forcibly, at angles, against either side of Jack's neck. Jack's eyes rolled back, and he began to crumple. The cowboy caught him and slid him back into his chair. He then turned to the stupefied Charlie and quickly removed the gun from Charlie's left-handed holster, before Charlie even knew what was happening. Motioning to Jack, he said to Charlie, "You'd better see to your friend here." Holding the guns, he added, "The bar-keep will see to these."

Before Charlie could recover enough to look after Jack, the cowboy was at the bar, sliding the guns across to the barkeeper. "You might want these," he quietly said as he did so.

"I surely do," the barkeeper replied, but he did so to the cowboy's back, as the cowboy had left the guns while on his way toward the door.

Luke and Molly, both in a kind of shock due to the nature and quickness of recent events, watched the cowboy's back as he made his way toward the door and out of it. Then they looked at each other, each of them seeing his or her own bewilderment reflected in the other's face. Luke turned away for a moment to look back at the slumping Jack, who was being tended to by Charlie. Then he turned back to

Molly. "What was that all about?" he asked her, a sort of innocent perplexity animating his features.

Molly answered by raising her eyebrows and shrugging her shoulders. Then, nodding toward Jack, she said, "He must have taken those dances a little too seriously. You know, when you boys all came in here, when the doors opened, and you all wanted to dance, and the girls and I danced with you without any music?" she said, recalling the arrival of Luke's outfit at the Lady Gay (most of whom had since left), and indicating, with a sweeping nod, the other women in the hall. Luke nodded. "Well," Molly continued, "he was pretty insistent that he dance with me. He must have made something out of that. Sometimes they do."

"Huh," Luke said, as he looked from Molly toward Jack and Charlie. Then he stepped toward them. Jack still slumped unconscious in the chair. Charlie hung over him, trying to open Jack's eyes with his fingers. As Luke approached, Charlie quickly stood upright and retreated to the other side of the table.

"What's this all about, Charlie?" Luke asked, the look of perplexity still on his face.

"Blamed if I know," Charlie answered, all color having drained from his face.

Luke turned and looked at Jack and put his hand in front of his face. Feeling Jack's breath on the back of his hand, he said, "Well, he'll be all right, I expect." Then turning back to Charlie, he asked him again, "What's this all about, Charlie? Jack just pulled his gun on me and appeared ready to burn powder, and you were sittin' right across from him. You've got to know somethin'."

"Well," Charlie began, a bit of annoyance beginning to mix with his fear, "Jack's an ornery cuss. You know that, Luke. Maybe you did somethin' to get 'im riled," Charlie concluded, looking off to his left, away from Luke, in a manner that suggested that Luke might need to examine his own conscience to resolve the matter.

Luke could see that this interview was going nowhere. He could see that well enough, having spent months on the trail with Charlie and Jack. He looked back down at Jack and said to Charlie, "You goin' to take care of Jack?"

"Yessir."

"All right then." Luke turned away and returned to the bar, and Charlie took his place in front of Jack. The barkeeper, smelling salts in hand, joined Charlie.

Luke said to Molly at the bar, as he gathered his letters together, "I've got to catch up with that man."

"Your friend?"

"I've never seen the man before."

"That doesn't mean he's not your friend, Luke."

"You might have somethin' there," Luke responded, with raised eyebrows, as he tied up his packet of letters, "but, regardless, I need to thank him, and maybe find out what it was all about. Thank you kindly, Miss Molly," he said, looking up at her after he tied up the letters, "for visitin' and readin' my letters." He was more sober now than Molly had yet seen him, in their brief acquaintance, though he was still far from fully sober.

"We didn't get very far on your letters." Molly's forced smile betrayed some of her disappointment.

"No, we didn't," Luke agreed, "but I thank you for the start." He tipped his hat to Molly and headed for the door.

When he stepped outside, the early afternoon sun nearly blinded him for a moment. He looked in every direction and finally saw the cowboy riding his horse down the street to his left. He followed in that direction on foot.

Though more sober after recent events, Luke was still in a state of drunkenness, which he found to be no great advantage in navigating down the street. He did his best to walk as straight as he could, but realized that he was staggering to some degree and that his head was swimming in the afternoon heat. Despite these symptoms, he managed to follow the cowboy and see him turn into the livery stable.

By the time Luke arrived at the livery stable, the cowboy was leaving without his horse, but carrying saddlebags over his shoulder and a bedroll under his arm. Luke jogged a few steps to catch up with him.

"Howdy," Luke greeted the cowboy as he came up on his side.

The cowboy stopped, turned to face Luke, and pulled his head back a bit, in surprise. "Howdy," he shot back.

"I just wanted to thank you for what you did back there," Luke said, jerking his head back toward the Lady Gay. The jerk of his head did little for his steadiness, and he was required to look down and shuffle his feet a little to keep his balance.

"I didn't do much really, but you're welcome all the same," the cowboy replied, recognizing Luke.

"You kept me from gettin' shot at, which is somethin' enough for me," Luke countered, as he regained his equilibrium and looked up at the cowboy. "But what was that all about, anyways?"

"Seems that fellow took exception to the attention you were showin' the lady."

Luke's brow wrinkled with the reception of this intelligence, and his head jerked back slightly. Slightly, but still enough to make him unsteady, and again he shuffled his feet a little to regain his balance. He stared at the cowboy for a moment as his mind worked through the mist of inebriation. The sun, combining with his last few drinks, was beginning to have its effect. "But I wasn't really showin' Miss Molly attention," he managed to tell the cowboy, not without slightly slurring the words, "I mean, not such as would be . . . I mean, I was just visitin' with her."

"That may be true," the cowboy agreed, "but she was showin' you attention, and through the eyes of jealousy the picture can become mighty distorted."

By this time, pictures were becoming mighty distorted for Luke as he grew more unsteady on his feet. The cowboy looked on the slightly swaying Luke, and a light smile worked itself into his face. He took a canteen from over his shoulder and handed it to Luke. "Here, have a drink of water to cut through some of that liquor. It's warm," he added, as Luke took the canteen and opened it.

Luke took a drink and nearly spat it out. He managed to swallow hard, and then blurted, "That's hardly warm, it's hot as coffee."

"Coffee would cure what ails you all the faster," the cowboy recommended. "I'm goin' to find some dinner and would be glad to have you join me."

"I'll not be buyin' any dinner," Luke said, handing back the canteen.

"Well then, how about joinin' me and havin' some coffee while I eat?"

"All right."

"I'm Tom Schurtz," the cowboy said as he stuck out his hand.

Luke grasped the hand, shook it, and completed the introductions. "Luke Stuart," he said.

Tom Schurtz smiled, then released the handshake and led off toward the north side of town. Luke fell in alongside him, staggering as badly as ever.

They walked across the Plaza, picking their way through the traffic of man, beast, buggy, and wagon, and angling a little to the east, toward the north end of Bridge Street. They talked a little as they walked, though Luke's need to concentrate on walking alone left little room for talk. Nevertheless, after crossing the railroad tracks, he asked Tom, "What was it you did to Jack, anyways?"

"Oh, just somethin' I learned from a Chinese man a few years back."

"A Chinese man?"

"Yessir, I met up with some Chinese folks back when I was workin' on the railroad."

"Huh," Luke responded, watching Tom for a moment as they walked along. Then he looked forward again to better navigate. His mind returned to the topic of the incident in the Lady Gay. "I can't figure out why Jack behaved the way he did back there."

"That says more about you than it does about him."

"What do you mean?"

Tom did not respond right away, so Luke asked him again, "What do you mean, it says more about me than about him? What do you mean by that?"

"I just mean," Tom said, "that the man appeared to have a seriously flawed character, and you seem to be able to look beyond that." Turning his head toward Luke, he clarified, "To be decent enough not to see it, or try not to see it; I don't know."

"Uh," Luke responded, pondering that thought for just a second before dismissing it as too much for his brain, in its present condition, to take on. "Well, you know," he then said, "I didn't mean anything toward Miss Molly. I'm not lookin' for a woman. I'm married to the finest woman I know."

Tom looked around, the smile again set into his features. "Well, it's good to know you honor that."

"Indeed, I do honor it. All I was doin' was visitin' with Miss Molly. The other boys put her onto me; jokin' they were. I had no intention of goin' into any dancehalls, but after a few drinks they persuaded me . . . ," he paused and smiled as he remembered, "well, almost forced me. Then she was goin' to read these letters from my wife." Luke held out the packet. "I really wanted to get my letters read. See, I can't read myself," he said, looking over at Tom. He saw no reaction, but did manage to bump into another cowhand as they entered into the north end of Bridge Street.

When he had caught up with Tom after the collision, he asked him, "Can you read?"

"Yes, I can."

Luke considered that answer as he walked along staring blankly at the ground out in front of him. After a few more steps, he said, "Would you, uh, consider readin' one of these letters for me?"

"Yessir, I would." Tom stopped, as he said it, and turned to his left, right there on Bridge Street (about midway up the second block from Front Street), to face a large, white, gable-faced house.

Luke kept walking, still talking to Tom and trying to untie the packet of letters as he walked. He had gone several yards before he realized that Tom was no longer beside him. He turned back to see Tom standing before the white house, apparently subjecting it to no little scrutiny. He walked back and, stopping next to Tom, joined him in the study of the house.

The orderly, well-kept appearance of the house regularly drew the admiration of passersby, as it now drew the admiration of Tom and Luke. Two full stories high, it had a covered, railed porch across its front and flowers planted in the yard in front of the porch. Above the porch hung a sign with large black letters that read: Krause House. Smaller letters below this title listed the amenities of the establishment: rooms, meals, baths. Under the sign, upon the porch, in a stout chair, sat a portly man, who regarded the two men regarding the house.

"You stayin' here?" Luke asked, as he turned his head with the question.

"I don't know yet," Tom replied, still eying the place.

"Uh," Luke rejoined, turning to look the place over again.

"But this is where I'd like to buy you dinner, if that's agreeable to you," Tom finally stated.

"No," Luke answered with immediate resolution, "I'm goin' to eat out at camp."

"Well, I'd ask you to reconsider," Tom said. "I realize that you had planned to eat out at your camp, but I would consider it a favor if you would allow me to buy you dinner, as I'd rather not eat alone and would appreciate your company. Besides," Tom continued, with a sideways glance at his companion, "that letter would read a whole lot better over a good, home-cooked meal, . . . unhurried."

Luke was hungry, after all, and in his drunkenness this appetite was more keenly felt, and not so easily put down. Besides, the man said he would be doing him a favor, and like his hunger, in his present condition, this rationalization was not so easily put down. And then, of course, there was his letter.

Luke looked for a moment at the bound letters in his hand and made up his mind. Whatever his earlier objection to dinner had been, it now dissolved. "All right," he said.

"Good," Tom exclaimed, and he led the way up the steps onto the porch. There they greeted the portly man, seated to the right of the doorway. He was about fifty years of age, large in every proportion. He was clean shaven and barbered and neatly attired in clean work clothes. Streams of sweat crept down the sides of his flushed face, despite the shade of the porch.

"Hello," the man said in response to their greetings. Then he continued in a heavy German accent, "I'll trrouble you men to leafe yourr guns viss me."

Tom indicated that he had left his guns at the livery stable as Luke handed over his six-shooter, in compliance with the city ordinance.

"Is dinner still bein' served?" Tom asked him, with little concern that *dinner* (the popular term for the midday meal in many regions of Texas) would be construed to mean *supper* in this town that catered to the Texas cowboy.

"It iss," the man replied, wiping his handkerchief across a sweat-moistened brow. "You vant a rroom?"

"I might."

"One of the girrls vill help you inside," the man said, still looking out at the street and waving the back of his hand toward the house.

"Thank you," Tom said as he entered. Luke nodded and followed him in.

They made their way down a narrow hallway, passing a closed door to their right and an open doorway into a comfortable parlor to their left. At the end of the hall, they entered a small foyer with a staircase to the upstairs on the left and a desk with a register on the right.

They turned to their right and stepped up to the desk. Tom set down his saddlebags and bedroll. As there was no one at the desk, they looked around. The room had one window, above the staircase. The rest of the light in the room came from the hallway through which they had come and through the doorway to their right, next to the hallway, which opened into a dining room with windows that looked out onto the porch and the street beyond. The closed door they had passed in the hallway also opened into this dining room. Another closed door, to their left against the back wall of the room, led to the family's living area, which included the kitchen. Behind the house were the laundry and bathhouse. Upstairs were the renters' rooms.

It was about those renters' rooms, as well as about dinner, that Tom wished to inquire, but still there appeared no one of whom to inquire, and glances into the open doorway behind the desk, which led to a small office, gave no more assurance that "the girrls" of whom the man on the porch had spoken were anywhere about. Consequently, Tom turned his attention to the doorway into the dining room. He stepped closer to the doorway, and without looking all the way into the room, he could see at least four people still seated at the large main table. He heard the opening and closing of a swinging door and presently saw a young woman, carrying plates of pie for the diners, come into view. She was a fair-haired young woman, of perhaps twenty years of age, neatly dressed in a dark skirt and white blouse and apron.

The young woman did not look up, at all, as she set down the plates and cleared away other dishes, and Tom could see that she was about to disappear without noticing him; so he managed to mix a sort of cough with the sound of clearing his throat, and the young woman did look up at him. Her fair face caught Tom's attention, but not for long, because she immediately lowered it again after catching sight of him. She quickly finished gathering the dishes and then whisked off in the direction from which she had come, after which Tom again heard the sound of the opening and closing of a swinging door. This door in the back corner of the dining room, out of Tom's sight, led to a pantry between the dining room in the front of the house and the kitchen in the back (which placed the pantry on the other side of the back wall of the office behind the desk).

A moment had barely passed after the sound of the swinging door, and it was heard again, and shortly the fair young woman whisked into the room from the dining room, breezing past Tom, who stepped back in surprise and to make way for her. Without raising her eyes to the two men, and with little expression, but with an air of business about her, she stopped behind the desk, examined the register, and addressed them.

"Would you like a room?" she asked without looking up.

"Yes, I would," Tom said, stepping back over to the desk from his place by the doorway. Luke looked at him.

The young woman looked up, for the first time, at Luke and said, "And you?"

"Uh, no."

With that reply, she very businesslike returned her eyes to the register and turned her attention to Tom. They made the arrangements of fees, rules, and schedules. Then Tom signed the register and paid for two nights in advance, which the young woman dutifully recorded in a ledger she had taken from the office behind her. And the young woman laid a key on the desk for him.

Tom responded, "Well, I thank you kindly, and we were wonderin' if we could still get a bite of dinner."

At this, the young woman did, at last, look up at him, still without expression, and Tom liked what he saw. She had wholesome good looks, with soft blonde-brown hair pulled back and up behind her head. The fair, lightly freckled skin of her face was fresh as a baby's, and the large, wide-open blue eyes that looked out from under her long, fine eyelashes invited deeper inspection. But this was denied, as she quickly looked down and efficiently turned and headed back to the dining room with the quiet command, "Follow me." As Tom reached down for his bags and roll, she said over her shoulder, "Leave your things. They will be taken to your room." Tom left them as ordered.

The men did follow her into the dining room. There, in addition to the large dining table, sat two smaller tables by the two bay windows that looked out onto the porch, the yard, and the street beyond. She led them to the one on the left, and they seated themselves.

"We've got roast beef with potatoes and gravy, carrots and onions and green beans," she informed them.

Tom and Luke looked at each other in agreement, and Tom voiced their mutual sentiments. "We'll both take a plate," he said. "What do you recommend to drink?"

"There's Father's own beer."

"Is Father the man sitting on the porch?"

"That's Father."

"Bring us each one," Tom said. And with that order, the young woman left them.

"A beer's integrity is a reflection of the man who brews it. I trust we'll not be disappointed," Tom said.

Luke managed a dubious smile.

"Ah," Tom sighed, "you probably didn't want another beer."

"Well, I do think I've stretched my limit," Luke replied, as he slumped down and turned away from the window to sit almost sideways in his chair, with his feet out in front of him and his elbow resting on the table.

"That's all right," Tom assured him. Then turning to the young woman, who had stopped at the large table to his left, he said, just loud enough to be heard, "Miss." She turned and looked at him. "Make it just one beer, please." She stared into him, then looked at Luke, then back at the table she was serving. After gathering some dishes there, she whisked to the kitchen.

Tom turned back to Luke and slightly shrugged his shoulders at the young woman's way of responding, or not responding, to them. "I suppose I just should've drunk it," he said. "I never did get to finish my beer in that dancehall."

Luke glanced over at Tom and then looked down. After a moment he said, "You know, I still can't figure out this whole thing with Jack MacNeil, back there. He's always seemed to carry some grudge against me. Seems ever since we met and started out on the trail, he's been on me, but I could never figure out what it was."

"Well," Tom replied, as he turned and looked out the window, "there are a lot of people who want to have the happiness that other people have, but don't want to commit to the kind of living it takes to get that happiness." He turned back to face Luke. "So, instead," he continued, "they live selfishly, squandering assets and, most important, time, which they can never recoup, and they grow bitter and fuel a hatred for those who remind them of their dissipation. I suspect that is the case with MacNeil. That anger was not just about your showin' attention to a dancehall girl. He's been nursin' it for a while."

Luke stared at Tom as he finished his assessment of Jack MacNeil. "How do you know all that?" Luke asked him.

Tom looked back out the window. "I know people," he said.

"Hmmh."

Silence hung too heavily over the table for a July afternoon in Dodge City, and Luke did not wait long to remedy the situation.

"You know," he began, "I don't generally drink much, at all. That's exactly why I came to be in the state I was in . . . ," he considered for a moment, "am in," he corrected himself, with a quiet chuckle. "We just got in from the trail from San Antone. The outfit is trailin' on to Montana, but it was understood that I would only ride as far as Dodge. So the boys decided to give me a sendoff, and they thought it would be great sport to get me to drinkin'. I don't know about you, but when a bunch like that gets a person goin', it's easy to lose track. I had no intention of visitin' any dancehalls, but with the drink and the forceful persuasion of the boys, there wasn't much left to choice. They had a high time buyin' me drinks and goadin' Miss Molly into tryin' to make me forget about my Elizabeth. They're good boys, but most ain't married, and with a little liquor in 'em, they were enjoyin' themselves at my expense, over my missin' Elizabeth and the kids. Miss Molly played along a little while, but then we got visitin', especially the more I drank. And those boys made sure I drank. After a while all those boys were gone, one way or another."

Tom had turned back from the window at the start of this narrative from Luke. The serious face that he had turned toward the window, just moments before, gave way to a light smile as Luke concluded.

After a moment, Luke asked, "When did you decide you were goin' to get a room here?"

"After we met the proprietor."

The door from the kitchen swung open, and the girl in the apron, carrying a mug of beer, passed through the doorway and over to their table. She looked from one to the other of them and then set the beer down in front of Tom. Then she glanced at Tom, who was watching her. When their eyes met, she looked back down, with little expression, and headed back to the kitchen. Tom called after her, finally catching her attention with a second call, his first call drowned out by the noise of two other diners, a drover and a buyer, leaving the large table. In fact, though Tom had only seen four men from the doorway, there were seven at the large table finishing their meals, and it appeared that earlier the dining room had been full of patrons.

She turned and returned to their table.

"Miss, could we get a cup of coffee for this gentleman?" Tom asked her, as he nodded toward Luke.

She looked up at Tom, then at Luke, then back at Tom. "Yes," she responded, and she turned and headed back toward the kitchen.

"His daughter merely confirmed my decision," Tom said. He looked across at Luke and said, "She is a handsome girl." Then he added, "She is also a good indication of how this place is run."

Luke considered that, and looked at the door to the kitchen as it swung closed behind her. "Yessir," he mused as he looked around, "neat and clean. And she is a handsome girl," he said, after giving it some thought, then added, "though not as handsome as my Elizabeth."

"Ah, yes, the fair Elizabeth," Tom said. "Let's see that letter."

Luke fumbled with the packet, a little more sure-fingered than he had been in the dancehall. As he did so, a swing of the pantry door produced the blonde girl with a cup of coffee, which she set before him. He acknowledged the delivery with a nod, and she was gone. Luke turned back to his packet and pulled out the letter that Molly had begun to read. Staring at it, he slowly handed it over to Tom, finally raising his eyes to Tom's, watching how Tom received it.

Tom received the letter with the same respect that Luke had shown. He slowly unfolded it and glanced it over. "You want me to read from where Molly left off, or the whole thing?"

Looking out the window at the great expanse of distance, Luke replied, "The whole thing."

Tom nodded, looked down at the letter, and began to read:

April 12, 1877

My dearest Luke,

You have only just left this very day, and already my heart yearns for you. I dread to think that tonight, and for nights on end, I will not hear your tread on the porch and see your kind, handsome face when that door opens. I do believe that this child of ours, who plays within my body, shares this same sentiment, because, though I have not mentioned it, as it would seem a mother's fancy, on more than one occasion, he did seem to stir upon your approach, much as did that blessed child, John, in the womb of another Elizabeth, at the approach of the mother of our Lord, those many centuries past.

It may well be that the sacred bond that unites a mother to her unborn child fosters communication beyond that normal kind we know of in spoken word. If this be true, then there would be no question or wonder at the notion that this child would stir in joy at the approach of one who brings such joy of love to his mother.

Oh, and I do believe he is a he, as only she who carries him could know.

Zachariah is already a great help to me, so young a boy, who tries so hard to fill his father's shoes while he is away. This, too, pays tribute to that man I miss, whose favor and approval are so earnestly sought by one so young and innocent.

Rachel does not yet understand why her daddy will not be home this night and asks constantly about you and where you have gone. She will have grown so upon your return.

My dear Luke, I must pause now and return to my work, as the sun seeks repose in the west. You will hear more from me than you will probably care to hear, but for now it is enough to say that our days will not be full again until your return.

Yours always,

Love,
Elizabeth

And with the name "Elizabeth," a net of silence fell upon their table. In that silence, Tom too looked out the window to the cattle-covered plains beyond town. Finally, he said, "San Antonio's home, then?"

Luke looked at him. "Down in Medina County, west of San Antone," he said. "You?"

"Well, I'm up from Corpus Christi, but I'm not sure I'd call it home," Tom said.

"So, you have two kids, then?" Tom resumed, carefully folding up the letter.

"That's right," Luke said, looking back out the window, "with another on the way. He might even be here by now. There were two others, but Elizabeth lost one, and another, Jeremiah, died after six months."

"Your wife must be a strong woman."

"Elizabeth is powerful strong," Luke affirmed, as he turned from the window. "I mean, she's a slender thing, but she won't give up. Has a strong faith. She's real smart, too. I don't know what I'd do without her."

Tom looked down at the letter in his hand and said, "She writes a good letter."

Luke looked back out the window and said nothing for a few minutes. Then, still looking out the window, he asked Tom, "You married?"

"No."

"Huh."

Tom handed the letter over to Luke, whose attention was thus drawn back from the window, and he returned the letter to the packet.

"When you headin' home?" Tom asked.

"Soon as I can, probably the day after tomorrow. I'm obliged to ride herd until the new man from Montana arrives to help pilot the outfit the rest of the way," Luke said. "I'll be leavin' right after that."

"I don't blame you. You goin' by rail?"

"No, I'm goin' overland. Figured I could make better use of that railroad fare than to spend it on a ticket to San Antone. I'm fixin' to purchase a packhorse for the return."

"I intend to buy a horse, myself, a mare," Tom said. Then, after a moment, he added, "How'd you like a partner on your ride south?"

Luke looked up, surprised. He stared at Tom for a moment and then asked, "You?"

"Yessir."

A smile spread across Luke's face. "You'd be most welcome."

"Then I'll join you."

"That suits me fine," Luke exclaimed. "I'll be down at the stockyards tomorrow, loadin' cattle. I'll stop by to let you know how things stand. Should I look for you here?"

"I thought you said your herd is trailin' north?" Tom asked him, ignoring his question.

"It is, but for four hundred head bound for Chicago, which we'll be puttin' on cars tomorrow."

"Huh," Tom replied, nodding his head lightly in understanding, though his eyes were cast down upon the foam of the beer his hand was raising toward his mouth. He took a satisfying sip of that beer, and savored it. Then he responded. "You'll be down at the stockyards?"

"Yessir."

"Try me at the Dodge House."

"All right," Luke agreed.

With that, the door from the kitchen flung open, and their waitress brought two steaming plates of ample portions of roast beef, potatoes, carrots, and beans, along with a loaf of warm bread, well balanced on her forearm.

As she set the meal before them, Tom watched her with admiration and said, "You are an awfully handy girl. Are you allowed to walk in the evening in the presence of a gentleman?"

She stopped for a moment and looked at Tom. Then her eyes went back down, and a light smile played about her features. She returned to her work with the reply, "The gentleman would need to look and smell like a gentleman first." The meal set and her work done, she glanced at Tom again, then turned and was gone, back to the kitchen.

"She is the most intriguing girl," Tom said, not only to Luke, if to Luke at all, but to himself and any other soul present. Then, rubbing his beard with his hand, he said, through his smile, to Luke, "She does have a point, you know."

Luke chuckled. "We are pretty ripe."

"Well, first things first," Tom said. "I'll have at this meal, and then it's on to cleanliness." And Luke agreed.

And thus the conversation slipped into a lull, as they "had at" the meal. When eventually they had finished, there was little evidence that the meal had ever existed. Both men, taking slow, deep breaths, leaned back in their chairs.

Their waitress returned to clear the table. "Will there be anything else?" she asked as she cleared.

"Could I know your name?" Tom asked her.

Without hesitating in her task of clearing the table, she replied, "Would not a gentleman introduce himself first?"

Tom smiled, his estimation of the girl rising with her every utterance. "Indeed, he would. I am Tom Schurtz, and this is my friend, Mr. Luke Stuart."

The young woman stood up straight, all dishes gathered in her arms, and looked back and forth from one to the other and said, "Mr. Schurtz, Mr. Stuart, I am pleased to meet you." Then she fixed her blue eyes on Tom and said, "I am Marta, Marta Krause." She looked at him, enjoying this as much as he, and again she turned and disappeared into the pantry.

"Intriguing," Tom said, "the most intriguing girl." He paused, contemplating the object of these comments, and then, as if coming around, said, "Well, I guess it's on to cleanliness."

The two men rose and left the table. At the desk, Tom met a younger girl of the Krause family, Gretta, by name. Through her he arranged to have the cost of Luke's meal added to his bill. He also arranged to have a bath drawn upon his return. Then he left with Luke, who received his gun from Mr. Krause, still seated on the front porch, as the two men paid their respects to that proprietor on their way out. At Front Street they parted, Luke to recover his horse from the livery and return to camp, and Tom to buy a new outfit of clothing in anticipation of his bath.

•   •   •

IT DID NOT TAKE LONG for Tom to return with a new outfit of pants, shirt, underwear, socks, kerchief, hat, and boots. These he donned at the conclusion of his bath, a bath that soaked out of him not only dirt, but also various aches and pains of the trail. Immediately following that bath, clothed in his new outfit, a rejuvenated Tom Schurtz returned to Front Street to visit the tonsorial parlor for a haircut and shave. Fresh from the tonsorial parlor, he struck out to visit the various establishments on Front Street, browsing and making some purchases, which included the latest three editions of the Dodge City Times, cartridges for his pistol and rifle, a comb, needles and thread, buttons, and at least two books.

These purchases also included a drink of fine scotch and a Monagram cigar, which Tom slowly savored in the subdued atmosphere of Henry Sturm's Occident saloon. The more he savored, the more convinced he grew of the propriety of such savoring, given the hardships and deprivations of the trail that had preceded his present indulgences. Accordingly, in the protracted enjoyment of the one premium cigar and one fine drink, he settled into a very warm and fluid comfort. And in that comfort, his body, possibly in alliance with the subconscious part of his mind, was made aware of the greatest deprivation of the trail, that blanket deprivation under which all the more specific deprivations could be squeezed, sticking and jutting out according to the specificity of definition. That deprivation was the deprivation of rest. Rest, that act characterized by the lack of menial activity and by the appropriate fulfillment of one's needs. To it the Creator had resorted after the vast creation of the universe, and to it was man commanded to also resort, in imitation.

So, the man, Tom Schurtz, now comfortably weighed down by a growing sense of his need for rest, with both cigar and drink consumed, and with his purchases firmly in his grasp, made his way out of Henry Sturm's establishment, through the heat, dust, and traffic in the streets, to his room at the Krause House. There, in the heat and light of his room in midafternoon, he propped himself up against the pillows on his bed, with some idea of restfully reading the newspaper. He started with the oldest of the papers he had picked up, the June 23 edition of the Dodge City *Times*, and his eyes immediately fell upon an item under the heading "CITY AND COUNTY," entitled "A Few Items For Our Friends In the East to Read." The article began:

> There are but few claims taken in the vicinity of Dodge City. The land is good, and we want the county settled with industrious farmers and stock raisers. Heretofore the business men have depended upon the Texas cattle trade for support, and have not tried to induce immigration. The railroad company has been anxious to settle the country and sell its lands east of us before putting this land into market. For these reasons no attention has been paid to settling the country.
>
> Dodge City is one of the most promising towns in Kansas, and the land and farms in its vicinity will rapidly increase in value.

The article continued, listing various pieces of evidence to support its claims about the promise of Dodge City and its surrounding lands. Then it mentioned a particular "large tract of Osage Indian land . . . in this vicinity, . . . subject to entry at the exceedingly low price of $1.25 per acre, one half of the price of governmental land." Tom was suspicious of why Osage Indian land would be available for entry. Still, he read on from that particular to the more general subject of the land in the thirteen unorganized counties attached to Ford County. The article went on to list the various attributes, water and rainfall being far from the least important, of those lands as well as the land surrounding Dodge City within Ford County.

From this article, Tom browsed some more until he came across another item entitled "Locations for Stock Ranches." It began:

> In answer to various letters lately received we would say yes, there are plenty of good locations for stock farms or homesteads within thirty miles of this city; both north and south of the Arkansas, on never-failing streams of water with plenty of timber for fuel and stock shelter.

Homestead. The word appealed to Tom, as did the policy. A man only needed to locate his 160 acres, file on it and pay the twelve-dollar fee, live on the land and cultivate it for five years, make the "final proof," pay the six dollars, and receive his patent, and it was his: his land, his home. He liked the idea. Let those have the land who would work it, develop it, and make good on it. And Tom was in good company. Thomas Jefferson had long ago expressed some of the sentiments behind the homestead movement with the words, "The earth is given as a common stock for man to labor and live on. . . . The small landholders are the most precious part of the state." And Galusha Grow of Pennsylvania, author of the first homestead law, had said, "Why should not the legislation of the country be so changed as to prevent for the future the evils of land monopoly, by setting apart the vast and unoccupied Territories of the Union and consecrating them forever in free homes for free men?"

Still, for his own part, Tom had no intention of homesteading, as he was in a position to be able to purchase land, if he should find any he wished to purchase. That had not always been the case, and there was a part of Tom that almost wished it were not the case at present. There was a part of Tom that almost wished he were in a position to homestead, to choose his land and earn it by his own husbandry, to make a home upon his land, to make his land a home, a place to be from and to return to, a place where, if all else failed, he could eke out his existence by the work of his hands and the sweat of his brow.

Land. His own land. A home upon the land. As Tom read in the newspaper about these lands, their streams, grasses, timber, rainfall, altitude, atmosphere, soils, topography, accessibility to railroads and the protection of forts, he gradually fell to dreaming a dream that had slowly crept into his mind over the past couple of years or so, and that had been recurring with greater frequency in the past several months. It was a dream of land, his own land, his own home upon his own land: land with good water; with timber for shelter, building materials, and fuel; with game and fruit; with plenty of grass for livestock and haying; with good soil for planting; and with varying terrain, just for the beauty of it.

Nevertheless, though this dream had crept up on him and was increasingly recurrent, he did not see its realization in sight. He had a feeling inside that it was near, that he was drawing toward it, that it was where he was being called to be, where he ought to be, where he truly desired to be; but try as he might, he could not determine anything about where or when or how, exactly, it was going to be. Furthermore, as strong as the feeling that this was to be was another feeling, a feeling that he could do nothing to bring it about, nothing to determine the when, where, or how of it, and this bothered Tom.

Tom wanted to do, to act, to bring this thing about, but any such attempt by him had ended in frustration. When he had thought about making a purchase of land or had even looked into it, by following up on leads like those in the newspaper, he had never been able to determine where to proceed from that initial interest or investigation. The world was a big place, and Tom did not discount the possibility that his home could be in any habitable place within that world. There was nothing holding him to any one place. How did he narrow it down? It was true that he had felt some pull back to Colorado, to the rugged lands he had known there, but he had had no clear sense that that was the direction in which he was being called. Still, in a vague, persistent feeling that pervaded the background atmosphere of his thought, he was sure that he was being called somewhere, however undefined, and that all he could do was wait and be available, and Tom found this situation unsettling.

But Tom was not to be bothered with it all now. He would be unsettled another time. Now he would rest, and in rest, he would dream. Such dreaming could be most intoxicating to one who had long been deprived of rest, as he had been, and so it was. Thus to dreaming he succumbed and, through dreaming, to deeper rest and eventually to the sleep that would no longer be denied. So the man slept, and the man dreamed, and he dreamed of a home upon the land.

Man making a home upon the land, a relationship as ancient as man himself. Indeed, it had been from the land, out of the very ground (*'adhamah*), up from the primordial "slime of the earth," that God had formed man (*'adham*), and he had then breathed into him "the breath of life," and man had become "a living being." God had planted a "garden of Eden," a "paradise of pleasure," and had placed man within it, "to dress and to keep it" and to take his sustenance from it. And when man, male and female, had estranged himself from God, through pride, distrust, and disobedience, God had cursed the land, the ground, the earth, because of man's sin, and had condemned man to wrest his sustenance from the earth in "labour," "toil," and "the sweat of thy face," and to return to the earth in death, "for dust thou art, and unto dust shalt thou return." Still, God had forgiven man and had allowed man to remain fruitful, and God had clothed man. And though man had been forced to accept the chief consequence of his sin, which is death, and other consequences, among which had been to be driven from the garden of Eden, man had been sent back to the land "to till the earth from which he was taken."

Thereafter, man had multiplied sin upon sin upon the earth, and this cycle of sin, punishment, and forgiveness had continued, with the land playing an important part in God's reconciliation with man. After man had almost been completely destroyed in the great flood, the land had been restored to man through a covenant with Noah. After man's language had been confused and man had been scattered over the face of the earth, a new land had been promised man, with the promise of a great nation, in a covenant with Abraham, through whom all the peoples of the earth would be blessed. After bondage in Egypt, that promised land had been restored to Abraham's nation, in a covenant through Moses. After centuries of bloodshed and warfare, a kingdom had been established in that promised land under Saul, and then David, with whom God had established a covenant promising that God would "establish his line forever and his throne as the days of the heavens," and God had come to dwell in the land, on Zion. Then, after Solomon, had come the split and, eventually, the collapse of the kingdom, and defeat upon defeat, and exile and reestablishment under foreign domination, and a brief period of freedom only to be followed by more foreign domination. Through all this, as the prophets had begun to look for the "New Covenant," an "everlasting covenant" that might be realized in ways beyond their understanding, and as some had begun to see that New Covenant realized in the "Son of Man," of "the line of David," who had "no place to lay his head," it was the promise of a "great nation" in a "new land" with an "everlasting reign" that they had seen fulfilled in his kingdom, "not of this world."

Man and the land. Formed from the land in God's created time, yet inspired by the very breath of God, man was placed in the paradise "to dress and to keep it" and to take sustenance from it, upon the earth to "fill" and "subdue" it and to "have dominion" over it. He was capable of fulfilling this exalted role in harmony with creation because of his elevation through the inspiration of the breath of God. But man's sin disordered all relationships. Man was disordered within his person, among his persons, and in his relationship with all of creation, because he disordered his relationship with God, upon which all other relationships depend. Where he had dressed and kept the paradise and eaten freely of the fruit of its trees, save one, now he would eat of the plants of the earth and, later, of the animals as well. The earth, itself, would thwart man's attempts at cultivation, bringing forth "thorns and thistles" to man. What food man could derive from the earth, he would do so in "toil" and "labour" and "the sweat of thy face."

Nevertheless, man seeks to do so. Man seeks to cultivate and harvest the produce of the land, plant and animal, despite the hardships. Man seeks his promised land in which to do it. It is true that, in his fallen state, man must do so to sustain himself physically. Still, though his nature is wounded, it is not entirely corrupted, and though he must now draw his material sustenance from the earth in hardship, there remains in man a vestige of that original, primordial relationship to the land that God intended in paradise. That vestige makes the working of the land, the cooperation with God in bringing forth the produce of the land, attractive, in a way that only those who so labor can truly know.

That vestige was making its presence felt in Tom. It was making its presence felt in a call to his promised land. Though that call remained as yet indistinct, Tom had become distinctly aware that following the call to his promised land of this world was not wholly unconnected with following the call to that promised land "not of this world."

Of that, Tom had become aware, but anyone looking in on Tom at this moment, as he lay back on his pillows, his eyes closed and his newspaper spread open across his chest, would have found him seriously lacking in anything resembling awareness. For now Tom rested, Tom slept, and Tom dreamed, and any cowhand who had ever been "up the trail," would have agreed that he had earned it.

•   •   •

CONSCIOUSNESS drifted into the wide ocean of unconsciousness, gradually displacing it, and Tom's eyes slowly opened. He stared contentedly at the recently painted white ceiling, long enough to be well acquainted with it, before his eyes turned to the wall, with its light print paper, to see that the angle of the beams of sunlight entering through the window had grown noticeably sharper. The realization that it was getting on toward seven o'clock came with the realization that he had better be getting himself over to the Plaza House, where Mr. Whittacker Dallen, the man who owned his outfit, had invited him to supper.

Swinging into a sitting position on the bed, he kicked aside the newspaper that had fallen to the floor. Then he pulled on his new boots, which he had had made at J. Mueller's boot shop on Front Street, experiencing the characteristic "pop" as his foot hit bottom. He rose and stepped into them a bit, getting his feet accustomed to them. He walked across the room and combed and smoothed his hair in front of the mirror that sat atop a simple chest of drawers. (That piece of furniture, along with the bed; two small tables, one with a bowl and pitcher, the other with a lamp; and two spindle chairs, tastefully furnished the clean room.) Tom's grooming took little effort because his hair was still slicked down with the aromatic application that had completed his session at the tonsorial parlor. Hair combed, he fitted his new hat atop his new hair and stepped back to survey the results in the mirror with the satisfaction of a man who was clean, shaved, and barbered; had just completed a long, arduous job; had money in his pocket, new clothes on his back, and the prospect of an excellent supper lying ahead. Survey complete, he left his room and the house, set his course for the Plaza House, and entered the streets of Dodge.

Even before he reached Front Street, he could see that it was alive again with cowhands streaming in from their camps outside town. Tom turned left at Front Street and, merging into the throng, directed his steps toward the Plaza House on the corner.

The Plaza House that welcomed him was famed for comfortable, if not elegant, surroundings and a menu that satisfied the powerful men from around the country who descended on Dodge to deal in cattle. The dining room was three or four times the size of the dining room at the Krause House. From its ceiling hung an eclectic mix of chandeliers, which were as yet unlighted, as sunlight still flooded in the windows that made up the front of the building and the smaller windows set into the east wall. A dark, flowered-print paper covered the walls down to a chair rail, and various framed pictures hung upon these papered portions of the walls all around the room. Mahogany-stained wainscot covered the walls below the chair rail. The floors were of bare wood.

Tom spied Whittacker Dallen, seated at a table near the back of the room, along with his boss foreman, Harvey Chapel. Tom made his way to the table.

"Mr. Dallen," he said as he approached.

Dallen had spotted Tom coming across the room and had already risen to greet him. He was a tall, trim, strikingly handsome man in his fifties, graying in both his moustache and his hair, and dressed in a suit. He spoke Tom's name as he extended his hand, and the two men shook hands. Harvey Chapel had also risen, and he and Tom shook hands, as well.

"Harv," Tom said as the men shook hands.

"Tom," the foreman responded.

A look at Whittacker Dallen and Harvey Chapel offered a distinct contrast. Whereas Dallen's appearance belied the years of hard work that had put him in the position he was in, Harvey Chapel, perhaps ten years his junior and a good eight inches shorter, showed every minute of his life of hard work. Still, aging and work had not so much worn as mellowed Harvey. This mellowing showed in a square, lean, and hardened body, in rough hands padded with muscle, in brown hair tinted with silver, in a pair of keenly observant, deep blue eyes set into a tanned face, creased with fine-line memorials of expressions that had conveyed the myriad thoughts and emotions evoked throughout years on the range and trail.

Having dispensed with the formalities, Dallen said to Tom, "Have a seat," as he motioned to the seat across from him.

Tom took the seat as Dallen and Harvey resumed their own.

"I'm glad you both could join me," Dallen began. "It allows me the opportunity to show my appreciation for the fine job you did in getting the herd to Dodge in an expeditious manner and with so little loss." As he said this, he pulled two small bags from his coat pocket and handed one to each of them. "Go ahead and look," he said.

Tom and Harvey glanced at each other and then guardedly pulled open the bags, each finding a generous amount of gold within. They both glanced at each other again and then offered their thanks to Whittacker Dallen.

"No, no, thank you," Dallen responded as he waved his hand. "Each of the men will get a little extra, but you two deserve a little more." This was typical of Whittacker Dallen. He was known for his fairness, generosity, and appreciation for hard work. He himself had come west from Virginia after the war. Though it was rumored that he had been of a landed, slave-owning, wealthy family that had lost everything in the war, one never heard much about such a past from Whittacker Dallen. He certainly had not tried to rest on such a history, had there been one. Through hard work and intelligent management, he had quietly built up a sizable cattle business outside of Corpus Christi.

Though grateful, Tom knew, and he was sure Dallen did too, that the greater responsibility for the success of the drive belonged to Harvey Chapel. Harvey was in his mid forties, and with Harvey it seemed that every year of experience seemed to count for two. Whatever lesson there was to learn from a situation, Harvey seemed to learn to a deeper degree. Harvey was truly a wise man. He led by humble example, manifested in hard work, which did not preclude him from issuing the orders required of a foreman. These were obeyed without complaint by the cowboys, who knew that Harvey knew his business, and that business was cattle.

Tom was Harvey's complement. More on the "bookish" side, Tom nevertheless appreciated Harvey's wisdom and delighted in the opportunity to learn from a man like him, and he took every opportunity to do so. Though Harvey could read, write, and figure, these were challenges for him that he was more than happy to leave to Tom, whose accuracy and integrity he could trust. Though separated by as much as twenty years, the two men had developed the mutual respect and appreciation for each other that is not always overtly displayed, but that withstands long separations of time and distance.

They had worked together now for four years since Tom had first arrived at the Dallen ranch as a cowhand in 1873. Harvey was the main reason Tom had stayed as long as he had in one place. Both Harvey and Whittacker Dallen had seen promise in Tom from the beginning, and within two years Tom was the *segundo*. This was their third trail drive together, and Tom was well aware of how invaluable a man like Harvey was to a successful drive. Few men were capable of the management of animals, finances, food, and equipment, and especially the management of men, demanded by the trail, and Harvey was more capable than any foreman Tom had ever met.

Thanks to the capability of both men and their herders, Whittacker Dallen was a richer man than he had been before, and he was in a mood to celebrate in his own reserved way. "You men order any and every thing you would like on that menu," he told them, "then we'll have a brandy and a cigar." And so they ordered.

The three men's conversation hovered over a meal that was as far from trail fare (as good as that was with the Dallen outfit) as Tom's new clothes were from his old. On Dallen's lead, they all partook of the oyster soup and the roast turkey and cranberry sauce, and differed only in how they complemented these dishes with their individual choices of relishes, vegetables, pastries, and desserts. All in all, it was a splendid meal that deserved the time they devoted to it.

From their table they could see well-known cattlemen, drovers, and buyers meeting over meals to buy and sell entire herds in the matter of minutes. Other tables might hold a whole trail crew being treated to a good meal by an appreciative cattleman. Dallen had so treated his outfit the night before, but tonight it was just Harvey, Tom, and he. In the atmosphere of the successful accomplishment of a long and difficult undertaking, the three enjoyed a relaxed conversation that comfortably drifted across a variety of topics. They were well into their cigar and second brandy, and Tom was speaking about the articles he had read in the paper concerning available land, ending with a lighthearted comment that he had half a mind to homestead himself, when the sound of a gravelly voice, directed at Dallen, interrupted their talk.

"Whit," spoke the voice.

The three looked up to see a square-shouldered, broad-chested, bearded man in a suit and tie loom over their table. The man's graying hair and beard suggested an age near that of Whittacker Dallen's or perhaps a little older. Dallen's eyes registered recognition, and he rose and extended his hand. "Henry," he said as the two men shook hands.

Dallen introduced Harvey and Tom to Henry Edwards, and the two also rose to shake his hand. Then, responding to Whittacker Dallen's invitation, Edwards joined them at their table, taking the seat between Tom and Dallen, and Dallen ordered a brandy and cigar for him, as well. These would certainly not be his first of either that evening, Tom was sure, due to the smell of alcohol and tobacco that emanated from the man. Nor did Tom have any doubts about the cattleman's ability to handle his share of both.

Dallen explained that he and Edwards went back in the cattle business, back to after the war. Edwards jumped right into the topics of his own herd in New Mexico and a herd, in which he held an interest, that had recently arrived in Dodge after a drive up from around Goliad. He then questioned Dallen about Dallen's herd, including its sale, and about his outfit, and then launched back into topics of his own choosing. Eventually, in the course of his remarks, he made a passing derogatory remark concerning some homesteaders whose paths he had crossed in Colorado.

"Homesteading," Whittacker Dallen spoke up, "Tom was just mentioning homesteading."

Dallen said this in the way that was characteristic of him, with hearty enthusiasm that Edwards had lighted on a topic that would bring Tom into the conversation, so that Tom and Edwards could get acquainted. As soon as he said it, though, Tom's insides experienced a slight twinge. Homesteading was not a policy that had universal support, and Tom had little doubt that it did not have the support of Henry Edwards. He correctly suspected that Henry Edwards hailed from the Old South and had participated on the side of that region in the War Between the States. Tom knew that if that were so, that history and his being a cattleman would likely place Henry Edwards among those least supportive of the policy. Here, Tom's intuition told him, was no Whittacker Dallen.

"And what did he have to say?" Edwards inquired, as he turned his intense, dark eyes on Tom.

Dallen responded in the same lighthearted humor that had animated the talk at the table before Edwards' arrival. "He was just saying that, with all the available land, he might even try homesteading himself."

The twinge dug a little deeper into Tom, as did Edwards' stare. Tom's brandy-lubricated tongue was talking before he was even aware of it. "I wasn't entirely serious," he said, "but I do think homesteading gives a man, who might not have a better opportunity, a chance to own and work some land of his own . . ."

"White niggers," Edwards interrupted, as soon as he had determined the tenor of Tom's comment. Then, with a slight sneer that uglified his otherwise ruggedly handsome face, he turned back to his brandy and took a drink.

Tom had stopped short at Edwards' interruption and now sat staring at the man.

Edwards swallowed his drink and, with the sneer set a little deeper into his face, glanced sideways at Tom, as if that were all the look he warranted. "White niggers," he repeated, "livin' in the dirt and bustin' up the sod on a meager quarter section that was never meant to be put under the plow."

"But they're makin' it," Tom countered in a simplistic reflex response.

Edwards froze as he was about to take another drink. With his glass held in front of his face, he rejoined, "Some are, east of here. You just let 'em move farther west and let 'em have a taste of drought."

"They've survived the locusts," Tom countered again, again freezing Edwards in his attempt to take a drink.

"Some," Edwards repeated, with no attempt to hide his irritation. "Give 'em locusts and drought." Again he turned to his drink.

Tom could have let it lie there, and he probably should have, but he had had his brandies and cigar, this was a topic that interested him, and he enjoyed having reasonable conversations with people who held opinions different from his own. So, he continued. "They've survived locusts *and* drought," he said. Then, thinking of the Eclipse Wind Engine Company (in Beloit of his native Wisconsin) that manufactured windmills of the design patented by L. H. Wheeler in 1867, he added, "Besides, they can use windmills and pump up water from wells to irrigate . . ."

"Windmills!" Edwards interrupted, and if he could have spat the word, he would have done so. Still not having been able to take his drink, which he still held before his face, he threw another sideways glance at Tom and said, with some vehemence, "That's what you'd want anyways, isn't it, windmills out in this cattle country." He lowered his drink to the table and then lowered and shook his head a little, not unlike a buffalo shaking off flies, and then suddenly turned on Tom, exposing him to a sneer set so deeply into his countenance that Tom could sense its origins in the very depths of the man's soul. He blasted Tom, "You're one of those nigger-lovin' Yankee Republicans, aren't you? White niggers or black niggers, it's all the same. Windmills." He shook his head, and with his voice still rising in volume, he launched more strongly into his argument. "You and your kind would have every lazy son of a fool out there with their puny plot of land and their sod-bustin' plows and dirt shanties and plow-lines and fences, and now with wind-mills too, and have 'em grubbin' around in the dirt and carvin' up the land that's fit for range alone . . ."

"I . . . ," Tom began, but Henry Edwards talked over him at a sound level that drew the attention of most of the others in the room, most of whom would have been, at least to some degree, in sympathy with the sentiments he was expressing.

"This is cattle country!" Edwards continued, with a pound of his fist on the table. "And you greenhorn Yankee dirt farmers and grangers better stay and dig in the dirt of your little farms in the North and leave this rangeland to the men who know how to use it. You Yankees aren't used to these man-size spaces, and if a quarter section is suffi-cient for your needs, maybe you ought to head back east, where you can root around in your black dirt and live safe and snug with your women . . ."

"I wasn't sayin' . . . ," Tom tried to explain, aware of the audience Edwards was building at his expense, but Edwards would allow no such interruption.

"You sent down your carpetbaggers and stirred up the niggers, and now you Yankees are pullin' out of the Old South, and where are the niggers goin'? They're comin' to Kansas. Who else is comin'?" Edwards asked, raising his eyebrows in feigned surprise. "Yankee white trash mechanics and grangers, and foreigners," he answered himself. "The Yankee government's goin' to give 'em all land. You Republicans love the niggers so much, let's see how your Yankee white trash likes it when your niggers get land before they do."

There was a lull in the rant, though Edwards had Tom fixed in his sights as if Tom were the embodiment of all the vices of the Yankee Republican government. Tom stared wonderingly at the man. He hesitated to respond due to his two previously failed attempts. Finally, after a moment, he said, "I wasn't sayin' all the land open to homesteading should be . . ."

"This is rangeland!" Edwards snarled, loud enough to drown Tom out. "Free range, open range! It's not for the Yankee government to cut up and parcel out to ignorant nesters. Farmin' a quarter section of the range west of here, even if you could get water, wouldn't produce enough for one man to live on, let alone a family, and then how do they expect to have anything left over to market? This land is fit for grazing, and it belongs to those of us who are fit for it, men who know better than to cut it up in little pieces, men with the dignity to know better than to be rootin' around in the dirt. We're the ones who've been out here. We're the ones who've made this land useful. We're the ones who've killed the buffalo and fought the Indians that were wastin' all this land. We're the ones who've fought the elements and have made somethin' out of this country. You Yankees come along and cut up the land in little pieces and put your little niggers on it, and now you're goin' to put windmills on it, and pretty soon you've got a quarantine line runnin' so far west that before long this whole town'll be dead, and there goes the railhead for Texas cattle."

Tom attempted one more time to interrupt and point out to Edwards that he was extrapolating far too much from the little bit that Tom had been allowed to say, but Edwards cut him off.

"You Yankee grangers and socialists want to revive Lincoln's income tax, too," Edwards continued for all to hear. "Invade a man's privacy and tax his earnin's!" he all but shouted, turning toward an embarrassed Whittacker Dallen, who sat staring at the top of the table. "They'll do it, too!" he warned. "You just wait and see!"

By now Tom's breathing had become short and shallow. A prickly red heat had begun to climb up his neck and face, and a red fog had begun to cloud in around the edges of his vision as he watched the words spew out of Edwards' face, a face that registered contempt for Tom, whom he did not know, as well as contempt for the argument that he himself was manufacturing and putting into Tom's mouth. And mingled with that contempt was a certain pleasure, a bully's pleasure of beating an opponent in a fight while the opponent's hands are securely tied behind his back.

"And you can't get away from these nesters," Edwards was now saying. "I move on to Colorado; here come the nesters. Then to New Mexico, and I'm just waitin' for 'em there." And so Edwards continued on his themes, which were continually adapted in any way to be a personal attack on Tom.

Tom had, by this point, given up on any further attempt to get in a word. It was apparent that, even if he could say anything at this point, it would not really matter. Any opportunity would present but a little opening, and so much had been said and was being said, and he had been so misrepresented, that he would only be able to try to formulate an entire clarification in the single instant that Edwards might allow before he recommenced his ranting. Furthermore, Tom had seen enough to know that any response on his part would be ignored or misconstrued to further the argument that Edwards was blasting forward at his expense for public consumption. Besides, Tom's anger was so aroused that rational reply would have been difficult, at best, even if rational argument had been relevant in this instance.

Eventually a drover came by the table and interrupted Edwards to remind him that he had intended to join that drover's table for a drink. Edwards said his good-byes, not without his parting shots at Tom, then left for the other table with the drover, Edwards loudly describing the misguided thinking of the Yankee greenhorn as they went.

Silence rushed in upon the table, one so vacuous that it created a buzzing in Tom's ears.

Whittacker Dallen, grimacing and unable to raise his eyes to Tom, quietly stuttered, "Tom, I . . . uh . . . am sorry that you were subjected to that."

"That was out of line," added the usually laconic Harvey, shaking his head.

Tom barely heard them. His neck and face still burned prickly hot, his vision remained clouded, his breathing short, and he knew that he must immediately leave the Plaza House. He quickly thanked Dallen for the supper, bid him and Harvey farewell, and made his way out into the evening, in desperate need of less crowded environs to help dissipate his fury.

He stalked east down Front Street through the lively Dodge City nightlife, nearly oblivious to it all, as responses to the Edwards barrage erupted in his mind. In that mind, words still poured out of Edwards' sneer, along with the derision both words and sneer conveyed. "Nigger-lovin' Yankee Republican." Yes, I am! Tom answered in his mind, as he would have liked to answer vocally at the time of accusation, had he been allowed. Yes, he was and proud to be so! A Yankee (not a northeastern but a northwestern one, it was to be understood) by the grace of God and the location of birth and rearing. A Republican by determination, determination based on principles, principles that a man like Henry Edwards would never understand. "Nigger-lovin'" because of those principles, principles that commanded that a man must love his neighbor, and if the Negro was a man, then a neighbor.

"Nigger," how Tom hated the term. All races of men had their representatives of high and low character. He had met intelligent, capable, and genteel black men, and he had met white men with none of those attributes, and he wondered how superior men like Edwards would believe themselves to be had they been the product of generations raised within the conditions of black slavery.

Regardless, "nigger" was a term of choice. One chose to use it or not, and thus chose to accept and convey, or not, all that the term implied. Appropriately then, it was by championing a specious right to choose, under the name of "popular sovereignty," that the Democrat party, in opposition to the Republican, had conveniently absolved itself of making the principled determination on the right or wrong of slavery.

The Republican party, on the other hand, had made that principled determination: in fact, the party had been founded upon that determination. The party had been founded in reaction to Senator Stephen Douglas' Kansas-Nebraska Act. By that law, Douglas, an Illinois Democrat, had sought to repeal the prohibition of slavery in the Louisiana Territory north of 36°30' (a prohibition guaranteed in the Missouri Compromise) in exchange for the southern states' abandonment of their quest for a southern route for a transcontinental railroad so that a midwestern route might be secured. This repeal, with the later help of the Dred Scott decision of the Supreme Court in 1857, had had the effect of dividing the nation over the question of whether or not the residents of a territory had the legal right to exclude slavery from within its boundaries before the formation of a state constitution. President James Buchanan, a Democrat, did little to heal the division when he championed the unpopular pro-slavery Lecompton constitution for Kansas.

The Republican Party had been born amidst this "hell of a storm" that Douglas had predicted his bill would generate. That party had arisen as an antislavery party committed to keeping slavery from extending into the territories, or, as the Republican Abraham Lincoln had put it in his famous House Divided speech in 1857, "to arrest the further spread of it, and place it where the public mind shall rest in the belief that it is in the course of ultimate extinction." Therefore, to preserve the Union, the Republicans would leave slavery alone where it already existed, in the belief that it would eventually die out there, but they would not stand for the extension of slavery. This, of course, had not been acceptable to southerners, who had demanded the right to extend their way of life into the territories, especially those won from Mexico in the controversial war with that nation. Besides that, southerners had not put much faith in the idea that abolitionists would stop at keeping slavery out of the territories. As Jefferson Davis had put it, "Abolitionism would gain but little in excluding slavery from the territories, if it were never to disturb that institution in the States."

Amidst all this, the Democrats had hidden behind their specious right of choice, popular sovereignty, allowing sectional factions to interpret, as they saw fit, whether that right to choose existed only at the time of making up a state constitution, or if it existed while yet the region remained a territory. But Mr. Lincoln had not let Mr. Douglas sit on that fence. At Freeport, Illinois, in 1858, Lincoln had forced the question, and had drawn forth from Douglas an admission that a territory could legally exclude slavery before that territory created a state constitution, putting Douglas at odds with both the South and with the Supreme Court's Dred Scott ruling.

And as for the Dred Scott ruling, that infamous case of judicial activism, it might best be considered in light of an admonition in Mr. Lincoln's first inaugural address:

> If the policy of the government, upon vital questions
> affecting the whole people, is to be irrevocably fixed by

decisions of the Supreme Court, the instant they are made, in ordinary litigation between parties in personal actions, the people will have ceased to be their own rulers, having to that extent practically resigned their government into the hands of that eminent tribunal.

Regardless, it had been nearly four years before Freeport that Mr. Lincoln had forthrightly cut through the Democrats' smokescreen of a right to choose, to get at the moral question that lay at the heart of the choice. In October of 1854, when Stephen Douglas had stopped in Springfield, Illinois, on his campaign to defend the Kansas-Nebraska Act and popular sovereignty, a particular version of the right of self-government, the right to choose slavery, the right to choose to treat another human being as something less than human, Abraham Lincoln had stepped up to challenge him in these words:

> The doctrine of self-government is right, absolutely and eternally right; but it has no just application, as here attempted. Or perhaps I should rather say that whether it has such just application depends upon whether a Negro is not or is a man. If he is not a man, why in that case he who is a man may, as a matter of self-government, do just as he pleases with him. But if the Negro is a man, is it not to that extent a total destruction of self-government to say that he too shall not govern himself? When the white man governs himself, that is self-government; but when he governs himself and also governs another man, that is more than self-government; that is despotism. If the Negro is a man, why then my ancient faith teaches me that "all men are created equal," and that there can be no moral right in connection with one man's making a slave of another.

Yes, his ancient faith, Tom thought, as he himself looked to the profound truths of the Christian faith to conclude the same, but even less than that, even the secular document upon which the nation was founded held "these truths to be self-evident: That all men are created equal; that they are endowed by their Creator with certain unalienable rights; that among these rights are life, liberty, and the pursuit of happiness." That was the strength of the nation: a foundation upon the equality of human persons and the recognition and defense of those unalienable rights endowed by the Creator. Thus, it was clear: if all men were created equal and endowed with the unalienable rights of life, liberty, and the pursuit of happiness, then either the Negro was not a man, or his enslavement had constituted a most heinous offense against his God-given dignity and rights.

The Democrats could not have it both ways, as they hid behind their right to choose, and Lincoln had pressed them on it. And he had been right, Tom demanded. The Negro was either a human being or he was not, at all times, in all conditions, not just when it was convenient for the white man to think him one or not. And if he was a human being, then he deserved, at the very least, freedom, and in justice, he deserved full legal equality with the white man. He deserved his pursuit of happiness.

Life, liberty, and the pursuit of happiness. Let one man's choice infringe upon another's legitimate pursuit of happiness, and it will eventually invade that other man's right to liberty, upon which the pursuit of happiness depends. Let one man's choice infringe upon another's liberty, and it will eventually invade that other man's right to life, upon which liberty, and indeed all other rights, depends. And when, if ever, in this land, it could get to the point that one's choice could supersede another's right to life, Tom would have to concur with Abraham Lincoln again, when, commenting on why he could not be a member of the Know-Nothing party due to its prejudices, he had said, "Our progress in degeneracy appears to me to be pretty rapid."

Yes, Abraham Lincoln, the Republican, of that party that had stood against slavery and for Union, to the point that it had been willing to allow slavery to continue where it was, to later die out of its own accord, so as to avoid the horror of civil war and the hostility that would have been visited upon the black man by the white man if abolition had been forced in that region. But civil war had come, in fulfillment of John Brown's prophecy, "I John Brown am now quite certain that the

crimes of this guilty land will never be purged away; but with blood."
And the war had lasted, leading President Lincoln in his Second
Inaugural Address to expand on that theme with these words:

> "Woe unto the world because of offenses for it
> must needs be that offenses come, but woe to that man
> by whom the offense cometh!" If we shall discern
> therein any departure from those divine attributes
> which suppose that American Slavery is one of those
> offenses which, in the providence of God, must needs
> come, but which, having continued through His
> appointed time, He now wills to remove, and that He
> gives to both North and South this terrible war as the
> woe due to those by whom the offense came, shall we
> discern therein any departure from those divine attrib-
> utes which the believers in a Living God always ascribe
> to Him? Fondly do we hope, fervently do we pray, that
> this mighty scourge of war may speedily pass away. Yet,
> if God wills that it continue until all the wealth piled
> by the bondman's two hundred and fifty years of unre-
> quitted toil shall be sunk, and until every drop of
> blood drawn with the lash shall be paid by another
> drawn with the sword, as was said three thousand years
> ago, so still it must be said, "The judgments of the
> Lord are true and righteous altogether."

And beyond the war, hostility against Negroes had also come. And
just when Mr. Lincoln's talents might have best served his country,
when his wisdom, magnanimity, and compassion might have directed
the forces of his legal, political, and moral acuity and the power he had
gained in office toward effecting a national reconciliation, his life had
been drastically ushered from this world, and the Reconstruction that
could have been had passed with him, to be replaced by that which
had been.

What could have been, Tom thought, as he pondered the loss of
the man of whom Ulysses S. Grant would later write, "I knew his
goodness of heart, his generosity, his yielding disposition, his desire to

have everybody happy, and above all his desire to see all the people of the United States enter again upon the full privileges of citizenship with equality among all." And Tom pondered Lincoln's own words on the matter:

> With malice toward none, with charity for all, with firmness in the right as God gives us to see the right, let us strive on to finish the work we are in, to bind up the nation's wounds, to care for him who shall have borne the battle and for his widow and his orphan, to do all which may achieve and cherish a just and lasting peace among ourselves and with all nations.

Such had not been the Reconstruction that had followed. Still, Reconstruction had had its successes, especially under President Grant, not the least of which were Negro suffrage and the formal education of hundreds of thousands of Negroes. But it had also had its publicized failures, evidenced if in no other way than that, now, after a convoluted presidential election and the ostensible end of Reconstruction, southern Negroes, the Exodusters, were, as Edwards had indicated, fleeing the old South and moving to Kansas to establish homes and colonies.

Regardless of its failures and imperfections, a result of having been created and animated by human beings with their own failures and imperfections, the Republican party had been founded to stand up for the unalienable rights of those who were powerless to demand them for themselves. How did Tom know this? He knew because Peter Schurtz, his father, a devout, practically religious German-immigrant farmer, had taught him. Peter Schurtz had hated slavery because he had believed his Christian faith demanded it, and because he had come to the United States, and had loved that nation even before he had come, for its great promise of freedom. For those reasons, he had rallied to the Republican party, in their home-state of Wisconsin, almost from its inception in the Northwest. He had been a Republican and had joined in that party's cry of "Free Soil, Free Labor, Free Men." And he had been a Lincoln man, even before Lincoln had become a Republican. He had first learned of Lincoln by reading newspaper accounts of his response to Douglas's defense of Kansas-Nebraska in

1854, and he had told his Irish wife, Aileen, that it would only be a matter of time before Mr. Lincoln would become a Republican. He had been right, proudly so, and had taken even more pride in reading from newspapers, or any other source, any shred of anything his protégé (for that was what Mr. Lincoln had become with the realization of Peter Schurtz's prediction) had written or spoken. And he would read them to his wife, and he would read them to his children, particularly Thomas, his oldest boy, who at an early age had an appreciation for language and was soon reading and memorizing, to his father's delight, excerpts from Mr. Lincoln's speeches.

Tom could still see his father reading the president's first inaugural address, pounding his fist on the arm of his chair and saying, "Dat's rrright, Dat's rrright," in his heavy German accent, as he read out loud:

> In your hands, my dissatisfied fellow countrymen, and not in mine, is the momentous issue of civil war. The government will not assail you. You can have no conflict without being yourselves the aggressors. You have no oath registered in heaven to destroy the government, while I shall have the most solemn one to "preserve, protect and defend it."
>
> I am loath to close. We are not enemies, but friends. We must not be enemies. Though passion may have strained, it must not break our bonds of affection. The mystic chords of memory, stretching from every battlefield and patriot grave to every living heart and hearthstone all over this broad land, will yet swell the chorus of the Union when again touched, as surely they will be, by the better angels of our nature.

But passion had broken the bonds of affection, and Mr. Lincoln had called for troops. Peter Schurtz had answered the call of his protégé president. And at Missionary Ridge, on November 25, 1863, Peter Schurtz had given "the last full measure of devotion," when Tom was thirteen years old. Peter Schurtz had fought and died for his country, an adopted country in which he had found the freedom to worship God, who was the center of his life, and to raise his family and provide for their welfare

in freedom. He had fought and died to prevent that nation's suicide and
to rid it of a great fundamental evil at the foundation of its suicidal inclination. He had died believing these sentiments Mr. Lincoln had
expressed to Congress in making his case for emancipation:

> We know how to save the Union. The world knows
> we know how to save it. We—even *we here*—hold the
> power, and bear the responsibility. In *giving* freedom to
> the *slave*, we *assure* freedom to the *free*—honorable
> alike in what we give, and what we preserve. . . . Other
> means may succeed; this could not fail. The way is
> plain, peaceful, generous, just—a way which, if fol-
> lowed, the world will forever applaud, and God must
> forever bless.

Peter Schurtz had died for love: love of God, and love of neighbor—in family, friends, and strangers he would never meet. He had
died for love of country, that country that had assured him the freedom to practice love. He had died for those and lesser virtues, truths,
and principles, and the thought of a self-centered brute like Henry
Edwards trampling over those virtues, truths, and principles galled
Tom exceedingly.

And, in his mind, Tom let Henry Edwards know that he was no
"greenhorn." He had taken over the role of man of the family and farm
at age twelve, when his father had left for war, and had assumed it with
greater conviction when he had learned that his father would not
return, and had continued in that role until he was sixteen. At that age,
he had passed on that role to his brother John, one year Tom's junior,
and had left Wisconsin with his Irish uncle to work his way west on a
railroad construction gang, sending money home, as did his bachelor
uncle, to his widowed mother and seven siblings. After the connection
at Promontory Point, he had worked on the Denver Pacific, and after
that, he had worked at other construction projects in the fast-growing
city of Denver. He had returned east for a while, but by 1873, he was
in Texas, working in the cattle business, and had been ever since.

And Tom was no socialist! He had strong reservations about any
attempt to revive the income tax. An income tax, especially a graduated

income tax, was clearly unconstitutional, and the government had only resorted to it in 1861 as a war measure, one that had been extended until it had finally ended in 1872. And to suggest that it was Lincoln's income tax was to ignore the substantial roles played by such legislators as Thaddeus Stevens, Justin S. Morrill, Augustus Frank, William P. Fesenden, J.B. Grinnell, and, later, John Sherman and Robert C. Schenck in the inception and perpetuation of the tax. It had been a deviation from law to support the deviation of war caused by the deviation of slavery. As such, it had been appropriate because citizens were called on to sacrifice everything, even their lives, in times of defense of the nation. But Tom had serious reservations about whether an income tax was acceptable for any nation of free men, especially this nation of free men, as the Constitution did not allow for it. Direct taxes were forbidden by the Constitution unless they were apportioned among the states according to population. This prohibition protected property rights and assured equality under law, even in taxation.

In its recent experimentation with an income tax, the country had had a taste of the threat such a tax posed to private property. For that reason, it was no surprise that communists and socialists advocated the income tax as a means for the state to usurp property rights toward the goal of the destruction of private property. In contrast, the strength of the United States was a foundation upon the equality of human persons and the recognition and defense of their unalienable rights, among which were "life, liberty, and the pursuit of happiness." In light of this strength, Tom's opposition to an income tax was related to his earlier opposition to slavery. Did not free men have the right to dispose of the fruits of their labors as they saw fit, rather than to have them confiscated by a government, especially in a country that had been founded upon a distinct distrust of government? Had not Jefferson, or one of the founding fathers, said, "That government that governs least governs best"? Thus, it was clear that the implications associated with an income tax included not only the confiscation of private property by the government but (in order to make such a confiscation acceptable, if not legal) an attack upon the very rights protected by the Constitution. Protected, not granted, as human beings "are endowed by their Creator with certain unalienable rights," and are not so endowed by any construction of men. Furthermore, experience had provided enough evidence to support Representative Justin S. Morrill's assertion that a graduated income tax "tends to undermine public morals," and that it "cannot be justified on any sound principle of morals. It can only be justified on the same ground that the highwayman defends his acts."

Again Tom bristled at the memory of Henry Edwards labeling him a socialist and lumping homesteading with an income tax as another socialist policy he would support. Of course he agreed that income taxation tended toward socialism and communism, and because of that, he tended to oppose it because he was opposed to socialism and communism. But Tom's mind was not going to construct the full argument for that opposition now. Instead, his mind was already examining the policy of homesteading, as he understood it, in light of Edwards' implication that it too was socialistic. In truth, Tom habitually considered himself insufficiently informed on any topic unless his knowledge of it was exhaustive, and because of that habit, he considered himself insufficiently informed on the historical debate over homesteading. Accordingly, he resented Edwards publicly portraying him as a champion of the policy. Tom merely found the policy an attractive one, at his level of understanding of that policy, in contrast to his finding the truly socialistic income tax unattractive. Tom's mind now examined why.

In the case of an income tax, he reasoned, the government laid claim to and confiscated private property from its citizens. In the case of homesteading, the government made available public property, not confiscated from its citizens, to those citizens who could benefit from it and were willing and able to improve the land and bring forth its produce to augment the production of the nation. The government did not retain ownership of the land, but turned over ownership to the private citizen after the citizen had earned it and, in the process, proven himself suited and worthy to own it, benefiting the nation in the process. Thus, whereas through an income tax the government confiscated private property, through homesteading the government created private property by distributing parcels of the public domain to those who earned them.

And, after all, was not the United States of America a nation of people in a geographic area with a system of government devised by that people: "We the people of the United States of America." The land did not belong to the government: it belonged to the nation, a nation of people. The representative government of that nation, that "government of the people, by the people, for the people," merely fulfilled the role of administering the nation's public land. Since the land of the nation belonged to the people of the nation, and since the land in question did not belong to any particular citizens, why not make it available to the greatest number of citizens or potential citizens (especially those without the capital to purchase it) who would earn ownership of it by improving that land and making a living from it, toward the end of making them productive, propertied citizens? Why not, where it was feasible, open the land to ownership by those citizens who would prove their worthiness to so own through their commitments of time and effort and their achieved improvement of the land? If an applicant could not improve it, could not make it, then he did not earn the property. The property would be open for another to attempt to earn. This process would continue until those who earned ownership of the land were those most suited to inhabiting and making a living from it. It was an investment of the nation in itself, to place upon the land those most suited to bring forth its produce.

Was it not in the best interest of the nation to place upon the nation's land the greatest number of deserving people who could benefit from it, rather than allow the land to be concentrated in monopolies by persons or entities? Did it not give more citizens a stake in the nation, give them more reason to participate as free citizens? And this was not a giveaway. It was a sale, in which those with little or no capital could purchase land through their labor by "proving up." And it would not contribute to dependence but to independence, as those who earned it were awarded ownership. And it was Republican. Though the roots of homesteading were older than the Republican party and could be traced back to a proposal by Thomas Hart Benton in 1825, and even further back to Thomas Jefferson, who had said, "as few as possible should be without a little parcel of land," it was the Republicans who had made it law. It had been a plank in the Republican party platform, and Republican Galusha Grow of Pennsylvania had authored the homestead bill that President Lincoln had signed into law in 1862. Lincoln had succinctly said of the policy, "I am in favor of cutting the wild lands into parcels, so that every poor man may have a home."

Still, Tom knew that the policy and law had their problems. Edwards was right: small farms farther west were impractical because the land was more suited to grazing, and large tracts of land would be needed to graze stock on it to any advantage. At least that was the case for the present, but he also knew that irrigation and improved varieties of crops might change that. Regardless, even if some land would always be best suited to open range, such realities could be taken into consideration, and the policy adjusted to accommodate them.

Nevertheless, Tom was fairly certain that Henry Edwards' vitriolic reaction to the subject of homesteading had a deeper foundation that went back to his days in the South before the war. It had not been until 1862, with the South out of the Congress, that a homesteading bill could be passed. Homesteading had been opposed by the South before the war because many southerners had been afraid that Edwards' "white niggers," his "Yankee mechanics," "grangers," and "foreigners" would populate those lands open to homesteading and thereby create antislavery majorities in the territories. This had tied the issue indirectly to the Democrats' popular-sovereignty doublespeak. It would have made little difference whether the northern-Democrat or southern-Democrat interpretation of popular sovereignty had prevailed, if northern industrial workers, northern farmers, and immigrants could have flooded into the territories as homesteaders and created anti-slavery majorities there. Even though statehood would have required the approval of Congress, southern legislators could have held back the force of those majorities only so long. The balance of slave states to free states would have been disrupted, sooner or later, and abolitionists would have gained more power toward the abolition of slavery in the South, further threatening the southern way of life. This, of course, had become a moot point with the election of the Republican Lincoln, pledged to disallow the extension of slavery into the territories, and the subsequent attempted secession of southern states. The war that had followed had allowed for the settling of the homesteading question, though it had hardly done away with the passions involved in it.

And passions had certainly animated Henry Edwards' defense of open range. But open range could not last forever across the expanse of the territories, Tom maintained. And from that perspective, Tom would have argued that the buffalo and the Indians had not been wasting the land, as Edwards had claimed. Theirs had been a different relationship to the land, which had served them well for a long period of time. Obviously, things had changed and the past was the past. Still, the future would depend upon what people learned from the past. Tom believed it foolishness to banish and disregard the wisdom of the people who knew the land better than any others, even if, in different circumstances, one might reach different conclusions about how the land would best be used. The Plains Indians had had a different land use. Theirs had been a different ethic. They had lived a nomadic life based on the migrations of the buffalo. Still, Tom would have questioned the notion, often proposed, that the Indians had not subscribed to an idea of ownership of the land. Though they may not have recognized private ownership of the land, had they not recognized ownership of the land, albeit of a communal nature, when competing peoples had fought bloody wars for the right to control various hunting, planting, or holy lands? Certain lands had been known as the lands of certain peoples. And, in some instances, one people had displaced another from its ancestral lands, as the Comanche had done to the Apache.

Similarly, the Indians' land use had been displaced by the land use of the more numerous peoples coming from abroad, who eventually established a new nation, from which their land use continued to displace that of the Indians as the newcomers grew increasingly more numerous and pushed ever farther beyond their former frontiers. It had been an ugly displacement with little assimilation, as such displacements throughout history have often been, with acts of treachery and savagery committed by those of the displacing land use and those of the land use displaced. Tom felt deep regret and shame over the way that much of that displacement had occurred, at the thought of massacres of even women and children, at the thought of ancient cultures destroyed, at the thought of the wanton, greedy, and wasteful destruction of the millions and millions of buffalo. (Unbeknownst to Tom, as he entertained these very thoughts, the three-month retreat to Canada by the Nez Perce under Chief Joseph was already underway in the Pacific Northwest.) Nevertheless, this regret was tempered, if only somewhat, by the personal knowledge of atrocities committed against white people by Indians and the acknowledgment that the land use of the Indians could not long be sustained in light of the filling of the land with more people. Regardless, Tom could not help but think that had virtue been more operative, even on one side only, it might have gone very differently.

Open range was one of the land uses that had displaced the more primitive nomadic land use of the Indians. But open range was not all that far removed from what it had displaced. Though open range did rely on domesticated cattle rather than the wild buffalo, the degrees of domestication of the Spanish and even the Texas cattle were not over-whelming. And although these cattle were owned and herded rather than hunted, they wandered far and wide and were hunted often enough. Open range also had its own nomadic, migratory character, though on a smaller, more individualistic scale than that of the Indians' land use. As such, open range would, in its time, need to give way to systems that would make more efficient use of the land to accommodate the growing population of the growing nation. As citizens of that nation, a distinction that had not restricted the Indians, open-range advocates would have to accept that. They could accept it as less a policy imposed by the government, that government of the people, than as a natural evolution in land use. And, in the case of open range, the citi-zens had every right to demand a change in land use because the land did not yet belong to any private citizen but was owned by the entire nation. In effect, open range (free grass) was subsidized by the citizens of the nation because it was as much their land that was being used as it was the grazers' who were using it. If, on the other hand, open-range cattlemen wanted to rent, lease, buy, or otherwise obtain legal rights to the land, especially that land best suited to grazing alone, and then graze their stock on it, let them do so.

"Buy rangeland!" Tom could just hear, in his mind, Henry Edwards shout those words as he would launch into another rant about how the land belonged to the open-range cattlemen. No, it didn't, Tom shouted back mentally; Henry Edwards merely wanted to use public lands with-out renting, leasing, or buying those lands. So, who was the socialist?

And Tom did realize that open range might be the only practical land use of some of the more rugged regions of the West. Where that was the case, so be it.

Such was the stream of thought that flowed through Tom's mind, a rapids, really, formed by the convergence of various tributary responses, sprung up in reaction to the Edwards barrage. Tom's mind had gushed out this rapids of thought as he had stalked through the busy street, alone in the crowds within his shell of anger, and had continued to gush after he had found himself out at the stockyards east of town. Once or twice he had caught himself forming the words of his responses with his lips and giving low voice to them, but he had checked himself. Now at the stockyards, as his mind kept churning through its reaction, he paced along the pens amidst the bawling of the cattle being held there to be shipped the next day. As he paced, the face of Henry Edwards loomed up in his mind, mixing in its features the man's contempt for Tom and his enjoyment of using Tom as an object at which he could hurl his vitriol for public consumption.

Tom knew that he could have articulated well enough his true responses to Henry Edwards in a rational and reasonable discussion, and that he would have been more than willing to listen to any reasonable responses that might have come from Edwards. Instead, Edwards had stifled any response he might have made, time after time talking over him to put arguments in his mouth that he would not have made. The man had misrepresented him and mischaracterized him with ad hominem attack. He had done so purposely and publicly to vent his long-lived and self-augmenting anger, to expose the error of positions opposed to his own, and to publicly denounce and humiliate their personification in Tom, however erroneous that personification might have been. And Tom was sure, too, that it had done nothing to lessen his suitability as a target for an Edwards' attack, that he, Tom, a young, fresh-faced (Tom looked younger than his years, all cleaned and shaved) cowhand would be sitting at table, alone, with a well-known cattleman like Whittacker Dallen and his respected boss-foreman Harvey Chapel. Who was Tom to be sitting and conversing on a par with such men as these? Hence, Henry Edwards had put the greenhorn in his place, and it galled Tom that he had been so used.

So used. There was the cowman's face again, the words spewing out, in loud voice, pouring out all over Tom and over the whole room at Tom's expense, loud and misrepresenting and wrong, and Tom would not have it. And so, he struck out. With his fist he punched hard and fast into one of the corral posts. The post was stout, and though the blow was enough to make some of the beeves back into the rest and rile them up a bit, it did little to the pen, except to leave a couple of knuckle prints in the face of the post. To Tom's fist, though, it did a bit more. The instant the blow struck, pain radiated from the large knuckle out all over his hand and up his arm. Tom cussed and shook his fist once or twice, but he refused to be mastered by this pain, the product of his anger and its servant stupidity, and he stalked off along the pens with gritted teeth, through which he released a few muffled grunts.

The blow and its resultant pain did its part, nonetheless, to help dissipate Tom's fury, and Tom was soon directing his steps back into town. Determinedly and skillfully he made his way through the throngs of cowboys. Though his fury had dissipated some, his mind still churned over the incident with Edwards. In time he arrived at Bridge Street, and he stopped and glanced up the street in the direction of the Krause House. For a moment he let a thought of Marta Krause cut through the churning over Henry Edwards, but the churning returned, and he let his head drop to look into the dirt. Again, Marta Krause entered his thoughts, and again he looked north up Bridge Street, but he could not hold it. Edwards returned and he let him stay. He turned, and with his back toward the Krause House, he walked south.

IT WAS ABOUT TEN O'CLOCK when Tom stepped across the threshold of the Lady Gay. The lazy, sun-lighted ambience of that afternoon had been transformed into the raucous, lamp-lighted atmosphere of a Dodge City dancehall at night.

Tom worked his way to the bar past the crowded gambling tables and through the sea of patrons congregated around them. At the bar, he eventually caught the attention of the barkeeper and shouted out an order for beer over the cacophony of band music, gambling calls, and all variety of shouting, laughter, and conversation. Shortly, Tom and the barkeeper were exchanging beer for money over the heads of the people at the bar.

Beer in hand, Tom started toward where he had been sitting earlier that day. As he worked through the crowd, he bumped into one cowboy who was leaning against the bar on his elbows. The man turned and looked over his shoulder and let his piercing dark eyes stab his annoyance into Tom. Tom saw in those eyes an intensity that, were it to erupt in anger, could bode no good for him. Nevertheless, Tom let his own eyes stab back the anger presently behind them, despite the injury it had already caused to his fist. In this way, the two men faced each other, locked for a moment in reciprocal stares of animosity, poised on the brink of the hostile activity which must ensue. Tom's muscles tensed as he readied himself for what must come, fully intending to give it his best. And then, suddenly, he saw a change take place in the eyes of the stranger. Though anger smoldered in the intensity found there, rather than erupt, it gave way, haltingly at first, to recognition, and then, all at once and completely, to elation, which did erupt with all the intensity that the anger had promised in potential.

"Tom!" the cowboy sang out, as he raised himself up from the bar and swung around, throwing his right hand out and bringing it back in, with force, to take a firm grasp of Tom's left shoulder.

"Bob!" Tom answered in his own level of intensity upon recognizing the intense one, though there should be little wonder that the recognition on his part was not immediate, for this was a transformed Bob Huber. Bob was the *segundo* of a neighboring outfit in south Texas that had sent some beeves and herders north with the Dallen outfit. He and Tom had ridden together for months, and both were accustomed to the appearance of the other as they had last seen each other. Since then, Tom had had a bath, shave, haircut, and was bedecked in a new outfit. Bob's transformation, though on the same order, was of a different magnitude altogether. The eyes, of course, were the same, but the lean, tanned, sculpted face, with its high cheekbones, had been shorn of its trail beard and was no longer framed by the fine straight blond-brown hair that had grown out on the trail. That hair had been neatly cut and trimmed up short above his ears. Still, neither the shaved face nor the cut hair qualified as the most notable feature of this transformation.

The most notable feature of the Bob Huber transformation was not really a single feature but more of an ensemble of two features, which offered an effect that made it difficult to separate the two. Both of these features, and their ensemble effect, can only be fully appreciated when contrasted to what they had replaced.

Starting from the top, Bob Huber had always been readily recognizable, even at some distance, by his weathered and distinctive plainsman hat. That variety of hat had a wide brim and low crown, and was typically nondistinctive. Not so Bob's.

Bob had developed a certain loyalty to his hat and would never fail to tout its advantages whenever challenged to do so. He had even been known to come to blows in defense of that esteemed piece of headgear. Such loyalty makes for long relationships, and as other cowboys would routinely replace their hats upon receiving their pay at the end of a drive, Bob would have none of such infidelity. Instead, he would have his hat cleaned and brushed up and treated with whatever application he was convinced would assure the hat's longevity, often visiting several establishments, including saddle shops and boot shops, until he had found the place and the person who would ensure the kind of treatment the hat deserved. But all such treatment had merely postponed the inevitable. In time, the plainsman had grown more faded and frayed. Its brim had drooped more and more, and had threatened to separate from the crown, and had actually begun to do so by the end of the most recent drive. The dents from hailstones had become more difficult to punch out, and the protection from hail and from the rays of the sun had increasingly diminished, particularly as more hailstones had succeeded in perforating the crown.

Such was the hat of Bob Huber. Nevertheless, on this memorable night, at the bar of the Lady Gay, in July of 1877, there was no sign to be found of the noted headpiece on or about Bob Huber's person. Instead, in its place, on the top of Bob's head—well, in truth, on more than just the top of his head, as it comfortably settled its way down the sides to his ears and down the back to his neck, especially pushed back as it was—sat a giant, bright-white felt sombrero, festively ornamented with a band of white-stitched red felt all around the edge of its extensive brim.

There was no mistaking it: it was Bob beneath all that hat. There were the dark eyes, now nearly sparkling, and the high cheekbones, now crowded with flesh, as, since recognition, the flesh of the face had been pulled up in one of the largest smiles Tom had ever come to know, and with as straight and white a set of teeth as would be appropriate for such a distinction. Yes sir, Bob Huber smiled with as much intensity as he did everything else.

And there, above the teeth of that smile, could be found the other of the two features that had so transformed Bob Huber. There upon

Bob's upper lip, where formerly had hung his long, dark, bushy moustache, sat a neatly trimmed version of the same, but one in which both
ends had been waxed and shaped to extend outward and up and
around, so as to form nothing less than what might be termed
curlicues, and large ones at that. The effect on Tom, of this whole picture—the familiar face, with its familiar, remarkable smile, beneath the
monstrous hat, and fitted with the outrigger curlicues—was nothing
short of a kind of shock, a shock which he could not hide, even after
he had recovered from its initial effects.

This shock did not go unnoticed by Bob Huber, and far from displaying any kind of disappointment because of it, the flesh of his face seemed
to pull up even higher than would have seemed possible, exposing even
more than would have seemed possible of those straight, white teeth.

He dropped his hand from Tom's shoulder and stepped back as
much as the tight space would allow. "Whadda ya think?" he said, in
the distinctive way he had of taking whole, rounded sounds and tones
and giving them definition in a sharp edge. "I gotta new hat!"

The size of Tom's eyes, large enough now to take in the whole hat,
still betrayed his shock. Bob's remarkable teeth separated, top from
bottom, as his smile gave way to a wide-open-mouthed laugh, which
surprisingly had little sound to it other than a dry, sharp, low, "hah,
hah, hah, hah."

Tom nodded his head cautiously, and finally said, "That's some
hat, Bob."

"Hah, hah, hah, hah."

"What did you do with the old plainsman, Bob?" Tom inquired
in a sort of reflex, almost regretting he had asked the question once it
was out.

But Bob showed no sensitivity to the subject and, with smile still
firmly intact, responded, "Buried it."

"Buried it?" Tom echoed.

"With all the solemnity the occasion demanded," Bob assured
him. "Right up there on Boot Hill," he continued, still smiling, with
a nod in the direction off Tom's right shoulder. "Gene was there, and
lent his hand to the interment."

At this mention of his partner's name, Bob swung around to a
blond man leaning onto the bar next to him. The man was turned

away from them, speaking quite intimately with a pretty young woman with light brown hair who stood against the bar to his left. Bob hit the man's right shoulder with the back of his hand and called out his name.

"Gene."

The man turned from the woman and directed his broad, though well-cut, face their way.

"Say hello to Tom, here."

"Tom!" Gene said as he raised himself from the bar and stuck out his hand.

"Gene," Tom said as he shook the hand of Eugene Heath, Bob's partner. Though of about the same height as Bob (which was about the same height as Tom) Gene had a broader, more squarish frame than Bob. Regardless, his physique did not exhibit the disciplined leanness of Bob's. Still, Gene could work hard, when pushed, and under the same circumstances could prove exceptionally strong.

Bob and Gene worked for the same outfit, though not for long, Tom thought, as he knew Bob had been building a herd of his own, with his boss's permission, and before long would be in business for himself. Gene might well go to work for Bob at that point, Tom thought, because the two had been partners for years. Tom found it hard to imagine Gene making his way through life without Bob's guidance and tutelage. It had been some time since Tom had seen Gene, as Gene had trailed north with a different drive while Bob had been trailing north with the Dallen outfit, overseeing the interests of his boss and himself. On that drive, Bob had readily recognized Harvey Chapel's authority as trailboss and Tom's authority as *segundo*. For their part, Harvey and Tom had not wasted Bob's talents, experience, drive, and discipline, never failing to rely on him as situations warranted.

All well and good, but the relevant point, for the time being, was that the two partners had been separated. And now, after months apart on the trail, they were reunited, and Tom knew the two well enough to know that Dodge City would feel the effects of their reunion. According to custom, after drinking their share of liquor, the two would generally devise their own unique brand of shenanigans, like burying hats and obtaining a curlicue moustache and oversized sombrero. Then they would drink some more and possibly shoot some lights out or try to ride a horse into a south-side saloon or something along that order. If, after that, they still had not been taken in—not without a fight on their part—to the calaboose, Gene would drift toward the gambling and the women, spending a good deal of what he had been paid before Bob could convince him to save it. (For Bob Huber, except for celebrations like these at trail's end, was a frugal man, and honest, too. It was a certainty that the day after his revelry he would make his way around to pay for any damages thereby incurred.)

Bob, on the other hand, would steal off to some quiet place where he would write a letter in Spanish to his Mexican wife, Lucia, who since their marriage had served as the cook at the ranch, near Corpus Christi, where he worked. Bob had learned Spanish, through assiduous study, after he had first met Lucia, intent on courting her and winning her hand. This was typical of Bob, this disciplined approach to accomplishing a task to which he had committed himself. It was due to that same discipline, Tom believed, that when Bob decided to cut loose, he did so with gusto.

And now, Tom too was about to feel the effects of that gusto, as Bob and Gene immediately drew him up to the bar and ordered him a drink, putting his beer to the side to serve as a chaser. Tom knew that it was not in his best interest to long associate with the partners in their present state. Still, he accepted the drink, as to do anything else would have smacked of gross ingratitude to those two gentlemen.

Tom's moderating influence on the pair had the effect of slowing their consumption of spirits. For that reason, they were only into their second drink together, when Bob, delivering a vocal dissertation on why his particular sombrero was the optimal hat to replace the recently interred plainsman, suddenly stopped short. It was a reference to that former apotheosis of headwear that had brought about this interruption of his thesis. Suddenly, seemingly oblivious to Tom's presence, Bob stood up straight and reached across Tom's back, as Tom still leaned against the bar, and shook Gene by the shoulder.

"Hey, Gene."

Gene had returned his attention to the young woman who stood at the bar to his left. At Bob's interruption, he turned his head Bob's way.

"We never did put up that marker, up at the grave," Bob said calmly, but with a seriousness that he might have used if he were telling Gene that a flood had just washed away the chuck wagon. "We forgot the marker."

Gene looked down at the bar for a moment, and Tom, now turned toward him, watched him to see what his reaction would be.

"You're right, Bob," he finally said, as much to the top of the bar as to Bob. "You're dead right. We plumb forgot the marker." So saying, Gene stood up straight to face Bob across Tom's back.

Bob continued in the same serious vein, not without a little mix of wonder. "We were on our way down to find us a board fittin' for the service, and we got sidetracked when you had that altercation with that muleskinner."

"You're right, Bob," Gene concurred, rubbing his chin at the point where the altercation had become physical.

"We were on our way to find a board for a marker," Bob said.

"That's right."

"Well, I think we ought to go, then," Bob concluded matter-of-factly.

"I think you're right," Gene agreed.

Bob then turned his curlicues and sombrero brim on Tom. "We're goin' to have to be leavin', Tom."

Tom straightened up and turned his back to the bar, so as to address both men. He indicated that he understood. He shook hands with the two men and bid them well. Then Gene said his good-bye to the young woman, with assurances that he would return, and the partners waded through the sea of patrons to exit the establishment, Bob's new hat clearing the way for the following Gene.

Tom considered himself fairly lucky to have escaped the encounter with only two drinks. He reached around and took up his beer, which was still cool. As he did so, the young lady who had been talking to Gene now turned her affections on Tom, but he politely declined them and again bumped along through the crowd, behind those leaning against the bar, toward where he had been sitting earlier that day.

The chair in which he had been sitting had since been moved to accommodate one of those patrons engaged in games of chance at the tables. It would have mattered little because the spot where he had been sitting was occupied by a standing patron, as was almost every inch of the area around that patron. Tom worked past these individuals to a spot beyond the window, where he found a vacant piece of wall. There he leaned, sipped his beer, and ran his eyes over the interior of the Lady Gay and those gathered within her.

The assemblage was a varied lot. Men outnumbered women about two or three to one. The Texas cowboys made up the single largest category of those men, though to try to find uniformity of appearance among that class would have been a challenge. Tall, short, thin, stout, dark, or fair they were. Some wore full suits, others, parts of suits, whether it be the pants, coat, vest, or tie. If they wore but a part of a suit, often enough it matched not at all with any other part of their outfit. Vests were common, and coats nearly as common. For pants, the cowboys wore wool trousers or jeans designed to stand up to the rigors of their work. Below the pants might be seen shoes or boots, laced or unlaced. Above it all, these outfits were topped off with hats that included plainsmen, Montana peaks, sombreros, bowlers, and even a top hat or two. Many of these outfits were new, purchased with the cowboy's trail-end pay. For some, many of whom looked like little more than boys—often enough because they were only boys—this pay might have been the first they had ever earned of any real quantity, though it was little enough for all the work it remunerated.

These cowboys ranged in age, as well, from those mere boys to gray-haired and gray-whiskered gentlemen, who looked far older than their spryness, particularly on the dance floor, would indicate. (In such cases, that spryness combined with their weathered, gray appearance to make these old cowboys look almost ageless.) Though the hair of the average cowboy, of any age, in the hall was neatly clipped, due to recent trips to the barber, still there were some men who declined the barber's arts and kept their hair long. Whiskers came in sundry arrangements or were missing altogether. Plenty of men were clean-shaven who had not been before they had arrived in town. Many others had retained a moustache, though they were otherwise clean-shaven. A smaller number kept beards of various styles and thicknesses.

Other men present included muleskinners and bullwhackers, often enough a burly and profane (at least in language) class, who were less particular about the appearance of their outfits than were the Texas cowboys. There were cowmen, as well, dressed as often in full suits as in work clothes, and yet, when in full suits, still easily distinguishable from the more polished, suited cattle buyers, also present. Full suits, bowlers or top hats, and fine polished boots bedecked the dandies or dudes, who were very often gamblers or confidence men. Other men included various visitors to town (land speculators, surveyors, hunters, passers-through) and the men of the town, whose descriptions ran the gamut. There were some soldiers from Fort Dodge present, though soldiers often enough avoided the establishment (and many other such in Dodge), so as to avoid fights with Texas cowboys and their repercussions, which would do nothing to help them keep or advance their stations in the army.

The women were as varied in shape and size as the men. Generally, they were young to middle-aged. Still, there were a handful who were at least pushing the boundaries of middle age and attempting, with liberally applied cosmetics, to appear younger than they were. In dress, most of the women wore gingham or calico dresses, of assorted colors, that reached to the ankle or floor and had a formfitting bodice, a tight neck, and tight sleeves that reached to the elbows or wrists. Some wore earrings, and some wore necklaces on the outside of the closed necks of their dresses. Most wore their long hair up behind the backs of their heads. A few wore hats of their own, and a few others wore hats belonging to cowboys.

This initial survey of the room instinctively singled out and drew Tom's attention to one of the women present. She sat at a table across the room from him with her back toward him. Although he could not see her face, something about her continued to draw his attention, even as he glanced about the room at its many attractions. Perhaps it was the long mane of chocolate-colored hair that was pulled up behind her head, or the posture of her slender, shapely back and her long, slender neck that captivated him, or the way that she effortlessly moved in her chair as she raised her slender arm to rest her chin upon her slender hand. Who could know? What could be known was that Tom's attention kept coming back to her and eventually settled on her, even though he still had not seen her face. That was soon to change.

A man sitting next to her, of the dandy class, threw in his cards at the end of a hand and turned to say something to her. Then they both rose and turned from the table and started toward the dance floor. As she stood, Tom could see that she was taller than average and indeed slender, though shapely. She wore an ankle-length, light-colored dress that contrasted pleasantly with her dark skin. The dress's high collar, formfitting bodice, and tight, elbow-length sleeves nicely complemented her figure. It was obvious, even from across the room, that hers was of a higher quality than the dresses of most of the other women present. A pair of elegant, high-heeled, laced-up dress boots showed beneath the hem of her skirts. As she turned, she glanced in Tom's direction, and in an instant, something seemed to register with her, something, perhaps, not unlike what had registered with Tom upon his first sight of her. Tom was struck by how very pretty her face appeared in the lamplight at that distance, with her fine brows arched above the dark eyes that had flashed his way. There was that slenderness again, or was it length?—but she was not unusually tall—or was it just a rare and natural gracefulness that made her appear weightless as she glided toward the dance floor, her swanlike neck accentuated by the rich silken arrangement pulled up above it? Whatever it was, to Tom it seemed that the elegance she conveyed could not have contrasted more with her surroundings.

Tom would have found it difficult to pull his attention away from this woman, had he been trying. Instead, he accepted his beguilement and wondered at it. What was it about this creature that drew and held his eyes, confused his mind, quickened his pulse, and weakened his limbs? What was it that held his attention so?—this different kind of attention stirred up by a beautiful woman, this attention of more than just the eyes and the mind but of the whole person drawn toward the object of that attention, drawn right out of the heart, though it could not be love, not at this superficial stage. Was it this particular assortment of physical traits, blended together in delicate proportions, as they were, to render this singular embodiment of woman? Whatever it was, the attraction had to be of a shallow nature, given the circumstances. The fascination she held for him—and most likely for a good many other men—fell somewhere outside the realm of reason, or perhaps, instead, took reason into a realm in which its powers of control and definition failed, and in which it fell into a confused subjugation to impressions, feelings, and instincts that left it swimming in a sea of irrationality.

Of course, the degree to which this fascination succeeded in taking reason into such a contradictory realm relied, in no small part, on the willingness of the free rational man to allow his reason to be so taken. Though it cannot be known exactly to what degree this fascination succeeded with Tom's reason, it is worth noting that Tom would later admit that, at that moment, the Henry Edwards incident was completely dispelled, if only temporarily, from his mind.

Tom watched her for a while, as she danced with her partner out on the dance floor, and he had the distinct impression that she was glancing at him whenever her position in the quadrille allowed it. If he was correct in this, and not imagining it, she was not being at all bashful in directing her attention his way.

Regardless, the Charley Lawson orchestra played on, and Tom sipped slowly on his beer, enjoying the lively activity going on all around him. Eventually, he caught sight of a chair being vacated, and he grabbed it, pulled it over against the wall, and sat down on it. From where he was seated, he was able to watch a poker game being played at the table in front of him, and as the stakes mounted, so did his interest. He was fairly absorbed in the game when a feminine voice invaded his concentration.

"Would you like to dance?" asked the voice, which was a little higher than average but softened by a slight huskiness. He turned to look at the woman in the light-colored dress whom he had been watching, now standing to his right.

"Uh," he said as he stared at the woman, in a way that gave a hint as to the state of his reason at that moment. Then recovering himself, he stood, nodded slightly, touched his hat with his left hand, and added, "Yes, I would." He then raised his beer with his right hand and said, "Let me just finish this off," which he did. Then he left the beer mug on the window sill and turned to face her. With the touch of a feather, she took his hand in hers and led him to the dance floor, where they flowed right into a waltz already underway.

Dancing had been a part of Tom's education that he had furthered in Denver and elsewhere, and it showed. His sure steps artfully guided her graceful form around the floor. When the music stopped (not long after Tom and the woman had entered the dance) to allow the players and dancers a rest, Tom and the woman stood facing each other.

She was about in her mid twenties and much prettier up close, almost too pretty to be real. Her features were fine, almost delicate. She needed no cosmetics, nor did she wear any. Her skin was of a darker hue than average, but it was a soft, light-brown hue with almost a glow to it. It was flawless, except for one small, faded scar, on her cheek under her left eye, that almost added to her beauty due to the contrast. The light from the wall lamp, which brought out the glow of her skin, also deepened the natural redness of her lips, and caught her chocolate hair, too, highlighting the soft strands that fell loose over her neck. The light caught her dark eyes, as well, and sparkled in them: those eyes that now looked into Tom's own.

"Would you like to sit down?" she asked, and Tom indicated that he would. The light hand again took his and guided him to two chairs at a small table against the far wall, just off the dance floor, miraculously empty and secluded, given the crowd that filled the hall. She slid into the chair on the far side of the table, and Tom took the other. And they looked at each other.

She tried to hide a slight smile, of straight white teeth, as she looked down at the table and lightly pursed her lips. Without looking up, she asked, "Would you buy me a drink?"

Now it was his turn to smile, remembering where he was, and with whom, and what her duties would be. "I would."

She stood up and said, "I'll get them; you don't even have to move."

He stood up anyway and said, "Thank you," as he reached into his pocket for a coin. She moved in close to him and looked up at him from under long, dark lashes, and, taking the money, said, "Um, it's a little expensive; it's a dollar a drink."

She did not look at him when she said it, obviously practiced at providing this information in a way that was both direct and least likely to cause embarrassment to the buyer.

"Oh," Tom said. He fished back in his pocket, trying not to show his shock at this price compared to the two-drinks-for-a-quarter that had been in effect at the bar. He brought forward the two dollars required and handed them over.

The woman received them with quiet tact, but in taking them, she noticed Tom's hand and took gentle hold of it, once the two dollars had been delivered. "What happened to your hand?" she asked him, with apparent concern, as she held his hand softly in her own.

Tom looked down at his hand. It had swollen quite a bit, so as to make the knuckles indistinguishable. It had also begun to color purplish red, and a small, fresh scab had formed where the impact had broken the skin. Tom had been conscious of stifling a slight wince when he had dug into his pocket for the money.

"It's nothing," he said, as he hastily pulled his hand away.

She looked at him for a moment. "Would you like a brandy?"

"Sure," Tom responded, not really considering the question but just being agreeable with this lovely woman.

"I'll be right back," she said, and she was gone. Tom slid back into his chair, conscious of how this woman's sensual attractiveness had overwhelmed him in a way.

He was just recovering his emotional equilibrium when she returned. "There you go," the voice said, as she slid back into her chair, placing his drink before him and hers in front of her. She sipped from her highball, which Tom correctly suspected to contain little or no alcohol. He watched her drink, enjoying every movement she made. Even the way she inconspicuously licked her lips and the way she straightened her neck were treats for a cowboy not long off the trail.

He took a drink of his brandy and noted how watered down a one-dollar drink tasted.

"My name is Julie." Her perfume wafted in with the name.

"I'm Tom."

"You've been watching me, Tom."

"I have been a bit," he admitted. "I've also flattered myself to believe that you've been watchin' me a little, yourself."

"That's true." She smiled a little and looked down with the admission.

The silence grew a little too thick for Tom. "Are you from Dodge?" he asked her.

She looked up and said, as if stating what she already expected him to know, "Well, . . . not originally."

Now Tom looked down, with a light smile, and nodded his head, as he realized the unlikelihood of a person Julie's age being from a town not yet five years old.

She looked sheepishly at him and laughed lightly, with him, at his embarrassment. She finally said, to alleviate that embarrassment, "I moved here from Wichita over a year ago."

"Where from before that?"

"My, you are full of questions, aren't you? I should be asking you the questions."

"Are those the rules?" he asked her, looking more intensely into her eyes.

She looked down, at this reference to the professional nature of their relationship. In truth, in making the comment, Tom was probing that professional nature to see how deeply it ran and to get a sense of just how much of the attraction, on her part, was professional.

After a moment, she raised her eyes to look at about the place where Tom's right elbow rested on the table. "I'm from a farm in east Kansas," she said, as if offering a confession.

"What brought you to Dodge?"

She looked down again and hesitated. Then, without raising her head, she looked up at him, from under those generous lashes, as she pondered whether to further expose herself. What she saw in him and felt from him did not dissuade her. She stretched out her arms and spread her hands on the table and looked at them as she continued.

"When I was seventeen, I left home with two of my brothers." She pulled her arms and hands back to herself and assumed a more matter-of-fact air than that which had characterized her side of their budding romance up to this point. Looking at him, she felt drawn to talk about herself in a way she did not often do with men. Before she knew it, she was telling him her story. "They were going to Wichita to make their fortunes in the cattle trade. That was in late 1870, and the next year the Santa Fe Railroad only came as far as Newton. Those were some rough times. There was a lot of wrangling and conniving with Park City, but finally the second bond issue for the railroad was passed, and the quarantine line was held back, and in May of 1872, the railroad came, and Wichita became a cowtown. My brothers did well."

"So your folks let you go?"

"Well, there wasn't much they were going to do to stop me," she let him know. "I wasn't going to marry the boy down the road and spend the rest of my life on a farm. I wanted to see city life, to meet interesting people. I've danced with rich men and mayors and gunmen and lawmen and even a congressman, since then," she said, intending to convey that she had danced with a variety of interesting or powerful men, though, except for her use of plurals, in the Dodge City of that era, it would not have been outside the realm of possibility to have said this and have danced with only one man. "I've visited cities like St. Louis and New Orleans and Chicago. I've received letters from all over the world. My parents knew they either had to let me go with my brothers, or some day I would go alone. Besides, I have three sisters at home to help out."

"And to marry the boy down the road?"

She checked him with a glance. "That's up to them."

They both looked down, and neither of them said anything for a moment. Tom finally broke the silence. "So, what do your brothers think about your workin' in dancehalls?"

"They don't like it. They quit talking to me when I started in Wichita. They let me stay at their place long enough to find decent lodging in the respectable side of town, but they haven't spoken to me since."

She looked at Tom. "Don't get the wrong idea; I'm just a dance girl. I don't do anything I'd be ashamed of, anything indecent, like some of these girls, but according to our religion, even dancing isn't allowed. They think I'm an evil woman," she admitted, returning to the subject of her brothers, her brow furrowed slightly, "but I earn my money honestly with my pay and gratuities and dancing fees. And I can't help it if men give me presents and won't take them back."

At this explanation of how she earned her money honestly, Tom found himself subconsciously staring at her highball, which was little more than tea, that had cost him a dollar.

"So, there's a fee for dancing?"

"No, not here, but I've worked in places where there was," she said. Suddenly, she seemed to recover something in herself, and she looked again at Tom in the way she had before they had got onto the topic of her life. She leaned forward on her elbows as she stretched out her hand across the table to rest it on Tom's, and opening wide her dark eyes, she coyly said, "Besides, for you it would be negotiable."

"Hmm," Tom considered that, as the soft hand and dark eyes made consideration of anything else increasingly difficult. Though feeling fairly negotiable, himself, he was not so far beguiled as to keep the talk of dancing fees from bringing a little reality back into this budding romance.

Tom smiled. "Well, you sure are pretty," he said, as he felt himself falling, in a way, into those dark eyes.

Julie looked down modestly. Then she brightened up, raised her eyes, and said, "Now, what about you? Where are you coming from?"

"I'm up from around Corpus Christi."

"How long are you staying?" she asked, leaning forward onto a pretty hand, the graceful fingers of which fell lightly on the side of a pretty cheek.

Pondering the question while trying to get a bearing on his situation, Tom looked off to his left across the room, and as he pondered, he realized that his line of vision had fallen upon a familiar face. There, at a table across the room, sat Miss Molly of Luke Stuart acquaintance, the dancehall girl who had begun to read Luke's letter from Elizabeth earlier that day.

"Well, I'm just not sure," he said, betraying his distraction, as he kept his eyes on Molly. Then, leaning closer to Julie, he asked her, "Who is that girl, at that table?"

Julie turned to follow his line of vision. "Which one?" she asked, unable to hide her bewilderment at this abrupt turn their conversation had taken.

Tom clarified, "The girl with the red hair at the end of the table."

"Oh, that's Molly." Looking back at Tom, and then down, Julie said, with a tone that suggested she had taken some offense, "Would you rather sit with her?"

"No, no," Tom responded, turning quickly back to face her. "From the minute I first saw you, I knew that I'd like to spend time with you." Julie relaxed and looked up, and Tom continued, "But, I'm just curious about her. Do you know much about her?"

"She came here a couple . . . a few weeks ago from around Caldwell, I think. She's a widow with four kids. Her husband was a farmer, and he was killed in some accident or something. She doesn't talk much about it." Leaning closer, Julie intimated, "I don't think she's going to last very long here, though. She complains about taking money to dance with the men and get them to drink and play the games. She says that's not what a lady would do, but she stays for the money. I just figure that's what the men want to do anyway; why can't I let them talk to me and dance with me and buy me drinks, if it makes them happy, and I make a little doing it?"

Tom smiled a little and looked down.

"But that's not why I came over to talk to you," Julie clarified.

"Oh."

"No, I just wanted to meet you. I could tell you were different."

"You could?" Tom responded without much inflection.

"A girl gets to know."

"I suppose she does."

Julie continued, "I'm just a dance girl, you know, nothing more than that. It's just a job."

Tom smiled wistfully at her, as reality further encroached upon their tête-à-tête. He leaned into her a bit, and asked her, "Would you like to walk with a gentleman in the cool of the evening?"

"Do you mean tonight?"

"Yes."

"It would be pretty out tonight," she mused.

"It would," Tom agreed, watching her.

But Julie's mind was not made up. She glanced around at her surroundings, and was gratified to find that other men looked at her in a way that made it clear that they envied Tom's present position. Some of them looked at her with more than just that envy, some looked with a desire that might have frightened less experienced women. Julie had learned the power she possessed as an object of such desire. Tom knew that, as he watched her glance around. She looked back at Tom, glanced back out at the crowd, then looked again at Tom. Then she leaned toward him, took his right hand in both of hers, and, with a quiet animation, said, "Well, why don't we stay here and get to know each other better. We can talk and dance all we want."

"Uh, well . . . ," Tom pondered aloud. Then quite suddenly he said, "No," as one who has made up his mind. "I'll not be stayin' longer."

"Why not?" she responded, taken aback.

"Because I really don't belong here."

"What do you mean?"

Tom leaned forward and brushed the back of his hand against her soft cheek. Fixing her with a steady gaze, he said, "Julie, I could sit here for all time just lookin' into your beautiful eyes and hearin' your pretty voice and touchin' your soft hand and cheek, but I have my qualms about patronizin' a place like this, probably for the same reasons Molly doesn't like workin' in 'em. It's a matter of principle. Thing is," Tom continued, taking in again, as he said it, the glowing, soft-brown skin, the lamp-lighted hair and lips and eyes, those sparkling dark eyes, "I like to dance with a pretty girl, and you're as pretty as any I've ever seen."

She looked down and smiled in reassurance.

"But, as I say, I don't belong here. So, I'll be leavin'," Tom concluded, as he started to lift himself from his chair.

Julie looked up suddenly, all reassurance gone, and reached out and clutched his right hand in both of hers, as a new expression pressed into her pretty features. "You can't go," she said, as if the idea were unimaginable.

Tom was pulled back into his chair by her reaction. Surprised by the suddenness of it, he looked into her face for an explanation. He saw there her new expression, and looking into it, he saw something else. He saw its cause. Looking into those dark eyes, changed now, he saw, deep within them, the tiny beginnings of a desperation with a pitiable potential for growth. Tom knew, though he might not have been able to explain it at that moment, but he knew, in a feeling, an intuition, that at the root of that desperation was fear, the fear of loss. And he knew, too, that the loss feared was not just the immediate loss of his attentions, but, rather, what that immediate loss portended.

Tom stared at Julie as these revelations settled into his mind, and she looked down under his stare. She loosened the sudden grip she had put on his hand, though she did not let it go. Tom realized that she was trying to regain the quiet confidence she had had from the beginning, a confidence of which he had not really been conscious until its recent flight, a confidence rooted in her beauty and its attraction.

Tom felt a pity for the beautiful woman, reduced, as she was, before him. Still, hers was a condition of her own choosing, but even that was pitiable. Had she chosen to be beautiful? True, she had chosen what to make of it, but how great the temptation for a girl from a dirt farm in east Kansas to take up some of what was laid at the feet of the beauties of the world. How great the temptation, and how great the cost.

Julie looked back up at Tom, her demeanor changed again, this time to one that feigned the confidence that had been there before. But she could not hold this new demeanor. As her eyes resettled upon Tom, she saw in him something frightening, something terrible. She dropped his hand and recoiled slightly against her chair, because, in Tom, she had seen his pity.

Tom, feeling her embarrassment, looked down at the tabletop and said, "Well, I'd better go."

"All right," Julie said, as she looked off to the left of Tom and straightened herself in her chair and checked her hair with her right hand.

Tom stood and looked down on her, feeling like he wanted to do something for her. He hesitated for a moment and then said, "Good-bye, Julie. Thank you for the dance and your time."

"You're welcome. Good-bye," she said, still looking off to the left.

Tom stood for a moment longer. Then, finally suppressing his desire to act on the compassion he felt for her, he walked away.

He waded through the crowd to where Molly sat at the table. Pulling his hand from his vest pocket, he leaned down next to her ear and said, "Here's for the kids," as he placed some coins in her hand. She turned to face him, and as her eyes met his, they registered understandable surprise that slowly gave way to a halting recognition.

"You're Luke's friend," she said, and he responded with a slight smile. She looked down at the coins in her hand and then looked back up at him. "What . . . ," she was saying as she looked up, but he was gone. She turned around to see the crowd close behind him as he moved toward the door. She watched him until he was completely out of sight, then watched in his direction a little longer. Then she lowered her eyes thoughtfully and turned back to the game at the table. She had not had the time, before he left, to entertain the questions and thoughts that were still springing up in her mind in response to his words and gesture. How did he know about her children? Did he remember her from earlier that day, though they had not even spoken or been introduced to each other? She could only wonder, and she did.

•   •   •

WITH MOLLY'S FACE and its wondering expression still in his mind as he crossed the Plaza, Tom could not help but think about how different the evening might have turned out if he had seen her before he met Julie. Already his mind had him walking Molly home and bidding her goodnight at the front of her house, that same wondering look in her green eyes. He dropped the notion, given its improbability, but still could not help but consider that it always seemed that women came in threes. A man could go for a spell without meeting one woman to pique his interest, and when he finally did, there were always two others to confuse the matter. The relevance of these thoughts needs to be seen in the context of his approach to the Krause House, home of the family Krause, of which Marta Krause was a member.

Tom entered the house, passing no one as he made his way through the hall, up the stairs, and to his room. His room, on the northwest corner of the house, retained the heat of the afternoon sun. Open windows on both the north and west sides allowed the wind to push through and drive out some of that heat.

He settled back, lit the lamp, and read for a while from his Bible, which he had extracted from his saddlebags. Then he extinguished the lamp and pulled a rosary from his pocket and knelt for prayer. He praised God and thanked God for the gifts from his bounty. He simultaneously examined his day and his conscience—which included no little consideration of his recent encounters, especially with Julie, but also with Henry Edwards—and shared the examination with the Lord, asking pardon for offenses and seeking direction in all that lay ahead. He asked blessings on many, beginning with his distant family, then on others, including Julie, Molly and her family, his new friend Luke Stuart and his family, Marta and the Krause family, Whittacker Dallen, Harvey Chapel, and the outfit, and Henry Edwards, whose memory still stirred the coals of his anger. Then, in words from Sacred Scripture and from the Tradition of the Church, with the invited aid of the Holy Spirit, he prayed the rosary, meditating on the mysteries of Christ through the heart of his mother. Eventually, he crossed himself, rose, undressed in the dark, and crawled into the first bed he would sleep in in months.

As he lay there, comfortable and content, thoughts rose up in his mind in a rapid and nearly involuntary manner, a manner quite familiar to him. The Edwards incident rose to the crest of the highest wave in his sea of thought, and Tom felt the anger rise again as the incident played itself out in his mind. Again his mind constructed the responses he had not been allowed to make, but he caught himself in this. As he lay there, sedated somewhat by earlier drink and, in a better sense, by prayer, Tom calmed his mind and took a more peaceful approach to the topics that had been raised.

In the resultant consideration, he acknowledged that it would be best if there were no need for the Homestead Act. The ideal would be that there would be no need for a law at all. The ideal would be that individuals would acquire property to the level of their talents, work ethic, and generosity. The reality was that that ancient, ugly capital sin, greed, never failed to work its way into human affairs of ownership, to the degree that the individuals involved were susceptible.

Regardless, he did not begrudge anyone honest acquisition of wealth, but he believed that those who so acquired had the responsibility to voluntarily do what was right with their acquisition. What exactly constituted what was right, God alone knew. It was essential, therefore, that each individual continually develop communication with God, so that each could come to an understanding of how to justly proceed in life. Nevertheless, given the situation in the American West, where a limited number of men had arrived early on the scene and had benefited from the use of public lands in circumstances that no longer existed, he did not see any reason to oppose a homesteading law that allowed newcomers with a good work ethic to have a chance to enter and try to succeed at *earning* land, without being prematurely squashed by some cattle baron, from that vast quantity of land that belonged to the entire nation. If people wanted more land, they could buy it, big and small alike.

Such did his mind work again on the Edwards incident. Still, that incident, and the passion it had aroused, could not hold its place in his mind as it had before. It had been overwhelmed by another incident, or, perhaps better, another meeting, one that had aroused very different emotions, emotions far subtler though more pervasive and lasting than pointed passion, albeit they combined in a passion of their own.

The meeting, of course, was the one with Julie, and the emotions were those which only such a meeting could bestir.

Edwards ebbed away, and Julie flooded back—from where she had been occupying a good deal of the area behind it—to the forefront of Tom's mind. In truth, she had occupied the greater part of his mind for most of the time since he had first seen her, and had at least wafted around somewhere in the back or bottom of his mind when she had not been occupying the greater part. It was not as if he actively thought of her. He did not need to think of her. It was less voluntary than that. He would have had to think to keep her out. There was a naturalness to the way she flooded his mind. Thinking of her was a natural reaction to the stimulus of her, and that thought had a naturally sensual character to it. The natural scent of her hair and skin, subtly enhanced by perfume, again delighted his sense of smell, in memory, intoxicating his mind through that most evocative of the senses. Her slender, lithe figure and the way that she moved played upon him in a way that no dance or drama could or, for that matter, could any imaginable movement of even the most graceful of the creatures of land, sky, or sea. Again he saw her eyes and, starting with those portals open wide to him, again ventured upon that journey into her beauty. Again her rich silken hair rested against the side of his face, as it had when they had danced; again the softness of her cheek glided beneath the light brush of his hand; again her delicate hands lightly enclosed his own.

He chuckled at how she had immediately attracted him and at how she still had a sensual hold on his mind. She was not the first to so affect him, and he doubted that she would be the last. He knew, from experience, that her absence would allow time to continually diminish the superficial though pervasive place she presently held in his mind, and he knew that, in this case, absence was the most prudent policy.

To get involved with a girl like Julie would be to give himself over to insecurity, because, since they did not appear to share common values, she could just as easily be interested in any other man who suited her (and probably would be), and he in any other woman. Julie was pretty enough to demand as much commitment as the willing man could afford, however illicit. Her knowledge of her power over men as an object of desire, and the pleasure such power obviously gave her, would only add to the insecurity of the relationship, as it would keep her ever watchful for that future man, better than the rest, who, too, would fall prey to her beauty and her charms. Judging from what he had seen of her values, Tom knew that he would not be this ultimate man, and he wondered whether any man ever would be, before her beauty would gradually succumb to the cosmetic applications so evident, at the Lady Gay, upon the faces of older members of her occupation. Regardless, such insecurity in a relationship could well lead to possessiveness or, paradoxically, to its contrary, disregard. Possessiveness could eventually lead to anger and resentment, disregard to indifference.

Tom considered further the development of a relationship founded on such shallow footings. How many times had he seen a man fall "head over heels" for a woman, only to see him, after that relationship had ended (and the fellow had been all but broken in half), fall equally in love with another woman nothing like the last. Such a thing could not then be love, Tom maintained, but some baser attraction. Love, instead, elevates desire between a man and a woman to its proper place, in a way that sets the human apart from the horse or the cow. Love elevates that desire into a consciousness of the need for moral and practical compatibility, which does not allow one to fool oneself into believing that selfish obsession with another can be love. This special love between a man and a woman must then require something of reason, which sets the human apart from the beast, to elevate this desire. The human creature must let reason rule desire and let love rule reason for them to be properly directed. Such is required by the dignity appropriate to the rational creature.

Therefore, Tom would never have considered that it was love that kept Julie in his mind. He had seen some men—and not just the young fellows fresh away from home and under the influence of drink—make that mistake often enough. But Tom knew that any fellow who would believe that he was in love in such a case, or even in a case more involved though equally shallow, was missing something. Otherwise, how could a man feel similar romantic feelings for different women, very unlike each other and of very different minds from the man himself?

No, such could not be love but merely infatuation. Tom knew love, and he would not have elevated infatuation to that height. It was because he knew love that he was also wary of over-romanticizing love between a man and woman. Love was plainer than glamorized infatu-ation, and yet, more profoundly beautiful in its plainness. It had its share of hardship, hard work, and pain. Love had a nakedness about it, compared to which the nakedness of infatuation was but a woefully shallow imitation. The nakedness of love could not be satisfied by the merely sensual. The nakedness of love demanded far more because it was far more: because it was the complete exposure, the complete shar-ing, the complete gift of the self, not just of the body. (And, in truth, given that the body is an essential component of human nature, one could never truly share the body without, at least to some degree, shar-ing the self, licitly, to one's benefit, or illicitly, to one's detriment.) The nakedness of love demanded commitment, with all that that word denoted and connoted, and a commitment not just to the other, but to the Other, Who is the Source of all love, Who is Love itself.

This awareness, on Tom's part, always brought him around to his belief that there must be far more than just the sensual attraction between a man and a woman before it is appropriate to move further into the sensual realm of the relationship. There must be something profound that puts the sensual in its proper place and elevates it. There must be a singular affinity between the minds and souls of the man and woman, an affinity that draws them toward the commitment of love. There it was again, commitment, an act of the will, an act of the will that is the gift of the self. That is love: an act of the will that is the gift of the self! The commitment of love, in this singular case, must be Matrimony, the only commitment that, as a sacrament, provides the grace for a man and woman to share the nakedness of the Garden of Eden while yet in a fallen world. The grace of the sacrament assures that, rather than become a selfish taking, the sensual intimacy can be a selfless giving: to spouse, to God, to the children thus begotten. Hence, the Sacrament of Matrimony is the only commitment worthy of the ultimate sensual intimacy, an intimacy through which a man and woman become one body and, as such, enjoy the profound privi-lege and responsibility of participating in and sharing in God's creation of another human being. It is in this commitment of the Sacrament of Matrimony that a man and woman are most capable, by design, of accepting their responsibility to raise to adulthood the human beings created through their union.

Given all that, Tom believed that it should follow, then, that a man should test his attraction to a woman for that affinity that draws a man and a woman into the Sacrament of Matrimony. He should do so because the attraction could lead to union, and union to procreation. The procreative result of this union is another human being, another material and spiritual creature with the capacity of union with the Infinite. Thus, the union of man and woman must command a most profound respect and commitment, because the procreation and upbringing of the product of that union, a child with a supernatural destiny, must carry a most profound responsibility.

He knew that no such affinity could exist between Julie and him. And yet she remained in his mind. He saw again the lose strands of her hair around her pretty ear and against her graceful neck. He saw again those long lashes and looked into those dark eyes. And again he knew that he could have been lost in those eyes, and that, past a certain point, he could have dissolved into her and enjoyed great pleasure in doing so, but for some little guide in him, a guide that could reach out and offer him the opportunity to return to shore from those waters into which he had begun to wade. Ah, but for this guide, conscience, what the contemporary Briton John Henry Newman would call "the aboriginal vicar of Christ." Yes, but for this guide, what further evil might be introduced into this world under the guise of pleasure.

In this way, Tom's mind examined the reality of the day against revealed truths and personal conclusions. That examination was part of a river of analytical thought that flowed through his mind seemingly involuntarily and almost incessantly. This flow of analytical thought was something Tom took for granted: he knew no other way.

"Hmph," Tom sighed out loud, in a kind of muffled chuckle. "All this from dancin' with a dancehall girl," he thought.

But he knew it was more than that. All human relationships have a beginning, and how and why they begin determine to greater and lesser degrees how and where they proceed. Julie may not have technically been a cyprian, like some of the dancehall girls, but she saw no problem with accepting pay to show her affections. And Tom knew that once a person decided that her affections were for sale, the object of those affections would be the highest bidder, whether the bid was in money or some other variety of tender.

Nevertheless, though he had thus disposed of this potential relationship, it was the nature of Tom's mind that, no matter what other thoughts ran through it, thoughts of Julie drifted around behind them and, often enough, advanced to the front, until he fell off to sleep.

TOM AWOKE THE NEXT MORNING, well rested. The sun had just begun to climb into its arcing course across the royal blue sky. Shakespeare might have said of the earlier sunrise, "The morn, in russet mantle clad, walks o'er the dew of yon high eastward hill," except that there was little height to the eastward hills, no dew, and the sunrise had been more of an orange color than russet. Other than that, Shakespeare had had the right idea, Tom thought, though from his northwest corner room, he could hardly have viewed that late astronomical event. That was beside the point. It was that kind of a morning, one that deserved classical description on a grand, timeless scale.

Tom lay back, clasped his hands behind his head, and took stock of his state of affairs. He had just slept the entire night in a clean bed in his own room, without having been awakened to ride guard over the herd. Only yesterday he had bathed and been shaved and barbered. He had new clothes and a full money pouch, and his future lay as open as that blue sky that was brightening with every passing moment. Gone were the twenty-four-hour work days, the exposure to every kind of weather: sun and heat, clouds and rain, hail, lightning, and wind, on scales unknown to most parts of the world, both during the day and night, work and sleep. Gone were the critters: the wolves, coyotes, rats, snakes, scorpions, spiders, flies, mosquitoes. Well, maybe not all gone, but far fewer in number, he thought, as he watched a fly circle the room. Gone was the dirt, thrown up by the living trail, the hooves, wheels, and wind stirring into the air a dry soup of it, that penetrated into every pore as well as did any saturating fog.

Tom did not now so revel in his present circumstances because he despised the trail, but rather because he had so well embraced it. The trail offered one manifestation of the rugged life beneficial to a man during the formative years of adolescence or early adulthood. Tom thought of the carpenter from Nazareth, honed by the ruggedness of his trade during his formative years, to serve him well on the ultimate trail to Calvary. In a man, that better part, that seasoned part, could be pulled up, to rise to the top, by the trail, with all its challenges and hardships, as well as its satisfactions and pleasures, which were often ground down to their simplest forms by deprivation, anticipation, and freedom from the more contrived attractions that so hamper the human spirit. Few meals would ever taste better than those soggy, hot beans, bacon, and biscuits, eaten with filthy hands while huddled under a blanket, soaked and shivering, following a cold bruising hailstorm and its companion northern wind. Few drinks would slake as well as that long draught from the creek, following a dry stretch of failed water holes, drunk while lying face down in the mud amidst the hoof prints and dung of the herded stock. Few sights would resonate so deeply as the hawk circling heavenward on thermals before the sharp, chiseled face of a weathered mesa escarpment. Even the herd itself, a living, undulating patchwork of senseless self-interest, became a thing of beauty, plodding through the sea of grass beneath the endless sky and its baking "eye of heaven." But that beauty rested largely in the eye and heart of the beholder, brought to life there, for the most part, by the noble dispositions of husbandry.

Tom let his mind's eye rest on this scene for a moment. "Undulating ungulates," he then said out loud. "It's time to get up."

He rose, washed, and dressed and stepped before the mirror to comb his hair. He noted gratefully how the dry climate of the Plains, so unlike his native Wisconsin or eastern Texas, left one's hair as dry as the night before and hardly mussed, easily reestablished with the comb. His toilet thus complete, he made his way to the dining room.

The attendance in the dining room, at this early hour, differed little from that at the time of Tom and Luke's late dinner of the previous day. A suited cattleman and a teamster sat on either side of one end of the long table. Tom's greetings were answered in kind by these men, as Tom passed them on his way to the vacant table he and Luke had occupied the day before. Still, the atmosphere was not the same. An almost palpable quiet hung over the dining room, a pervasive quiet that draped the entire city of Dodge at this time of early morning.

Daybreak brought with it a time of rest for Dodge City, during which the condition of her persona matched that of her revelers of the night before, who had lately dragged themselves off to their dens of rest. Thus, Dodge City slept, and the quiet of the dining room was part of a larger quiet that had descended upon the entire town. It was not a silence, as it was not complete. Nor would it ever reach the point of silence, for Dodge was a city of business. But the business now conducted was more like the work of a dream within the slumbering city, a more peaceful, stabilizing work, that put order to the work of the city's waking and prepared that city for when she would rouse herself and operate again as the queen of cowtowns that she was.

This morning atmosphere and Tom's bright outlook may have combined to draw forth Tom's gentlemanly qualities, because the efficient Marta Krause, who seemed to be created for this dream-time part of day, appeared noticeably more responsive to his attentions than she had been the previous day, though his clean, barbered appearance should not be discounted for the part it may have played in effecting this conversion. Whatever the case, in the interchange that attended the ordering and serving of his breakfast, Tom made arrangements for Miss Krause to walk in the cool of that evening in the presence of the gentleman she now supposed him to be.

AFTER BREAKFAST, Tom spent the morning visiting many of the establishments on Front Street and made some additional purchases. Among these was a cooking outfit, consisting of two frying pans, a coffee pot, two cups, plates, forks, and spoons. He also bought some books at Collar's bookstore, including *A Tale of Two Cities* by Charles Dickens and *The Adventures of Tom Sawyer* by the American Twain and some of the *McGuffey Eclectic Readers*.

After stowing his purchases in his room and enjoying a satisfying dinner at the Krause House, he returned to Front Street and purchased a pack saddle, which he would pick up within the next few days. From the saddle and harness shop, he walked east the length of Front Street, keeping an eye out for Luke as he made his way toward the Dodge House. At the Dodge House, he glanced in the front door, then checked in the front door of the billiard hall next door, and saw no sign of Luke in either place. He turned and looked back to the west, the direction from which he had just come, and saw no sign of Luke. Then he looked to the east and studied hard the men working at the distant stockyards, but could not be sure that any one of them was Luke. Regardless, he concluded that Luke had probably not yet finished his work of loading cattle, so he turned up Railroad Avenue and headed toward the Dodge House livery stables.

At the stables, Tom purchased a mare, a promising brown, which would serve well as a packhorse on his ride south. Then he returned to the Dodge House for a beer and a game of billiards.

One game of billiards turned into several, without any sign of Luke. Tom enjoyed the diversion, nonetheless, but, after a while, removed himself with a cold beer to the front porch of the billiard hall. There he chose to sit down in the chair to his right, rather than on the bench to his left, on the other side of the door, as it was already occupied by two Texas cowboys. To these he nodded greetings, and they nodded in response, one touching his hat, as well. Besides a "howdy," little else was said. But, then, it was hot, and unlike matter, personalities have a tendency to contract in high heat, like eyes squinting against the intense light from the sun, which was still well in command of the sky at this time of midafternoon. And it was dry, as if the heat had baked any thought of moisture from the air. This left the dust as free as ever to ride upon the rising and falling wind and to settle, however briefly, wherever it would, which was everywhere.

Tom's hand felt the gritty dust on the arm of the chair, as he lowered himself into it, though the chair could not have been vacated very long. He felt the heat, too, in the air and in the wind, but he was grateful for the porch roof, underside of the balcony above, that kept direct sunlight off much of the porch, at this time of year, even though the porch did face south. Still, it was a scant and weak shade thus provided, and Tom was again compelled to marvel at the phenomenon of scarcity of shade on the plains. (Just earlier that afternoon, he had found himself checking for his shadow as he was walking to the livery stable.) Even where it appeared there ought to be shade, given some object above, direct sunlight encroached to an excessive degree beyond its apparent natural limits, as if the sunlight were in the very air itself. Therefore, the shade thus provided was not of that strong, sharp, black quality of some of the better examples of summer shade that he remembered experiencing in other parts of the country, but of a weak, pallid quality, pitiful in comparison.

On the other hand, though this pitiful shade did allow one some escape from the direct rays of the sun, it still provided plenty of light.

Plenty of light allowed one to read. And reading was exactly what Tom intended to do, as soon as he found a spot for his beer.

He tried the windowsill behind him, but, in testing it, found it too awkward to make retrieving the beverage very comfortable, and so he settled on placing the beer on the floor below his chair and his right hand. Then he pulled from his vest pocket the recent July 7, 1877, Dodge City *Times* and began to read.

He read that over one hundred thousand head of cattle were at that time "in the immediate vicinity of Dodge City," and that just one of the herds numbered forty thousand. The previous Saturday, alone, twenty-five thousand head had been sold. It was expected that by the end of the year the total drive from Texas to Dodge would run about two hundred thousand head.

He read in "Items of Interest," among other things, that girls would be allowed to study at Harvard the following year. This information prompted him to look up from the newspaper and out into the sunny street in front of him as his thoughts drifted to a different time and place. A heavy wagon rumbled by and brought him back to the present, and he returned his attention to the paper.

He read on. He learned about soap from cottonseed in Georgia, about an unsinkable lifeboat that could be "used as a refrigerator when required." He learned that the northern Texas wheat harvest was expected to be double what it had been the year before. Then he read about a new horseshoe of compressed, chemically treated cowhide that had been invented by a Mr. Yates of Manchester, England. Tom was impressed with what he read. The item reported of the horseshoe:

> It lasts longer and weighs only about one fourth as much as the common shoe; it never splits the hoof, and has no injurious influence on the foot. It requires no calks; even on asphalt, the horse never slips. It is so elastic that the horse's step is lighter and surer. It adheres so closely to the foot that neither dust nor water can penetrate between the shoe and the hoof.

Tom pondered this new invention and wondered how one might contact Mr. Yates, to inquire into the possibility of investing in the manufacture and sale of this work of genius. He imagined himself as part of the enterprise that would provide the shoes for every member of the genus *Equus* that labored in the service of man. As he did so, his eyes scanned the several members of that genus within his immediate view, while his mind's eye scanned all those at work for man just in his occupation alone. He thought for a moment longer, then thought he might just do what he could to look into such an investment. Then he returned his attention to the paper.

He read an article entitled "Alcohol in Hot Weather," which correlated sunstroke to drinking alcoholic beverages when the weather was hot. He then peered dubiously over the arm of his chair at his beer sitting on the porch floor below. After scrutinizing the beer for a moment or two, as if scrutinizing the face of an old friend, made stranger, for signs of ill intent, his features relaxed with the consideration that such might just well be more temperance propaganda. He then picked up the beer and took a healthy draught. Setting it back on the floor, he returned to the paper and read on.

Eventually, at the bottom of the "Local Brevities" column, Tom came across this item, which piqued his interest:

> DODGE CITY, July, 1877.
> EDITORS TIMES: - Will you please inform the citizens of Dodge City through your paper that Catholic services will be held at the Court House, on Wednesday, July 11th, at 9 1-2 a. m. The Catholic community is invited to be present for the purpose of transacting business of importance relative to a church building. A lecture will be delivered the same day at the same place, at 7 p.m., on the "Influences of Christianity over Civilization." Services at the post on the following day at 9 o'clock.   Resp'y,
> Felix P. Swembergh

Tom was quite pleased to find this notice of services and a lecture, and he immediately determined to attend all that was offered. Wednesday, the 11th, was the very next day. A certain exuberance stirred in Tom at the thought of receiving the sacraments of Penance and Holy Communion, as he had had no opportunity to do so for the long months on the drive. He looked forward to the lecture, as well, as he expected it to be more stimulating than anything he had heard for some time. Tom had heard Fr. Swembergh preach at Mass at Fort Dodge in previous years, and knew him to be an educated man with a great deal to offer for the education of others in matters of the Faith.

Fr. Swembergh had been appointed pastor of Wichita and the western missions in 1873, and had accomplished a great deal, and would accomplish even more before his untimely death. His intrepid approach to the frontier was not only made evident in the several churches he would build, but in his commitment to his ministerial duties, including a trek of over one thousand miles from Fort Elliott to Mexico and back, across unknown and dangerous territory, with only one other priest, neither man armed with anything more than a knife. Robert Wright, one of the founders of Dodge City, would later write that Fr. Swembergh was "a little fellow with a big heart, with charity for all and malice towards none, no matter what the denomination. He was very highly educated, could speak fluently more than a half-dozen different languages, and visited Fort Dodge to look after his flock and minister to the needs of his people, years before Dodge City was established."

Wright would sometimes drive Fr. Swembergh between his mission posts, and claimed that the two "became warm friends." Wright later lost that friend when, in 1878, Fr. Swembergh sacrificed his life to care for those suffering in the epidemic of yellow fever that had gripped Memphis. Of that death, Wright would later write, "When the great call was made from the South to North, for aid and nurses to subdue the terrible scourge, Father [Swembergh], with twenty-odd other priests, nobly responded, well knowing that they were going to their death. Very few ever returned and Father [Swembergh] was among the number that went down. His was a noble life."

That noble life still graced the Kansas of summer 1877, and Tom looked forward to the effects it would have on his own. Gladdened by the prospects of receiving the sacraments, Tom returned his attention to the newspaper and read on.

He read where the *Times* had taken notice of Wyatt Earp's return to town and had expressed its hope that he would again join the city

police force. He read about the city's centennial Fourth-of-July celebration, held the previous Wednesday, one year late. Then he noted
the following weather information for the month of June 1877 out of
the exhaustive report from the U.S. Signal Service: the warmest reading had been 98 degrees; coldest, 42; total precipitation, 3.9 inches;
prevailing wind, southeast; highest wind velocity, 60 m.p.h.; and 1 cloudy
day "other than those on which rain fell."

Tom looked up from his paper and scanned the sun-bleached sky
for even a hint that this day might qualify as the one cloudy day in the
month of July 1877. Finding no hint, or even a hope of a hint, Tom
returned his attention to his paper. There, at the top of the next page,
he came across an article by Mr. G. C. Noble of the Atchison
Champion, in which he related his observations of Dodge City after a
recent visit. Mr. Noble challenged popular depictions of the wild city
and the cowboys. He wrote, "The Texas cattle men and cow-boys,
instead of being armed to the teeth with blood in their eyes, conduct
themselves with propriety, many of them being perfect gentlemen."

Tom had no sooner finished reading this sentence than his attention was drawn away by the sound of a horse pulling up to the rail in
front of him. The stocky rider of this horse dismounted and carelessly
wrapped the horse's reins around the rail. He spat into the dust. Then
he stepped up onto the boardwalk and halted there as a group of cowboys, exiting the billiard hall and fanning out in the process, impeded
his advance. During the brief period of time that this rider stood
halted by the exiting cowboys, Tom took a good look at him. Perhaps
two or three inches shorter than Tom's six feet, the man was indeed
stocky, well-muscled, and trim, which one could tell even though his
clothes did nothing to accentuate his physique. These worn and baggy
clothes hung about him, dirty and stained, wet with sweat, and covered, as was the entire man, with a fresh supply of prairie dust. His
boots, too, showed their wear, as his feet were doing their best to break
out of the sides of those boots, and they were making headway.

The man waited for the cowboys to pass, nodding lightly to their
greetings, though he did not raise his face to them. Still, he did not
hold his face low enough for Tom to miss noticing a slight indication
of annoyance in his features. Eventually, the cowboys all passed, and
the man laboriously dragged his sturdy frame over the boardwalk, up

the steps, and onto the porch of the Dodge House Billiard Hall. There he turned around and slumped heavily, with a primal grunt and a cloud of dust, onto the bench to Tom's left (on the other side of the doorway), now vacant. He removed his hat and rested his sweat-soaked head against the wall behind him. The cowboy Luke Stuart had finally arrived.

Tom had watched Luke all the way to the bench. Now he turned to look out into the street, his features betraying his amusement. "A bit warm," he said from the comfort of his chair.

A weary, though somehow forceful, "huh," escaped from the person of Luke Stuart in response.

"It's been pretty rough out here on the porch," Tom added, as he raised up his paper and again turned his attention to it.

Luke turned his head toward him. With his fatigue evident, if in no other way than in how his mouth hung slightly open, allowing for a light panting, he scrutinized Tom.

Tom glanced over at Luke, and seeing him staring at him in the manner described, he indicated the paper by raising it a little higher and said, "I mean readin' the paper and havin' a beer out here in this heat. Wearies a body some," he added in an accent closer to Luke's.

Luke turned his head back to face out into the street. "Hmph," he sighed, "in all this town I'd have to pull up next to a comedian."

Tom chuckled. He noted that there was little sign of the more timid Luke Stuart of the day before. Hard work and a hot sun had a way of reducing things to a more basic form. He knew, too, that this reduction of Luke Stuart had occurred with the help of the ample quantity of alcohol consumed by that cowboy the day before.

"You all done playin' cowpoke?" Tom asked him.

"Yessir."

"Then, I'll buy you a beer."

"No," Luke protested, "I owe you one . . . ," but it was too late. Tom had ignored him and was already inside the doors by the time Luke had finished his protest. Luke turned and looked in the doors after Tom, then turned back and again rested his weary head against the wall and just let the matter go.

Tom returned with a cold beer.

"Thank you," Luke said, as he took the beer.

"You bet," Tom said, as he slid back into his chair.

Luke drank from the beer like the thirsty man he was. Tom picked up his own and finished it off.

"So," Tom said after a moment, glancing Luke's way, "when you figurin' to leave?"

"Soon as I can; tomorrow, I guess."

"Any way I can get you to consider leavin' the day after tomorrow?"

Luke turned and looked at Tom. "Why?"

"There's somethin' I'd like to do tomorrow mornin' and evenin'," Tom replied, thinking of the church services and lecture.

"Well," Luke said abruptly, turning to face back out toward the street, "I've got to tend to some things of my own. I reckon we could leave the day after instead."

"I'll tell you what," Tom said. "Since it is because of me that you're holdin' up a day, when I know you'd prefer to be on your way home, I'll stake you for a room at the Krause House."

Luke looked at Tom for a moment, then turned back to look out into the street. "No, I'll be stayin' out at the camp."

"Tonight you will," Tom responded, "but you're stayin' an extra day on account of me, so let tomorrow night be at the Krause House on me."

Luke hesitated, but held his position.

Tom pushed further. "Look, I'd sure feel a lot better about keepin' you an extra day if you'd let me put you up. Kind of clear my conscience."

Luke glanced sideways, at this last comment, and saw Tom smiling and managed a slight one of his own with a "huh."

"And you'd be right in town," Tom continued. "You could get around and get some business done, make purchases, whatever you'd want to do."

Tom could see that Luke was considering the proposition.

"Besides," Tom added, "after all this time on the trail, you could use a bath and a night in a clean bed. Let it settle those nerves jarred about by the vicissitudes of the trail. And besides that, I'd consider it a good investment. I don't want for a trail partner some old cuss, ornery from lack of refined rest."

The expression of these last sentiments appeared to make some sort of impression upon Luke as he sat studying Tom as the latter was making them. With the last comment about the effects of the lack of rest on his disposition, Luke chuckled a little bit, though he continued to stare at Tom, for a moment, with something of the wonder that had more characterized his dealings with Tom the day before.

"Well . . . ," Luke said, as he turned to look back out into the street.

"You'll do it," Tom finished for him.

"All right," Luke finally agreed, bowing his head a little.

"Good," Tom said, "I'll arrange it. Come around probably after noon tomorrow and settle into your room and have 'em draw you a bath."

"All right," Luke said, turning back to face him. "Thank you. I can't repay you."

"Well, like I said, you'll be doin' me a favor, relievin' my conscience for holdin' you up and restin' your body and soul so as to make you agreeable company on the trail. Besides, there's the whole good works thing. Good works beget good works, so you never know what's repayin' what. And you never know in what way you might repay me directly in the future. So, repayment's not really good for much but to make the repayer feel better, like he's not receivin' anything. But we're all supposed to be receivers. Mark 10:15: 'Amen I say to you, whosoever shall not receive the kingdom of God as a little child, shall not enter into it.' That bein' the case, I figure we can use all the practice at receivin' that we can get."

Tom's mind had been well rested, and, along with his tongue, was slightly lubricated by the cold beers, and such a stream of talk was the result. In fact, in such cases, he often had the feeling that that which issued from his mind and tongue did so before he was fully aware that it had.

Luke, his brows slightly knit and his mouth slightly open, stared again at Tom. He did not know, exactly, what to make of the man.

Tom sat staring good-naturedly at Luke. After a moment, he said, "Can you sit and visit awhile?"

"Little while," Luke said, adding, as he turned his head and nodded toward his horse, "got to get ol' Arbuckle there out of that saddle and bridle and into some water and grass."

Tom nodded in understanding and looked over the dark brown horse, as sturdy as his rider. "Your horse?"

"Yessir. I brought my own along, besides the remuda. Brought some of my own beeves, as well. Sold 'em with that bunch we loaded today."

"Your own beeves?" Tom responded, with something of surprise.

Luke nodded without looking at him.

"How many head?"

"Just twenty-five head, but my herd's grown considerable since that first crop."

"It has?"

Luke nodded that it had, and the two men talked for a little while about Luke's herd down in central Medina County. Luke seemed a bit evasive about going into too much detail about his operation, and so Tom let the matter lie, as a person did in the West of that time.

"Want the paper?" Tom said, after the conversation had died down. He held out the paper to Luke.

Luke looked at the paper for a moment, then, looking back out at the horse, he said, "No sir. Thank you."

Tom realized his blunder, in forgetting that Luke could not read, and pulled the paper back to himself. He recalled earlier thoughts he had entertained, since he had arranged to return south with Luke, that such need not remain the case.

By now it was late afternoon, and the traffic of patrons, who had been passing periodically between Luke and Tom during their conversation, was increasing. Luke was anxious to get his horse to camp and turned out to pasture. He and Tom rose and shook hands, intending to see each other the next day. Then they went their separate ways.

THAT EVENING AFTER SUPPER, Tom returned to Front Street. He stopped in among the pleasant and well-managed surroundings of the Saratoga saloon to enjoy a cigar and some music. In time, he left the Saratoga and returned to meet Miss Marta Krause, who had indicated that she would need time to clean up after the supper crowd and then to change for their engagement.

The Marta Krause who met him was one transformed. Tom had recognized, since their first meeting, an understated attractiveness to Marta, in her daily habit of blouse, skirt, and apron, but now, as he beheld her, that very understated quality glowed softly through in a mellow-toned beauty. Though as tall and straight as ever, the shapely nature of Marta's slim figure was now accentuated by a floor-length, blue dress of simple good taste. A white collar peeked out around the high neckline of the dress, which was held closed with a tastefully ornamental pin. Above that neckline, Marta's blue eyes, enhanced by the blue of her dress, shone out from her fair face. That fair face, with its faded freckles and light-blue eyes and pale-red lips, had a pastel quality to it, beautiful in its muted hues. Above it all, her soft blonde-brown hair was pulled up behind her head, as it always was, but with a distinction that Tom could not quite determine.

She waited for him, with her mother, in the parlor off to the left of the hallway. Tom entered and visited with the two women. Mrs. Krause liked Tom, though they had only spoken on one or two occasions. Still, on one of those occasions they had spoken for some time, which had seemed to annoy Marta somewhat, as if her mother's involvement with Tom had compromised her own mystique. Undaunted by this apparent reaction on Marta's part, Tom had listened and asked many questions of Mrs. Krause, with sincere interest, and had thus learned a good deal about her home in Germany. Mrs. Krause had appreciated Tom's interest and had felt an instinctive trust of him, partly because, as she later told Marta, he reminded her of her brother Wilhelm in Germany.

On this occasion, too, Marta, though quiet, seemed somewhat annoyed at her mother's presence, though Tom and Mrs. Krause enjoyed a warm visit. Nevertheless, Marta was eventually relieved of her discomfort, when Tom excused Marta and himself, and the two left the house bound for the Plaza House and a bite of dessert.

Though one of the more subdued establishments on Front Street, the Plaza House endured its share of the boisterousness that accompanied the height of the cattle season. Hence, though they did so with the reservation appropriate to their surroundings, many of the men present did little to hide their admiration of Marta's appearance. This Marta enjoyed. In fact, she seemed to enjoy it to distraction and annoyance—her distraction, Tom's annoyance. The couple's conversation over dessert revealed that Marta was further distracted, almost to preoccupation, by a certain peerless wonder of the town named Joseph Sutter. Joseph Sutter was just eighteen years old, which, Tom now learned, was Marta's own age. By the time Marta revealed this, Tom was not at all surprised and might have even guessed younger, though when he had first seen her on returning to the Krause House to meet her, he would have supposed her at least twenty-one.

Now, eighteen was a perfectly respectable age for a woman that a man Tom's age (twenty-seven) might court in the West of that time. Indeed, much older men had married even younger women, in fact, girls, of just fourteen. Age was not the matter here, but behavior, and that behavior was making the hour that Tom was spending with Miss Krause interminably long. The behavior was capped off, upon leaving the Plaza House, with Marta's sudden need to free herself from Tom's escort and hurry across the street to greet and exchange pleasantries with Joe Mason, Dodge City policeman, known as the "Apollo of Dodge," due to the ladies' assessment of his outward appearance. As she spoke with Mr. Mason, she glanced back at Tom to monitor his reaction. Tom merely followed after her in an unhurried fashion and introduced himself to the policeman. Marta hung her head as the two men politely engaged in a short introductory conversation. Then Tom and Joe Mason wished each other well, shook hands, and separated, and Marta answered Mr. Mason's farewell without raising her eyes to him. Tom and Marta then continued on toward the Krause House.

At last the evening was over, and Tom was relieved to return Marta to her home. Mrs. Krause had fallen asleep in her chair in the parlor, and Marta strongly resisted any suggestion of awakening her, but instead had Tom walk her to the door to the family's quarters beyond. There Tom politely, though clumsily, sidestepped Miss Krause's condescension to allow him to call upon her again and to correspond with her once he had left town. Tom did nothing to deflate Marta's overestimation of his affection for her, because he was embarrassed for her. Beyond that, he understood intuitively that such was the reaction of a girl, often complimented by men for her appearance, whose pride, circumstances, and traditional old-world mother allowed her little opportunity, other than the limited one of waiting on them at meals, of interacting with men in a mature and wholesome way.

Whatever the case, after returning the young Marta, Tom felt a need to go out on the town in a manner more consistent with his age. And so, instead of returning to his room after Marta closed the door to the family's quarters, Tom sneaked back to the front door, tiptoeing past the sleeping Mrs. Krause, and left the house.

Meanwhile, Marta had been waiting behind the door to the family's quarters to hear his footsteps on the stairs above her. When she did not hear them, she listened intently for the opening and shutting of the front door. She finally did hear the familiar pattern, though it was muffled due to Tom's best efforts to exit noiselessly: the turning of the knob, the creaking of the hinges, the slight jarring of the door, with the slight shaking of its glass, and, again, the turning of the knob. Upon hearing the door close, she came out from behind the door to the family's quarters and crept to the front-door window. There, she stared after him, and it would have surprised Tom greatly to know that moisture clouded her eyes and a pain clamped itself around and dug into her heart as she watched him walk away from her toward Front Street.

Once on Front Street, Tom wandered up and down the north side. Eventually he settled onto a bench outside the Saratoga, where he could listen to the music, watch the crowd pass, and not feel any obligation to buy a drink or a cigar. In time, he drifted back to the Krause House and quietly made his way to his room and to bed.

IN THE MORNING, he rose and left the Krause House without breakfast, as he intended to receive the sacraments. He arrived at the Court House early and was able to receive the Sacrament of Penance, and then he stayed for Mass and received Holy Communion. He remained after Mass, because, although he was not a citizen of Dodge, as a member of the Catholic Church, he wanted to be present while the Catholic community of the town transacted "business of importance relative to a church building."

After the meeting, he meandered through the north side of Front Street, feeling in his heart an exuberance that shown on his face as a well-founded joy. He had received the sacraments, the Lord himself, after having been so long removed. All that that meant he could not have expressed in hours of vocal explanation, and he would not have wanted to try. He was content to let it settle into him, to shine out from him, this further participation in the Lord toward the furtherance of his own conversion. And he had also been able to witness the work of this local community of the Church, to witness it as a member of the same universal communion. Participation, participation, participation, he thought.

Shortly after noon, he returned to the Krause House to see if Luke had arrived. He found him in the dining room, though he had to look several times to make sure it was he. Here was the gentleman "cow-boy" of Mr. G. C. Noble's article, at least in appearance. Gone were the dirt, the sweat, the whiskers, and a good part of the hair. Replaced were the clothes and the hat, but not the boots, those bedraggled boots, which stuck out under the hem of his new dark trousers.

Tom slid into the chair across from Luke, where he sat at the other small table in the other bay window, to the left of the one they had first shared.

"Tom," Luke said.

"Luke," Tom replied, as he took in the revised version. He just looked so clean. His blue-and-white-striped shirt hung stiffly upon him. His rigid new hat had been removed from his head to the table, exposing Tom to the full effect of the shortened, slicked black hair and the perfume of the slicking agent.

Tom stared for a moment and said, "You are Luke Stuart?"

"Hmph," Luke allowed quietly, "what a comedian."

The room was busy, so it took the two men a moment to order dinner, and when they did, Tom was relieved somewhat to find that Marta's sister, and not Marta, would wait upon them. He still felt awk-ward about the night before and preferred not to have to deal with her in her role as one waiting upon him. He even suspected, correctly, though he could not have known it, that Marta had set it up that her sister would wait upon him. Still, Tom felt guilty about the way he felt about the whole affair, and he found himself making attempts to catch Marta's attention, any time she was turned in his direction, so as to offer some slight form of greeting or recognition. If Marta ever saw one of these attempts, she managed to hide it well.

Despite this distraction, Tom and Luke enjoyed their dinner and talked of their plan to leave in the morning. Luke said he was trying to wrap up some things but hoped to have it all finished by then, including picking up the boots that were being made for him, which were supposed to be completed by that evening.

After dinner, Tom accompanied Luke as he visited the various businesses of the town. Each man reminded the other of this thing or that to which he might want to give his attention before he left town.

Tom enjoyed sauntering through the busy, sun-blanched and sun-baked town with his new friend. Luke had a child's enthusiasm about

things that interested him that Tom found refreshingly honest and rejuvenating. And, despite Luke's new apparel (which, given the state of his
old outfit, could hardly have been considered extravagant, though it was
of good quality) and his other purchases, Luke still betrayed a certain
concern about overspending the money he had earned for his family.

They supped together at the Krause House, still without the benefit of Marta Krause's waiting, and then Tom was off to the courthouse
for Fr. Swembergh's lecture, "The Influences of Christianity over
Civilization."

IT WAS DARK when Tom left the lecture and the civilities that followed.
He had made a point of thanking Fr. Swembergh for the edifying lecture and had taken the opportunity to visit with the good priest for a
moment. Then he had departed with various other Catholic citizens.
Now he exchanged pleasantries with those citizens as they all walked
together toward their separate destinations. At First Avenue, they
turned left toward Front Street, and shortly thereafter, Tom's companions dropped off on the way to their homes.

At Front Street, Tom merged into the crowd and turned east to walk
toward the Dodge House. At the Dodge House, he turned around and
walked west through the lively throng, his mind pondering various
points made by Fr. Swembergh in "The Influences of Christianity over
Civilization," as he made his way through that sample of civilization
immediately surrounding him.

When he had walked out into the western outskirts of town, he
turned around and headed back. As he arrived at Bridge Street, he still
felt a bit restless and felt like walking more, or at least doing something
more, but inexplicably he felt, at the same time, strongly drawn back to
the Krause House. Though part of him nearly overruled this strange sensation, nevertheless, he turned up Bridge Street toward the Krauses'.

As he entered the gate, Tom saw a figure rise from one of the chairs
on the porch and move toward the steps. The way the figure moved
and then its outline in the lamplight shining through the front door
confirmed that the figure was that of a woman (and what a remarkable
figure it was).

"Mr. Schurtz," Tom heard the figure say, as he neared the steps.
Though he still could not make out her face, due to the silhouette

effect created by the light behind her, there was something familiar in her voice and appearance.

"Mr. Schurtz," she said again.

"Yes," Tom said, squinting into the darkness surrounded by light, as he continued to approach, trying to make out the identity of this woman who knew him by name.

The woman stepped back and slowly turned to the side as Tom ascended the stairs. She began to explain herself, "I apologize for waiting for you, but Luke told me that you were leaving tomorrow, and I knew I would have no other chance to see you."

The light from the hallway lamp was lighting part of her face by now, and recognition stirred in Tom's brain as he stepped up onto the porch to face her. "Miss Molly!" he said.

"Yes."

"From the Lady Gay."

"Yes," she said again, this time lowering her face and her green eyes to look at the floor.

It was Molly, all right, Tom could now see, turned as she was with the light falling on her left side. She was fairly tall, a revelation to Tom, who had never seen her except when she was sitting. She wore a floor-length, high-necked green dress. Inside the green collar of the dress, a white, slightly ruffled collar enclosed her neck. These collars were clasped and ornamented with a cameo brooch. It was an attractive dress, of almost the same green as her eyes, and it appeared to accentuate her hourglass figure, though it would have been difficult for a dress to do anything less. Still there was little fleshy about Molly. Rather, she had a certain trimness to her, except in her face, which was only lowered slightly, not too low to prevent Tom from studying it as she looked down at the floor. Tom enjoyed the effect of the whole as he distinguished its various elements, the softly rounded cheeks, the full cupid-bow lips, the small slightly upturned nose, all of it, except for the lips of course, covered with that lightly ruddy peaches-and-cream complexion, warmed by the low golden light of the lamp from the hall. Above it all, her thick, more-red-than-auburn ringlets, neatly arranged and pulled back on the top of her bowed head, completed the picture.

Without raising her eyes, she said, "I hope you won't think ill of me for finding out where you were staying and coming to see you." As she spoke, she lightly pulled at the fingers of her left hand with those of her right.

"Not at all," Tom said, pleasantly surprised to see her, "but how did you find out where . . ."

"I saw Luke," she said, raising those green eyes to meet his. Then she corrected herself. "I looked for Luke, or you, but finally found Luke at Rath's, and he told me where you were staying."

"You were lookin' for me?"

She lowered her eyes and, blushing (which was evident even in that low light), said, "I wanted to return the money you gave me."

Tom waved his hand and began to reply, "Oh, . . ."

"But, I can't." Her eyes came up with the blunt statement, and Tom's gaze involuntarily fell into them.

She looked down again, blushing more. "I need the money, Mr. Schurtz. I'll be honest: I need it, and I am accepting it as charity."

"Well, that's . . ."

Her eyes met his again as she interrupted him. "I don't know how much Julie told you. You see, Mr. Schurtz, I am a widow with four young children. My husband was a good man, and we were building a homestead. He borrowed for equipment and seed, but then the drought came, then the locusts, and prices went down and costs went up. Then one day, when he was riding back from helping a neighbor, his horse, which was a wild young thing that he had bought at a bargain price, threw and dragged him . . ."

Her eyes had misted up as she was telling this, and now she looked down and sniffed. Tom swallowed a lump that had suddenly risen in his throat. His brow furrowed, and he too looked down as he felt a light perspiration break out from his pores.

But Molly was not long delayed. She sniffed again, then dabbed at her eyes quickly with a handkerchief that had appeared as if out of nowhere, and she raised her misted eyes and continued. "I couldn't stay out there with him gone, but I did manage, with the help of neighbors, to salvage what I could of the crop and to prove up on the homestead. I ended up giving the homestead and the crop to a neighbor, who then assumed our debt. He let me stay until spring and made me keep some of the money from the sale to get back to family, but I don't have any family living. My parents were immigrants, and they've both passed on, and both my brothers died in the war. I don't know much about my husband's family, other than that they disapproved of our marriage and that we never heard from them."

"You don't owe me any explanation, ma'am."

"I do, Mr. Schurtz. I've taken your money. I'm ashamed." She looked down and turned to face out toward the street, leaving Tom to view her profile. "I took the job in that place," she continued, "because I was desperate and scared. I was afraid of how I was going to feed and house my family." She turned back to face him. "And I was tired of seeing my children dirty and barefoot. I was tired of living in dirt. The first time I saw our soddie, I broke down and wept. Here my good husband had worked hard to make it the best it could be, and I just stood there and cried. But I made the most of it. But that was done now, and I was tired of flees and bugs and rats and snakes. I wanted a real house for my family."

She looked back out at the street. "In truth, I could have found other kinds of work and made less and got by. But the pay was so much better, and I just thought I would work there for a little while. When I was hired, they made the work sound almost honorable, just dancing with men away from home, like at a social, and they made the money sound good, too."

"Ma'am, I know that most of the girls there are good girls," Tom interjected.

"Most?" Molly said, sending a dubious sideways glance his way. "I don't know about 'most,' maybe 'some,' but that's beside the point." She looked back toward the street. "I knew the kinds of things that go on with some of those girls. I also know that even just enticing the men to drink and gamble was wrong. Many of those men leave without their hard-earned pay. Some go home empty-handed to families. Besides, it is a misuse of my sex, to be an object of enticement, a professional flirt. It may not be as bad as what some of those girls were doing, but it is at best a lower form of prostitution, and one for which I should be more accountable, considering how I was raised in a good Christian home and am trying to raise good Christian children."

She turned back toward him. "After speaking with Luke and reading his wife's letter, I felt more keenly the shame I was trying to hide, the shame I was trying to justify away."

She looked down again. "When you gave me that money, I was thoroughly ashamed. At the end of my shift, I quit my job. The next morning, I went to see my pastor." She looked at Tom. "He has already found me a position at Fringer's Drug Store and Post Office. Better yet, he has found me a living situation with a couple who adore children but were unable to have any of their own. We'll be moving in at the end of the month. I will help with the housekeeping and kitchen and, in return, be given a very light rent. And my pastor is going to recommend me for a schoolteacher position opening this coming term."

"Congratulations," Tom said, expressing his sincere happiness for her.

She blushed and looked down again, and Tom noticed how nicely her full eyelashes complemented the other features of her face.

"Anyway," she said, "I just wanted you and Luke to know that I am not a Dodge City cyprian."

"We know that, Molly," Tom said, unconsciously calling her by her first name.

"You do?" Those green eyes were upon him again.

"Of course we do."

"How did you know?" she beseeched him.

"A person can just tell."

"Mr. Schurtz, you cannot know how good those words sound to my ears. I had begun to think that when people saw me they saw a 'soiled dove.' It is so good to hear that that is not the case." She had moved closer in her earnestness, closing, but not crowding, though close with Molly didn't quite seem like it could be crowding. Her eyes were closer too, clear, glistening.

"No, that's not the case," Tom said, and he found himself leaning into those eyes a bit.

"Ma'am," he said, leaning a little farther.

"Yes," she said, leaning a bit herself.

"Would you like to sit down?"

"Yes," she said. Then she gave her head a slight shake and said, "No, . . . no, I must be getting home." She was blushing again, stepping back and smoothing the skirts of her dress. "I've been waiting a little while and need to get home to the children. My neighbor is watching them, and I really do need to get back. She's a dear, and I hate to make her wait any longer."

"Naturally, I'll walk you home," he said.

She stopped still and turned a pleasant light smile upon him. "That would be nice."

So they descended the steps together and proceeded up the walk. Tom opened the gate for Molly, held it as she passed through, then passed through himself. Then, stepping off down the road, the lady walked with the gentleman in the cool of the evening.

TOO SOON, they arrived at Molly's humble dwelling on Walnut Street, where she profusely thanked and politely dismissed her neighbor. Then Molly went into the house and checked the children. This house, too, had a porch. This porch, too, had chairs, and it was to one of these that Mr. Schurtz retired, when he was asked to wait while Molly attended to the children. And it was to a chair just like it, right next to it, as a matter of fact, that Miss Molly soon retired, herself. And it was from these chairs that Mr. Tom Schurtz and the widow Mrs. Molly Banks got better acquainted, in a quiet talk that lasted perhaps a little beyond what would have been considered a decent hour for such a visit, but both had long since lost much concern for time. For Tom, measured time had dissipated upon his first sight of Molly standing at the top of the Krauses' porch steps. For her, it had happened some time later, after her initial embarrassment and shame had ebbed away under the fixed gaze of his blue eyes.

At last they bid each other good night, not without a little piece of each one's heart refusing to proffer good-bye. He had assurances that she would write to him as soon as he left; she, that he would answer, and that he would see if he could possibly delay his leaving one more day, so that he and Luke could enjoy a home-cooked meal, cooked at her home, cooked by her. Then he pulled away and started for the Krause House, periodically looking back to see her lovely silhouette in the doorway, until the sharpening angle obscured her from his view.

Tom made his way to the Krause House, and once there, to his room. Shortly after he closed the door, someone knocked on it. Tom opened the door to find Luke standing there in his stockinged feet.

"Hey," Luke said, "I was wonderin' if we couldn't leave the day after tomorrow instead of tomorrow mornin'."

The pleasant feeling that had grown up in Tom's heart during his time spent with Molly expanded with the request.

"Day after tomorrow's fine."

Luke noticed that Tom appeared to be far from disappointed. Curious, he watched Tom as he explained further. "They're not finished with my boots, and there are some other things I could use a little time for."

"Sounds good."

"All right," Luke said. He hesitated for a moment, then added, "See you tomorrow, then."

"All right."

Luke departed, and Tom closed the door.

AT BREAKFAST THE NEXT MORNING, Luke noticed a certain distraction in Tom's manner. Luke would start a topic of conversation, and though Tom might respond, there was little substance to his response, and sometimes it had nothing to do with what Luke had said. Luke found himself occasionally looking at Tom as if searching for something, but Tom offered little to find.

Eventually, Luke said, "I saw Miss Molly last night on the front porch."

"Huh," Tom offered without looking up.

"She said she was waitin' for you."

"Huh."

"I told her we were stayin' here when I saw her at Rath's yesterday. Hope you don't mind."

"No, I don't mind."

"She wasn't there when I came back last night, and I wondered if she got a chance to see you."

"Yehp, she did."

"Just wanted to make sure; in case she didn't, you might want to go see her."

"No, she saw me."

"That's good," Luke concluded.

Silence hung between them for a moment. Then Tom finally spoke, and Luke listened with piqued interest.

"As a matter of fact, . . ."

"Yeah."

"Miss Molly invited you and me to supper tonight, after she's put the kids to bed."

"That right?"

"Yessir," Tom responded. Then he did look up at Luke, raising his eyes, in a somewhat sheepish manner, as his face was still tilted down. "You want to go?"

"You want to go?"

"I do."

"I reckon I'd like to go too," Luke decided.

And that night they did go. They enjoyed a delicious chicken supper and then a delightful visit afterwards, which was interrupted by Molly's youngest, who had awakened during the talk and had begun to cry. The child eventually fell asleep in Tom's arms, presenting a picture that impressed itself into the memory of Molly's heart, not soon to be forgotten.

In time, Luke left, and Tom and Molly removed themselves to the chairs out on the porch. There they remained even later beyond what would have been considered a decent hour than they had the night before. And at their parting, they made even more promises of future correspondence, and even larger pieces of their hearts refused to proffer "good-bye." And then Tom took her hand to bid her goodbye, and as their eyes met, something between them made Tom so bold as to kiss her lightly on the mouth, and she let him. Any concern he had about the forwardness of the gesture dissolved when he drew back and looked into her eyes again. They kissed again. Then he took himself away, with no words left to be spoken, glancing back at her and finally just turning around and walking backwards away from her, to see as much of her as he could as he departed, fixing in his memory, as his final vision, the lovely silhouette of the widowed Mrs. Molly Banks.

THE SUN HAD ALREADY BEEN UP for an hour when Tom and Luke met at the breakfast table the next morning. They said little, their thoughts caught up in the journey that lay before them. Luke's thoughts centered on their destination and the growing proximity they would be making to it. Tom's centered more on their place of departure and the growing distance they would be making from it. Luke's manner betrayed his eagerness for that proximity. Tom's betrayed his hesitation about that distance. Nevertheless, despite this hesitation on Tom's part, which was compounded by the realization that he had no obligation to be in any specific place at any specific time, the tender feelings for Molly that had been developing in his heart were being overruled by a deep, resonating intuition that his path, his life path, his vocation, wherever it would take him, required, at that moment, that he ride south with Luke rather than stay to plumb the depths of what had begun to develop between Molly and him. At the same time, he had no sense that such a course would exclude Molly from his future. Instead, ironic as it seemed to him, he sensed that Molly had a place in a future that included his riding south with Luke. He was sure he would see her again.

Though this was Tom's present state, Luke was in a more active than reflective frame of mind. His eagerness translated into impatience, as he shifted about in his chair and fidgeted with his silverware and plate and glass, while Tom tried to finish his breakfast. Tom appreciated his companion's mood, nonetheless, and so he made quick work of his breakfast. At last, he was finished, and the men headed for their rooms to assemble their things. Tom was fortunate to catch Marta Krause at the desk, on his way to his room. He had not had the opportunity to speak to her since the night they had gone out to the Plaza House. This gave him the opportunity not only to check to make sure that his bill was settled satisfactorily, but also to tell Miss Krause that he had been honored to meet her and to wish her farewell.

Marta, without looking up, assured Tom that his bill was settled. Then, in response to the following civilities, she raised her eyes to him, for just an instant, and Tom saw in that instant the vulnerability she tried so hard to hide. He saw, too, her relief in discovering, in that glance, that his expression of these civilities was in earnest. With eyes back down, she responded in kind, and Tom was glad to have been able to make this friendly closing.

Tom climbed the steps to his room, where he gathered his things. On his way back down, he was not surprised to see no sign of Marta Krause at the desk. Out on the porch, he met up with Luke, and the two men departed for the livery stable.

On their way to the livery, they saw, here and there, members of the Cheyenne people, from the band of Cheyenne then camped on the opposite side of the Arkansas River from Fort Dodge, east of town. In dress, these Cheyenne generally wore a blanket over a knee-length shirt and leggings, moccasins covered their feet, and one or two wore a hat. They were, for the most part, good-sized, muscular men, "at least 6 feet high," and "average about 180 pounds weight," as the *Times* would later report. The *Times* would further report that the band had about 995 members, "300 males and 300 females over fourteen, and 395 children." Under the charge of 1st Lieutenant H. W. Lawton and soldiers of the 4th Cavalry, they were coming from the Red Cloud Agency in Nebraska, on their way to be settled in the Indian Territory.

Tom and Luke would not remain in town long enough to see members of the band flood into town later that day. They would not see the colorful and lively dance that young Cheyenne braves would perform in the middle of Front Street. They would not see the hundreds of Cheyenne in ones or twos visiting the homes of Dodge City. Nor would they see, in September of the following year, the panic that would be caused when the noted Dull Knife would lead many of those same Cheyenne past the city in a desperate attempt to escape sickness, famine, and ill-treatment in the Indian Territory and return to their ancestral lands in the Black Hills.

None of this would they see, as they, especially Luke, were in no waiting mood. At the livery they settled up their bills. Then they saddled their horses and loaded their packhorses. With preparations complete, they mounted and rode toward the river. Passing through Dodge, this terminus of a major episode in their lives, each man silently entertained his own thoughts. They crossed the bridge, and the wide gate of Dodge City fell behind them as they advanced along the narrowing ways into their futures.

Chapter Two

A PLAN SHARED

A faithful friend is a sturdy shelter:
he that has found one has found a treasure.
—SIRACH 6:14

HEAT.

South Texas heat.

Sodden heat, gravity's accomplice, weighing all things down.

Down were Tom and Luke, down by a creek, down by the water, down in the shade, down upon a bed of grass and moss: Tom stretched out on his back under a towering elm; Luke resting his back against the trunk of a nearby ash; both taking refreshment from the creek, earlier in drink and bath, presently in attendance to the cool song of its fluid roll over impediments to its course.

Down, too, were their horses, down the creek, down where it widened, down where they could stand unsaddled in its bracing flow, beneath the verdant canopy of arboreal giants.

The horses had earned it. Well had they borne their masters, and their masters' belongings, down the long trail from Dodge City, and in this thick heat of mid-August, neither Tom nor Luke wished to push them. So the men extended their noon stop. Each settled into his shaded spot, quiet in the heat, in the company of a book.

Tom's boots and his towel, still damp from his bath, made up the pillow under his head. Next to his side lay his book, still bearing the perspiration imprint of his fingers on its cover. Perspiration had played no small part in Tom's abandonment of the book. As he had read, he had found himself distracted by the perspiration forming on the back of his hand. He would wipe it off to watch it immediately form again, and again, until the book had fallen into his right hand, which had slid down to the moss at his side, where it had left the book. From the book, the hand had gone to his hat, lying just beyond it, which it had retrieved and rested on Tom's forehead, down well over his eyes. There the hat now remained. Wherever the hat touched his skin, it crushed beads of sweat together, which then fed the rivulets running down, down, off his face.

Sweat. Sweat stood out on every pore of his exposed skin. It saturated his clothing of wool and cotton, which stuck to his skin or sagged and hung on him, requiring greater effort for even the slightest movement. Sweat on his face, and on his neck, on his chest, back, and the backs of his knees. Sweat-soaked he was, in the shaded heat, in the languid, liquid, shaded heat, and down, down he fell into sleep.

No less so Luke, hot and perspiring, but not languid. No, there was a restlessness there, a fidgety restlessness, that would have brought him to action had he not agreed to rest the horses during this, the hottest part of what must have been one of the hottest days in the history of Texas, or so Luke was sure. His book, an advanced level McGuffey reader, though it attested to the advancement he had made under the tutelage of Tom and Mr. William Holmes McGuffey, was not the sort of work to keep one's attention when one's attention needed keeping. Accordingly, it had been first laid on the moss, then picked up, and again left, and picked up again, and on and on, until finally consigned to the moss. Now he fidgeted through Elizabeth's letters, deciphering much more of her neat script than he would have thought possible, though not enough to quell a rising frustration. When he would look out beyond their shady retreat, out into the intense diffused light of the steamy day, toward his home, just hours away, he could not help but see the faces of his wife and children, and then silently censure himself for not seeing them more clearly. He was eager to remedy that deficiency, but he had agreed to wait out this hottest part of this hottest day. And so he would wait, one hour more.

So deciding, he rested his head against the tree trunk and tried closing his eyes; then he opened them and tried closing them again; then he read Elizabeth's letters, then closed his eyes. In short, Luke Stuart used up an hour's worth of patience in five minutes.

With patience exhausted, he wrapped up his letters, picked up his book and hat, and rose to his feet, as he replaced his hat on his head. He walked over to Tom and stood over him.

"Hey."

Tom did not respond.

"Tom," he said sharply.

Tom stirred and removed his hat from his face.

"Time to get movin'," Luke said, which is exactly what Luke did, for on finishing this sentence, he was on his way to the horses.

Tom looked around to reorient himself after this abrupt end to his nap. Then he sat up and looked around some more, trying to shed the hold that sleep still had on him despite his jarring ascent from her depths. He saw Luke tramping toward the horses. He turned his eyes from Luke and peered out beyond the shade to find that the sun still held a lofty place in the sky. He looked back toward Luke, who had already caught his horse and was leading him to his saddle. Once again, he turned to look out past the shade, this time in the direction they were riding, the direction of Luke's home. Once more, he turned back toward the active Luke, and he realized that it was indeed time to go. He pulled on his boots and replaced his hat, and after removing his sweat-saturated bandanna from around his neck, he washed it out in the creek, wrung it out, and replaced it around his neck, with no little appreciation for its cooling effect. He took a drink, and then, with his book and towel in hand, he headed for the horses.

Luke was already cinching up his saddle when Tom dropped his towel and book near his own. It did not take long for him to catch Ross, his exceptional bay. Ross was short for Frederick Barbarossa, named after Frederick I, the Holy Roman emperor. The horse was so named because of the deeper red of his lower jaw, which looked to Tom like a beard, and for his intrepid and indomitable spirit, and for his intelligence. Tom could not remember if Frederick Barbarossa had embodied all these traits, but he had some recollection that he might have, and with the red beard, that was close enough.

Tom led Ross over and began to saddle him.

Luke spoke up as Tom hoisted the saddle. "There'll be plenty of creeks where we can stop and hole up if we need to. No need waitin' any longer."

"No need," Tom agreed.

Luke was now mounted and waiting, and Tom was shortly mounted too. Without saying another word to each other, they walked their horses out of the shade toward the south.

They did stop a few times at creeks along the way, making the most of the shade and water, but each stop lasted only as long as Luke could bear to wait, and then they were back on the trail.

There was little of the talk to which they had grown accustomed on their long journey. The heavy heat seemed to absorb even the energy for talk. Besides, Luke had nearly talked himself out, concerning the topic of his home, during the past weeks on the trail. Beyond that, he seemed to lack the will to say much of anything, so distracted had he grown the closer they had moved toward his home.

At last, they climbed out of a mesquite thicket onto a rounded hill. The sun sat lower in the sky to the west, but it still had plenty of light to spread in the remaining hours till sundown. Before them, now, it spread its light across a neat arrangement of buildings, fences, and trees, wrapped by a pretty wooded creek, all sharply streaked by length-ening shadows. The focal point of the arrangement was an inviting white house with dark trim, plenty of windows, a covered porch that ran the full length of its front, and a yard shaded by tall mesquite, elm, and cottonwood trees. All of it was set at the top of a gradual slope that ran down to the creek north of the house. And all of it was still a good distance away from them, but not so far that they could not make out a small figure bending over to retrieve a bucket from the creek and then lifting and carrying it, balanced by another in the other hand, up the slope toward the house.

"Zack," Luke said quietly, insensibly, as much a confirmation to himself as to all reality. "That's my boy, Zachariah!" he nearly shouted, and with a kick into the sides of his mount, the sun and the heat were fully forgotten as man and horse flew across the country at the speed of love.

Tom watched the scene unfold silently before him, its sound swallowed in distance. He watched Luke grow speedily smaller, as the boy with the buckets made his way up to the gate of what appeared to be a fenced garden in the yard of the house.

By now, Luke was merging into the scale of the small figure. Crossing the creek and pulling into the shaded yard, he dismounted on the run at about the same time that the boy put down his buckets in front of the gate and turned in Luke's direction. The child stood motionless for a suspended moment and then suddenly burst into the charging run of a little boy to dive into his father, who caught his son and swung him around clasped against his chest.

Shortly, a flurry of excitement spilled from the house in the figure of a woman and another figure smaller than the first. These ran to the father and son and joined the embrace.

And Tom watched, and he watched. Then he nudged Ross and slowly walked him toward the scene.

As Tom further nudged Ross into a canter, the group suddenly hurried into the house, the woman pulling Luke by his arm, the boy still hanging on his father's neck, and the little girl dancing along excitedly by her mother. They entered and remained in the house.

In time, Tom reached the creek and crossed it. He was just pulling up into the yard in front of the house when Luke stepped back into the doorway, holding a figure far smaller than the rest.

"Tom," Luke said, as he stepped out of the house and gestured with a jerk of his head for Tom to come nearer. "Come on," he said, as he jerked his head again and stepped off the porch into the yard.

As Tom dismounted, Elizabeth stepped tentatively out of the house, her face registering her curiosity about the recipient of her husband's remarks. The children came out with her, Zachariah watching closely his father and the baby, and Rachel keeping close to the back of her mother's dress. By now, Elizabeth had had time to recover from the excitement and to wonder what sort of picture she presented to her long-departed husband. Thus, she emerged from the house hurriedly tucking up some of the loose hair that had fallen from where it was held up behind her head and smoothing her apron and the skirts of her light calico dress. Her hurried toilet could not hide that she had been working in a warm house on a hot day.

"Tom," Luke said, nodding toward his shoulder to direct Tom's attention to the baby whose head rested there.

Tom slowly approached.

"Robert Turner Stuart," Luke said, with another nod, turning his shoulder, and the tiny human face that rested against it, toward Tom.

Tom was drawn to the face. His slow approach now forgotten, he stepped right up and looked fully into it. Robert Turner Stuart opened his moist steel-blue eyes to Tom and rolled them around as he pushed his tongue in and out and sent a gentle wave of movement through his small torso and limbs, then closed his eyes against the light of the late afternoon.

Tom patted the boy's back lightly. "He's a fine boy, Luke."

"He sure is," the father responded.

Elizabeth stood watching this stranger who was her husband's friend. Finally, she stepped forward and said, "I am Elizabeth Stuart," and she put forward her hand.

Tom took a light hold of the hand and, removing his hat, bowed slightly over it and said, "Tom Schurtz, Mrs. Stuart. It's a pleasure to meet you."

"I'm sorry, uh, Tom, uh, Elizabeth," Luke stammered, "this is Tom Schurtz. We've been ridin' together since Dodge City. I've asked him to stay with us for at least a little while."

"Ma'am," Tom said, still holding his hat, "that's only if you're agreeable. I made that clear to Luke. Won't be any trouble for me to keep movin' on."

Elizabeth sized up the man and liked him. "You are welcome to stay with us, Mr. Schurtz."

"Thank you, ma'am."

"I told him so, Elizabeth, told him how you two would get along real well. He reads all kinds of books. He even read me your letters."

Elizabeth looked down and stared off at a point somewhere off Tom's left side. "Well then, Mr. Schurtz," she said, "we're hardly strangers."

Tom involuntarily stared at the woman who would not look at him. Dressed simply in a calico dress and apron, she was a petite, pretty woman with fine, soft features, fair of complexion and eyes and hair, which was tucked back behind her head. The light blush natural to her cheeks deepened now. Tom finally noticed and looked down in some discomfort of his own.

Elizabeth recovered herself and turned to gather her children before her and, that task completed, said, looking down at first one then the other, "These are our children, Mr. Schurtz. This is our son Zachariah, who just turned five years old, and this is Rachel, not quite yet three."

Tom offered his hand to the blond-haired, blue-eyed, square-shouldered Zachariah, who took it, as he rolled his tongue along the corner of his mouth and his lower lip. "Pleased to meet you, Zachariah; I've heard a lot about you."

"Zachariah," Elizabeth said, nudging the boy.

"Pleased to meet you, sir," replied the boy so nudged.

"And it is a pleasure to meet you, too, Rachel," Tom said, not even bothering to offer a hand to the brown-haired, blue-eyed little girl, who was busy trying to seek refuge behind her mother's skirts, despite her mother's attempts to hold her out front.

"And you've met Robert." Elizabeth nodded toward the baby in Luke's arms.

"Little Bob, Tom," Luke said. "You look at this young'un and tell me he don't look like his father."

Tom looked and said, "A mite short."

Luke chuckled. "You're right; we'll hold off teachin' him to ride till he's stretched some." He chuckled again.

"He will have stretched quite a bit before that," Elizabeth said, still holding her other two.

"I can ride, Daddy," Zachariah said.

"I know you can, Zack. You ride real well." Turning to Tom, Luke added, "You ought to see him, Tom. Boy's a natural." At which comments, one son did stretch some.

Elizabeth said, "Well, Mr. Schurtz, you're practically one of the family now. And this family is going to sit down to eat."

"Elizabeth's got a big tom turkey in there roastin', over the fire, Tom." Luke stopped for a moment and looked at Tom and said, "No relation I hope." Again Luke chuckled, as Tom looked down and shook his head, trying not to smile at the simple humor, and failing, to Luke's enjoyment.

"Anyway," Luke said to those assembled, "let's get in there and eat. You young'uns know where to get washed up." Luke looked at Zachariah and Rachel, Rachel sticking close to her mother and Zachariah watching Rachel to make sure that she, too, would be required to depart from the scene and wash up, before he was about to succumb. "Go on now," Luke said.

With Elizabeth's gentle push, Rachel ran from her mother toward the back of the house with Zachariah right behind, and soon, in front of her.

"You men can take care of those horses and wash up, yourselves," Elizabeth said, "and prepare yourselves for a real meal."

"We will," Luke said, looking into the eyes that were looking into his, as he stepped toward her. Suddenly remembering something, he turned slightly and briefly toward Tom and said, "Tom, you mind turnin' out the horses in the corralled pasture by the barn?" He nodded toward a barn west of the house. "Zachariah can show you."

"Good enough," Tom said, as he immediately gathered the reins of the horses and took them around the side of the house, relieved to find a reason to leave the couple alone.

Luke turned back to look into Elizabeth's eyes and put his free arm around her waist. He drew her closer to him as she rested her hand lightly on the back of little Robert, still resting on his father's shoulder. For a moment they looked deeply into each other's eyes to find there what only they could see. Then they kissed and hugged each other close, Elizabeth laying her head upon Luke's chest and snuggling her face into the side of her sleeping baby.

"I couldn't stop thinkin' about you and the kids," Luke said, his cheek resting against the soft hair on top of her head. "So many times I just wished you were there to talk to."

Elizabeth smiled playfully against his chest. "Well, Mr. Schurtz seems like able company."

Luke held her out and looked at her, with a smile of his own. "It's not the same, Elizabeth, you know that. Besides missin' just bein' close to you, you know there ain't nobody I like talkin' to more than you."

"Ain't nobody?" Elizabeth asked him, with a mock scowl.

"Isn't anybody, . . . anyone, . . . isn't anyone," he corrected himself, and the scowl melted into a smile. They kissed and hugged close again.

"Sure was good to have Tom along to read your letters though."

Elizabeth pulled back from against Luke's chest and, with her arms still wrapped around him, said, "And that means that you owe me a good deal of news. I am all but wrung out of what I had to say up to that point. It's your turn to correspond with me."

"What do you want to know?"

"Now, Luke Stuart, you know perfectly well that I want to know everything. Everything that concerns you is of interest to me, and I will delight in your telling it." She hugged back against him. "I'll delight in just hearing you tell it. It is so good to hear your voice."

They stood there thus, hearing no voices for some little time, neither of them aware of time.

Finally, Luke said, "It's good to be home, Elizabeth."

"It's good to have you home," she responded, still hugging up against her husband and her baby.

Pulling away, she said, "But now you go wash up, and I'll put supper on. And you'll have to tell me more of this Mr. Schurtz. But that will wait. You go and wash up."

So saying, Elizabeth gently removed young Robert from Luke's shoulder, which made the baby frown and turn red and scrunch up his face and rub his face severely with his fists and look like he was about to cry. But Elizabeth quickly and gently turned him and laid him against her own familiar shoulder, and after a few squawks and frowns and squirms and fist rubbings, and without ever opening his eyes, he settled back to his infant slumber.

"You git," Elizabeth said.

"Yes, ma'am."

They looked into each other's eyes again, and Luke kissed her. They hugged again, sensitive to young Robert's presence, then broke apart, and he departed to the back of the house as she went inside.

As Luke neared the corner of the house, a little body came running around it and nearly right into him. "Whoa," he said, as he bent down and picked up Rachel. "What's the hurry there, little girl?"

Rachel looked down and away from him, pulling back as he held her.

"I don't blame you, Rachel, for bein' a little shy. Your daddy's nearly a stranger. But I'll be around for good now. We'll have plenty of time to get reacquainted."

Rachel glanced at him once and then looked quickly down. Luke smiled and put her down. "You go on and help your mama," he said. The girl scampered off toward the door. Luke watched her, chuckled, shook his head, and continued to the back of the house.

At the back of the house, he found Tom and Zachariah on the small porch set into the house between the two main rooms. Tom and Zachariah had just arrived there, after unsaddling and turning out the horses, and Zachariah had just begun his ablutions at the little washstand not much lower than his chest. Pitcher, water, and soap were all supplied, and a towel hung from a dowel on the table. Luke stepped up onto the porch near Zachariah and tousled his hair.

"You wettin' down the trail dust proper, Zack?"

"Yessir, Daddy."

Turning to Tom, Luke asked him, "Find everything all right, Tom?"

"I did, thanks to your boy Zachariah here."

"Yep," Luke acknowledged, "my Zack's a fine boy; ain't you, Zack?"

Zachariah, who had stepped away from the washstand and was now drying his hands with the towel, ran his tongue over the corner and bottom of his lips. Seeing the boy's reaction, Luke could not resist the urge to pick him up. This he did, squeezing Zachariah in a hug. Then he loosened his hold and said quietly to the boy in his arms, "Your mama wrote in her letters that you were a great help to her while I was away. I'm right proud of you, son." Luke hugged him close and said, "I missed you an awful lot, boy."

"I missed you, too, Daddy."

"You'll make a good man some day, son."

"Why, Daddy?"

"'Cause you're a good boy," Luke said, and he set Zachariah down on the porch. "Now, get yourself in the house and get set for supper."

"I will, Daddy," the boy said, and he disappeared quickly through the open door into the kitchen, whence came the sounds of clinking and clanking of dishes and cookware.

Tom had glimpsed the show of affection between father and son, but had turned his attention to washing up out of respect for their privacy. Still, as he had picked up the towel, he had seen the young Zachariah, energized by the personal affirmation from his father, disappear into the house. Finished with the towel, he gave it a shake and hung it back on the dowel as Luke began to lather up.

"You've got a fine family, Luke," he said.

"I sure do, Tom," Luke said, looking back at him. "The Lord has truly blessed us." Luke turned back to his task and, leaning down, bathed his face in the soapy water, which he then dumped out into the yard. Then he rinsed his face in fresh, clear water and reached for the towel.

As Luke dried his face, Tom stepped off the porch and surveyed the rolling land. Though it was obvious there had been a dry spell, the grass, mainly mesquite grass, looked fairly good. Still, the range had its share of chaparral, but even that offered grazing for cattle, with plenty of black brush; and plenty of guajillo and mesquite, with its beans, to further supplement that; and plenty of prickly pear if the rest failed. Post oak, live oak, and, to a lesser degree, cedar were also in evidence.

"Looks like pretty good range," Tom said.

"For now," Luke said, stepping down beside him.

Tom looked at him.

"Herman'll tell you there's more brush and less grass. You know, there's a lot of sheep around here, too, and more all the time, and they're hard on grass. Sure they nibble the grass way down, but cattle'll do that too. The difference is there's just so many of those little sheep; when they're grazin', they just trample down the roots with their numbers, all those sharp, little hooves."

"Huh."

"But Herman'll come out all right. He always does. He watches and studies and works as hard as a body ever did. He'll come out all right. He doesn't run sheep on this range anymore. With the creek windin' through here, there's plenty of water for beeves, and there's still plenty of grass, and cattle'll eat the brush: black brush, guajillo, and mesquite beans. Even with that, he tries to keep the herd down to no more than 750 on this range. Still, you get a better return on the sheep, sometimes twice as good as cattle, what with the wool, especially with these merino crosses, but sheep require a greater outlay up front, and they *are* hard on range," Luke said.

Tom nodded his head. He knew some of this about sheep, and he had learned about Herman on the trail from Dodge. Herman Richter was a cousin of Luke's mother. He had come from Bavaria in the 1850s, with his wife, Elise, and their first two children, and had gone through Galveston and Indianola and had settled and built a cabin near where the Stuarts now lived in central Medina County. There he and Elise had raised their seven children, and the whole family had worked together farming, capturing and trading mustangs, herding a neighbor's cattle on shares, and raising sheep and cattle of their own.

Though he abhorred slavery, Herman had served in the Confederate frontier military to protect the frontier against Indian attack, a serious threat since the federal troops had been pulled out of, if not evicted from, the Texas frontier forts at the beginning of the war. At the conclusion of the war, he and his sons had built the house that the Stuarts now occupied. The Richters had continued to work hard, but they had been able to expand only so far due to the rangeland of other herds of cattle and sheep all around them. So they had moved most of their operations to lands farther west and north, though they had kept the house and the original range. Luke had estimated that Herman controlled over fifty thousand acres of land to the west and north, and would not have been surprised if it were over one hundred thousand acres. On all that land, he raised thousands of cattle and sheep and an ample number of horses.

That the Stuarts now occupied the house that Herman and his sons had built was a blessing that Luke and Elizabeth did not take for granted. It had come as a result of Luke taking the advice of his older sister, Linda, that he contact their cousin Herman Richter, a rancher in Medina County, and inquire after a job. Linda had for years kept up a correspondence with Herman's daughter Birgitt. Though she had never met her pen-pal cousin, the two had developed a warm and informative correspondence, and Linda regretted that they had corresponded less and less as they had grown older. Still, judging from what she had learned of Birgitt and her family, she was sure that Luke's inquiry about a position would at least meet with some consideration.

Luke had known less about the Richters than had Linda. He knew that his mother had corresponded with her cousin Herman before Herman had moved from Bavaria to Texas, and for some time after that, and that Linda had begun to correspond with Herman's daughter when she was young. But Linda was five years older than Luke, so Luke knew little more than that. In fact, Luke did not know all that much about his mother. He knew that she had been raised in the Shenandoah Valley of Virginia and had moved with Luke's father to Tennessee some time after they had been married. He knew that she had been a kind, hard-working mother, but at about the age when Luke was beginning to grow more curious about the larger picture than just their small world in Tennessee, Luke had lost both his parents. His father had been killed fighting for the Confederacy in the war, and his mother had died of illness after the war, when Luke was about twelve years old.

At the death of his parents, Luke's older sister Linda and her newly-wed husband, Robert Glenn, had assumed the roles of guardians for Luke and his brothers and sisters. While still in his teens, Luke and his three younger siblings, in the charge of Linda and Robert, had moved to Texas. (Two other older siblings, an unmarried brother and a married sister, had decided to stay in Tennessee.) They had moved with a number of other families, one of which was Elizabeth's, who were escaping the conditions in the Old South after the war. The families had settled not far from Dallas, and there Luke and Elizabeth had grown to adulthood near each other. They were married in Dallas in 1871, when Luke was eighteen, Elizabeth seventeen, and had subsequently accepted the position in Medina County offered by Herman Richter, on a trial basis, in response to Luke's inquiry. Thus, in the spring of 1873, they had moved to the stone house, which the Richters had vacated in 1872 when they had built a larger house on lands farther to the west. Luke was to manage a herd and range on shares, receiving one calf of every four born, as recompense, plus the use of the empty house and a modest stipend for food and expenses. The trial period was to have lasted several months, but it had soon passed, as Luke had worked hard to keep such a beneficial placement for his family, and he and his cousins had grown to like and respect each other.

Tom now looked over the stone house that the Richters had built. It was a solid, handsome house, made of native stone that was mortared over and whitewashed. Dark green trim surrounded the windows and doors. The porch posts and rails were painted this same green. Above the small inset porch on the back of the house, where he had lately washed his hands, a small dormer with a small window jutted out of the roof. To the right and left of the porch, on the first floor, each room had one window. Recollecting what he had seen of the rest of the house, he recalled three downstairs windows and one upstairs on each of the two gabled ends of the house. On the front of the house, the north side that they had first approached, he had noticed two second-floor dormers, each with a window. A railed porch ran the entire length of the front of the house. Under the roof of that porch, five windows—two to the left and three to the right of the front door—graced the north wall.

"Let's eat." Luke's words broke into Tom's observations, and he and Tom entered the house into the kitchen.

The house was warm from the heat and the cooking, but a breeze cut across the kitchen from windows open all over the house. The stone walls and floor of the large kitchen helped to take some of the heat out of the room. Tom glanced through the doorway on the southern end of the western wall of the room and saw a hallway and a staircase beyond it. Another doorway, farther down the wall to the north, opened into a foyer between the kitchen and the main room, a foyer into which people entered when using the front door. The back of this foyer accommodated the hallway and staircase Tom had seen.

Regardless, Tom had only glanced through the doorway, for it was the table in the kitchen that had attracted most of his attention. Set with china and silver and glassware, Tom had not seen anything like it in some time. But beyond that was the food, the turkey, vegetables, breads, and all their complements, spread out on the table.

"Mrs. Stuart," Tom said, "this looks grand."

"Thank you, Mr. Schurtz," Elizabeth said, surprised at his choice of adjective. "Would you take the place there next to Luke?"

"Yes ma'am," Tom said, as he sat in a chair on the side of the table to Luke's left. Luke sat at the end of the table toward the back of the house, and Zachariah sat across from Tom on the other side of the table. (Tom could look beyond Zachariah and over the counter against the wall and out through the windows at the range beyond.) Elizabeth took her seat at the other end of the table from Luke. Rachel sat to the left of her mother on Zachariah's side of the table. Robert lay fast asleep in a cradle on the floor against the wall at his mother's end of the room.

Now, with all seated for the family meal, the Stuart family participated in a tradition that had been handed down in Elizabeth's family of devout Baptists for generations. Just as had her father and his father before him, so Elizabeth called for the Bible to read from God's own Word before partaking of the gifts they had received from his providence.

"Zachariah," Elizabeth said, "would you fetch the Bible, please?"

"Yes ma'am." Zachariah left his seat and retrieved the Bible from the buffet under the china cabinet and carried it toward his mother.

As Zachariah passed Luke, Luke reached out and caught him by the shoulder and said, "I'll take that, Zack."

As Luke took the Bible and began to page through it, Tom watched Zachariah stare intently at his father, then look at his mother in surprise, then back at his father, and then slide back into his place, still looking. Tom glanced down the table at Elizabeth, whose own expression betrayed a myriad of emotions constraining themselves in potential, shifting, mixing toward appropriate display.

Meanwhile, Luke paged without looking up, and then he stopped. He laid open the Sacred Scriptures, and he read. Before his family, from the Sacred Scriptures, Luke Stuart read: "'And, behold, a certain lawyer stood up, and tempted him, saying, Master, what shall I do to inherit eternal life?'"

It came forth deliberately, though somewhat haltingly, as Luke concentrated on that which he had practiced.

Tom heard and watched him read what he had heard and watched him read many times before. He looked at Zachariah, who watched his father work through the sacred words, worthily proclaiming them in his concentrated effort. He looked at Elizabeth, who leaned all the way back in her chair now, her arms crossed across her breast, her one hand raised to her mouth, holding it, tears pooling in the bottom of her eyes, through which she took in this vision of her husband.

"'A certain man went down from Jerusalem to Jericho, and fell among thieves. . . .'"

And the tears overran their pools out onto Elizabeth's cheeks, down, down, and Elizabeth raised her apron to her eyes to wipe them. She sniffled, and Zachariah looked from his father to his mother, and stared, his brow furrowed, and then back to his father with the same intensity.

Little Rachel, alarmed at watching her mother, said, "Mama, why are you crying?"

Elizabeth, holding her apron up to her face, pulled in a stuttering breath and turned a tearful smile on her daughter. She held her finger to her lips, to still her child during the reading of the Word of God, and then reached out to her and rested her hand on her small head, and then slowly stroked her hair as she looked back to her husband. Rachel spoke not another word, but she too turned to watch and hear.

"'But a certain Samaritan, as he journeyed, came where he was: and when he saw him, he had compassion on him,

"'And went to him, and bound up his wounds, pouring in oil and wine, and set him on his own beast, and brought him to an inn, and took care of him. . . .'"

So Luke read, and he read, and all watched and listened and heard.

"'Go, and do thou likewise.'"

And Luke closed the Sacred Scriptures, without looking up, and after a little wait, he began to slide the book toward Zachariah. But Elizabeth rose quickly from her chair and hurried over to take up the Bible and return it to its place on the buffet, where she stood, with her back to the room, wiping her eyes and nose with a kerchief. She turned and came to Luke's chair and bent down and hugged him and kissed him on the cheek as he sat. Luke raised his arm to embrace her too, but she pulled away and left the room. Rachel immediately left her chair and ran out of the room after her mother.

Luke sat staring at the table as Tom did the same, neither saying a word. Zachariah stared at his father, now and then looking at Tom or at something else, but mainly stared at his father.

Elizabeth's husband, the head of the household, had read from the Scriptures before supper; her husband, whom she had often in the past begun to tutor, even well before they were married, only to have him give up in frustration and embarrassment each time; her intelligent husband, whose difficulty with reading had long proved an enigma to her; her committed husband, who had secretly determined, even before leaving on the long drive to Dodge City, that he would return from that drive able to read, for her. And so, he had striven, with the help of a kind and discreet bunkmate, who had carried books and magazines with him and had frequently read from these. He had practiced and memorized some words and had tried to remember what Elizabeth had taught him about the letters and their sounds. He had tried to ask the well-meaning bunkmate about these, pawing around in the dark for the system of the whole thing, and the bunkmate had answered specific questions, but Luke had only been getting bits and pieces. He had known that he was not getting the basics of the system that Elizabeth had many times tried to teach him. Those times he had failed. But now his boy was learning to read, and for that boy and his other children, but, most of all, for Elizabeth and for what it would mean to her, he was going to learn, regardless of frustration. Still, by Dodge City, frustration was most of what his efforts had amassed.

Enter Tom Schurtz. On their first night on the trail, Luke had confided to Tom his goal and had humbly asked Tom to try to teach him. So, Tom had begun. He had first asked Luke why it was important to him to learn to read. From Luke's answer, Tom had decided to start Luke, from the very beginning, on practicing his choice of a reading from Scripture, regardless of how much of it would be memorization at first. Luke had chosen, without hesitation, the parable of the Good Samaritan. At the same time, Tom had started Luke on a relentless regime of fundamental phonics and basic reading, with the help of the *McGuffey Eclectic Readers* he had bought in Dodge City with this very possibility of tutoring Luke in mind. Relentless, indeed, Tom quizzed and drilled Luke on the rules of phonics as they rode, and on the simple readings when they camped. "Sound it out. Sound it out," Luke had heard until he was about ready to sound Tom out and ride on without him, but he had endured. For over three weeks, Tom had almost badgered Luke with the rules of phonics, phonetics, and grammar, all that Tom had thought Luke could handle and a little more, over and over, day in and day out, in the saddle and out of it, until

Luke was full up beyond his hat line and sick of the matter and regretful to think that he had ever asked Tom to teach him at all. And then, Tom had stopped.

With something like a week left in their journey, Tom had just stopped. For one whole day, he had said nothing about reading; nothing about phonics, phonetics, or grammar; no rules, no sounds, nothing. Then he had done so for another day. At the end of that first day, in their camp, Luke had refrained from taking up his readers or his Bible to read. He had done so cautiously, watching Tom for his reaction. He had seen none. The second night, after another full day on the trail, he had tried to leave his reading alone again, but eventually an inexplicable restlessness had caused him to pull out his readers, and his Bible. Then he had sat down near the fire in the twilight, and he had read. He had read. No forcing the rules or the sounds, he had just read. His mind had absorbed the system, and though no more smoothly than his earliest attempts at riding, he was reading, and he was progressing. The whole thing, including all the work he had done with the help of the kind bunkmate on the way up the trail, was falling into place. He was grateful to Tom, and Tom could have known no greater reward than to see the wonder with which his student was reading everything he could find, working his way through difficult passages of Scripture, passages he knew, opened to him in a way they had not been before. From then on their tutoring had taken on a different pace. No longer did Tom badger, but rather, he answered the questions and guided Luke's voracious ambition to learn more. They had only just begun working on cursive before they had arrived at the Stuart home, where they now sat, looking down at the top of the table.

A few minutes passed, and Elizabeth, leading Rachel by the hand, came back into the room. Without looking at anyone present, she lifted Rachel and placed her in her seat and then went over to the counter under the window for some final preparations for the meal, preparations previously completed. Once or twice she raised the bottom of her sleeve to dab at her eyes, but in a short time, she returned to the table. Luke then led them in prayer, and they commenced with a sumptuous meal, throughout which a quiet Mrs. Stuart regarded her husband anew. Occasionally Luke would look toward Elizabeth, and their eyes, those of husband and wife, would meet, but he would look away, as he was unprepared, outside the realm of marital privacy, to deal with all that was being communicated to him: all the emotion, the questions, the love.

Nevertheless, both Luke and Elizabeth tried to make polite conversation with Tom and with the children. But their palpable distraction hung over the meal, and the conversation amounted to nothing. Tom did his best to make the most of the exceptional meal, as he sensed that it would not last very long. And it did not. Nearly as soon as all were finished, which was fairly soon, Elizabeth began clearing the table, with the help of the children, and Tom left with Luke, who took with him a reviving Robert, to be shown around the grounds before the fading twilight faded altogether.

The tour was also short. Luke showed him the barn and some log corrals, but it was getting late for Robert, and before long, the men and baby were back in the house.

With darkness almost fully upon them now, Elizabeth and Luke put Zachariah and Rachel to bed. Tom, meanwhile, sat awkwardly at the kitchen table, not exactly sure what he should be doing, where he would be sleeping, when he ought to turn in.

Eventually, Luke returned to the kitchen followed by Elizabeth, who was holding Robert.

"We were goin' to sit out on the porch, Tom, if you want to join us," Luke said in lowered voice.

Attuned to the couple's need for private communication, Tom responded in the same hushed tone, "Well, I thought I'd just turn in. It's been a long day."

"All right. Elizabeth's got the young'uns' bed all made up for you. They're campin' out on the floor."

"You didn't need to go to that trouble," Tom said to both of them. "I can sleep outside."

"No guest of ours will be sleeping outside, Mr. Schurtz," Elizabeth whispered. "Your bed is made up."

Tom knew the matter was closed and thanked Elizabeth. He passed from the kitchen into the foyer and climbed the stairs to the second floor, where he saw, to his right, Zachariah and Rachel camped out on a rug at the foot of their parents' bed. He smiled at their adventure and turned to his left, where he found his way to his bed, in an area separated from the rest of the room by a wardrobe and chests of drawers. He undressed down to his underclothes and turned in.

He did not sleep for a while, due to the humid heat and the discomfort of having entered a family's intimate space. He heard the sounds of the night, including a wolf, coyotes, insects, and an owl, and the low murmuring of Mr. and Mrs. Stuart getting reacquainted on the front porch of their home. They were interrupted once by the indignant wail of an awakened Robert, whose cries were shortly silenced by what Tom correctly assumed to be a feeding. In time, the sounds of the night coaxed a quiet from Tom's mind, and he was asleep.

TOM AWOKE to morning before the sun. As quietly as possible, he peeked up over the chest of drawers to see all still asleep. He slipped into his clothes, and carrying his boots, he tiptoed down the stairs and out the front door onto the porch, where he put on his boots.

From the porch, he walked down to the barn, where he retrieved a book from his saddlebag. Leaving the barn, he looked at the milk cow. He thought for a moment, then laid aside his book, picked up a pail, and milked the cow. On his way back to the house with the milk and his book, he heard first a rooster and then Robert cry, and by the time he returned to the house and set the milk in the kitchen, the whole house was astir. He sat out on the porch and read for a while, allowing the family to rise and dress. Eventually Luke stepped out onto the porch, wearing only his pants pulled on over his cotton flannel underclothes.

"You milk the cow, Tom?"

"I did."

"Thank you. You needn't have done that."

"Well, you're welcome."

Luke sat in a chair. "How'd you sleep?"

"Real well."

"You ready for some breakfast?"

"Sure."

"Elizabeth's feedin' Little Bob. It'll be just a little bit. You'll like Elizabeth's breakfasts. Sure beats what we been feedin' on."

At that moment, Zachariah and Rachel came running out of the house, Zachariah in the lead, carrying a basket, and Rachel close behind.

"Don't you be runnin' like that when that basket's full, now," Luke called after them.

"We won't, Daddy," Zachariah called back, as he disappeared around the side of the house.

"Fresh eggs, Tom, what do you think of that?"

"I'm lookin' forward to it."

And well he should have. Breakfast consisted of ham and eggs, pancakes with molasses, greens, and plenty of coffee. At its conclusion, the men were content to sit and let it settle, and the children were dismissed to run outside. Elizabeth cleared and washed the dishes.

"Thank you for the excellent breakfast, Mrs. Stuart," Tom said from the same seat he had occupied the night before.

"You're welcome, Mr. Schurtz. Thank you for milking the cow."

"You're welcome."

"It was most satisfying, Elizabeth," said Luke. "It is good to be home."

Elizabeth turned her head to look at him over her shoulder and smiled warmly, then turned back to her work.

"It is a fine home," Tom said.

"It is that," Luke said, now staring at the floor, though seeing a far greater distance. Elizabeth turned her head again to look at him over her shoulder. He looked up from the floor to her, and they remained thus for a moment. Then Elizabeth turned back to finish her work, and Luke's vision fell to the top of the table as a serious expression took control of his face.

"Tom," Luke said to the top of the table. Tom looked at him, and Luke raised his eyes to meet Tom's. At the same time, Elizabeth turned around and leaned back against the counter, wiping her hands on a towel as she did so, and she faced Tom from across the room. "We're fixin' to leave here," Luke said.

"Huh," Tom responded, revealing little emotion other than a slight wonder as to why.

"We're goin' to the Panhandle to start a ranch."

"Huh."

"We're wonderin' if you'd want to come with us. To be our partner."

"Huh." This time Tom slightly raised his eyebrows and shifted his head to let his gaze fall upon the tabletop.

"We'll have somewhere around three hundred head of cattle, a merino ram, and some Mexican ewes. We've got hogs and chickens. We've got a wagon, and we're fixin' to get a bigger one, for haulin'."

As Luke spoke, he watched Tom, trying to read some kind of reaction, positive or negative, to what he was saying. Without seeing any, Luke continued, "I know it probably sounds loco, Tom, to leave all this, this whole setup, but I just want to get out on my own, to make my own stake, to be able to start somethin' and make it grow."

"You're young enough to fail," Tom said without looking up from the table.

"What's that?"

"You're young enough to fail," Tom repeated. "A fellow I worked with years ago said that to me when I was considerin' settin' out on a venture."

"Did you fail?" Luke questioned.

Tom raised his eyebrows again without raising his line of vision from the top of the table. "No," he said, "I wouldn't say that." He smiled lightly and added, "But things didn't turn out the way they were expected to." Tom considered this for a brief moment, then abandoned that consideration and raised his eyes to Luke's. "Of course," he added, "I didn't have a family." So saying, Tom glanced from Luke to Elizabeth. Elizabeth looked down.

"Why the Panhandle?" Tom asked, turning back to Luke.

The Stuarts again raised their eyes to each other. Then Luke looked back at Tom. "Well . . . uhm," Luke began, "well, uh, Tom, it sounds kind of strange, but I've got to, uh, to ask you to promise not to say anything to anyone, especially if you don't become our partner."

Tom gestured "fair enough" with his face and said, "All right. I give you my word."

Luke and Elizabeth looked into each other's eyes once more, a little longer this time. Then Luke looked back at Tom. He had made up his mind. He leaned back in his chair and opened what he had to say with a question, "You heard about Charlie Goodnight and the Palo Duro Canyon?"

"Yessir," Tom said with a nod. He had first heard rumors and then had heard more of the story while in Dodge City. Goodnight, a seasoned cowman known for, among other things, the Goodnight-Loving

Trail, had begun drifting some sixteen hundred head of cattle out of Colorado in 1875, settling into winter camps on the Canadian River in eastern New Mexico. From there he had continued drifting his herd east along the Canadian River. Eventually, on the intelligence of a Mexican mustanger, Goodnight had located the extensive Palo Duro Canyon on the eastern edge of that great plateau of the high plains called the Llano Estacado, the Staked Plains, and had moved his herd into it in the fall of 1876.

"Well," Luke continued, "there's another canyon, some ways south of the Palo Duro, not near as big, but plenty big enough. It has all the grass and springs and creeks and timber the Palo Duro has, and all the protection in winter, being nearly as deep. There's even fish in the creeks. All kinds of game: buffalo, deer, antelope, . . . bear, turkey, . . . quail."

"How do you know about it?"

"A *vaquero* just south of here, a sheep *vaquero* named Sean Grady, and his wife, Maria. They came this way from New Mexico. Even though he's been herdin' sheep for years, seems he's done just about everything else, includin' minin' and herdin' beeves. Pretty interestin' fellow. And Maria's family were what they called *ciboleros* and *comancheros*. The *ciboleros* were Mexican buffalo hunters, and the *comancheros* were traders that used to trade with the Comanche and Kiowa, Cheyenne too, I think," Luke explained, as Tom nodded his head as if to indicate that he knew this. "They used to trade up in the region called the Quitaque," Luke continued. "Maria heard tell of this Escondido Canyon, or Cañon Escondido, which was real hard to find. That's why they called it '*escondido*,' because it means 'hidden,' or 'mysterious,' or somethin' like that. Weren't many *comancheros* that ever really saw it."

"What makes you think it's real then?" Tom queried.

"Well, Maria's father did see it. He was privileged because he got on real well with some chief or some such. He claimed there were mesas that stood at the canyon's mouth, and they made it look like there was no canyon at all. Besides that, there are two smaller canyons on either side of it, some miles off, that confuse people. They think they're the same one, so it's like the land in between doesn't even exist.

"Supposed to be that even that explorer, uh, that Spanish explorer, uh, . . ."

"Coronado," Tom and Elizabeth said at the same time.

"That's right, Coronado," Luke said, looking back and forth between Elizabeth and Tom. "Supposed to be that he or one of his men wrote about the canyon in his diary or journal or somethin'. Said it was real mysterious, hard to find and just mysterious, haunted, or somethin'."

"Haunted?" Tom asked with surprise.

"Well, that's what Sean said, or somethin' like that," Luke explained.

"So, he's read this journal or diary?"

"Well, no, I don't think so, but he heard tell of it somewhere along the way," Luke said, looking down and feeling less secure in his presentation after Tom's questioning. But Luke had more information to bolster his presentation and his security in it. "Besides," he continued, "Sean's half-Apache. His mama was Apache, and he claims that long ago, over a hundred years ago, or two hundred years ago, or somethin' like that, the Apache used to control that area up there, until the Comanche pushed 'em out. He says there's probably ghosts up there, because if an Apache is just plain bad or mean, like a traitor or a witch, or if he dies an untimely death or is killed by violence, his ghost doesn't go to the happy place, the happy hunting ground, you know, . . . heaven, I guess," he said, glancing at Elizabeth with a shrug. "He sticks around to bother people. Anyway, Sean says that is probably why people cannot find the canyon; it's, uh, . . . well, he said it's haunted, but he used another word too. How did he say it, Elizabeth?"

"Enchanted," his wife said without conveying any of the enthusiasm for the story that was animating Luke.

"That's right, enchanted."

"But," Elizabeth added, "*haunted* is probably the more accurate term for what Sean describes."

"And you want to move there?" Tom asked, noting his friend's fascination for the unexplained, for the supernatural, for a good ghost story, common enough among the people Tom Schurtz had met in his life.

Elizabeth spoke up, "We're Christians, Mr. Schurtz. We do not partake in pagan superstition." She paused for a moment and added, "Are you superstitious, Mr. Schurtz?"

"Well," Tom considered, "I don't think I am superstitious, but I am half-Irish, which I suspect is the other half of your friend Sean Grady. And if I am correct in this, however much of the story comes from the Apache half, there can be little doubt that the interest in the canyon being haunted or enchanted and the legend from the journal have at least some basis in the Irish retelling."

Tom meant what he said. Nevertheless, he believed that there was far more to know about the spiritual world beyond what he knew, and beyond what he knew was appropriate to investigate. He was content to seek blessings and prayers to protect himself and others from evil, and not to dabble in areas that could lead one into serious error. This line of thought he did not deem prudent to raise under the circumstances, and so he did not. Instead, he continued, "Still, if his wife has her information from a *comanchero* father, that seems especially worth considerin', especially if it correlates independently with this legend of Sean's."

"That's what I figure," Luke said.

"Huh." Tom thought a moment and then said, "What about Indians? Comanche and Kiowa are still up that way. Comanche are pretty well known for . . ." He refrained, in Elizabeth's presence, from mentioning anything regarding the Comanche renown for imaginative torture and killing. "Well, they're not necessarily known for bein' best of neighbors to white settlers."

"They've been on the reservation at Ft. Sill since Colonel Mackenzie ran 'em out of Palo Duro in '74," Luke responded. "They might come off the reservation now and then, but they'd be pretty careful not to cause trouble, I imagine. Besides that, the army's been bringin' in more and more of those still on the loose, like Captain Lee's been doin' out of Fort Dodge. And just this spring, a band of buffalo hunters out of Dodge City broke up one of the last bands of Indians still out on the Staked Plains." Looking at Elizabeth and receiving a light smile of confirmation, he said, "It's a chance we're willin' to take."

"Huh," Tom responded. For a moment a heavy pause blanketed the three. Tom also knew of Ranald Mackenzie's reduction of the Comanche and Kiowa by the destruction of over a thousand horses and mules, and he had heard, while in Dodge City, of the more recent military campaigns and of the exploits of the buffalo hunters on the Staked Plains. These had not taken the Indians out of the equation, as far as Tom was concerned, but he said no more about it. Tom broke the heavy pause, "So you only know about this canyon through this Maria and her husband, Sean?"

"That's it, Tom," Luke confirmed, "but neither of them are the kind to make things up. What they say you can pretty well count on."

Tom considered that. "But they could believe it themselves, and it wouldn't have to be true."

Another pause followed this comment. Luke broke this one.

"Well," Luke said, revealing a sudden determination not to let Tom dissuade him, "even if there's no canyon, there's liable to be plenty of land up there now, before all the white men start headin' that way. Goodnight's story's been out a few months now. It's time to move, now or never. Get there now, get in while the gettin's good. Wait on it, and who knows what'll be left. If we leave as soon as we can pull everything together, we might be able to make it to the protection of the canyon before any northers hit."

"What about this place?"

"We'll have to let Herman know about it. He already knows we're thinkin' of leavin'; just haven't made it formal. He's been awful good to us. I can't even tell you. We won't be leavin' him in the lurch, though. His youngest boy, Will, is gettin' married, and this is probably just the spot for him. The older boys've been in business with their daddy for years, but young Will kind of came along later, and this place would probably suit him and his new wife just fine."

"Did he ride line on this place while you were gone?"

"No, he worked for his daddy on their operations to the west. Won't be movin' over here till we've moved on and the house is free. No, Sean Grady's boy, Andy, rode line here. Sean's got three of his boys workin' as *pastores* for him, but his oldest boy Andy's not real fond of shepherdin'. Would rather work cattle, and he was real happy to have the chance. Besides, that made room for his brother, little Pedro, to fill in as a *pastore*."

"How many kids does he have?"

"Eight, I think. Is it eight, Elizabeth?" Elizabeth nodded. Still looking at Elizabeth, he added, "Five boys and three girls?" She nodded again. He turned back to Tom. "They've lost two since we've known 'em, and I think one or two before that.

"I'll tell you what," he continued. "That boy Andy's been quite a help to Elizabeth while I was gone. He shot that turkey we had last night. He's been ridin' line on the herd, earnin' some of a cowhand's wages from Herman, just for that time. I kept gettin' the shares, with the expense money, for pay, even though I was on the drive. Andy earned what Herman would've paid a hand on the trail. I imagine he was pleased to earn a stake. He set up his own *jacal* on the south end of the range as his headquarters. He's just seventeen, so probably felt pretty good to get out on his own, still a safe distance from home. Elizabeth had him stay here, often enough, when he was on this end of the range, though." Luke smiled at Elizabeth, to think of her looking after the thoughtful young man who had been looking after her.

Luke turned back to Tom. "Sean told me, before I left, that they would keep an eye on the family and check in. Herman and his family did the same. Herman's wife, Elise, and one of his girls, Anna, and his daughter-in-law Katie came over for Elizabeth's birthin'. Maria and her oldest girl, Teresa, came, too, and helped and watched the young'uns and were even prayin' the uh, what was it they call it, Elizabeth?"

"The rosary," Elizabeth said. Luke stared at her as if he had not quite understood, and Elizabeth elaborated for Luke and Tom, "To Mary the mother of Jesus."

"Yeah, the rosary," Luke confirmed.

"They all were very good to me," Elizabeth said, as if to herself, as she looked at the floor, corroborating Luke's report of what he had learned the night before. "And while I labored, Maria, Teresa, and Katie prayed the rosary. They prayed in English, out of deference to Katie, who did not know Spanish, but Maria and Teresa said some prayers in Spanish. I did not understand this praying to Mary, but I do remember that, at that time, I did not question it. I know that I just began to think about the birth of our Savior and of his mother and her young motherhood of God's only Son." She had said enough. "That is all I know."

Tom eyed her more intently. Still looking down at the floor, she continued, "Andy has been such a fine young gentleman, always checking in on us in his quiet way, doing little things you'd never think to ask him to do. Zachariah loved it when Andy would come, and he would follow him around and 'help' him, and Andy was so patient."

Tom noted the real affection Elizabeth conveyed in her expression of these sentiments. He noted too the wistful look that spread across Luke's face at the mention of his son following in the footsteps of another man.

Eventually Luke spoke again. "We've been hopin' and prayin' that the Lord would send us someone to go in with us. We'll be all alone out there, at least at first. There'll be a lot of work to do. Besides, there's just the matter of trailin' the herd, small as it is, and the horses and the wagons, and just havin' an extra man in case of trouble. Elizabeth and I were talkin' last night, and we know that you're the right man, Tom."

Tom pondered this offer of a home upon the land. "What could I bring to this partnership? I mean, you're contributin' the cattle, and the rest."

Luke looked at Elizabeth, then back at Tom. "Tom, we need money. We want to buy the land, as much of it as we can. We buy it at the head of the canyon, at the source of the springs, we got the water rights. Then if we keep buyin' it as we go, pretty soon we could own all the land in the canyon, and beyond. We could have quite a ranch. We could pass it on to the young'uns and everything."

Tom nodded his head slowly, ruminating on what he had heard, impressed at Luke's reasoning (and, he suspected, Elizabeth's, too).

"Free grass ain't goin' to last forever. There are too many people movin' onto the land, and open range, free grass, just ain't, uh . . ." Luke looked down, searching for the word. "It's just not, uh, . . . It's just not . . . efficient." His head came up with the word. "Those old maverick cowmen out there can control a range, as long as there's not many on it and they're all in agreement as to whose range is where, but you get more folks movin' out there for their share of the public land, and then those old mavericks can only control by bullyin', that is, unless they're willin' to buy the land, which sooner or later they're goin' to have to do to keep it. The way things are goin', with the Indians gone and the land fillin' up with settlers, it's the only secure thing to do," Luke said.

Tom's mind immediately conjured up the run-in he had had with the open-range cattleman in Dodge City, thinking that, here, in the person of Luke Stuart, was one more witness to the unsoundness of that man's position.

Unaware of Tom's musings, Luke continued, "Besides, I saw this fence they were showin' up there in Dodge. It has barbs on it, so the cattle won't go near it. Of course, Herman has talked about it, but I'd not seen it before. Only a few strands of this wire on some posts and you can hold entire herds. Won't be long before folks start usin' it. It might be expensive now, but you know how things change."

Tom was familiar with the wire. "Yep, with that barbwire fencin' you could really control breedin' and improve your stock."

"That's right," Luke said. "Course, that is down the line a ways, but the day will come."

Tom nodded his head some more and then said, "So what kind of money are we talkin' about here?"

Once more Luke and Elizabeth exchanged glances. Then Luke looked Tom straight in the eyes. "Tom, we're thinkin' in the neighborhood of about a thousand dollars."

"Huh," Tom responded. He considered the amount for a moment. Then he said, "How much land you intendin' to buy with a thousand dollars?"

"Well, we figure about twelve sections," Luke said.

"Twelve sections?"

"Well, Herman'll sell us some of his railroad certificates for fifty dollars a section: that's around eight cents an acre," Luke explained. "We ought to be able to locate 'em for anywhere from ten to twenty cents an acre. When we locate those sections, we have to survey the alternate sections for the state school fund. Those alternates then belong to the state. They become part of what's called the 'appropriated public domain,' but they'll be part of our range. So we buy six sections, but we end up with twelve."

Tom thought for a moment. "When did you decide all this?" he asked them, as he considered that they had been apart for months.

"We've been thinkin' about it for some time. I learned a lot from Herman about usin' certificates to buy land and how the whole thing worked," Luke told him. "The idea's just been fleshin' out over time, so that we had our minds pretty well made up before I left in April, and the situation keeps lookin' better all the time. I truly do not think there is a better time than now. The dangers are lower than they've been in the past, and I do not believe that the kind of opportunities available in that virgin land will last much longer."

Tom pondered this. He knew something about what Luke had described concerning the railroad certificates, as he had considered buying such certificates in the past, but because he had had no idea where he might locate them, he had passed on the opportunities. Still, he well knew that they were available, if ever he should change his mind. The trade in land certificates was a lively one. He had heard of some certificates selling for five cents an acre, or even less, at one time or another.

This low cost of land was a result of the unique history of the state of Texas. Ever abundant in land, Texas had seen land grants character-ize its settlement and improvement from the time of Spanish rule, through Mexican rule, through the period of the Republic, and well into its statehood in the United States. Concerning its lands, even the state's annexation by the United States was unique. Due to its great potential for destroying the fragile balance of slave states to free states, as well as its potential to bring about open hostility with Mexico (which involved further implications for the free-state/slave-state bal-ance), many in the United States—especially abolitionists, many of the Whig party, and residents of the North—opposed the annexation of Texas. Accordingly, in one attempt at annexation, when Texas offered its 175 million acres of remaining public domain in exchange for the assumption by the United States of ten million dollars of the Republic's debt (estimated to have been as much as thirteen million dollars at the time), the proposed treaty was defeated by the United States Senate.

Nevertheless, the idea of a vast independent republic—with the potential for expansion and for alliances with other nations—right on the very border of the United States raised concerns, even among those opposed to slavery. With the prospect of occupation by the United States of the entire Oregon territory in the north and with the election of the pro-annexation James K. Polk to the presidency of the United States, Texas was admitted to the United States by a controversial joint resolution of Congress, as proposed by then President John Tyler, which required only a simple majority in both houses, rather than by treaty, which would have required a two-thirds majority ratification in the Senate. By virtue of this action, Texas became the only state to enter the United States with both its debt and its public lands intact, when it was annexed on December 29, 1845. Later, the Compromise of 1850 settled boundary disputes between Texas and the United States, and Texas gave up its claims to lands that later became parts of Colorado, Kansas, New Mexico, Oklahoma, and Wyoming, some seventy-nine million acres. In exchange, Texas retained some ninety-six million acres of remaining public domain and eventually received almost $15.5 million, which solved its debt problem, with money left over to begin a permanent school fund and to build a capitol, a governor's mansion, and more.

Still, as when it had been an independent republic, so now that it was a state, Texas had extensive lands to fill with settlers and to use as capital for the internal improvements Texas would need in order for its citizens to prosper. Consequently, land continued to be distributed, and internal improvements earned their share (and sometimes more than their share in the many instances of fraud). Among these internal improvements, railroads earned the greatest allotment of land—sixteen sections of land for every one mile of track completed—in the form of scrip, land certificates that could be assigned. And so they were assigned, with railroad scrip and other certificates for Texas land flooding the market, so that land could be purchased and located (that is surveyed, registered, and patented) often enough for less than twenty-five cents an acre.

But even in the case of railroad certificates, Texas did not abandon a principle that went back all the way to its Spanish days: to use public lands for the establishment and support of a free education system. The impact this had on railroads and other internal improvements was to require those that had been granted land certificates in exchange for internal improvements, or those to whom those certificates had been assigned, to survey, for every section of land they surveyed for themselves, an adjoining section of land for the state to be added to the state's permanent school fund. These sections were often referred to as public school lands, school lands, school alternates, alternates, or the alternate sections. This was the background of the situation Luke was describing.

Tom further considered the Stuarts' offer and the prospect of a home upon the land. A thought of the potential investment in the cowhide horseshoe of Mr. Yates of Manchester, England, flitted weakly through his mind, but was overcome by this new possibility. A home upon the land, his land, a place where he could bring forth produce from the work of his hands and the sweat of his face, a place to be from and to return to. Was this the realization of the dream that had been creeping deeper and deeper into him? Was this what he had not been able to bring about? Was this what he had been waiting for, what he had been leaving himself available for? Everything in him seemed to be saying "Yes!" But Tom said something else.

"Well," he said, still looking at the top of the table, "it all sounds pretty good. Sounds like you've put a lot of thought into it." He raised his eyes to Luke and Elizabeth and added, "Still, it's all pretty new to me. I'd like to mull it over some, to sleep on it."

"I expect you would," Luke said. "You let us know as soon as you've got an answer, Tom. Don't rush none, but just know that the sooner we get goin' the better."

Tom drew his head back slightly as he looked at Luke. "Well," he said with his eyes wide open, "I won't rush then."

They all remained frozen for a moment. Then Elizabeth broke into laughter, with Luke and Tom falling in immediately behind her. They all laughed together, and it was good, good laughter; healthy, full laughter; the laughter of friends, of compatriots.

Nevertheless, Luke sought to explain. "I just meant," he began, as he tried to rein in his laughter behind a smile that would not be subdued, "you ought to take your time, but we've got to keep in mind . . ." What exactly they needed to keep in mind, he never did make clear, as Elizabeth and Tom laughed all the more, and he could not finish what he had been trying to say. As laughter again threatened to overwhelm his smile, he managed to send a look Tom's way and shake his head and say, "What a comedian," before his smile gave way, and he fell into the hilarity enjoyed by Elizabeth and Tom, and the discussion was over.

Breakfast was over too, or had been for some little time now, which meant the day was well underway. With the effects of their mirth still hanging lightly about them, Luke and Tom made their way out to the barn and saddled their horses to ride the line of the range of the Richter homeplace.

•   •   •

ONCE OUT ON THE RANGE, they found that Andy had been conscientious in his care of the cattle, with not a few indications that he had doctored for screwworms. As a shepherd, Andy would only naturally be diligent in watching and treating for screwworms. These larvae of the screwworm fly parasite would hatch about eight hours after the female screwworm fly had laid her eggs on the edge of a wound. If left untreated, they could do considerable damage and even kill, especially sheep, which were often nicked in the shearing process and their wounds hidden by their fleece. Cattle too were susceptible, especially if the wounds from dehorning and castrating were not healed before the warm weather brought the flies. Still, there were plenty of wounds cattle could incur other than those from the roundup, and even the smallest wound could invite the pest.

The treatment for screwworms was not a pleasant one. It was an exercise in putridity that could rob a cowboy of his appetite for hours, the stench invading and laying hold of the olfactory sense, as well as the sense of taste. Nor were the senses of sight, touch, and hearing spared in this intimate encounter with maggots and decaying flesh. The treatment consisted of rendering the animal immobile—in the case of cattle, roping and tying it down—then pouring kerosene or a "medicine" (often enough, chloroform) into the wound to kill the larvae, then digging those larvae out with a stick or some other instrument, and then applying tar or some other agent to the wound to close it against subsequent infestation and allow it to heal. Luke had seen Sean use a mixture of coal oil (kerosene), charcoal, and ashes for this purpose, and had used it himself.

Andy had used it, too, to keep these cattle healthy. Besides that, Luke and Tom saw not one case of pinkeye, another serious problem for range cattle, and they needed to rescue only two beeves bogged in water holes made low by the dry summer.

Some time after noon, Luke and Tom crested a rise, and they stopped to look off to the east, out upon the range that, for over four years, Luke had worked and come to know.

"Good land, wouldn't you say, Tom?" Luke submitted.

"It is," Tom agreed, contemplating the rolling expanse of blond and green grass, with its brush and streams and trees.

"We were so young when we came here, four, . . . four-and-a-half years ago."

"Huh."

"Seems like a thousand years ago," Luke mused.

The two men gazed upon the land, spread out beneath the cloudless sky, all bleached, land and sky, to lighter, brighter hues by the August sun.

"You know," Luke continued, "in that first roundup when I got my shares, that fall of '73, you know, I had exactly seventy calves. Seventy," he said again, as he turned his head to look at Tom, who was leaning upon his arms crossed over the horn of his saddle, his own head turned so that he could look at Luke. "With all the loss from weakness, disease, wolves, coyotes, even panthers, with all that, I had exactly seventy head. Not sixty-nine, not seventy-one, exactly seventy."

"Hmph," Tom quietly responded, nodding his head in appreciation of the import Luke assigned to this fact.

"It was an established mixed herd," Luke continued, "and I worked hard to keep 'em healthy, so I expected a good return, but exactly seventy."

Tom hmphed and nodded some more in further appreciation.

"You know," Luke said, looking out and then back at Tom, as Tom all the while watched him, "Elizabeth said that that seventy was a sign. She said it was an important number in the Bible. She said seventy was the number of the descendants of Noah after the flood, and that all the people of the world came from those seventy."

Having said this, Luke watched Tom to see his reaction. Tom merely pressed his lips together and offered another "hmph," while nodding his head slowly in consideration of this Biblical allusion.

Luke found the reaction satisfactory, and so he continued. "She said that before the Lord brought all those quail to the Israelites, when the people were tired of eatin' the manna in the desert, the Lord told Moses to pick seventy men. And the Lord gave some of the spirit he had given to Moses to these other seventy men, and that was just before the people were goin' to eat meat again, you know, the meat of the quails, like our beeves are for meat."

Another "hmph" emerged from Tom as again he nodded.

Luke looked back out upon the land as he continued. "And Jesus sent out seventy, two by two, before him. And Jesus told Peter that he was supposed to forgive his brother seventy times seven times, to teach him that he had to forgive without limit. Elizabeth says all this points to a good sign for our herd startin' out at seventy." Luke looked back at Tom, who had turned to gaze out upon the land again. Luke continued, "Like the seventy descendants of Noah and the seventy sent out two by two and the number of times we're supposed to forgive, the number seventy is a great sign of expected increase."

But it was as if Tom no longer heard Luke, for before Luke had completely finished speaking, Tom proclaimed, though in a quiet, low tone, as he looked upon the land, "'Then came Peter unto him and said: Lord, how often shall my brother offend against me, and I forgive him? till seven times? Jesus saith to him: I say not to thee, till seven times; but till seventy times seven times.'"

Then Tom was silent, his gaze still fixed on the land, on this cattle range before him. Luke, too, was silent, as he continued to look at Tom. Then he, too, looked back out upon the land, then again at Tom, then back to the land. After a little while, Tom spoke up. "Well, you think we ought to be movin' along."

"Yessir," Luke replied, and they nudged their horses and rode down from the rise into the land they had been contemplating.

It was shortly after this, as they were approaching one of Luke's older cows, that something jarred in Tom's mind. As he settled his eyes on this four-year-old cow, its brand seemed to jump out at him. First, on the left hip he saw a vented brand, one that had been marked out with a slash, that read LES. Below it he saw the brand that Luke referred to as Seven Ox Seven, which appeared 7OX7, but now he saw it differently.

"Seventy times seven," he said to Luke as they approached the cow.

"What's that?"

"Seven Ox Seven is seventy times seven!"

"That's right," Luke admitted, pleased, which was evident in his smile. "Seven Ox Seven is easier on the tongue and sounds more like a brand. It kind of keeps it our secret, Elizabeth's and mine. This cow was one of our first calves." Luke rode up alongside of her and said,

"How are you, old red cow? That's a fine calf you've dropped for us, old cow. Thank you, old cow." Pointing to the brands on her left hip, he said to Tom, "See that there, that marked out LES? That's what we first branded that first bunch. It was for our names, Luke and Elizabeth Stuart. We didn't really know what to brand 'em, so that was as good as any. But after we branded that first seventy, and Elizabeth got to thinkin' on it, we decided the next spring to change it, kind of in honor of the Lord's goodness to us, and a reminder, and a sign of hope in an unlimited increase. So that's where the Seven Ox Seven brand came from."

Tom liked it, and he thought about it. For the rest of that day, as they rode and worked the range, Tom pondered the Stuarts' offer. He pondered into the night as well, with prayer to guide his pondering. He did not sleep as well as he usually did. Yet, in the morning after breakfast, with the children gone outside—but for little Robert, who nestled quietly in his mother's arms—Tom was ready for further discussion.

"About these school lands," he was saying to Luke, "what about buyin' those. I mean, are they available to buy or for someone else to buy out from under you?"

"No, not accordin' to Herman, and Herman would know. As I understand it, school lands are available for sale, but a person can only buy, at the most, a quarter section, and that they can only buy at a minimum price of $1.50 an acre. So, you got 160 acres at $1.50 an acre compared to the unlimited acres at fifteen to thirty cents an acre you pay for the unappropriated land, sometimes less. Now, you only need pay ten percent of the purchase price for the school lands, and you have ten years to pay off the rest at ten percent interest, but why waste your money that way when the certificates are such a better value?"

"What about leasin' the school lands?"

"No way I know of, yet, least not for state school lands. Some county lands can be leased, I think, but we won't be dealin' with any of those. As far as I understand it, there is no way, as yet, to lease the school lands, and no way to buy them for less than $1.50 an acre, and then for no more than 160 acres," Luke summarized.

"Huh," Tom responded, meditating as he ran his tongue back and forth against his back molars. Then he said, "Well, I've got to say that I am a little uneasy about not bein' able to buy those school lands. Like you," he said before Luke could interrupt him, "I think the days of free grass are limited. I believe it is wise to purchase the land, to invest in it, and I just don't like the idea that half the range—in pieces scattered throughout, not just on the outside of the range, but probably checkerboard after some fashion—may some day come open to some-one else, that we might not have any control over it, that someone else might be able to gain control of it."

Luke nodded his head and looked down at the top of the table. "I know," he said, "Elizabeth and I have had the same concerns. But," he continued, as he turned to look at Tom, "everybody else is in the same sit-uation, and true range men would not move in on another man's range."

"That's true range men, principled range men. Them I'm not wor-ried about. It's the unprincipled that concern me," Tom concluded.

Luke again was looking at the top of the table. "Well," he said, "that's just the way it is, one of the risks, but a lot of folks are takin' that risk, and we think it's worth it."

"So do I," Tom declared.

Luke and Elizabeth both turned hopeful, expectant faces on him.

"I've thought about it, and just wanted to know the whole situa-tion with these school lands, but I've decided, if you folks would have me, I'd be honored to be your partner in this venture."

"We're glad to have you, Tom," Luke said, with a smile that spread over his face in the release of a certain tension and the replacement of that tension with a sudden joy at this good fortune. He reached out and shook hands with Tom.

Elizabeth, meanwhile, deflated somewhat in her own release of tension. The degree of that release, and the degree of relief that came with it, took her by surprise, as she had been a good deal more tense about their pending venture than she had realized. Tom's involvement in the venture would mean a great deal. He would double their man-power, as far as work and protection were concerned, as they made their way into the frontier. His monetary help would mean that they would not need to turn over some of their herd to Herman in exchange for the certificates. The relief she felt was conveyed, to some extent, in her reaction to Tom.

"You don't know, Mr. Schurtz, how welcome your words are," she said as she rocked little Robert in her arms. "We're honored to have you as a partner," she added, sincerely, because she had learned from Luke his positive appraisal of Tom Schurtz.

"Now that we're partners, you two might start callin' each other by your given names," Luke said as he glanced from Elizabeth to Tom.

Tom nodded ascent and said, "Mrs. Stuart, please call me *Tom*."

"I will, Tom," she said, adjusting to the change. "And you please call me *Elizabeth*."

"*Elizabeth* it is," Tom agreed.

And Elizabeth rose, with the baby in her arms, and poured coffee in all three cups. The young friends then raised their cups, up before their warm smiles of joyful hope, and toasted the birth of their bold partnership.

AFTER ELIZABETH, LUKE, AND TOM finished their coffee that morning, Tom and Luke saddled their horses and rode south to the range where Sean Grady's family pastured their sheep. They rode leisurely, alternating between a walk and a canter, and in a little over an hour, they were upon the Grady's range. Tom noticed that post oak and live oak were more in abundance in this area.

Eventually a large *jacal* came into view. It was situated on a rise near enough to two large live oaks to derive some benefit from their shade. Sheep pens spread across the rise below the *jacal* to the south. They approached the camp from the east, having crossed a stream at a ford almost directly east of it. As they approached it, Tom could see that the *jacal* had a stone front that included a chimney. Behind this front, the walls were made of sticks in picket fashion, chinked with mud. The roof was thatched with tules. A sort of awning protruded from the front of the house. It was supported by four posts: two against the rock front of the dwelling and two farther out in front. Across each of these pairs of posts was laid a long tree branch, parallel to the front of the *jacal*. Smaller branches were laid perpendicular to the two long branches so that their ends rested on the long branches. Sticks and brush were heaped up on this crude frame to shade a packed-earth area in front of the *jacal*, with a counter and tables arranged within it, which appeared to serve as a kitchen.

A woman and three girls were working beneath the awning, between the counter and the fireplace. A little boy played in the yard in front. As Luke and Tom approached, one of the girls noticed and brought their approach to the attention of the woman, who then sent the smallest girl running off toward the pens below the *jacal*.

As they drew closer, Tom's attention was drawn to the tallest of the girls, though he could not get a clear look at her as she moved between the fireplace and the counter, usually with her side to him and often with her luxuriant hair hiding her face.

Luke called out to the woman as they dismounted, "Maria."

"Luke," she replied.

"This is Mr. Tom Schurtz," Luke said as both men approached the *jacal* on foot and tipped their hats in the presence of Maria and her daughters. At Maria's urging, they stepped in under the edge of the awning.

Then Tom saw. The oldest girl, really a woman of maybe eighteen years of age, looked up at him with brown eyes far darker than her flawless brown skin, the pure whites of her eyes all but shining as she looked. She quickly looked away, much too quickly for Tom.

"Mr. Schurtz," Maria said in her heavy Mexican accent.

"This is Maria, Teresa, and Brigid Grady," Luke said, pointing out mother, the tallest daughter, and her younger sister, respectively, "and that was Marina who you saw running away. And that's young Patrick over there," Luke added, pointing out the little boy playing in the yard, who stood and stared at the two men and then ran to his mother's side.

"Mrs. Grady," Tom said, lifting his hat and executing a slight bow, almost a nod. He then nodded his respects all around.

Luke proceeded to inquire after Maria's and the girls' health and the health of the family in general. He then thanked Maria for her family's watch over his own family while he was away and, in particular, thanked her and Teresa for the help they had rendered Elizabeth when her time had come. As Luke visited, Tom could see a man approaching from where the youngest girl had found him working on an extension of the pens below. A boy remained behind, continuing to work on the fence. As they awaited this man's arrival, Tom and Luke leaned against opposite poles of the awning. Luke continued to visit with Maria and the girls, and Tom listened politely, involuntarily glancing, now and then, toward the oldest girl, to find out if he had really seen what he thought he had seen.

Before long, Sean Grady arrived at the *jacal*. He was a tall, dark, broad-shouldered, long-legged man with a broad face of striking features, and shoulder-length, dark hair. As he arrived, he stuck out his hand and said, "Luke. Well, it is grand to see you," in a whole-toned voice of reserved depth.

Luke shook hands with Sean Grady, and the men inquired after each other's well-being. Then Luke turned toward Tom. "This is Tom Schurtz," he said, stepping aside so the men could shake hands.

"Tom," Sean said as they shook.

"Pleased to meet you, Sean."

"Pleasure's mine to meet a friend of Luke's," the man responded in a singular accent that well mixed the man's ethnic heritage. "Have you met my wife, Maria, and my daughters?"

When they assured him that Tom had, except that he had not met Marina, Sean introduced the girl, who was already back at work, baking with her mother and sisters. Formalities completed, Sean asked, "Would you have something to eat, then?"

When they had both assured him that they had not long ago eaten a large breakfast, he said, "Coffee, then?"

They both said that they would, and Sean said to his oldest daughter, "Teresa, would you bring us some coffee, please."

The young woman brought over cups and placed them on the table, then glanced up at Tom with those eyes. She returned with the coffee and another glance for Tom, confirming, without a doubt, that she was, indeed, one of the most beautiful women he had ever seen anywhere. Tom was immediately struck by the seeming incongruity of her appearance to her humble setting.

Sean was no less struck by Tom's involuntary attraction to his oldest daughter, for which he made no judgment of Tom. He had seen it from men before and was not unaware of his daughter's beauty, and of all that it could mean. It was for that reason that he had eagerly accepted a proposal of marriage for her, from a young *vaquero* from another sheep ranch to the south. As a *vaquero*, the man would provide for her, and he was of the mettle to advance beyond that station to *caporal* or *mayordomo*. And he was a good man, and handsome, the better to keep a woman of beauty from temptation.

"Teresa will be leavin' us soon," Sean said.

Tom could not hide his interest.

"She will be marryin' Fernando Gomez, a *vaquero* at the ranch to the south of here."

Teresa glanced at Tom again. Tom looked down, with a light smile for reality.

"Congratulations, Teresa," Luke called out. Tom offered a nod and the light smile.

"Thank you," she answered demurely from beneath her hair, with a light smile of her own, revealing teeth no less white than the whites of her eyes, to complete the vision for Tom.

Those sentiments expressed, the men changed the topic to the drive to Dodge City from which Luke had just returned, then to how the summer had passed for the flocks under Sean's care, and to Andy's experience of working for Herman while Luke was away, and to Luke's appreciation for that work, and to various other matters that had a way of making for good conversation whenever Luke and Sean, and now Tom as well, began to visit. Finally, they got to the matter of the Stuarts' move.

"You are goin', then?" Sean confirmed, after Luke had said they were.

"We are, and Tom's goin' with us."

Sean looked at Tom as if he were now sizing him up anew. After a moment he said, "Well, I am glad of that. I didn't like the idea of sendin' these folks off alone," he said to Tom. "And it's not for me to be goin' with them."

"You know you folks are more than welcome to join us," Luke reminded Sean of past encouragements.

"I know," Sean responded, "but it's not for me. We're here now. This is for us," he said, looking down and nodding his head slightly with an air of contentment. Then looking up quickly, he said to Luke, "When are you leavin'?"

"We'll be roundin' up early, to cut out our herd, in four or five days, I expect. Herman and his boys'll help. Shouldn't take long with help."

"Andy will want to help," Sean said.

"He'll be more than welcome," Luke replied. "By the way, could you let Andy know that we're back? I haven't had the chance to round him up yet."

"He knows," Sean said.

"How does he know?"

"I don't know. I just know that he came back yesterday and went out with the sheep. So I've got Pedro workin' with me today."

"Huh," Luke said as he pondered. "Hey, do you think Andy'd want to ride line for these next few days? I'd pay him whatever Herman's paid him, per diem. We're goin' to ride into San Antone, and the less scattered those beeves are before the roundup, the easier it'll go."

"He'll be glad to do it," Sean assured him.

They talked some more, and at last, with Luke's help of bringing the subject around to Escondido Canyon, Tom was able to ask Sean about its "enchantment."

"Well, you know," Sean said, leaning back in his crude chair and fixing Tom with a steady gaze, "the Apache are a very religious people. Like the Irish," he added. "The Apache—or Indeh, as they call themselves—believe there is only one God, Ussen, and they pray to him and have laws from him. And there is an afterlife, a 'happy place,' a 'cloud land.' But just by sayin' a dead person's name, you summon his spirit, no matter what he is doin' in the happy place. Vengeance is important to the Apache religion too, and the Apache have a lot of ideas about ghosts and what they can do, and I've only heard about it in bits and pieces," he said. "Now, I'm a Christian, raised Catholic by my father and my mother: my mother had converted. Though I do not subscribe to the Apache religion, I do not take it all lightly. What a people believe and practice can have its spiritual effects, and I do not take any of it lightly."

Tom had the sense that Sean said this as if he thought Tom might need convincing, but Tom was of the same mind that the spiritual realm was not one to toy with. Prayer to God and seeking the help of saints and angels was good, as the Church taught, but delving into anything beyond what was appropriate was not for man to play with.

"So," Sean continued, "I don't know all that much about the Apache tradition concerning the Escondido, but from what I've heard, there were some old tales of this enchanted canyon, and I believe it was supposed to be the same one as the Escondido. I know more about the Escondido from Maria, whose father saw it with his own eyes, as Luke has probably told you. That's about all I know, though the tellin' of it gets embellished on occasion," he concluded, with the hint of a smile and a bit of an Irish twinkle in his eye that Tom recognized readily enough. Tom smiled and looked down in a manner that led the half-Irish Sean to wonder if the half-Irish Tom, who had heard his share of Irish tales, had understood more than he had expected.

Then they talked of sheep and of how far the boys were out with the flocks. Tom listened and tried to strain, from the mix, Sean's various accents: Irish, Apache, and Spanish, too, as he was fluent in it.

"You goin' to be able to sell me a merino ram and some Mexican ewes, like we talked about last spring?" Luke asked him.

"I can," Sean said. "Mr. Jones said fifteen dollars for the ram and three dollars apiece for the ewes."

"Agreed," Luke said. "Why don't we make it five ewes and make it an even thirty dollars."

"All right."

Luke counted out thirty dollars, from the money he had pulled from his pocket, and handed it to Sean. Luke would have liked to buy more, but he and Elizabeth had budgeted their money, and their main interest would be cattle. Still, sheep produced wool, a valuable commodity that in six months was worth as much as the sheep and was always and everywhere in demand. It would be greatly appreciated in the Panhandle, known for its northers.

Luke's purchase demonstrated the knowledge of sheep he had gained from his association with Sean Grady. An owner of Mexican sheep (the Spanish *churro* or "common sheep") would be happy to get two pounds of wool per head per year, but it was a hardy animal that mothered its young, endured periods of poor grazing, and could take the heat of the south Texas summer. When bred with merinos from the northeastern United States (originally from Spain), the cross would lose some of that hardiness, but would produce three or four pounds of wool per head per year, with further grading raising yields to as high as eight pounds per year.

"You think Andy could bring 'em on up when he comes for the roundup?" Luke asked Sean.

"He can."

Then Sean suddenly sat up straight and stuck a finger into the air as if something had just occurred to him. He stood up and led Luke and Tom back past the *jacal* to a small shed. There they found, around their mother, a litter of Border collie puppies, some of them asleep.

Sean picked up one of the sleeping puppies and said, "He's ready to be weaned. Should be one hundred percent. Shannon, the bitch that bore 'em, descends from the original bitch my father brought with him when he sailed from England. He bred her whenever he could find a collie male, and I've done the same. The one breed of dog bred for intelligence. One hundred percent or not, he's a far cry from these mongrels they use all about us here. They take 'em from the bitch and stick 'em on a goat or sheep's teat and think they've got a sheep dog. This is the real thing."

He handed him over to Luke and said, "He's for young Zachariah. Train him right, you'll have a fine herder, sheep or cattle. He'll do the work of several men and horses. Keep mum about that, or we'll put some cowboys out of a job."

Luke looked down at the black puppy with its white chest and nose and stockings. "This is awful good of you, Sean."

"'Tis nothin'," Sean said, as Tom noted the distinctly Irish delivery from the very Apache-looking man.

"It sure will be somethin' to Zachariah," Luke replied.

"Who knows," Sean said, "he might even have some help trainin' him."

Luke looked at Sean with a slight smile, curious about what he might mean, but he thought little of it when Sean did not respond.

Finally, Sean, Luke, and Tom sauntered back to the *jacal*, where Luke and Tom, especially Luke, bid those present of the Grady family a warm farewell. Then Luke and Tom mounted and road away, Luke cradling the puppy in front of him and Tom, after one last glance, appreciating the wisdom of a father who put more store in the beauty of his daughter's soul than in that of her body. For Tom believed that Teresa would be far better off the wife of a local *vaquero*, potential *mayordomo*, than the toast of society circles, where she could indeed attain a high status based on her outward appearance, but on that alone.

LUKE AND TOM pulled up in the yard of the Stuart home and dismounted. Elizabeth was working in the fenced garden off the northwest corner of the house, with little Robert asleep in the shade on a blanket.

He was asleep under netting because Elizabeth had heard stories of screwworm eggs being deposited in the noses of sleeping people, and she would not let that happen to one of hers.

Luke called out in a hushed voice, "Elizabeth."

She looked up.

Luke, with Tom behind him, was advancing on her, cradling something under his vest. She met him at the fence, where he slipped out the puppy for her to see. "From Sean," he said, still in the hushed voice. "Where's Zack?"

"He's down by the barn with Rachel," she said, and she oohed and petted the puppy.

"Come on," Luke said.

"Wait," Elizabeth called, in her own hushed voice, and Luke turned back to her. "I've got to show you something," she said, and she hurried over and retrieved the sleeping Robert and returned to the fence, where Tom held the gate open for her. She thanked Tom and then led the way around to the south side of the house. There on the inset porch, still in a crate, was a brand-new cook stove, with several joints of stovepipe resting on top.

"Where'd this come from?" Luke asked incredulously.

"Herman," Elizabeth said.

Luke looked at her, the surprise showing in his face.

"He and Franz were returning with two full wagons from San Antonio, mostly with wood for a house they're building for Franz and Katie," Elizabeth began to explain. "He stopped to see if you were back and to see what we had decided about moving. I told him you were back and that we were moving to the Panhandle. He raised his eyebrows at that, but I explained that we had thought it out and were sure. And I told him that we had a new partner, a good man," she said, smiling at Tom.

"Vell, he t'ought dat vas goot," Elizabeth continued, "and then he said that we 'vill neet to eat vell und be varm up dere in de nort,' and he and Franz unloaded this stove and left it on the porch. He said that they had intended to order three, one for the new house (Franz and Katie's), one for the house that Anna and James had built, and one for Elise and him to put in the big house. He said that with each stove they had added to their order the price per stove had gone down, which made this fourth stove 'almost frree': so they ordered it."

Luke just stared at the stove. "You know," he said, turning to Tom, "that Herman, he knows where every cent goes, and will not waste a cent, can come across as tight, you know, . . . stingy, but then he does somethin' like this. And he does it often enough, too."

Tom bent and looked over the stove through the grate. "This is a high-quality stove," he said. "It's got to weigh four hundred pounds."

"It would be quality," Luke said. "With Herman, it would be."

"This is better than the stove we've got here," Elizabeth said enthusiastically. "Here, I was expecting that I'd have to go without a stove for some time. I couldn't tell Herman how much it meant. I was speechless. He knew. He knew what it meant. And you know how much Herman hates to have any displays in his presence. I think he was glad that I was holding Robert, or he might have been afraid that I would hug him. He waved off my thanks, and he and Franz headed right back to the wagons."

"Did he say anything about the roundup?" Luke asked her.

"He did say, 'Vell, I suppoze you'll be vantin' to roundup soon, t'en,'" Elizabeth said. "And I told him you were planning to go to San Antonio for two or three days, and were planning to ride over before you went. He said not to bother, that we had much to do and that he would plan on a roundup in four or five days, and he would talk to you then. I told him that you had gone down to the Gradys' to talk to Andy and Sean. He said that 'vas goot.'"

"We didn't see Andy," Luke told her. "He was out with the sheep, but we did see Sean and got filled in. Andy'll ride line for the next few days and will help out on the roundup. He'll bring up the sheep when he comes for the roundup." Luke paused for a while. "That Herman," he finally said, looking from Elizabeth to Tom, "he is one rare gem. I'll tell you what." Luke looked at the stove some more and just shook his head. "Well," he said, "this saves us a ride over there. We can ride into San Antone this afternoon."

Tom nodded.

Luke suddenly stepped back and held the puppy out from him as it began to wet. "Aw, little fellow, I forgot all about you," he said as he held the puppy at arm's length and turned to hold him out over the ground, where the puppy finished his business. He looked down and surveyed his front. "Well, damage is minimal," he said. "Looks like I'll need a washin' up and change of shirt before we ride into town."

"Before you eat dinner," Elizabeth corrected him.

"Anyways," Luke said, "let's get this little one taken care of." With that, he stepped off the porch and started toward the barn, with Elizabeth (holding Robert) and Tom falling in behind him. Damage done, Luke brought his arm around and held the puppy behind his back.

When they neared the barn, Luke called out, "Zachariah."

Zachariah and Rachel looked up from where they were playing with a toad.

"Come on over here."

The children came running toward the three clustered adults.

"Mr. Grady wanted me to give you somethin', Zack," Luke said as he pulled his hand out from behind his back and revealed the puppy.

Zachariah's eyes and mouth opened to their limits as he viewed the puppy. "Daddy, is he mine? Is he mine, Daddy; is he mine?"

Rachel was not to be forgotten, as she added, "Is he mine, Daddy; is he mine?"

"Now easy with him, he's just a young'un," Luke warned them as he handed the puppy over to Zachariah.

"He's a fine puppy, Daddy. He's a fine puppy," Zachariah was saying as he alternately squeezed the puppy against himself and held him out in front to look at him. Rachel had her hands right in there with Zachariah's, to the point that she was pulling on the puppy, trying in a child's way to have her share of him, while the puppy sought to gnaw on any fingers available.

"Better let Zachariah handle him, Rachel. He's Zachariah's puppy, but you'll be able to play with him too," Luke told her in an effort to save the puppy from being pulled apart.

Rachel pulled her hands away and put them behind her back, as she would if a stranger—which her father almost was—had admonished her. She retreated to her mother's skirts to watch from there, with a finger in her mouth, as Zachariah petted and held his puppy, and then put him on the ground, letting him move away a little, and then caught him up again.

"He is a fine puppy, Daddy, just a fine puppy," the boy said again. He added, "Thank you for my puppy, Daddy."

"You thank Mr. Grady next time you see him. That's who gave him to you."

"I will, Daddy."

"What are you goin' to call him?" Luke asked him.

"Charlie," Zachariah said without hesitation.

Luke looked over at Tom and said quietly, "Boy's always wanted to fix the name 'Charlie' to some animal. Have no idea why that name. Go ahead ask him."

Tom's curiosity was too aroused to reject this invitation. "Why you want to name him 'Charlie,' Zachariah?"

"I like the name 'Charlie,'" the boy said without looking at the visitor.

Tom's curiosity was further aroused. "Why do you like that name?"

"I just like it, sir," Zachariah said, telling the full truth and remembering the manners his parents had taught him.

Tom glanced over at Luke with a smile and slight shrug of his face and shoulders. Luke answered in kind. "He just likes it," he said to Tom in a low voice. "Always has."

Then Luke turned back to Zachariah and said in full voice, "And he's a first-rate purebred Border collie, and if you train him well, he'll be a herder. He'll help you watch over those sheep we been talkin' about, without any trouble," Luke said, reminding Zachariah that he would be helping out on their new ranch with the herding of the sheep.

"I will, Daddy. I'll train him well."

"I know you will, son," his father replied. Then the father turned and picked up his little girl and hugged her and said, "You'll be able to play with the puppy, too, Rachel; just need to be plenty gentle." He held her out and looked at her, as she looked down. He hugged her close again and said, "That's all right, Rachel; we'll be gettin' reacquainted as time goes on." Then he slipped the girl to one arm, and she rested her head on his shoulder, as she watched her brother with his new puppy. Her father slipped his free arm around her mother's shoulder, as they too watched.

And Tom Schurtz watched it all, this family with whom he had become partners, and he realized that it was all very good.

THE STUARTS AND TOM ate an early dinner, and immediately after, Tom and Luke saddled their horses and rode toward San Antonio, some forty miles distant. They arrived in town by late afternoon and managed to get to a bank before it closed. There, Tom wrote a check for a thousand dollars off a bank in Corpus Christi. He and Luke would need to wait two or three days for the money to come in, which they had expected.

In the meantime, they visited the office of a lawyer, who drew up a contract for them according to their stipulations: Tom would supply the money (a thousand dollars) for an initial outlay for land, the Stuarts would provide the stock, and Tom and Luke would jointly manage the affair. Certain items needed for the ranch were to be provided from an operating account to which each would contribute four hundred dollars, for a total of eight hundred dollars—Luke's share coming mainly from the money he had made from the sale of his beeves in Dodge City. Profits from the first sale of cattle were to go exclusively to the Stuarts. Thereafter, all profits, after operating and expansion expenses, were to be divided in half between the Stuarts and Tom Schurtz. The contract was to stand until both parties decided to renegotiate or terminate it. Luke and Tom signed the contract and made their contributions to the operating account.

This completed, the two men made their way around town looking for horses and mules in one of the best horse markets in the West. They also priced a large wagon and some oxen. But purchasing would wait until tomorrow. Now, with the day coming to a close, Luke and Tom sought out the tables of the chili queens and enjoyed one of the great delights of San Antonio: chili, served by young Mexican women, at communal tables, in the open air of the city squares, within the ambience of warm light from oil lamps set out on the tables. After the chili, they rode out to camp on the outskirts of town.

In the morning the men returned to town and purchased the large wagon they had priced the day before. During the next two days, they also bought three yoke of oxen, two stout mules, a promising colt that they expected to use as a stud upon maturity, a good brood mare, and two riding horses to round out their small remuda. The men also purchased supplies, which included plenty of flour, beans, bacon, coffee, sorghum molasses, salt, soda, sugar, dried fruit, canned goods, and kerosene, and a twenty-gallon barrel for water. They bought tools, too, the most substantial of which was a good plow, not only for farming purposes but also for plowing fireguards out on the distant grassland.

And they bought ammunition and a Sharps .50 rifle, a buffalo gun, for which they expected to find good use in the land to which they were destined.

During their time in San Antonio, Tom confessed and attended Mass. He also wrote and posted a letter to Whittacker Dallen, to let him know of his partnership with Luke and that he would not be returning to work for him. And he did something else. On the afternoon of their second day in the city, while he and Luke were separated for Luke to attend to purchases stipulated by Elizabeth, Tom wrote another check, of a substantial amount, for a purpose that would have surprised his new partner. This he sent in a letter to his brother John in Wisconsin.

THE ROUNDUP that followed the men's return from San Antonio yielded the Stuarts 307 head, with Herman substituting older calves for those few newly born, to the consternation of calves and mothers alike. These older calves would not slow up the drive, as would the new ones. The roundup also gave Luke one last opportunity to work with cousins and neighbors who had become true friends.

On the afternoon that they finished the roundup, the men did not disperse and go back to their separate homes. Instead, they all rode from the branding pens to the Stuart home. Here the women of their families, many of whom had been preparing their meals throughout the roundup, had already gathered with intentions of having a celebration, to give the Stuarts an appropriate sendoff for regions north. And celebrate they did, German style (with a little Irish thrown in), with food, beer, music, and dancing. Luke even enjoyed one or two of the home-brewed lagers, with no opposition from Elizabeth, under the circumstances. Those same circumstances allowed Elizabeth to let her husband whirl her around the floor in a polka, on more than one occasion, despite her usual scruples against dancing. Men, women, and children were coming and going from the house, dancing where they could, in the living room or on the porch or in the yard. Food kept flowing from the kitchen, as did beer and coffee.

Later in the evening, after many of the children had finally succumbed to sleep upstairs on beds, mattresses, or on the floor, and as the adults continued their revelry, Luke, standing next to Tom in the kitchen as Tom helped himself to a cup of coffee, gave Tom a light backhanded blow to his arm. Tom looked around at him. "Tom," Luke said, and he nodded toward the door to the backyard. He then sauntered to the door and out of it, looking over his shoulder to make sure Tom was following.

Once out in the yard, Luke led the way to the raw picket fence that closed off their yard from the range, and he leaned against it. Tom pulled up next to him and leaned against it, too.

"This is some place, wouldn't you say, Tom?" Luke began.

"Yes it is."

"You know, Zack was just a baby when we moved in here, and Rachel and little Bob were both born here."

"Hmph."

"All this land, Tom," Luke said, as they looked off to the south through eyes adjusting to the light of the moon and stars, "I've been over it all, time after time. And these folks," he continued, nodding over his shoulder, "you don't find these kind of folks every day."

"No," Tom agreed. "No, you don't."

Suddenly a quiet voice invaded their musings. "Luke, Tom," said the voice, and the two men turned their heads to look upon Andy Grady, who had come up silently behind them. The men straightened up from the fence and turned around to face the seventeen-year-old. He was tall, like his father, square-shouldered, though not as broad. He was not as dark as his older sister, Teresa. He had lighter eyes, too, somewhere between brown and green, and high cheekbones. His hair, cut by his sisters, was short, unlike his father's.

"I want to go with you," he told them.

Tom and Luke glanced at each other, then looked down, as each considered.

"Your folks know you want to go?" Luke asked him.

"My dad does."

An expression of understanding came over Luke's face. "That's why your daddy said Zack might have some help trainin' his puppy. You plannin' to bring ol' Rita?"

"I am," Andy responded, referring to his own Border collie, several litters and six years older than Charlie. Rita was short for Senorita.

Luke and Tom looked at each other again. Luke had known Andy for years. Tom had known him since the beginning of the roundup. Both men saw the potential Andy had to be an asset to the venture. Their looks communicated the mix of emotions each was experiencing in reaction to this request. Luke looked back at Andy, and Tom looked down.

"You are pretty good with horses, aren't you?" Luke asked him.

"I'm all right."

"You know we won't be able to pay you much," Luke made clear, "maybe shares or somethin'. This is all pretty sudden. We'd need to think up some kind of payment for your work."

"That's all right with me."

Luke nodded at the ground a little more and chewed on Andy's answer and even more on the main question under consideration. Finally, he said, "All right, Andy, I'll tell you what. You go on home tonight and talk with your folks. You get their blessing, both of 'em, and you make your good-byes. Then you come on back here tomorrow night, and we'll let you know whether we'll take you along or not. And there's no guarantee we will. Now, we'll be loadin' those wagons tomorrow, and pullin' everything together so as to leave early the mornin' after. You be here tomorrow night, and if it's all right with your folks and with us, you can stay over and head out with us in the mornin'. Fair enough?"

"Fair enough," Andy said. Then he shook hands with Luke and Tom and started walking off toward the south, a whistle bringing his dog Rita from the barn to his side.

"Andy," Luke called out to him, "take ol' Stonewall for the ride home."

"All right," Andy replied, and he redirected his course toward the barn, where he would saddle the gray he had ridden for much of the roundup. "Thanks, Luke."

"That's all right. We'll see you tomorrow night."

"All right."

As Andy drew out of earshot, Luke said to Tom, "What you think about that, Tom?"

"Well, he is good with horses, cattle too, a natural. He'd be a real asset. But he is young. Still, he's no younger than I was when I left home."

"And it could be a real opportunity for him."

"Could be."

"And we could sure use the help with the herd and wranglin' our small remuda. And that dog of his would make short work of those sheep. He would earn his pay in shares," Luke added.

"I believe he would," Tom agreed, "as long as it's good for him."

"That's right."

The men considered Andy's request a little longer. Then they let the matter lie for the time being, and they returned to the house and to the party.

THE CELEBRATION LASTED WELL INTO THE NIGHT and into the morning. As people slowly drifted out of the party, they made their beds on most of the floor of the house, on the porch, in the barn, in wagons, and on the ground. Nevertheless, it was not long after the rooster crowed that most were roused, ready to eat the hearty breakfast the women were already turning out.

After the breakfast, the men lent their hands to loading the wagons, though Luke and Tom could have used less help from these determined men who had celebrated into the early morning. Regardless, soon all the items to be loaded on the wagons had been carried to as near a wagon as they could get before Luke or Tom could halt the carriers from loading them aboard. The packing for a move that would include a trip of several weeks demanded some careful planning and positioning. So plan and position Luke and Tom did.

The smaller wagon carried boxes of clothes, dishes, and other household items, bedding, medicines, and food. Food and cooking utensils were packed to be easily accessible for every stop. The large wagon carried what furniture could be brought, the new cook stove, the new plow, other tools, guns, ammunition, harnesses, as well as all else the Stuart-Schurtz party had discerned they would need to carve a ranch out of the unknown wilderness. Beneath the wagon was suspended the stovepipe and a possum belly for wood, cow chips, and buffalo chips for fires. A chicken coop was attached to the back. Secured to the side was the twenty-gallon barrel for water.

The loading was finished, except for odds and ends, in not much more than two hours, thanks, in good part, to the packing that Elizabeth had done before, while Elise Richter, her daughters, daughters-in-law, and the neighbor women had cooked for the roundup. Luke and Tom would shift some of the load around later, but for as much as cousins and neighbors could do, it was done. Thus came the time to say good-bye.

The women made their good-byes with many tears and demonstrations of affection and promises of correspondence. The men made theirs more stoically, with handshakes and quiet words and silences. Still, when it came time to say good-bye to his older cousin Herman, just a stranger when the Stuarts had arrived four and a half years earlier, Luke felt a bit of emotion rise in his throat. Herman Richter was the closest thing to a father that Luke had known in his maturity, and the lean, round-shouldered, hard-muscled man with the sharply cut jaw, the bushy moustache and eyebrows, and the bright blue eyes would be sorely missed in Luke's life. They were bright blue eyes, indeed, into which Luke now found it difficult to look, bright blue eyes of a man who had been so good to him.

"Thanks for everything, Herman," Luke said.

"And t'anks to you, Luke." Herman's hard, strong, calloused hand crushed his emotion into Luke's, and Luke's reciprocated.

"Our home will always be open to you and the family," Luke added.

"And t'is vill alvays be home for you," Herman assured him.

More was said too, much of it repetition, but the men slowly, awkwardly pulled themselves apart and joined their wives and children. Then wagons and horses and mules pulled away from the Richter homeplace, the Stuarts' home for these four and a half years, and the Stuarts and Tom Schurtz were soon alone.

A low somberness fell over them, as they continued their work that day, punctuated now and then, quietly, with sighs from Elizabeth, sent out through silent tears. By evening, they were all packed, except for those items they would need for breakfast the next morning. Luke and Tom rounded up the cattle, which they had let graze throughout the day, and herded them into the fenced pasture behind the house.

The house was empty. The cattle were penned; as were the horses, sheep, and hogs. All that was ripe had been picked from the garden. All was in readiness to leave, to leave their home, to leave it all behind. It was a quiet supper they shared that night.

But the evening did not remain quiet. Not long after supper, in the late evening sun, a wagon could be seen approaching from the south.

Two men on horseback were also discernible. It did not take long for the Stuarts to recognize the Grady family approaching, with Sean and Andy riding horses out in front, and Juan and Matthew walking alongside. Rita the collie, never very far from Andy, padded along with the party.

In time the Grady family was in the yard and unloading from the wagon. They did not come empty-handed. Besides unloading themselves, they unloaded a Mexican feast, which they soon brought into the house. The somber Stuarts were somber no more, as celebration again filled their house and yard. It was a more subdued celebration than that of the night before. The Gradys appreciated that the Stuarts and Tom had worked hard on the roundup, had packed everything, had celebrated the night before, and would be leaving in the morning. With a sense of propriety, like that which Tom had witnessed in his own Irish mother and uncle (though it was not shared by all the Irish, Tom could attest), Sean Grady managed the gathering so that it served the needs of the Stuarts and Tom, and did not tax them at all. Not long after all had eaten their fill, he gave silent indications, and the family gathered up what they had brought, cleaned up anything that needed cleaning up, and began to repack the wagon.

The Stuarts well appreciated this opportunity to gather with the Gradys one final time before their move away. The Gradys would have been welcome at the roundup and its festivities, but they did not mix much with the "Anglo" cattle families, preferring the sheepherding families of Mexican descent. Sean, and Andy too, appeared to be at ease in the company of either group; so it was Maria, the Stuarts believed, who placed this limitation on the family's society: the Stuarts failing, in their naiveté, to give due credit to the roles played by strangeness, pride, and prejudice in the segregation of the two groups. Regardless, here were the Gradys, and now it was time to say good-bye.

Elizabeth and Maria exchanged emotional farewells. Elizabeth had grown to love this wise woman, who, in complementing Sean's quiet fulfillment of his role as head of the household, had revealed a quietly matriarchal character of her own. Maria and the entire Grady family had seemed so foreign to Elizabeth at first. Luke had met Sean while out riding the range, and had developed a friendship with him, and had visited the Grady home several times before Sean had first visited theirs. Then the families had visited each other. In time, with familiarity and mutual charity, Elizabeth's initial resistance to the Gradys' blend of different cultures had given way to respect, as the better values of those cultures—to which the Gradys inclined—were seen and appreciated, especially as they were practiced.

She would miss Teresa, too, the beauty she had watched grow to womanhood, who would sometimes visit her to spend time with a woman other than a mother or younger sister, and a woman raised in the Anglo world. She would miss the younger girls and boys, in their turns, whom she had also watched mature. She would miss the little ones, whom she had held in their infancies and many times since. And she would miss Sean, that tall Apache-Irish gentleman with the touch of a Celtic brogue.

But she would not miss Andy. Andy, the quiet young man who, at thirteen, had first come to visit with his father; who would, thereafter, silently show up at the Stuart home, with no regularity to such visits; who would, whenever possible, ride line with Luke, or hunt with him, or skin the winter die-off with him, or just spend time with him, whatever Luke was doing, until he would quietly depart on foot for his home miles to the south. No, she would not miss Andy, who had ridden line for Luke while he had been away, and who had often hunted for her or carried for her or done any kind of work that she might have needed done, and who had sometimes stayed at the Stuart house, when Elizabeth had deemed it too late for him to go or he had had any concern about the family's safety, making his bed on the porch or in the living room, as he had pleased, though usually on the porch.

No, Andy she would not miss, because Andy would go with them. She, Luke, and Tom had decided it, contingent upon his parents' consent. They would not be able to pay him much, but they would be able to pay him something, and would be able to pay him more after the sale of some cattle. Beyond that, there were plenty of ways to pay for work on the frontier other than with money.

His parents had agreed, and now they took their leave of their oldest son. His mother held her boy hard and cried over the first to leave her nest, to leave it for far distant regions, regions over which her father and Sean's grandfathers had traipsed in earlier and different times. Then Andy and his father shook hands firmly and, after a moment or so, drew into a firm hug, then pulled away, the father imparting words by which the young man could live honorably and reminding him to write to his mother as often as was possible on the Panhandle frontier. Then Teresa hugged, then Juan, then Brigid, Matthew, Pedro, Marina, and even little Patrick, who did not really understand that he might never see his kindly older brother again.

Sean had followed his farewell to his son with a farewell to his companion collie, vigorously and affectionately petting and rubbing the fur of Rita, the pick of her litter and an exceptional herder for these several years. Each of the others bid the dog farewell in similar fashion. Then the Gradys loaded themselves up again, and Sean climbed back into his saddle, and the family drew away toward the south. The Stuarts and Tom and Andy stood and watched them go. Everyone was waving, those departing and those soon to be departing in the opposite direction, until the Gradys were out of sight and hearing. Andy, with Rita sitting on the ground beside him, watched a little longer than the rest, his emotions known to him alone.

In time, after the others had gone into the house, Andy, with Rita falling into step beside him, left from where he had been watching his family disappear into the distance and the night, and led the gray Stonewall off to the barn. As he unsaddled Stonewall, Luke came up.

"Uh, Andy."

"Luke," Andy responded without looking at Luke.

"Andy, we can't pay you as much as we'd like to."

"That's all right."

"Well, it's not," Luke replied. "So we'll be payin' you as much as we can, and keepin' track, so that, with stock or some way, we'll try to pay you what Herman was payin' you this summer, with maybe a bonus or somethin'."

"All right."

"Now, between you, Tom, and me, we'll be drivin' the big wagon, herdin' the cattle and stock, and wranglin' the horses," Luke said. "Now, you know you can be helpin' yourself to any of the horses, but you really ought to have a horse of your own."

Andy looked at Luke.

"So, we were thinkin', how about, for your first wages, you take ol' Stonewall here as your own?" Luke petted the animal on his back and side and said, "He's nearly nine years old, so he's no colt, but he came with us when we moved here, and he's from good stock, has maybe twice as many years yet ahead of him, and if his line is any indication, will have as much spirit as he does now for most of those years."

Andy had taken off Stonewall's bridle and now stood facing the horse. He began to pet the animal's face and neck and to look at him in a new way, as one who was now fully responsible for him.

"That suit you?"

"Suits me fine, Luke."

And Luke could see, in the boy's look, that it did indeed suit him "fine."

IN THE MORNING, on the final day of August 1877, the Stuart-Schurtz party, with its fully packed wagons and all its stock, pulled away from the Richter homeplace in Medina County and headed north toward the frontier of the Texas Panhandle. As they did so, they merged onto the great Western Trail, further merging, in the process, their individual stories, lived out in this singular land, into that larger composite story of Texas.

Chapter Three

JOURNEY OF CONSEQUENCE

The country, your companions, and the length of your journey will afford a hundred compensations for your toil.
—OVID

ANY WERE THE WAYS, BROAD AND STRAIT, trod out upon the trails of Texas. Trails renowned and trails obscure emerged upon the land, born of the myriad imprints of foot, hoof, and wheel: first a single set of prints, then another, and another, countless prints matched to human wills, wills intent on their separate ways, some to loom large in the annals of history, multiples more to be forgotten. Remembered or forgotten, these ways shared a profound importance, as each determined the ultimate success or failure of a singular human being graced with a supernatural destiny. The trails were but lines worn into the face of the wilderness, now province, now state, now nation, now state; but the ways trod out upon those trails, each determined by a human will reaching through intentions toward desired ends, with allowance for circumstances, were journeys of consequence.

At the end of August 1877, members of the Stuart-Schurtz party joined their individual ways in a common goal to journey toward consequences common and individual. Pulling away from home and its holds of love, of memories, of the fruits of labor, they merged their ways onto the Western Trail, their great journey made somehow small upon a trail renowned for epochal migrations of man and beast.

Small upon the trail, small upon the land, small against its time, and yet their souls opened large enough for all of it. The key, of course, was freedom. They were free, at least relatively free for human beings still bound in the temporal phase of life. They owed nothing material to any other human beings. What they had was theirs, and they had enough, enough to supply their needs and even some desires beyond need, though not so much as to compromise freedom with excess. They had broken abruptly with the past, its concerns falling farther away behind them with each passing mile, each passing hour. The concerns of the future lay far off in a place and time unknown to them. Still, this was not a false freedom without responsibility, which becomes the most subtle and insidious bondage, but the true freedom of accepting responsibility, indeed of taking responsibility for their destinies, and of accepting the incumbent lesser responsibilities meted out in the routine and manageable doses of the trail's daily chores, each with its immediate and visible reward, however humble, and all, in combination, laying the groundwork for the potentially life-changing reward at trail's end.

Nor were those lesser responsibilities all there were to accept in the larger taking of responsibility, for the trail offered challenges of a far graver nature as well. There were rivers to cross, which could provide the dangers of drowning or loss of property at any time, but most especially when a flood surge, begun far upstream at a place and time remote from those of the traveler, would sweep through and carry away whatever might be in its path, leaving in its aftermath debris scattered as high as the treetops. There would be rattlesnakes, and skunks carrying hydrophobia. There would be predators: coyotes, wolves, panthers. There could be outlaws and rustlers and hostile Indians.

There could be stampedes, caused by anything that might spook the cattle—rustlers, Indians, a predator, some errant sound, the wind, the rain, the hail, the thunder, the lightning—stampedes that could send the cattle running in any direction, at any time, in any condition, leaving the attendant herders little option but to ride with them at full gallop, often enough into the dark unknown of night and storm, with no sense whatsoever of the potential perils toward which they might be hurtling. Such stampedes could carry the cattle and herders for miles before the herders could turn the cattle into a mill to stop their flight. At daybreak the herders would be required to gather the herd, often scattered over miles, and try to find the location of the camp and then herd the cattle in that direction.

It was weather, often enough, that caused such stampedes: rain that could pound and flood in moments, hail that could injure and even kill, thunder that could shake the earth, and lightning that could terrify and electrocute. This lightning the trail made available in an uncommon assortment: scattered lightning bolts electrifying the night simultaneously in awesome profusion; lightning arcing across the horns of the cattle, across the ears of a horse, running along one's skin and lifting one's hair; or lightning balls shooting through the air or across the ground. And there was the wind, that fickle prairie wind that came with all of it, varying from the pleasant waft from any direction that brought pleasant coolness into heat or pleasant warmth into cold, varying from that to the deadly tornado. Then, too, any wind could shift suddenly around, without warning, to come down from the north and become the dreaded norther, plummeting temperatures in its path in a matter of minutes, and far more in hours, freezing to death stock and human beings caught unawares.

Still, Luke and Tom knew these challenges of the trail from experience. Andy had had his share of experience with most of them, as well, from his days of herding sheep and cattle. They were all prepared to accept them. Elizabeth, too, was prepared to accept them, though her experience of such challenges might not have been as profound. The children, too, were prepared to the level of their ability. They would all accept these challenges, as such challenges arose, and they would overcome them, as God willed, to experience even more of the freedom available to their souls.

Thus, the members of the Stuart-Schurtz party had loosed the hold, to some degree, of the tethers and weights that bind man to this world, manifested in no small way by their present mobility. In this liberating mobility, they challenged even the bonds of time. Matching the elusive present as it moved through time, rendering time tangible from the future, for an instant, then intangible again as past, they moved with the present, making it spatially ever new. No time or place held them, especially no place belonging to someone else, and yet, it was the promise of a place in time, a place in the future, a place of their own, that motivated their travel. Their freedom was manifested in and exercised in a committed movement toward a discerned good: freedom within the context of freedom, movement within the context of movement, their earthly free movement but a small step farther into the boundless free movement available to their spiritual souls.

Still, their earthly movement, how slow, how small: free human souls checked and humbled by space and time. Inching their way across the giant land at the pace of the plodding cattle, averaging less than fifteen miles a day, they followed the trail to the north, their slow progress dwarfed by the petrous testament below. They climbed up over the Balcones escarpment, where the three-hundred-million-year-old Ouachita Mountains lay buried under thousands of feet of stone beneath them. From the Balcones, they entered the Texas Hill Country, carved into the earth over millions of years by the timeless cycle of water—rain, percolation, trickles, creeks, streams, and rivers—dissolving and cutting through the limestone caprock of the Edwards Plateau into softer limestone and sand beneath, which it cut through with greater effect, sculpting hills, their tops protected by remnants of the Edwards limestone, as the water eroded the land from around their descending bases.

They climbed out of the Hill Country onto the formation that had at one time covered it, the Edwards Plateau, a massive formation of amazingly intact limestone, thrust up two thousand feet by geologic forces some ten to twenty million years before, having been formed under Cretaceous seas some one hundred million years before that. Once held by water, now holding water itself, the porous Edwards limestone served as a vast aquifer, which would in later years supply the water needs of millions, but for now would lie largely untapped, its potential unknown to those who passed above.

Once out on the Edwards Plateau, they skirted the western edge of the rugged region of the Llano Uplift. Raised up at the same time as the Edwards Plateau, this region featured deposits of the most ancient rock exposed in Texas, laid down over one billion years before and metamorphosed in the crush of continents and the building of mountains. Eventually descending from the plateau, they continued out onto the North Central Prairie, over sedimentary rock laid down over millions of years, some 250 million years before, as sediment washed down from ancient mountains, now long buried.

Buried, buried, all buried beneath ancient layers of stone. Stone upon stone, the structure of the face of the earth, covered by the earth's derma, soil. From this soil sprouted vegetation, much of it green now from recent rains, in patches and patterns of varied hues, alive in the winds of the present.

And Tom watched it all as they moved along toward the north. He watched the land, its contours, shapes, and shadows, the features carved by the creeks and rivers that twisted through it, the texture lent it by the native flora: mesquite, chittam, sumac, hackberry, soapberry, willow, live oak, post oak, elm, cedar, cottonwood, pecan, and other trees, the ubiquitous prickly pear cactus, and, always, the grass—short and tall, tufted and in straight patches, from blond to fiery red to the deepest green, protector of the soil and sustenance for their stock and their very way of life.

Over it all they moved, now out across the North Central Prairie. Here, as Tom watched, his interest was drawn toward a familiar feature of the land off to the west, as it came and went from view according to the roll of the land across which they traveled. It appeared to be some escarpment, which continued to stand out solid against the western sky for several days, as they made their way past it. Mesas or peninsular protrusions of this seemingly endless escarpment appeared to stand out before it, each such formation passing on the role of western horizon to the mesa or protrusion to its north as the travelers passed that way.

Tom had seen this feature of the land on past trail drives and had often wondered about it: its actual height and depth, its extent, its provenance, its deterioration, its ageless secrets. Now he wondered about it anew, with a future in mind that would take him to a far more formidable escarpment, but one that from a distance would look little different from the one about which he now wondered. What relationship, if any, existed between these two escarpments, this one now visible to the west and that of the Llano Estacado? How far away was this one? How far did it extend? How much farther the Llano Estacado?

Tom could not know that the escarpment about which he now wondered, part of the Callahan Divide, was capped and protected by Edwards limestone, remnants of the plateau lately traversed. He could not know that the escarpment of his destination, hundreds of miles to the northwest, owed its existence to a much younger caprock of sandstone and caliche, laid down and formed from erosion of the Rocky Mountains and the percolation and evaporation of water. He could not know; so much about these two escarpments he could not know. Nevertheless, the escarpment now visible to the west did its part to keep him mindful of the one toward which he and his companions traveled and the future home upon the land they sought to make there.

On toward that home, that life, the Stuart-Schurtz party inched, passing between ridges of the Callahan Divide, on east and west, and rolling up and over the cuestas to the north. On over the trail they went, down into draws and valleys cut by creeks, crossing where most advantageous. On and on, over the trail, until, in the latter part of September, about three weeks after setting out, they arrived in the vicinity of Fort Griffin.

FORT GRIFFIN was one of a line of frontier forts reestablished in Texas after the conclusion of the Civil War. During that war, due to the expulsion and evacuation of federal troops from Confederate Texas and the consequent increase of Indian raids upon settlers, as well as the increased vulnerability of settlers to such raids, the Texas frontier had retreated one hundred miles or more, depending upon how strictly was interpreted the term *frontier*. With the war concluded, settlers again sought to push the frontier farther to the west, and Indians sought all the more to oppose that advance. The army was again free to protect the settlers in their advance, as well as to protect those who sought to cross the lands beyond the frontier or to hunt, trap, or graze there. And so the army sought to do.

Strangely enough, as the two cultures of settlers and Indians clashed, the army often had as its object the protection of Indians, as well. As long as the settlers and Indians could be kept apart, which included the confinement of Indians to those lands to which they had been removed, there would be less danger to settlers, Indians, and soldiers. Though paternalistic and contradictory to the way of life of the Plains Indians, this policy was often the best a commanding officer could realize in the evolving larger picture of warfare, treaties, and sporadic, deadly individual clashes between two radically different cultures with radically different conceptions of land use.

To protect, the army would need forts, and one such was Fort Griffin. In truth, Fort Griffin may have been more accurately labeled a cantonment, rather than a fort, as there were no fortifications, and the intention of the Quartermaster Department that all of its buildings be constructed of stone had given way to a reality of structures hastily constructed of green wood, which subsequently shrank. This left the pitiable soldiers quartered therein subject to extremes of temperature variation, and to the very wind itself, while yet indoors. Though these were supposed to be temporary, the stone buildings that were to replace them were never built. In the end, only key buildings (like the headquarters, hospital, commissary building, bakery, and magazine) were constructed of stone.

All of this construction, such as it was, had taken place upon a bluff that rose out of the land between Collins and Mills creeks, about a quarter mile south of the Clear Fork of the Brazos River in Shackleford County, about 120 miles west of Fort Worth. This had not been the original site of the fort. Originally, in early 1867, troops had been ordered to reoccupy Fort Belknap, to the northeast, which had been closed in the late 1850s, but the location's poor defensibility, the dilapidated condition of the buildings, the lack of an adequate water supply, and the rotting carcasses of old bull buffalo that had rallied enough strength for one more migration from the north but not enough to pull themselves from the bogs of the region had all combined to induce Lieutenant Colonel S. D. Sturgis to seek another location for a fort. This he had done, and based upon the report of Lieutenant H. B. Mellen, whom he had sent out to scout, he had moved his four troops (F, I, K, L) of the Sixth Cavalry thirty-five miles to the southwest to a mesa with a commanding view of the valley of the Clear Fork and the surrounding country. There they had established

Camp Wilson, named after a deceased lieutenant. This was soon changed to Fort Griffin after General Charles Griffin, the former commander of the Military Department of Texas.

At the base of the mesa, a flat land stretched northeast to the Clear Fork. On that land between the mesa and the river, the Tonkawa Indians had subsequently made their camp. The Tonkawa had earlier been moved to Indian Territory (later-day Oklahoma) in the 1850s, after the Brazos Reservation at Fort Belknap had been closed. In Indian Territory some quarrel had arisen with other tribes, and these tribes had slaughtered the Tonkawa. Fewer than one hundred had escaped the massacre by flying to the protection of white settlers. As a result the Tonkawa remnant and their offspring hated the Comanche and other Plains Indians. They thereafter made their home at the edge of white settlement in the shadow of Fort Griffin and provided the army with exceptional scouts. By the date of the arrival of the Stuart-Schurtz party, the Tonkawa's primary camp consisted of roughly twenty-five tepees situated on the flat land northeast of the fort along the banks of the Clear Fork.

The Tonkawa were not alone on that flat land. Beginning in 1867, white settlers had begun to move to what came to be known as "the Bottom" or, more popularly, "the Flat." In time, the Flat took on the name of the fort, but in a way that distinguished it from that establishment, which looked down upon it from what had come to be known as Government Hill. So the scattering of various establishments and residences of the Flat came to be called Griffin, though it was still called "the Flat" by those who knew it best. And those who knew it best knew that Griffin had as good a claim on being the roughest, wildest, meanest, wickedest town in the West as did any other, and a far better claim than most.

By the time of the arrival of the Stuart-Schurtz party in September of 1877, Griffin had established itself as the major outfitting and trading post for buffalo hunters, who in little more than two more years would nearly extinguish the great southern herd of the American bison. The town had also taken on the role of a major stop for cattle outfits trailing north on the Western Trail. Surveyors, too, used Griffin as a base for their land-locating expeditions out into the public domain of west Texas. Hence, those who sought to have land located by surveyors

were also among the transient population there, as were hide merchants, teamsters, and various other men of business. The Flat provided
for all of them: soldiers and local ranchers, and hunters, skinners, trap-
pers, cattlemen, drovers, cowpunchers, surveyors, merchants, drummers,
muleskinners, bullwhackers, and more. Among that provision was an
ample supply of vice in the form of gambling, prostitution, and too much
alcohol. Lawlessness was a common feature of this frontier town, with
theft and murder committed in broad daylight, and thieves and mur-
derers coming and going from the town and fort with impunity. A vigilance committee preceded organized law and kept up its work of
nighttime lynchings even after organized law, such as it was, had arrived,
then left, then arrived again. Nevertheless, with the most lawless element of the frontier regularly passing through or spending time in
Griffin, the prospects for the town's conversion were slight.

It was with this in mind that Luke had weighed whether or not to
take Elizabeth and the children into Griffin on the morning after they
had arrived within the vicinity of that place. The evening before, they
had made camp to the south of town in a good pasture of rich mesquite
grass, with water provided by Mill Creek. Tom and Luke had determined that Luke would go into town to get some supplies. Though they
had made most of their purchases of supplies at wholesale houses in San
Antonio, so as to avoid the higher prices of Griffin, still, they would at
least try to replace what they had used over the last three weeks, as well
as supply a couple items they had neglected, before they continued on
to their destination some two hundred miles beyond this last major
frontier outpost. More important was Luke's other mission, which was
to seek out a reliable surveyor to locate the land certificates they had purchased, according to plan, from Herman Richter.

Tom would have preferred to go with Luke, but that would have
left Andy alone with the stock, and though he was very capable, neither Tom nor Luke wanted to leave this young man, for whom they
felt responsible, alone to watch over the stock in a place where theft
and unprovoked murder were not uncommon. As for Elizabeth and
the children, Elizabeth wanted to visit the Occidental Hotel and Mr.
and Mrs. Henry Clay (Hank) Smith, who owned and ran that establishment. She had heard about them from Tom and Luke, who had
both been through Griffin, both up and down the trail, and she wanted

to enjoy, one more time, the company of a good woman, in a more refined setting, before she left civilization behind. For his part, Zachariah had made it clear to Luke, in his persistent though quiet way, that he would very much like to visit a real fort. Furthermore, wherever Elizabeth went, Rachel and Robert would need to go. Luke took into consideration that people like the Smiths, the officers and their families, and other families of the town and surrounding ranches did their part to add some civility to the place with Sunday religious services, camp meetings, picnics, dances, and socials. With all this in mind, it was decided that Luke, Elizabeth, and the children would venture into the town of Griffin during the daylight hours, while Tom and Andy tended to the stock and the large wagon.

And so they did. On the morning after their arrival in the vicinity of Fort Griffin, the Stuart family rolled into the town of Griffin in the smaller wagon, which had had some of its cargo unloaded and left at the camp and the rest lashed snugly down as preventative measures against theft. Luke steered the team immediately for the Occidental Hotel next to the telegraph office at the base of Government Hill. The Occidental was a large cottonwood-log structure: double-picketed (the logs having been put up vertically instead of horizontally and doubled for better protection against the elements of every season), plastered and whitewashed, and covered with a cotter-shingle roof. This hotel was part of a compound that also included a dining room with an adjoining bar, and a wagon yard and livery stable. All of it was surrounded by a fence.

Mrs. Elizabeth Smith—a trim, large-boned woman with a full, kindly face, and dark tresses pulled up on the back of her head—stood in front of the hotel tending to vines that she had trained to climb willow pickets placed there for that purpose. As the Stuarts pulled into the yard, Mrs. Smith turned and graciously greeted them, in enough of a brogue to betray her native Scotland. The Stuarts returned Mrs. Smith's greetings and then introduced themselves. Mrs. Smith seemed to remember Luke from his passing through that summer. When Elizabeth Stuart indicated that she had hoped to meet and visit with the Smiths, Mrs. Smith explained that her husband was away, had just left earlier that morning, as a matter of fact, but that she would very much enjoy their visit. Luke then said that he would not be staying,

but would be seeking a surveyor, if any were in town, and he asked if
Mrs. Smith knew of any and if she could recommend any one in particular. Mrs. Smith told Luke what she knew of surveyors in Griffin at
that time. Luke thanked her and then pulled away with the wagons to
tend to his errands. Mrs. Smith then ushered Mrs. Stuart and the children into the Occidental's celebrated dining room for a good breakfast,
despite Elizabeth Stuart's assurances that they had already eaten a substantial breakfast at camp.

The dining room that Elizabeth Stuart entered was all that she had
expected, with its finished wood; its framed pictures; its china, silver,
and crystal displayed on shelves built into the wall on both sides of
lace-curtained windows; and its place settings on its linen-covered tables
with their matching chairs, each set of which comfortably seated ten.
Many of these articles had been gifts presented at the Smith wedding
three years before, which had been attended by officers, professional
men, merchants, ranchers, and cowboys—and the wives, daughters,
and sisters of any of them—from the surrounding area. Elizabeth
Stuart and her children quickly settled into the places to which Mrs.
Smith had directed them, and Elizabeth settled even more into the
spirit of this visit with the good Mrs. Smith.

Luke, for his part, had pulled out of the yard of the Occidental, first
steering the wagon across the already busy main thoroughfare of Griffin
Avenue to the post office, where he mailed letters and picked up others
that had already arrived for members of the party, including a few
addressed, in a feminine hand, to Tom. From the post office Luke proceeded to Conrad and Rath's general merchandise store, where he purchased the needed supplies. (The Charles Rath of this partnership,
which also served as the sutler at the fort, was the same of Charles Rath and
Co., Dodge City, Kansas.) From Conrad and Rath's, Luke maneuvered
the mules and wagon down Griffin Avenue through the congestion of
horses, people, and other wagons, which nearly choked traffic to a stand-
still in front of the supply houses, toward the camp of the Tonkawa at
the northern edge of town. Past the restaurants, stores, shops, boarding-
houses, and wagon yards he drove, and past the saloons, dancehalls,
gambling houses, and the even less reputable shelters down near the
river. Many of these structures, like the Occidental, were constructed of
pickets and plaster, and others, of pickets and mud.

Luke's mission in this drive toward the camp of the Tonkawa was not an interview with members of that people, but rather an interview with their current neighbor, Mr. Matthew Colmey, of the firm of Hill and Colmey, Dallas, Texas, with an office in Eastland, Eastland County, Texas. This firm specialized in locating land, with Mr. Hill specializing in the office end of the business and Mr. Colmey in the field end. Accordingly, Mr. Colmey was a bonded deputy surveyor for the Jack Land District.

The Jack Land District of the state of Texas was one of three districts of land west and north of the western boundary of Taylor County that had not yet been divided into separate counties. The other two districts were Young Land District with its office at Graham and Bexar Land District with its office at San Antonio. Jack Land District, with its district office in Jacksboro, consisted of those lands north of a line that extended west from the northwest corner of Young County all the way to the state's western boundary with New Mexico.

Each of these districts was under the supervision of a district surveyor, who at that time for the Jack Land District was Mr. Wesley Callaway. A bonded deputy surveyor like Mr. Colmey would have been appointed to the position by the district surveyor and would have had a five-thousand-dollar bond on file with the district office. As a deputy surveyor, Colmey was free to survey and locate lands in the district and sign the field notes of such surveys, as well as the field notes of surveys made by other surveyors working under him. His signature was required before the field notes could be submitted to the district office for recording. There the field notes would be reviewed and approved or not approved. If approved, the field notes would be signed by the district surveyor and recorded. The field notes would then need to be filed, along with the land certificates, in the General Land Office in Austin. After submission to the General Land Office, a period of ninety days was allowed for conflicting claims or surveys. After the expiration of that ninety days, a patent for the land was issued by the land commissioner and the governor.

Matthew Colmey had been recommended to Luke by several people of whom he had inquired that morning in his business at the post office and supply house. Colmey had been recommended even before that by Mrs. Smith at the Occidental, in answer to Luke's query of her.

Colmey was reported to be honest, accurate, and hardworking. He was also reported to be a little more expensive than some of the other surveyors, but recommended before them, nonetheless.

Luke found Colmey's camp beyond that of the Tonkawa on the bank of a bend in the Clear Fork. The camp consisted of a large wall tent and a wagon. Colmey was seated on a folding chair in front of the tent, hunched over a small folding table, writing up field notes from recent surveys that had taken him out onto the Llano Estacado. Only two of the seven other men who made up his party were in camp. One of these was a man named Stillman, the cook, who also doubled as a guard against Indians. The other was Robert Wilson, a chainman. The other chainman, the transit man, the two flagmen, and the corner builder were away, looking into what Griffin had to offer.

Colmey stood and received Luke graciously with a strong handshake. He was a man of average height and build with brown hair and blue eyes scrunched up to what appeared to be an unnatural degree under bushy brows. An equally bushy moustache hung over his top lip and down along both sides of his mouth. He was dressed in a gray flannel shirt, wool pants, a wool vest, and stoga boots. After introductions, he turned and entered the tent and returned from it with another folding chair, which he unfolded for Luke. Luke was seated, and soon the cook, Stillman, had a cup of coffee in Luke's hand.

Luke explained that he was there to see about having some certificates located. He showed Colmey the certificates and asked how much he would charge to do the locating.

"Ninety-six dollars a section," Colmey said. "That's fifteen cents an acre."

Luke was prepared for this price, but he was also prepared, or at least he thought he was, to bargain.

"There are other outfits that'll do it for less than one-third that price," Luke said truthfully, as Colmey nodded his head. "What makes your survey worth more than theirs?"

"Well, sir," Colmey responded, "for one thing it will be accurate. That is a far sight more than I can say for some of the surveys that are being . . . ," he paused as he scrounged for the word he wanted, until he continued with, "perpetrated," after which he paused again to let the word have its effect, "upon unsuspecting certificate holders by some so-called surveyors. It won't be any 'office survey' that you'll get from us, where the surveyor never goes out onto the land under survey. With us you'll get a deputy surveyor himself, that is, me, making the survey. We'll put up the corners and give you a full description of your land, and we'll deliver the patents."

Luke was impressed with the man's apparent competence and his confidence in the quality of his work. Still, Luke had come to bargain, and so he would. "How about eighty dollars a section?"

But Colmey *was* competent and confident, and so he responded. "No sir, we'll do it for ninety-six dollars a section, and we've got plenty of business at that price. You'll be able to get it done for the price you've offered—or for far less, for that matter—but not by us, and not without concerns about accuracy and reliability."

Luke considered this. He had not really had his heart in the bargaining. He believed what Colmey had said and what others had said about him. He had merely begun to bargain because it had seemed that he should. Now, somewhat relieved, he put aside the bargaining and agreed to Colmey's price, and the men shook hands on it.

Luke then gave Colmey as good a description of the land he wanted located as he could, despite the fact that he had never seen the place and that there was good reason to question whether the place even existed. Colmey questioned him about it, as he had been to the Llano Estacado, though not as far north as the land Luke sought to have surveyed, and he wanted as accurate a description of the location of the land as possible. This he would need, not only to find the place, but also to give a description of it for the initial file he was required to write out and have recorded in the district office. Colmey then drew up a contract, in duplicate, which he and Luke both signed, each taking one of the copies. Luke gave Colmey certificates for six sections, for which he had paid Herman Richter $300 of the original $1000 that Tom had supplied for the purchase of land. Luke also paid Colmey $288, one-half of the $576 for the locating. Colmey wrote Luke receipts for the certificates and the money. Luke, according to their contract, would pay the remaining half for the locating upon receipt of the patents.

Colmey told Luke that he was on his way to Jacksboro to have the field notes of his recent survey approved, signed, and recorded. His partner, Mr. Hill, would meet him there to give him more certificates to locate and to receive the certificates and field notes of the recent surveys, so that he could take them to Austin to file with the General Land Office. While in Jacksboro, Colmey would write out the preliminary file for the Stuart-Schurtz survey and record it. He suggested that Luke or one of Luke's party seek out his surveying party in late October, by contacting Hank Smith at his stone house in Blanco Canyon, about 150 miles northwest from Griffin on the Mackenzie Trail. The Colmey party would leave word of their whereabouts with Smith. Luke expressed some confusion about Hank Smith's residence in Blanco Canyon, having just come from Smith's Occidental Hotel where Smith's wife appeared to be very much in residence. Colmey explained that Smith had taken possession of a ranch being established in Blanco Canyon, because the man who had been establishing the ranch had defaulted on debts owed to Smith and had fled the country.

Luke wondered about Hank Smith's move to Blanco Canyon, as he steered his wagon back up the busy Griffin Avenue toward the Occidental. He would learn more of the story of the Smith "rock house" in Blanco Canyon from his wife on their return trip to their camp, but first they would visit the post above town. Earlier that morning, during his stop at Conrad and Rath's store, he had struck up a conversation with a Lieutenant Flaherty, and the lieutenant had invited Luke and his family to be his and his wife's guests for lunch. The lieutenant had seemed very eager to meet the family and to have his wife meet the family and to enjoy their company. Life at Fort Griffin for a young officer and a young wife was such that they might well make the most of any opportunity to enjoy the company of a family like the Stuarts.

Luke pulled into the wagon yard of the Occidental and sought out his family. He found Elizabeth helping Mrs. Smith and the cook prepare for the lunch that they would shortly be serving to the hotel's guests, as a young black girl watched over and entertained the children, including Mrs. Smith's own son George, now nearly eleven months old. (George had been born on October 29, 1876, just two days after the one-year anniversary of the death of the Smiths' first son, Henry, who had died at five months, and four weeks after the death of Elizabeth Smith's father on October 2, 1876. The year before, Elizabeth

Smith's brother had drowned in the Clear Fork. Thus, by the time of the Stuarts' arrival, in less than four years in Griffin, Elizabeth Smith had buried her father, brother, and son in the Griffin cemetery.) When Luke announced their appointment with the Flahertys, Elizabeth expressed disappointment, as she had intended to help Mrs. Smith with lunch. Mrs. Smith assured her that no such help was necessary and encouraged them to keep their appointment, because she knew the Flahertys and thought well of the lieutenant and his young, home-sick wife. Consequently, the Stuarts left the dining room, all of them thanking Mrs. Smith as they drifted to the wagon and climbed aboard.

Mrs. Smith followed them to the dining-room door, where she stood to watch them depart. As they were pulling out of the yard, Luke noticed three or more dogs in various places in the yard. He had noticed these earlier and now remembered to ask Mrs. Smith about them. They were full-blooded border collies, she assured him, of those raised by her father, who had come from Scotland after his wife had died to join his four sons and his daughter in America. Since his death, the Smiths had sold or given away some of the dogs. Luke arranged with Mrs. Smith to hire, for overnight, the better of the two males to take out to camp. Andy's collie, Rita, had been in heat for two days, and they had all tired of chasing off the stray dogs that had been drawn to their party because of it. Here, Luke thought, was a solution. He arranged to pick up the dog on their way down from the post.

Luke then drove out of the yard into the very busy Griffin Avenue and turned left into the road that climbed up to the post. Lieutenant Flaherty, a tall, lean, dark-haired fellow with blue eyes, met them at the post trader's, the sutler's store of Conrad and Rath, at the top of the hill, and led them to the quarters he shared with his wife on the north corner of the small parade ground. It was a frame house of two rooms with a detached kitchen. The Flahertys had done what they could with furnishings to make it a home. Mrs. Flaherty, a dark-haired, dark-eyed, fair-skinned young woman from Pennsylvania, was indeed very home-sick and hungry for the kind of company she found in Elizabeth and the children. Her husband had apparently made his invitation to the Stuarts in no small part out of consideration for her, and he exhibited, throughout the Stuarts' stay, no little concern that she be comfortable and enjoying herself.

After a long lunch with much conversation, the lieutenant took Luke and Zachariah for a tour of the fort, while the ladies and other children remained behind to visit. At the bakery, the baker treated Zachariah, Luke, and Lieutenant Flaherty, too, to some fresh hot bread. At the powder magazine, Zachariah could no longer keep quiet, but had to know of the officer how there could be small windows that let in air but did not let in fire or bullets. The young officer promptly picked up Zachariah and showed him how the windows angled down into the wall to prevent such an occurrence. At the cannons, Zachariah stood in awe of the big guns and their potential.

When the tour was complete, they had visited the saddle shop, the wheel shop, the carpenter's shop, and the blacksmith shop. They had seen the library, the hospital, the mess halls, the administration office, the guardhouse, the commissary, the stables, and the barracks. At Luke's request, they had even walked down the hill to the lime kiln east of the fort. They had seen practically all of it, and they had seen the men.

Zachariah wondered at these men. He had never seen so many black men, never black soldiers. These soldiers were members of the Tenth Cavalry, a Negro regiment, currently assigned to Fort Griffin. The officers of these "buffalo soldiers," as the Indians called them, were white men, with one notable exception. That exception was Henry Ossian Flipper, who earlier that year had become the first black man to graduate from the United States Military Academy at West Point and receive a commission as an officer in the United States military. Lieutenant Flipper was, at that time, at Fort Sill in Indian Territory, awaiting the arrival of his troop. Lieutenant Flaherty told Luke and Zachariah of Flipper, in answer to Zachariah's naive question about whether there were any Negro officers. Flaherty had known Flipper at West Point, though he had been one year ahead of Flipper, and he spoke regretfully of the way he and the other cadets had completely ignored him, to the point of ostracism, and admirably of how Flipper had held up under four years of such isolation.

When the tour concluded at the stables, Lieutenant Flaherty excused himself from Luke and Zachariah to look in on a mount that had suddenly pulled up lame earlier that day. Luke walked Zachariah away from the stables and the smell of the latrines of the enlisted men, toward the southwest end of the large parade ground. There he and Zachariah gazed off toward the west as they waited for their host.

Luke looked up at the young autumn sun, and he thought of the commanding hot, bright, overhead sun of summer. He noted the contrast between that summer sun and this autumn sun, which seemed to struggle against the seasonal forces that diminished its heat and light and held it lower in the sky, closer to the southern horizon as it passed overhead, waiting to tug it ever more quickly and definitively below the western horizon in the evening. Autumn had its grip on old Sol, and Luke felt it, too, in a wistfulness for the year that had been, the home that had been left. And he felt it in an insecurity about the unknown that would be home: the unknown, the unsure, into which he was taking his family. He looked down at the top of his towhead son, whose face pointed west toward the hills beyond. Then he looked out at those hills, himself, hills that marched to the western horizon; hills that obscured the view of the trail they would follow; hills that seemed to pull at old Sol, that seemed to want to pull old Sol down into obscurity behind them. He looked back down and studied the top of the towhead and thought of the person beneath it. Suddenly that person turned back toward him, and the back of Zachariah's hand hit lightly against his thigh. "Look, Daddy," the boy said, "those mountains go on and on."

Luke smiled at the wonder of the boy, at his innocent trust and security, at his innocent ignorance of his parents' doubts and concerns. Luke's smile grew fuller as he was impressed by the goodness of his son. He reached out and tousled the boy's hair.

"What are you seein', Zack?"

"Those mountains, Daddy," Zachariah replied, pointing out at the hills beyond, "they go on forever."

"Forever," Luke said, picking up his son and giving him a squeeze and laughing.

"Why are you laughin', Daddy?"

"Because I have such a fine boy for a son," he said, and again he hugged the boy, who hugged him back.

"Come on, boy," Luke said, putting Zachariah back on the ground. "It's time we went huntin' up your mama." And he led the boy toward Lieutenant Flaherty, who was walking toward them from the stables, and the small party of two men and a boy made their way back to the Fort Griffin quarters of Lieutenant and Mrs. John H. Flaherty.

•   •   •

MRS. FLAHERTY, BESS, hated to see Elizabeth and the children go, to a degree that made Elizabeth feel sorry for her, and a little concerned for her as well. Therefore, the Stuarts visited with the Flahertys for another hour or so after Luke, Zachariah, and Lieutenant Flaherty had returned. Nevertheless, go they must; so the good-byes were made, with invitations from both families to visit the other. Finally, the Stuarts pulled away, and after picking up the male collie from Mrs. Smith, were on their way back to camp. As they rode, Elizabeth related to Luke what she could remember of what she had learned from Mrs. Smith, including what she knew about Hank Smith's removal to Blanco Canyon.

The Mrs. Smith of whom Elizabeth Stuart would speak—who in the lore of the West would become "Aunty," "Aunty Smith," "Aunty Hank," and finally just "Aunt Hank," in an evolution of titles conferred on her by the great variety of frontier characters who would experience her kindness and hospitality over the years in Griffin and, later, at the "Rock House" in Blanco Canyon—had been born Elizabeth Boyle in the wool-manufacturing town of Dalry in Ayrshire, Scotland on July 12, 1848. She had studied for seven years at Blairmains School, which had included a daily study of the *Westminister Shorter Catechism* of the Presbyterian Church. In response to the suggestion of an older brother who had come to America, Elizabeth Boyle had joined her other brothers in immigrating to the United States, when she was twenty years of age, so that she could "keep house" for all of them.

The family had settled in Missouri, until the brothers had answered the inner call to move farther west, which had brought them to Fort Griffin, Texas. Elizabeth and her father, who had moved to America after his wife had died, had joined the brothers in Griffin in late December 1873. In all, Elizabeth, her father, and her four brothers (Joseph, John, James, and Andrew) had all emigrated from Scotland to live, at one time or another, in Texas.

At the end of 1873, twenty-five-year-old Elizabeth attended the annual Fort Griffin New Year's Ball, the community's major social event. There she made the acquaintance of Henry Clay (Hank) Smith, who, at thirty-seven years old, was already a seasoned frontier veteran.

Smith subsequently courted her with weekly Sunday visits. These visits expanded to twice a week. All of it expanded to a proposal, and on May 19, 1874, the couple were married.

At that time, Hank Smith held the contract to supply hay to the fort, besides working as a clerk at Conrad and Rath's during the slow winter months. In 1875, he quit his job at Conrad and Rath's and built the Occidental Hotel on the Flat at the base of Government Hill.

At that Occidental Hotel, in late 1875 or early 1876, depending upon the account, arrived the young and handsome Mr. and Mrs. Charles Pennick Tasker, whose fine dress, retinue, and provisions might have better suited their life in Philadelphia, where the family business was iron and steel. As if the Flat were not sufficiently ennobled by their arrival, they had, in their company, an Irish Lord of the name Jamison, to make the work complete. This distinguished party pulled up in an impressive new coach behind a pair of magnificent bays driven by a liveried coachman. Their needs were apparently to be well met, and exceeded, by what filled the number of wagons that followed the coach, provisions that included quality wines, spirits, and cigars.

From the start, Tasker spoke loudly and openly about his desire to found a great ranch and to hunt buffalo. He also made it known that he was an expert at gambling, which, in this wild frontier town, was music to the ears of the true experts, who eagerly sought to have him display his expertise. His subsequent free wheeling at the gambling tables and high spending both in Fort Griffin and Fort Worth, as well as his assurances that he was backed by a millionaire uncle in Delaware, generally convinced the inhabitants of Fort Griffin and its environs that he had the means to do all of it.

Jamison, on the other hand, had made quite a different impression on Mrs. Smith, as not only a man of high intelligence, but one of high learning, which he had accomplished at the University of Dublin. Mrs. Smith would later recall that Lord Jamison and her brother, who had graduated from the University of Edinburgh, used to compete against each other at solving challenging mathematical problems.

If Jamison's intelligence showed forth in these mathematical contests, a greater show of intelligence may well have been displayed when he pulled out of his association with Charles Tasker. This occurred after Tasker had hired Hank Smith to locate for him a ranch with a view, situated so that it would have year-round water, good grass, fire-wood, and seclusion. While Tasker and Jamison were on their way to inspect the place that Smith had selected in Blanco Canyon, 150 miles or so west of Fort Griffin, Jamison seriously injured his hand by an accidental gunshot, which required his return to Fort Griffin, where he received medical treatment for several weeks. During this time, the "sensible fellow," as Hank Smith would later refer to him, "became disgusted with the whole project, and especially with Tasker, and abandoned the whole thing to Tasker."

With land certificates, Tasker purchased four sections of land (which, with the school alternates, amounted to eight sections) at the site Smith had chosen for him. In early 1877, he hired hunters to kill the buffalo, and herders to manage the cattle and horses he had placed on the ranch. He hired masons, carpenters, cooks, teamsters, hayers, and any other workers needed to create a great ranch and buffalo park, his *Hacienda de Glorieta*, the center of which was to be a mansion of stone, from which he would reign over the whole estate.

In the meantime, a two-story ranch house rose up from the floor of Blanco Canyon, built of stone quarried locally and lumber freighted from Fort Worth at great expense. Along with the house, rose a stone barn and corrals. Meanwhile, Tasker continued his lavish living and spending on credit, credit for his employees as well as himself. Eventually, his financing from the East was cut off, and he was left penniless and seriously in debt to the many who had extended him unlimited credit.

With money borrowed from Hank Smith, who would later estimate Tasker's debt to him at over eleven thousand dollars, Tasker moved with his wife out to the unfinished stone house in Blanco Canyon. But even the wilderness of Blanco Canyon could not provide Charles Tasker a refuge from his financial problems. His employees at the ranch expected that they should be paid for their work. These were led by the man Tasker had hired to boss his ranch, a man of very sorry reputation, known as, among other things, the Chief of Red Mud, because he led a gang of men, described by the contemporary Edgar Rye as "cowardly cut throats," who made their camp along Red Mud Creek in that region. Rye further related that this same "Chief" had once tried to terrorize the town of Griffin by stalking down Griffin

Avenue with his belly full of liquor and his hands full of Colt .45's, which he fired indiscriminately as he stalked, calling out as he did so, "Coyotes, hunt your holes! The biggest wolf on the range is coming down the trail!" When the trail took this biggest wolf into a local saloon, the barkeeper, a former acrobat, cut that trail short by pulling tight the loop of a lasso he had deftly placed on the floor. The loop closed around the Chief's legs, and before he knew what had happened, his feet were off the trail, and he was upended and suspended, upside-down, from a hammock ring in the wall, so that he had to hold his head off the floor with his hands, while the barkeeper juggled his .45s for the amusement of the gathering crowd.

But there were no ex-acrobat barkeepers at *Hacienda de Glorieta*, and the Chief of Red Mud felt perfectly free to bully the improvident Tasker and his wife. This he did, with the result that, by the dark of night, with the aid of a young cowboy, the Taskers escaped the ranch and fled the region. Tasker was eventually found and brought to justice, though that justice may have been called into question by his creditors, who were left to divide the meager spoils. Of those spoils, Hank Smith received the ranch, at a further cost to him of hundreds of dollars. To this ranch in Blanco Canyon he had just moved to complete the unfinished stone house, which would come to be known as the Hank Smith Rock House.

As much of this story as she could recall, Elizabeth shared with Luke as they rolled along toward their camp south of Fort Griffin. When the Stuarts arrived at the camp, they found that Tom had already started a fire and was all prepared to cook a meal of venison, from the deer he had shot the day before, and biscuits, while Andy was out watering and grazing the herd. Elizabeth was relieved that most of the preparation for supper was out of the way, and she manifested her appreciation by producing fresh pies, one pecan and one apple, that she and Mrs. Smith, with the help of Rachel, had baked, and which Mrs. Smith had insisted that Elizabeth take with her when she left. After Luke, Tom, and Andy had tended to all the stock, and after Andy had inspected the Smith collie, named Lad, and heartily approved of him, the men, with night horses saddled and picketed nearby, left the contented cattle to themselves, and to the distracted dogs, for a change. This allowed the entire party to sit down to supper together as an orange sun hung above the western horizon, spreading warm light and lengthening shadows across the cooling landscape.

It was fair to say, with all due respect to the work that Tom had begun and Elizabeth had finished, that the venison and biscuits, along with the green vegetables that Elizabeth had purchased from Mrs. Smith, were not accorded the full attention they deserved by some of the members of the party, who hurried through those more substantial elements of the supper, while their thoughts rested on the two pies waiting in the wings. When the apple pie was produced, cut, and distributed, it was met with absolute satisfaction, so that not a sliver of it remained in the pan, out of which Tom scraped with a spoon, and then ate, the sweet, partially burned, crusted fragments that had stuck there, undeterred by Luke's good-natured chiding for doing so.

As Tom finished off the last remnants of the pie, Luke changed to a new topic deserving comment. "You plannin' on a trip to town, Tom? You look mighty spruced up."

Elizabeth, too, had noticed this, but had said nothing, feeling uncomfortable about commenting upon the almost unimaginable possibility that Tom might be intending to enter such a den of vice as Griffin after dark. She had noticed that Tom had bathed and shaved, and that he was wearing a shirt she had only seen once before and a clean pair of pants. Still, as upsetting as such a possibility might be, there was a far graver concern. Andy, too, was shaved, bathed, and dressed in his best. Surely, Tom could not possibly be considering taking Andy into Griffin at night.

Elizabeth's reaction, since she had returned from town, was not lost on Tom. He had noticed how she had quietly taken note of his change of appearance. Indeed, long before the Stuarts had arrived, he had begun to anticipate, with no little discomfort, some form of reaction from her upon her return. And then she had been so stiflingly quiet during supper, not that she was usually loud or chatty, but Tom had learned, in the three weeks that their small party had been traveling and living together, that Elizabeth was capable of producing an almost oppressive quiet that could descend upon their little community with greater effect, at least upon him, than if she had begun to rant. Curiously enough though, Tom had also observed that Luke was often oblivious to this reaction from Elizabeth until it developed into something more than quiet. Not Tom though; he was aware. He had noticed her lack of participation in the supper conversation. He had noticed the furtive glances that she had shot his way, when she was not awkwardly concentrating on her food. More important, he had noticed the glances she had shot toward the "spruced-up" Andy and how those glances had been immediately followed by glances directed at him, glances that, short as they were, effectively communicated her silent rebuke. All of it combined to the effect that Tom's supper was not settling as well as it might have, and he was more and more regretting having agreed to fulfill a certain request made by Andy.

Still, Luke's question required an answer. "I was thinkin' about it," Tom said to the empty pie tin.

Then Luke—amazingly aloof to his wife's present disposition, as far as Tom was concerned—charged straight into the matter, adding a certain annoyance to Tom's discomfort, as he silently wondered at Luke's injudicious appraisal of the situation.

"Andy, you're lookin' pretty dolled up, yourself," Luke said. "You also plannin' to trip the light toe fantastic?"

The disapproval that fell upon Andy, with the look that Elizabeth raised up from her empty plate, was all but palpable and only to be exceeded by the disapproval that shifted to Tom when Andy responded that Tom had said he would take him into town that night.

Tom winced as Andy said the words. The conditions for Elizabeth's full rebuke, for her complete disapproval of him, were realized. His eyes still on the pie tin in his lap, Tom sat defenseless before Elizabeth's look of censure and melted before it as if he were butter on a glowing rock around the fire.

"Children," Elizabeth said, still looking at the melted Tom, with her jaw set in a way that Tom had come to recognize even without looking up to see it, "it's time for bed."

There was relief for Tom, as Elizabeth rose and gathered the children to ready them for bed well before their usual time, but Tom knew that it was only a temporary relief that merely postponed manifestations of disfavor that would, for some time, maybe forever, characterize Elizabeth's dealings with him. Elizabeth had lost respect for Tom, and he knew it. Still, Tom could not help but feel that it was unfair. After all, Tom had hesitated when Andy had first asked if he could go into town with him. He had hemmed and hawed whenever Andy had brought up the subject throughout the day. If the usually laconic Andy had not caught him off his guard and worn him down by asking him over and over throughout the day, Tom might well have considered not visiting Griffin at all.

Besides the unfairness of it, what aggravated Tom was that the real problem was not so much Andy's going to town as it was concern over Elizabeth's evaluation of the matter. Andy was now eighteen years old. He had ventured out on his own with an outfit trailing toward the frontier. Granted, this trail outfit was more like family, and Elizabeth treated Andy like her younger brother, a youth still innocent, whom she would do all she could to keep that way, but if Andy were with most any other outfit, he would be going into town. Andy was old enough to be deciding for himself, but what Andy had done, by getting Tom to agree to take him into town, was to shift the responsibility for his going onto Tom, in Elizabeth's eyes. In fact, Tom had realized, without forming it into words in his mind, that when Andy had been asking if he could go to town with him, he had been, in effect, seeking Tom's sanction of his going, in anticipation of Elizabeth's expected disapproval. With that sanction, Tom would take on the responsibility for Andy's going to town, as far as Elizabeth would be concerned. Tom had finally given in to Andy, after his repeated requests, especially since Andy had made the case that he might never have the opportunity to visit Griffin again. Though Tom did not think that Andy would suffer for not having visited Griffin, still, the boy was young and wanted to see the town, and Tom had finally convinced himself that maybe he could take Andy into town and give him some sheltered exposure and keep him out of trouble. Now Tom looked across the fire at Andy, for whom he too had developed a fondness as for a younger brother, and communicated in his look his own displeasure at the position in which his young friend had placed him. Andy responded with a shrug of his shoulders, as he raised his arms and held his hands open and sent a wide-eyed "What did I do?" expression toward Tom. Tom shook his head at the pathetic gesture and resigned himself to his fate.

Before all this, Tom had been looking forward to Fort Griffin for many days and many miles up the trail, but once within its proximity his enthusiasm for going to town had all but vanished in a way that was becoming more familiar as he grew older. The idea of a visit to a town like Griffin had lost much of its allure, as its growing proximity had brought a greater sense of reality to his expectations. Time and experience had made Tom more aware of the actualities of visiting the Griffins of the West and less inclined to be swayed by fanciful expectations and memories. He did not care to waste his time, energy, and money to prove those expectations hollow and those memories flawed. Besides, he was tired. He had ridden the second watch the night before. This would be his night for a full night's sleep. And he had not felt particularly inclined to go to the trouble of shaving, bathing, and dressing up to visit a town like Griffin. It was no Dodge City, after all. Griffin could brag that it had all the bad that Dodge had, but what it did not have were the alternatives that Dodge offered. This brought to mind another concern that had been nagging at Tom: did he really want to leave Luke, Elizabeth, and the children, with all that they owned, outside one of the most notorious frontier towns in the West?

After all, Tom could take or leave the gambling. He would play a little now and then, but a practicality set deep within his bones never let gambling take a strong hold of him. He could enjoy a drink, especially a cold beer after a hot day working cattle, but he rarely drank for the sake of drinking. For Tom, drinking beer, wine, or spirits, other than as a complement to a meal, had its greatest value as a stimulant to good conversation, or, in the case of wine, as an enhancer to a romantic mood while dining with a lady. In such a case, it was always best to keep within the bounds of moderation, to stay well short of crossing the line to excess, though that line, in Tom's experience, often seemed to shift more than the course of the Rio Grande, especially when in a romantic mood, or engaged in good conversation, or just under the influence.

And what would Griffin be after all? Tom knew: he had seen it. It would be dusty or muddy or both. The saloons would be loud and raucous, allowing little opportunity for conversation. And it would be populated by the most licentious of the frontier element. Besides all that, the smell of buffalo hides, staked or stacked even this early in the season, would permeate the atmosphere of the town, invading all other aromatic formulas with its putridity, a condition that had not been lost on Elizabeth and the Stuart children earlier that day.

And as for the women? Well, that was really the point, after all. The greatest attraction that a town held for Tom was feminine companionship. A man did not think lightly about passing up the opportunity to visit a town, with its share of female inhabitants, when the ratio of men to women in much of the West was ten to one or worse. But what quality of companionship would it be? There were some good women in Griffin, like Mrs. Smith, but most of these would be married like Mrs. Smith, and most, especially the unmarried, would not venture out into the town in the evening. There was always the chance that there might be a church social or something like it, but what was the likelihood, even if there were such a social, that they, as strangers in an area full of outlaws, would be admitted. The reality was that, in Griffin, a good share of the women who would be available for a man to meet would be cyprians. There might be some dancehall girls who were not prostitutes, but in Griffin that was probably less likely than elsewhere. Even if there were women who were not prostitutes among the dancehall girls, what were the chances that meeting a woman in a dancehall in Griffin would develop into anything beyond that? And if there was no potential for anything beyond a night of dancing in a loud and wild dancehall, why aggravate oneself?

Tom thought about that for a moment, realizing that he had met Molly in a dancehall. But Molly was different. And that raised another reason why Tom would have just as soon remained at camp. Luke had given Tom letters from Molly that had been waiting for him at the post office, and Tom had stashed them away to read when he would be alone. Tom wanted to read those letters from that woman of substance, rather than venture into a night of superficial embellishment, entertainment, and companionship.

Still, the letters from Molly were not Molly. That woman of substance was a long way away in distance, time, and probability. Griffin was here, now. He would not see another town of Griffin's size for some time. Once past Griffin, a woman's company, other than that of Elizabeth's, would be rare, if not nonexistent. As for the safety of the Stuart family, outlaws were part of frontier life, and Luke was as capable of defending himself and his family as any man Tom knew. Besides, Elizabeth was as good a shot with a rifle as most men, and with the Smith collie, there were two dogs at the camp. Beyond all that, he had told Andy he would take him into town, as much as he now regretted it. He would keep his word and try to do so in a way that would keep that youth as far from corruption as possible.

So, he was going into Griffin; and Andy was going, too; and Elizabeth was mad; and he figured they might as well make short work of it and get going as soon as possible. Thus, he began to gather the dishes to wash them, and he glanced over at Andy to indicate, with that glance, that Andy's help in this matter of dishes was expected, given his central role in their current disfavor. Andy wasted no time gathering his share of the dishes on receiving Tom's silent communication, and they headed over to the washtub and the bucket of water by the wagon to wash them.

This was not unusual work for cowboys at that time. With the lop-sided ratio of men to women on the frontier, cowboys, buffalo hunters, and other frontiersmen did not enjoy the luxury of dividing up daily chores into those for men and those for women. Whether there were women around or not, cowboys needed to eat and be clothed, and this required that they be able to cook, wash, sew, or do any other task that daily living required. Even when a woman was in their midst, especially in the early days of frontier cattle raising (women being so scarce), she might be waited on by men rather than be expected to wait on them. Nevertheless, women also took on, as necessity required, some of the tasks traditionally ascribed to men, like hunting and skinning. Still, where the ratio allowed for it, men and women fell into traditional roles, for the most part, with men more often performing the heavy, outdoor work, and women performing more of the domestic work, which had a heaviness all of its own. However the work was distributed between men and women, members of both sexes toiled hard and long to make a living on the frontier.

Tom and Andy were now beginning to toil hard at the domestic task of washing the supper dishes. Suddenly Elizabeth was there, stepping in between these men and their task, and she said, "You'd better go bed down the herd."

There would be no argument with the order, nor with the way in which it was delivered, and the two men left to bed the herd. Often enough only two of them bedded the small herd, as the other tended to the other stock or helped Elizabeth. And sometimes only one of them accomplished the task, but tonight all three rode out. They drove the watered and grazed herd around in a circle, a mill, as close to the wagon as they could, until all the cattle settled down and eventually lay down, with acknowledgments of their contentment in the sounds of grunting and blowing and the grinding of teeth on cud. The men continued to ride in a circle around the bedded cattle for a short while, Luke going one way and Tom and Andy the other, until they all pulled up together, on the far side of the herd from the wagon, in the fading light of the setting sun.

Luke spoke up. "Don't bother hurryin' back for your guard, Andy. I'll stand it this night. They're all pretty docile, and if I get too tired, I'll just lie down near the wagon and picket my horse. Besides, the dogs are here to help, and Rita will alert me to anything that demands my attention." Andy nodded his appreciation, as Tom wondered about such an arrangement, thinking of outlaws and Luke's well-earned reputation for being a heavy sleeper.

Tom voiced his concern. "What about outlaws?"

"Ah, with the herd this close to the wagon, I'll be right handy. Besides, Elizabeth has the Winchester, and I'll picket Lad right next to the wagon. I'll post Rita out on the far side of the herd. Who knows, I might even catch up on some sleep this night."

Tom knew better, and he was truly concerned and feeling no little guilt about leaving the Stuarts. He further expressed his concern, but Luke assured him all the more that they would be all right.

Luke was convincing, and Tom was ready to be convinced. He did appreciate Luke's offer to take the entire watch. It would be the first time since they had left Medina County that they had adjusted their guard schedule. They had worked it out at the beginning and had agreed that they would rotate, with one man riding guard from sunset to midnight, another riding from midnight to sunrise, and the last sleeping a full night and taking over the herd after breakfast, to relieve the last watch so that he could eat before they started out. They moved forward in the rotation every day, with the "sleeper" going to the night watch, the night watch moving to the early-morning watch, and the early-morning watch moving to the "sleeper," and all had found the arrangement satisfactory.

Luke went on, "You all might as well head straight into town without goin' back to camp, as Elizabeth is in no good mood at all. You notice she didn't say a word at supper, and she chased the kids to bed early? I'm not sure what burr is under her saddle, but it's best to give her a little room when she's like this."

Tom did not even bother to look at Luke. This was a phenomenon he had seen in married men before, that he could not explain or understand. He wondered if it was a survival mechanism triggered in all men just before marriage that would allow them to be least perceptive to what was festering inside their wives. Tom and Andy knew, but Luke had no idea, and yet Luke was an otherwise intelligent and insightful man. Tom wondered if he himself would be like that once married. He had seen others who were not. He wondered if it was not a trait that made Luke and Elizabeth compatible.

Whatever the case, regardless of Luke's assessment of the situation, Andy and Tom would need to return to camp, because Andy would need to get some money from a sock in which he kept the little money he had. Luke rode in with them to get a cup of coffee.

Elizabeth, sitting by the fire, paid no attention to them as she rocked the now fed and nearly sleeping Robert in her arms. Andy went about the task of finding his money, and Luke and Tom stepped up to the fire, across from Elizabeth, where Luke crouched and filled his cup from the pot. Soon Andy joined them, ready to go. As he and Tom started to step away from the fire, Tom said sheepishly, ostensibly to Luke, "Good night."

"Good night," Luke responded. "Don't paint the town too red, now," he jokingly admonished.

Jokingly or not, Tom cringed slightly at this statement, as he would have at anything that might worsen his crime or punishment. Still, he took courage. "Hmmmm," he cleared his throat lightly. "Good night, Elizabeth," he said, as much to find out where he stood as to wish her well.

She did not answer. He had never had any hope for absolution, but he had to know where he stood.

"Hmm," he cleared again. This time a little louder, he said, "Good night, Elizabeth."

"Good night, Tom," she said without looking up.

It was bad. She had not even acknowledged Andy, not even acknowledged his participation in the crime. It was all Tom's responsibility.

Andy was just an innocent succumbing to persuasion and bad example. Tom knew where he stood.

"Uhmm, well, we better get goin', then," he said.

Luke nodded, as he caught the reins of his horse. Then he climbed into the saddle without spilling a drop of coffee. As he rode out to circle the herd, Tom and Andy caught the reins of their own horses, mounted up, and slunk out of the campfire's glow into the night.

"You think she's pretty mad?" Andy asked quietly, when he judged they were out of earshot.

Tom turned his own look of censure on the newly corrupted, who had remained comfortably silent until now. "What's it matter to you, Silent Sam?" he said before he turned back to look down the trail toward Griffin.

Andy accepted this rebuke with good humor, not completely avoiding a smile. He knew that Tom would bear the brunt of Elizabeth's disfavor and that Tom's annoyance with him would only be temporary. He could see the humor in Tom's current state of disgrace, all things considered. He knew that the state of disgrace could not last long, considering that Tom was a decent fellow, after all. Beyond all that, he, Andy Grady, just eighteen years old, was riding into one of the most notorious frontier towns at night, with an experienced and trusted friend, hundreds of miles from his parents and family. He thought that he had good reason to smile.

The moon had risen and was nearly full, and its light dispersed through thin, white clouds that lent a sort of glow to the night. The men's eyes adjusted quickly to this lower light, as they made their way toward Government Hill. As they rode, Tom's uncertainty about the wisdom of his decision deepened. The reality of Fort Griffin, particularly the reality of the Flat at night, began to impress itself more forcefully upon his mind, crowding out any haziness concerning its true character. The disapproval of Elizabeth registered more forcefully in his mind as they went, especially as he questioned more and more the impact that Griffin might have on the young Andy. Tom knew Griffin. He knew trail towns. He knew that he could enjoy them but guard against being fully seduced by them, that he could be in them but not of them. But what about this impressionable young man in his charge. Tom knew that Andy was a young man of good sense, but others of good sense had been known to lose it. Did Andy really need to be exposed to the vices of Griffin, however guarded that exposure might be? Did he need to be exposed to them while more or less under Tom's guardianship? An uneasiness began to rise in Tom's stomach as concerns about complicity in Andy's corruption rose in his mind. There was Elizabeth, too, in his mind, inflicting her silent rebuke.

They reached Government Hill and started around it. As they did so, a group of cowboys from a ranch in that region rode up behind them at a dead run and passed them with little reduction in their speed. Their six-shooters were drawn, and no sooner were they around on the Griffin side than they began to shoot those .45s into the air, "shooting up the town," a custom among many such visitors to the Flat, and one that did nothing to put to rest Tom's doubts.

Tom and Andy rode around the base of Government Hill until they found themselves at the top of Griffin Avenue, where they stopped and took in the scene. Horses crowded the hitching rails all down the street. Wagons were parked anywhere they could fit, but done so as to allow at least enough room for people to pass by. And pass by they did, in wagons, on horseback, and on foot, in a hodgepodge of humanity that all but defied description. These people, of widely varied descriptions and backgrounds, moved ill-defined within the moon's low light, until definition and color would fall upon them as they passed into the brighter light pushing out through the doorways and windows of the nightlife establishments, out, out, to where it dispersed in the fair light of the moon. Sound pushed out with the light to meet the lower sounds of the street, those of the wagons and horses and mules and oxen and the farther sounds of the woods and plains, those of the coyote, owl, and the wolf. Out from the inside pushed that sound of lighted night, the sound of piano, fiddle, mandolin, of gambling devices, of clinking glasses, and even a gunshot, now and then, and just the sound of people gathered, that hubbub of individual voices and personal sounds, blended into a sonance of its own, continuous though pointed and pitted by the varied contributions of the many. And there were the many, composed of the individuals, coming and going, men and women—the buffalo hunters, the cowboys, the soldiers, the surveyors, the dandies and gamblers, the Tonkawa and other Indians, the dancehall girls, the laundresses and cyprians—all of them moving within the light, within the sound, within the light and sound of the Griffin night.

On the edge of that light and sound, Tom hesitated. He could not wait long. Andy had looked long enough at the scene of the Flat. Now he looked at Tom. It was time to move into the Griffin night. Tom could not avoid it. He nudged his mount forward, and with the possibility of corrupting an innocent weighing heavily on his conscience, he started their movement down Griffin Avenue into the Griffin night. But there was hesitation in his night horse's advance, as the black mount sensed the hesitation in his rider. Horse and rider both experienced a tension of moving forward while at the same time holding back. Then, suddenly, the tension broke with a jerk of the reins, and horse and rider turned abruptly to the right.

They turned into the wagon yard of the Occidental Hotel, with Andy following. Tom swung down from his night horse, Othello, and headed toward the dining room. There he found Mrs. Smith and introduced himself. She was sure she remembered him from the summer before and now more clearly remembered Luke from that time, as well, as Tom and Luke had visited Hank Smith's bar (of a more respectable character than the saloons of the town) together. In response to his inquiry regarding respectable social events in the Griffin area for that evening, Mrs. Smith informed him that there had been a wedding that day at the Higgins ranch, north of town, between a Miss Laura Higgins and a Mr. Barney Kendall, and that it was a huge affair, and that she regretted that her duties had kept her from attending. She assured him, though, that she intended to attend, if even for a short while, the infare to be held two days later at the Kendall ranch.

These infares were a type of reception for the bride by the family of the groom and could even rival the wedding celebration in terms of "feasting and dancing." But Mrs. Smith made it clear to Tom that the Kendall family would have quite a task ahead of them to rival the wedding celebration prepared by the Higgins, but still, if any family could do it, those Kendalls could, they surely could.

More to the point, Mrs. Smith assured Tom that the Higgins would be glad to have Tom and Andy as their guests at the dance, and that, should any question arise, they should merely say that they were guests of hers, as she had been duly invited. With that assurance and with directions to the Higgins ranch, Tom thanked Mrs. Smith and departed from her and returned to the yard, where he mounted Othello.

The usually inscrutable Andy could not hide the curiosity that now showed on his face. Tom glanced at him and said, "Follow me."

Tom could have been more prudent in his choice of a route out of town, so as to completely avoid exposing Andy to the Flat, but he was so relieved at the alternative he had discovered for that evening, that a ride down Griffin Avenue hardly seemed to present a problem, considering the possible scenarios for that night presented to his mind just moments before.

Thus, with Andy trailing behind—trying to take in as many of the sights as possible—Tom rode toward the crossing of the Clear Fork of the Brazos River at the end of Griffin Avenue. The two men rode past the various saloons, gambling houses, and dancehalls, passing one of the most notorious, the Beehive, before which Andy slowed down to read the infamous poem posted outside:

> In this dive we are all alive,
>   Good whiskey makes us funny,
> And if you are dry
> Step in and try
>   The flavor of our honey.

As he read, a tall man, of about Luke's or Tom's age, passed behind his horse, while crossing the street, and strolled toward the Beehive. He had been gambling at Shaughnessy's saloon, on the corner of Fourth and Griffin Avenue, and was ready to try the Beehive's tables. As the man stepped into the light from the Beehive's windows, Andy could see that he was finely dressed in a well-tailored gray suit and a clean shirt, obviously starched and pressed, with a carefully tied cravat around his collar, and that his blond hair was neatly barbered and combed. This man was John Henry Holliday, a Georgia-born dentist, well trained for that occupation at the Pennsylvania College of Dental Surgery in Philadelphia, and in five years of practice, first in Georgia, then Dallas, and since then in various frontier towns. He would have been a handsome man, and had been considered one when he was younger, with his blond hair, blue eyes, and nearly six-foot frame, except that now there was a hollowness about him, in his pallid, sunken cheeks and his thin body, that bespoke consumption. And consumption did have its grip on "Doc" Holliday. The consumption of tuberculosis had brought him west to Dallas. Then other consumptions had set in, gambling and alcohol among them. The gambling had begun to consume him when business had been slow in Dallas and he had put into practice, in the local establishments, gambling lessons he had learned from a young mulatto woman who had been a servant in his uncle's household. It was probably concurrent with the planting of those seeds of the gambling consumption that his consumption of alcohol began to consume him. By the time of an earlier visit to Griffin, two years before, his bill for liquor at the Occidental had been nearly six times the amount of his bill for room and board.

Holliday would remain for a few months on this visit to Fort Griffin, during which he would begin a friendship with Wyatt Earp, who would stop in Griffin while hunting an outlaw. Earp was a friend of John Shaughnessy, who owned the Cattle Exchange Saloon where Holliday would be dealing faro by the time of Earp's visit. It was in that establishment that Wyatt Earp would become acquainted with Doc Holliday.

Doc would also come to know "Big Nose Kate" Elder, also known as Kate Fisher, but whose given name was Mary Katherine Harony. The two would pair up, and later, when Doc would be put under "house arrest" in his room at the Planter's Hotel for a stabbing that appeared to be self-defense, Kate would set a shed ablaze to divert attention, draw a gun on the man guarding Doc's room, and flee with Doc, eventually to Dodge City in early 1878. There Doc would develop his friendship with Wyatt Earp and his brothers. Doc's association with the Earps and with Kate Elder would last the rest of his life, the story of which would develop into a notorious mix of indistinguishable fact and fiction.

Tonight, though, when Doc Holliday was still just another temporary resident of the Flat, one who practiced dentistry in his room during the day and played the faro and poker tables at night, he was heading into the Beehive Saloon. He may very well have been looking in to see if he could find the mysterious Lottie Deno present at the gaming tables. The beautiful, well-dressed, well-mannered, redheaded, black-eyed

Deno, who had a certain association with the Beehive, was known to be an exceptional gambler, and, as such, to prefer the gambling houses to the saloons, as she was not known to drink. She was seen almost exclusively in the gambling halls, the store (when in need of provisions), or on the way to or from her shanty near the river, where she received no visitors. In the same silent manner in which she had come to town, she would leave one day, after her "sweetheart" had been killed by deputies after his arrest. Some time later, law enforcement would enter her abandoned shanty to find it well furnished and to find a note instructing them to sell those furnishings and to give the money to someone in need. She would eventually settle in New Mexico, where she would marry and, after her husband's death, join the Episcopal Church and distinguish herself in acts of philanthropy.

Ah, but that was yet to come. For now these characters were temporarily set in the town of Griffin, just as Andy was. But they, for their part, moved into the Griffin night, as he, in the company of a true friend, passed through it.

Yes, he and Tom passed through. Beyond the shanties at the edge of town, they left Griffin behind and entered the waters of the Clear Fork of the Brazos River and came up out of the waters on the other side, heading north.

Locating the Higgins ranch was made considerably easier than it might have been due to the light provided by the lanterns and fires that lit the great affair and, even more so, by the first of three fiddlers who would play in shifts until dawn the next day. Tom and Andy rode up into this music and light, dismounted, and tied the reins of their horses to a picket line not far from the house.

As they approached the party, they could see that there was little need to be concerned about being invited. People were everywhere about the grounds. Officers and their wives were in evidence, as were many cowboys and ranchers, and even some buffalo hunters, and nearly every woman of good reputation within a fifty mile radius and beyond. Closest to the house, the yard had become an extension of the dance floor inside, where men and women danced to square dances, waltzes, quadrilles, polkas, and the schottische, notwithstanding that the inside dance floor had been expanded by removing a partition from between the two front rooms of the large stone house and moving all the furniture outdoors.

As they approached, Tom was drawn to the linen-covered tables set up next to (or, more likely, moved to make room for) the outside dance floor. Though the tables had been well picked over, there was still plenty left of the original seventy roasted chickens and the dozens of turkeys and the barbecued beef and the boiled hams. Indeed, a woman was replenishing the meats as they approached. Pies, too, covered a substantial portion of the tables, along with custards, and cakes— enough cakes to last, with the coffee, until well after dawn.

Tom stepped up to the table and was intercepted by an older woman in an apron holding a coffee pot, which she had filled from a wash pot of coffee in the fireplace in the kitchen.

"Coffee?" she said as the men approached.

"Yes, ma'am, thank you," Tom said.

The woman picked up two cups from the table and filled them and handed them to the two men.

"I'm Mrs. Higgins, mother of the bride," she said, unable to hide a little of the fatigue that had begun to set in after days of preparation and, already, one long day of celebratory work. "What ranch you boys in from?"

"Well, ma'am," Tom said, as he and Andy tipped their hats, "I'm Tom Schurtz, and this here is Andy Grady. We're drivin' through with a small herd to start a ranch west of here. Mrs. Smith at the Occidental directed us your way, sayin' that we could attend as her guests."

"Oh," said Mrs. Higgins, with a wave of her hand, "there's no trouble at all in that. As you can see, there's plenty, and the more the merrier."

Saying this, she did scrutinize Andy a little bit, but gave it up. Andy's Irish, Apache, Mexican ethnic mix, especially with his hair cut short, as it was, left people with little certainty about whether he ought to be excluded from their company or not, though it was enough to draw their attention. His striking good looks, as well as his height and his erect posture and his quiet (though not bashful) demeanor, had a way of quashing prejudice, especially on the part of women, before it had much time to develop beyond a hint. These attributes worked that way on Mrs. Higgins.

"And there are plenty of eligible girls that are looking to do some dancing, so don't you all be shy," she said.

"Thank you, ma'am; we won't be," Tom assured her.

"And help yourself to all this food. There's plenty."

"Thank you, ma'am; we will."

Mrs. Higgins shone a tired smile upon them both, allowing it to linger a little on the handsome Andy as just a bit of curiosity rose up behind it. But that curiosity was then immediately dismissed as she pulled herself away to attend to her many duties.

Though it had not been that long since they had partaken of a supper of venison, biscuits, vegetables, and pie, Tom and Andy each took a healthy sampling of the meats, and they had no trouble consuming them, as they stood on the edge of the dance area and watched the festivities. Healthy samplings of desserts followed, which they were just finishing when the fiddler announced that the second candy pull of the event was about to take place. There had been an earlier pull for the children, in which some of the adults had participated, but this one was for adults only, mainly young adults, mainly unmarried young men and women.

Two women who had been making the molasses candy in a wash pot at the other end of the dance area brought forward the pot and carried it up onto the porch. They placed the wash pot on a small table near a group of older men, who cleared away from it, perhaps reliving painful experiences from earlier in life.

As the calls were made for the young couples to come forward for the candy pull, Tom's attention was drawn to a blonde girl of fair complexion, perhaps fifteen or sixteen years of age, not too far from Andy and him, who kept turning her head to look their way and then turning it back to look at the scene developing around the wash pot on the porch. Finally, she made up her mind and started their way. She was short of stature, around five feet tall, and though she was pretty enough, she was not so confident in her appearance, especially in light of the appearance of some of the other pretty young ladies present, to expect that the man of her choosing would come to her.

"Pardon me;" she said to Andy, when she had come to stand in front of him, "my name is Susie Kirkland, and I noticed that you had only arrived a short time ago, and since you don't appear to know anyone, I wondered if you would like to join me in the candy pull?"

Andy looked down upon the young lady. He smiled at her spunk. Then, in the manners he had learned from his father (who had learned them from his father), he introduced himself and Tom and added, "I'd be delighted to join you, Miss Kirkland," at which the Kirkland maiden beamed.

Andy turned and left his plate on the table, then turned to say, "Excuse us, Tom," to a smiling Tom. He was then led off like a prize pony by Miss Kirkland.

Ah, but the candy pull merely served as Andy's debut and Miss Kirkland merely as his discoverer, which, despite its merits, could not assure her of sole possession. The other young ladies, in ways consistent with the customs of the times, were not long in making Andy's acquaintance, which inaugurated a full night of dancing for Mr. Andrew Grady.

Tom enjoyed no little amusement at Andy's social success, relishing it all the more considering that it had been brought about without exposure, other than a ride through town, to the ways of the Flat. Not only was his own conscience celebrating this turn of events, but he could also be assured that, despite whatever concerns Elizabeth might have had, she could hardly object to the wholesome entertainment of a wedding party. She might have her objections to the dancing, but at a wedding party in that country, even dancing was excusable.

Thus was Tom so agreeably disposed that his own mind, cleared now of the concern over Andy, began to settle into the reality of being at an extraordinary wedding dance with many eligible young ladies. And, in time, after some dancing of his own, Tom's mind settled some more, to finally rest upon an exceptional maiden visiting from Kentucky, a Miss Nancy Hawkins.

Miss Hawkins was a tall, shapely girl with long brown hair, pulled up, and a light complexion, faintly freckled about the nose and high cheeks. It was a good nose, slightly rounded at the end, above full lips, which nicely framed her white teeth, which so often showed forth in smile after nearly any comment Tom made that even bordered on what might be considered witty. But for all that, the smile that came from her eyes outshone that of the teeth. Clear eyes of light brown, she had, in which Tom could see nothing but good.

And if there were anything else to see there, one would think he would have found it, because he certainly looked long enough. For though Miss Hawkins had a full slate of dance partners, as the night wore on her dances were more and more taken up by Tom. Interestingly, she danced less and less, the pair finding themselves sitting for longer and longer periods of time on chairs on the porch, talking, watching the dancing, or just sitting in each other's presence. She was, at the present, unattached, even though she was already nineteen years old, due, no doubt, to her parents' demand that she pursue higher education. Hence, she was not only bright, but educated, which information she had not volunteered, but Tom had managed to get out of her in conversation. And that conversation developed pleasantly amidst the celebration of the marriage of Miss Laura Higgins and Mr. Barney Kendall.

So the night wore on until a roseate glow on the eastern horizon signaled its impending end. Tom was loath to tear himself away from the Kentucky beauty, and she from him, and they promised each other they would write. Andy promised, too, to a number of girls for whom his dancing and well-mannered conversation had made the night particularly memorable. Tom's promise took on a fuller meaning when he asked Miss Hawkins, in light of the probability that he would not see her for some time, if he might kiss her. The beauty blushed and smiled lightly and lowered her head. She confessed, in a quiet voice, that as much as she might like to be kissed by Tom, it went against her religion to kiss a man before marriage. Tom responded that he respected such noble convictions, and that those convictions only deepened his admiration for her. She did allow him to take her hand, though. This he held for a moment, until she was again looking at him. Then he kissed that hand, which she did allow, and he was off.

As the sun pushed the beginnings of its light above the horizon and out over a much subdued Griffin, Tom and Andy rode up Griffin Avenue, reaching its beginning at the base of Government Hill just as the sunrise gun was fired at the fort above. As they continued around the base of Government Hill and passed out of Griffin, they heard the bugle sounded and the shouts and noise of the troops assembling on the parade ground of the mesa above them. Loud enough, though still barely audible to minds occupied with memories of the long night, these sounds faded, faded as the two men passed out of Griffin.

WHEN THEY NEARED CAMP, Andy rode immediately out to the herd without stopping in camp, so that he could relieve Luke, who had taken his watch. There he found a very tired Luke. Luke had slept some, when he had lain down after settling the cattle after their midnight stretch. Still, he had awakened to a restlessness in the herd not long after that, and he had been in the saddle ever since. With Andy riding out to spell Luke, Tom was left alone to face Elizabeth.

Elizabeth looked up when Tom entered the camp. She was alone, as the children were still asleep. "Are you ready for breakfast?" she asked him coldly, without looking up.

"I am, thank you. I could cook it if you'd like," Tom said, nearly ready to kick himself at this obvious attempt at ingratiation.

Elizabeth merely ignored him and started some biscuits from the dough she had made and slapped bacon into a pan and placed it on a grate over the fire. Fresh eggs were ready to follow the bacon in the pan. As she prepared this breakfast, Luke rode into camp.

Luke's lack of sleep, no stranger to a cowboy on the trail, was evident in his drawn face with its heavy eyelids. He said little more than enough to greet Tom and Elizabeth, who was no more happy at Tom and Andy's trip to town in that it had caused her husband to spend a nearly sleepless night in the saddle. Tom, too, now that the adrenaline from attending the party was wearing off, was beginning to feel the effects of a sleepless night, and he was no more talkative than Luke. Still, after the two men had sat down on the ground around the fire and Elizabeth had served them breakfast, while consuming that hearty breakfast of eggs, biscuits, bacon, and plenty of coffee, Luke opened up the breakfast conversation.

"Well, Tom," he said, "Andy tells me you all found a right respectable wedding party to attend last night."

Elizabeth's ears perked up, though she did not look up from her work of preparing more food over the fire around which the men sat.

"That's right," Tom said, as much for Elizabeth's hearing as for Luke's. "It was a fine gathering."

"Andy said there was quite a table spread."

"There was indeed: roasted chicken after roasted chicken, turkey, barbecued beef, ham. There were cakes and pies—you cannot imagine all the desserts—and plenty of coffee. And it was such a fine gathering of people." This last note was also thrown in for Elizabeth's benefit.

And benefit she did, as she was relieved of the burden of meting out the appropriate punishment for Tom's—Andy's too, but particularly Tom's—transgression. Still, there was no indication that Tom had known that they were going to a wedding dance when they had left, so he might not be entirely deserving of reprieve; luck may have come to his aid. Nevertheless, he had chosen a respectable wedding party over the disreputable Flat, and Andy may have been preserved from corruption. She listened further as she appeared to pay little attention to the men.

"How'd you find out about this weddin' dance?" Luke asked.

"We stopped at the Smith hotel and asked Mrs. Smith, and she told us about this wedding at the Higgins ranch, and we headed immediately for the ranch. Andy met a whole passel of nice Christian girls." Though Tom was aware, to some extent, that he might be laying it on a little thick, his enthusiasm for getting the truth out to Elizabeth and for clearing his guilt in her eyes fueled his doing so.

Elizabeth listened, and the seeds of forgiveness began to sprout. Of course, there was no indication of whether or not Tom had taken Andy through Griffin, so there was still some room for concern, but all in all the report was a far cry from her worst fear. She filled the men's coffee cups, and as she was filling Tom's, without looking at him, she said, "There are plenty more eggs and biscuits, Tom, if you'd like some more."

"I would, Elizabeth. Thank you," Tom said, handing her his plate and grasping at the significance of the offer.

And so it began, with extra helpings of breakfast. Eye contact would follow, which would grow in duration along with the duration of pleasant conversation, so that, in the course of a few days, all was forgiven, and things were back to normal.

OF COURSE, THOSE DAYS OF RECONCILIATION were spent on the move, and the normalization of relationships took place amidst the normality of the daily driving over the trail and the nightly herding of the cattle. That morning, after that breakfast, Tom rode swiftly into town with the collie Lad across his saddle and returned him to Mrs. Smith. When he arrived back at camp, the Stuart-Schurtz party headed out and crossed Collins Creek without incident and entered the Mackenzie Trail, credited to Colonel (later General) Ranald Mackenzie, from the period of his campaigns against the Comanche and Kiowa (1871 to 1875), and used by just about everyone else in that region afterward, and even by some before. Ten miles west of Griffin, they stopped at the Ledbetter Salt Works to purchase as much salt as they could fit in their wagons, as pioneers could not have too much of this essential commodity on the trail and the frontier. From there they continued west to where they crossed the Clear Fork of the Brazos River (the same that flowed past the town of Griffin), before making camp for the night, as was their custom. They well knew that if they waited until morning to cross a stream, they ran the risk that the water could rise suddenly during the night, due to rains several miles away, making the stream unfordable.

Also according to custom, after supper and bedding down the herd, the night guard, who was Tom this night, stayed with the herd while the rest of the party retired to their beds. The children would turn in earliest, of course, with the adults often lingering about the fire, exchanging stories, or sharing information or observations, or participating in a communion of meditation evoked by the dancing flames stretching into and pulling back from the surrounding darkness, the personal fruits of that meditation known to the individual participants alone.

In time, the adults too would seek their beds. Elizabeth would join the children under the canopy of the smaller wagon, to sleep upon the mattresses that lay on top of all that was packed in that conveyance. Little Robert would sleep next to those mattresses in a cradle right behind the seat of the wagon. Luke, when he was not sleeping in the wagon with his family; Tom, when he was present; and Andy would also retire to their beds. These were spread out upon the ground, each (since Luke had bought Andy the proper makings of a bedroll in Fort Griffin) consisting of a doubled-over wagon sheet; a pair of wool blankets; and a pillow of clothing, boots, or a saddle, or whatever else might fill the need, according to preference. And all would sleep—after the day's working and walking and running and exploring, while the wagons had rolled on at their bumpy pace; and after the evening's supping and sitting and talking and singing, while the campfire had burned on to just flickering coals. Yes, all would sleep, under the dark, star-studded firmament stretched above, amidst the cool, dry autumn air, with its smells of grass and trees and smoke and cattle, and its sounds of beeves and owls and coyotes and wolves and, even sometimes, a panther, after whose unnerving scream some would not sleep quite so well as they had before.

And there were antelope, too, pronghorn, though these were not
heard in the night, but they were seen in the day, during the party's
waking westward advance, and often seen in large numbers, great
herds. And they would draw surprisingly close, close enough to sate
their curiosity: for these were curious creatures. And fleet! Though
bound to the earth, their flight across the ground, through the grass,
had more of the flight of a bird of the air than of other grounded creatures. Deer, too, were seen, though not as often, and in fewer numbers,
and usually toward evening, near a creek or river, to which they would
steal down for a drink.

Still, it was not for lack of creeks or rivers that the deer were less
often seen. Of such streams there were plenty: Collins, Trout, Limpia,
Clear Fork, California, Paint, and later, Double Mountain Fork, Salt
Fork, Salt, Duck, South Fort, Red Mud, Freshwater Fork (also known
as Catfish, Blanco, or White), and others. The trail crossed them all,
whether running or dry, and so must those who would follow the trail,
and so must their wagons and stock, at crossings made less difficult by
the former passing of troops and other westward travelers, and especially, by the passing of many buffalo hunters with their many wagons,
wearing down the banks of the streams through which they rolled,
heavy wagons carrying their tons of hides.

Thus it was that as the party rolled deeper and deeper into the
West—down through tree-lined streambeds, with their deer, wildcats,
beavers, muskrats, otters, and turkeys; and over grass-covered divides
and prairies, with their pronghorn antelope, wolves, coyotes, jackrabbits, prairie dogs, prairie chickens, and quail; and into breaks and
draws, with all of it, including shinnery hogs and the reclusive bears
and panthers; and under a cloudless sky, with its eagles, hawks, scissortails, larks, and doves—there was evidence of imbalance. For those
skies held buzzards, too, and those too-numerous winged scavengers
pointed to that animal most in evidence, though not most in sight, the
quarry of those hunters, the original wearer of those hides, the
American bison, the buffalo.

The buffalo was in evidence early on the trail, in skeletal remains
of the great beasts, bleached white skeletons, many, many skeletons,
often over fifty or even one hundred or more in a small area of just a
few acres. At such places, hunters had "held a stand" on the animals.

To gain and hold a stand on a herd of buffalo, a hunter, staying downwind of his quarry, would sneak as close to the herd as was practicable. This need not be all that close, and was often several hundred yards away, as the Sharps rifle (.50, .45, and .44 caliber), the principal weapon of the buffalo hunter, was accurate and deadly at legendary distances. Once established, usually with the barrel of his heavy Sharps resting in the crotches of two sticks brought along for that purpose, the hunter would single out the leader of the herd, usually a bull, then aim, and fire. His aim would not be to shoot the animal through the heart. If this were done, the animal would be likely to buck and kick and pitch, which would break the stand. So, instead, the hunter would aim farther back, behind the animal's ribs, and shoot it in the belly. If the herd were on the move at the time the leader was shot, they might begin to run, then slow down and stop behind that leader. Whether on the move or still just grazing, once the leader was shot in this way, he would start to walk around, while the rest of the herd would graze, until he would just lie down. Then others of the herd would gather around the downed leader and bellow, which buffalo hunters often likened to similar behavior observed among domesticated cattle. Nevertheless, the herd would eventually begin to graze again. When the successor to the downed leader would lead out of the herd, he would meet the same fate as the last, and so would the next and the next, until the leaderless herd would begin to mill around and around, and the hunter would be free to shoot one after another. In this way, the hunter could often kill dozens or scores of animals, until all were down, or the stand was broken and the animals stampeded away under a new leader or just scattered. Either way, once the hunter had shot all that he could, the skinners would go to work.

Though many of the hunters would do their own skinning, those who had made a great enterprise of the hunt had in their parties men who specialized in skinning alone. These would move in on the downed animals as soon as possible, so as to skin them before rigor mortis set in, or before the carcasses froze, a real concern since winter was the main season for buffalo hunting. With his Bowie knife for ripping and his Wilson knives for skinning, as well as a large steel or whetstone for frequent sharpening, a practiced skinner could skin up to fifty carcasses in a day, sometimes more.

This the skinners would do, as circumstances would allow, leaving in their wakes millions of skinless, rotting hulks of flesh and bone. For though it is true that some of the meat would sometimes be taken from these carcasses by some of the hunters (usually the tongues, the hams, and the humps, which would then be cured, packed, and sold), still, most of the meat, tons and tons of it, would be left to be gorged by glutting scavengers, or to rot, as much of it did. Thus was the buffalo in evidence, farther down the trail, in countless buzzards circling over distant kills.

In flies, too, was the buffalo in evidence, in swarms of green blowflies that grew thicker the deeper the party moved into the buffalo hunting range, despite the lateness of the season. The flies came from the decaying flesh of the buffalo carcasses, where the adults would deposit their eggs and the larvae would feed and develop into flies, which effectively continued the cycle. In fact, this process continued the cycle so effectively, that it became difficult for the members of the Stuart-Schurtz party to eat their meals without having them covered with flies.

And the buffalo was very forcefully in evidence in the almost over-whelming stench of putrefaction. This odor, depending upon the direction of the wind (which blew often enough from the southwest, right through prime buffalo hunting territory toward the Stuart-Schurtz party), long preceded the actual sightings of the rotting carcasses of recent stands. It also preceded the buffalo camps, which the party passed and, on more than one occasion, camped near. The stench emanating from these camps came mostly from "green hides" staked out to cure, though the notorious squalor of some of these camps added its own spice to that stench. These green hides would be staked out over a large area of flat ground. This was done, when the hide was still fresh from the carcass, by stretching out the hide, flesh side up, and driving several small pegs through small holes cut around the edges of the hide. After a few days, the hides would be turned over and pegged wool side up. Then they would be turned over every other day or so, until completely cured. Once cured, a hide was hard and stiff and hence referred to as a "flint hide." These flint hides would then be folded, stacked, and tied in bales to be hauled off to Fort Griffin or Fort Worth, or to be sold to buyers on the range.

Therefore, the buffalo was also in evidence in the hides stacked in wagons that were already rolling back along the trail toward the east, even though the season had only just got underway. Although this season was recognized to run from fall to spring and was at its peak in the winter months (when the animal's hide was at its best for robes, and the southern herd had migrated into the region to the west and southwest of Fort Griffin), still, some buffalo hunters remained on the range throughout the summer, hunting all that time. And a good many of the hides taken by buffalo hunters on the range, in any season, passed through Rath's City, also known as Camp Reynolds, Reynolds' City, Rath's Station, Reynolds, Rath, Rath's Store, or Hide Town. Through that same frontier outpost, the Stuart-Schurtz party also passed, on their sixth day out of Fort Griffin, and there the buffalo was very much in evidence. The buffalo was in evidence in the stench and the flies and the hides staked and stacked in the Reynolds and Rath hide yard.

Reynolds was of Lee and Reynolds (Fort Elliott, Texas), and Rath was of Rath and Wright (Dodge City, Kansas), and these two concerns had formed a partnership to profit from the great buffalo hunt in west Texas. They would do so by selling supplies to the hunters and by purchasing their hides and later selling them to businesses in the East and in Europe, where they would be made into robes, and lap robes, and leather goods, among which would be thick leather belts to drive the machines of industry. The partnership had followed the buffalo south in 1876. Charles Rath himself had led this following, and many had followed him, first his own freighters driving several freight wagons loaded with supplies, then some sixty hunters with their sixty wagons, all loaded with supplies and each drawn by six yoke of oxen. They had traveled directly south from Fort Elliott, with the help of a compass attached to the horn of Rath's saddle, creating, as they did so, the Rath Trail, over which many of the hides, of the buffalo they had followed, would travel directly north to Fort Elliott and from there to Dodge City and on to destinations in the East. At the end of the trail, the partnership had set up its supply store and hide yard, south of the Double Mountain Fork of the Brazos River in southwestern Stonewall County, Texas, about sixty-five miles west of Fort Griffin. With them had come the hunters, two saloons, a dancehall, and a Chinese laundry, and the personnel associated with each, including about forty women.

And so it was that on the day that the Stuart-Schurtz party passed through—which is exactly what the party did—what met their eyes, amidst the stench and flies, was a dusty, filthy outpost of a handful of sod buildings strewn about on both sides of the road, the north side featuring a sod corral and, in front of one of the sod saloons, a cistern full of water, the south side boasting Reynolds and Rath's and the Chinese laundry. Since, by design, it was in the early morning, not long after dawn, that the party passed through, most of those present in the "City" had either just retired for their sleep or were too played out after their night of drinking, dancing, card playing, and brawling to pay much attention to the two wagons and the small herd rolling west along the road from Fort Griffin. So the party passed on and out of Rath's City/Camp Reynolds, Texas. Two short years later, the City would be abandoned and would pass on, itself, along with the great buffalo herds, into the history of the West.

But for now, Rath's/Reynolds boomed, and it did so because of another boom, a sound in which the buffalo—and the entire basis for the existence of Rath's or Reynolds—was very much in evidence. This was the boom of the Sharps rifle, heard more clearly and frequently now by the members of the Stuart-Schurtz party, as they advanced deeper into the West over the low rolling plains of Texas toward their destination. There were Springfields and Spencers and Henrys, too, but there were mainly Sharps, and it was the Sharps rifle that came to stand as the weapon symbol of the great buffalo hunt. Fast, accurate, powerful, and deadly, the Sharps .50, .45, and .44 had been designed for the buffalo hunt by Christian Sharps Rifle Company of Connecticut, at the request of John Mooar, brother and partner of J. Wright Mooar, one of the earliest participants in the great buffalo hunt. Hence, in the frequent boom of that excellent weapon, the buffalo was very much in evidence, and so was the hunter, the broker, the manufacturer, the merchant, and the consumer. So also was the slaughter and the waste and the greed.

This realization most impressed the members of the Stuart-Schurtz party when the buffalo was in evidence in the strictest sense. Yes, despite the great slaughter, the buffalo was still there to be seen in its true living form. It was to be seen in several small herds, as the party proceeded westward along the trail. One time, in particular, it made its presence felt in a most convincing way. On the second morning after they had passed through Rath's City, in the low light before sunrise, they awoke to find themselves surrounded by a herd of buffalo, which promptly stampeded through their camp, as Tom and Andy scrambled from their beds to take refuge behind the wagon in which Elizabeth and the children still lay in bed and were thus secured. Luke was farther out with the cattle, which had begun to run when the buffalo had, and he managed to turn them away from the buffalo and get them to mill before they had gone very far. Back at the camp, Tom and Andy stood behind opposite corners of the wagon, enthralled by the power of the charging mass of the small herd as it passed by, several individuals at a time, just arm's length away. Tom was especially struck by the look of vulnerability in the small brown eyes of the massive beasts, which were cast back, as if in fear of whatever they might be running from.

They had plenty from which to run. But where could they go, what with the slaughter and the greed behind it that caused the wanton waste? Where could they go?

Nowhere. That was obvious. As long as greed continued to inflate demand and corrupt supply—without any regard for the wanton waste of thousands of tons of meat left to rot or the extermination of the preponderant species of the North American Great Plains—the buffalo had nowhere to go, except to extinction.

The members of the Stuart-Schurtz party, especially the adult members, who could better appreciate the implications of what they were witnessing, shared a common regret over the profligate slaughter of these native beeves of the prairie. Still, as they rolled deeper into the reality of that slaughter, the overwhelming magnitude of it all constricted the expression of their reflections on the matter to an occasional comment or just a shake of the head. Nevertheless, whether expressed, unexpressed, or underexpressed, reflections did continue to rise up in their minds as they rolled through that land of carnage, or, if reflections had been exhausted, at least impressions continued to rise up, and these were unfavorable ones.

Tom, for his part, still reflected as he rode along through the region in the dust of the trailing herd. One thing of which he was sure was that the slaughter was wrong. The hunting of the buffalo was not wrong. The skinning of the buffalo was not wrong. The sale and use of those skins for clothing, industry, or any other legitimate use was not wrong. Even the reduction of the vast buffalo herds to make way for other uses of the land was not necessarily wrong. What was wrong was the greed behind it all and what that greed had wrought.

What that greed had wrought was the waste of untold tons of meat (and even the waste of many of the hides for which the animals had been killed, due to hasty skinning, curing, or both). It had wrought a slaughter that, if it continued apace (and there was every reason to believe that it would), was sure to wipe out the species without due consideration of all the ramifications of that extermination. It had wrought further enmity between whites and the Plains Indians and the further reduction of those peoples to a pathetic dependency.

It had wrought all of those things and more, Tom could see. And yet, as disturbing as all that was, there was another work of that greed that encompassed all the rest, and that was the work of perverting freedom into license. Tom believed that such a large-scale perversion of freedom was detrimental to, and indicative of, the relative health of a nation, especially of one that had been founded with the security of the inalienable right of liberty as one of its central tenets and had recently fought a bloody civil war to preserve itself and abolish the singularly most glaring and festering contradiction to that tenet. Where freedom degenerates into license, he mused, man has already relinquished the mastery of himself to his passions, and it only remains to be seen who or what will succeed his passions as his master. In such circumstances, a free society is very much in danger.

There is no true freedom without responsibility. In light of that truth, Tom thought of some of the buffalo hunters he had met along the trail and before. Despite the common characterization of the buffalo hunter, some of these hunters were respectable people, some of them whole families, and many of them regretted the wasteful slaughter of the buffalo, actually lamented the part they were playing in it. Yet, they licentiously continued in it, killing as many as they could as quickly as they could, before there were no more to kill, because they were desperate to get as much as they could out of the slaughter, desperate to secure their part of the fortune that the buffalo hides represented. Had a law been passed to stop the slaughter and preserve the breed (and there were several attempts at such legislation throughout the 1870s), they would have gladly obeyed it and been glad for it, and yet, as long as there was no law, they would continue to play their part in the slaughter up to the very extinction of the animal.

Due to greed, and the pride behind it, these hunters were willing to reject their God-given stewardship of the earth. They were willing to relinquish their own judgment of what was right and wrong, as well as their freedom to act upon it, because they wanted to get all that they could get, and they did not want to fall behind anyone else who might be profiting from the same motivation and the same refusal to govern himself according to right and wrong. Tom thought about how that tendency was not so uncommon, how that tendency was, indeed, universal. Still, there were individuals, call them the *conscientious*, who, through prayer, reflection, or both, came to know such tendencies in themselves and to see the evil in those tendencies and, with the help of grace, to overcome or check those tendencies, to greater or lesser degrees. In doing so, the *conscientious* were forming their consciences, and in doing so according to objective truths, these individuals were subjecting themselves to "the laws of nature and of nature's God," cited in the *Declaration of Independence*, a subjection without which a free society must degenerate into anarchy or tyranny or the ugliest amalgamations of both.

A free society depends upon the will of the individuals in that society to take personal responsibility for their freedom, to govern themselves according to objective truths of right and wrong, Tom reasoned. When the individuals of a free society refuse or even just neglect to take responsibility for their freedom, when they refuse or neglect to form their consciences and to be ruled by those consciences attuned to "the laws of nature and of nature's God," then those individuals choose license over freedom, and they give in to a progression toward disorder or toward being ruled by something other than the self guided by conscience.

Tom saw just such a progression in this matter of the buffalo. He considered those hunters, not the lawless element of that occupation, but those respectable ones, call them the *lawful*, as they were willing to submit to the laws of the state. He considered those *lawful*, who would willingly and gladly stop the slaughter, and even feel relieved to do so, if only the state would enact a law requiring it. He considered how those *lawful* were passing on the responsibility for their actions to the state, and with it, they were passing on their freedom, their right of liberty, their right of self-government. He thought of all that it had cost in human sacrifice to establish and preserve a nation that had been founded to protect freedom and other human rights. Then he thought of how such shirking of responsibility and freedom and relinquishing of rights was unworthy of that sacrifice, and of how it would be better to have one's freedom and rights usurped rather than to have them so carelessly discarded.

Interestingly enough, even the *lawless* element of the buffalo hunters (those apparently most opposed to being ruled by others), though they might refuse or neglect to discern the wrongness of the slaughter that the *lawful* had discerned, and, in fact, because they refused or neglected to do so, they too were passing on their freedom to the state, because they would not even accept responsibility for their freedom to discern. These *lawless* too were giving the state greater power with which to rule over them, even if they intended to defy that power. Both kinds of men, those who had some respect for the law and those who did not, were willing to let their freedom be overwhelmed by the dictates of the state.

And to whom or what were the *lawful* and the *lawless* passing on their responsibility and freedom when they passed them on to the state? Well, at least in the United States of America, a republic, they were passing on their freedom and attendant responsibility to a seemingly innocuous form of government, a representative government, a government of elected peers. But those peers, too, were human. They, too, only ruled as well as they were willing to form their consciences to the rule of "the laws of nature and of nature's God," and to act in accordance with those consciences. Besides, once a matter like the slaughter of the buffalo was referred to the state, the state, in regard for all its citizens, was required to rule at a higher degree of generality than that of the individual conscience with its single subject, so that the general law of the state would be less adaptable than the more immediate and specific law of the individual conscience. Ergo, the individual lost freedom. For at that point, even if circumstances presented a situation in which the individual could act in a certain way in good conscience according to "the laws of nature and of nature's God," he might no longer be able to do so according to the laws of the state, because he had relinquished his responsibility and freedom to the state and was the more subjected to it.

Tom considered a simple hypothetical case in this matter of the buffalo. In that case, those hunting the buffalo, *lawful* and *lawless* alike, would continue the slaughter despite the obvious signs of it being wrong, if in nothing else than the prodigious waste of meat. Elected representatives of the people, outraged at the waste and the precipitous reductions in the numbers of the animal, would eventually pass a law to forbid the killing of the buffalo. Given that scenario, the following case unfolds. A man out on the prairie comes upon a lame buffalo bull that has been left behind by its herd and is obviously going to die. The man has a family who, though they have some food and are not starving, could make good use of the meat from the bull. Now, however, according to the new law, the man with the family must not kill the bull, and so the lame buffalo moves on to die in some remote place where the meat will go to waste. Before the law, the man could have legally killed and butchered the bull and fed his family with the meat, and he could have done so in good conscience. Now, after the law, his only legal option is to *not* kill the bull. His conscience must now weigh the law against the hunger of his family and the waste of the meat. If the man decides in good conscience, after weighing the matter, that it is better to kill the bull to feed his hungry family rather than to let the meat rot, he has decided, in good conscience, to break the law. This is no small matter, because in a free society laws should exist to protect the inalienable rights of the citizens; therefore, the conscientious person, in good conscience, should normally obey the law.

In such a case, then, the law, the conscience, or both have been compromised. This conflict between conscience and law comes about as a result of the refusal of earlier hunters to form or obey their consciences. It is a result of those earlier hunters' failure to rule themselves, a result of their having handed over responsibility to the state, which, by its nature, must rule in a more general way than the conscience. That the man in the hypothetical case is not a hunter illustrates another point: when citizens turn over responsibility to the state, not only do they turn over, with it, their own freedom, but also that of every other citizen, even the most conscientious.

Tom reflected on how his hypothetical case also illustrated the communal nature of man, the latent sacramentalism awaiting men's acceptance of and cooperation with grace. "No man is an island," wrote John Donne. "Never send to know for whom the bell tolls; it tolls for thee." If one is diminished, all are diminished. So John Donne let the world know in poetry, some two and a half centuries before, what the Church had been teaching for some sixteen centuries before that, having been taught it by Christ. Neither man nor a man lives in a vacuum. The act of a single man changes the world, the universe, regardless of how private or public the act. A good act has the capacity to yield good consequences far beyond the immediate effect; so does an evil act have a similar capacity to yield evil consequences. Therefore, for man (the creature in whom matter and spirit are combined in one nature, created with free will, in the very image of God), all his actions entail responsibility. Responsibility is a natural concomitant to human actions. To shirk responsibility is but an illusion, as the shirker is responsible for that shirking. And because human actions entail responsibility, each human action deserves its due consideration. When humans fail to accept the responsibility for their actions; when they refuse to give those actions due consideration; when, after such consideration, they refuse to act on the conclusions of an informed conscience, then events like the slaughter of the buffalo result.

Thus, Tom considered three broad categories of men: the *conscientious*, those who formed their consciences and acted according to them; the *lawful*, those who waited for the state to pass laws to legislate their behavior and thereby relinquished their freedom and its attendant responsibility to the state; and the *lawless*, those who had no respect for the law and would defy the law as they saw fit, until they were prevented by the state from doing so, thereby passing on all of their freedom and its attendant responsibility to the state. Consideration of these led Tom's mind onto consideration of another category of man, call them the *semi-lawful*.

Like the *lawless*, the *semi-lawful* did not respect the laws of the state, though not to the point of disregarding them altogether as the *lawless* would. Like the *lawful*, the *semi-lawful* relinquished their responsibility to the state, though not in the passive way of the *lawful*, but rather in an aggressive way. The *lawful* just went along with what

they were doing for their own benefit, without regard for their consciences, their free wills, their responsibilities, their places within the
human communion, and their roles of stewards of the earth, until the
state passed a law to stop them. The *semi-lawful* also went along with
what they were doing for their own benefit, without regard for their
consciences, their free wills, their responsibilities, their places within the
human communion, and their roles of stewards of the earth, until the
state passed a law to stop them, but the *semi-lawful* would go further.

The *semi-lawful* would then defy the law, often enough within the
bounds of the law, by challenging the law, by pushing it to its limits,
by finding and using every loophole in the law, by defying the spirit of
the law to get around the law through legal trivialities, which would
require more laws to be passed to close the loopholes and address the
trivialities, which would serve to further restrict the freedom of the
people. Or sometimes the *semi-lawful* would even break the law, where
the chances of their being held to account were slight. The *semi-lawful*
would not just submit to letting the state legislate their morality, thereby
relinquishing their responsibility to the state, as would the *lawful*, but
they would actually go so far as to ascribe to the state the role of conscience, and, even then, rather than obey that surrogate conscience,
they would fight it, stretching it, in any way, to allow them license,
which they would mistake for freedom. Even then, the *semi-lawful*
would blame any moral failings on the imperfections in the laws of the
state, which had borne their steady attack. This was not to be confused
with the *conscientious* who might responsibly oppose a law and seek to
have it changed because it contradicts their informed consciences.
Instead it was the *semi-lawful* rejecting the conscience and then ascrib-
ing the role of conscience to the state and then opposing that surrogate
conscience to enhance their license.

Interestingly enough, as soon as these *semi-lawful* would see a competitor (which to one of the *semi-lawful* was almost every other person)
reaping a better benefit than they were from an area of endeavor where
there was no law, or there was a loophole in the law, or there was a law
that favored the competitor, the *semi-lawful* would demand a law to
curb the success of that competitor, even if the law restricted the
license of the *semi-lawful*. Once such a law was passed, the *semi-lawful*
would go about finding a way around that law, until another competitor

did so better than they, at which time the *semi-lawful* would again demand another law.

These *semi-lawful*, like defiant children against their parents, could grow very proud of themselves as they battled against their surrogate consciences and their ubiquitous competitors and made their little victories here and there. They could believe themselves quite superior to all others because of how well they played the game they believed life to be.

Tom thought about that and wondered how superior the *semi-lawful* would consider themselves if there were no *lawful* or *conscientious* or even other *semi-lawful* over whom they could triumph. Put them in among the *lawless* only, among those who had a more honest disregard for the law, and see how well the *semi-lawful* would fare. There would be the real game; there would be the fair match, with all law stripped away and all participants equally unrestrained. How long would the *semi-lawful* remain superior without the law they so abused and without the *conscientious* and the *lawful*—constrained by conscience, law, or both—upon whom the *semi-lawful* could prey?

Regardless, the irony was that a good many of those to whom the *semi-lawful* felt so superior, especially the *conscientious*, were not only not playing the game, but they were not even in the game. A good many of those over whom the *semi-lawful* believed they were triumphing, did not even know there was a game. These, especially the *conscientious*, would have been surprised to know that the *semi-lawful* lived life as a contest against imaginary competitors and a surrogate conscience, rather than as the wholly gratuitous gift of existence, the unimaginable opportunity to *be* in the vast universe of time and space, the preciously limited opportunity to seek perfection rather than trivial victories over self-created foes.

The *conscientious*, to varying degrees, knew life as this gift, this opportunity. They knew the importance of forming their consciences and being ruled by those consciences attuned to "the laws of nature and of nature's God." They knew that a free society demanded that its citizens be disciplined, that they be virtuous, that they be responsible. They knew that if the citizens instead rejected virtue or did not seek it, and if they did not form their consciences, and if they substituted for the conscience some construct of man, then they set themselves up for anarchy or for tyranny by a power-hungry elite, often enough composed of the *semi-lawful*.

In considering these examples of the *conscientious*, the *lawful*, the *semi-lawful*, and the *lawless*, Tom considered the problem of a free society where not all the citizens valued virtue, where not all were conscientious. As a result, Tom concluded that the best system of government on earth was a representative government like that of the republic of the United States of America, which he loved. And he believed that such a representative government, founded by the *conscientious*, was best because it allowed for the possibility of having a government made up of the *conscientious*, limited in terms so as not to corrupt their conscientiousness. And he believed that, with a republic so founded and sustained, there was a chance that the government would respect and sustain the free will of its citizens, and, at the same time, protect, from abuses of free will, those citizens' God-given rights.

Such was the ideal, but Tom had just been considering the categories of the *conscientious*, the *lawful*, the *semi-lawful*, and the *lawless*, and he knew that the ideal was far from realization. For one thing, the representatives were elected by the citizens, and there was no guarantee that the citizens would elect only the *conscientious*. Instead, there was a good probability that they would not elect only the *conscientious*, and plenty of history to support that probability. For another thing, even if only the *conscientious* were elected, they would only be conscientious to the degree that they would form and obey their consciences. Experience suggested that this formation and obedience would not be perfect. One only need look at the founding of the great United States to see that its conscientious founders allowed it to be conceived within the context of its original sin of slavery, a context radically contrary to the exalted principles instrumental in its conception.

Ah, there it was, the nation's original sin, but that was only a relatively recent manifestation of the root of the problem. The root of the problem lay in the original sin of the human race that left man with a wounded human nature, which, though it was not totally corrupted, was thereafter inclined to sin, the result of proud opposition and disobedience, in a garden, that led to a tree of forbidden knowledge and deprived man of access to the tree of life. Therein lay the font of destruction for any free society. And that destruction was inevitable but for one quiet though superabundant hope, the result of humble submission and obedience, in another garden, that led to a new tree of knowledge that became the tree of life.

Therein lay the problem and the solution, Tom thought. And as he rode through the stench and the flies and the carcasses and the bones and the hides and the hunters and the booms of Sharps rifles, Tom thought of how much better the world could be if people accepted the truths presented in figurative language in the story of the first garden and then accepted the Truth made accessible because of the submission in the second garden. Such was his hope, and such was his prayer, as the Stuart-Schurtz party progressed along the Mackenzie Trail, drawing ever nearer the escarpment of the Llano Estacado.

THEN THEY SAW IT. But not just like that. No, it was a gradual sighting. While yet some twenty miles distant, the dark, low line of the Llano Estacado, to the west, began to lift off the low rolling plains, which had long served as the western horizon for the party. Ever so slowly did it lift, as the party inched steadily toward it. What they approached, in this Llano Estacado, was a great plateau that towered as much as one thousand feet above the low rolling plains, over which the Stuart-Schurtz party had been traveling, and stretched some 150 miles east to west, well into New Mexico, and, from the Canadian River in the north, some 250 miles north to south.

It now rose five hundred feet or so above the land over which the Stuart-Schurtz party approached. By that evening, when the party made camp, still several miles from the escarpment of the Llano Estacado, the line it presented had risen well off the low rolling plains to define a new, elevated horizon, flat, but with varying levels of flatness, where land met sky. These varying levels on the horizon were but illusions, caused by recesses and protrusions in the escarpment, that belied the relative uniformity in elevation of the land above. The grandest of these recesses lay directly in their path, a wide opening, perhaps as much as ten miles wide, bordered on either side by the stone face of the escarpment, rising well over three hundred feet above the floor of that opening.

The opening was Blanco Canyon, a thirty-mile-long gash, running northwest/ southeast, gouged into the Llano Estacado by the erosive forces of nature, particularly those of water cutting through stone over millennia, water from as far away as New Mexico, periodically coursing across the Llano Estacado through Running Water Draw into Blanco Canyon, where it would plunge into the spring-fed Catfish Creek and rush down the length of the canyon and out of its mouth to empty into the Salt Fork of the Brazos River. There were those who, in recognition of the creek's contribution to the Brazos, referred to it as the Freshwater Fork of the Brazos or Freshwater Creek. Still others would refer to it as Blanco Creek or River, after the canyon itself. This name would last, in translation, as, in time, the stream would come to be known as White River, but at the time of the Stuart-Schurtz arrival in that country, it was known popularly as Catfish Creek, and on its sandy bank, within seven miles of the entrance of Blanco Canyon, on the evening of their tenth day out of Fort Griffin, that party made camp.

Excitement saturated the atmosphere of the camp that evening, as the members of the party carried out their chores and ate their supper and bedded their herd in the waning light of an early sunset behind an elevated horizon, which offered a most impressive sign of their journey's progress. That excitement made for a bit of restlessness that was not conducive to sleep, so that, after the children had been put to bed and Tom had left to ride his watch, talk of the canyon ahead and of the escarpment and of the nearness of their destination and of many such things passed among the three adults sitting around the fire. Talk also emanated from the covered wagon, where the children were supposed to be asleep. This night, though, the children were not told to quiet down and go to sleep, but rather they were indulged and answered by the adults, until they spoke no more, and only the adults' voices drifted, with the crackling of the fire, out of the fire's light and mixed with the sounds of the night.

The excitement roused with the party in the morning, too, as the light of the rising sun poured color into the motley face of the escarpment, and into the red soil, and into the variegated green of the grass and brush and trees, and into the bleached white of the clusters of buffalo skeletons all around them. And as the sun poured forth its light, the darkness pulled back into shadows that crept along the low places and ducked into the recesses and crevices of the escarpment.

That motley escarpment marked by early morning shadows was the "caprock" of the Llano Estacado, or so it was called. In fact, the caprock was not really the escarpment, but only part of it, consisting of a thin layer of white rock at the top of the escarpment, which therefore served as the rim of the canyon before them. Still, thin as it was, it was caliche, and it was hard, and as such, it had a good deal to do with why the escarpment of the Llano Estacado presented as dramatic a sight as it did. This caprock was the top layer of the Ogallala Formation, a light-colored layer of rock that had been formed over some six million years, ten to four million years before, from sand and gravel washed down from the erosion of the young and growing Rocky Mountains. Percolation of calcium-rich water probably converted the top layer of this sandstone into the hard limestone caliche layer, the "caprock." Though this formation served as the top layer of rock, resisting erosion while erosive forces cut away the rock layers below it to render the cliffs of the escarpment, still, the formation extended under the surface of the entire Llano Estacado and was not only present at the escarpment. Nevertheless, it was most visible at the escarpment, and so the terminology stuck. Where the Stuart-Schurtz party now camped would have been said to be "below the caprock" or "below the cap" or "off the caprock" or something similar. Were they to ascend onto the Llano Estacado and camp on the surface of that great plateau, they would have been said to be "above the caprock" or "on top of the caprock" or "up on the cap" or something similar. Any approach to the escarpment from above or below would have been said to be "nearing the caprock" or something similar.

And the Stuart-Schurtz party was nearing the caprock now, having made quick work of breakfast and of the hitching up of steers and mules and of the other morning chores. But as they rolled along the Mackenzie Trail, they could not make quick work of the distance, and so they were still a mile out from the entrance to the canyon when they made their noon stop for dinner, again along the wide, sandy bank of Catfish Creek.

Like breakfast, dinner too was hurried, and as it was for man, so it was for beast. Accordingly, the usual noontime grazing time was cut short, and the steers and mules were soon back in the harness, and the whole outfit was soon on the move.

As the travelers drew nearer, the cliff walls at the opening of the canyon rose ever more magnificently, their rock faces ever mutating at the rate of the changing angle of the sun and of the travelers' position. And then, the party was between them. Insignificant seemed their entrance into the canyon between three-hundred-foot-high walls, ten miles apart. These canyon walls were less sheer than they had appeared at a distance, their sides sloping down from the the initial straight drop at the caprock rim. The varicolored surface of these walls could be picked apart at this closer distance to distinguish the white caprock layer and the tan, orange, and red layers of stone beneath it, peaking out through growths of juniper, shinnery oak, elbowbush, sumac, salt-bush, and short and medium grasses.

Slowly they moved into the canyon, lilliputian amidst its great expanse. Slowly, slowly they moved, and gradually the land began to change. The width of the canyon gradually narrowed. The road grad-ually improved as it rose out of the sand of the lower canyon. And gradually the effects of a specific abundance became apparent. That abundance was of water.

Water flowed from various seeps and springs and found its way into the Catfish, and life blossomed all along its course. Large trees (cotton-wood, hackberry, willows) grew along streambeds. Fruit was abundant, too, or would be by next summer, on the grapevines, that draped lavishly from the trees, and on the many plum trees. And there were acorns, in the mast beneath the oak shinneries, to which the party's hogs were espe-cially partial. There were mesquite trees, as well, and the plentiful juniper, and there were sumac and soapberry and wafer-ash and lotebush and even a stand of oak trees. And there were the spiky yucca and the spiny prickly pear. And there was grass, in a rich assortment that the cat-tle and sheep lost no time in sampling. Tall grasses (switchgrass, Indian grass, and big bluestem) grew along the streams and bogs and in the floodplains. Medium and short grasses (little bluestem, side-oats grama, sand bluestem, mesquite, curly mesquite, and buffalo grass) grew along the canyon floor and up its slopes.

This rich assortment of grasses fed not only the party's cattle and sheep, but buffalo, too, though not as many as the party had seen on their approach to the canyon. There were plenty of antelope, though, just as there had been out on the low rolling plains, in large herds that drew away from the trail as the party advanced. And there were beeves, which they rightly suspected to be part of what Hank Smith had acquired from the Tasker estate. These were scattered here and there, but gathered in more of a herd farther along the trail. There were some deer, too, though not so many, and these kept more to the woods. There were rabbits, the cottontail; and hares, the jackrabbit. And there were prairie dogs, whole towns of them, bustling in and out of their holes, standing sentinel and throwing their heads back and whistling, then diving for their holes, as the party passed by. Not only for human travelers did the prairie dogs take to their holes, but for coyotes as well. And the party saw some of these, and a wolf, which reminded them of a pack of ten or so wolves that they had seen early that morning as they had approached the canyon.

Birds too filled the canyon, and their songs filled the air: larks, doves, plovers, scissortails, finches, buntings, woodpeckers, and road-runners. There were ducks, geese, and cranes, as well. Hawks rode the thermals above, and burrowing owls popped out of the ground below. Quail trotted in lines along the ground, and turkeys strutted in flocks wherever they would.

All of it, and all of its abundance, was due to the water. Even the water, itself, held life in abundance, in the form of carp, catfish, and crawfish, and frogs and turtles, too. And the water could do so because of its own abundance, which it showed off to great effect at Silver Falls, less than three miles inside the mouth of the canyon, which the party reached by late afternoon. There water poured from the sandstone and fell, in a glistening cascade, twenty feet to the canyon floor. There, too, in the heat of the late afternoon, under the shady spread of trees and vines, amidst the tinkling and bubbling melodies of the chill water, a familiar odor reached the noses of the members of the Stuart-Schurtz party, and they knew what to expect on the trail ahead. They found it an hour later.

Just off the trail, at Dewey's Lake, a pond created by an old beaver dam, the remains of 200 or so skinless buffalo lay in a fairly advanced state of putrefaction, not an unfamiliar sight to the travelers. These carcasses must have been cows, because around them were the bodies of about 150 calves. In truth, not all the calves' bodies were around the cows. The party had seen several bodies of calves along the trail, as they had approached the pond. They attributed this to the tendency of a buffalo calf to follow along behind the wagon that held its mother's hide. Sometimes, if calves proved enough of a nuisance, they were shot. Otherwise they were left on their own. They did not live long after that.

Dewey's Lake would have otherwise provided a most fitting site for a camp, but due to its present condition, the party passed it by and proceeded another hour up the trail before making camp. They chose a spot just off the trail, which at that point was about half a mile from Catfish Creek. Still, the spot was well watered, situated as it was on a level area on one side of a rolling divide between two spring-fed streams. The grass was good and the wood plentiful, from the cotton-woods and hackberrys that lined the stream near which they made camp. The stream was also lined, at this time in the evening, with turkeys, two of which—after Andy's well-aimed single shot from the shotgun—were soon roasting over the party's fire.

The day had been sunny, warm, and dry, as had most of the days of the trip. Interestingly enough, whereas the grass showed green from the recent rains of September, the party had experienced little rain along the trail, only two showers, though they had seen several storms at various other places in the distance. Now, as the sun edged ever closer to the elevated horizon of the Llano Estacado above, the day's warmth slowly slipped away, displaced by a pleasant coolness drifting in with the evening. Soon, within this process, the men would need to bed the herd. This they did, in a good pasture on the other side of the stream.

Then Tom and Luke returned to camp and joined Elizabeth around the fire, but they did not share the kind of talk those around the fire had shared the night before, while still outside the canyon. No, they had little to say, as speculation had been answered and expectation overwhelmed in the day's experience. They did speak a little of the morrow and decided that, since Tom had met Hank Smith on several occasions, and therefore Smith might remember him, Tom would ride ahead in the morning to announce their arrival. Soon they crawled off to their beds, and night draped its sleep over the weary travelers. Andy, a lone mounted sentinel beneath the stars and rising moon, remained awake, circling slowly around the bedded herd, singing softly to the beeves, as steam rose off their bodies into the cooling night.

•   •   •

MORNING BROUGHT with it the usual routine, except that, after coming off his midnight-to-dawn watch, Tom unsaddled Othello, ate breakfast, then saddled and mounted Ross, and rode for the ranch that had formerly been Charles Tasker's *Hacienda de Glorieta*. The morning was about half over and the party three miles farther along the trail when Tom returned from the ranch. He related that Hank Smith was at the house and that they were very welcome there. Smith had offered to let them bed the herd for the night in the stone corrals at the ranch, and he had offered to let them stay in the nearly completed stone house.

It was with anticipation, then, that the party made its way up the Mackenzie Trail and up Blanco Canyon, as a warm, dry breeze blew in from the southwest, waving, beneath the sun, the sea of green and blond grass through which they passed. They anticipated learning what there might be to learn of the epilogue of the Tasker ranch story. They anticipated learning what Hank Smith, lately of Fort Griffin, was making, and intended to further make, of the ranch that had been deeded to him, in what initially appeared to be a very poor return on a very substantial investment. They also anticipated learning what this frontiersman could tell them about this land, in which he alone—save for Charles Goodnight, some eighty miles to the north, and maybe less than a handful of others—was settling. And they anticipated learning more about the man himself, who, at forty or fifty miles south of what they hoped would be their home, would be their nearest neighbor.

That anticipation, however, could not sate the hunger that the morning's hike had whetted, and so, about three miles up the trail from where Tom had rejoined it, the party stopped for noon dinner at the canyon narrows. Here the canyon had constricted so that its walls were only two miles or so apart. Here, too, suggested some contemporaries, Charles Tasker had intended to build a stone wall to close in buffalo to create a kind of buffalo park. Whether true or not, at this place, on a rise beneath a rounded peninsular protrusion of the caprock, the Stuart-Schurtz party made their noontime stop, and they gazed forward, beyond the narrows, into the wide open space to the north.

That was the wide-open space of the canyon. Yes, here, farther up the canyon, where one might have expected it to grow increasingly narrow, it widened out again. On the right, the canyon could be seen to open up to the east, even though other peninsular protrusions of the caprock obscured the party's view of the extent of that expansion. Nevertheless, they could see that, on this right side of the canyon, directly to the north, beyond the widening, the escarpment created a northern wall to the canyon, a barrier to expansion in that direction, for about a mile and a half, until that wall turned toward the northwest, allowing the canyon to further extend in that direction. On the left, toward the west, the canyon opened up even more than it did on the right. In fact, it opened into another canyon, Crawfish Canyon or Crawfish Draw, which also extended to the northwest. This tributary canyon accommodated a tributary stream, Crawfish Creek, which emptied into the Catfish about a mile and a half to the northwest of where the party had stopped for dinner. A most striking feature, a towering mound of gleaming white rock called Mount Blanco, stood above and between Crawfish Draw and the northwest extension of the main canyon. In fact, that landmark rose a good twenty-five feet above the high plains of the Llano Estacado itself.

With that landmark in view, the party set out again after dinner. They climbed with the Mackenzie Trail to higher ground, to avoid the boggy pond at the confluence of Crawfish and Catfish Creeks, which, with its thick cover of willows, cottonwoods, and hackberrys, supported a rich assortment of aquatic life and invited an assortment of terrestrial life that fed upon it. As they rose with the trail, something else appeared to rise up from behind the trees that lined the creeks, something they all recognized—Tom by sight, the others according to descriptions they had received. It was the Tasker, now Smith, stone house, beaming yellow-white in the afternoon sun, on a level area of the upper canyon off to the northwest of them, about a half-mile north of Mount Blanco.

The house stood out there, not only in its brightness, but also in its precision—its square angles and straight lines. And in that precision, the house, along with its partially constructed stone barn and its corrals, stood out in its incongruity. This large stone structure of man stood small and exact within the larger stone structure of nature, "and of nature's God," gnarled and jagged, chipped, bent, and broken, spreading miles wide, rising, in cliffs behind the house, easily ten times the house's proud height, to the high plains above. The travelers gazed upon the house, not having seen anything like it since they had left Fort Griffin. There, anything like it was rare enough, and anything like it would stand in proportionate contrast with the structures of that civic setting, but out here, amidst the structures of this wild and rugged canyon, the contrast was extreme, and to Tom's mind, as he pondered it, fittingly so.

Toward that contrast the party steadily moved. As the trail took them down again toward the Catfish, the house again settled behind the trees of that creek with their descent. They crossed the Catfish north of the mouth of Crawfish Canyon, in the shadow of Mount Blanco, which would eventually lend its name to the ranch of Hank Smith, to the post office that would be run by his wife there, and to the small community that would develop on top of the caprock about three miles to the northeast. That was all yet to come, and though some of it may have been envisioned by the new owner of the *Hacienda de Glorieta*, he faced the more immediate concern of making something out of what "had been left to him," as he would later write, "as a result of placing too much confidence in the wrong man."

There was every reason to believe that this Henry Clay Smith, who stood awaiting the party in the yard of the stone house (visible again to the travelers as they emerged from the trees), was the right man for just such a task. Born Heinrich Schmitt on August 15, 1836, the eleventh of twelve children born to Johann and Margareta Schmitt in the village of Rossbrunn in northern Bavaria, he had emigrated along with two older sisters from Germany to America in May of 1851, when he was fourteen years old, to live with another older sister already established in Peru, Ohio. After a few months of formal education, he had abandoned it for the life of a sailor on Lake Erie. In less than a year, after the wreck of the boat on which he had been working, while still a very young man of fifteen or sixteen, he had decided to go west. Thereafter, he had traveled and worked throughout much of the West: Iowa, Missouri, Kansas, Nebraska, Colorado, Wyoming, Utah, California, New Mexico, Arizona, Texas, and Mexico. He had held various occupations, including chainman for a surveying outfit, bull-whacker, muleskinner, broncbuster, cowboy, miner, freighter, scout, wood and hay contractor, and sutler's clerk. He was familiar with several

Indian peoples, having crossed the paths of the Yankton Sioux, Paiute, Apache, Coyotero, Kiowa, Comanche, and others. He had lived with some, fought others, and still spoke some of their languages, besides also speaking English, German, and Spanish. He had served, in one capacity or another, first the Confederate, then the Union side of the War Between the States. He had traveled the Santa Fe, the Mormon, the Oregon, and several other trails, including, more recently, the Mackenzie. He had settled and married and then built, owned, and operated, along with his wife, a hotel, restaurant, bar, livery stable, and wagon yard in one of the wildest frontier towns in the West. And now he had been forced to receive, in lieu of payment of a debt of over eleven thousand dollars, the foundation of what had been intended to be the dream-ranch of an improvident spendthrift from a wealthy family in the East. Having moved out to the ranch to take over and make the most of what Charles Tasker had left him, he now stood in the yard of the residence of that ranch as the Stuart-Schurtz party approached.

In his early years in the United States, Heinrich Schmitt had become Henry Clay Smith, or Hank Smith. In the years that would follow, he would come to be known by many in the west as "Uncle Hank," with or without the "Smith." That Hank Smith impressed those approaching as a particularly long man. Though only an inch or so over Tom's six feet, length seemed to hang from him—in his face: down from his high forehead through his long, straight nose and out his trim beard; and in his body: down his sloping shoulders through his solid torso and long arms and into his sturdy legs and tall boots. So, long and tall, he stood awaiting them, and weathered, too, from having lived almost two-thirds of his forty-one years on the frontier.

Tom led the party into the yard of the stone house. He dismounted and shook hands with Hank Smith and then made introductions as the rest of the party pulled into the yard. Andy would be introduced later, as he, with Rita's help, had continued up the canyon with the herd to where Tom had showed him Hank Smith had recommended they graze and water the beeves before bedding them in the corrals. Smith soon had Elizabeth in the stone house—which, from now on, would slowly come to be known as Hank Smith's Rock House—and was showing her the larger of the two downstairs rooms (about fifteen by twenty feet), which was cleared out for her family.

Then he led her to the kitchen next door (about fifteen feet square) and let her know she was free to use it, if she were so inclined. She indicated to the big, quiet man with the intelligent eyes that she was very much so inclined. He expressed his appreciation and, from that moment, looked forward to the supper that this pleasant Mrs. Stuart might prepare for that evening.

Quiet though Mr. Smith may have been and pleasant though Mrs. Stuart may have been, they raised their voices at each other, for a good part of their short tour, to make themselves heard over the sounds of sawing and hammering coming from the second floor of the house. The source and purpose of this upstairs construction was soon revealed to the travelers. After they had carried in all that they would need for the night, Smith led Elizabeth (holding Robert and with Rachel following), Luke (with Zachariah following), and Tom upstairs to where a Mr. Berry was laying maple flooring over a plank subfloor laid across two-by-ten joists. Smith introduced Elizabeth, the men, and the children to Joseph Berry, the only one of the men hired by Charles Tasker who had stayed after Tasker had fled. Berry, a graying, powerfully built man of average height, bowed slightly to Elizabeth and shook hands with the men. Smith indicated that ever since he had arrived a few days before, he and Berry had been rounding up and herding the cattle Tasker had left and finishing off the house—setting windows, laying flooring, hanging doors, and doing any other finishing work that still needed to be done.

Joseph Berry was a carpenter. His skill at the trade made that apparent to Tom. It was also apparent that some highly skilled masons had worked on the project. When Tom asked about them, the names Emmen and Sullivan were offered. The stone had been well quarried locally, and well laid, leaving an imposing structure, two stories high, forty feet long, nineteen feet wide, with walls twenty-two inches thick. The roof had been shingled some time ago, as it should have been, soon after the trusses had been set on top of the stone walls and the lathing attached to the trusses.

But this was only to have been a temporary residence for the Taskers. As Elizabeth arranged the things that had been brought in and prepared to feed Robert and make supper, Smith led Tom and Luke, with Zachariah and Rachel in tow, to an excavation on a nearby mound that

rose above the level of the stone house. Here was already laid the foundation for a mansion that would have dwarfed the stone house. When
Tom asked incredulously if Tasker had really intended to build a house
of such proportions at that time out in the wilds of Blanco Canyon,
Smith assured him that he had and then smiled quietly, knowingly, and
understandingly at Tom's incredulity. From there he showed them the
large dugout where the hands and workers had lived. Smith indicated
that he might turn the dugout into a store for hunters and for those passing by on the Mackenzie Trail on their way to Fort Sumner or Fort
Bascom in New Mexico. Then he showed them the rock barn, under
construction, the corrals, also under construction, and the well. Finally
he showed them where they could pull up the wagons, and the men did
so and then unharnessed the mules and oxen and let them graze.

In the meantime, Smith was saddling his own horse, so that, when
Tom and Luke were finished with their chores and had left Rachel with
Elizabeth, they all mounted up, Zachariah in front of Luke on Luke's
horse, and Smith led the group farther up the canyon. They stopped
where Andy was grazing the herd to introduce him to Smith and to
bring him along, leaving Rita in charge of the cattle. They could not
have known, as they left the herd and rode toward the head of the
canyon, that they were leaving the cattle to graze upon land that had
been camped upon by Francisco Vasquez de Coronado and his expedition of a thousand men in 1541, during his search for the fabled city
of gold, El Dorado, which he had hoped to find realized to the north
at Quivira, in what would become Kansas. It would be another 120
years before this camp of Coronado's would be located with the discovery of a chain-mail glove and some crossbow bolts, not the regular
equipment of Indians, buffalo hunters, or cowboys.

Smith led them about eight or nine miles up the canyon to where
it widened again, forming a kind of basin with a towering butte in the
midst of it. The bluffs here were still some 150 feet high. From here the
canyon narrowed to its head, about five miles farther to the northwest,
where it was only fifty feet deep, and the waters from the Running
Water Draw and Callahan Draw watersheds, combined now in Catfish
Creek, dropped into it.

They took the Mackenzie Trail out of the canyon and up onto the
Llano Estacado and followed it, in the waning pink and orange twilight,

to where it descended from the plains into Crawfish Draw near Mt. Blanco. At the mouth of Crawfish Draw, they turned to the north and were soon riding into the yard of the Rock House, as the evening pulled away the last of the fading light of day. Luke stopped at the house to let Elizabeth know that they would soon be returning. Then the men rode up the canyon and retrieved the beeves and led them to the corrals at the Rock House, where they bedded them. In time, they were out of their saddles, and the horses were too, and the men were on their way toward the house and a hot supper.

The men ate in the large room where the Stuarts were to sleep, and where the children were already in their beds—Zachariah and Rachel laid out on a mattress a safe distance from the fire, and Robert asleep in the cradle between the mattress and a love seat that had been brought to the house by the Taskers. It was turkey again, shot by Andy, but no one was complaining, because the meat of that fowl was so delectable and the quantity provided so manageable for those on the trail. (Regardless, the variety of game all along the trail assured that, should they ever weary of one kind of meat, they could easily provide another.) Elizabeth had also made a cobbler out of apples that needed to be eaten, which Luke had bought in Fort Griffin almost two weeks before. The men offered various vocal expressions—some intelligible, others not—of their appreciation of Elizabeth's culinary accomplishments, which, together with the eating that had roused that appreciation, left little room for any other vocal expressions in the form of talk. Soon, though, the last of the cobbler was consumed, the dishes were washed and dried, and over the ample coffee that remained after the cobbler no longer did, conversation began to flow.

Hank Smith was a reserved man who did not waste words; still, he made good use of words when he had something to say. He had had something to say, now and then, throughout the tours he had earlier given the members of the party. Each member of that party had been impressed by Smith's assessments of the canyon's potential and by his immediate ideas about what steps he might take to realize that potential. Though Smith had not been at his Rock House much longer than they had, they had heard him speculate about raising cattle, hogs, sheep, and even buffalo. They had heard about hay and various potential crops and even orchards. They had heard about dams, wells, and irrigation. They had heard much about the future, and now, after they had added some wood to the warm coals of the fire, and as their suppers settled and they drank their coffee, they would be blessed to hear about the past.

Tom, on several occasions, and Luke, when he and Tom had passed through Griffin the previous summer, had enjoyed some of Hank Smith's recollections from the treasure of his experience. Elizabeth and Andy, for their part, had enjoyed Tom's and Luke's reports of Smith's accounts. They all now sat united in expectation in the presence of this man, whose forty-one years had seen so much. Elizabeth, with a wool throw over her shoulders, sat on the fireplace side of the love seat, next to Robert's cradle. Luke sat on the other side. Hank Smith, Joseph Berry, Tom, and Andy occupied other chairs (ranging from those brought by Tasker to two that had been roughly constructed from native woods) loosely arranged in a semicircle centered on the fireplace, with the love seat at the far right end.

And yet, it was Joseph Berry, not Hank Smith, who commenced with a reminiscence of his own, not without a twinkle in his smiling blue eyes, and quite adept he was at reminiscing, too, and quite a treasure of experience he also had, not uncommon among people of that time and place. Then Smith followed with an account of his own. Then Berry offered another that had some relation to the one Smith had just related, and then Smith to the one of Berry's, then Berry to Smith's. And so it went, one story begetting another for the attentive listeners. Tom and Luke knew the custom well from their experiences around campfires along the trail and out on the range. But the others knew it, too, as an integral part of a time when people took the time to be interested in each other, to visit their neighbors, a time when people saw the value in sharing their stories, in listening, and in learning from those older and more experienced than they were.

After several rounds of stories, Mr. Berry excused himself and retired to the room above the one in which they were sitting. He had removed his things to that room in anticipation of the party's arrival. It was the room in which he had been laying the flooring, the largest of three bedrooms upstairs. Like the bedroom on the other end of the house, it had a fireplace on the end wall, which shared a chimney with the fireplace below. Intending to use that fireplace to take some of the night chill out of the room, he took some firewood with him when he left.

With Berry gone, Luke ventured to share a story. Smith listened as well as he spoke, sitting back with his left leg crossed over his right knee, puffing contentedly on his pipe as he did so. Luke exhibited a certain sincerity, a kind of innocent enthusiasm, manifested, among other ways, in a quiet chuckle that seemed to be beyond his ability to control. Tom had appreciated this quality in Luke from the beginning, and as he watched Luke relate his story, he could see that Smith appreciated it, as well. This did not surprise Tom, and it confirmed his good opinion of the man.

Luke finished his story. Then Smith offered another. Then Tom had one. And around it went, as the logs in the fireplace turned to embers, to be replaced by more logs, and the aroma of mesquite smoke, mixed with that of tobacco, wafted with the conversation through the warm room.

Again it was Luke's turn, and he described his experience of watching a cowhand rope a buffalo and the antics that followed that roping. The cowboy had survived the incident, so there was plenty to laugh about. Still, Luke managed to contain his chuckling, for the most part, until the end of the story, when he let go with what might best be described as a chuckle-laugh, characteristic of him. It went something like, "Ehhhh, heh heh heh heh heh heh heh heh heh," each syllable in rapid succession behind the other. It was one of those laughs, peculiar to a certain individual, that draws laughter, or at least a smile, from any other person present. Those who knew Luke knew this laugh. Hank Smith had not known it, but he was becoming well acquainted with it now. With the conclusion of his story about buffalo roping, Luke called on Tom to relate another story involving a hapless buffalo, one that Tom had heard Robert Wright, partner of Charles Rath, telling some customers at their store in Dodge City.

Tom looked down and offered a little chuckle of his own and then began to tell this story: "It seems Mr. Wright and a compatriot by the name of Harris—a long, thin, and particularly lanky fellow—started out to bring in some buffalo meat. Whether the buffalo had got wind of this venture or not remains a mystery, but what can be known is that there were no buffalo to hunt. After a good day's effort, they couldn't scare up a single one. By now the day was gettin' late, and they decided to give it up and turn back. On the way home, with no prospects for buffalo, they practiced their marksmanship at any movin' target—skunks, prairie dogs, rattlesnakes, and the like—exhaustin' their store of cartridges in the process."

Smith's eyes were smiling, as were Andy's. Elizabeth's head was tilted a little forward. Luke was sitting forward on the love seat, leaning out over his elbows resting on his knees, his mouth open, as if in anticipation of the laugh he expected to be arriving shortly. Luke's posture might have also served to facilitate a certain intensity of involvement in another's telling of a story, evinced in a running commentary of huhs and reallys, and the like, and short low chuckles and the quiet mouthing, here and there, of some of the words of the story itself, whether he had heard the story before or not.

"Then, all of a sudden," Tom continued, "a big bull buffalo jumped to his feet from where he'd been lyin' in the top of a sand hill that'd been hollowed out by the wind. With their cartridges gone, Wright and Harris relied on their six-shooters, which they both emptied into the animal. Though Mr. Wright related that the bull was 'bleedin' profusely at the nose,' he would not go down. He did stagger some, though, enough to make them think he might go down. But the stubborn old fellow just would not give in. Finally, with darkness comin' on and the two men losin' their patience, Mr. Harris decided to creep up on the bull with the intention of cuttin' his hamstrings with a butcher knife. By now the bull was lyin' down, and Mr. Harris proceeded with his plan. He crept up ever so slow and quiet." Tom's lowered and measured speech reflected the stealth of Mr. Harris's approach, as his hunched shoulders and slight rocking back and forth conveyed a sense of its motion.

All were leaning a bit into Tom's story by now, in spirit if not in body.

"Suddenly!" Tom exclaimed, sitting up and giving a start to his listeners, "without any warnin', the old bull jumped to his feet, but this time he didn't stand still. Instead, he started chargin' around the top of that sand hill, with his head down, in what Mr. Wright described as 'a perfect circus.' And he did so with a little more weight than he was accustomed to carry; for, it seems that, though Mr. Harris had not succeeded in cuttin' the old fellow's hamstrings, he had got close enough to get a good hold of that gentleman's tail."

"Ehh, heh heh heh heh heh heh heh," shot out of Luke, as he rose up and his hands replaced his elbows on his knees. Elizabeth's eyes closed, as she jiggled with quiet laughter at the scene presented to her mind's eye. Even Andy and Hank Smith had to open their mouths to let out the laughter that was more than their eyes alone could hold.

"And he intended to hold onto it, too," Tom explained, "because, as he later told Wright, he knew that if he let go, he was 'a goner.' For that same reason, his great fear, during the whole episode, was that he might pull that tail out by its very roots and then face consequences graver than those he'd face if he'd let it go."

Quiet, squeaky sounds were escaping from the jiggling Elizabeth, as she held her hand to her mouth.

"So, there he was, this tall, lanky fellow attached to the tail of this old bull buffalo, bobbin' along behind the beast, with his legs flappin' over his head, as the bull charged around and around and around the top of this old sand hill, while Robert Wright looked on. Wright said that he couldn't 'help him in the least, but had to sit and hold his horse and judge the fight.'"

Elizabeth broke open, adding her sharp punctuation of laughter to Luke's chuckle-laugh and to the easier, steadier laughter of Andy and Hank Smith. And this mirth was not readily extinguished. For some little while after the story, the fire served as a focal point for those gathered, as the scene played itself out in their minds, more than once, and occasioned low chuckling, laughing, or smiling to rise to the lips of now one, now another.

Eventually, the laughter and chuckling subsided to the point where Elizabeth could ask, with real interest and some concern, "What finally happened?"

Tom looked up at her, facetiously expressing in his features his surprise at anyone having an interest in more of the story than he had related. "Well," he said, "the old bull eventually did slow down, and Harris did cut his hamstrings, and Harris and Wright left with the tongue, the hump, and the hindquarters, and a good story to tell over the meal."

"Well, at least they took some of the meat," Elizabeth responded. This comment met with a quiet commiseration from the men of the party, who, nevertheless, felt an immediate hesitation to raise that serious topic amidst the jolly atmosphere that had prevailed, especially in the presence of Smith, whose sentiments on the topic they did not know. "The waste of all that meat is just sinful," she added. "I am just sick to think of all those cows and calves down at that lake that we saw yesterday."

Hank Smith shifted in his seat a little and turned an intense gaze on Elizabeth, which was noticed by Luke and Tom, who were beginning to feel a little uncomfortable in the presence of their host. Finally, taking the pipe from his mouth with his left hand and lowering it until it rested on his knee, Smith said to Elizabeth, "That joke was principally on me."

They all looked at him, not sure what he meant by the remark, Tom and Luke wondering if he had not taken offense at what Elizabeth had said.

Smith continued, still looking at Elizabeth, "I had planned to capture and domesticate those calves, or at least some of them," he explained, to the relief of Tom and Luke. "I'd been told, by one of the men that had worked for Tasker, that that herd of cows and calves had made their home here in the canyon, and I started having visions of a herd of the bison tribe, marked and branded."

They were all looking at him now with no little curiosity. He raised his pipe to his lips and took a long draw on it. Silence, except for the crackling and popping of the burning logs and the dull puffing of Smith on his pipe, pervaded the warm room, lit by a kerosene lamp turned low and by the flickering orange light of the fire's licks and embers. Smith withdrew the pipe from his mouth and continued, "An outfit of British army officers, led by a Captain Howell, visited the canyon a week or so ago. They were accompanied by some of the local talent, to whom I'm indebted for this story. It seems a couple of the local hunters had killed all those cows and taken their hides, and when Howell's high-toned outfit happened upon the surviving calves, they killed every one of them. But that wasn't the end of their fun. It seems that this Captain Howell was evidently something of a sport and a daredevil blowhard, and as such, he had expressed a determination to ride a buffalo bull."

Smith let that bit of information settle on his audience, as he paused to take another draw on his pipe. Smiles were already beginning to curl the corners of the mouths of at least two listeners, with even a "huh" or two escaping from between those curled lips.

Smith continued, "After reaching Blanco Canyon, a party was selected to especially aid the captain in his wild desire. Charley Hart, one of the greatest hunters and shots in this country, was of this party, and the plan was for him to crease a buffalo bull, and then, while the bull was stunned, the captain would run up and get on his back."

By now Luke was glancing from Smith to Tom, chuckling lightly as he did so. Tom's face was uncontrollably pulling into a grin. Elizabeth was tilting her head a little lower in concentration on her host. And the grin in Andy's eyes was nearing the point of overflowing into the rest of his face.

Smith noted these reactions, as he deliberately puffed away during an extended intermission that had the effect of heightening the suspense of his listeners.

Presently, he resumed his story. "Up on the cap, about four or five miles west of where you saw those cows and calves, they found a bunch of buffalo, and Hart creased a big bull and stunned him sufficiently for the captain to mount his back. The captain went ahead and did so."

All eyes were upon Smith as he puffed some more.

"Well, this was an altogether new game for the bull," Smith continued, as Luke chuckled again. "So, the bull got to his feet, knowing something was on his back that didn't belong there, but, instead of running and snorting and pitching, he proceeded very deliberately to figure it out."

Now Elizabeth and Tom each added a single-syllable laugh to Luke's chuckle, and Andy's mirth overran his eyes and began to curl his lips into a grin. Uncle Hank Smith fixed his eyes on Elizabeth, and there was laughter in those eyes, though the rest of his face betrayed none of it, as he drew again on his pipe. Again he took the pipe from his mouth and continued.

"Well, the old bull was mad enough, to be sure, but he was cool and deliberate and was evidently planning serious mischief in his own way. This procedure greatly angered the captain, who proceeded to liven things up by sliding down behind the bull and grabbing his stubby tail."

Smith settled back deeper into the chair and puffed but once before he continued. "Then things got livelier than the captain had contracted for. The bull proceeded to go round and round with a mighty whirl, while the captain, with a death grip on the stubby tail and both feet off the ground most of the time, went popping around like the tail of a kite in a storm, yelling, 'W'y the bloody 'ell don't somebody shoot the beast.'"

Laughter burst from Elizabeth, who had been trying to contain it, in no small part out of sympathy for the bull. Luke's staccato "Eh, heh heh heh heh heh heh heh . . . ," rang out long and loud, loud enough for Elizabeth to check him with a hand on his arm to remind him of the sleeping children and Mr. Berry. Tom rocked forward as laughter spilled out of him. Even Andy was laughing, quietly shaking out a "heah, heah, heah," as he looked at the floor.

Smith puffed away at his pipe, his eyes expressing no less merriment than that enjoyed by the rest. When the laughter had subsided just to the point where he could be heard, again, he concluded, "Of course, owing to the whirling motions, about the only thing that could be positively distinguished from the bull was the captain's yells, and a shot into the revolving mass was about as liable to hit the captain as it was the bull. Finally, Hart took a chance and shot the bull. After this incident, the boys declared that they couldn't even get the Englishman to ride a brown horse."

New waves of laughter burst forth, even louder than the rest, and Elizabeth's concerns about the children were realized, as both Rachel and Robert stirred and began to cry. Zachariah, who slept as hard as his father, shifted around on his mattress and was soon as oblivious to the world as he had been before. Elizabeth reached down and lifted the baby Robert from his cradle, and Luke went over to pick up the softly crying Rachel, sitting up among her covers, not yet fully awake. Rachel wanted her mother, so Elizabeth shifted Robert to Luke, and Rachel crawled up on her mother's lap, as the rest of the party realized that the evening had come to an end. Bidding the parents, with their crying charges, good night, Hank Smith, Tom, and Andy ascended the stairs to the second floor, where they laid out their beds. Shortly, the crying ceased, and the low talk of Mr. and Mrs. Stuart died away, and sleep settled over all within the warmth of the Hank Smith Rock House.

THE PARTY DID NOT RISE until the sun did the next morning, as all took the opportunity of sleeping indoors to garner a little more rest.

But, at last, that celestial orb greeted the new day and then, too, did all the inhabitants of the Rock House, with the aid of the party's rooster.

Tom and Andy rolled out of their beds and began to roll those beds up, so that they could take them out to the wagon. After stowing those bedrolls in the wagon, they would unpen the cattle, sheep, and pigs, to let them graze, and round up the horses, mules, and oxen, while Elizabeth made breakfast. But before all that, as Tom was shaking out his bed, preparatory to rolling it up, he heard something drop to the floor with a characteristic sound that made him immediately aware of what it was, even before he saw it. And so, he hunted for his rosary under the bedding, found it, and picked it up to put in his pocket. As he did so, a chill feeling crawled up his spine and induced him to turn around. When he did, he saw Hank Smith watching him put the rosary into his pocket. Tom looked at Smith and Smith looked at him. Then they both looked away, and Smith left the room and went downstairs.

Smith may have left, but the look he had given Tom remained in Tom's mind, and that mind, in a reaction that seemed all but involuntary, was already reviewing the look Smith had given him, at the sight of his rosary, to try to determine what that look had conveyed. This was no small matter. Anti-Catholicism was still widespread and consequential in the United States of that time. Memories of the anti-Catholic riots of the 1830s, '40s, and '50s contributed to an insecurity among Catholics in the United States, which had been kept alive by later developments. One such development was the rise and relative success of the anti-Catholic American or Know-Nothing party, which had been considered a serious national party just twenty-one years before. At that time, these Know-Nothings had contributed to the defeat of John C. Fremont, the first Republican candidate for the office of president of the United States, by accusing him of being a Catholic. Many candidates of the various parties, like the Democrat Stephen A. Douglas and the Republican William H. Seward, had suffered politically due to accusations of associations with, or just toleration of, Catholics. More recently, the Ku Klux Klan, the "Invisible Empire of the South," already intimidating and terrorizing blacks and white Republicans, would include Catholics and Jews as targets of its terror. In Fort Griffin itself, Smith's recent home, land had already been acquired for a Masonic lodge. And there were far subtler manifestations of

prejudice, in such things as employment or service at places of business, that Tom had experienced directly or had seen directed toward
people with German or, worse yet, Irish names. As a result, Catholics,
especially where they were a clear minority, often did not go out of
their way to advertise their fidelity to Holy Mother Church and the
Catholic Faith.

Thus, this look from Smith had given Tom pause. But Smith had
said nothing, so Tom tried to put the matter out of his mind. He rolled
up his bedroll, made his way down the stairs and out of the house to
the wagon, and proceeded with his morning chores.

Elizabeth produced a good breakfast of pancakes and sorghum,
bacon and eggs, and coffee, all of it in quantity. All of that quantity
was soon consumed. Then she cleaned the dishes and the kitchen and
saw to the children, as Andy began to drift the herd back down the
canyon, and Tom and Luke loaded the wagons, filled the water barrel
from the well, and harnessed the teams.

Soon the party—except for Andy, who had said his thank-yous
and good-byes before his departure—was assembled in the yard of the
Rock House in the early morning light. The sun had risen as a blazing
red ball and had broken free of the horizon, below a bank of thick,
though perforated, clouds of pastel purple, edged with pink-white
highlights, hunkered just above the eastern edge of the earth. As the
sun had risen, it had faded and had slipped in behind the pastel clouds
to shout its bright orange through their perforations and to deepen
their pastels to rich pinks, reds, purples, and oranges, too, as it pushed
to rise above them into the cloudless blue above. In the light of that
sun, streaked by long shadows from the east, and in a cool, rising wind
that seemed to come from everywhere, Berry had bid them all good-
bye, before he had returned to his work in the house. Smith had
remained in the yard to see the party all put together and safely on its
way. Now, all put together, the members of the party once more proffered their thanks and once more invited Hank Smith and his family
to visit them when they were settled. Again he let them know that they
were always welcome. Then they all bid good-bye.

As Tom climbed into the saddle on his favorite Ross, Smith
stepped up next to the horse. "You'll want to head down the road a few
miles, to a shinnery off to the left," he said, looking down the Mackenzie

Trail rather than at Tom. "There you'll be able to climb up on the caprock on a gradually ascending trail. You ought to be able to see some tracks. There's a surveying party been up and down there a few times lately, and there's an old trail, another trail of Mackenzie's, I believe, up on the caprock, that heads north, keeping a few miles back from the escarpment. It's seen little use in the last few years and is pretty faded, but you ought to be able to make it out, and it ought to take you into the country you're seeking."

"Thank you," Tom said.

Smith nodded a reply. Then he did look up at Tom, and he added, "*Dominus vobiscum.*"

Tom had been looking at Smith, but now his look intensified. He *had* read something in the look that Smith had given him when he had dropped his rosary.

"*Et cum spiritu tuo,*" Tom responded, as one Catholic reciprocated another Catholic's wish, expressed in liturgical language, for him to remain in the presence of God. Then the two men shook hands and bid each other farewell, and the Stuart-Schurtz party rolled out of the yard of the Hank Smith Rock House and rejoined the trail.

BACK DOWN THE TRAIL, they had decided, was their best route of progress. They could have taken the Mackenzie Trail to the northwest, up out of Crawfish Canyon onto the Llano Estacado, then back across Blanco Canyon farther to the northwest, and then gone on their way to the northeast. This, though, would have left a good deal of the escarpment unscouted, and they did not want to take the risk of passing their mystery canyon, with their imperfect knowledge of its location, their imperfect knowledge (if not complete ignorance) of the region, and the canyon's dubious claim on existence.

It would seem strange to people of a later age (who would have easy access to aerial photographs and maps and would routinely travel in less than fifteen minutes the distance the Stuart-Schurtz party was traveling in an entire day) that there should be so much question about the existence and location of a geographic feature as large as the Escondido Canyon was reported to be. But it must be remembered that, in this time of the Stuart-Schurtz party, without the aerial maps and high speeds and established roads, this region appeared almost

limitless, in space and time, and remote to white civilization. It is true
that members of the Apache, Comanche, Kiowa, and Cheyenne peoples had lived in this region. It is true that some white men had already
traveled the region, in military, hunting, or surveying expeditions, and
that other white people, including whole families, had traveled
through it on their way to somewhere else. It is true that others, from
Mexico and New Mexico, had not only traveled the region as hunters,
but as traders and shepherds, as well. But it is also true that those who
knew the most about the region, the Indians, had little incentive to
share what they knew of it with others not of their people, even if those
others had been interested. And it is true that most of the Mexicans
and New Mexicans who knew the region were separated linguistically
and culturally from most of those approaching it from the east.
Beyond all that, those who had traveled the region had little reason or
opportunity to share what they had learned of it with any outside their
circles of soldiers, hunters, traders, shepherds, surveyors, or passing
pioneers. Hence, not only was there no great single pooling of information about the region, there was little connecting of one body of
information to another.

These circumstances made it possible to have a case like that of
Charles Goodnight's discovery of the Palo Duro Canyon. Goodnight had
scouted the region of the escarpment of the Llano Estacado extensively
in the early to mid 1860s: for the Minute Men of Texas before the Civil
War, and for the Frontier Regiment of Texas during the Civil War. The
army, albeit without Goodnight's participation, had scouted and cam-
paigned in the region in the 1850s and throughout the 1870s. In 1874,
the army, under Mackenzie, had routed the Indians in the battle of
Palo Duro Canyon. Nevertheless, in 1876, Goodnight, an exceptional
scout with extensive experience, had learned of the existence of the
Palo Duro Canyon from a Mexican mustanger who was familiar with
the canyon, and, with the help of that mustanger, had searched for
days for the sixty-mile long canyon before he had finally found it.

Goodnight had come to settle. And that pointed to one more reason for the region's obscurity. He was the first white man, of note, to
do so. Others had traversed and exploited the region, but none, except
a very few, had come to stay. Those who had—Goodnight, and now
Hank Smith—had settled in canyons, great canyons with water and

shelter for livestock and, possibly, crops. Above those canyons stood the Llano Estacado, and that great plateau had already been saddled with a reputation.

One individual who had contributed to the establishment of that reputation was Captain Randolph Marcy. Marcy had encountered the Llano Estacado in the summer of 1849, while escorting a wagon train from Fort Smith to Santa Fe. Of it, he had written the following:

> When we were upon the high tableland, a view presented itself as boundless as the ocean. Not a tree, shrub, or any other object, either animate or inanimate, relieved the dreary monotony of the prospect; it was a vast, illimitable expanse of desert prairie—the dreaded 'Llano Estacado' of New Mexico; or, in other words, the great Zahara of North America. It is a region almost as vast and trackless as the ocean—a land where no man, either savage or civilized permanently abides; it spreads forth into a treeless, desolate waste of uninhabited solitude, which always has been, and must continue, uninhabited forever; even the savages dare not venture to cross it except at two or three places, where they know water can be found. The only herbage upon these barren plains is a very short buffalo grass, and, on account of the scarcity of water, all animals appear to shun it.

This perception was shared by other early explorers. For that matter, just two years before, in 1875, the *Texas Rural Register and Immigrants' Handbook* had said of the Llano Estacado that it would probably never "be adapted to the wants of man," that it was "the only uninhabitable portion of Texas."

The derivation of the name "Llano Estacado" or "Staked Plains," can no longer be established with certainty. Still, many have been suggested. One explanation for the name is that Spanish explorers marked their way across the expansive plateau with stakes driven into the ground. This explanation is not wholly unconnected with another that holds that these same travelers marked springs with mounds of white stones. Another explanation is that the "stakes" of the Staked Plains refer to the tall stalks of the yucca plants that clutter some areas of the plains like a forest of stakes. Another explanation depends upon interpreting the word *estacado* as "stockaded," which would then refer to the escarpment's resemblance to a fortification. Yet another explanation depends upon the possible corruption of the term for prominent or elevated plain, "*Llano Destacado.*"

Whatever the derivation of its name, the Llano Estacado, the Staked Plains, soon provided the setting for the continuance of the Stuart-Schurtz party's journey. In the early afternoon of the day they left the yard of the Hank Smith Rock House, in early October 1877, they climbed up out of Blanco Canyon, through the shinnery Smith had described, and emerged onto the Llano Estacado.

Vast was this flat land under the blue dome of sky in which white clouds would, on some days, materialize and grow and aggregate at places, here or there on the horizon, darkening in the process, until, very dark, they would send out their lightning and send down their rain. This the party could watch, often enough in perfect dryness, as there was room enough under a sky far more vast than the vast land to see more than one such storm in the sky and yet remain under a portion of the sky that threatened no rain. Under that sky, they progressed through the short and medium grasses—green and golden and red blond—dusted with other hues (depending on the light and the nature of the sky through which that light passed) ranging from fiery orange to light lavender, the colors most abundant and varied in those taller grasses that grew in the basins of dried playa lakes. They killed a few rattlesnakes, and they saw buffalo and mustangs and coyotes and prairie dogs, hawks, owls, larks, and other animals, though sometimes they saw no such life at all, standing alone as the only representatives of animated life in their vision. But then a bird would flit by, or a snake would slither past, or a prairie dog or two or a dozen would pop up, and they would be reminded of the subtlety of animal life on the great grassland plateau.

Across that plateau, in the early morning of the fourth day of the party's travel upon it, Tom, who had ridden ahead to scout, came galloping toward the party from the northeast. He rode up to Luke, as he walked alongside the oxen pulling the large wagon, and reined his night horse Othello into a walk alongside Luke, who raised an expectant look to him.

Tom, unable to fully check the excitement that had been rising within him, reported, "Found a small canyon up ahead, less than two miles ahead. It's maybe two miles or so long. Cuts into the cap toward the northwest."

Luke looked down as he kept walking. Then, after checking the oxen, he looked up at Tom. "Could be one of the bookend canyons," he said, using the term Tom had coined for the two smaller canyons that were supposed to be one north and one south of the Escondido.

"Could be," Tom said. "There's a game trail off the cap, just before the canyon, where we could get the wagons down with little difficulty. We might need to chain the wheels, but maybe not. There's a spring-fed creek down below with plenty of water in it."

Tom had learned that a low-level excitement lay ever beneath Luke's surface; now it rose above it, and Luke's eyes locked on Tom and exposed the wonder behind them. Tom, for his part, now shifted his eyes to the oxen, then to Luke, then back and forth between the oxen and Luke, as Luke—with his attention now focused on Tom and on the canyon of which he spoke—seemed to have lost all thought of the draft under his management.

Regardless, Tom continued, "Thought it might make a good place to noon over; that is, if we wind up findin' it's worth makin' our way down off the cap. What I mean is, we might as well hold up, up on top, and we could scout on ahead and see if the Escondido is up there. If it is, and we don't see any better trail, rather'n go around this canyon, we could drop off the cap and make our way toward the Escondido from down below."

"Right, right," Luke said, still looking at Tom, whose concern about the oxen Luke shortly put to rest, when, without looking at them, he raised his right hand and, with the snap of his wrist, unfurled his whip to send it out to crack over the ears of the plodding steers, as if he had never taken his eyes off them. Tom silently marveled at this ability of Luke's, which he had seen before. He could drive a wagon or buggy, or ride a horse, all the while looking at the person next to him, except for a periodic quick glance, and still know when and where to direct the horse, mule, or oxen, when directing was needed. Without noticing Tom's reaction to his singular steering ability, Luke continued, "I'll tell you what. I'll saddle up ol' Arbuckle, and you take Ross, and we'll make short work of any distance and be on top of that canyon before we know it."

Tom smiled at this immediate enthusiasm, which was characteristic of Luke, and accepted the plan, but after thinking about it, he suggested another. Having seen a full playa lake directly north of where they were, he suggested they water the cattle there and make camp and have an early dinner, and then he and Luke could scout out the canyon, while Andy, Elizabeth, and the children rested and saw to various small chores around the camp.

And so they did. When they had finished their midday dinner, Luke wasted no time in catching and saddling Arbuckle, and Tom did the same with Ross. Then they rode off toward the west, a little to the north, in a path that would take them near the beginning of the small canyon that Tom had described. When they reached it, they crossed a shallow draw, just above where it cut through the caprock and dropped over two hundred feet into the canyon.

They picked up more speed after crossing the draw. Then Luke called out to Tom above the noise of the wind and of the horses' hooves against the ground and through the grass. Tom looked over to see Luke smiling mischievously at him. Luke nodded a little as he slightly spurred his mount, and Tom understood. He returned the smile, which spread into a full-face grin that threatened to break into a laugh, and he nudged Ross, and the gallop was on.

They flew toward the northeast, under the open blue sky and its bright sun, across the golden-grassed prairie, seemingly endless before and around them, the edge of the caprock being far off to the east. Tom fell into a familiar rhythm with Ross, and he pushed him, leaning out over the horse's neck, at one with the animal in its full stride. He glanced at Luke, and Luke glanced at him, and both looked out ahead again. There was more that the horses could give, and it was urged from them now. The glances—to the other, now ahead, to the other, now ahead—continued, and the ground blurred past beneath them. More speed, more push, more stretch, and the land passed away. Ross began to pull ahead a bit, as he was the superior horse, but Arbuckle was a fine horse himself, and Luke a good rider, so Ross's gain was kept to a minimum.

Mile after mile, the ground passed away, until, seven miles or so north of the small canyon, as the riders glanced to the other and then out ahead, the scene before them took on a subtle change, hardly noticeable at first, but gradually more definite as they charged toward it. Their glances toward the other met, and they both knew that the other saw. They allowed the pace of the horses to slacken a little, not much, as the vision before them drew them toward it in haste. This was no longer the haste of the racer, but rather that of the seeker, of the searcher on the threshold of discovery, of one tempted to ignore thought of anything other than the discovery, but a haste, in the case of these fairly reasonable seekers, tempered by caution before the unknown and by awe before that which could well be the thing sought, the existence of which had often seemed beyond the reach of the faith they had invested in it.

They slowed even more, as they both stared in wonder at the scene before them. The sea of grass had broken open, up ahead, in a faint, dark horizontal line above a deepening horizontal line of tannish white, bright in the afternoon sun, that cut neatly across the prairie, from right to left, as far as the eye could see. Slowing a little more, they rode toward the white line, both looking intently ahead. Then they looked at each other, this time with expressions of awe and incredulity that were mixing with expressions of a hope that, until now, could easily have been mistaken for a dream. Those expressions broke into smiles of wonder, and each turned back to look ahead, as he urged his mount forward.

As they rode, the band of white continued to deepen across the horizon, but only to a certain depth, until the earth opened before them in a fissure that zigzagged away from them through the grass, widening and deepening as it opened toward the white band, revealing a hint of what lay below it. They slowed to a walk, as they approached this gash in the earth, and finally stopped at its pointed beginning. Here the land fell abruptly away, thirty feet or more, in worn rounded shoulders down peninsular arms that draped to the scree below.

Beyond these shoulders of land lay the mouth of this draw, through which the men saw clearly the white band beyond and saw it for what it was—rock, the caprock of the Llano Estacado, brilliant in the bright sunlight. Though two miles distant, on the opposite wall of an impressive canyon, the caprock was now distinguishable, as the men could now see the rock layers beneath it. Layers of color were these layers of rock below the white, first a variegated layer of pink, gray, white, then another of purples, browns, yellows, and tans, then a glimpse of red.

Luke turned his face on Tom. "You think this is it, Tom?" he asked, the excitement in his voice apparent.

Tom glanced at Luke, then looked back out into the canyon. "I don't know, but it sure could be," he responded, not yet allowing himself to be fully convinced.

They nudged their horses into a walk to the right of the draw, toward the edge of the canyon into which it opened. As the horses walked on, the men saw more and more of what was promised by the glimpse through the draw. Their vision dropped deeper and deeper into a wide canyon that opened fully before them when they reached its southern edge. Here they stopped lest they plunge hundreds of feet into it.

"Whoa!" Luke exhaled, as the immensity of the canyon sucked the breath out of him.

"I think we've found it, Luke!" Tom exclaimed. "I do believe we've found it."

"It's the Escondido! It's got to be, Tom!"

There was the red, beneath those upper layers, in a thick layer of its own, cut by fine lines of white gypsum. There was the green, too, that speckled the other colors wherever the escarpment was not too steep for vegetation to gain a toehold.

The canyon lay some two miles wide at this point. Its bottom, some five to six hundred feet below, lay deeply carpeted in grasses, the subtle color variations of which, from green to golden and even russet, were teased out by remnants of wind that had dropped off the high plains so far above. Mesquite spotted the vast carpet, and at least two streambeds could be made out by the dark line of cottonwoods, willows, hackberrys, plums, and grapes that defined their courses. Stands of juniper, cedar, shinnery oak, and sumac darkened the breaks along the base of the escarpment, with soapberry, wafer-ash, sumac, yucca, and cactus growing in greater abundance farther down.

Luke's voice again entered the scene, conveying his wonder and a certain reverence. "We found it," he said. "We did find it."

"This has got to be it, Luke!" Tom concurred. "It all fits!"

"Yessir, yessir," Luke said, almost to himself. Then after surveying the canyon a moment he exclaimed, "Do you believe it, Tom? It's real! It exists! It's starin' us in the face!"

Tom was nodding his head in response, a serene expression having taken hold of his features, as the evidence that lay at his feet slowly purged from him the remaining shreds of disbelief. Then, after a moment, he exclaimed, "This is awesome!" The statement was reactive, reflexive, its speaker fully aware of its inadequacy, but it had just risen up out of him, its very inadequacy offering further testament to the indescribable grandeur of the spectacle before them.

Tom removed his hat, bent his head, and crossed himself. Luke followed Tom's lead by removing his own hat and bending his head in prayer. After a moment, Tom crossed himself, raised his head, and exclaimed, "Praise God!"

"Amen!" Luke affirmed, as the men returned their hats to their heads.

Having acknowledged its Creator, they now tried to judge the extent of the canyon. Looking off to the west, they could not clearly make out the head of the canyon, two miles or so distant, the jagged canyon walls making definition difficult. To the east, though, the canyon widened, making the view somewhat less obstructed. Still, it was obstructed enough by juts of its walls, north and south, and by buttes and mesas, to render the canyon mouth, some six or seven miles distant, completely blocked from view.

Luke pointed to a large herd of pronghorn that covered an extended high pasture on the canyon floor toward the east. "Look at all those antelope," he said. "And those buffalo," he added, scanning his finger across the rest of the canyon floor, over which two or three small herds of buffalo were scattered in smaller bunches. Tom nodded. Both men were aware, as well, of the richness of fauna not presently visible to the eye, which would include threats to their enterprise in the form of the coyote, mountain lion, even the bear, but potentially most decimating, the lobo or "loafer" wolf. Then they saw a wolf, then three, and they saw several coyotes.

Luke nodded off to the east, and the two men nudged their mounts away from the edge of the escarpment, back some distance, and rode toward the east, skirting various draws that opened into the canyon, as they continued to offer exclamations expressing the wonder and gratitude they were experiencing. They rode several miles, at a pace commensurate with the awe that gripped them before this pristine work of the Creator, to which they were ready to make a far more superficial claim of ownership than his own. (And how much more superficially would they occupy it?) As they rode, a pair of red-tailed hawks circled high above the canyon, riding thermals, a lazy, though potent, extension of the life of the canyon far below.

Finally, the men reached the southern lip of the mouth of the canyon, where the escarpment cut sharply around to the southwest. There, though hardly believing what they were seeing, they found the conditions that had been roughly described by Sean and Maria Grady. These conditions, and their making, accentuated all the more the superficiality of the small mortals' intended occupation and ownership.

Water, long a tool of the Maker, had flowed here eons before. About two hundred million years before, during the late Triassic Period, it had flowed in sluggish streams that had carried and deposited sediments washed down from ancient highlands to the southeast. Mud, clay, sand, gravel, and silt, laid down in floodplains and streambeds, had accumulated over the millennia and had risen as the highlands to the southeast had worn down. As rivers through the deltas they create, these streams had cut their channels through the beds of sediment they had laid down, laying down more sediment in the process and rising with the higher floodplains around them.

One such stream had flowed northward across the land that had lain above the land now exposed at the mouth of Escondido Canyon. There the currents of the stream had conspired, for a relatively short distance, to carve a narrower, deeper channel into the sediment.

A far older stream, in the vicinity of where the younger one would carve its deeper channel, had previously carved its bed, which was long dry and filling with sediment by the time of the younger stream's flow. This older stream had turned for a short distance to course toward the northeast, suddenly splitting its streambed, after the turn, to force its entire volume through two narrow channels—one on each side of the island created by its split—channels carved ever deeper by the rush of the concentrated flows. These two channels had rejoined to form one streambed beyond the island, just before the stream had corrected itself in a great bend to resume its general direction of flow to the northwest. After this older stream had dried up, its streambed, including the deeper channels that had split around the island, had received deposits of sediment from the flooding of younger streams. Nevertheless, those two deeper channels, as well as the deeper channel from the younger stream, still had plenty of depth by the time erosive leveling and climate change had caused the water and its sediment to flow no more.

Time had passed, about 180 or 190 million years of it, and during the late Tertiary Period—beginning about ten million years before Luke and Tom would witness its results—as the Rocky Mountains had risen to the west, water had flowed into the region again, carrying the sediment from those young and rising mountains. This time it had flowed from the west, across the ancient streambeds of the Triassic rather than through them. Thus, as the deposits of gravel, mud, sand, and clay had risen upon the land—over the course of the next eight million years or so—to form the Ogallala Formation topped with its limestone caprock, they had risen thicker where those channels had lain. The thickness of the caprock over those ancient channels had predisposed it to better withstand the erosive forces that had cut the caprock back some two hundred miles, over the succeeding millennia, from its farthest extension to the east. The thickness of the caprock over those channels had therefore protected the rock beneath the channels, as water had cut away the surrounding rock, to leave behind the formations that had kept the Escondido hidden, had kept it a mystery.

Luke and Tom, from the edge of the caprock, some eight hundred feet above the floor of the canyon, now looked upon those formations in wonder. The older of the streambeds, that which had run a short distance to the northeast and had split around an island, had left as its legacy two linear, parallel mesas, outliers of the Llano Estacado, themselves eight hundred feet high, that ran southwest to northeast, where the channels of the split streambed had cut the deepest and the Ogallala Formation had filled in the thickest. The eastern of these two outliers, the larger of the two, stretched about a mile and a half in length. Its southwestern end stood off about a quarter mile from the escarpment of the Llano Estacado and extended about a quarter mile south of the mouth of the canyon. The western of the two outliers, something less than a mile and a half in length, stood inside the mouth of the canyon, more than a quarter mile west of its larger twin. Still, its southwestern end stood a quarter mile short of the southern wall of the canyon, while its northeastern end extended about a half mile farther north than the northeastern end of its twin. Consequently, between the two of them, despite the fact that they allowed entrances of a quarter mile in width, these outliers effectively blocked from view the southern mile and a half of the mouth of the canyon.

The channels upon which the tops of these outliers had been built, it is to be remembered, had reunited to form a single streambed, which had then turned again toward the northwest in a great bend. On the outside of that bend, the flow of water had cut the deepest. This had since filled in the thickest with the Ogallala and its caprock. For that reason, northeast of these two outliers, the north wall of the canyon, at its most eastern point, about a mile farther east than that of the south wall, hooked back around toward the two outliers, in a short, curved peninsula of the Llano Estacado that partly closed the mouth of the canyon. Therefore, though inside its mouth the canyon was three miles or more in width, at its mouth it was less than two and a half miles.

Those formations had been built upon the older, split streambed, but they were not alone. The younger stream, the one that had flowed north over the land that had lain above that now exposed at the mouth of the Escondido, had left its legacy, as well. Where its currents had carved a deeper channel, the gravel, mud, sand, and clay of the late Tertiary Period had filled in to form an even thicker portion of the Ogallala than had formed over the other two channels. The results of all this flow and fill stood about a quarter mile outside the hooked north lip of the mouth of the canyon. This outlier, well over eight hundred feet high and all of two miles long, ran in a north-south direction. Its northernmost point extended about a quarter mile beyond the northern lip of the mouth of the canyon. Its southernmost point extended at least three quarters of a mile beyond the northernmost point of the smaller of the twin outliers. At their closest point, the larger outlier stood about a quarter mile to the east of the twins. At its southern end, the larger outlier was nearly a half mile to the east of the larger of the twins.

Whatever the distances, it became clear to Luke and Tom, even from their place on top of the caprock, that from the low rolling plains, without close examination, the mouth of Escondido Canyon was completely obscured from view by overlapping walls of solid rock. Even upon closer examination, the entrances into the canyon would appear to run into other walls of solid rock, unless the examiner would persevere and push his way over the breaks and through the passages between the giant rock formations to well inside the mouth of the canyon. And who would go to all that trouble, the two men reasoned between themselves, unless he already knew that the canyon was there? Otherwise, as their later observations from below would verify, the true entrance to the Escondido looked as unlikely to have a major canyon behind it as any section of the escarpment that did not have one.

And Tom had noted something else. When they had left the head of the smaller canyon some six or seven miles to the southwest, they had ridden to the northeast. When they had arrived at the southern edge of the Escondido, its head had appeared to be about two miles to the west. As Tom had reckoned their angle and distance, he had approximated that the head of the Escondido was no farther to the west than that of that smaller canyon. Tom figured, correctly, that the caprock jutted out about six or seven miles farther to the east between the smaller canyon to the south and the smaller canyon he believed existed to the north, so that even though the Escondido was six or seven miles longer than the two smaller ones, its head was no farther westward than either of them. In fact, Tom reasoned, if there did exist another small canyon to the north (and there did, about four or five miles to the north), and if its head were also as far west as the Escondido's (and it was actually another half mile farther to the west), it was easy to see how anyone riding up above on the Llano Estacado would miss seeing the Escondido. If he were riding far enough to the west to skirt either or both of the smaller canyons, he would skirt the Escondido as well. And any rider on the Llano Estacado, especially in that section of it, was rare enough. It was no surprise, then, that there was confusion about whether there was one, two, or three canyons.

In this way was the Escondido Canyon obscured from above and below. Add to that obscurity the fact that it was situated in a remote area of a remote region (some forty miles north of Hank Smith's Rock House and some fifty miles southeast of Charles Goodnight's Home Ranch and even forty miles northwest of the trading post of Tee Pee

City, the closest settlements, all recently established), and it was easy to see how the canyon maintained its dubious claim on existence. So obscure and remote was it, that it appeared that, despite its suitability to their occupations, not even rustlers or other outlaws had discovered the canyon.

As if to punctuate the remoteness of the canyon, a few small herds of buffalo grazed lazily, unmolested by hunters, right out in the open on the low rolling plains beyond the entrance to the canyon. These must have lagged behind when the others had continued their migration to the south, lending credence to Charles Goodnight's belief that buffalo migrated to find new grazing rather than for reasons of weather and the change of seasons. Goodnight would later point to the buffalo's failure to migrate once the great southern herd had been decimated to the point that those few remaining, in several small herds, could be maintained year-round, each herd in one place, on the grass available there. The current hunting season would nearly accomplish that decimation and would certainly assure that no such scene would present itself at this same season of the succeeding year.

Whether or not Tom and Luke were considering that possibility, only they could know. Regardless, they both watched in silence, for a long time, the great beasts, small at this distance, speckled across the golden rolling prairie. Then they turned their horses and began to search along the escarpment to the southwest, until they found a game trail, which they descended to the base of the escarpment, where they turned back to explore the canyon that was to become their home.

It was far later in the day when Tom and Luke rode southwest under the stretching shadow of the Llano Estacado, the unseen sun sinking ever closer to the western edge of the earth, far below and beyond the far western edge of that great plateau. Though their intention in returning to their camp along the base of the escarpment, rather than above it, was to reconnoiter a trail for their return to the canyon with the entire outfit, their minds were not wholly concentrated on that task, as their thoughts remained, at least in part, in the canyon behind them.

"It's our canyon, Tom," said Luke. "It's all ours."

"Yeah, . . . well, it will be."

"Sure it is, Tom, what with no one knowin' that it even exists and us havin' contracted with Hill and Colmey. In fact, Matthew Colmey has more than likely already recorded our preliminary file in Jacksboro."

"All the same," Tom responded, "I'll feel more secure in our ownership when Colmey's outfit is out here runnin' their lines, and even more secure when we've got the patents in our hands."

"I reckon you're right, Tom, but will you allow that there is a good likelihood that the canyon is ours and indulge me in entertainin' thoughts of ownership?"

Tom looked over at Luke, as they stopped momentarily to determine the best way through an arroyo, and met in his face the humorously pleading expression that well represented the sentiments he had just expressed. Tom laughed and said, "All right, I guess I'll allow it."

"Good," Luke responded, and they turned to their left toward a game trail that, they could see, would take them in and out of the arroyo. "It's our canyon, Tom, all ours."

"That's right," Tom concurred, with a firm nod of his head.

"You want to build a house on the south side, you build it. You want to build on the north, you build it," Luke continued, looking over at Tom. "We want to raise beeves, we raise 'em. We want to raise sheep, we raise 'em. We want to raise elephants, we raise 'em. We raise whatever we want. You see that place, Tom? You see all that grass and water? You see all those trees? Did you ever expect to see all that timber up here, even oak, and those black walnuts at that spring? Grapes and currants, plums. Who'd've ever thought it?"

"And the game," Tom said with a smile, permitting himself to be overwhelmed, in his own way, "I mean you've got buffalo, antelope, deer, turkey, quail, . . . bear, jackrabbits, . . . ducks and geese, and beaver, too. It's a lot more than I ever counted on way out here. I mean," he continued, turning toward Luke, "I've been up through this region on drives, you know, east of here, in Indian Territory, and I've chased down stampedes and hunted strays well inside the Texas border. You know, you've done it, too," Tom added as Luke, now looking down seriously, nodded to the back of Arbuckle's neck. "And never," Tom continued, "would I have thought you'd find such an Eden as this up in these parts. It's just as you say, and so blessed beautiful. God's own brush painted the walls of that canyon. Imagine bein' able to look at that every day."

"And our own creeks, Tom, the Schurtz and Stuart creeks," Luke said about the two major streams that ran through the canyon eventually to exit the canyon in opposite directions: the northern Stuart Creek to turn north and wend between the canyon wall and the largest, northern-most outlier; and the southern Schurtz Creek to turn south to flow out between the canyon wall and the southernmost of the outliers. "Would you ever think you'd have your own creek?" Luke continued.

"No sir," Tom responded, with a shake of his head.

"Named after you and everything?" Luke continued.

"Nooooo sir."

"Full of fish just waitin' to be caught."

To this statement, Tom responded with a broad smile.

"Won't Zack like that?" Luke speculated. And Tom agreed that he thought Zack would.

And so it went. Few features of the canyon were neglected in this review, and most were revisited more than once, so that by the time the two men reached the game trail below the area where they had made camp that day, and they rode up and into camp, there hardly seemed any more to say. But say they did, doing their best to paint in the imaginations of their riveted listeners, young and old, the pictures of what they had seen, so that what sleep did come to those excited minds was visited by visions of the dream-canyon of their tomorrow.

THAT TOMORROW ARRIVED EARLY THE NEXT MORNING, and the eager travelers hurried through breakfast as part of their hur-ried preparation for what could possibly be their last day of travel. But such hopes faded as the trail down from the caprock did demand that the wheels be chained, lest the wagons run over the mules and oxen in front of them. Even so, it was a grueling and tension-filled task to get the wagons down the steep trail without mishap. Another option would have been to dismantle the wagons and take them down in pieces on the backs of the mules. The thought of all that such a plan would entail, not the least of which was a substantial delay, was enough to make Luke and Tom lean a little beyond the bounds of safety and take a substantial risk in driving the wagons intact. Thus it was that the members of the party breathed a considerable sigh of relief when the second wagon, the smaller one drawn by the mules, reached the base of the escarpment, and the party was forced to settle for nooning at the spring-fed creek that Tom had originally recommended for the day before. Still, they were down off the caprock, and no one of the party was going to make light of the dangerous work that had been safely and successfully completed that morning, least of all Luke and Tom, who, as the engineers and main participants in the task, were the most aware of how close they had come to disaster several times. That knowledge, and the experience behind it, along with the grueling work, had all but drained them of their strength.

They needed all the strength they had left, as well as that gained from a hearty dinner and the rest that accompanied it, because in the afternoon they struck out across the land at the base of the escarpment. That land was threaded by creeks; those creeks had banks; and those banks had not been worn down by the wagons of buffalo hunters. Tom, Luke, and Andy, therefore, spent a good deal of time shoveling trails through steep banks and chaining wheels to get the wagons up and down those banks safely.

Still, they did make progress. They found, too, what Tom and Luke had confirmed on their ride back the evening before, that Tom had been correct in his reckoning that the Llano Estacado did jut out here, in a long rounded extension that allowed for the length of Escondido Canyon. For this reason, after the party had pushed a little ways out onto the rolling plains to avoid the roughest areas of the breaks at the base of the escarpment, they were required to travel to the northeast to maintain their distance from those breaks.

Despite the creek beds, the party now made good progress, due in large part to the way they pushed the teams and herd across the land in between the creeks. They pushed to make the canyon by nightfall, even after they realized that they would not make it. Finally, after that extra push, of the kind that often occurs between realization and acceptance, they decided to make camp. They did so along a low-banked creek, within sight of the outliers at the mouth of the Escondido, or so they thought, but they had thought that they could see the outliers, in rock formations up ahead, at other times and places that day, only to be disappointed. And although Tom and Luke believed that this time they recognized certain landmarks to indicate the vicinity of the Escondido, the shadows of the plateau were lengthening and deepening towards night, and they could not be sure. They did consider the possibility that they might have missed the opening, but Tom ruled that out because they were still moving toward the northeast, and as he reckoned it, the Escondido opened at the caprock's farthest extension to the east in that region. Regardless, they marveled at the canyon's elusive character, and more than once had to check themselves against questioning their own sighting and exploration of the canyon the day before.

They rose early again the next morning. In fact, Luke and Tom had slept hardly at all, due to a restless night in which, first, skunks had harassed the camp, then, wolves had harassed the cattle, so that both Luke and Tom had ridden guard from midnight until sunrise. They breakfasted hurriedly, and then, leaving Elizabeth and the children with a Winchester, Tom, Luke, and Andy rode ahead to scout out the Escondido. As they rode toward the northeast with the protrusion of the escarpment, what they had thought were the two largest outliers (the larger of the twins and the single north-south one farther to the east) turned out to be only partly correct. What they had seen was just another section of the deceptive face presented by the escarpment of the Llano Estacado, along with a portion of the southern end of the larger of the twin outliers. They realized this as they rode closer and began to see the largest of the outliers, that one farthest to the east, come into view around the eastern edge of the large twin. It was all so big, all this rock, and deceptive, with its recesses and protrusions. They were so confused by what was presenting itself to their eyes, in contrast to what they remembered they had seen, that they were not sure that they had found the right place until they had made their way between the southern end of the larger twin and the escarpment, and then between the southern end of the smaller twin and the escarpment, and then found themselves on the floor of the canyon itself.

Mere crumbs within this closed mouth, three miles wide, the men sat their horses for a considerable moment and marveled—Andy at his first sight of the awesome canyon, and Tom and Luke at not only what they were seeing, but at the Escondido's singular faculty for guarding the secret of her existence. From where they sat, if they looked back to the east, toward the mouth of the canyon, they saw what appeared to be a solid wall of rock, but by riding toward that wall and turning in one direction or another, they could find one of the broad corridors that opened onto the low rolling plains beyond the canyon.

Luke and Tom did not allow much time for this marveling. They were tired and had business in this canyon, which they straightaway sought to carry out. With Andy falling in with them, they rode up the canyon. They noticed and noted much of the varied flora and fauna, as well as the topography of the canyon, as they went. Still, they did not stop or slow down to explore, but rather kept on at a determined pace.

In time they pulled up short of the head of the canyon. Because they knew that buffalo tended to avoid the narrower sections of a canyon, and since they could see no more buffalo farther up the canyon, they determined that they needed to go no farther. They pulled out their guns. Tom had the Sharps .50, as he was the best shot. Luke had his Winchester. Andy had a six-shooter that Luke and Tom had given him as part of his pay. The men checked their arms. Then they spread out, with Tom in the center and Luke and Andy a few hundred yards on either side of him—Luke on his right, toward the south, and Andy on his left, toward the north. Then Tom started his horse forward down the canyon at a walk, and after allowing Tom to get a little ahead of them, Luke and Andy did the same.

After a short distance, Tom spotted a large bull buffalo partway up the incline at the base of the escarpment of the canyon's south wall. He stopped his horse, took careful aim with the big gun (which felt particularly heavy to his tired hands and arms) and fired. He saw a tuft of dust pop up near the great animal, and then he saw the bull run down toward the canyon floor in the direction of the mouth of the canyon. A perfect shot. He lay the gun across the saddle in front of him and resumed his forward progress, until he saw a buffalo similarly situated and shot into the ground near it, as well, to scare it down onto the canyon floor. In the same way, but with weapons of far shorter range, Luke and Andy also persuaded buffalo down toward the canyon floor and mouth. Soon they came upon buffalo in front of them on the canyon floor, and by yelling, waving their hats, throwing their ropes, riding at them, or shooting at the ground near them, when necessary, the men began to scare them to make a retreat for the mouth of the canyon, an increasingly hurried retreat as more of their kind joined in. In time, it was a full stampede, of several hundred of the huge animals, that shook the very ground and sent up a rumble that reverberated off the walls of the canyon with deafening effect. In this way, Tom, Luke, and Andy chased the buffalo out of Escondido Canyon.

The three men followed the buffalo out of the canyon: Luke exiting between the southern ends of the twins and the escarpment; Andy, between the northern end of the largest outlier and the escarpment; and Tom, by weaving, first to the northeast to get around the northern end of the twins, then to the southeast to get around the southern end of the largest outlier. The men met up on the plains beyond the canyon and watched the distancing buffalo as they began to slow and then to graze out on the rolling plains. The men watched for a while with quiet admiration: such large, powerful, and dangerous animals, but at the same time timid and vulnerable, their timidity and vulnerability earlier betrayed by the eyes of the fleeing beasts, eyes that bore an unsettling resemblance to the eyes of a frightened child. Now they grazed contentedly, delivered from the annoyance of the men on horseback, the recent stampede apparently forgotten. But in that same present, three other creatures, those men on horseback, looked forward, as was the prerogative of their nature, to the future for these animals they had just exiled from the protection of the hidden canyon. As they looked forward, they wondered how long it would be before these buffalo out on the prairie would be discovered and destroyed. To what fate had they sentenced them?

The men sat and watched them for a while. Then they turned toward the southwest and headed back toward their camp.

WHEN THEY ARRIVED AT THE CAMP, everything was long packed and ready. Elizabeth was eager to hear of that morning's reconnaissance, and as the men related what they had seen, the two older children—even little Rachel, but especially Zachariah—crowded around her to hear the men's report. They had indeed found it, about two miles up ahead, and though Elizabeth entreated the men to tell her more and more of it, her anticipation got ahead of itself, so that she could no longer bear to be standing still while the canyon lay just ahead, even though she had not wrung from the men all the details she sought to hear.

Consequently, the teams were soon hitched; the cattle, horses, sheep, and pigs soon gathered; and the Stuart-Schurtz party was soon on its way. That way carried them over a trail that the men had scouted out on their way back from the canyon, improving on what Luke and Tom had scouted out in the fading light of the night before the last. The trail passed through some breaks, but required only one time that the wheels be chained while crossing a creek bed. Before long they entered the broad sandy bed of the now gentle Schurtz Creek, which flowed down the middle of the bed in a stream not more than ten feet across at that point. They rolled down into the gradually sloping streambed and crossed the stream and climbed up its other gradually sloping side to where the grass held the sand more firmly, allowing for better progress by the wagons.

They followed the streambed, finally passing beneath and between the towering escarpment (which became the south wall of the canyon) and the grand twin outliers standing sentinel at the mouth of their future canyon home. Small and slow did their passage through this magnificent corridor seem, until, at last, they were inside the canyon, pulling up out of the streambed onto firmer ground, flatter ground too, offering much less challenging terrain than the rugged breaks through which they had traveled to get there.

They rolled along deeper into the canyon, wondering all the while—especially Elizabeth and the children, with this their introduction—at the canyon's rich blend of stimuli, which neglected not one of the senses. It was all a bit overwhelming for those just arrived from the prairie, those who intended to make this environment their home.

Farther into that intended home they rolled. With the firm, level ground making the travel easy, they had rolled on about a half mile into the canyon before Tom rode up alongside the heavy wagon, where Luke sat uncharacteristically driving from the seat rather than walking alongside. As Tom rode up, he could see that Luke was absorbed in thoughts of his surroundings and all that those surroundings signified. Tom had come to learn that, in such a state, Luke would very well go on, without any sense of time, until made aware by either the passing of a good deal of time or some interruption. Tom intended to interrupt.

"We could noon any place along here," Tom said, as they moved along.

"We could," Luke agreed, coming suddenly out of his reverie. Nodding out ahead, he indicated how abruptly he could depart from such reverie by adding, "How about a sandy spot on the banks of the beautiful Stuart Creek?"

Tom dropped his head and shook it slightly, trying unsuccessfully to keep from giving Luke the satisfaction of drawing a laugh from him. Satisfaction given, Luke laughed his chuckle-laugh, and Tom tried to hide his no more, the two men laughing unchecked on this glorious autumn day.

Glorious, indeed, it was, even had those appreciating it not just entered their promised land. The sun, angled seasonally lower toward the south, poured out its pure light through the dry air, air of the temperature just warm enough to let the periodic cooler breeze waft it to perfection. The birds sang, the cattle lowed, the grass swayed, the cottonwood leaves fluttered, and the members of the Stuart-Schurtz party would have agreed that the Creator reigned as he should and that indeed, "all was right with the world."

The settlers did pull into a sandy spot on those banks of that beautiful Stuart Creek, and there they stopped. With the reins still in her hands, Elizabeth sat unmoving upon the seat of the smaller wagon, transfixed by not only the effect of the whole canyon upon her, but by the particular effect of a herd of pronghorn grazing on a hill beyond, their markings standing out against the blond-green grass like the patterned artwork of a primitive people.

Suddenly Luke was beside her on the seat, taking the reins from her hands. "I've got to show you somethin'," he said, as he slapped the reins against the backs of the mules. The mules pulled on for a little while, along the south bank of Stuart Creek, until Luke reined them to a stop. Looking to his right, beyond Elizabeth—who was looking at him—he said, "Look yonder."

Elizabeth did turn and look, out beyond the creek, beyond the canyon wall, into a draw of multihued green, tinged here and there with yellow and gold. The shimmering leaves of towering cottonwoods dominated the green, supported by hackberry, willow, and other leaves as well. Luke made mention of others.

"This is just one draw like this, Elizabeth. There're any number of 'em, especially a big one farther on up the canyon, near where I'd like to build our house. There's a spring back in there waterin' all this, same as the other one. There's plums in there, and grapes, and currants, and even a few black walnuts at that spring, for makin' furniture. It's all ours, Elizabeth. It's all ours," he concluded, looking out into the space and time before him.

Elizabeth kept her head turned away from Luke, her gaze fixed on the draw. She had removed her bonnet when they had stopped for dinner, and now the strands of her hair that had fallen loose, from where she had it all pulled up, shifted and changed color from golden to light brown, playing in the sun at the whim of the prairie wind dropping down off the high plains. Her beauty, set as she was, even turned away from him, suddenly impressed itself upon Luke as much as it ever had. He could not see her face, but each knew, each knew in that depth of intimacy of their sacramental bond. She reached around and found his hand without looking back. Then she turned to face him, her gray-blue eyes releasing slow, crystalline tears down cheeks softly reddened by sun and wind. Their foreheads met, pushing back his hat, as she bowed her head and reached up to brush away the tears with the back of her hand.

"We're home," Luke said.

That was all the trigger her emotions needed.

"I know," she said, her weight slumping more heavily against him as the tears now flowed freely, silently, her hand up to cover those flowing eyes. Luke ran his hand over her back and leaned her head against his shoulder as he ran his eyes over their promised land.

"Let 'er run, Elizabeth; you've earned it."

Rachel, who had been sleeping with the baby behind the seat, woke to this scene, and as alarm hastened her usually extended waking period, she blurted out, "Daddy, why is Mama crying?"

Elizabeth looked away from the child and wiped her eyes on the sleeves of her dress, then reached around and lifted Rachel over the seat and set her on the edge of the seat between her parents. With her arm tightly squeezing her only daughter and while smiling and choking laughter among her tears, she pointed into the canyon and said, "Look here at your new home, Rachel."

Rachel did look into the draw, but then looked back at her mother in wonder at this mixture of laughter and tears. The child might well have wondered, as she in her youth, and the others in their sex, had not the capability to fully empathize with Elizabeth, who was experiencing her own mix of the emotions visited upon the pioneer woman. Elizabeth sat within her canyon, before the beauty of her dream, this draw aptly depicting its many aspects and nuances, like a play within a play: the stark ruggedness and jaggedness of the broken rock, the serenity of the sluggish stream, the fecundity of the earth, the fruitfulness of the vines and trees and grass. Add the shimmering cottonwood leaves, the golden sands, the ample game. Add it all, and present it in light and darkness.

All about them now, the autumn sun pushed its light through the dry air to sharply define all upon which it fell, in contrast. Hence, the green of the trees stood out in an almost surreal way against the bright red of the cliffs, the bright blue of the sky. It stood out also against the sharp darkness of autumn shadow. Darkness, dappled by the light that sifted down through the wind-shaken foliage. Darkness that blanketed scattered areas in shapes of objects blocking light. Darkness that, more than any color behind another color could ever do, contrasted starkly with the light. In beauty lies that contrast in balance. It is not the balance of equal portions, but the balance of appropriate portions of light and darkness that stirs an appreciation of beauty in the human soul, itself ever struggling with the fluctuation of the light and darkness of the human condition. Light by which we see, but, unchecked, capable of bleaching all definition from the world. Darkness by which light is tempered to render definition in color, line, form, and texture, but, unchecked, capable of drowning all in the toneless, lifeless cloak of gray, or far worse, inky black.

Thus, Elizabeth sat before their dream in light and darkness, a panorama on a stage oblivious to its audience. Life as she had known it behind her; feminine companionship as far away as the distancing past or possibly the future of her own child's maturity. Life before her a promise of contrast endowed with the potential for beauty. Land, water, wind, light, darkness—yielding and resisting, sustaining and inundating, caressing and blustering, illuminating and bleaching, enhancing and eclipsing. And so she cried, and she laughed, and after some time, she picked up the reins from her husband's hands and steered the wagon into their noon camp and the rest of her life.

Chapter Four

A HOME UPON THE LAND

*Home, in one form or another,
is the great object of life.*
—J. G. HOLLAND

THE REST OF ELIZABETH'S LIFE COMMENCED WITH her preparation of the party's first meal in their canyon home. With that dinner of turkey, shared on the broad, sandy bank of Stuart Creek, the party joined a long history of meals shared in that same locality. Back, back, some twelve thousand years before, PaleoIndians had first shared meals of mammoth, then of giant bison, and then modern bison, the buffalo. Later, MesoIndians, some seven thousand years before the party's dinner, had first, during a three-thousand-year drought, shared meals of small game and gathered food from plants, then again, after the drought, had shared the buffalo. Later, NeoIndians, some eighteen hundred years before the dinner, had first shared meals of buffalo and of gathered food from plants, then had added more and more of cultivated beans, squash, and corn. Later, Apache—Andy Grady's paternal ancestors among them—some five hundred years before the dinner, had shared the buffalo. During the time of the Apache, a reconnaissance party of the Coronado expedition had too shared the buffalo there. Later, Comanche, some two hundred years before the dinner, had shared the buffalo among themselves, then had shared it with their Kiowa and Cheyenne allies. During the time of the Comanche, expeditions of Pierre Vial, Jose Mares, Francisco Amagual, and Randolph B. Marcy had not shared the buffalo in the canyon, not having discovered the canyon, but certain *ciboleros* and *comancheros*—Andy Grady's maternal grandfather among them—had shared the buffalo there. Hence, though he made no show of acknowledging it, Andy's participation in this history enjoyed a legitimacy foreign to that of the rest of the party.

Luke broke the lull that had fallen over the party at the end of the meal. "Well," he said, "I suppose we ought to look out a spot for our abode."

"Suppose so," Tom agreed. "Then we'll need to locate what land we want to purchase."

Luke took up the matter from this point. "That's right. You figurin' fifteen, twenty sections for the whole canyon, Tom?"

"I'd say it's in that range," Tom said. "Figure eight or nine miles long, maybe average two miles wide, say around sixteen sections, maybe eighteen, . . . maybe twenty," he said, adding the last part with a shrug.

"And we'll control twelve of 'em, with what we buy with our certificates and the alternates," Luke said. "We'll have practically the entire canyon. Then there's the plains beyond, and once we're past winter, plenty of grass up on top of the cap. Free range makes that available until we buy more. These Seven Ox beeves'll be fat, the cows droppin' calves before we know it."

These sentiments drew various facial expressions from the adults. Andy's variation involved pressing his lips together and nodding lightly.

This reaction from the often inscrutable Andy did not go unnoticed by Luke. "Look at ol' Andy, there," Luke said, grasping at the gesture. "He's all set to be a cattleman."

And they did look at Andy. And he looked back. And all laughed, Andy included, at the very real possibility.

AFTER DINNER, Tom and Luke rode out to scout for a place to build their homes, their headquarters. Andy rode out to hunt antelope. Elizabeth milked the cow and cared for the baby. She and the children then gathered firewood—not without a stern warning from Elizabeth to the children that, even this late in the season, they should keep a sharp watch for rattlesnakes. Then they further set up the camp for the evening meal.

Tom and Luke rode toward the head of the canyon, scouting all afternoon for places to locate their headquarters. By evening, when they rode into camp, they had decided to take the next morning to explore a little more before deciding on a spot.

A natural excitement animated the otherwise weary travelers as they supped that night, and the talk bounced around among sundry plans and ideas. The volume of ideas may have been expanded by a surprise bottle of wine that Elizabeth served with supper. This was one of three bottles that she had acquired, in a rare purchase from Mrs. Smith at the Occidental Hotel in Griffin, and had secreted away in the wagon to await special occasions, none expected to be more special than the discovery of, and arrival in, the canyon. It had been a rare purchase in that Elizabeth's lips—and Luke's, too, when Elizabeth was around—rarely touched alcohol. But, on this night, even Elizabeth could see celebratory benefit in the fermented fruit of the vine, given this most special occasion.

Elizabeth had nursed little Robert before supper, and the baby was now soundly asleep. Rachel sat under her mother's arm, a blanket over them both. Zachariah sat up against his father, his eyes large in the light of the fire, as he enjoyed the festive atmosphere that enlivened the camp.

Tom spoke up. "Elizabeth, I believe that was the best meal of the entire journey."

"You'll have to thank Andy, as he supplied the antelope," she replied.

"That's right," Luke said through his chuckle, and he and Tom nodded their appreciation to Andy, who smiled at their good-natured mockery.

"But Tom's right, Elizabeth, there was somethin' special about tonight's supper," Luke continued.

Andy nodded his silent agreement.

"It must be the surroundings," Elizabeth said. "Or the wine," she added with a tipsy giggle.

Luke chuckled at the light intoxication of his lovely wife, intoxication of joy as well as spirits. "Yes ma'am, the surroundings," he said. "Antelope does taste a mite better when it's your own," he added, returning to a favorite theme.

"It won't be long before I'll have a garden, and we'll have greens and vegetables all season long," Elizabeth declared.

"Think of that, Tom, Andy," Luke said, adding, as he looked down at his son and across at his daughter, "Zack, Rachel, greens and vegetables all season long." To this, Rachel stuck out her tongue and wagged her head back and forth as her father chuckled.

"Sounds fine," Tom replied. "They'll taste the sweeter for havin' been grown on our own land."

"That's right," Luke heartily agreed, happy to have Tom take up the theme.

"Yessir, a man certainly could entertain thoughts of settlin' for good out here," Tom said.

"Are you going to settle down without a girl, Tom?" Elizabeth teasingly inquired, in a way that she would not have done fully sober.

"Well, I haven't met any of the local girls yet, Elizabeth," Tom admitted, drawing another Lukan chuckle and even a "huh" and smile from Andy. "But I don't worry much about that anymore. I guess I'd rather be unmarried than badly married, and I know that if the Lord intends a woman for me, he'll bring us together, no matter what. And you know, my soul truly feels that the good Lord will provide."

Luke chimed in. "We are some distance from civilization though, Tom. You expect there's a woman keepin' herself over in those trees?"

"The Lord works in mysterious ways," Tom responded.

"I'd like to see the mystery that sneaks up on you out here," Luke rejoined.

"Now, Luke," Elizabeth interjected, "you know Tom is right. All things are possible to him who has faith."

Luke leaned back against his bedroll and said, "Well before we go marryin' this drifter off to a phantom, we'd better help him plan his honeymoon cabin. Ain't that right, huh?"

"Don't know about the honeymoon part," Tom replied, "but a fine cedar-log house would be a little bit of all right. A house of fine crafts-manship," he added, speaking out as if to a vision of the Platonic ideal of house.

"We can look out a location for just such a house, tomorrow," Luke said, his eyes brightening as he leaned into his delivery.

"That's a good place to start," Tom agreed.

"I'll start planning my dream house," Elizabeth said with a wistful air.

"You do that, Elizabeth," Luke said, a sudden vehemence charging his voice. "You can start plannin' in your dreams tonight." Luke looked over at Tom and smiled a bit, then continued to Elizabeth, "You better start plannin' for ol' Tom here, too. He's goin' to need a woman's touch for when he brings his gal home."

"Mysterious ways," Tom said.

"You think this'll be the first miracle I'll ever see?"

"Mysterious ways."

Luke, still smiling at Tom's last rejoinder, found his eyes resting on Andy, whose eyes communicated his expectation of comment. Luke delivered it. "With all that mystery, there might even be hope for ol' Andy here."

The laconic Andy answered with a bit of defensiveness and an ani-mation rarely seen in him. "You never know," he said.

At this the other adults exchanged glances of surprise and then broke into laughter, which was joined by the children copying the adults, and finally by Andy himself, who could no longer hold it back.

And thus laughter wafted out of the ring of firelight into the black-ness of the night, out over the gurgling of the creek, the hoot of the owl, the cries of the wolf and coyote. The sights and sounds of man had returned to Escondido Canyon.

IN THE MORNING the men checked the stock, after which Andy and his collie, Rita—with the help of Zachariah, on the old mare, and his own puppy, Charlie—began moving the cattle and sheep up the canyon. Luke and Tom rode up the canyon again, as well, exploring various draws and other features of the land as they scouted for a place to build.

At noon, the two men stopped on a grassy knoll along Stuart Creek, built a fire of mesquite, and made biscuits, beans, bacon, and coffee. They were quick to clean up and return to their scouting, so that by midafternoon they had settled on a location.

It was a high bank more than a half mile down from the head of the canyon, where the canyon walls still towered two to three hundred feet above the canyon floor. Still, the shadow from those walls to the south (in this region where the sun journeyed across the sky in so high an arc) would not encroach upon their location, as it was just south of the middle of the canyon, on the north side of the more southern of the two streams, Schurtz Creek. The bank rested well above the flood-plain of Schurtz Creek. This was an important thing to consider, as evidence of the creek's potential—when torrential rains had sent water flooding off the high plains to channel through the canyon—was etched into the land well below the bank. Set on the north side of the creek, the bank faced south, with a broad level area of grass before it (also above the floodplain) that would serve as a yard for the family.

Tom located a place for his house, as well. It was easily reached from the Stuarts' by proceeding directly toward the head of the canyon, nearly due west, through a mesquite thicket and up a game trail that climbed a slope of long-ago eroded material, to an extensive level area with a Trujillo-sandstone base, a good fifty feet or more below the rim of the canyon. This elevated flat would provide plenty of room for a house and corral. It would offer several other advantages as well.

One such advantage was the flat's proximity to a notch (which nature had sculpted almost to perfection) leading out of, or into, the canyon. Ancient waters had cut this notch into the caprock and the softer layers of rock beneath it, so that it opened onto the north end of the flat. The game trail that the men had followed up to the flat continued westward up into this notch and very comfortably climbed out of it onto the Llano Estacado. The notch could easily accommodate a buggy, and possibly a wagon. With a little improvement, the trail would make an excellent road.

Water, too, was in good supply, as a spring flowed out of the base of the caprock, a little south of the center of the flat, and out over the flat, pooling here and there as it drifted toward the flat's abrupt southern edge. From there, its water flowed over, dropped in front of, and crashed against rock, on the water's descent to where it joined the waters of other springs, far below, to create the beginnings of Schurtz Creek. These spring waters were not alone responsible for the abruptness of the southern edge of the flat, nor always for the full volume of the creek at its head. Copious runoff from the Llano Estacado had periodically, over the millennia, contributed to the erosion of the flat, and of the rock beneath it, that had created the drop-off on the flat's southern side. Distant and proximate rains would still send this runoff to cascade down through a draw cut into the caprock, south of the flat, and plunge nearly one hundred feet to where it would join the spring-water source of Schurtz Creek. In examining this drop-off at the flat's southern edge, Tom found that, below the level of the flat, in the short distance between the edge of the flat and the drop-off, the spring's water had carved a pool, hidden from view, that Tom noted for its apparent convenience for bathing and washing.

In addition to the water from the spring and the runoff, more water flowed out onto the flat farther to the north, near the trail, from a seep at the base of the cliff. The water from this seep flowed across the northern edge of the flat and off to the east, down the slope, creating a muddy trickle that wound through the trail, as the water sought its own level, meandering down the canyon to where it eventually evaporated. This flow of water illustrated how the land fell off in a gradual slope from the northern and eastern edges of the flat, in stark contrast to the drop-off at the southern edge.

Tom intended to cut a pit into the flat, in which the water from this seep could pool, to supply the corral he intended to build. The more abundant spring to the south, on the other hand, Tom would use to supply his own water needs. Accordingly, he would build his house to the southeast of the corral, south of the center of the flat, guaranteeing a supply of water from the spring. And he would build it well out from the cliff at the back of the flat, out on the eastern edge, to avoid any falling rock and to get as much as he could of the evening sunshine. Furthermore, that situation would allow him a clear view of the Stuart home, a half mile down the canyon to the east, an advantage that was not lost on Luke.

"I am glad to know that you'll be able to see our place from up here, Tom. You know Comanche and Kiowa've been known to leave the reservation at Fort Sill and pass through this country. With

Elizabeth and the young'uns, it's gratifyin' to know your house won't be far," Luke said with a grave sincerity that, especially coming from the person from whom it came, struck Tom as slightly humorous.

Looking down and failing to stifle a slight smile, Tom corrected him, "You mean my honeymoon cabin."

Luke's gravity dispersed in a chuckle and a smile. "There you go," he responded, "you'd need to be close enough for Elizabeth to help you set up for that gal of your'n."

"I reckon I would have to be close."

"Positively."

Tom changed the subject. "You know, we ought to take another look up on top before that storm yonder reaches us here. Tomorrow we'll be too busy for any more scoutin'." He was already riding off toward the trail that went through the notch as he said it.

Luke followed, calling after him, "What are we doin' tomorrow?"

Tom yelled back over his shoulder, "We're diggin' you a house."

"Before the honeymoon cabin?" Luke hollered, catching up.

"You've got a family to shelter."

Luke shook his head with feigned seriousness. "I don't think it's fair to make that girl of your'n wait."

"You're loco," Tom declared.

"Poor gal."

"Loco . . ."

"No, I mean it, Tom. We can sacrifice for your happiness."

"Chewin' on the loco weed."

And occupied by this invaluable discussion of the pressing matters of life, the two men climbed the natural trail through the notch in the rock and passed through that notch out onto the high plains of the Llano Estacado.

ONCE OUT ON THE PLAINS, the men rode to the north along the edge of the head of the canyon. They followed that edge as it curved back to the east, so that they were eventually riding along the northern edge of the canyon. They skirted the draws and small canyons cut into the caprock as they continued to the east, until, finally, they neared the mouth of the canyon and came in sight of their camp and stopped at a spot above it. They could see Elizabeth, Andy, and the children, far below and away, going about various tasks in preparation for supper.

Off to their right, the yellow-white sun, surrounded by a yellow halo, alighted upon the straight, black western horizon of the spreading tableland. Radiating out from the sun, a belt of brilliant orange settled atop the black horizon, the color dissipating into the light gray-blue sky as it pushed up and out. Nor was brilliant color confined to the western horizon. The sun's light, waning though it was, still painted the high layers of the opposite wall of the canyon, far to the south, in yellow and red, blotched here and there with vegetative green. Above that painted canyon wall, deep multihued purple and gray massed in an advancing storm that slid across the sky in a northwesterly direction like a giant ship upon a calm sea, growing ever larger, ever more defined, as it passed before them. Lightning bolts periodically, not often, struck silently through the purple and gray to the ground, save for a jagged rebel bolt that shot horizontally across the storm's upper colors. Now and then, a remnant of thunder, barely audible, carried as far as the men's hearing.

The northwesterly course of the storm suggested that it would pass by them to the southwest, but its great mass made it impossible to be certain of escape from its effects. Hence, could Elizabeth be seen, antlike below, to be gathering the children into the wagon. Still, the men sat fixedly upon their mounts, with no more thought of moving from their vantage point than any patron of the arts would move from his seat before the unfolding of a masterwork of drama. Though the storm threatened to displace even the sky above them, they sat calmly transfixed, as observers of the magnificent.

A giant, gray anvil cloud, towering into the sky's soft but vibrant blue, served as the bow of this ship of a storm. Brilliant white highlighted the anvil's front and top, highlights from the setting sun, which managed to throw an orange tinge into the gray behind the white. Orange tinged the gray-blanket base of the storm, as well, which extended beneath the entire storm far back to the eastern horizon, and upon which the white-edged anvil rode as it cleaved steadily through the soft vibrant blue.

Above the men, feathery wisps of white led the northern edge of the storm into their sky. Behind these the clouds piled up to a cobalt blue. Rows of thick, puffy, cotton-ball clouds, brilliant white as the face of the anvil, hung low from the cobalt blue sliding past overhead. Behind these first rows of cotton balls hung a second set of rows, which did not hang as low as those in front and, blocked by those in front from the sun's light, remained the cobalt blue. Behind these hung yet another set, lower like the first. These ranged from lighter to deeper orange as they extended to the eastern horizon, the cobalt blue swirling above, behind, and among these more wispy orange balls to deepen their color and definition in an arresting contrast of advancing and retreating hues.

Winds from the southwest had managed to keep the day comfortably warm, even as the men had ridden along the edge of the canyon, but with the advance of the storm came a soft, cool, easy breeze, from out of the southeast, that brushed the men's faces with a taste that strangely mixed moisture and dry cedar. The breezes picked up with the storm's advance, like child breezes pushed forward by a mother wind. Constant now, these cool breezes gently pushed forward the ship of a storm.

And all deepened as the sun slipped slowly behind the black horizon: the sky—deeper blue; the now larger and less-defined anvil to the south, and the wispy edge above—deeper white and orange against the blue; the white, cobalt blue, and orange cotton-ball rows—deeper, deeper. And deeper sank the sun, eventually to pull back its light after deepest color, slowly, to leave all above the men in pastels and then varying hues of blue and gray.

In this way did acres of moisture slide above Tom and Luke, rain draping gray from gray far to the south, yet did not a drop fall upon them as the gray clouded out the remaining blue of sky.

Luke looked out across the teeming canyon. "It's ours, Tom," he said.

"That's right."

"We can plant it, graze it, hunt it, if we want."

"Yep."

"We can cut the timber, hunt the game. It's ours, Tom."

"Yes, it is."

"There's so much promise here," Luke concluded.

"There is that," Tom agreed.

As the two men looked down upon the canyon floor, hundreds of feet below, and watched Elizabeth emerge from the wagon to prepare the supper for which they would be late, they thought much, spoke less, of the potential way their stewardship would manifest itself in this, their home upon the land.

THE NEXT MORNING the party broke camp and began moving the wagons and stock up the canyon to the site Luke and Tom had chosen for the Stuart home. In truth, they broke camps, not camp, since Tom and Andy had made their own camp near the cattle and sheep, at the pasture farther up the canyon to which Andy and Zachariah had moved them the day before. Zachariah had wanted to camp with them, but Luke had brought him back to the main camp, as he would need him and Charlie to keep the hogs moving along the next day.

With the stock up ahead, and with much of the travel over fairly level prairie in the middle of the canyon, the party made good time, taking in all that they could of the land through which they passed and gradually rising in elevation several hundred feet, as they did so.

It was not long after noon when the party reached the site and pulled the wagons onto the level area that would serve as a yard for the Stuart home. Luke halted and braked the large wagon and then jumped down from it and ran back to the smaller wagon and climbed up alongside the seat on which Elizabeth sat. "There's your new home, Elizabeth," he said, pointing to the bank he and Tom had selected.

"It's lovely," Elizabeth said, gazing at the bank, and then at the surrounding land, especially the sandy creek bed with its abundance of timber and fruit trees. "This is home, then," she said, pondering with quiet hope, and near incredulity, the reality of it.

"That's right," Luke said, as he jumped down from the wagon. "Let's unload this thing."

Elizabeth handed Rachel, who had been sitting beside her, down to Luke. Then she reached behind and pulled out young Robert from his cradle and handed him down, and he began to cry. Luke put down his daughter and then received Robert from the hands of his wife and immediately began to try to soothe the infant as Elizabeth climbed down from the wagon. Upon reaching the ground, Elizabeth took Robert from his father, and she shortly had the baby sighing against her shoulder. Luke put his arm around wife and child, as Rachel hugged her mother's leg on the other side. Elizabeth nestled in close to Luke, as they both looked over the land, the stock, and the people with whom they were sharing it.

"The Lord has truly blessed us, Luke," Elizabeth said.

"He has, Elizabeth. He surely has."

"We should pray," Elizabeth said.

Luke took off his hat, and the couple offered simple thanks for these gifts of God's providence.

Having prayed thus, Luke squeezed his wife closer to him, then let her go and turned his attention to the oxen and mules that had served them so well.

Eventually the beasts of burden were relieved of their harnesses— most for a period longer than one night, for a change—and were turned out to graze and rest. In a similar way, the human element of the expedition shed the major share of its own burden: a quiet yoke of concern and subtle anxiety attending the departure of the familiar for the wild unknown, further weighted by the responsibility for young dependents and the possibility that the unknown could well be the nonexistent. With such weight lifted, and with the additional buoyancy of enthusiasm for all that they had suddenly acquired, it was with a light air that dinner was prepared as the tent was set up and the stock attended to. All shared that enthusiasm during the noon meal with hopeful talk of the kind that had characterized their meals of the two days before.

In the afternoon, they unloaded the smaller wagon (which they would be needing for various projects), setting what could be set outside on pallets and covering it all with a wagon sheet. Some of it they placed on one pallet inside the tent. Anything else they loaded into the heavy wagon, which they did not unload and would leave unloaded until they had a home into which they could move its contents. (They had previously rummaged around in the large wagon to find and extricate such things as extra tools.) They then—with everyone's contribution, including even the blurted sentiments of young Rachel—selected and plotted, upon the chosen bank, the spot for their new home, which they would begin constructing (or excavating) the next day.

For the remainder of this day, they tended to sundry chores. Luke mended harnesses. Elizabeth tried to finish sewing gloves from an antelope hide. The children attended to whatever chores they were assigned and, along with the puppy, Charlie, played or visited one adult after another to watch each in his individual pursuit. Tom staked out a wolf hide that he had taken that morning from a "loafer" he had shot along the breaks, while moving the cattle. He had saved the skull for the brains, with which he would tan the hide. Andy was tanning an antelope hide with the brains of that animal. He had squished up the brains into a pot of water and was now forcing the stubborn dried hide into the mixture. This he was trying, for the first time, as an alternative to rubbing the brains into the hide. He would let the hide sit in the brains and water overnight, then wring it out and lay it to dry in the sun. After it had dried a little, he would pull it out all around and lay it in the sun some more, and he would repeat the process of drying and pulling until he had a beautiful, soft hide. At these and other tasks did these new settlers spend the rest of their third day in the canyon.

As people of faith characteristically do, the settlers saw providence in the mild weather that they continued to enjoy even though they were nearing the middle of October. They rose early the next day and, with the rest of creation, shook off the effects of the cool evening as the sun continued its warming ascent. Elizabeth milked the cow, while the children gathered the eggs. They all breakfasted quickly, and then Luke, Tom, and Andy rode out to check on the herd, while Zachariah watched over the sheep and Rachel helped her mother. Elizabeth cleaned up after breakfast, nursed little Robert, and then scouted around the bank that was to be her new home, and scouted beyond it, for a spring or a place in the creek where they might construct a springhouse to keep her eggs and butter from spoiling. Then she and Rachel gathered firewood to add to the dwindling supply that they had unloaded from the possum belly of the wagon, Elizabeth once again reminding her daughter of that which her husband often reminded her: to watch out for rattlesnakes, which, at this time of year, would be returning to their dens in preparation for winter. Though Luke had assured Elizabeth that the many tarantulas crawling about the canyon posed little risk to anyone, she, nevertheless, found them no more attractive than the dreaded rattlesnake.

The men found that the cattle were spreading out among the grassy knolls and hills and back up into the draws. Andy would be tending to the herd and riding line, for the most part, for the next little while, as Luke and Tom planned and built up the headquarters and ranch. Andy would help with the other work, but his first priority would be the herd.

The men returned to camp for the noon meal. When dinner was finished, Elizabeth cleaned up, with the children's help. Andy hitched up a team of mules to the smaller wagon and headed off to a spot where Luke and Tom had found a good deposit of limestone. There he would quarry the stone that they would later burn and crush for mortar. He would also quarry building stone. Meanwhile, Luke and Tom set out to dig a house.

The dugout was, and would be for some time, a common dwelling on the Texas frontier, particularly in places where timber was scarce. Even though there was plenty of timber in this canyon, the dugout would readily provide shelter and warmth against the cold of winter. Dugouts varied from the crudest holes in the ground with barely enough room for a person to sit up, no door, and vermin very much at home, to large affairs with plenty of height, stout doors, and walls coated with mortar to keep the vermin out. Those walls might have first been lined with mortared logs or rocks. A log, rock, or sod wall often stood as the front of the dugout, with windows serving, with the door, to complement that face. (Still, a dugout could get by without a window, a door, or even a face, relying on a trap door through the roof for ingress and egress.) Fireplaces were often built into the back wall and vented by high chimneys of wood, stone, or sod. Half-dugouts were only partially excavated, the rest of the walls being built up by logs, stone, or sod to a desired height. Dugouts generally had roofs consisting of a long ridgepole with lesser poles laid on either side of it to the tops of the walls. Hay or such material would be laid over the poles, and then dirt, a foot or more of it, would be laid and packed down on top of that. Of a similar kind of roof, Mark Twain once observed, "It was the first time we had ever seen a man's front yard on top of his house."

Luke, with the enthusiasm that he characteristically brought to the beginning of any project, had grand designs for his dugout—Elizabeth's term "dream house" still fresh in his mind. He had decided nothing less than twenty by twenty feet would do. It must be stone lined, with a stone front with windows (to let in light) and a stout door.

Tom thought Luke's plan a bit ambitious, if not unrealistic, but figured that the reality would make itself felt in the digging. So he said nothing to dampen his partner's spirit.

The men picked up their shovels and a pick and bar, and they made their way to the selected spot along the bank, nearly oblivious to the small figure, and that figure's puppy, who tagged along behind them. Elizabeth was not oblivious to that small figure, having noticed right away how Zachariah had abandoned his customary task of hauling the water for the after-dinner cleanup so that he could follow his father and Tom to the dig. She smiled, glad to see her son spend so much time with his father and such men as Tom and Andy (though she resisted the idea that young Andy was yet a man), especially after watching Zachariah pine away for his father for the several months that Luke had been away on the drive, months made considerably more bearable for the child due to Andy's patient indulgence.

So Elizabeth let him go, and go he did, right on the heels of his father and Tom, as if physical proximity would place the boy inside that important world of men. Once or twice or more, he asked questions about the impending process, to which Luke and Tom, both absorbed in Luke's review of his plan for the dig, would try to offer answers, however distracted and incomplete those answers proved to be. When the men finally stopped in front of the bank for Luke's final survey of the spot that would, in time, yield a home, Zachariah stood off to the side of Luke and finally cut through his father's distraction by pulling on the leg of his pants and asking a question.

"Daddy, can I help dig?"

Luke turned and looked down at the boy, so desirous to help the men, who stood pulling at the fingers of his left hand with his right, his tongue moving back and forth across his bottom lip, unable to look at his father as he awaited the answer. His usually playful puppy appeared to await the answer, as well, as he sat next to Zachariah, his black and white head, with its inquiring eyes and draping tongue, tilted, as if in attendance on what Luke would have to say. Luke smiled. He looked over at Tom, who was smiling too, and then back at Zachariah.

"Come on, Zack," he said, and he turned around and headed back to the pile of tools, the boy now doing his best, with an occasional jog, to keep up and walk alongside him, as his puppy bounded along beside, before, and behind them both. They reached the tools, and Luke picked out a sod shovel and handed it to Zachariah, whose face, with its tongue sticking out of the corner of its mouth, could hardly have registered a more balanced blend of contentment and importance.

As they walked back to the site, Luke said, "You can help, Zack, but you'll need to keep out from under Tom's and my feet. I'll show you a spot where you can dig, and you can have at it, but you've got to stay there. You understand?"

"Yes sir," was the child's reply.

They returned to the site, where Luke offered Tom a light smile and nod in regard to the newly be-shoveled status of his son. Tom smiled and said, "You goin' to help us dig, Zack?" In response, Zachariah, still looking straight ahead at the bank, pulled in his tongue just long enough to say that he was. Then all three, and Charlie, climbed the bank and—after Luke assigned Zachariah his spot to dig, which was at the other end of the area to be dug—they began to dig into the alluvial soil, long packed by time and the elements.

In this way, two men and a boy started out to dig a home. Tom and Luke worked their way through the crusty surface and into the soil beneath, each starting at an opposite corner. Before long, they were working into the ground. Zachariah, meanwhile—with Charlie alternating between sticking his nose into the boy's work and bounding off a distance to play at or investigate something else—worked himself into a sweat of exertion and frustration as the stubborn ground yielded but divots to his determined efforts. Periodically, Zachariah compared his progress to the substantial progress of the men and returned to his efforts that much more determined. After a while, Charlie gave up on the digging game, preferring to chase after birds and ground squirrels, leaving Zachariah to his determination. Still, a child is a child, and as his progress proved limited so too did his attention to the unyielding spot assigned him by his father. Consequently did Luke—as of some distraction that slowly worked its way into his consciousness— become aware that Zachariah had moved his efforts over to the looser soil laid bare by his father and was very nearly digging under one of the two pair of feet that he had been expressly warned to stay out from under.

Luke stepped back and took advantage of the opportunity to wipe the sweat from his brow with the back of his hand, and then he cupped his hands over the top of his shovel handle to rest his arms. He watched his son, unmindful of his father's absence, attack the earth.

Luke looked over to Tom, working away at his own spot, and shot a whispered yell, "Tom." Tom did not hear him, so he waited until Tom had emptied the next shovelful and shot again, "Tom."

Tom looked up, the sweat glistening in his eyebrows and running down his face. His mouth was open in a questioning attitude that allowed for a welcome pant for breath. Luke motioned toward Zachariah with a nod of his head and point of his finger, and Tom stepped back, as a smile spread over his features, to take in his view of the youngster. He too leaned on his shovel and watched Zachariah, head bent to his work, resolutely applying himself to the task at hand. Memories of his own boyhood and the perspective of a boy in similar situations immediately rose up in Tom's mind. By this time, Zachariah's exertions had put him squarely in front of Luke, in the very spot in which Luke had been digging before he stepped back.

Exchanging smiles periodically, the two watched, for a while, the boy working in his father's footsteps. Finally, Luke spoke. "Zack."

The boy continued to wrestle his shovel into the ground.

"Zack," Luke said louder.

Zachariah stopped and stepped around on the other side of his shovel to face his father. At first squinting and shielding his eyes against the sunlight that outlined his father's form, he ducked his head, picked up his shovel, and stepped closer, farther into his father's shadow, so that he could see.

"Zachariah," Luke said, "don't you have your own spot to dig?"

"Yessir."

"Where is that?"

"Over there." Zachariah pointed to the spot. He noticed Tom watching and looked down. Tom looked back to his work, stepped back into it, and started to dig again.

"But you're diggin' here," Luke said.

"Yessir."

"The ground a little slow where you were workin'?"

"Yessir." Zachariah looked down, with his tongue sticking out of the corner of his mouth. He turned his ankle up and down.

"Kind of lost your patience with it?"

Zachariah made no answer.

Patience should be a virtue in greater supply in the older than in the younger, as the older have had more opportunity to appreciate its necessity, by observing and experiencing the rhythms of time and process, and to pray for it in greater abundance. Luke's response indicated that such was the case with him.

"You can dig here in the looser dirt, but you try to keep out from under foot."

"Yessir," Zachariah agreed, as he stepped back around his shovel to resume his work, his back now turned to his father. Luke put a hand on his son's shoulder and pulled him up against his leg and patted him on the chest.

"You keep workin' hard like this, Zack, and you'll have all kinds of muscles."

Zachariah smiled, looked down, and blushed a little. Not able to look at his father after such a grand compliment, he again took a more determined look at the ground and went back to work, soon to be joined in that work by his father. Of course, the boy did get underfoot now and then, though he tried, as well as a five-year-old might (and he did do pretty well), to stay out from under. Eventually he asked Tom if he could dig by him, for which permission was granted, and for a while he continued to work with the two men.

Patience is enlightened by wisdom, and it was in wisdom that Luke and Tom both knew that a five-year-old's attention to a project would dissipate. In time, Zachariah had abandoned his shovel to reunite with the frolicsome Charlie, and he was off to other pursuits like chasing quail and prairie dogs, searching out tarantulas, floating sticks down the creek, and playing with his sister. In the days that followed, he would return to his digging, then to play, then again to work. He sometimes would ride off to work with Andy, though he was expressly warned to stay out of Andy's way when he was working with an axe or a maul. Though he watched Andy, as was allowed, he heeded his parents' orders in this regard. Then, again, he would return to work with his father and Tom.

Still, patience is no constant, and more than one time over the following days, as the men labored diligently, Zachariah was turned away from their work. And yet, for the most part, he profited from the experience of participating with the two hard-working men in carving out a house from the resistant earth. Slowly it took shape, a square box cut into the side of the bank.

The laborious task of digging and a timely suggestion from Tom persuaded Luke to moderate his design from twenty feet by twenty feet to twenty by sixteen, especially considering that they were committed to digging deep enough so that even Andy could stand upright inside with room to spare. Directing as little of their time to other tasks and chores as possible, it took the men several days to finish the excavation, while Andy tended the stock, hunted, quarried limestone and building stone, or cut timber.

Meanwhile, Elizabeth cared for the children, cooked and washed, and made a home out of their large tent, which had been little used on the trail. She milked the cow and tended the chickens. She leached lye from ashes saved from campfires and made soap from it. She churned butter, storing it with eggs in covered pots that she placed in a cool place in the creek, near where a spring flowed in. She worked, when she could, at carding, spinning, and knitting the remainder of the wool that had been provided by their sheep the spring before. She continued to work at making gloves and vests for the men, as well as other articles for them and the children and herself, from the hides the men had provided. She also helped in the preparation of pelts and skins, preferring to tan with an ooze of soft water, laundry soap, soda, and lard rather than with the animal's brain. Still, she considered either preferable to the chemical treatments that were sometimes used on hides, as either the brain or the lard treatment produced a superior hide and one that would last at least twice as long, she was sure. She also helped smoke and dry and otherwise prepare meat that Andy brought in: antelope, deer, turkey, quail, catfish, and even a buffalo.

The biggest project in this regard was the buffalo that Andy shot one day when he set out in the wagon for that task. He and Luke and Tom had all decided that they would each kill at least one buffalo, despite the buffalo carnage they had witnessed on their journey, and, perhaps to a greater degree, because of it. It appeared that the hunters were well on their way to exterminating the species. It was entirely possible, the men believed from what they had seen, that soon there would be no buffalo to hunt. They would each kill at least one buffalo to make a robe from its hide and to butcher it for meat, intending to waste as little as possible. Luke and Tom would hunt theirs later, some time after the dugout was complete and the animals' coats were thicker. Andy would hunt his now. The animals' coats were thickening in this early autumn, and now would be a good time to bring in all that meat: it would provide for the party for some time and avoid the oversupply of meat that would occur if all three men were to shoot their buffalo at the same time.

He had seen, while out riding line, that some buffalo from the herds out on the rolling plains had been grazing ever closer to the mouth of the canyon. Thus it was that one day he loaded the Sharps, some ammunition, the ripping and skinning knives, the sharpening steel, some ropes, a couple pulleys, and a wagon sheet into the wagon and drove toward the mouth of the canyon. He was gone about an hour, when Luke and Tom took stock of their situation. Having been digging daily for almost a week, they had let Andy go without them so that they could dig some more. They stood considering the situation, especially in light of their most recent encounter with some stubborn rocks. Looking out over their hands resting on the ends of their shovel handles, they questioned the wisdom of giving up the opportunity to participate in Andy's first buffalo hunt so that they could continue at the digging that would be there just the same for them tomorrow, when Andy's hunt would not. It did not take long for the shovel-wearied philosophers to see the value in experiencing that which could not be experienced again. Minds made up, they stuck their spades in the ground and ran off to catch their best horses. As they led the horses in to saddle them, Luke yelled out to Elizabeth.

"Elizabeth, we're goin' to run out and see if Andy doesn't need our help," Luke said without looking for more than a glance at his wife, so as to avoid any possibility of his professed aim being thwarted and of having his more boyish unprofessed aim, that of joining in a comrade's first buffalo hunt, being discovered.

"Oh, I'm sure he'll need your help," Elizabeth responded, drawing both men's attention away from saddling their horses to look back at her. There they saw her smiling over her wonder that they had lasted as long as they had, and they realized that they were discovered, and they smiled too.

Zachariah then ran into the scene, asking if he could go with them. Luke threw a glance over his shoulder at Tom, as if to say, "Ah, the complications of fatherhood." Then he looked down at Zachariah and called out to Elizabeth, "I'll take Zack with me; he can ride back in the wagon with Andy."

Elizabeth admonished Zachariah as Luke and Tom swung into their saddles, and Luke reached down and pulled Zachariah up to ride in front of him. "You mind your father and Uncle Tom and Andy, Zachariah. Don't you get in the way, especially with that gun and those buffalo."

"He'll be all right, Elizabeth," Luke assured her.

"I'm sure he'll be all right, Luke," she said, as she drew near to Arbuckle, on whose back Luke and Zachariah were seated, and looked up into her husband's face, "but I want you to remember that he is just a little boy, and he's got plenty of time to grow up. Sometimes I think we might be mindful that we don't rush him."

"All right, Elizabeth," Luke said, lowering his head in deference to these sentiments and to the person who spoke them, his wife, the lone woman in their little community. But then his head came up, and he smiled down upon her. "But he'll be all right this one time, Elizabeth."

Elizabeth smiled in resignation and looked down and shook her head lightly. "Yes, yes, he'll be all right this one time," she said as she waved the three off.

And off they went with that wave, down the canyon at a good pace, riding across the grassy pastures and around and through the sculpted mounds and draws. In time they spotted Andy's wagon, and they caught up with him.

Andy did not appear to be at all surprised to see them and kept right along at his pace, until Luke suggested they stop so that he could hand Zachariah over to Andy to ride with him on the wagon seat. This they did and then continued on.

Near the mouth of the canyon they saw a small herd of some thirty buffalo that had started to graze back into the canyon. These buffalo were downwind of the men and boy approaching from the west, and it did not take them long to pick up the scent of man and charge off out of the canyon, through the central corridor between the outliers, and disappear from sight.

Andy kept along at his steady pace, despite Luke's attempts to hurry him into pursuit, and Tom just followed along observing the two very different personalities and approaches to this hunt.

Once out of the canyon, Luke continued to encourage pursuit of the herd that had just fled the canyon and was continuing to flee, then graze, then flee toward the east. Andy chose instead to turn south and head toward another small herd in that direction, farther away than the other, but one that was contentedly grazing and not downwind from their approach. At about four hundred yards from the herd, Andy pulled the wagon down into a draw and parked it. He climbed down, took the Sharps from the wagon, and loaded it, as Tom and Luke climbed down from their horses. He then took the cross sticks from the wagon and headed on foot in the direction of the herd to the south. Luke pulled Zachariah down off the wagon seat, and the two men and the boy followed Andy, giving him the distance appropriate for his role of hunter.

Andy stealthily encroached upon the herd—with Luke, Tom, and Zachariah not far behind—until, about 150 yards from the herd, Andy lay down at the top of a small knoll, set up his sticks, and rested the barrel of the Sharps across them. With the rifle in his hands, he scouted the herd for a considerable amount of time. Then he shifted to bring the rifle stock snugly against his shoulder and looked down upon the herd through the gun's sights. He took careful aim. Then—*Boom*! The sound of the Sharps broke open the warm stillness of the autumn day.

He was no hide hunter intent on holding a stand, this Andy Grady, and so he shot for the heart, and immediately the big young bull he had selected began to pitch and buck and kick, causing the rest of the herd to stampede in several different directions. Then the big bull dropped heavily to the ground, and Andy—and Luke, Tom, and Zachariah behind him—stared at the massive body that had just been a vessel of stubborn, combative life, now dead.

After a moment, Andy stood up. Luke and Tom congratulated him on his good shot, which he accepted with his usual equanimity. Then the men and boy all headed back to the wagon.

Andy, with Zachariah at his side and Luke and Tom riding their horses alongside, drove the wagon to where the carcass lay. There he stopped and jumped down from the wagon. He took the knives, the sharpening steel, and the wagon sheet from the back of the wagon, and he walked to the carcass.

He had chosen well. A young bull like this would render the best meat and the best hide for a buffalo robe, and yet it was a large bull for all of its youth.

As Luke, Tom, and Zachariah looked on, Andy gutted the carcass with the Bowie knife, keeping the heart, liver, kidneys, lungs, paunch, small intestines, and sweetbread. Then, with Luke and Tom's help, he managed to work the wagon sheet under the carcass. He then tied two ropes to the wagon sheet, and under his direction, Tom and Luke took the other ends, wrapped them around the horns of their saddles, and dragged the wagon sheet with the carcass on it to the edge of a shallow but steep draw nearby. Andy followed with the wagon, with Zachariah aboard, and drove up next to the carcass, climbed down, and approached the carcass again.

This time he took two large stones and wedged one under each side of the carcass to make it stand on its back with its legs in the air. Next he cut the hide around the four feet, and then around the neck. Then, from where he had ripped open the animal's belly, he extended the cut through the hide to both ends of the animal, and then ripped the hide down all four legs to that main cut. This done, he laid aside the Bowie knife and took up one of the two Wilson skinning knives and began to skin the legs down to the body.

Luke and Tom, still in their saddles, watched Andy work as they visited with each other and with Andy, to the degree that his concentration on the task at hand would allow. Zachariah, now on the ground as close to the buffalo as he was allowed, watched the skinning attentively, occasionally asking his father or Andy a question about the process. Andy continued skinning the body of the carcass, changing and sharpening the Wilson knives frequently. Once he had the sides skinned down to the ground, he kicked one side of the skin as far under the carcass as he could. Then he leaned the carcass over on that side, onto the wagon sheet still beneath it. With the back of the carcass now exposed, he finished skinning it, pulled off the skin, and took it over and laid it in the wagon.

Andy then climbed onto the wagon, as Zachariah did the same, and drove the wagon down into the shallow draw at the point where he had crossed it earlier, where the bank was not very steep. Once in the draw, he drove to where the carcass lay up above on its bank, and he backed the wagon up against the steep side of the draw and braked it. He tied the pulleys onto the front end of the wagon bed, took the two ropes still attached to the wagon sheet and fed them through the pulleys, and then handed one end of rope to Luke, the other to Tom. These they wrapped around their saddle horns again, and under Andy's direction, they neatly pulled the nearly eight-hundred-pound carcass into the wagon.

It had taken Andy over an hour to gut, skin, and load his buffalo, which was not bad for a novice. Still, there were some skinners out on the buffalo range who were reputed to be able to skin sixty or more carcasses in a day.

As they drove back to the camp with the buffalo in the back of the wagon, Tom considered again this matter of the over-hunting of the buffalo. Here in this wagon was enough meat to last their party a considerable amount of time, as well as a good hide that would provide Andy with an exceptional robe. Ergo, here the buffalo provided food, clothing, and possibly shelter. Why not take the buffalo for what it had to offer, rather than waste most of what it had to offer to make a lot of money? What was money, after all, but a means of exchange one used to provide for oneself. And what more did one need to provide for oneself than food, clothing, and shelter, like that lying in the back of the wagon, available as it was without the terrible waste?

Granted, Tom admitted to himself, such a perspective presupposed a primitive economy and one that did not much allow for some of the finer things of life. Still, he agreed with himself that, in light of the profligate slaughter of the buffalo, it was a good idea to sometimes consider the primitive, the simple, the fundamental when taking stock of the world in which one lived, not with the aim of going backward, but rather with the aim of going forward wisely. Such consideration could be part of making a cultural examination of conscience, more or less, so as to head off that culture in its headlong run into wrong. But, Tom considered, would not a cultural examination of conscience properly demand the examinations of consciences of the constituents of the culture, and would not that come down to the individual constituents making their individual examinations of conscience? And then, for any good to come of those examinations, would not those constituents need to make them honestly and then submit to their honest conclusions and live them out? Ah, Tom considered, there one returned to the matter of the *conscientious*, the *lawful*, the *semi-lawful*, and the *lawless*, and to the matter of the tree chosen in the first garden in disobedience and the tree embraced in the later garden in obedience. And Tom considered those two trees and those two choices, and he prayed silently, as he and his friends made their way, with their buffalo, into and up the canyon toward home.

Back at the camp, as Andy pegged out his hide, Tom and Luke selected three heavy logs out of the many that Andy had harvested for their building projects. When Andy had finished pegging the hide, the three men arranged the logs into a kind of tepee, and they hung the carcass from it. Andy saved the head for the brains, which he would use to tan the hide once it was cured. The liver, kidneys, lungs, sweetbread, paunch, and intestines were soon cooked by Elizabeth or Andy—or fed to the dogs, depending on the item, as Elizabeth had not quite developed Andy's appreciation for all of these delicacies. Later the men butchered the carcass, and after Elizabeth selected certain cuts of meat (including the tongue) for meals for the next few days, she soaked the remaining meat (hundreds of pounds of it, including the heart) in a brine in whatever suitable containers she could find, the largest of which consisted of hides that the men had stretched across poles driven into the ground. After four days, she added sugar and saltpeter to the brine and let the meat cure in that for two more weeks, during which time Andy constructed a small, simple smokehouse of poles and hides. When the meat was thoroughly cured, Elizabeth and Andy smoked it for almost two weeks in Andy's smokehouse.

For at least the first few days of this whole meat-curing process, Luke and Tom kept digging at the house. Throughout their days of digging, the weather cooperated, offering pleasantly warm days with dry winds from the southwest that, at times, rose to substantial gusts. Still, no windstorms or rainstorms or cold weather hampered their efforts. Coolness seeped into their world each night, as the sun slipped behind the caliche cliffs, making for pleasant evenings of rejuvenating sleep.

The afternoon of the day they finished their digging saw a drastic change in the weather. The wind switched around to bear down from the northwest. Temperatures plummeted as the men scrambled to cover with wagon sheets the excavation that would be their home. They were not about to watch it be eroded by rain. And rain threatened, as a line of deep gray clouds descended with the wind from the north, creeping ever farther into their cliff-bordered horizon. And they watched, after covering the dugout and anything else that needed covering, to see the advance of this norther: a meteorological phenomenon that was not unheard of down in Medina County, but that was more common, and potentially more deadly, in this region of their new home.

Elizabeth, too, scrambled to cover—to cover her children, Luke, and herself. She gathered the children into the tent, where she dug into the trunks, set on the pallets, in search of the woolen items that she had packed to outfit them all against the cold. After first wrapping the baby in a wool blanket, she soon had Rachel and Zachariah dressed in woolen caps and mittens and wrapped in wool blankets. Then she pulled out wool coats for Luke and herself, and opened the tent flap to look outside. The wind tore the tent flap from her hand, as she spied Luke, Tom, and Andy standing near the excavation, looking toward the north.

The approaching grayness was palpable, as it sent its messenger gusts across the high plains to drop off into the canyon below and shoot among the draws and breaks and strike the vulnerable pioneers from all directions. Elizabeth called for the men to come in, but Luke, intent on watching the storm, ignored the call. Elizabeth persisted until Tom said, "I guess we'd better go inside," and Luke grudgingly gave in to his wife's concern.

They all managed to get inside the tent and tie down the flaps before the ice-cold drizzle began to pelt at its sides. Warmth was gone. Cold now permeated their world. Not a frozen cold—no, that would come at night—but a freezing cold, a more liquid cold, spitting and saturating through the flesh into the very marrow of the bone.

Tom dug into his bedroll and brought out a wool coat and a slicker. Andy dug into his own roll to pull out a heavy woolen poncho that his mother had knit. Luke sought to dig out his own layers, but Elizabeth had already done so. And Luke tolerated, for a moment, her fitting sweater and coat on him, before he gruffly took them from her and put them on himself, as Elizabeth stepped back a little and continued to assist him in unconscious pantomime. Luke satisfactorily clothed,

Elizabeth hurried over to a flour sack and pulled from it pairs of fur-lined gloves, which she had made from deer and antelope pelts for just such weather as this, and handed out a pair to each of the men. They gratefully acknowledged the surprise gifts and commented profusely on their good quality and timely utility, to Elizabeth's delight.

Luke looked at the huddling children and, seeing an opportunity to work on a new metal appliance, said in an aside to Tom, "We could set up that stove."

Tom pondered the suggestion, weighing the likelihood of a quick return to warm weather and the greater efficiency of waiting until they could set up the stove permanently in the new house, and he did not feel so cold. Still, he too looked at the children and then at Elizabeth and replied instead, "We could."

Luke then lightly backhanded Andy's arm and nodded toward the door of the tent. Then he untied that tent-flap door, and he departed with Tom and Andy into the miserable blowing drizzle, securing the tent flap behind them. They fought through the wind to the large wagon, where Luke and Tom climbed inside and began to maneuver furniture, tools, and anything else, to try to get the stove out in a way least injuri-ous to any other items or to the men themselves. Tom thought occasion-ally of the children to remind him of the worthiness of the venture. As Luke moved one item after another from here to there in the tight space and dug around for stove lids and other loose pieces of that appliance, Andy stood outside the crowded wagon, the drizzle soaking into his poncho and collecting in the rim of his hat to drip off in various places and contribute to the further saturation of the poncho. At last, he too climbed up into the wagon and under the shelter of the wagon sheet, and he managed to find a place to stand by working his feet into two small spaces between some of the items packed there. Tom looked back from his place among furniture and stove, still not convinced of the necessity of the undertaking, and his eyes met those of Andy. "That's all we need, Andy," he said, "just one more body in here."

Andy responded without batting an eye, "It's wet out there."

"Huh," Tom offered in the form of a light laugh, "I suppose it is. Here," he said, passing back stove lids and other parts of the stove that Luke had managed to pull out from the well-packed cargo, "why don't you take these into the tent?"

Andy took those pieces of stove, put them down on the end of the wagon, and then jumped off the end. He loaded them up in his arms and departed for the tent.

Before long he was back, and at Luke's command, he unloaded the stove piping from under the wagon and took that into the tent. He returned again to help unload some of the tightly packed items that would need to be removed from the wagon to make room for the stove. Once Luke and Tom would get an item, like a chest of drawers, to the edge of the wagon, Tom would hop down from the wagon to help Andy on the ground. And on the ground, Tom and Andy would try, as best they could, to keep the item covered with a sheet against the rain, as they removed it from the shelter of the wagon and carried it through the elements to load it onto a pallet. Finally, the stove itself could be unloaded and hauled into the tent, and it was. There Luke began to set up the stove (though Tom would have taken a more care-ful, systematic approach to it) as Tom and Andy returned to the wagon to reload the items that had been unpacked, drying much of them with towels once safely returned to the wagon.

By the time Tom and Andy returned to the tent, Luke had the stove set up, the piping hooked up and vented out a tent flap designed for that purpose, and the beginnings of a fire crackling in the stove. But Tom and Andy were not going to enjoy that fire just yet. Instead, with Luke, they went back out into the rain and hauled firewood over to the outside back wall of the tent, where a flap would allow easy access to it. They brought into the tent a healthy supply of that wood and, before long, were enjoying a fire sufficient to warm the coldest tent.

The rain varied from drizzle to downpour for the rest of that after-noon and evening, changing to snow in the wee hours of the next morning, before it stopped altogether. The pioneers woke to a gray day, a full gray that covered the sky with pregnant clouds hanging low, looking as if they were huddling and holding back their rain against the cold. The earth too, with its own gray cast, held on to its moisture in the cold. Thus did a dampness permeate the start of this canyon day, a chill dampness that held and slowly absorbed the thin speckling of snow dispersed among the grasses and scattered upon spots of rock and earth least hostile to its delicacy.

Into this cold gray ventured Luke, Tom, and Andy, with hats tied down over their heads and slickers covering the layers covering their bodies. Even Andy wore a slicker, an old one that the Stuarts kept for Elizabeth, or anyone else who might need it. And each of the men wore his new fur-lined gloves.

They caught their mounts and mules and, in time, had them saddled or hitched up to the wagon. Luke drove the wagon, while Tom and Andy rode. They headed for the breaks that lined the base of the escarpment. They sought cedar. They knew of one particularly promising spot, farther down the canyon, where a stand of large cedar and juniper stood. There Andy had begun to cut some timber, though, up until now, he had mainly concentrated on quarrying stone.

Andy's efforts had been fruitful. A pile of good-sized stones already lay near the dugout awaiting the mason's craft. He had also quarried and collected a good deal of limestone, which he had left near where he had quarried it, as Luke and Tom had told him to do, because the site offered a good location to burn and crush the lime.

There was no point in burning and crushing lime in weather that threatened so much moisture. The burned lime would only reabsorb the moisture burned out of it, and the crushed lime, doing the same, would set up as it lay. Furthermore, with the freezing temperatures at night, the mortar that they would use in the rock front of the dugout could freeze and then crack, and be worthless.

Naturally, the men hoped for dryer, warmer weather in which to finish the dugout, but in the meantime, the grasses were being watered, and they could still harvest wood for the dugout, other buildings, and the pens. The breaks were full of cedar, and oak was also available, and no better woods could be found to meet their construction needs. Where lesser woods would do, the ample supply of cottonwood would suffice.

The men cut and hauled wood that entire day. The next day, with no improvement in the weather, Luke and Andy cut and hauled more. Tom, in the meantime, dug out from the large wagon the woodworking tools he had purchased in San Antonio. These he would use to convert the wood from logs to lumber and to make use of that lumber in the building of their ranch, relying on skills he had learned in Wisconsin and developed while constructing buildings for the railroad and while working on other construction projects in Denver. With his tools he began to cut, rip, and rive lumber from the logs. As he generated the lumber, he stacked it with plenty of space for curing.

ON THE AFTERNOON OF THE THIRD DAY of the norther, the wind shifted around to come from the southwest. Dry warmth again drifted into the canyon and soon swept up the telltale moisture of the previous two days' precipitation, so that the next day the men could burn and crush lime. It was also nearing the end of October, the time when Matthew Colmey had said that his surveying crew could be sought out by way of Hank Smith in Blanco Canyon. The party agreed that the next day Tom would ride to Hank Smith's Rock House to find out where to find Colmey so as to lead his crew to the canyon.

Hence, the next morning, as Luke and Andy headed down the Escondido to make lime, Tom left for Blanco Canyon. Having bid Tom farewell, Luke and Andy drove the wagon to the site where Andy had quarried and collected the limestone, and they found there a good flat-rock surface on which to crush the lime. Nearby they dug a kiln, which they filled with mesquite wood. Then they piled limestone on top of the wood, and, with a little help from some coal oil, lit the wood on fire. The fire blazed up. In time, the fire settled down, the mesquite producing excellent coals, and did its work on the limestone, even making some of it explode as the expanding moisture sought its escape. Eventually, when the limestone was sufficiently burned, they removed it and crushed it with sledgehammers on the selected surface nearby. In this manner, they burned and crushed enough lime, over the next few days, to make the mortar necessary to build the stone face of the structure, and, in addition, to make a good start on rendering (coating with mortar), at Elizabeth's request, the floor, and possibly the walls, of the structure against penetration by vermin.

They hauled the lime back to the camp. There they mixed it with sand, sifted wood ashes, and water to produce a good mortar. With that mortar, they laid up the double-layered stone front of the dugout, with stone lintels over the openings for the door and windows. The front completed, they reinforced the inside dirt walls with cedar logs, chinked with mortar, and began to render the floor, leaving a bare walkway for access to the back wall, where they intended to build the fireplace. While the mortar cured, they dug a fireplace and chimney at the back of the dwelling, which they rendered, as well, and built up the chimney with stone and mortar to achieve a good draw. They even stuck a piece of stove pipe through the wall into the chimney to accommodate the stove, which they would set up next to the fireplace. Then they rendered their walkway and allowed it time to cure. Meanwhile, they went to work on a stout cedar log and some lesser logs, cleaning and dressing them for the roof, and on other logs to be used for the fence-posts and rails of planned corrals.

It had now been almost two weeks since Tom had left, and as Luke and Andy cut fence posts, Tom led the surveying party of Hill and Colmey, Dallas, Texas, through the notch near the intended site of his future house and into the Escondido. Though Luke would joke that Tom had taken his time in fetching the surveyors so as to avoid the work that he and Andy had put into the ranch in his absence, Tom had been doing some work of his own. After he had learned what he had been able to about the surveyors' whereabouts from Hank Smith in Blanco Canyon, he had caught up with the crew where they were locating lands to the northwest of Blanco Canyon in central Hale County. They had lost one chainman, who had left them after an Indian scare the week before. Tom had volunteered to serve as their chainman to expedite their work. They had completed that survey, but still had needed to locate more certificates farther to the northeast in Hale County, which was as close to the Escondido as they would be on this outing. Accordingly, Colmey had intended to make the survey in northeast Hale County on his way to the Escondido, and then run a line to the east and then north from it to locate the canyon. And this the Colmey party had done, with Tom serving as chainman.

Tom had assured Colmey that he would serve as chainman for their survey of the Escondido, as well. Nevertheless, this duty was postponed for the first few days after their arrival, as the surveying party left the canyon to search several miles to the north for some corners established by Jot Gunter and John Summerfield of Gunter, Munson and Summerfield, surveyors and foresighted land speculators working out of Sherman, Texas. The Colmey party also took time out to check and write up some survey notes from the previous surveys, to check and maintain instruments, and to take in a hunt.

As the Colmey party was thus employed, Tom joined Luke and Andy in their work on the house. The three men laid the stout cedar ridgepole from the back of the structure to the slightly peaked stone front. This they further supported with two vertically standing cedar poles, each set equidistant: one from the front wall, the other from the back, and each from the other. To complete the structural base of the roof, they laid, close together, smaller cedar poles from the ridgepole to the top of the walls of the dugout. These they then chinked with mortar. Then they covered this roof structure with hay, then covered the hay with nearly fifteen inches of dirt, which they packed down.

Tom helped with all of this, but most of his time went to fashioning and setting wooden jambs, lintels, and sills, and to fashioning and hanging a door and some shutters, using the lumber he had processed some two weeks before. At last, a solid plank door of oak covered the doorway, hinged with heavy steel hinges that had been purchased in San Antonio. Hinged shutters of like design and substance covered the windows. Door and shutters alike were fitted with hardware, also acquired in San Antonio, that would allow them to be barred with thick oak planks.

Finally, their house lay complete: a neat edifice of stone set into the bank, square to the top of the walls, with a squat stone triangle above that. And above that lay the earth-covered roof, presenting little more than a ripple in the contour of the bank, so well did it fit in. This, as Luke had intended, was indeed a first-rate dugout. In fact, as dugouts went, this one—with its stone front; chinked-log walls and roof; mortared floor, fireplace, and chimney; hinged oak-plank door and shutters—was all but opulent. And now, it was ready for occupancy.

They moved in the stove first and situated it next to the fireplace and hooked up the piping. Then they began to move in much of the rest of their belongings, which included a bed, a dresser and mirror, two old trunks, a larder, a table and chairs, dutch ovens and other cooking utensils, canned goods, china, and heirloom silver. They reassembled what had been disassembled and built crude shelves and furniture, which included stacked bunk beds for the children and for Tom and Andy. These beds they covered with wolf pelts.

They placed the table and chairs centered between the east and west walls in the back third of the dugout, the kitchen end. The beds were placed along the outer walls. Zachariah and Rachel's stacked bunks, Zachariah's on top, ran along the west wall of the room, with the heads of their beds about four feet from the back wall. At the foot of their beds rested Robert's cradle. Elizabeth and Luke's bed made up the distance along the west wall from Robert's cradle to a foot or two from the outside rock wall. On the other side of the room, Tom's and Andy's stacked bunks (Tom's on top) ran along the east wall, with the heads of their beds a good twelve feet from the back wall to allow room for a kitchen and eating area, the stove, against the back wall, being on their side of the room. The feet of their beds were kept about a foot from the southern rock wall. All of this was set up, and suddenly their dugout was very full.

They had all agreed to share this one dwelling through the coming winter, with the plan to construct separate dwellings as time and weather would allow. Elizabeth would take care of the children and manage the domestic chores, especially the cooking. The children would assist her as they were able, with Zachariah taking a guided responsibility for the domestic stock of pigs, chickens, and milking cow, and for the few sheep. He and Rachel would also help collect firewood. The men would manage the stock and the range, and hunt, butcher, and skin game. They would also quarry stone and cut timber and work on corrals, dwellings, and other buildings.

This arrangement would prove to work remarkably well. Though this group consisted of seven strong personalities, conflict would be seldom and insignificant. Even the children would behave well, with exceptions usually due to tiredness or illness. Often enough the baby would cry in the night, and Elizabeth or Luke would pace the floor holding young Robert, trying to soothe him, but none would complain, as all the adults had been raised in families and expected no less from a helpless infant.

This harmony was not uncommon upon the frontier. Perhaps in such a setting, where the starkest loneliness surrounded the pioneer at all times, kept at bay only by the one or few human beings with whom the pioneer might come in contact, those few human beings took on a preciousness closer to the ideal intended by God and sought by all religions in seeking their harmony with him. Hence, harmony became necessity, as faults and weaknesses were overlooked (and often enough embraced) in the human need for friendship toward the human destiny of communion.

Complementing that need, in developing that harmony, was an enthusiastic commitment to a shared goal. These members of the Stuart-Schurtz party were building. Together they were building. They were building a home, a way of life, with a commitment to a common stewardship of the land. And they were discovering, as well, discovering various aspects of their new home and way of life. They were too busy in this positive exertion, in this positive work and discovery, to allow much room for the negative energy that begets and fosters discord.

And so they moved in, to live in harmony and continue to build toward a common goal. That goal included ownership of land. Toward that end, Luke and Tom, with suggestions from Elizabeth and Andy, had scouted out, as their work had permitted, the best parcels of land to purchase to make the best use of their certificates. It was with this in mind that, on the day before the surveyors would start their survey, Luke and Tom rode out into the canyon.

A mile or more down the canyon from the headquarters, they stopped at a familiar spot on a bank above Stuart Creek, and looked down on the plentiful grass that grew throughout the floodplain.

"We'd want to buy this for the hay," Tom said.

"Yessir," Luke concurred.

"All right, then," Tom continued, "we'll be purchasin' the head of the canyon, a good legal claim on the water with that. We'll purchase those sections with the best pastures that we've looked out. We'll get this hay, and those other hayfields we've looked out. That'll give us legal ownership to about half this canyon."

"That's right."

"The rest we can just claim as range, and have a better claim to it than most of the ranches in west Texas have to their own ranges," Tom concluded.

"That's right," Luke quickly assented, with the stronger emotion that accompanied ownership.

"That is," Tom added, "until we can buy it."

"That's right."

After a pause in which the men looked out over the land and pondered this ownership, a not-so-common concept in the open-range mentality of west Texas at that time, Tom said, "Well, I guess we've looked out the best of it."

"I reckon so." Luke slowly nodded his head in agreement. Then they sat quietly until Luke added, "It's hard to believe, ain't it, Tom?"

Now Tom nodded his head and answered with an affirmative, "Hmph."

"I mean," Luke continued, "all I owned five years ago was a horse, then, over time, a few head of cattle. Now I'll own a canyon, a ranch."

"We," Tom corrected him with a grin.

"That's right, 'we,'" Luke corrected himself, "but, I mean, this was outside the realm of possibility, Tom. You look out there now, and you can imagine pastures covered with Seven Ox cattle. You can even imagine neighbors within twenty miles. Who knows, some day even a church and a school. That would be Elizabeth's dream come true."

Tom nodded thoughtfully, respecting and appreciating his partner's musings. After a moment he said, "A school would need a teacher, wouldn't it?"

"That's right," Luke said with his chuckle-laugh, as he turned toward Tom. "A lady teacher lookin' for a honeymoon cabin."

"You're startin' again."

"Don't tell me your thoughts weren't tendin' that way."

"You're startin' again."

"There's some mysterious ways, right there, right under my nose, ain't there?" Luke continued.

"Well, mysterious ways aside," Tom said, "there won't be any mystery as to who owns this canyon, and some of the land above it, as well. Now we just got to stock it."

"That's right," Luke said. "It's happenin' as we speak, but won't be long before we get some blooded stock in here, and then we'll see things grow. As long as we can keep those lobos at bay."

"They'll take their share before we've finished with 'em," Tom conceded, "but we've got our share of pelts already, and there's plenty more to come."

"That's right," Luke said, and they both looked out over the land again, in silence.

After a pause, Tom said, "We're buildin', Mr. Stuart."

"That's right, Mr. Schurtz. We surely are."

TOM WENT BACK TO WORK for the surveyors the next morning.

As the days passed, while the canyon was being surveyed, Luke and Andy plowed a fireguard around their ranch headquarters. Prairie fires were a serious threat, particularly during the fall and winter months, and could easily destroy the ranch's grass and timber, along with much of its stock and any wooden constructions. Though they had caused no fires, the surveying party had provided Luke, Tom, and Andy with a visible reminder of how campfires and smoking tobacco added their potentials to that of lightning for starting prairie fires. And so, Luke and Andy lost no time in beginning their work of plowing two furrows in a loop, roughly three miles around, that would enclose the dugout ranch site, the site farther up the canyon on which Tom would build his house, and the land in between and around these sites. The men would then plow two more furrows, a few feet inside the first two, leaving a strip of land in between the two sets of furrows. Then, on those rare days that were not windy, they would set fire to the grass on the strip in between the inner and the outer loops of furrows. On those days, at least until Tom could return, even Elizabeth would help. One of the men would fire the grass between the furrows; the other would stand by with a wet sack to prevent the fire from jumping the plowed furrows; and Elizabeth—with the baby in the wagon with her and the other two children not far away—would drive the wagon carrying extra sacks and a barrel full of water, in case there was a need to fight a fire that had jumped the furrows.

Fireguards were not all that kept the settlers busy while Tom worked as a chainman for the surveyors. Luke and Andy also worked on building corrals, riding line, and hunting for food and for the protection of their livestock from wolves, coyotes, and even a couple of panthers. Luke also shot a large bear during that time, not as much to protect the stock as for the meat and the hide. Meanwhile, Elizabeth continued to make the dugout into a home.

The surveyors benefited from all of this during the time that their camp was set up near this home, a period which they tried to extend as long as possible, as far as their work would allow. It was while they were camped near the dugout that they enjoyed some of the fruits of Luke's and Andy's hunting, and Elizabeth's cooking and baking—and darning and washing, too, for that matter. Elizabeth's heart went out to these men, so long in the field without the comforts of home. So, she provided what she could, which may not have been in the best interest of expediting the survey of the canyon.

Still, there was no evidence that the settlers' hospitality in any way slowed the surveyors' progress. If their progress was slowed at all, one might first have suspected the canyon terrain with which they had to contend. Or one might have suspected the trouble they had with the transit, which required repair and the need to correct lines they had already run, or with the wagon, which broke a wheel when it jarred through some breaks and required repairs of its own. Or one might have suspected the norther that descended upon them halfway through the survey and swept the high plains with its raw, frigid winds for two days, letting those winds deposit their cold into the canyon as they rushed by overhead, dropping frequent errant gusts to stir up that cold below. Or one might have suspected Tom's insistence that the surveying party run around and close the survey, as much as this was practical. Such closure was more the exception than the rule in Texas frontier surveying of that time, because there was such a rush to locate certificates on the best lands available as quickly as possible before someone else could do so. Still, Matthew Colmey, despite his own concessions to the expediency of hurried location, did not balk at Tom's insistence on closure, as it better fit his personal surveying ethic, though it took more time. All of these causes, and others, might have been more rightly suspected than that of the settlers' hospitality, if the surveyors' progress was indeed slowed. Nevertheless, if one considered how much the surveyors valued the settlers' hospitality, then one's suspicion of that hospitality as a possible cause for slowing their progress, if indeed their progress was slowed, would have been better founded.

But again, there was no reason to believe that the surveyors' progress was slowed by any cause. The pace of progress of a survey depends upon so many variables that it is truly relative, and there was every reason to believe that Matthew Colmey's survey of the Seven Ox Seven Ranch in Escondido Canyon was progressing at the pace that was appropriate for the conditions and expectations. And then one day, it was complete, and the Matthew Colmey surveying party packed up their instruments, broke camp, made their farewells to the settlers, and started back to Hale County to locate more certificates. When they would be finished in Hale County, they would return to Jacksboro, where Colmey would finish writing up the field notes of his surveys, sign them, and have them approved, signed, and duly recorded by Mr. W. Callaway, district surveyor of Jack Land District. Then Colmey would take all his field notes and certificates to Austin to have them filed in the General Land Office. After ninety days, to allow for conflicting claims or surveys, the patents to the land would be issued to the Stuarts and Tom by the land commissioner and the governor. Considering that Colmey intended to be out in the field for at least three more weeks, the Stuart-Schurtz party, owners and managers of the Seven Ox Seven Ranch, would not see their patents for several more months. Such was the nature of time on the frontier of the Texas Panhandle in late 1877.

In that time, Tom rejoined Luke and Andy in the work about the ranch, and the members of the party settled into more of the pattern that had characterized their participation in time before the arrival of the surveyors. And time passed, but not very much of it before the settlers disrupted their pattern of participation in time for a reason that, like the surveying, held promise, but promise of a far more universal nature.

FAR OUT IN THE FUTURE lay the end of the several months that must pass before the Stuart-Schurtz concern would receive its patents for its land. The immediate future held its own promise, as the settlers prepared to celebrate the birth of their Savior, Christ the Lord. Toward that end, Tom invited the rest of the party to join him in keeping an Advent wreath, which he fashioned out of cedar branches and candles, to mark the Sundays of that season that anticipates the birth of the Lord. And in more immediate anticipation, on the day before Christmas, in the face of a norther that dropped temperatures and also moisture in the form of snow, Luke, Tom, and Andy rode out—the weather contributing to the appropriateness of their task—to choose a Christmas tree.

The snow had begun early that day, after the wind had shifted around to come down from the northwest and a pillowy blanket of gray had slid into their canyon sky. The thick fall of heavy flakes hinted at the possibility of blizzard, and so Luke and Tom had thought it best to secure a Christmas tree before that blizzard materialized and they were bound to the dugout. Andy joined Luke and Tom, because he had a significant role to play in this venture, and all three saddled their horses and headed out into the snow that had already begun to accumulate.

Andy had been told, some time before, to watch out for a well-formed cedar that they could cut for a Christmas tree. When Luke had asked him, the day before, if he had found such a tree, Andy had indicated that he had, and now he led the way to it. Hence, three dark figures of man on horse moved through the whiteness, the men bundled and wrapped, their hats secured with wool scarves, the loose ends of which flapped and fluttered about them as they bent their heads over their mounts, whose heads also bent against the worsening storm. Whiteness thickened, deepening beneath them, swirling ever tighter around them, sticking ever longer upon their hats and clothing and the manes and coats of their horses, and yet the horses plodded forward into that encompassing whiteness. Andy's course led along Schurtz Creek, a landmark ribbon of darkness winding through the white. Once Andy stopped and looked intently at the creek and then out beyond it at the land on its other side, lost now in the opaqueness of distance in the swirling snow.

Luke rode up beside him and yelled out from his wraps over the sound of the wind, "We there yet?"

Andy shook his head "no" and continued on along the creek. Luke stayed where he was as Tom pulled up alongside him. "You think he knows where he's goin'?" he shouted to Tom. "It's gettin' pretty bad."

"He probably knows where he's goin'," Tom yelled back, "but do we want to go there? I mean, it's not gettin' any better out here, and if we just cross the creek and ride in among the breaks, we can gather us a cedar and head back."

Luke nodded his head and looked out ahead at Andy's dark form, nearly invisible, and then invisible, and then nearly invisible again, through the snow. He nudged his mount, and Tom followed, and they headed toward Andy. They caught up to him finally, partly because he had stopped again and was again looking intently at the creek.

Luke called out, "Andy, maybe we ought to just pick a tree and head back out of this."

Andy shouted back, "We're here." He looked out across the creek toward the land beyond, that he could not see.

Andy led the way across the creek, and Luke and Tom followed. They continued to follow, as Andy worked his way into the breaks over a light, and now covered, trail that he had developed while harvesting timber. Luke was about to call a halt to the expedition and select any one of the cedars they had been passing, when Andy pulled up in front of a particular specimen. Tom and Luke pulled up beside him. Andy dismounted and pulled out a saw from his saddlebag and trudged to the tree. Luke looked over at Tom, who looked back, and they too dismounted and trudged to the tree. There all three stood: Andy in silent consideration of his tree, Luke and Tom indulging in silent consideration of their own.

Finally, Luke spoke out to Andy, "This is why we came all this way in this storm?"

"Yes sir," Andy said without looking at him. Then he went around to the side of the tree, to an open spot low in its form where he could reach in with the saw, and he knelt in the snow and began to cut at the trunk of the cedar. Luke looked at Tom and shook his head, then turned and plodded through the snow to his horse and removed his rope from the saddle and returned to the tree.

It did not take Andy long to cut through the trunk, and once the tree was down, they wrapped an old wagon sheet around it, and Luke fastened his rope around its base. Standing up, he yelled to Andy, "Now, you think you can find your way back in this?" as the snow was even closer around them than before. Andy nodded his head, and the three men mounted their horses, and Andy led off, followed by Tom, followed by Luke, followed by the cedar, wrapped in the wagon sheet, being dragged at the end of his rope.

The storm had worsened, and if it had not been for the creek and Andy's excellent sense of direction, the men might never have found their way back. As it was, Andy, at a number of points along the way, doubted that he was on the right path, but he followed his instincts and kept his doubts to himself.

At last they arrived at the dugout, and they unsaddled the horses and turned them out into the picket corral that they had constructed for them, a corner of which was covered. Then they dragged the tree toward the dugout.

Inside the dugout, a fire crackled in the fireplace, and lamps burned on the table and in the kitchen area, warming and lighting the earthen home to a mellow coziness. Zachariah and Rachel sat at the table making ornaments for the tree out of magazines, cloth, ribbon, and dried flowers. Robert sat in his highchair, asleep at the moment. Elizabeth stood at the stove, where she was popping corn in a pan. A bowl of dried currants and juniper berries awaited the popcorn. These were all to be strung together with needle and thread into garlands for the tree.

Suddenly, a heavy pounding fell upon the door, and Elizabeth hurried to the door and lifted the heavy oak bar that secured it against Indians or white renegades. She flung open the door, in disregard of the caution that Luke had demanded of her whenever he, Tom, and Andy were not at home. Three dark, wrapped figures stomped into the light and warmth from the cold and swirling white, bringing it with them as they came, the penetrating storm trying to penetrate this haven of warmth and light, but failing, as Elizabeth pushed shut the door against it, leaving the last flakes that had managed to invade the room to waft to the floor and immediately melt. With the figures had entered a tree, a cedar of good height and girth.

The men stomped and brushed off snow and untied scarves and removed gloves and hats and coats. Elizabeth was there to receive Luke's wraps and shake them out. She hurried them over to wooden racks by the fireplace, where she hung them. She returned for Andy's and Tom's, and hung them over chairs, which she slid near the fire.

Robert had been awakened and had begun to cry with the sound of the pounding at the door. Elizabeth removed him from his chair and, holding him, returned to the men gathered around the tree. Zachariah and Rachel were up from their chairs and around the tree as well. "Is that our Christmas tree, Daddy?" Zachariah asked Luke.

"That sure is," Luke replied, and throwing a glance at Andy, who held the tree, he continued, "and a rare specimen it is, too. We rode all over this canyon just to bring home this prize."

Tom looked at Andy, whose light smile belied all other appearances that he had ignored the comment. Andy merely picked up the tree, which stood about six feet tall, and moved it over against the east wall between the head of Tom and his bunks and the back wall. There he stood it up straight and stepped away from it to hold it at arm's length for all to behold.

The tree did have a fullness to it, with height, and a certain balance that was pleasing to the eye.

"It's a lovely tree, Andy," Elizabeth said.

"Thank you," Andy said. "I thought so," he added, turning his eyes on Luke.

"It's the best tree in the canyon," Luke corrected. "We ought to know, we saw every one, or would have, if there weren't a blindin' blizzard ragin' all around us the whole time out there."

Tom chuckled at this comment, and Andy laughed with his eyes, and Luke added his chuckle-laugh. But then Luke remembered something. Turning on Elizabeth, he said, "Why didn't you check through the hole before you opened the door?" Luke referred to a small hole they had bored through the oak door and fitted with a sliding cover, so that they could open it and peer out to see who was at the door.

Elizabeth responded, "Well, I knew that you would not be out very long and that you had been out plenty long already, and I was worried. Besides, who would be out in this storm this far from any other place?"

"No tellin' who might be out there," Luke said with a seriousness that registered in his face, particularly across his eyebrows. "Elizabeth, don't ever open that door without checkin' who's out there first." Looking at her intently and not finding serious enough consideration in her face, he added, "I mean it, Elizabeth, not just for your sake, but for the sake of the young'uns."

"All right," Elizabeth responded, without looking at him. "I won't open the door. Now let's get on with our Christmas preparations."

Luke looked at her still. "I mean it," he said more quietly, though no less intensely.

"I won't," she said, bumping his arm with her own and looking at the tree and wishing to drop the subject.

"All right, then," Luke said. Then he looked at young Robert in Elizabeth's arms. He reached out and tickled Robert in the ribs with his finger, and Robert squirmed and squealed. "Little Bob," he said, "this'll be your first Christmas. Hey, Elizabeth, little Bob's first Christmas."

"That's right," his wife answered, looking into the eyes of her baby son, whose steely eyes looked back into hers.

Luke, with a wistful smile at this time of Christmas, when time is measured and remembered and projected, turned again to Andy and his tree. "So, this is our Christmas tree," he said. "What do you think, Tom?"

Tom looked over the tree for a moment, then stepped back and said, "I think it is a fine tree." And Andy's eyes shot a smile at Tom.

"Well," Luke said, "it'll have to do, because I'm not about to go out there after another one."

With that said, Andy leaned the tree against the wall and stepped to his bunk, as all the rest of the party watched him. There he reached under the foot of his bunk and retrieved a wooden stand he had made for the tree. It was constructed in such a way as to allow the base of the tree to be suspended in a bowl of water placed beneath it. He began to fit the stand to the tree, and Tom and Luke stepped forward to lift the tree up to make his task easier. Once the stand was secured with rawhide thongs, they stood the tree up. All admired Andy's ingenuity and the beauty of the tree. Elizabeth fetched a bowl of water, and Andy lifted the tree so that she could set the bowl under it, and then he lowered the base of the tree into the water.

The tree was admired again, and then all turned their attention to their own preparations for the celebration of the next day. The children, under Elizabeth's direction, returned to making ornaments. Luke joined in to string popcorn and berries. Tom began to carve ornaments from pieces of cedar he kept at the foot of their bunks. Andy lay on his bunk writing letters. Elizabeth began to prepare the noon meal and to make preparations for the meals of the next day, Christmas.

And so the day went, inside the warm dugout, safe from the blowing storm. The ornaments were made, the tree decorated, foods prepared, and a host of details completed for the next day. At supper that evening, Luke read from the beginning of the Gospel according to John. He read God's own Word:

> In the beginning was the Word, and the Word was with
> God, and the Word was God.
> The same was in the beginning with God.
> All things were made by him; and without him was not
> anything made that was made.
> In him was life; and the life was the light of men. And
> the light shineth in darkness; and the darkness com-
> prehended it not. . . .

He was in the world, and the world was made by him,
and the world knew him not.

He came unto his own, and his own received him not.

But as many as received him, to them he gave the power
to become the sons of God, even to them that
believe on his name:

Which were born, not of blood, nor of the will of the
flesh, nor of the will of man, but of God.

And the Word was made flesh, and dwelt among us,
(and we beheld his glory, the glory as of the only
begotten of the Father,) full of grace and truth. . . .

And of his fulness have all we received, and grace for
grace.

For the law was given by Moses, but grace and truth
came by Jesus Christ.

Following this reading from the very Word of God, they feasted on
the eve of the birthday of the Word made flesh. The feast was long and
full of the talk of people who share their life in a meal before God.

In time the meal ended, and they began to clean up. Finally, it was
time for the children to go to bed. They were excited and hardly
seemed capable of sleep. They had hung their stockings over the fireplace and now awaited, with much anticipation, what Santa Claus
would bring them. Reminded that Santa Claus would not come until
they were asleep, they finally resigned themselves to rest and were
shortly asleep.

Then how old Saint Nicholas did his work, stealing into this warm
dugout, far removed from any other human habitation, at the bottom of
an untamed canyon cut into the remote and wild tableland of the Llano
Estacado. How he did his work. What gifts did he stir up from hiding
places, ever so clever? What presents did he bring forth, true labors of
love? In what spirit did he participate as he gave and gave and gave?

And some time in the wee hours of the morning, the final lamp
was extinguished, and the quiet work gave way to sleep, only the glowing embers in the hearth remaining awake and working, adding their
warmth to the immeasurable warmth of spirit. But embers tire, too,
and as the early morning hours wore on, their crackling grew less constant,

their glow less bright. Eventually the embers retired to their own sleep, beneath their blanket of ash, still adding their subdued warmth to the warmth of spirit, itself subdued in sleep, the sleep of the denizens of this happy home.

FIRST ASLEEP PROVED FIRST AWAKE, and the children's expressions of excitement and joy served to wake the rest. Soon Elizabeth's feet joined those of the children already on the floor. She roused the embers from their sleep, and shortly after that, the smell of coffee served to rouse the men from their beds and bring them to the table, where they sat over cups of coffee and warmed sweet rolls (which Elizabeth had made the night before) as the cold, snowy norther whistled, howled, and moaned outside.

Elizabeth had earlier taken down the children's stockings from above the fireplace for them, while the embers within the fireplace still slept. Now those embers were wide awake, stirred to life as soon as the stockings had been removed and reinvigorated with a healthy supply of mesquite wood from the well-stocked woodbin in the corner. Once again the dugout glowed.

The children had emptied their stockings on the table and were showing the grownups the contents. There were molasses candy and hard candy, and sweets and toys made by familiar hands, all from that grand giver, St. Nick. Then there was the tree, and what was to be found in its branches and beneath? Well, among it all, there were moccasins from Andy; and gloves, vests, britches and a dress from Elizabeth; and pelts from Tom and Luke. There was a wooden version of a Winchester rifle that fit Zachariah just right, and there was one very lonely little doll who could only be comforted by darling Rachel. These had come from the combined efforts of the children's parents. There was more too, including, there amidst the branches, a rolled up paper, wrapped in a red ribbon, that no one seemed to know anything about.

No one, except maybe Tom, who encouraged Luke to take the paper down and unroll it. This he did. Then Luke looked at it, with Elizabeth, who was seated next to him and leaning against him so as to peer at the paper, as she sought to sate her own curiosity regarding its contents.

"It's a contract," she said, "from Mr. Colmey, the surveyor."

"What does it say?" Tom asked her.

Elizabeth perused the document. "There must be some mistake," she said at last, "this contract is for twelve sections, not for six."

"There's no mistake," Tom said.

Luke and Elizabeth raised their faces to Tom, their expressions of bewilderment meeting, in his face, an expression of exuberant joy that he could hardly contain. "There's no mistake," Tom said again. "We own twelve sections, which, with the alternate school lands, gives us control of twenty-four sections."

Luke and Elizabeth continued to stare at him in their bewilderment, their mouths open in unspoken questioning.

"I bought six more certificates from Colmey and had him survey the entire canyon and some land up on the cap above and some out beyond the mouth below," Tom told them. "We agreed on a reasonable price," Tom said of the twenty-five cents an acre ($160 a section, total $960) that he had negotiated with Colmey for the extra six certificates, located and registered with patents delivered. "I'm sure my runnin' chains for him and our all-around hospitality helped with that. Besides, Colmey's a good man, and I think he just likes us generally. He located all twelve certificates and will do all the registerin' and will deliver the patents. He'll be out on the Staked Plains with crews locatin' land for two- or three-month stints, and can deliver them while out on one of those. He knows where we are. Of course, it will be some time before the patents are issued, as he won't register these surveys for another few weeks, I imagine, and then there is the ninety-day wait for conflictin' claims, but he says there should be no concern about that, as no one has been into this specific region. He did say somethin' about how it was a good move to secure this land before Gunter and Munson, land agents out of Sherman, moved into this area, since they're hard at it securin' a good deal of the land to the north of here, up in Charlie Goodnight's territory.

"But, as it is, we've got the entire length of the canyon and, of course, some overlap of the land above the cap, on the sides; a section, two with the alternate, down beyond the mouth of the canyon out on the rollin' plains; and a section, again with an alternate, up on top of the cap, northwest of the head of the canyon. And, of course, I purchased this section," he added, pointing to the ground under them, "which means we own clear and outright the land that our homeplaces rest on, yours here and the place I intend to build up on the flat. They don't fall on any school alternates, on any appropriated public domain, but on our own privately owned property, which makes me rest a little easier about all this appropriated school land that'll lie checkerboard throughout our entire ranch. This sets us up pretty well to purchase more land if and when we want to expand out onto the low rollin' plains beyond the canyon mouth or onto the high plains up on top of the caprock. There's plenty of good grass, either above or below, for grazin' in the warm months before we drive the beeves back into the canyon for winter, and plenty for hay, especially in some of those playa lakes above. Of course, if these school alternates come up for sale, we'll want to buy 'em before we do anything else."

Luke and Elizabeth—and Andy, too, for that matter—still stared. Even the children, though not fully comprehending the message, appeared to comprehend its gravity, as they too stared. Finally, Luke and Elizabeth looked at each other and then looked back at Tom, and Elizabeth said, "But Tom, how did you . . . How were you able . . ."

"Yeah, where did you get the money, Tom?" Luke translated for Elizabeth.

"Well," Tom said, "as you all know, the first six sections come out of what I contributed to this enterprise for the purchase of land. For this second set of six sections . . ." Tom paused after saying this. Then he said it again, "This second set of six sections—there's a bit of a tongue twister for you." Then he chuckled, and then so did the others, and Luke, Elizabeth, and Zachariah all took their turns at the phrase before Tom resumed his answer. "Anyways," Tom finally said, "these new six sections I'll pay for off some holdin's I have in a bank in Denver. I wrote Colmey a check for the first half of payment for the new six sections, payable immediately, and sent with him a letter for the Denver bank instructin' them to hold the other half in his name and to give him notice that such has been done, the money to be forwarded upon receipt of a second check, which will be issued by me upon receipt of the patents for the land. That should just about clean me out. Fact is, I'll be about broke, busted. I guess I'll be what they call land rich and money poor. I should say 'we.' That land is registered in the name of the partnership."

In this way, Tom accurately related the state of affairs of the ranch and himself. His once considerable savings were now all but wiped out. He had contributed some twenty-four hundred dollars to the partnership. In addition to all that, there was that mysterious check for a substantial amount that he had written and sent to his brother John, back in Wisconsin, while he and Luke had been outfitting in San Antonio for their move to the canyon.

Luke and Elizabeth had listened intently to what Tom had related and were now more overwhelmed than bewildered. Again, they looked at each other. Then Elizabeth looked down.

"But Tom," Luke said, "our agreement was for you to supply just that first thousand for land, besides the four hundred apiece we both put up for operating expenses . . ."

"That's right," Tom said, "but you folks supplied the beeves, and most important, you supplied the idea. We took a risk. Now the risk is gone. We know what we have, and it is better than what we hoped for. I have this to offer the partnership right now, for the good of all of us. Won't be long before some land agents get in here and start crowdin' us out of this canyon. Now we need to buy, and I am able and am satisfied in the fairness of addin' this to my contribution to the partnership. So, there's really no more to say about it."

Naturally, the Stuarts did not readily accept that there was no more to say about it, but in time, they said little more, except for expressions of appreciation, which Tom waved off. Slowly the reality that they owned the whole canyon settled in upon them, and that realization permeated their experience of Christmas, enhancing their joy even beyond the bountiful joy that they would normally experience at that sacred time of celebration.

Celebration, indeed, flowing, in its traditional way, through Scripture, prayer, and the singing of hymns and carols, to the table and the feast to be enjoyed there. The food for the meal had been provided by the Creator, prepared by human hands, and now would be shared in the human communion of need and sustenance. Having themselves hunted, gathered, or raised, and then prepared what the Creator had provided for the meal—and thus having an intimate, working knowledge of whence came their sustenance—these feasters, far more than those of a later more comfortable era, may well have had an innate understanding of the belief of their Jewish Savior's own people that to share one's table, one's meal, was to share one's very life. At this Christmas celebration, meal had appropriately become feast, as sustenance had swelled to bounty, and what bounty. There were turkey, venison, buffalo, and bear. There were preserved vegetables and fruits. There was honey. There were pies and cakes and sweetbreads. And there was the second of the three bottles of wine that Elizabeth had bought from Mrs. Smith and secreted away, the first of which they had enjoyed on their first night in the canyon. There was even brandy, for the men, which Elizabeth would allow after the children had gone to bed.

Before the meal, of course, it was time to remember whence came their sustenance and salvation, and the party turned to Scripture and prayer. The Stuarts, still overwhelmed by Tom's surprise gift, handed him the family Bible and invited him to read from Sacred Scripture. Tom received the Bible with reverence, turned to the Gospel according to Luke and read:

> And there were in the same country shepherds abiding
>   in the field, keeping watch over their flock by night.
> And, lo, the angel of the Lord came upon them, and the
>   glory of the Lord shone round about them: and they
>   were sore afraid.
> And the angel said unto them, Fear not: for, behold, I
>   bring you tidings of great joy, which shall be to all
>   people.
> For unto you is born this day in the city of David a
>   Saviour, which is Christ the Lord.
> And this shall be a sign unto you; Ye shall find the babe
>   wrapped in swaddling clothes, lying in a manger.
> And suddenly there was with the angel a multitude of
>   the heavenly host praising God, and saying,
> Glory to God in the highest, and on earth peace, good
>   will toward men.

And so this very active Word of God graced their table, working on them, in them, as they allowed it, feeding a far brighter, warmer glow within each of them and among them all, far brighter and warmer than even that bright, warm glow that radiated from the lamps and hearth to saturate their atmosphere of feast. And as that glow from the lamps and the hearth mellowed to deeper tones, so too did that glow within each and among them all, with the help of food, drink, and communion. Eventually, the children mellowed toward sleep and finally were in bed, and Elizabeth and Luke, and Tom, and Andy all sat before a mellow fire indeed, the men, even Andy, each with a glass of brandy, mellowing, mellowing.

They talked and they listened and they further mellowed with the day deeper into night. Eventually, after a comfortable quiet had descended upon them all, as they sat bathed in the warm glow of the hearth(the only light in the home, as all lamps had been extinguished) Elizabeth, sitting back in her chair, her legs drawn up and a blanket around her, quietly said into the fire, "'For God so loved the world . . .'"

Quiet again. Then, after a pause, Tom's voice broke into the quiet.

"It is amazing," Tom, warmed by communion and fire and a touch of brandy, said toward the fire from his comfort of satiation. "It is amazing," he said again, this time closing his eyes and nodding his head forward with emphasis on the penultimate syllable, "that God, the Creator of the universe, should entrust his only Son to man, in the form of a helpless infant. I mean, I have met many men that I do not trust, but God, who knows the very hearts of men, knows all the evil that can be found there, all the evil that is in us, and still, he entrusts his Son to mankind, in the form of a helpless infant. He offers his Son, in the most dependent and helpless form a human being can have, to mankind, places him in the hands of the most innocent girl in a world of sinful man. That is love," Tom emphasized by leaning his head forward and raising his voice, "to give oneself over. Can we even imagine givin' ourselves over in helplessness to those we do not trust, for their own good, to aid and abet them, to save them. Talk about 'divine condescension.'"

The others looked at Tom for a moment, pondering the unfamiliar terminology used in his conclusion. They were not surprised at this, as they had grown accustomed to Tom, every now and then, expressing himself in ways that they did not completely understand without some thought. After a moment, they looked back at the fire, and Elizabeth picked up on the theme with which Tom had concluded, as

far as she understood his conclusion. "'While we were yet sinners . . . ,'"
she said into the fire.

"That's right," Tom said. "It would be like handin' little Bob over
to a young girl surrounded by a band of renegades, out of love for the
renegades, except that God's love for his Son would be infinitely greater
than ours for little Bob, or yours for little Bob," he said, nodding
toward the Stuarts. "It would be like trustin' little Bob to the renegades,
out of love for them who did not deserve that love. That's how much
he loves us. That's how we can so completely trust in his love. That!"
Tom emphasized, "is beyond comprehension."

And all agreed in quiet affirmation and meditation, meditation
that sought that transcendent comprehension, meditation that eventually gave way to sleep and dreams as Christmas day 1877 slipped slowly,
slowly from present to past.

AS WITH CHRISTMAS, so with the days that followed, each sliding
at its own pace from future through present into past. The settlers slid
with those days, with *time*, working, eating and drinking, resting and
worshipping in greater docility to and in greater harmony with that
integral attribute of creation, realizing the truth, in living out the reality, that "for everything there is a season, and a time for every matter
under heaven."

Undoubtedly their occupations of husbandry, hunting, gathering,
and homemaking, in this land so unfettered by man's control and yet
so comfortably in their possession, allowed time to subtly communicate more persuasively her natural rhythms, cycles, and seasons. And
yet, the celebration of the Christmas season in their new canyon home
must not be discounted for its possible effects upon their receptiveness
to time's subtle communication. Perhaps, in that place, at that time,
under those circumstances, with the settlers engaged in their present
occupations, the celebration of the Incarnation—that event in which
almighty God, in the Person of the Son, humbled himself to enter into
his own creation, to be bound by its limits, to be subject to its time—
and all that it meant, worked deeper into their hearts, stirring up a
deeper humility in deeper appreciation of divine providence, rousing a
deeper contentment with the unfolding of time according to the
Creator's will, in the rhythms, cycles, and seasons he set within his

creature *time*. Perhaps in that deeper appreciation of the Incarnation, which has as its culmination the Paschal mystery, through which "all that Christ is . . . participates in the divine eternity, and so transcends all times while being made present in them all," perhaps in that, however well or poorly they understood it, the reality of the sanctification of all time settled more deeply into their beings and made their participation in sanctified time more amenable to its rhythms, cycles, and seasons. For Tom and Andy, this celebration and deeper appreciation also brought with it a growing sense of missing the celebrations of the liturgical year and of the sacraments.

Nevertheless, if this celebration and deeper appreciation improved their participation in time, if it sweetened and made more fulfilling their acquiescence to the rule of time in God's creation, then it did so through their participation in the motivating principle of the Incarnation and its resultant Paschal mystery. It did so through their participation in that principle, the greatest theological virtue, that perfect prerogative of God, in which man was created to share. It did so through their participation in love.

This was real love, not an easy, weak, groundless, and ostentatious attraction, too often mistaken for love (especially in a time far in the future from that of the founding of the Seven Ox Seven Ranch). This was love, not a feeling, but an act of the will, involving commitment, sacrifice, duty, and work, lived out in the day-to-day relationships the settlers enjoyed with each other within the larger context of their relationships with God. This was love, often communicated, silently enough, through a communion of several labors directed toward a common goal of living a good life in time, with the hope that they might enjoy an infinitely better one beyond time.

Still, for now, they loved within time, and the season in time was winter. Winter weather in the Panhandle of Texas varied greatly. Most days were cooler, growing increasingly so as the season progressed. Nights would be cold, dropping below freezing often enough. Though sunshine was a common commodity in the Texas Panhandle, still winter had some overcast days, with some of those days offering rain or snow. More frequent were the days of wind, which were common to any season in the Panhandle, often enough gale-force wind, kicking so much dust into the air, at some times of the year, that teeth crackled with grit whenever one closed them, and eyes could burn and swell shut and crust over. Exceptionally warm, sunny days would occasionally creep in among those more evident of winter, sometimes a few in succession. Then too would come the cold, bone-chilling cold that could snap down upon them in the form of a norther. The norther might last several hours or several days, but then the wind could shift and warm winds could return and melt the snow, drying up any evidence of its late blanketing. Snows were as infrequent as summer rains, but they could be as torrential when they hit. In short, the land lay subject to a wide range of varying weather that often manifested itself in capricious, agile shifts to extremes.

The settlers, including the children, enjoyed the winter weather, and all enjoyed, more when of choice than necessity, the opportunities to wrap up against the cold and venture out into it. The men further enjoyed the winter weather because it was freeing their cattle of Texas fever, deadly to more domesticated stock. When the worst of the weather precluded outdoor work, there was plenty for the men to do indoors, like working hides, mending harnesses, cutting and tapering cedar shingles, sharpening tools, cleaning guns. And Elizabeth always had plenty to do with cooking, baking, and otherwise working in the kitchen, carding, spinning, knitting, sewing, and cleaning, among other things. All could read and respond to letters, which the surveyors had conveyed to them from the post office at Fort Griffin. Their responses would not be sent until the surveyors returned with the patents, unless someone else passed through on his way to a settlement before that. Besides letters from various members of the various families and from the Richters, there were also letters from Mrs. Molly Banks and Miss Nancy Hawkins for Tom, and several for Andy from the young ladies he had met at the Kendall wedding near Fort Griffin.

Still, there were few days that did not allow some outdoor work, and the settlers accomplished much during their first winter in the canyon. Throughout the winter, the men hauled timber and rock from which to construct houses, corrals, and outbuildings, and they began some of that construction. They rode the line of their range, which amounted to little more than riding a survey of the canyon and a little beyond, both above and below it, as the canyon's walls did most of the work of containing their herd. Nevertheless, riding line did allow them to check for bogged cattle and to turn back any cattle that might have strayed too far out onto the plains beyond the canyon.

Riding line also allowed them the opportunity to assess the toll the local predatory population was taking on their stock. And it allowed them the opportunity to do something about it. Often enough, they shot and skinned lobo wolves and coyotes that were taking their toll, especially the wolves, on their stock. They would see a puma, which they called panther, now and then, but shot very few of that elusive quarry. More often they would hear the puma in the darkness, its womanlike scream cutting through the night air of the canyon, right into the spines of any who heard it. They shot few bears, with Andy shooting none. He had had his opportunity to shoot a bear, though, early on, not long after their arrival in the canyon. In that incident, a large bear had broken out of a thicket of currants near where Andy was felling cedars. Andy had grabbed the Winchester he had laid nearby. The bear had charged to within a few yards of him, while he had leveled and held the gun on the animal. Finally, the bear had stopped and risen up on its hind legs, stretching to its full height, as it had run its eyes over Andy and voiced its loud complaints at his intrusion. Andy had had a perfect shot at the large bear, but he had not taken it. Eventually, the bear had lowered itself back onto all four legs, and had turned and ambled off into the brush, as Andy had watched it go. After the bear was out of sight, he had returned to his work.

There were plenty of other bears to shoot, but the men of the Seven Ox Seven did not bother them much, unless for protection of selves or stock. It was not that the meat was not good. On the contrary, it was exceptional. At least most of the party thought so. But Andy did not eat it. Characteristically, he never said anything about not liking bear meat, nor did he make any show about it; he just did not eat it. Neither would he use bear grease along with the brains of an animal to tan its hide, as Tom would do. The fact that one of such a small number of people would not eat its meat gave Luke and Tom little reason to hunt bear, given the variety and quantity of game in the canyon. So, they relied mainly on turkey, quail, antelope, and deer for meat, all of which were plentiful, especially the turkey, several of which could often be taken with one shot of a shotgun, they were so thick.

From the furred animals they took the pelts. These they cured and tanned either with the animals' brains or with Elizabeth's ooze. This left the settlers with some excellent skins and hides from wolves, coyotes, wildcats, antelope, deer, and the few from panthers and bears. Many of these they tanned with the fur intact to yield warm coverings for beds, floors, or walls, or to be sewn into warm coverings for the body. Others they stripped of their fur—by scraping it off with the back of a knife or a tool, or by pulling the skins back and forth around a post or the trunk of a tree, or, when weather permitted, by pegging the skins down in the creek and letting the current take off the fur. These supplied a variety of leathers that the members put to use according to the properties of each. In addition to those hides and skins the pioneers could use, they continued to accumulate others to sell, when the opportunity would present itself, as they were first-rate, well cured, and well tanned to last many years.

THE SETTLERS WOULD NOT SELL THEIR BUFFALO ROBES, though. These were highly prized, and they made warm coverings for beds in winter, sometimes too warm in the well-insulated dugout. Nor would they sell the large buffalo hide, the thick leather of which they used to mend reins, bridles, and harnesses.

Yes, Luke and Tom had shot their buffalo. They had taken them in January, one of the four months when they were best for robes. They had butchered them, too, wasting as little meat as possible (though not as little as Andy had), and had cooked, salted, and jerked, or otherwise preserved the meat. They had taken another buffalo, too, a huge old bull on his last legs. His hide, not of the quality to make a good robe, had been of the quality to provide the tough, thick leather for reins and harnesses. His meat had been of about the same quality as the hide. Still, they had made the most of what they could eat of it, and had shared with the dogs and scavengers much of what they chose not to eat.

The men had seriously considered taking another buffalo each, while the season for a good robe lasted, and they finally agreed that Andy would shoot one more buffalo, so that he could have a robe at its best. That buffalo, too, they butchered, and they preserved as much of the meat as possible. Beyond that, they could not justify shooting any more that season due to the waste of meat that would inevitably occur if they did so, as they had committed to a conscientious stand on the matter in light of the wasteful slaughter they had seen en route to the canyon. Ironically, it was because of that very slaughter that they even considered shooting more buffalo. In light of what they had witnessed, they seriously wondered if there would be another opportunity to take a buffalo robe if they waited until the next winter. Thus, they were tempted to take their chances with wasting meat now to get one more robe before there were no more to get. Instead, they decided to stand on principle, and they shot no more buffalo that winter.

That there might not be buffalo the next winter was difficult for them to imagine, as they would ride their lines down into the mouth of the canyon and out onto the low rolling plains beyond. There they would see several small herds grazing contentedly and naturally, the dark sturdy bulks of their members dotting the great windswept and undulating sea of grass made golden by the sun, set in a sky of cloudless blue. This was but a sample of the great southern herd of untold millions of buffalo, the mass of which had continued to the south, with herds the size of those in the region of the Escondido dropping off at various grazing grounds along the way, on this perennial migration that had begun as far north as the Platte and could reach all the way south to the Pecos.

Periodically though, when the wind and air were right, the distant boom of a Sharps rifle would carry as far as their hearing, and the men of the Seven Ox Seven would be reminded that that great migration of beasts was followed by a great migration of men. Still, they never did see a buffalo hunter in their region that winter. In the Escondido, they were far enough away from the prime hunting grounds that any hunters in their vicinity would be few and scattered. There would be no reason for buffalo hunters to seek out the Escondido, even if they had known that it existed. Theirs was a quest for the buffalo, and when in the field, they had little interest in anything that would distract them from the pursuit of their quarry. Nevertheless, when the men of the Seven Ox Seven would hear the reports of a far-off Sharps, they would be reminded of what they had seen on the trail and of the slaughter that was taking place at the same time on the grazing grounds to the south, and they would wonder anew about the survivability of the great southern herd, if not of the entire species.

Others had wondered before them. As early as 1835, Josiah Gregg, the noted traveler and resident of the southwestern United States and northern Mexico, had already recorded his concerns that the "continual and wanton slaughter" of the buffalo by "travellers," "hunters," and "Indians" was "fast reducing their numbers, and must ultimately effect their total annihilation from the continent." In 1841, the Osage Indian agent noted in his annual report that the reduction in the numbers of buffalo would soon make it necessary for the Osage to learn to farm. Later, in 1854, W. B. Parker, a member of one of Captain Randolph B. Marcy's expeditions into western Texas, wrote of the buffalo that "this animal is rapidly disappearing from the plains." Still later, after the Civil War and the resumption of the buffalo hunt, citizens and legislators wondered, too, as bills were drafted and proposed throughout the 1870s, at both the state and national level, to stop the slaughter, but to no avail.

There was foresight in this wondering, because this season of 1877–78 would be the last of the great buffalo hunt in Texas. A disappointing season would follow in 1878–79, marked at its beginning by the wondering of the hunters, who would set up and wait on the plains of Texas for that ageless grand migration that would never come again. They would shoot what they could of the buffalo that remained, but there would not be enough to accommodate them all. So most would leave for other occupations, while a few would continue to pursue the bison remnant, and still others would leave for the north to hunt the great northern herd of buffalo, until they had all but exterminated that by 1884.

Few would have imagined that such a diminution was possible in any amount of time, let alone within the period of a few short years. Many had witnessed, until those few short years, the massive annual migration of these massive beasts of the southern herd, which Charles Goodnight said, "would probably average a hundred and twenty-five to a hundred and fifty miles long, and twenty-five miles wide. The buffaloes in it were as thick as they could conveniently graze and left not a particle of grass behind them." At a much earlier time, the buffalo had ranged from Canada to Mexico, and from the Blue Mountains of Oregon to the Appalachians in the East. Even after the buffalo had been reduced to that number inhabiting the Great Plains, General Philip H. Sheridan, Major Henry Inman, and Robert M. Wright had estimated the great herd to contain at least 100 million head of buffalo, being over one hundred miles wide and of unknown length. Of the buffalo, William T. Hornaday, who served as the superintendent of the National Zoological Park, would write in 1889:

> Of all the quadrupeds that have lived upon the earth, probably no other species has ever marshaled such innumerable hosts as those of the American bison. It would have been as easy to count or to estimate the number of leaves in a forest as to calculate the number of buffaloes living at any given time during the history of the species previous to 1870.

Such numbers could presumably withstand considerable reduction before raising any serious concerns about extinction. It has been estimated (based on statistics that Captain John C. Fremont received from a member of the American Fur Trading Company, which he published in 1845) that the Indians of the Great Plains had killed in the preceding decade some five hundred thousand buffalo annually. And the buffalo population was sustainable at that rate of reduction, according to Dr. Hornaday, who claimed: "As the buffalo herds existed in 1870, 500,000 head of bulls, young and old, could have been killed every year for a score of years without sensibly diminishing the size of the herds." And yet, by 1878 in the south, and 1884 in the north, the hunt would be all but over.

The buffalo would be all but gone. And the buffalo would be missed. Even now, while the slaughter of the southern herd was at its peak, the buffalo were already missed, and were thus the more sought after. And here, right out on the plains beyond the mouth of their canyon, were buffalo. That knowledge contributed to a certain vigilance among the Seven Ox Seven men, so that, while they were out riding their lines, they did not watch for straying cattle and for predators only. They watched, as well, for a potentially more serious threat to their home upon the land. They watched for man.

The buffalo would be missed by the buffalo hunters, to be sure, but only as a means to quick monetary wealth, for the most part, which, however strong it might be, is not an attachment that roots very deeply. Regardless, it was not the buffalo hunter for whom the

Seven Ox Seven men primarily watched, as most were much farther
south, and those few in their vicinity would have little reason to seek
out the Escondido Canyon, even if they knew that it was there. Even
then, they would need to find it. That is not to suggest that they would
be treated inhospitably if they did find it. Though the members of the
Seven Ox Seven Ranch would make known their opinions about the
buffalo slaughter, and though they would disallow, as far as was possible, the slaughter on their range, still, they would practice, as was their
wont, that generosity to the stranger that was common on the frontier.
They would also practice the wariness that was necessary for survival
on the frontier. It was in that wariness that they were not unmindful
that, though there were some fine people, even families, among those
hunting the buffalo on the plains of Texas, there were also some of very
sorry reputation, some of the worst of the criminal element, hunting
out on the frontier under assumed names in a land where people knew
enough to ask few questions.

Nor was it the genuine outlaw for whom they primarily watched,
though they did watch for outlaws, as few places would have provided
a better base of operations for a band of outlaws than the Escondido
Canyon. Nevertheless, they believed that few white men had ever
heard of the Escondido, and of those few, they believed that most
regarded it as a place more of legend than of reality. Then, too, if some
outlaws had heard of it and did regard it as real, they, like the buffalo
hunters, would still need to find it. Beyond that, there was the remoteness of the place. This had to be taken into account, considering that
criminals were somewhat reliant upon the proximity of people, and
their property, upon whom to perpetrate their crimes. The Escondido's
location in a kind of no man's land, even more remote than the wilderness settlements of Hank Smith to the south and Charles Goodnight
to the north, offered little incentive for men bent on a life of crime to
sojourn there, especially since there were still relatively remote and hidden places much farther to the east that could offer the outlaw some
degree of proximity to the towns, ranches, stagecoach lines, and cattle
trails. Still, the men of the Seven Ox Seven took into account that
remoteness, especially with plenty of water and game, might be just
what some of the more desperate outlaws would be seeking. They also
considered that knowledge of Charles Goodnight's ranch in the Palo

Duro might draw some of that element, who might seek to make a quick profit off that gentleman's loss.

What the Seven Ox Seven men did not know was that they might well have had Charles Goodnight to thank for the lack of the outlaw element in their vicinity. Goodnight, the winter before, on a trip from Dodge City to the Palo Duro, had ridden into the camp of Henry Born on Commission Creek in the northern Panhandle, not too far inside the Texas boundary with the Indian Territory. Born, known as Dutch Henry, led a band of as many as three hundred outlaws. Once in his camp, Goodnight had let Dutch Henry know that he wanted to keep the country around the upper Red River, where he was building his ranch in the Palo Duro, "peaceful and lawful," and that he had the men to do it, though he did not like using his hands in that way. He had told Dutch Henry that if he would stay north of a designated creek about twenty-five miles to the north of the Palo Duro, Goodnight would stay to the south of it. Dutch Henry had said something like, "Well, old man, you are plain about it, but it is a fair proposition and I will do it." French brandy had sealed the deal, which both had kept from that day on.

Still, it was neither buffalo hunters nor outlaws for whom the men of the Seven Ox Seven watched primarily. It was, instead, for those by whom the buffalo would be most missed, those whose very life and culture had depended on the buffalo, those whom General Philip Henry Sheridan had sought to subdue by encouraging and supporting the extermination of the buffalo and opposing any measure to stop it. It was the American Indian, and in the region of the Escondido Canyon, that meant the Comanche. There were Kiowa and Kiowa-Apache, as well, allies of the Comanche, and, more lately, the Cheyenne, but it was the more dominant Comanche for whom the region had been called *Comancheria*, and for whom the New Mexican traders were called *comancheros*, and whose language had become the lingua franca of the South Plains, and whose name had long struck fear into the hearts of various peoples, red and white alike.

The Comanche are a Shoshonean people. At the time that the Comanche were first "definitely identified" by white men, the Shoshone could be found across a vast area that included most of Wyoming, a large portion of Idaho, and parts of Nevada, Utah, Colorado, and Montana.

The Comanche apparently separated from the Shoshone some time before the beginning of the eighteenth century and thereafter migrated toward the south. They may have moved southeast down the Arkansas River from the region of its headwaters in the Rocky Mountains, so that, by around 1700, they were situated in eastern Colorado and western Kansas. And they never stopped moving.

A nomadic people, the Comanche continued to drift to the south and east, pushing out anyone in their way (predominantly the Apache) to eventually occupy and dominate a region that measured roughly six hundred miles (north-south) by four hundred miles (east-west), bounded roughly by the Arkansas River on the north, by the Pecos River on the west and southwest, by the settlements around San Antonio and Austin on the southeast, and by the Cross Timbers (or just west of the ninety-eighth meridian) on the east. And yet the Comanche ranged far beyond this *Comancheria*, as far as the upper Missouri River as late as 1802, and nearly as far as central Mexico as late as the first half of the 1800s. They ranged within *Comancheria*, as well, each band of the tribe forever moving its main camp within a general area associated with it.

Three main elements of the Plains Indian culture contributed largely to the mobility of the Comanche. These were the tepee, the buffalo, and the horse.

The tepee, a portable dwelling of a dozen, or two, long pine or cedar poles arranged conically and covered with tanned buffalo hides, sheltered the Comanche against every kind of weather. Tight against the prairie sun, wind, rain, sleet, snow, and cold, it also incorporated venting above and below to allow for a fire in winter or a cooling draft in summer. It could be erected in fifteen minutes and taken down in less time than that, then loaded travois-fashion on horses, with the other household belongings, and soon be ready for a move.

This portability of the tepee was one of the main reasons for its longevity as the shelter of choice for the Comanche. For the tepee's portability served the Comanche's mobility, and the Comanche's mobility depended a good deal upon the mobility of the migratory bison, the buffalo, from which they took the hides that covered those tepees, and from which they also made clothing, bedding, tools, weapons, and shields. They took a good deal else from the buffalo, as well, to answer a good many other needs and wants. They took its flesh and organs for food; they took its bones for tools; they took its paunch for containers; they took its dung for fuel; they even took its blood for drink, when there was no water to be found, which may best illustrate the nature of the Comanche's reliance on that great beef of the prairie for their sustenance. For it was a vital reliance, not just of the individual Comanche, but of the Comanche people and their way of life.

In the summer months, when the buffalo were fat and their hides fully shed of the spring molt, and again in the late fall, when the buffalo were still fat and their hides fully clothed in the winter coat, the Comanche people participated in the communal buffalo hunt. In an assembly led by the war chiefs of the band, but to which all were welcome, the time for the hunt was determined. Then runners went out to locate and prepare a site for a temporary hunting camp. These were followed by the young men and women and the older children, but not before they had enjoyed at least one night of the Hunting Dance, in which both men and women participated. This nighttime dance might be celebrated at least one more time by the hunting party after they had left for the hunting camp.

Lacking the military fraternities or soldier bands found among the other Plains Indians, the Comanche trusted the organization of their hunt to a hunt leader and to the respect that the participants had for the rules of the hunt. Under the hunt leader's direction, once a herd had been located by scouts, the Comanche men—most often stripped of all but a breechclout and mounted bareback on horses trained to be rope shy and to respond to knee pressure alone for guidance—closed in on their quarry. Riding in against the wind, arranged in a semicircle (if the terrain allowed for it), the hunters suddenly closed in upon the buffalo, surrounding and circling them and killing them with bows and arrows or with lances, as the buffalo bulls circled the cows and calves in defense.

When the killing was done, the Comanche men dismounted to skin and butcher their kills, unlike the men of many Plains Indian tribes who delegated these tasks to the women. Leaving only the spine, rump, head, and the heart (the heart was left as a religious observance), the men returned to camp with the meat wrapped in the hides. There the women cut up and dried the meat and pegged the hides out on the ground to cure, in preparation for their eventual tanning. Then the hunt was on again, and the cycle continued until enough meat and hides had been procured, and it was time for the hunting party to return to the main camp with the fruits of the hunt. There the hunting party might enjoy a Buffalo Tongue Dance, a feast that, ironically, included no dancing or singing. The ceremony, hosted by a married couple of noted virtue, culminated in a noon meal of buffalo tongue, after a morning of ritual preparation. Thereafter, the people subsisted on what the hunt had provided, supplementing it, when needed, with smaller hunts until the semiannual communal hunt came round again.

Round again and again and again, the buffalo provided for the Comanche, season after season, generation after generation: man attuned to the rhythms set into creation, man reaping from the bounty of creation in respect to the natural order, man deriving sustenance therefrom. Preparing for the hunt, carrying out the hunt, processing and living off the fruits of the hunt—such was the life of the Comanche; such was their way of life, a way of life that depended upon the buffalo.

But the buffalo would soon be all but gone. More than three years before, Indian Agent J. M. Haworth had written down how Kicking Bird, a chief of the Kiowa (close ally of the Comanche), had described the place the buffalo held in Indian life and the impact the buffalo slaughter was having on the Indians of the Southern Plains:

> The buffalo was their money their only resource with which to buy what they needed and did not receive from the government. The robes they could prepare and trade. They loved them just as the white man does his money, and just as it made a white man's heart feel to have his money carried away, so it made them feel to see others killing and stealing their buffalo which were their cattle given them by the Great Father above to furnish them meat to eat and means to get things to wear.

General Philip H. Sheridan, commander of the military department of the Southwest, did understand the place the buffalo held in Indian life, but in light of that understanding, he took a very different perspective on the matter of the buffalo slaughter. To a joint meeting of the Texas Senate and House of Representatives in 1875, Sheridan had this to say about the buffalo hunters:

> These men have done more in the last two years and will do more in the next year, to settle the vexed Indian question, than the entire regular army has done in the last thirty years. They are destroying the Indians' commissary; and it is a well-known fact that an army losing its base of supplies is placed at a great disadvantage. Send them powder and lead, if you will; but, for the sake of lasting peace, let them kill, skin, and sell until the buffaloes are exterminated. Then your prairies can be covered with speckled cattle, and the festive cowboy, who follows the hunter as a second forerunner of an advanced civilization.

Thus Sheridan had spoken of the importance of the buffalo to his enemy. Yes, his enemy; and the enemy of the United States troops stationed in the frontier forts of Texas; and the one-time enemy of the frontier settlers of Texas, Kansas, Colorado, New Mexico, and Mexico, as well as most of the Indian tribes that had inhabited any of those regions over the years. To the Ute after 1726, they had become *The Enemy, Komantcia,* or more precisely, "anyone who wants to fight me all the time," which, in time, passing through Spanish and English, came to be rendered as *Comanche.*

To themselves they were *Neme-ne* (The People), and they had a strong sense of being The People as far as culture and identity went, and in that sense the Comanche were a tribe. And yet, the Comanche, as a people, were not a tribe in the sense of a single political entity. In historical times, they did not come together as a united body until they borrowed the tradition of the Sun Dance from their allies, in 1874, to unite around a young medicine man and against their white enemies, especially the buffalo hunters, which began a disastrous stage for the Comanche in a period of rapid decline.

Instead, the Comanche were organized in bands, though loosely organized. Even so, each band identified with a given region of

Comancheria, though no boundaries restricted a band to, nor other bands from, a given region. These bands ranged from the size of one family to that of several hundred people. Still, individuals or groups could come and go from one band to another without ceremony, and Comanche bands readily cooperated with each other and almost never warred with each other, with the notable (and long-remembered) exception of the Wasp band scouting for the United States Army in its final campaigns against the Comanche and their allies.

Reports of from three to thirteen major bands have been proffered by various sources across the years. Among those major bands were the *Penatekas* (Honey-eaters) or *Penane* (Wasp), the southernmost band, who occupied the region closest to the settlements of the whites; the *Yamparikas* (Yap-eaters [the yap being a potato-like vegetable]), the northernmost band, who occupied the region between the Arkansas River and the Canadian River; the *Kotsotekas* (Buffalo-eaters), who occupied the Canadian River valley; the *Nokoni* (Wanderers or Those Who Turn Back) later *Detsanayuka* (Wanderers Who Make Bad Camps), who ranged just north of the Penatekas; and the *Kwahadi, Quahadi,* or *Kwahari* (Antelope), who occupied the region that included the canyon-lands of the eastern escarpment of the Llano Estacado, the region in which lay the canyons Palo Duro, Tule, and Escondido, the canyon in which the Stuart-Schurtz party had made their home.

In appearance the Comanche people made different impressions on various white people. Early contact between southern Comanche and white people of the Republic of Texas did not always draw from the whites a favorable impression of these Indians. In the *Telegraph and Texas Register* in 1838, one writer described these southern Comanche as "diminutive, squalid, half-naked, poverty-stricken savages." Another, even less inclined to temper his evaluation, described them as "naked, half-starved savages; and of the very lowest order of the human species. They appeared to be but one remove from the brute creation, and infinitely inferior to any other nation of Indians which has come within our knowledge."

One might conclude from these descriptions that the living conditions of the southern Comanche contributed to the poor impression their appearance made on some white people. Though that may be, it should be taken into account that the appearance of the Comanche bands farther to the north, who were still in their prime, did not much more impress some of their white observers. George Catlin, the artist, wrote of these Comanche: "In their movements they are heavy and ungraceful; and on their feet one of the most unattractive and slovenly looking races of Indians I have ever seen." Colonel Richard I. Dodge described them thus: "In stature they are rather low, and in person often approach to corpulency. . . . The men are short and stout, with bright copper faces and long hair, which they ornament with glass beads and silver gewgaws." Captain Randolph B. Marcy was more specific and more complimentary: "The men are about the medium stature, with bright, copper-colored complexions and intelligent countenances, in many instances with aquiline noses, thin lips, black eyes and hair, with but little beard. They never cut their hair, but wear it of very great length, and ornament it upon state occasions with silver and beads."

Marcy's description fit the northern Comanche well. The men averaged five feet six inches; the women, five feet. Hence, in their "medium stature," their height exceeded that of their kinsmen Ute and Shoshone, but did not measure up to that of the other Plains Indians like the Cheyenne, Crow, Blackfoot, or even the Kiowa. In general, the Comanche had broad bodies with deep chests, round heads with broad faces, and features much as Marcy describes them.

As for clothing, the men commonly wore breechclouts of cloth or skin and fringed buckskin moccasins and leggings. Though the men generally wore no clothing above the waist, long, v-necked, fringed deer- or antelope-skin shirts and buffalo robes (worn over the shoulders) protected them against cold weather. The women wore dresses of supple buckskin that reached from neck to ankle, often ornamented with highly valued elk teeth, as were their moccasins. In winter, women switched to knee-length dresses, and leggings, with buffalo robes worn over the shoulders. Winter also occasioned the wearing (by members of both sexes) of knee-high boots made from buffalo hides with the fur turned inside.

Though the Comanche were not considered by many whites to be one of the most attractive of the Indian peoples, still, descriptions of the appearance of Comanche men and women by whites could range from "ugly" to "handsome," which might merely suggest that the Comanche, like all peoples, varied in appearance and in the degree of physical beauty possessed by individuals. Nevertheless, observers agreed that in one respect the Comanche, as a people, possessed a beauty that was rarely, if ever, rivaled, and that was as equestrians.

On horseback, a Comanche was a creature transformed. Colonel Richard I. Dodge witnessed to this: "On foot slow and awkward, but on horseback, graceful, they are the most expert and daring riders in the world." And the George Catlin quotation, cited above, concludes: "In their movements they are heavy and ungraceful; . . . but the moment they mount their horses, they seem at once metamorphosed, and surprise the spectator with the ease and elegance of their movements." And Captain Marcy wrote:

> It is when mounted that the Comanche exhibits himself to the best advantage: here he is at home, and his skill in various manoeuvres which he makes available in battle—such as throwing himself entirely upon one side of his horse, and discharging his arrows with great rapidity towards the opposite side from beneath the animal's neck while he is at full speed—is truly astonishing.

Hence, it was to this other quadruped, as dear to the Comanche as the buffalo, if not more so, that the Comanche owed much of their success and reputation. As horsemen, the Comanche were unsurpassed, and the impact of the horse on their culture is incalculable, as is the impact that the Comanche on horseback had on the cultures of all the peoples with whom they came into contact. Exactly when the Comanche acquired the horse is not known for certain, but it is known that in 1724, when Bourgmont, the French explorer, visited a Comanche camp in Kansas, the Comanche were well supplied with horses, claiming to have got them from the Spanish, and they were already enjoying an established horse culture and were excellent horsemen. How the Comanche acquired their horses from the Spanish was not specified, but it is documented that residents of New Mexico, as early as 1705 and 1706, were already suffering from Comanche horse raids, the Apache of that region especially so in the latter year.

The value placed on horses by the Comanche is inestimable. At the time when a wealthy member of the Sioux nation would own thirty to forty horses, Captain Marcy wrote of successful Comanche warriors owning fifty to two hundred horses. One Comanche chief was reported to own three thousand horses. In 1867, the Kwahadi band, though only about two thousand in number, owned some fifteen thousand horses and three to four hundred mules, compared to whole tribes—like the Pawnee, Osage, and Omaha—which owned twelve hundred to fourteen hundred per tribe.

As the Comanche valued their horses, so they treated them. A favorite horse was often picketed near the tepee for the night, rather than left out on the plains with the rest of the herd. The animal was indulged in other ways, as well, being treated more like a pet than a mount, and sometimes more like a member of the family, rivaling a man's wife and children for his love. Regardless, those children, boys and girls, soon had horses of their own, which they learned to ride early, by the age of four or five. Comanche boys were expected to be trick riders. Their practice at trick riding progressed over the years, until they were able to pick up a full-grown man from the ground while riding past at top speed. This was to assure that these young men could fulfill the duty of rescuing a fallen comrade, which ranked above all others of the Comanche warrior.

The horse allowed the Comanche to own more possessions, being able to pack them on horses rather than dogs. The horse allowed them to move farther and faster, to hunt better and return with more meat and hides. The horse allowed them to further enhance themselves by trading horses.

The horse also, and perhaps most especially, allowed them to better raid and plunder and fight, the main objects of which were the acquiring of more horses and prestige, the extension of the region under their control, and revenge for any defeats or losses they had suffered. Though often of secondary importance, unless the Comanche were on a vengeance raid, scalps and captives were also taken in large numbers, often of nearly defenseless settlers, like those of northern Mexico.

Reports of Comanche horse raids along the Rio Grande frontier went back to at least 1744. The Comanche continued to raid in the region, left all but defenseless and weaponless by the Spanish and Mexican governments due to fears of revolution, so that George F. Ruxton, who traveled through northern Mexico in 1846, described the results of the Comanche raids thus: "For days together, in the Bolson de Mapimi, I traversed a country completely deserted on this account, passing through ruined villages, untrodden for years by the foot of man." He further claimed that from the fall of 1845 until September 1846, "upward of ten thousand head of horses and mules have already been carried off, and scarcely has a hacienda or rancho on the frontier been unvisited, and every where the people have been killed or captured."

In time, things changed. White settlements in Texas encroached ever farther upon the lands claimed by the Comanche, but, more important, white hunters threatened to exterminate the buffalo. The Comanche responded by shifting the object of their fighting to that of retaining supremacy over the Southern Plains and preserving a way of life, a way of life that had long incorporated the plundering and murdering of others, red and white. In this way, the Comanche had finally been forced to fight more on the defensive than on the offensive, after having long enjoyed more of the offensive side of the fight. The Comanche had fought and defeated, at one time or another: Spaniards, Mexicans, Texans, Americans, Ute, Pawnee, Osage, Tonkawa, Apache, and Navaho, as well as Jumano and Pueblo Indians. They had warred until 1840 with their later allies the Cheyenne and the Arapaho, and had even warred with their closest allies, the Kiowa and Kiowa-Apache, before beginning their long-standing alliance with those two peoples around 1790. Fierce and hated in battle, the Comanche gave no quarter and expected none, to the point of fighting to the death against overwhelming odds. They raided the settlements of Indians and whites, alike, stealing their stock (especially horses and mules), and killing the men, and sometimes the women and children too, though the women and children were often carried away to various fates, such as ransom, adoption, sale, marriage, cruel slavery, heinous torture, or death.

Though the behavior of some whites toward the Indians was brutal and indefensible, still, the brutality of the Comanche did not need to be predicated upon some action of the whites. Nevertheless, it could be so predicated, and then, even the defensive killing of a warrior of a Comanche raiding party by an overwhelmed white settler was enough to instigate a vengeance raid on some other unsuspecting white settler.

The Comanche were nomadic buffalo hunters; they were also raiders, plunderers, and warriors, who valued the theft of horses, mules, and cattle; the killing of the enemy; and the taking of captives. They especially valued all of that when performed under difficult circumstances, though they often preferred to outnumber and surprise their enemy. Their enemies varied depending upon whether enmity or alliance better served their needs and wants. Such was their culture. They did not need the provocation of the white man to live as they did, though the provocation of some whites did nothing to lessen Comanche brutality. The enmity between whites and the Comanche was the result of a clash of cultures, exemplified in, and exacerbated by, the slaughter of the buffalo. That enmity was also the result of misunderstanding, dishonesty, treachery, bad faith, and brutality on both sides. As the Comanche had done to other peoples in the past, most notably the Apache, the more numerous and more powerful whites were now doing to them—extending their way of life into the vast lands that the Comanche claimed. Both sides exhibited virtue and vice—some of the vice provoked, some not provoked, but none of it, as vice never is, justifiable.

Therefore, the Comanche were not the Noble Savage sought for among the American Indians by some romantics, nor were the Kiowa, nor the Apache, nor the Sioux, Pawnee, Cherokee, nor the Cheyenne, nor the Arkansas, nor were any of the peoples of the earlier eastern Iroquois Confederacy, nor were any of the other aboriginal peoples of the Americas, nor were the aboriginal peoples of Australia, Asia, Africa, South America, or any of the world's islands. There was no Noble Savage. Still, there were those romantics who desperately sought to find the Noble Savage in some remote location as yet untouched by the evils of civilization. And some, when they could not find the incarnation of this concept, would try to create it by imposing upon some unsuspecting aboriginal people romantic criteria for the Noble Savage, making allowances where the subject did not quite make the mark. Nor would reality's refutation of the concept spell its doom. Though the concept of the Noble Savage might fall on hard times for a short while, romantics of the latter half of the twentieth century would be all too willing to re-create the American Indian, the "Native American," to fit their own criteria for that concept.

This search for the Noble Savage predates the Romantic period and even the Romanic period, with evidence of the concept in the mythical Golden Age of the Greeks and in Greek writers' treatments of the Arcadians and others. Later, the Romans, too, found the Noble Savage in this mythical Golden Age and in some of their contemporaries, like the Scythians and Germans. Still, it was the eighteenth-century Romantic Jean Jacques Rousseau who came to be especially associated with the concept, though others before and after him may have more strictly adhered to it. With the belief that man was naturally good, Rousseau (like Montaigne before him) believed that man had been corrupted by civilization. Rousseau believed that man had originally been a solitary creature and naturally good, as such, but then men had begun to build dwellings, allowing men and women to live together and to form families and then societies. "The moral part of love," the directing of the reproductive instinct toward a particular woman, was a new ingredient in this development, which led to jealousy, inequality, and pride; which brought on competition and industry; which led to the creation of property; which led to further inequality and the need to develop the laws and governments of civil society; which legitimized and institutionalized inequality, to the real detriment of all.

Besides revolutionaries like Marx and Lenin, who would seize upon such reasoning in support of their errors, a large part of an entire generation of Americans in the latter half of the twentieth century—some eighty or ninety years after the founding of the Seven Ox Seven Ranch—would reach similar conclusions, whether with the help of Rousseau or not. This spoiled generation, upon reaching the age of maturity (though not maturity itself), would wake up to find, to their dismay, that the world was not perfect, and would then violently stomp their feet against this intolerable reality, demanding the worldly perfection to which they believed themselves entitled, blaming their parents and ancestors for "the Establishment," or the civil society that tolerated and even institutionalized the imperfection that so vexed them. Faced with this intolerable reality—which they were sure they did not deserve because they did not want it to be so—and overwhelmed by the futility of their own attempts to change it with every variety of temper tantrum, the spoiled generation characteristically would run away from reality into drugs, licentiousness, entertainment, cults, the occult, communes, and sundry other escapes. And though this generation would eventually do more to embellish the

Establishment with ever larger government and corporations, and ever more yielding submission to lavish luxury, they would first look to nature for the solution to all their problems, and find, in that escape, the cult of the natural man, who, for some, would be the Noble Savage.

Accordingly, many of the spoiled generation would make attempts to live closer to nature—few if any without many of the trappings of the civilization they decried or without the immediate availability of return to that civilization when desired. As time would pass, most would "sell out" more and more to the Establishment they had so hated. Among these would be many who would increasingly hate the Establishment the more they would sell out to it, especially as they would build ever more luxurious barriers between themselves and nature, and demand ever more of nature to be set apart from the use of other people (and, indeed, demand fewer people, too), so that the spoiled might visit these nature reserves, or just know about them, without much threat to their luxurious barriers against nature. As such, they would see themselves as the great protectors of nature, indeed as the great lovers of nature, and see that love of nature as an end in itself rather than as a means to the proper end of loving the Creator of nature. Rather than a proper respect for nature that would engender good stewardship, they would succumb to varying degrees of worship of nature, which would engender a most unnatural spiritual subservience to nature, expressed forcefully in vocal ideological demands for the absolute protection of nature, but belied, at the same time, by a material exploitation of nature expressed more forcefully in the actual physical demands placed upon nature by their increasing appetite for luxury.

To these especially, though to others of the generation as well, the American Indian of the past would prove the embodiment of the natural man in the form of the Noble Savage. Thus would they create a mythology of the American Indian as man without vice, because he was a man perfectly at one with nature, and therefore at peace with all men, until the spoiled generation's ancestors had ruined that peace. Thus, too, would the spoiled generation be able to conveniently look to their own ancestors, forefathers of the Establishment, to find the villains who had wrecked paradise. Who better to shoulder the blame for their deepening enslavement to luxury?

The Noble Savage had not been, in the end, the solution for Rousseau. The mature Rousseau had not advocated a return to the forests, but rather the establishment of a genuine social contract in which men would exchange natural rights, instinct, and independence for civil rights, justice, and republican liberty, to create a society held together by the "general will," according to which the people would legislate collectively and obey individually, possibly under the direction of a qualified lawgiver (who might even claim divine inspiration), who could set up a constitution and legal system, and be supported by a civil religion. Rousseau's natural man would not be sacrificed to such a society. Rather, the natural man should be able to progress in civil society, with the help of an educational method that, interestingly enough, would not be above employing manipulation and deceit to bring out the natural and good attributes of man without the vices. For the natural man, "living in the whirl of social life it is enough that he should not let himself be carried away by the passions and prejudices of men; let him see with his eyes and feel with his heart, let him own no sway but that of reason." So wrote the mature romantic.

Given Rousseau's conclusion, would not the future spoiled generation of Americans have reason to be disillusioned? Would they not have been raised in a constitutional republic that had incorporated, from its very early days, many of Rousseau's ideals? In that case, would not that republic, after nearly two hundred years, have had enough time to reach the civil perfection that should have been possible to attain?

The spoiled generation, and Rousseau as well, might have found it helpful to look back to a far earlier attempt at societal perfection, that of the ancient Hebrew people, whose Lawgiver was not only divinely inspired, but divine. God, having written his law and covenant in stone, had continually called upon his chosen people to write it in their hearts. And the people had failed and failed and failed, generation after generation after generation, to live according to a social contract infinitely better constituted than that of the later Americans or any construction of Rousseau. And each failure had brought destructive repercussions upon their society. Even after they had been pulled together into a great nation under a great king, the king's failure, along with the failures of the rest of the people, had spelled the doom of that earthly achievement.

Nevertheless, that king had touched upon the cause of the people's failure, when he had lamented to God, concerning his sinfulness: "Behold, I was brought forth in iniquity, and in sin did my mother conceive me" (Ps 51:5). And he had touched upon the solution: "Create in me a clean heart, O God, and put a new and right spirit within me" (Ps 51:10).

Still, time had passed, and when, after many more generations of failure, it had appeared that God's chosen people had finally reached the point of despair, when all had appeared to be lost due to their failure to keep his law and covenant, when it had looked like their entire society was on the brink of destruction, the Lord God had saved them from despair with a promise. Rather than give up on his people, who, instead of his law, had their sin "with a point of diamond . . . engraved on the tablet of their heart" (Jer 17:1), God would go right to the heart of the problem, and he would deliver them from it. And so he promised through his prophets:

> A new heart I will give you, and a new spirit I will put within you; and I will take out of your flesh the heart of stone and give you a heart of flesh. And I will put my spirit within you, and cause you to walk in my statutes and be careful to observe my ordinances. You shall dwell in the land which I gave to your fathers; and you shall be my people, and I will be your God (Ez 36:26–28).

Into that new heart, God himself would place his law, so as to make a wholly new covenant with his people:

> Behold the days are coming, says the Lord, when I will make a new covenant with the house of Israel and the house of Judah, not like the covenant which I made with their fathers when I took them by the hand to bring them out of the land of Egypt, my covenant which they broke, though I was their husband, says the Lord. But this is the covenant which I will make with the house of Israel after those days, says the Lord: I will

put my law within them, and I will write it upon their hearts; and I will be their God, and they shall be my people. And no longer shall each man teach his neighbor and each his brother, saying, "Know the Lord," for they shall all know me, from the least of them to the greatest, says the Lord; for I will forgive their iniquity, and I will remember their sin no more (Jer 31:31–34).

That new heart, with God's law divinely written upon it, would be the heart of a New Man, God's Incarnate Word, his uniquely natural Christ, uniquely so because he would have not one nature but two, a human nature and a divine nature, in the single person of Jesus of Nazareth, "who, though he was in the form of God, did not count equality with God a thing to be grasped, but emptied himself, taking the form of a servant, being born in the likeness of men. And being found in human form he humbled himself and became obedient unto death, even death on a cross" (Phil 2:5–8). This New Man—who would empty himself of his divine privilege, though not of divinity itself—would remedy the sin of the old man, begun in the first man, Adam, who though he was *not* in the form of God, nevertheless *had counted* equality with God a thing to be grasped, and had grasped at it, in disobedience, trying to elevate himself to be like God "without God, before God, and not in accordance with God," in the words of St. Maximus the Confessor.

Therein lay the problem for the myth of the Noble Savage and for Rousseau's belief in the natural goodness of man. Man had indeed been created naturally good, but, more than that, he had been constituted supernaturally good, that is, graced: with original justice, which meant that he was in harmony within himself, between his persons (male and female), and between himself and the rest of creation; and with original holiness, which meant that he had a supernatural destiny to share in the very life of God. But, being deceived by the devil and reaching up in pride, distrust, and disobedience to grasp at equality with God, man had abused his freedom and had fallen far below his original state. Thereafter, human nature would be "deprived of original holiness and justice," and without these, though not totally corrupted, human nature would be, in the words of the Church, "wounded in the natural powers proper to it;

subject to ignorance, suffering, and the dominion of death; and inclined to sin—an inclination to evil that is called 'concupiscence.'"

Consequently, neither the Comanche nor any other people could be the Noble Savage. Nor could Rousseau's natural man attain perfection by cultivating his natural virtues and steeling himself against the detrimental effects of society. For the spoiled generation of Americans would get it partly right. The problem did lie in the sins of their parents and ancestors, but they would need to look farther back. The problem lay in the sin of our ultimate ancestors, our first parents, and in the wounded human nature, deprived of original justice and holiness, that they passed on to the rest of the human race. The problem is *original sin*, and human beings, though still deluding ourselves despite millennia of experience to drive home the reality, cannot solve the problem of original sin, and all the personal sin that follows upon it, by re-creating a primitive way of life; or by establishing some perfect political, social, or economic system; or by just electing the right political leaders. None of that will remedy the plight of a creature who had originally been constituted to join in the very life of God but had rejected that supernatural destiny for the deception that he could attain such an end by himself. Such a deception did not work for the first humans in the state of original holiness and justice; it certainly will not work for man after the loss of that state. Man's proper end, by the grace of God, was divinization, to share in the very life of God. Having freely rejected the grace that makes divinization possible, man certainly cannot thereafter achieve it.

The spoiled generation, and others of generations before it, might demand that such a situation is not fair, or that it is not the way they would do it. Yet, how futile is such a protest by all-too-finite man before the infinite Author of justice. The spoiled might further insist to know whence came this evil in the first place. The answer must ring loud and clear: Not from God! Never from God, who is never author or promoter of evil. Evil is the result of the rebellion from good of God's free creatures, some of his angels and the first man and woman, and their descendants. But why does God permit evil? In answer to that question, St. Thomas Aquinas gives a hint about the solution to the problem of original sin. He writes: "There is nothing to prevent human nature's being raised up to something greater, even after sin; God permits evil in order to draw forth some greater good."

Still, how can the God of superabounding love, who loved man into existence, bring man back to the end for which he was made without compromising man's freedom, necessary to man's dignity because it allows man to love? How, other than for God to enter into humanity to live it to perfection, so as to bring humanity back to God? And so it was.

Hence, rather than the natural man, there is the "natural" Christ, of natures human and divine: the true Man, because he is also true God, who nevertheless, "did not count equality with God a thing to be grasped, but emptied himself, taking the form of a servant, being born in the likeness of men" (Phil 2:6–7). Perfecting human nature in love, humility, and obedience unto a horrible death, Christ graced human nature to make it once again capable of a supernatural end, but an end even better than that originally intended for man, as St. Paul put it, "Where sin increased, grace abounded all the more" (Rom 5:20), and St. Leo the Great explains, "Christ's inexpressible grace gave us blessings better than those the demon's envy had taken away."

So, even though humanity freely rejected its originally graced state, God's own Son took on human nature and entered into a fallen world, a world hostile to his goodness, and subjected himself to that world's limitations and hostility, even to the point of undergoing death in its most cruel form, so that he might not only return man to his original potential but to an even greater potential. Fair? And all man is asked to do, to enjoy the rewards won by Christ, is to join himself to Christ—normally by joining himself to his Church, which is his Mystical Body on earth—and to abide by his commandments, based in love, that demand discipline in a fallen world, but that promise a superabundant reward. For the new Spirit that God promised is his own, with which he anointed his Christ. And when Christ, the Son, returned to the Father, he sent his Spirit upon his Church to animate his Mystical Body on earth, which is the graced and inspired communion of God and man. Therein lies the solution to the dilemma faced by Rousseau and the rest. St. Irenaeus expressed it thus: "For this is why the Word became man, and the Son of God became the Son of man: so that man, entering into communion with the Word and thus receiving divine sonship, might become a son of God;" or St. Thomas Aquinas: "The only-begotten Son of God, wanting to make us sharers in his divinity, assumed our nature, so that he, made man, might make men gods;" or St. Athanasius: "For the Son of God became man so that we might become God."

Thus is the continuing reincarnation of the Noble Savage exposed as a rejection of the revelation of original sin and a rejection of the mystery of the Incarnation of the Son of God as the remedy for original sin. Therein lies the basis for the durability of the myth of the Noble Savage. Honest acceptance of the revelation of original sin demands acceptance of the Incarnation as the sole means of man attaining the end for which he was created, which is divinization; and yet, man (male and female) seeks to divinize himself. The first man sought to do so in Paradise, and man, thereafter in the state of original sin, has sought to do so ever since, in ways subtle and gross. The myth of the Noble Savage, whatever its reincarnation, invites man to divinize himself in some mythic ideal, still attainable by man returning to nature in some manner or other. It allows man to delude himself about his condition and thus about his need for salvation. It allows man to pretend that the reality of sin, and man's proclivity to sin, can some day be remedied by an improved relationship between man and nature. It also allows some—who believe that that improved relationship rests in the return of man to some primitive state—to despair and grow bitter, because no one will join them in that return to the primitive that they believe would be the salvation of all, a return that, in truth, they are not willing to make themselves, especially as long as others are not willing to make it with them, which only deepens the despair and bitterness.

Such erroneous thinking flows from a departure from the balance of orthodoxy. For sin and corruption had created the conditions for the ship of orthodoxy to be rocked, and amidst those conditions, she had been rocked, until many of the rockers had departed in a flotilla of crafts of their own making, leaving the mother ship to settle herself, as those departing continued to rock their hastily constructed crafts. In that rocking shifted such matters of importance as: original sin, grace, nature, authority, human dignity, free will, predestination, responsibility, faith, works, sacramentalism, reason, revelation, inspiration, intuition, and truth, to name but a few. As the rocking of the flotilla continued, and these matters continued to shift from one extreme to the other, one craft after another slowly departed from the flotilla, each to seek its separate balance, jettisoning what it must to do so. Smaller crafts departed from these, and smaller from those, and so on.

In the wake of all this departure, and its attendant relativism, could various erroneous ideas like the Noble Savage be taken seriously, as could the malleable imbalance of naturalism that accommodated it and found a place in Deism, Freemasonry, Rationalism, Romanticism, and various other imbalanced *isms* before, after, and around those. So, too, could dehumanizing determinism, which snaked its way through its own share of *isms*. In this wake, also, could rise the imbalance of Kant's transcendentalism, from which Hegel departed to propound his imbalance of dialectical idealism, from which Marx departed to propound his imbalance of dialectical materialism. Of this last imbalance, built around Marx's atheistic theory of the self-creation of man, millions of men, women, and children, who would directly experience its various practical applications, would have good reason to wonder if it might not effectively result in the self-destruction of man, instead.

Of all this imbalance that followed in the wake of the great departure from orthodoxy, G. K. Chesterton would write, in his "popular sketch" of Thomas Aquinas, "that paradoxy has become orthodoxy." He would elaborate upon the effect this has had on philosophy:

> Since the modern world began in the sixteenth century, nobody's system of philosophy has really corresponded to everybody's sense of reality; to what, if left to themselves, common men would call common sense. Each started with a paradox; a peculiar point of view demanding the sacrifice of what they would call a sane point of view. That is the one thing common to Hobbes and Hegel, to Kant and Bergson, to Berkeley and William James. A man had to believe something that no normal man would believe, if it were suddenly propounded to his simplicity; as that law is above right, or right is outside reason, or things are only as we think them, or everything is relative to a reality that is not there. The modern philosopher claims, like a sort of confidence man, that if once we will grant him this,

the rest will be easy; he will straighten out the world, if
once he is allowed to give this one twist to the mind.

Twists of the mind or straightening out the world had little to do
with Luke, Tom, and Andy's regard for the Comanche, as the three
men rode the line of the Seven Ox Seven Ranch in the fall and winter
of 1877–78. Reality, rather than an idealized romantic myth, occasioned their vigilance. In the travels and associations that had been
part of their work in the cattle business, Luke and Tom had learned
plenty about what the Comanche could do. Andy, for his part, had
heard from his parents various accounts of Comanche atrocities that in
one way or another had affected their lives, especially when they were
younger. He could add to those accounts stories of atrocities that had
filtered down from various sources of his Mexican ancestry. Most
poignant, though, were his Apache grandmother's firsthand accounts
of Comanche raids, which she had recalled from vivid memories of
when she had been a little girl, recounted in the perspective of a terri-
fied child.

It was true that back in 1874–75, troops under the commands of
Colonel Ranald Mackenzie, Colonel Nelson Miles, Colonel G. P.
Buell, Lieutenant Colonel J. W. Davidson, and Major William Price
had taken to the field and fairly well subdued the Indians, in the wake
of the second battle of Adobe Walls and its aftermath. At that battle of
Adobe Walls in June of 1874, a large band of Comanche and
Cheyenne, under the influence of a charismatic young Comanche
medicine man named I'satai, in an effort to put a stop to the destruction of the buffalo, had attacked the buffalo hunters' deepest incursion
into their hunting grounds, a settlement near the ruins of an old trading post in the Canadian River Valley of Texas. Though unsuccessful
at Adobe Walls, the Indians had gone on from there to raid settlements
in Kansas, Colorado, and Texas, leaving behind them a trail of death
and destruction. The troops under Mackenzie, Miles, Buell, Davidson,
and Price had spent months in the field in an all-out effort to quell the
Indians of the region once and for all.

In that campaign, in late September of 1874, Mackenzie had discovered an extensive Indian camp in the Palo Duro Canyon. Though
most of the Indians had managed to escape, the element of surprise

had allowed Mackenzie to seize and destroy their lodgings and belongings. Among these had been a large herd of horses, of which he had
had over one thousand shot, so as to keep the Indians from retaking
them. Other results of the campaign had been similar, with low casu-
alties among the Indians, but high losses of horses and supplies, so that
the cold weather eventually forced most of the Comanche, Kiowa, and
Cheyenne onto the reservations in Indian Territory by the spring of
1875, with Quanah Parker's band of Kwahadi being the last major band
to surrender in early June of that year. These Kwahadi had been among
the most elusive and independent of the Comanche bands, often completely unrepresented in treaties between the state or federal government and the Comanche. They had been the most resistant to the idea
of accepting life on the reservation. Furthermore, they had, until their
surrender, long occupied the region of the eastern escarpment of the
Llano Estacado, the region in which lay the Escondido Canyon.

The Comanche, once settled in Indian Territory (later-day
Oklahoma), had not been content to remain there. Inspiration from
the Sioux and Cheyenne destruction of Custer's Seventh Cavalry at
Little Bighorn, in June of 1876, did nothing to put to rest the hope of
some Indians that they might still stop the buffalo slaughter and return
to life as they had known it. As late as the previous winter and spring
of 1877, a band of Comanche had left the reservation, under a leader
called Black Horse, and, along with some Mescalero Apache, had done
some serious and deadly raiding of buffalo hunters' camps. The buffalo
hunters had retaliated in "the Pocket Canyon fight," in which they
may have killed over thirty warriors, near later-day Lubbock, Texas.
Company G of the Tenth Cavalry, under Captain P. L. Lee, had then
taken to the field in mid-April, from Fort Griffin, and had returned in
mid-May, after little action, with a few women and children captives,
and some captured supplies and horses.

That had been in May. For all the settlers of the Seven Ox Seven
knew, there could be several bands of fugitives from the reservations out
in their region at that very time. As it was, the Indians were sometimes
allowed to leave the reservation, with a military escort or a pass from
the Indian agent, to hunt buffalo. Regardless, experience had shown
that the Indians were not averse to leaving the reservations without
authorization. Even if they were now settled, however imperfectly, on

the reservations, was it not reasonable for the settlers to be prepared for the possible return of the Indians to the Escondido, even if it were only temporary? Having shown contempt in the past for the disciplinary actions that had been threatened for those who might leave the reservation, what would keep the Indians from disregarding such threats now? They had seen the great buffalo slaughter and had gone on the warpath several times in the past to try to stop it. Why would they not—especially the Kwahadi Comanche, who had formerly inhabited the region of the Escondido Canyon—consider taking advantage of their fleeting opportunity to participate in the communal hunt of the buffalo in the lands in which they had been accustomed to do so? What disciplinary action could be so great as to keep them from participating, very possibly for the last time, in that occupation that had for generations defined their culture, had defined who they were, by serving as the basis for their very way of life? How might those Indians, still known for sporadic raiding during their early years on the reservations, respond to the discovery of a white settlement in the canyons region that had once been their home, especially if they thought that that settlement had anything to do with the buffalo slaughter? How much worse might they respond if they believed those now settled in their former home were Texans, whom they truly hated? And, considering that revenge killing was an integral part of Comanche culture, what vengeance—for loved ones lost in battles with white soldiers, hunters, or settlers—might a band of Comanche visit upon the little settlement of the Seven Ox Seven, if they believed that no one would ever find out about it, remote as it was? And, remote as it was, Luke, Tom, and Andy all kept two things ever on their minds: the Comanche and their allies knew the Escondido, and they knew where it was.

Thus were the Seven Ox Seven men vigilant and with good reason. One warm winter day, when Andy had been cutting sign for cattle out on the low rolling plains south of the mouth of the canyon, he had come upon a site where Indians had killed and butchered half a dozen buffalo. He could tell it was a Comanche kill because, among other things, all the meat, along with the hides, was gone, except for the rumps. The hearts, though, had been left, along with the spines and skulls, much in the way that a Comanche kill had been described to him by the man called Stillman, a man of no little experience, who had served as cook and rifleman for the Colmey party that had surveyed the canyon.

Besides this buffalo kill, on three separate occasions the men had found tracks from Indian ponies down in the lower part of the canyon. One set of tracks of a dozen horses or so, which they had followed, had gone all the way up the canyon, passing to the north of the dugout and corrals and up and out of the canyon through the notch at the canyon's head. These tracks, unlike the others, had not been discovered in the lower part of the canyon, but rather, they had been discovered one morning by following the tracks of three horses that had ridden up to their horse corral during the night. By following these tracks, Luke, Tom, and Andy had been led to the other tracks and had then followed those in both directions. Nevertheless, the Seven Ox Seven men had not seen one Indian. Nor had they lost any horses, as they had taken to locking them up with a padlock at night in their high-walled picket corral, long a common structure on the frontier of Texas to guard against Indian raids. These corrals did not always keep the patient and ingenious Comanche from earning the prestige that went with stealing horses under such difficult circumstances, but they thwarted the attempts at such stealing often enough. Theirs may have done so that night in the Escondido, but Luke, Tom, and Andy believed that part of the reason they had lost no horses that night was that the Indians had been in a hurry, or they would have made more of an effort than their tracks had indicated. As it was, they had killed a Seven Ox Seven steer and butchered it and made off with its meat and hide without even being noticed.

WITH THIS PRECAUTION of confining the horses and mules in a padlocked corral, the men had tried to lay up as much hay as possible, in the late fall, from several spots they had located along the stream bottoms in the canyon or in dry playa lakes on top of the cap. Though they had intended to corral the horses and mules, due to their concern about Indians, they had earlier been lax about it, often leaving the animals out to graze. After the first signs of Indians, the horses and mules were regularly corralled for the night.

Besides hay, they had been cutting, curing, and laying in firewood from the time of their arrival in the canyon. This required as much a shovel as an axe, because mesquite offered the best wood to burn, and the greater amount of it lay underground in the roots, which they dug and cut up.

And they were building, building a home in their canyon. The quantity of cedar and oak in the canyon precluded the need to rely on cottonwood for a building material, though there was plenty of cottonwood for whenever they wanted it. Accordingly, they continued to cut and haul cedar and oak logs for construction. The best of the cedar logs would be used for buildings. Of the remaining cedar, they fashioned fence posts, and dug and set them to construct corrals and pens. They fenced a pasture for the horses and draft animals. They would be making good use of that enclosure, at least while concern about Indian raids lasted, after which they would allow at least some of those animals to graze unfenced like the cattle. Their plans included pens for roundups, for protecting hay pastures and gardens and yards, and for the eventual breeding of cattle. They also continued to cut and haul rock, an inexhaustible building material in the region, adaptable to almost any construction need.

The rock would be used, along with the wood, in the buildings they would construct. Crushed, the rock could also be used in the construction of roads, though, at this early stage, most of their road-building efforts were confined to cutting down creek banks to make for easier and more direct passage between principal points in the canyon.

And they were building houses to serve as the nuclei of their canyon home. Luke had begun a house of stone, a "rock house," the foundations of which Tom and Andy had helped him dig and set. He was laying up limestone with lime mortar, laying up the rock double thickness for structural soundness. He had considered building the house over the dugout—as many pioneer families did, allowing the dugout to serve as a cellar—but rather than bother with beams, supports, wooden joists, and flooring, he had decided to build it a little to the southeast of the dugout, to face south onto the same yard that lay before the dugout. That way he could install a floor of stone and mortar, and later a floor of wood—should they desire it and it become more feasible. At the point where he began to build, the bank in which the dugout was constructed sloped down to just a little bit of a rise behind where his house would be. Therefore, the north-facing windows of the house would allow a fairly clear view, above and beyond the rise, in that direction. Windows on the other sides of the house would provide unobstructed views of the east, south, and west. The dugout to the northwest of the house would obstruct the view in that direction, but upstairs windows would help to remedy that shortcoming. The dugout would not at all obstruct the view of Tom's house from the western windows, because Tom's house would be so slightly off to the northwest as to be almost directly westward.

Andy's contribution to this construction included not only his labor but also his attendance upon the stock, in which he enjoyed the help of the collie Rita—despite the birth of five puppies to her around the beginning of December, resulting from the mating with the Smith collie. Zachariah, with his own collie Charlie (a natural herder like his mother, nearly full grown now, though still a puppy at heart), helped Andy whenever he could, though he well knew that his responsibility for the sheep outweighed his desire to accompany Andy in his line riding. Nonetheless, he was allowed to accompany Andy now and then, and Andy was ever patient, though firm, when it came to work, and Zachariah benefited from the association. Hence, did Andy's help allow Luke and Tom to spend more time on the construction of dwellings.

Tom continued to help Luke and Andy with the construction of the Stuart house, but he had also begun the planning and construction of his own house, a cedar-log house, up on the site he had chosen the day he had ridden out with Luke. On that level area, he had located a spot toward its eastern edge, far enough out to avoid falling rock and to benefit from as much sunlight as possible and still have a bit of yard between the house and the lip of the flat. The southern wall of the canyon was far enough away that his house would escape its shadow even in winter. The proximity of the western head of the canyon would hasten evening shadows, but not enough to detract from this ideal site.

He would build a horse corral to the northwest of the house, out away from the cliffs and nearly up against the trail out of the canyon. That would make it far enough away to keep the horses from contaminating the spring he intended to use as his water supply. The seep in the area where he planned to build the corral, though its volume of flow was far lower than that of the spring, would still provide plenty of water, when channeled, to fill a small tank he would excavate in the corral for the use of his horses.

As Tom looked over the site and settled on a plan for his house, he realized that it had been some time since he had really thought of a place as home. Indeed, he did not believe he had done so since he was a boy on the family farm in Wisconsin. Even the family farm had no longer felt like home to him long before he had left it. While still a boy, he had felt a pull toward some unknown place, unknown to him in his present, now past. And, as pulled, he had moved, and moved, and moved. He had been at another point of moving when he had met Luke Stuart in Dodge City. Something about Luke had pulled Tom, and when he had finally learned of the Stuarts' plan regarding the canyon, a certain surety of direction had settled upon him, actually bringing a settledness to him that he had not known since his boyhood. Now here he was in a place of destination, a place of settling, a home.

Finally at home, Tom set out to build his house. He would rely on the knowledge and experience he had accumulated in the course of his life: from his early years in Wisconsin, working on the farm and working with a German immigrant building log houses and outbuildings, to his later years, working on the railroad, on construction sites, and on ranches. He would apply this knowledge and experience, as well as the skills honed by them, to the wealth of raw materials available, and he would commit the time and energy necessary to build a structure worthy of the name *home*. There would be no hurry, no compromising. He would work on it when he could. He would dedicate himself to the process and see in that his ongoing reward, and he would hold up, as his motivating principle, the goal of embodying the ideal of *home* in this house.

Thus, Tom began to build, and he would continue until he had attained his goal. First, he plotted out an area about twenty-two feet by sixteen feet. This site was not exactly true to the cardinal directions. His home would face mainly east, but slightly to the southeast, so that it would look down into the canyon and down upon the Stuart home. He cleared this site and leveled any high areas.

With the site ready, Tom needed logs. Plenty were already available, as, at first, Andy, and then later, Andy, Luke, and Tom had been felling and hauling select logs since they had arrived. The canyon offered virgin stands of timber, which provided exceptional cedar logs of good length and girth. Of those they had cut, the Seven Ox Seven men had been saving the best for buildings. These better logs they had not cut early on, but had waited to cut them until winter had set its teeth a bit, so that their sap was down. Furthermore, Luke had demanded that they cut them during the dark phase of the moon to better assure good seasoning of the timber and to avoid later infestation by insects. As time allowed, using mules or oxen, and sometimes with Luke's or Andy's help, Tom hauled the best of these logs up to his site and laid them out in an area adjacent to the exact site of his house.

Here Tom prepared the logs for building. He had decided to plank the logs: that is, to hew two sides of them. He had considered hewing all four sides, but this would be exceedingly time consuming, which he did not mind as long as it produced the optimum results, but he was not convinced that it would. The wood that Tom was using had been cut recently enough to preclude thorough seasoning. With planking and chinking he could allow for warping. The planks would also give more coverage with fewer logs, and their unfinished tops and bottoms would accommodate chinking. Certainly in this canyon, with its unlimited supply of lime for mortar, chinking would not be a problem.

Tom planked one log at a time, amidst the fresh cedar aroma released by his work, a pleasant reminder of the wood's natural resistance to insects and decay. First he would score the log, regularly all the way down its length, with his broadaxe. Then he would snap a chalk line along the base of the scores, and straddling the log on one end, he would work his way backward down the log with his foot adze, chipping out the wood between the scores down the line. This completed, he would turn the log over and do the same to the other side. One log after another, he worked them—scoring, straddling, chipping—so that the fresh chips trailed slowly along either side of the several logs, and the subtle spice of cedar pushed out beyond the immediate area of work to season the air of the upper canyon.

Like Luke, Tom put in as much time as he could on his house, weather and other work permitting. The weather was more of a concern for Luke, as he was, almost from the start of actual construction, working with mortar, and he could not afford to let it freeze. Tom would not need to use mortar until the later stages of his project, and so had no such early concern.

Soon, Tom had all his logs planked. Next, he gathered or quarried stones to use as the foundation of his house. He had not wanted to rely on the stone Andy, Luke, and he had already quarried, as Luke would need all of that and more. Accordingly, he had been gathering and quarrying for his project from its very beginning, when not working on the logs. Now, with the logs all planked, he set out to complete this task. He did not need to travel far to do so. Behind the site for his house, nearer the cliff, there were plenty of stones from the erosion resistant caliche layer of the Ogallala Formation. These chunks of caliche had broken off from the formation due to their own weight, after the rock layers beneath had been caved out by erosion. These chunks lay scattered about at the base of the formation. Otherwise there was plenty more rock to be quarried. Besides some scattered chunks of caliche, Tom collected some large solid sandstones (eroded from the Trujillo formation) that lay farther down the canyon toward the Stuarts. He chiseled all of the stones that he finally selected into fairly regular rectangular shapes and placed them—caliche at the corners and in the middle, and sandstone in between these—and leveled them using a level and a line strung taut.

Finally the day came to start laying up some logs. From the logs, Tom selected the stoutest and straightest to use as sills and plates. These he hewed on the remaining two sides to render each square hewn. Then, with Luke's and Andy's help, and using small logs as rollers, he rolled the three sills into place—to serve as the bases of the front and back walls, and as a center support of the floor—and set them on the foundation stones. In this way, they set three sills, running slightly northeast-southwest of north-south, each log twenty-two feet long, with the two outside sills sixteen feet apart and the one in the middle, exactly in the middle. (The size of Tom's house hardly required three sills, but the wood was available, and Tom was building for solidity, stability, and durability.) With the sills in place, Tom began to shim them to make sure they rested solidly on the foundation stones.

As Tom began to methodically check each point where a log rested on a foundation for the need to shim, and as he began to shim with wedges of cedar or stone where needed, Luke expressed his readiness to make quick work of the project.

"We could have half of these logs laid up by the end of the day," he announced to Tom, who lay on the ground beside one of his stones engaged in his precision shimming.

"Huh," Tom responded, acknowledging Luke's comment but in no way making answer to it and certainly not assenting to the course recommended by it.

"You want to notch out those ends, and Andy and I can have the next log up there before you know it, and you just keep notchin' and we'll keep layin'," Luke continued.

"Aahhh," Tom stalled as he tapped the shim on which he was concentrating into place, until he had it just right. Then he stood up. "Well, uh," he said, "I still need to check all these stones for shimmin' and to shim wherever it's needed."

"All right, then," Luke said, "Andy and I can start movin' these logs into place, while you're doin' that."

"Well, uh," Tom said, again, "then I was goin' to mortise these sills for sleepers, and tenon the sleepers . . ."

"That's all right. We'll not rush you. We'll just move the logs. That'll save you some time, and we'll lay 'em up when you're finished," Luke tried again.

"Well, uh," Tom began again, "I have an idea of which logs I would want where."

By now Andy was smiling, standing off to the side waiting for his next assignment. He knew Tom, and he knew that this was a one-man project. He knew that Tom had compromised on various specifications on different construction projects that he and Luke had worked on together, but there would be no compromise on this, Tom's house. Luke was beginning to realize it too.

"And I'm goin' to full-dovetail notch the corners," Tom continued.

"Full-dovetail notch the corners?" Luke responded, pulling up a bit as he did so. "That's some serious craftsmanship. And with cedar?"

"I've seen it done. Besides these are stout logs, and they planked up real nice. No reason they shouldn't dovetail well," Tom replied.

"So, you're sayin' you don't want our help," Luke concluded with a wry smile.

"I didn't say that; I appreciate . . ."

"No, no, that's all right. We can tell when we're not wanted. Andy and I've got plenty to do. There's that rock house down yonder that demands our attention," Luke said, nodding down at the Stuart home below, "and it may not be as fancy as a full-dovetail-notched cedar house, but it'll keep the elements out for the likes of the rest of us."

By now Andy had to look down to hide the attempts his smile was making to break out into a laugh.

"I know," Tom tried again, "I appreciate your takin' the time out to help . . ."

"Come on, Andy, ol' Tom here won't have any more of our help," Luke said, as he walked to his horse. He swung into the saddle, and as Andy swung into his, Luke added, "Sure, we're all right to grunt a few sills into place, but we're no craftsmen of his caliber; that's plain enough to see. I just hope he'll let us cross the threshold into this palace when it's all complete."

By now Tom had no response except to shake his head as he smiled and allowed light laughter—which he tried to stifle as much as possible—to escape. Luke, too, was stifling laughter, though he continued to feign hurt feelings, as he and Andy turned their horses and started down the canyon. Tom was left with his work, and he went back to it.

He checked and shimmed wherever log met rock, until he was satisfied that no further shimming was needed. Then he turned his hand to the floor joists, or sleepers. To accommodate the sleepers, Tom cut mortises into the three sills, two feet on center. The sleepers consisted of smaller logs that he had hewn flat on one side. Into the ends of these he cut tenons and snugly fit them into the mortises in the sills, to effect a very solid floor foundation, which he intended to cover with oak. But that would have to wait. As it was, the day he laid up the first logs of his house was drawing to a close with the sun's setting and the fast fading of twilight. He had not yet finished tenoning and fitting his sleepers, but that and a good deal more work would wait for tomorrow, and for many tomorrows after that.

The next day he was back at work on the sleepers, and for that and days subsequent he continued to build his house, his home. He notched a half-dovetail into the ends of the three sills. Then he notched full-dovetails into the ends, and half-dovetails into the middles, of the two logs that would serve as the bottom logs of the side walls. These he fitted onto the ends of the sills. From then on he continued to select one log at a time, first for the front wall, then for the back, then for one side wall, then the other. Each one he would notch full-dovetail on each end, move it into place (with the help of rollers, his horse, Andy or Luke or both, if they were present), trim the notches to a tight fit, and set the log.

These full-dovetail notches required some time to cut and fit the way Tom intended them to fit. Using his axe, a ruler, a square, and a chisel, he would first cut the notches in the ends of the logs as they lay on the ground. (After cutting the first few notches, he cut a pattern from a piece of board and used that to help make the initial cut.) Then he would raise the logs onto the walls, where he would use the axe and chisel to precision fit the joints. He set carefully and trimmed meticulously to create neatly squared "boxed" corners.

To raise and set the logs, he relied on a skid on each side. The skid consisted of long poles, one end of each resting on the ground and the other end on the top of the wall. Up these poles he would roll or slide each log until it reached the top of the wall. He had notched these poles at various points to help prevent the logs from rolling or sliding back. He kept a running measure of the height of the corners and used a level and plumb line to make sure that all sides of the structure rose evenly and were plumb. He also made sure to make saw cuts into the top logs of the openings he intended for the door, the windows, and the chimney.

Finally, from the top of the sill, the logs lay up about one log above his own height. At this point, Tom had to decide whether or not he would use his longest logs to cantilever out over the front and the back (or just over the front) to provide the bases for the roof structures for a front porch and back shed. Tom decided against any cantilever roof, front or back, because he had never liked the look of them. He preferred to wait until he could return to a town and buy some milled lumber and construct a more finished-looking porch. Hence, he continued to lay up his logs until they were eight feet above the top of the sills. At that point, he cut mortises into the top logs, two feet apart on center, and cut tenons into logs that he had square hewn, and he began to insert the tenons of those logs into the mortises in the walls, so that the logs could serve as joists for the upper floor. The tenon ends of these logs, two feet apart from each other, showed as rows, one across the front, one across the back of the structure. He laid up five more logs above these joists, and then he was ready for the plates.

The logs he had chosen to serve as plates were nearly as thick as the sills. These, like the sills, he had square hewn. They were longer than the sills by four feet, so that they could cantilever out over the end walls to provide the base of a roof that would extend two feet beyond each gable end of the house.

Luke, Andy, and one of the mules helped Tom set the plates. With the plates in place, Tom could cut out the doorway to make it easier to get inside the pen. The doorway would not be centered, but would be positioned toward the northern end of the front wall. Before he cut this doorway, he pounded wooden wedges into the wall, along where he would cut out the doorway, to keep the logs from moving from their places once the portion cut out was removed. Then he sawed out the opening, making the doorway a little less than seven feet high. He cut straight, beginning at the cuts he had started when he had laid up the wall, right down to the sill, without cutting into the sill. Then he framed out the doorway with thick, wide oak boards that he had ripped (jambs) or rived and worked with an adze (lintel and threshold) and planed and sawn to fit. These he secured with countersunk lag screws. He did not, at this time, cut out any of the openings for the windows or the fireplace. These he would cut out later if he determined that he wanted them.

Through the doorway, Tom stepped into the dense skeleton of his house. He catwalked across a sleeper to the center sill and there looked at his work, turning from one wall to the next to the next until he had turned all the way around. There he stood looking. The planks were firm, the corners sound. The chinks lent the solid structure a contrasting airiness, as, through them, light and sound and wind passed between the dense, immovable logs into the pen. Tom stood and looked. The day was sunny though cool, the kind of cool that invites work. The wind, softer than those pushing around the grasses up on top of the caprock, made its presence known by leaning against the layered planks, and by whistling through the chinks in a song of rising and lowering pitch that told of the temporality of things. Tom smiled at the reminder within the context of his striving for permanence.

As if in reassurance of the soundness of his striving, he stepped out onto a sleeper and walked from one to the next to the next, often walking up and down them, and shifting his weight as he did, testing their solidity. Here and there he would push up against the walls, reveling in their firm resistance. This he did all the way around the inside of the pen. It was indeed a solid structure: solid, but still open. Having pushed against all the walls, Tom finally leaned up against the western wall, across from the door, and looked skyward.

He gazed into the heavens above, framed as they were by his structure. Thoughts of Molly Banks of Dodge City, and then of the Kentucky beauty, Nancy Hawkins, crept up in his mind, as he recalled the words they had written to him in their letters, which had been delivered by the surveying team the previous autumn. He knew their words well, having read them over and over, several times responding to those words, and each time editing the previous version of his response to better reflect his thoughts and feelings at his latest reading. None of these versions had yet been sent to either lady, as there had been, as yet, no means of conveyance. With his mind thus pleasantly occupied, he continued to gaze into the heavens. He drank in their blueness, lightly decorated with cotton-white clouds, lighted by the winter sun. His thoughts of the Dodge City and Kentucky belles gradually gave way to other thoughts that had been creeping up from the back of his mind. Consequently, as he gazed into the heavens and drank in their beauty, he found himself planning how he was going to shut them out. In time, after gazing, thinking, drinking in, and planning long enough, Tom left the structure of his house and rode down to the Stuarts' for dinner.

After dinner, he started on the roof. He chose thirty-two logs and began to hew them to about six inches square. Four of these he ripped in half with a saw. From the twenty-eight square logs, he chose two. Into one end of each, he cut a 45-degree angle, leaving a tenon protruding from one of them, perpendicular to the angled cut. Into the angled cut of the other, he chiseled out a mortise. Then he cut the other ends of these two rafters to make them twelve and a half feet long, making the cuts at a 135-degree angle from the tops of the rafters to provide vertical surfaces for the fascia boards. He chiseled notches into the bottoms of the rafters at the points where they would rest on the plates, allowing the rafters to overhang the plates so that the roof could do the same. This, he expected, would require some chiseling work on the plates to assure proper fits. He laid the rafters out, and joined them at the mortise and tenon, and adjusted these with a chisel and hammer until they fit snugly. He then drilled a hole into this mortise and tenon joint for a wooden pin, which he would insert when he finally assembled the rafters in place. As this set was to be one of the gable-end set of rafters, he cut studs from the boards he had ripped, which were stout three-by-sixes, for extra support and for nailing surfaces for the faces of the gables.

For the rest of that day, and for days following, he worked on his roof. He constructed a scaffold that rested on the plates and on supports based on the middle sill. Then he pulled up his first set of rafters and assembled it temporarily and put it in place. Except for slight adjustments, the rafters fit well. So he disassembled them and returned to the ground, where he used them as a pattern to cut and drill the other rafters. When all the rafters were cut and drilled, he took one set at a time up the scaffold, where he assembled it, pounding the wooden peg into the drill hole, and fit it into its place, nailing the base to the plate. The first set of rafters, that of the north gable, he held in place with the three-by-six studs that would provide the structure for the gable. These he had tenoned, and he fit them snugly into mortises that he had chiseled into the top log of the north wall and into the bottom of the rafters. After erecting the second set of rafters out at the end of the plates, two feet beyond the gable, he temporarily tied it to the first by partially nailing a piece of lathing between the two. Then he erected the gable and end rafters on the south end, and temporarily braced them in similar fashion. Thereafter, he began filling in the space between the gables with sets of rafters (each two feet on center apart from those on either side), assembled and installed with the same precision and care. He temporarily braced each of these with lathing as well.

With the rafters all in place, he added fascia boards to both sides, across the ends of the rafters that overhung the plates. Then he began nailing lathing across the rafters, beginning at the bottom, from one end of the roof to the other, on both sides, and continuing one row of lathing above the last, with spacing in between each row, all the way to the ridge of what was becoming his roof.

Both sides of lathing completed, he began to shingle. The shingles he had been cutting with a froe from pieces of cedar. To guard against warping or curling, at Luke's insistence, he had cut many of them during the dark phase of the moon. He had then tapered them, using a draw knife, and had laid up quite a pile of them, for both his own house and that of the Stuarts. He now shingled both slopes of the roof all the way to the ridge, capping the ridge joint by allowing the tops of the shingles on the western side to extend nearly a foot above the ridge.

With the roof complete, Tom returned to the pen of the structure. He cut out holes for the chimney and windows. He knew that too many openings cut into a log structure tended to weaken it, but he liked a lot of light to enter a building. So, although he cut the holes, he made sure to firmly wedge the logs, to secure them in place, before he cut them. The chimney hole he cut into the southern wall, and he cut a little window next to it. Into the western wall, toward its northern end, he cut a window, almost directly across from the door. This western window could easily be extended into a doorway, should he care to do so at a later date. He cut a window into the north wall, as well, which gave a good view of the road into and out of the canyon. Into the eastern wall he cut a double window to the south of the doorway. This window looked down upon the canyon and the Stuart home below. He framed all the openings with stout oak boards that he had rived or ripped from logs. He then shuttered all the windows with solid oak and closed the doorway with a solid oak door. He hung the shutters and door with heavy hinges he had bought in San Antonio. Over the chimney opening he hung a wagon sheet.

It was time to return to the lime kiln, which he did. There he burned and crushed enough lime to make enough mortar—when mixed with sand, ashes, and water—to chink the logs. He first filled the chinks with pieces of stone, then daubed these with the mortar. The result was a certain permanence: a very solid house.

Next, Tom went to work on the floor. He rived puncheons from oak logs with a froe and mallet. These boards were about two feet long, six to ten inches wide, and two inches thick. At the ends of each puncheon, Tom chiseled out wood from its underside, so that he could fit it onto the sleepers with lap joints. The puncheons would then meet in the middle of the sleepers. Tom meticulously cut and shaped the puncheons to create tight joints, then augered holes into the ends of each one and, with wood pins, pinned the puncheons down to the sleepers. He smoothed the floor with a foot adze and planed, polished, and varnished it. The blond, finished oak floor offered a handsome contrast to the walls of planked cedar logs and red mortar, complementing a beauty based in natural elements, retaining much of their natural qualities, but now squared, straightened, and plumbed, having been cut, shaped, and assembled into a structure of functional strength and stability, according to a design of man.

In time, Tom would lay up a rock chimney, and add a porch along the entire front of the house, and a floor to the upper story inside, and other amenities. Of course, all this would take time, and during that time, Tom and the Stuarts and Andy would accomplish other things too, not the least of which would be the simultaneous construction of the Stuart rock house.

BUILDING, BUILDING, THE SETTLERS PROGRESSED in the construction of their canyon home. More important than the building of physical structures was a building that had begun long before they had entered the canyon. It had begun in places like postwar Tennessee and central Medina County, Texas and Dodge City, Kansas. It was the building of human relationships, within the larger context of the human relationship with God, without which even the richest of physical structures can never make a home.

The same work that produced the physical structures contributed to the building of the relationships among them, as they all took their parts in the work of the ranch according to their individual aptitudes and abilities and the needs of all. Thus, though it was not always pleasant work, it was, in a real sense, happy work, because it was wholesome work directed toward a common goal of benefit for them and benefit for others beyond their small community, whom they hoped to feed from the produce of their ranch, the bulk of which they intended to be a superior quality of beef.

Besides working together toward a common goal, these pioneers lived together. As part of that living, they shared their meals, at which they also shared prayer and the reading of Sacred Scripture. They prayed privately for each other, as well, especially on Sundays.

Sundays they had agreed to set aside. On Sundays, they avoided work and directed their thoughts and attention more determinedly toward God. In an arrangement that had developed while they were yet on the trail, the settlers would rise, dress in their better clothes (usually having bathed the evening before), then gather together and sing a hymn or two (acceptable to all) and then share a general prayer.

Then Tom and Andy, declining breakfast out of respect for the pre-Communion fast, would go apart and read through the Mass for that day, out of Tom's missal, and make a spiritual communion. Having done so, the two men might supplement the scriptural selections from the Mass with further reading from Sacred Scripture. Then they would pray the Gospel, meditating on the sacred mysteries in the life of their Savior, along with his mother, by praying the mysteries of the rosary, quite often praying all fifteen decades. Usually, then, they would talk for long periods of time about matters of the Christian Faith, pondering the mysteries, great and small, and delving deeper into "the sacred deposit of the Word of God" in Sacred Scripture and sacred Tradition, guided by the authentic interpretation of the Magisterium of the Church. Tom had several books to aid them in these exercises, among them the *Roman Catechism* and an eclectic collection of works of the fathers, doctors, and saints of the Church, some of which he had had his brother send to Fort Griffin for him to pick up upon his arrival there the previous fall.

Meanwhile, as Tom and Andy usually spent their Sunday mornings in this way, the Stuart family spent theirs according to their own custom. After the first hymns and prayer, shared with Tom and Andy, the Stuarts would eat their Sunday morning breakfast, prepared by both Elizabeth and Luke. Then they would continue with more hymns and prayer, and with the reading and expounding of a selection from Sacred Scripture. Then Elizabeth would lead the family in a Sunday school session.

Eventually, by midafternoon, all would gather together again for Sunday dinner, thanking God for his bounteous providence and enjoying that providence in a spirit of thanksgiving, not least of all for Elizabeth's skilled preparation of the routinely sumptuous feast. On days when weather permitted, and even invited, this dinner might become a picnic at some select site, possibly under a spreading cottonwood tree near one of the creeks or one of the many springs. Or, even if the meal were eaten indoors, the settlers, all together or not, might take a ride to, through, or out of the canyon, and just enjoy the beauty of the land in which they had made their home. In the colder weather, in particular—as autumn had sunk deeper toward winter, and winter deeper into itself before slowly climbing back out toward spring, and as shorter days and colder nights had slowly lengthened their hours spent in the dugout—especially later in the day, after some supper, the settlers might join each other in singing, or playing dominoes, or reading. Reading aloud to each other was a valued pastime, and Tom's and Elizabeth's collections provided an interesting assortment of books for it. Sometimes this reading would include acting out some of Shakespeare's plays. *Julius Caesar* was a favorite.

And they would talk. And they would listen. Sunday dinners provided a most fruitful setting for this intercourse, but it could occur at other times. On any other day, if the weather were especially wet or cold or both, one of Elizabeth's delicious midday dinners might stretch a little longer, as the men and Elizabeth might tarry in conversation at the table, with its warm food before the warm hearth in the warm home, before returning to work. Or such weather might occasion an early supper, allowing plenty of time for sitting around the table and visiting long after the meal had been finished, the room still aglow from the warm fire and the kerosene lamps. Or at other times, more common, after work had stretched late into the evening, regardless of the weather, the men would drop themselves into chairs around the table, where Elizabeth would serve them a late supper and join them in it. The children would already be in bed, though often not yet asleep, and the adults would linger, long after their appetites had been sated, to sate the human appetite for fellowship.

They would talk of thoughts and ideas, of that day's work, of dreams and plans for the future, and they would remember. Sharing a meal around the table, the center of their domestic life, they would remember. They would remember their common story, in relating memories of experiences shared, and would enrich that story by sharing memories from beyond the realm of their common story, memories particular to individuals, memories woven now into the common story through the communal remembering.

Each participated in this communal remembering in his or her own way. Luke and Tom, having gained plenty of experience in cowboy life, proved the most natural vocal contributors: the one would share a story that would rouse the memory of an experience in the other, which would then be shared as a story only to rouse a memory in the first, which would then be shared, and around and around. This cycle, enhanced now and then by contributions from other participants, could last for hours, often drawing requests from participants for a favorite story that had been shared in the past but that might well be enhanced, itself, in the retelling, the rehearing, or the re-imagining.

Occasionally, Luke and Elizabeth would offer a story together. In such a case, it was not unusual for one or the other of them to begin the story solo. Then, very shortly, the one who had not begun might make a correction to the rendering begun by the first. Then the first might respond to the correction defensively, with something like, "No, no, it was [such and such]." The second would counter with something like, "No, it was [such and such]." And this argument would continue, without any expression of anger on the part of either participant, but not without each one's expression of incredulity at the other's flawed memory. Eventually, one would either concede the point with something like, "All right, you're right, you're right," or would not concede the point, but would concede the argument, with something like, "That's not the way it happened, but you tell the story." At that point, whoever had received the concession would continue the story until the next interruption, which by then could be quite animated, "[Name], that is not the way it happened! Don't you remember that . . ." If this interruption, or the response to it, would not draw some kind of concession from one or the other, the story could dissolve into a humorous relating of two separate accounts of the same event, dissimilar in anything from fine points to major ones, offered by two people joined in marriage, who, barely able to contain varying degrees of potential laughter, could only relate their versions in ever deepening incredulity at the flawed recollection of the other, to the amusement of not only themselves but of all those present, including their children.

Apart from occasions like that just described, Elizabeth left most of the Stuart family storytelling to Luke, as she was acutely aware of how much better their stories were translated through the medium of

Luke's singular delivery. Still, she could be coaxed on occasion to offer a story, and on such an occasion would deliver her story competently, though her obvious lack of confidence in the appeal of her story, or in the appeal of her telling of it, or just her lack of enjoyment in telling it would rob the story of the life natural to it. That was part of the reason that it was not only Luke's natural gift for telling stories that prompted Elizabeth to leave them to him, but also the fact that she was just not as inclined to tell stories, especially as the only woman in the company of all men, as she was inclined to listen to them. And she was never more inclined to listen to a story than when her husband was telling it, her husband whose gift she had so long recognized and reveled in, especially through years when his failure to learn to read had discouraged him and puzzled her. Through all that time, and more so now, she had been proud of this creative ability in Luke and, to some degree, amazed by it. And so she was content to enjoy it, and to enjoy his enjoyment of it, and her children's enjoyment of it, and the enjoyment of Tom and Andy, too, as she loved them all, her family very deeply, and Tom and Andy in a deepening wholesome affection. Accordingly, she enjoyed her listening, and, in doing so, enjoyed an integral component of communal remembering. Still, though it was by this integral component of listening that Elizabeth best participated in the party's communal remembering, neither she, nor anyone else, so participated better than Andy.

Andy would listen with a quiet intensity that gave more of an active than passive quality to that receptive form of participation. A glistening in his deep eyes would communicate his appreciation for the story, the teller, and the telling, an appreciation that was well grounded in his multiethnic heritage. Nevertheless, now and then, though not often, his quiet, manly voice would enter into the cycle of storytelling, arresting the attention of all other participants. At such times, as he would offer a thread of his story to weave into the fabric of their common story, that uncommon thread, and its telling in subdued intensity, would hold all his listeners suspended upon every word that he would deliberately bring forth in a vocal composition masterfully phrased.

Still, even more than Andy or Elizabeth, the children usually confined their participation to listening, often with their eyes wide, whether still at the table or already snug in bed in the quiet and warmth and glow of the earthen home. If still at the table, Zachariah would sometimes nudge a parent or make so bold as to speak up and request a favorite story of his father or Tom. He rarely requested a story of his mother, who was so apparently content to leave the storytelling to others. And he almost never requested a story of Andy, unless he was alone with him, as Andy's stories, and the manner in which he delivered them, inspired a respect as of the sacred, which inclined one to leave the when and where of his storytelling to the discretion of that inscrutable teller.

At times, even the children would contribute, usually after coaxing by the adults or after they had roused enough courage to speak up. Then the adults would listen intently—light smiles softening their faces—encouraging the child, tongue-tied though he or she may be, to the end of the story. In fact, among those adults, both Luke and Tom, by far the most frequent talkers, proved also to be good listeners, not only to the children, but to each other and to Elizabeth and Andy. They listened with interest and, truly, with an eagerness proportional to the infrequency of the teller's contributions.

Thus, each participated in the remembering in his or her own way. And thus were various threads exposed and contributed to the weaving of a common story, particular threads from separate lives and common threads from a shared life, all weaving together, as were those lives, each contributing to the common story being composed in the living and kept alive in the telling, in communal remembering.

And no less should have been expected, for these were Christians. Tom and Andy, in particular, as members of the Catholic Church, were participants in the unbroken Tradition begun with God's call and promise to Abraham, which led through the Passover and the Sinai Covenant ultimately to the Paschal Mystery of Jesus Christ and the New Covenant in his blood made with the new People of God, the Church: the "instrument for the salvation of all," the sacrament of the mission of Christ and the Holy Spirit, "the sacrament of the Holy Trinity's communion with men." As such, they were rememberers, participants in the most essential remembering: the inspired and graced communal remembering that makes present, remembering around a table, in thanksgiving, in a shared meal, a sacrificial meal, the salvific remembering handed on in the Sacred Liturgy of the Catholic Church.

A type of that sacrificial meal with its own type of remembering is the family meal. And the family meal, shared in thanksgiving around a common table, was still important to the Stuart-Schurtz settlers, as it often is to those who, upon the land and amidst the elements, must hunt, gather, raise, grow, and harvest the food that sustains them and those whom they love. Just so, the ancient People of God had known the importance of the common meal shared in thanksgiving. They had known famine, hunger, want. They had known manna and quail in the desert. They had not had the luxury of insulating themselves from the reality of divine providence, and they had suffered grievously for those times when they had tried to do so. To share their table, their meal, had been to share their very life. It is no wonder that the defining event of their history, the Exodus from bondage in Egypt, has ever since, according to God's own command, been remembered around the family table, remembered in a sacrificial meal, the Passover, that had originally anticipated the redemptive event of the Exodus. For the People of God of the Old Covenant, the redemptive event becomes present in that memorial, so that the participants in the memorial participate efficaciously in the event made present in the remembering of their common story of redemption by God.

In the context of that Passover (that meal, that feast, that sacrifice, that memorial), the Jew, Jesus of Nazareth, the Messiah, gathered at table with his friends, his apostles. There he took bread, blessed it, offered thanks, broke it, and gave it to his apostles to eat, and he took a cup of wine, gave thanks, and gave it to his apostles to drink, declaring these species of bread and wine to be his body and blood and commanding his apostles to do as he had done, in remembrance of him. In so doing, he instituted a new meal, a new feast, a new sacrifice, a new memorial, a new sacrament, and included his apostles in it, anticipating, in his prophetic word-action, the redemptive event of the Exodus from the bondage of sin, which he would accomplish for mankind in his sacrifice on the cross, and incorporating that sacrificial meal into his Paschal mystery, which "participates in the divine eternity, and so transcends all times while being made present in them all."

In that new sacrificial meal, he also anticipated the institution of the New Covenant in his blood, which was "poured out for many" in his sacrifice on the cross, and he "instituted his apostles as priests" of that New Covenant, which had been promised by God through the prophet Jeremiah. That New Covenant is made with a new People of God, the Church, a convocation, a communion of Jews and gentiles alike, who are not one "according to the flesh, but in the Spirit," built upon the foundation of the apostles, and animated by the Holy Spirit, and called to remember. This Catholic Church is the Mystical Body of Christ, with Christ as its Head. It is in the Church's liturgical remembrance of the abiding event of Christ's sacrifice, in thanksgiving and blessing, around a common table, in a sacrificial meal, with a successor of the apostles or one of his ordained representatives as priest, by the power of Christ and the Holy Spirit, according to God's own command, that the salvific event of Christ's sacrifice is recalled and made present, so that the participants in the memorial participate efficaciously in the saving event of Christ's Paschal mystery, the Exodus from the bondage of sin and death. By the graces of that sacrament, the separate threads of the lives of the participants in the communal remembering weave together into the fabric of the life of the Church, as they become one in communion with God and one another.

The vocation to this communion is rooted in the very heart of man. The essential nature of this communion is illustrated in an everyday type of this communion that is essential to physical life and the life of the family. That is the family meal, in which the participants take their sustenance in sharing a meal around a common table, in thanksgiving for their share in God's bounty, remembering how God has worked in their lives, and sharing their separate stories in the making of their common story, partaking of the life-sustaining food in the making of their common life as a family. Just as this communal meal is central to the earthly life of the family and its members, so is the memorial, sacrificial meal of the Eucharist, and its communion, central to the eternal life of the Church and its members. Those who respond to the vocation to this communion are called Christians. Therefore, it should be no surprise that the Christians of the Stuart-Schurtz party would naturally weave their separate stories into their common story by remembering around a common table in a shared meal in a spirit of thanksgiving. Nor should it be any surprise that a bond had grown up among them and was gradually strengthening and deepening. Nor should it be any surprise that in that bond they were building a home.

So, that building that should have been no surprise continued; and structures of wood and stone rose up in houses, outbuildings, fences, and roads; and structures of the human spirit deepened in the settlers' relationships with each other and in their relationships with the munificent Creator (whom they were growing to know more deeply in all this building) and in their relationships with the rest of creation through their relationships with its immediate presentation in the land in which they were set. And in that land in which they were set, the results of their building, both physical and spiritual, became gradually more apparent as the cold night of winter slowly gave way to the cool, but warming, morning of spring.

Chapter Five

COMINGS AND GOINGS

Look abroad thro' Nature's range,
Nature's mighty law is change.
—ROBERT BURNS

SPRING 1878 BUDDED AND BLOSSOMED IN THE canyon as did every type of its native flora. Nor was the native fauna to be outdone, as miniature copies of various canyon animals could be seen following in their mothers' footsteps. Everywhere was new life, so much so that the exotic human inhabitants of the canyon stood in awe before the reality that their dormant canyon of winter had contained the fecund potential budding and blossoming ever fuller every day, life springing out in a world opening up large enough for all of it.

Just so, the Seven Ox Seven Ranch appeared to be blossoming from its potential. Pens or corrals graced the pasture just to the north

of the Stuart house, with a picket barn attached to the pens northeast
of the house, just at the point where the bank behind the house leveled into the pasture. At the head of the canyon, up on the flat that
Tom had chosen for the site of his house, a corral stood to the northwest of the Schurtz house.

The houses themselves stood ever closer to full blossom, though
they had not sprung from any winter dormancy, but rather had risen
deliberately from any winter industry the exotic humans had been able
to devote to them. As a result, a neat, two-story, stone building stood
where Luke, Tom, and Andy had set the foundations for the Stuart
house. It consisted of a large main room and a smaller room on the
western end, Luke and Elizabeth's bedroom, in which a staircase led to the
second floor, where the children would sleep. "Would sleep" because
the house was not yet complete, and the Stuarts had not yet moved in.
The double thickness walls stood complete with a completed roof atop
them, but the upstairs had no floor, at least not a complete one. Luke
and Andy were still at work nailing down a plank floor atop the joists
that Tom had recommended be mortised into the walls as the walls
went up. Tom had not only recommended the mortising but had
directed its execution. When the upstairs plank floor would lie complete, the men would lay the downstairs flagstone floor. Then they
would lay up the chimney. After that they would shutter the windows,
hang the door, and eventually attach a porch.

Up at the head of the canyon, the Schurtz house lay at the point
where Tom was installing his puncheon floor. He would yet need to
rehang his door, which he had taken off to more easily install the floor.
Then he would need to lay up his chimney and eventually build on his
porch (which would look out to the east, a little to the southeast, down
upon the canyon and the Stuart house below). With his porch completed on the front of the house, he would attach a lean-to shed on the
back. After that he could lay a floor across the second-floor joists of his
house, if and when he felt the need.

As their industry produced these additions to their ranch, other
important additions, for which they could take only limited credit,
were generated in an ongoing fashion. In the dark of night or light of
day, morning, noon, or night, they were generated, sometimes quietly,
sometimes not. When not quietly, these additions could include a

lighter version of the bovine bawl, an immature version, which signaled the natural increase of the Seven Ox Seven herd. Despite loss to predators (with whom the settlers waged continual war), disease, exposure, and other causes, the herd was increasing at a good rate.

It was nearly time to take inventory of that increase, and thus, with the spring came the roundup. The settlers were impatient to round up to see how the cattle had fared, to better acquaint themselves with their canyon, and to cut out those beeves ready for market. They had been hoping to sell the cattle to Charles Goodnight at the JA Ranch in Palo Duro Canyon, even though they had as yet had no contact with him, and by that transaction relieve themselves of the need to drive such a small herd to market and, at the same time, receive some money to put toward furthering the development of their ranch. They hoped to have money in hand when one of Matthew Colmey's crew would deliver their patents to the land Colmey had located for them. Then they would pay for the purchase and location of more certificates to expand the boundaries of what they owned.

Beyond that, Tom planned a trip to Dodge City, Kansas, as soon as possible. He had decided not to wait and see if he could join a JA drive to that city, as he was impatient to attend to business, both professional and personal. In Dodge City, he would be able to sell the hides and skins that he, Luke, and Andy had been accumulating from wolf, deer, antelope, bear, wildcat, coyote, raccoon, skunk, hare and rabbit, and even panther. He also hoped that he could act as a broker for any of the hands at the JA who might have accumulated their own surpluses of hides and skins and who might appreciate having them sold in Dodge City. He would sell bones, too, from the tons that littered the prairie in the wake of the buffalo slaughter. These he could pick up as he walked along beside the wagon, and he could fit them into any empty space in the wagon. (They would be used to make combs and other utensils, or they would be burned or ground and used in the making of fertilizer, bone china, or polishing compounds, or in the refining of sugar.) Of course, an important part of his trip to Dodge City would be to acquire things needed and desired at the ranch. Among these would be molasses, salt, coffee, canned and dried goods, material from which Elizabeth could make clothes, as well as some clothes themselves, and boots, shoes, tools, ammunition, and,

possibly, windows, doors, and milled lumber. There was one other purchase he intended to bring home from Dodge City, a purchase about
which the Stuarts and Andy knew nothing. He had been looking forward to bringing this purchase home for some time, and he continued
to look forward to surprising his fellow settlers with it.

As for the personal business he was impatient to attend to, besides
the secret purchase, this bachelor had his "honeymoon cabin," as Luke
would have it, and it was time to see just what lay between Molly
Banks and him. They had been writing to each other since they had
parted the summer before. The last letters he had been able to send
had gone back to Fort Griffin with the Colmey surveying party before
Christmas. He had continued to write but had had no opportunity to
send the subsequent letters back to civilization. Now, he intended to
deliver them himself.

He had received some letters from Molly before Christmas, as well.
The surveying party had brought them out with the rest of the mail
destined for the Seven Ox Seven party. Those letters—and the ones he
had picked up in Fort Griffin the fall before, and the ones he had
picked up in San Antonio the summer before that—had revealed an
intelligent, warm, wholesome, family-oriented woman, who would
like to see him again, as soon as circumstances would allow. Such sentiments, expressed by a woman like Molly Banks, can often do their
part to hasten the circumstances that would allow. And so they did,
helping Tom to decide on an earlier date for his trip and on making it
to Dodge City rather than back to Fort Griffin (the less attractive,
whatever the circumstances, of the two options, especially since he had
learned from other letters that had arrived with the mail carried by the
Colmey party that Miss Nancy Hawkins of Kentucky had left Griffin
well before Christmas to return to her native state).

Tom was not the only one planning on a change. Andy, too, had
been doing some serious thinking along those lines. One day Andy
made known the fruits of this thinking. He and Luke had begun to lay
the stone floor of the Stuart house. Tom was there, too, to help with
shaping and laying the stones, and to mortar. At one point, late in the
afternoon, when the men took a break to pass a bucket of water and
ladle around, as they looked over that portion of the floor that they
had already completed, Andy spoke up.

"Luke and Tom," he began, drawing both men's attention, as, coming from Andy, it sounded like the beginning of a formal address, which they were not accustomed to receive from that source, "I've been thinkin' that I might like to join a drive this spring."

Neither of the men said anything. They both just froze, their staring at the floor immediately intensified with Andy's announcement. Tom stood for a moment, his lips pressed tightly, nodding his head slowly at the news. Luke bent, picked up a stone, and placed it on the sand nowhere near that portion of the floor already completed. Then he stood up again and attempted to position the stone with his foot in a place where it did not belong.

"You've thought about this, then?" Tom said, turning his head toward Andy, though only looking at him for a short glance and then looking down again.

"I have," Andy said. "The railroads are movin' ever farther into the country. Won't be too many years before the railroad is close enough to make a trail drive nothin' but a couple days' ride. Besides, people will be movin' into the country. Mr. Goodnight's already here. Mr. Smith in Blanco Canyon was talkin' about his great plans to get people out into that country. With the buffalo all but gone and the Indians on the reservation, herders will move out into these ranges, and all the good land will be taken up. Right now, you two can handle this outfit by yourselves. We got most of the foundational work done. From here it's mainly just buildin'. In a couple years, expandin' as you are, you won't be able to handle this alone. If I leave now and take the opportunity to ride in a drive or two before it's too late, I'll have that experience and I can maybe save up enough to start my own herd and come back to work with you with my own stake and startin' my own brand."

Tom kept looking down, nodding his head deliberately as Andy delivered this uncharacteristically detailed response. Luke shifted the rock a time or two with his foot.

Finally, Tom raised his eyebrows as he shook his head. He could almost feel Andy's conscientiousness about leaving the Stuarts and Tom at this time, and his need to make a short, quick, and solid case for doing so, as much for himself as for them. "Well," Tom said, "you have thought it out some. You fixin' to try the Goodnight outfit?"

"Figured I would. That's what's available."

"Huh," Tom responded.

"Well, you sure will be missed around here," Luke said, turning partly toward Andy but finding it difficult to look at him.

"You sure will," Tom agreed. Then he sighed a little as a light smile spread across his face, and he said, "I do remember my first drive, and that sure is somethin' a man shouldn't miss if he can help it. Goodnight and his outfits are as good as they get, too. You'd be trailin' with the best." Tom smiled wistfully again. "How old are you now, Andy?"

"Eighteen."

"Huh," Tom responded. "Well, I surely can't blame you for wantin' to head up the trail. Now's the time, too, while you're young and got so much ahead of you."

Luke kicked a little here and there at the rock. Finally, he said, "Andy, I wish we could pay you more than we have been payin'. We had planned to give you a bonus after the sale of the beeves. We've been plannin' it all along."

"I've got no complaints. It's been a real privilege to work with you all in the startin' of this ranch, and I hope to work with you all again. It's just that now's the time for me to go, or maybe I never will." Andy's words and his delivery conveyed a maturity deeper than that Tom and Luke had known in him, a maturity commensurate with the decision he had made and intended to carry out.

"I understand that," Luke responded in a serious tone, as the rock failed to rest in any one position under the influence of the toe of his boot, "but know that you will be receivin' a bonus."

"It's not expected, but I thank you."

"You plannin' on leavin' right away?" Luke asked him.

"No. You all said you're plannin' on an early roundup. I figured to work that with you, then try for a spot with a Goodnight drive. If I can get on a drive, there may not be work for me later; so I could wind up returnin' here after, though I do hope to work for Goodnight if I get the chance."

"Understood," Luke said.

"And understandable," Tom added.

"As I say," Luke continued, as he headed out the doorway to the pile of rocks, "you will be missed, not only in your work, but Elizabeth and the young'uns will miss you, especially Zack." He passed Tom and Andy and set down a pile of rocks on the sand subfloor; then he stood and made his way back past them, and they fell in behind him. As he was about to stoop down to pick up more rocks, he paused and thought for a moment. "No," he said thoughtfully, "especially Elizabeth."

And Luke was right. Upon receipt of the news of Andy's future departure, that night after the children had gone to bed, a deep, hollow sigh escaped from Elizabeth, as if it had been pulled out of her very soul. Elizabeth, the lone woman for miles, was losing one of her own. Though all three men had always been most accommodating to Elizabeth, Andy had more often been available to help Elizabeth directly, as Luke and Tom had more often been caught up in a managerial approach to the work about their infant ranch. Besides, years before, Andy had begun coming around the Stuart home in Medina County not long after they had first moved in, when he had come to visit with his father. Ever after that, on days when his father would let him take a break from the sheep, he might drop in at any time, and hunt with Luke or help with the cattle. Then, while Luke was away on the drive, he had checked in on Elizabeth frequently, making sure she was all right, hunting for her when she needed food, helping her with any work around the ranch, taking the children out from under foot when she needed time to work on other things or if she weren't feeling well due to her pregnant condition. It was Andy who had gone for his mother and sisters when little Robert was about to be born.

Often enough since the arrival in the canyon—especially after hunting, when he was butchering or preparing a hide—Andy was closer to home in work, and he was closer to home in age, too. He was like the younger brother Elizabeth had left back in the Dallas area when they had moved to Medina County in 1873: in truth, a man, but a man very lately a boy, a boy she herself had watched grow into this manhood, a boy she still knew within this manhood, one for whom she had cooked, toiled, and worried, one of her own, and he was leaving.

THE NEXT DAY AT THE NOON DINNER, Luke told Zachariah and Rachel about Andy's pending departure. Rachel appeared to be somewhat mystified by the announcement, but Zachariah expressed his reaction in words.

"You're leavin', Andy?" he said incredulously.

"I am, Zack."

"But where're you goin' to?" Zachariah asked him.

"Probably north of here."

"Why're you leavin', Andy?" Zachariah asked this young man who had been a part of his life for as long as he could remember. "Don't you want to stay with us anymore?"

This last comment, asked as it was from one so young, had its effect on the adults sitting around the table. Luke shifted in his chair and looked down. Tom looked down and pressed his lips together and nodded his head a couple of times. Elizabeth sniffed, batted her eyes a couple of times and, looking away from the table, dabbed at her eyes with the edge of her apron. Even the unflappable Andy needed to look down and clear his throat before he could answer.

"Well, Zack," Andy eventually said, after he had looked back up, "it ain't that I don't want to stay. It's that I've been wantin' for as long as I can remember to join a cattle drive north. Now I can do so, and I don't know how much longer I'll be able to. Besides, Tom and your mama and daddy," he thought for a second and added, "and you and Rachel and little Bob can handle this ranch all by yourselves. Won't be long before you can't. Then, maybe I'll head back this way."

"You'll be comin' back then?"

"Maybe."

"When you comin' back, Andy?"

"Well, I don't rightly know, Zack."

"Are you comin' back soon?"

"Well, most likely not, Zack."

"Aren't you goin' to miss us, Andy?"

Again heads bowed or turned, sniffs were heard. Andy's bowed head finally came up, and he said, his eyes looking directly into Zachariah's, "I will miss you, Zack, and I will never forget you. Besides, I won't be so far away as I can't come and visit sometimes."

With the news that Andy would not be leaving right away and that he would still be able to visit after he had left, the situation did not appear so bleak to young Zachariah, though it appeared plenty bleak enough. Nevertheless, they finally put the matter of Andy's leaving to rest for the time being and finished dinner, after which all returned to their work.

•   •   •

THE SPRING RAINS provided green grass already in early April, much to the settlers' delight, and they began the roundup not long after that. The good grass would provide the calves with plenty of nutrition to help them recover from their ordeal. Among various other reasons for an early roundup was the consideration that with so many buffalo carcasses lying rotting out on the plains, especially as the weather warmed, there would be blowflies and screwworm flies and their larvae, and the earlier the roundup the less likely those parasites would complicate the healing process, especially after castration. Beyond those pests, the men expected little complication to the roundup, in general, as they had kept the small herd well in check by conscientious line riding, which had been facilitated by the natural corral of the steep-walled canyon with the outliers at its mouth. Their line riding had had the added benefit of better acquainting them with the canyon, which would also contribute to a better roundup.

The settlers moved down to the lower end of the canyon, where Luke and Tom had chosen a steep, wide draw that formed a box canyon and had fenced off its mouth to serve as a holding pen for the cattle. Elizabeth drove the smaller wagon, pulled by a team of mules, and the men brought a small remuda of horses to use in the roundup. Rachel and little Robert rode in the wagon, and Zachariah rode a mule bareback alongside the wagon. Not far from the fenced draw, Elizabeth set up camp. The men set out to round up the lower end of the canyon.

With the help of Zachariah and Rita, and her five five-month-old puppies (already showing signs of their herder heritage), and Charlie (now about eight months old, who was becoming quite a herder in his own right, under Andy's and Rita's tutelage), the men managed to round up all the beeves in the lower canyon, with its many draws, in a few days. At the end of the day on which they finished rounding up, late in the evening, as the adults sat eating their supper in the light of the fire, the children already fast asleep on the ground near them, Luke made a particular point to Andy.

"Andy," Luke began, "as I said, we had intended to give you a bonus. We've been talkin', and since we don't have much for cash right now, and since you were so much a part of our beginnin's, we'd like you to share in our increase. Besides your pay, we'd like you to pick out ten calves to brand in your own brand. You'll be startin' your own herd, and can keep 'em right here on our range."

"And if old Colonel Goodnight lets you start a herd on his range," Tom added, "you can throw these beeves over onto that range or keep 'em here, whatever you like. In time, you might even locate your own range, right alongside ours if you like."

The spark that always burned deep in Andy's quiet, green-brown eyes grew a little brighter as he contemplated his future.

"Thank you, Luke, Elizabeth," he said, shaking hands with Luke and nodding toward Elizabeth.

"Thanks, Tom," he added, as he shook Tom's hand.

"You're welcome," Elizabeth and Tom said one after the other. "And thanks to you," Tom added, as Elizabeth nodded.

"That's right," Luke said.

THE NEXT DAY, they cut the calves out of the herd in the draw and had the dogs hold them against the fence they had built across the draw, which was not especially difficult because the calves tried to stay as near the calls of their mothers, on the other side of the fence, as they could. The next step was to have one man on horseback rope a calf out of the herd and drag it out to where the other two men would flank, throw, and hold it, while the first man would jump down from his horse and brand, castrate, and earmark the calf. It was hard work, given that Herman Richter cattle bred stout calves.

Andy started out on horseback so that he could select the six calves he intended to brand from the lower canyon. He selected meticulously and with a good eye, which caused Luke and Tom to smile at each other in approval of Andy's judgment (and not without a sense of their own loss) with each of the fine specimens he chose. He chose four heifers and two bulls, both of which he castrated. He had thought about what he would choose the night before. Six in the lower herd (four heifers, two bulls) and four in the upper herd (two heifers and two bulls). He had a pretty good idea of even the individual calves he would choose, because he had had plenty of opportunity to get to know them through his line riding. He would castrate all bulls because he did not need bulls: Tom and Luke's bulls would provide where needed. The heifers would assure that his herd would continue to increase, while the steers, as few as they were, would assure that in four years' time he would have a few head to sell should he be in need of cash.

He used dotting irons to apply his AG-connected brand. Thereafter, for the Stuart-Schurtz cattle, he switched to the Seven Ox Seven stamp iron that had been fashioned for Luke by Herman Richter while down in Medina County. The men rotated from flanking, to roping and branding, to flanking throughout the day. Zachariah was there to help, collecting in a bucket the testicles that would later be converted into the delicacy calf fries. Meanwhile, Elizabeth, Rachel, and Robert watched the process, Elizabeth keeping these smaller children well out of the way until they withdrew to the camp. There she prepared a hearty noon dinner for the hungry men, and later, a hearty supper for the same. By the end of the day, they had branded 87 calves, counting Andy's 6. Besides these, they had rounded up 158 head of previously branded cattle. Out of those 158, they cut out 35 four-year-old steers, which they left penned in the draw. These they would drive up to the upper canyon, to be held there until sold. They freed the rest of the steers and any calfless cows and heifers. They drove the newly branded calves and their mothers out to a pasture at a leisurely pace, allowing calves and mothers to find each other on the way. At the pasture, the men oversaw the reunions of mothers and calves, until they were satisfied all were reunited. Then they left them there to recover and graze.

The next day, the settlers broke camp and started for the upper canyon. Elizabeth drove the wagon, with the younger children aboard, ahead to the house, as the men, Zachariah, and the dogs herded the 35 four-year-olds ahead of them, rounding up all other cattle, save the bulls, as they went.

Over the next few days, they rounded up the upper canyon and penned the animals in the pens built for that purpose behind the Stuart house. They cut out all the four-year-old steers and put them with the four-year-olds from the lower canyon in a pasture watched over by the dogs. Then they began the same process of cutting, branding, castrating, and earmarking that they had finished in the lower canyon. Andy selected his four calves at the very beginning, to complete the beginning of his herd, and then they continued with the rest.

On the day that they were branding, they were surprised to see a lone rider enter the canyon by the trail near Tom's house. They watched him ride over to Tom's house, where he lingered for a while before he returned to the trail and rode toward them.

As the rider drew nearer, they halted the branding. Tom and Luke climbed out of the pen and awaited his arrival. Andy remained on his horse inside the pen, and Zachariah kept his place sitting on the top rail of the pen. The men watched the rider with interest and not without cognizance of the six-shooters in their holsters, as rustlers and outlaws were known to find their ways to the frontier. Though he was only one man, they could not be sure of what sort of man or of how many others might be waiting at a safe distance.

Shortly, the rider pulled up on a large sorrel. He was a powerfully built man, with broad shoulders and a full chest. His hair and beard were dark, though beginning to gray. His eyes, too, were dark, and piercing, as they took in the sight of the men and boy and indeed the whole setting before him.

"Name's Charlie Goodnight," he said as he dismounted and approached in a determined, bowlegged stride that indicated just how accustomed he was to saddle work. He thrust out his hand at Tom, who shook it and offered his name, then at Luke, who did the same.

"This is a fine place you have here. How long you been here?" he queried.

"Since last October," Luke answered.

"Did you build that log house up there?" Goodnight nodded back over his shoulder.

"That's Tom's," Luke said.

"You built it?" he inquired of Tom.

"I did."

"That house is the work of a true craftsman. Those mortises on the corners are as good as any I've ever seen, and I've seen plenty, have cut plenty myself."

"Thank you, sir."

"I've been cutting some lately. I run the JA Ranch in the Palo Duro Canyon, north of here," Goodnight said of the ranch he was building in partnership with the Briton John Adair, the financing behind the concern, "and we've been doing some building of our own. I'm out scouting the territory. You're the only folks in this country, other than rustlers. Had any trouble with 'em?"

"None to speak of," Luke responded.

"None to speak of," Goodnight repeated. "We've had our share of trouble. But I've got good men, which keeps any losses to a minimum. Still, you'd think you'd have some trouble. Probably haven't found the place, as I could hardly believe it when I happened upon it. I scouted out this country in 1863 with the Frontier Regiment of rangers," Goodnight said of those who fought to hold back the frontier after the Union troops had pulled out or been forced out of Confederate Texas, "and I don't recall ever coming across this canyon."

"It is well disguised from the rollin' plains," Tom explained, "as its mouth is blocked from view by outliers."

"That must account for it," Goodnight said, "though I find it hard to believe we missed it. It's almost as if it weren't here. If rustlers knew of it, they'd be here. And you can bet the Indians know of it, and they might be here yet."

Tom and Luke nodded their heads in agreement with these senti-ments of the noted cattleman. He looked at them as they did so. Then with an energy that seemed to belie his stocky physique, he turned his attention to the cattle in the pens.

"These are good-looking cattle," he said.

"Well, sir," Luke said, "we're glad you think so, as we were hopin' to sell you some four-year-olds."

"You were?" Goodnight responded, with a quick look at Luke that almost gave away his appreciation for Luke's straightforward approach.

"Yes sir, we were. And we planned to send back to you two of your own that drifted this far south," Luke said of two beefy steers bearing the JA brand that they had rounded up with the rest.

"Couple of my own, eh? Drifted this far, did they? Where are they?"

"They're yonder, with the four-year-olds, beyond that rise," Luke said, nodding to the northwest.

"Well, let's take a look at those four-year-olds," Goodnight said. And in moments all three men were mounted and heading toward the herd. Andy had let himself out of the pen, and Zachariah had called to go with him. So, Andy rode up alongside the pen and pulled Zachariah off the top rail and swung him into the saddle in front of him and rode to catch up with the men.

When they arrived at the herd of the four-year-olds and the two JA steers that were being held by the dogs in good pasture, Goodnight looked them over.

"These are first-rate Texas cattle," he said. "Where they from?"

"Medina County," Luke responded.

"That far south?"

"Yes sir. They were bred by a man named Herman Richter, who knew what he was doing."

"He certainly did," Goodnight concurred. "They wintered over in this country?" he asked, expressing a concern about Texas fever.

"Been here since October," Luke assured him.

Goodnight looked the cattle over again. Then he said to Luke and Tom, all the while still looking at the cattle, "I've brought in Durham bulls and am crossing the Texas stock with those. The cross has extra bone and weight without losing the Texas stock's superiority for trailing and the open range."

"We're plannin' to grade our herd," Luke told him.

"You are?" he said, looking at Luke and Tom. "Well, don't lose that Texas foundation." He paused then asked, "You interested in shorthorn bulls? There are more Durhams where those came from, and if you're interested, just let me know."

"Well, sir," Luke said, "to be plain, we're not quite sure what we'll cross with yet. Hear good and bad about shorthorns."

"I'll tell you," Goodnight responded, "in the winter of '71, on the Laramie Plains, I saw some Aberdeen-Angus that came through that winter in good shape, while plenty of cattle froze to death. That would be a good cross, if a man could get it, but they're hard to come by."

Tom spoke up. "I've heard some good about Herefords," he said. Upon hearing this, Goodnight lowered his head and looked down as a slightly amused, knowing look took hold of his features. Tom continued, "Hear they're good rustlers in any conditions, put beef on fast on grazin' alone, mature early, and produce superior calves . . ." His litany of the attributes of the Hereford drifted off as he watched the famed cattleman add a slight shaking of the head to his amused, knowing look.

Goodnight looked out over the steers and spoke as one who knew better. "A certain T. L. Miller out of Illinois has been making a lot of noise about those white-faced Herefords, but I saw some of his Herefords in Las Animas in '76, and they were no good. I told him so, too, and he got as hot as a wolf."

Tom glanced down at this intelligence. A sudden intensity came into his eyes and a wrinkle set into his forehead as his face took on a bit of color. After a moment, he seemed to realize that he was wasting this look of intensity on the back of his horse's neck, and he pursed his lips and rearranged his other features and raised his face to look out over the steers with a more contented look that required some effort.

"Well," Goodnight said, shifting from the topic of Herefords, "what do you got, sixty, sixty-five head?" He began to count. "I count sixty-four," he said after a moment. "Sound about right?"

"That's what we reckon," Luke said.

"I'll give you twenty dollars a head," Goodnight said, "in gold, provided one of you trail 'em back with me and receive payment." Goodnight knew, as did Luke and Tom, that this was a good price for a range buy, but he knew, as well, that this was as much an investment as a purchase, as these were apparently good people who intended to make good of this unsettled country.

Luke looked over at Tom, who pursed his lips and nodded, and Luke looked back at Goodnight.

"We accept your offer, Mr. Goodnight," he said.

"I'll take these for now, but I'll tell you, I may be interested in more than just steers in the future, given the quality of your cattle. I would be interested in talking to you about cows and heifers, as well. So don't count that out. As it is for now, though, we'll be trailing some to Dodge after roundup, so these beeves will suffice."

"We'll keep that in mind," Luke said.

Goodnight sat and looked over the cattle, then watched as one steer began to wander off a ways from the rest. Rita watched it, too, and in a moment was on her way toward him and shortly had him turned and trotting back toward the herd.

"Looks like you've got a good herder in that dog there," Goodnight noted.

"Thank you, sir," Luke said. "Rita, the bitch, and her puppies there belong to Andy here." Luke nodded toward Andy. "And Charlie," Luke glanced up at Goodnight as he pronounced the name that the cattleman and the puppy shared, "belongs to my boy, Zachariah." Luke nodded again, and Goodnight looked at Andy and Zachariah upon the horse.

"Where'd you get those dogs?" he asked Andy.

"They're descended from a bitch my grandfather brought over from Ireland or England."

"They full blood?"

"As far as we know."

"Would you be interested in selling any of those pups?"

"I might be," Andy considered.

"One of my men returned from New Mexico not long ago with a couple of New Zealand pups," Goodnight informed them. "He'd seen two adult New Zealand dogs herding two flocks of sheep each, and he begged a couple of the pups off the *pastores*.

"I know myself about the value of a herding dog. In the spring of '69, I was carrying thirty thousand dollars, riding alone from Colorado into New Mexico, trying to catch a Texas herd before they all began moving north, so as to buy one. I took with me a shepherd dog named Shep, that I had trained to sleep at the foot of my bed, in case of outlaws.

"After buying a herd on the Canadian, I hired three of that outfit's men to drive the two thousand head just purchased. As I had seen them gambling the night before we left, I told them I did not allow gambling, and they agreed that they would not. Well, it did not take long for them to go back on their word, more than once, and finally, though I tried to talk reasonably with them, the fighter in the bunch, thinking he had me in a hole, looked up and said, 'Well, what are you gonna do about it?'

"'One thing I can do; I can pay you off,' I told him.

"'What'll you do with your cattle?' he asked me.

"'Listen here,' I said, 'that's none of your business. They're my cattle and I paid for them. See that trail? Get your horses and get on it blamed quick.'

"I happened to have plenty of silver in my pocket, and just pitched their wages down to them without getting off my horse, made them saddle their own, and saw that they took the back-trail then and there.

"With the dog alone, I kept two thousand head drifting in the right direction for two days before I could hire another man, and then only one. The next day I hired one more, a known outlaw with whom I had already had a run-in, but I was desperate, and he repentant. At that point, it was just three of us and that dog. And up till those hires, it had just been me and that dog. The point is that dog was worth several men.

"There was another sheep dog that I remember showing exceptional mettle. Not long after we entered the Palo Duro in '76, along came these hombres, Casner by name, two brothers, who brought sixteen hundred head of sheep, along with some cattle and horses, into the canyon. Well, this Sostenes Archiveque, a particularly bloodthirsty outlaw, waylaid the Casners, and . . . ," Goodnight hesitated, glancing over at Zachariah (who was obviously tuned in to everything being said), and then continued, "dispatched them both, along with their Navajo herder. He didn't figure on their dog, though. That dog attacked him viciously, and he, uh . . . ," again he hesitated, glancing at Zachariah. He looked back to Luke and Tom and continued, "He shot out one of the dog's eyes, to save himself. Then he left for Tascosa, where he himself was promptly dispatched by Colas Martinez (an honorable *comanchero* and sheepman and Archiveque's own brother-in-law) and Colas' friends, who had got a report of his deeds. The Mexican boy who Archiveque had taken along to the Casner camp had deserted him, when he had witnessed the nature of Archiveque's dealings with the Casners, and had fled to Tascosa and given a report. The twenty-dollar gold pieces the Casners were reported to have with them never did show up.

"Well, nearly a week later, two of my men came across that camp. That dog, one-eyed and nearly starved, had held that herd together, all sixteen hundred head.

"Those are but two accounts of the many I could give of the value of a good dog," Goodnight concluded. "So," he said to Andy and Zachariah, "you take good care of those dogs, and they'll not disappoint you."

"Yes sir," Andy said.

Zachariah offered an almost whispered "Yessir," in imitation of Andy, the young boy mainly just staring in a sort of wonder at the seasoned cattleman.

"Mr. Goodnight," Luke said, "we were about to break for dinner. We'd be honored if you would join us."

"I'd be honored to join you."

Goodnight did join them for dinner. Then he assisted them with the rest of their work that afternoon, doing the branding and doctoring so that Andy could stay on his horse and rope, and Luke and Tom could flank, throw, and hold the beeves. Even though this was not his outfit, the cattleman could not help but take on a supervisory role, which the other men tolerated because they knew that few men had earned as much right to such a position as this man had in his forty-two years.

A count of the cattle at roundup showed that the herd of 307 head that the Seven Ox Seven had rounded up in Medina County the August before had grown to number about 464, a testament to Luke's selecting choice heifers when taking his shares while working for Herman. Of that number, Goodnight would be taking 64, leaving the Seven Ox Seven with an even 400 head, 10 of which were Andy's, a remarkably round number, they all agreed, given all the variables to be considered in the herd's increase and reduction.

With the roundup completed, the men ushered Goodnight through a twilight tour of the grounds, outbuildings, and the not-yet-completed rock house. Goodnight then joined them for supper in the dugout, and he stayed the night. In the course of that time, the Stuart-Schurtz party was treated to authentic tales from this singular individual, who, at forty-two, had not yet lived half his lifetime. He listened, too, learning as much as he could about their story, asking questions about their settlement and the purchase of their land. He agreed that it was wise to purchase the land and was glad to know law-abiding settlers like them, with the foresight to buy the land rather than just rely on grazing rights, were moving into that country. He mentioned names of others, too, who were moving into the country to the north: Bugbee, Bates and Beals, Cresswell. He pointed out that there was good range in the Quitaque to the north, but warned that it would not last long, as the surveyors Gunter, Munson and Summerfield were already locating railroad certificates and school lands there. He discussed the improvement of stock, as well, impressed with their plans in that regard, letting them know of his own method of keeping his blooded cattle in the upper canyon and removing inferior individuals to the common herd. Of cattle he bought for the common herd, he culled and spayed inferior cows and let them graze and fatten to be trailed and sold with the beeves in the fall.

In time the talk died down, and Goodnight accompanied Tom and Andy on their ride to Tom's house. Andy had moved in with Tom, when the house had been deemed habitable, to give the Stuarts more privacy and just to be able to enjoy less of what felt like supervision, especially from Elizabeth. Tom had finished the floor and had rehung the door. He was nearly finished laying up the rock chimney. Goodnight was even more impressed with the house once inside. He questioned Tom about the wisdom of so many windows, but Tom maintained his conclusion that whatever he lost in sturdiness—which he did not reckon to be too much, given the soundness of the construction, especially in the heavy framing of the openings—he gained in peace of mind, being able to look out on such arresting landscapes, and more than just landscapes, "skyscapes," too. That was the word Tom used, "skyscapes," as it was what came to his mind when he sought to convey what one could watch in the skies of that region: clouds coming into being out of nothing, before one's very eyes, so white against such a blue; white collecting, growing and molding, piling and deepening into grays, then purples, blues, black, greens, yellows, irradiated by the sun into brighter or deeper hues of those colors, splashed too by the sun with bright oranges, reds, pinks, yellows, and purples. Tom had been to many places, but he had never seen skies like those of the Panhandle and South Plains of Texas, and as much of those skies as he could let into his home, he would let in.

Goodnight went over every aspect of the structure, much impressed with the oak puncheon floors that Tom had finished to a shine. In time, the men went to bed, Goodnight refusing one of the two rough-wood beds that Tom and Andy had made, which were situated in opposite corners of the chimney wall (the south wall) with the heads against that wall. Instead he chose to take his place on the floor, on the bedroll he had taken from his saddle. He seemed to take a certain pleasure in sleeping upon a floor of a quality he admired; otherwise, Tom was sure, he would have preferred to sleep on the sandy ground outside.

•   •   •

IN THE MORNING, after an excellent breakfast by Elizabeth—which was not far removed from her everyday breakfasts—Goodnight and Andy, accompanied by the collie Rita, left with the four-year-olds and the JA steers. It would take them four days to move the cattle to the Palo Duro, after which Andy would return with the gold. Elizabeth had worried about Andy going with Goodnight, in particular about his returning with the gold, especially after hearing some of Goodnight's stories about his experiences with rustlers and other out-laws, and with Indians, the night before. Still, Luke and Tom had not wavered in this decision, because they had confidence in Andy and they had much work to do. They knew that Andy would want to talk to Goodnight about joining a drive, and they knew that it would give Goodnight and Andy a chance to get to know each other, for Good-night to see Andy at work, and for Andy to get an idea of how Goodnight ran his operations. Elizabeth knew all this, too, but her resistance to let go of Andy (subconsciously and consciously, as well) intensified her objections to Andy's going with Goodnight to move the cattle and to receive and return with the gold.

But go they did, Goodnight and Andy. In the days that followed their departure, Tom and Luke both finished their chimneys and started work on their porches. Luke still needed to frame out his windows with lumber, but he would wait until Tom returned from Dodge with some milled lumber to do so. In the meantime, he had fashioned rough wooden shutters that could be placed in the window openings against the bolts he had set in the mortar. The wall that would sepa-rate the main room from his and Elizabeth's bedroom would also wait for milled lumber: studs for the structure that would be covered by laths and plaster on both sides, and car siding to cover the lower parts of those sides. The Stuarts could have moved into the house at this point, but with Andy and Tom both leaving, Luke preferred to have the family remain in their formidable dugout until the house was fin-ished with sound shutters. As Goodnight had said, rustlers did prowl the area, and Indians might not be that far away. Comanche and Kiowa, in particular, who had not forgotten that they had controlled this region before they had been pushed onto the reservation, were not always content to stay on the reservation, particularly when food ran low. Then there were renegades, red and white, who gravitated toward the frontier, having deserted tribes or armies or civilization for a life of depredation. Yes, for now, the Stuarts would remain in the dugout.

In a few days, which was by now the beginning of the fourth week of April, Andy returned with the gold and with an excitement that could be seen in his eyes. Goodnight had hired him, to start with the roundup in a week, if that would suit the Stuart-Schurtz "concern." Luke and Tom readily agreed. The habitually laconic Andy waxed nearly loquacious as he recounted for the Stuarts and the Schurtz his experience with Goodnight. As uneventful as the short drive had been, still, there was the JA ranch with all its expanding and building and grading of herds. Andy was a young man stepping out into the world, a young man who had a distinct sense that he would be participating in what would one day be recorded history. And so he talked, and so the others listened, excited for this young man who reminded them so much of that age in their pasts, or who made at least one among them think a good deal about that age in his future.

Despite his obvious eagerness to begin his new adventure, Andy, true to the character instilled in him, worked hard that entire week. He had always had a certain steadiness and patience about his work that gave it an easygoing appearance, and yet, he did hard work, did it well, and did it in good time, which presented a certain incongruity to the observer's innate sense of time and space. It was as if Andy worked in a different dimension, one that allowed a slower, calmer pace to accomplish more than it should within the confines of time and space. So it seemed.

All seeming aside, time passed in relation to the space occupied by the settlers. In time, in their space, eventually it was Sunday, the day before Andy would leave. The settlers went about their Sunday as they normally would. Since Tom and Andy had moved up to Tom's log house, they had been worshiping together according to their own custom first and then joining the Stuarts later to sing hymns. This day was no exception. With the weather being quite pleasant at this time in late April, they had set up chairs outside the dugout and were seated and singing there.

When they concluded their worship, the entire group started to move en masse toward the new rock house as if it were the most natural thing to do, though it had never been done before. Tom and Luke (holding Robert) and Elizabeth and Zachariah and Rachel all talked to Andy—one after the other, and sometimes more than one at a time—as they moved along, Andy being almost insensible of the group's motion, including his own, as a result. Shortly, as (on one side) Tom and (on the other) Elizabeth were speaking at Andy about the recent roundup, on the one hand, and about the condition of his animal hides, on the other, Andy finally became aware that he stood before the threshold of the Stuart rock house, with Luke (little Robert still in his arm) standing in front of him inside the house holding open the heavy oaken door.

Andy's vision shifted from Luke and Robert to focus on what lay beyond them. There, within this new room of stone and mortar—which had been scrubbed well with brush and water, making it as clean as only washed stone and mortar can be—sat the table and chairs from the dugout, the table set with Elizabeth's fine china and silver. One chair, the large chair at the head of the table, was decorated in ribbons and prim-roses. On the table was a sumptuous spread of turkey and venison and bread and baked goods and various fruits and vegetables: as much food as that season and canned goods could offer. A bottle of wine, the last of the three that Elizabeth had purchased and hidden for most special occasions, stood on the table, and the aroma of fresh coffee filled the air, as it brewed in a pot on a grate in the new fireplace—which, use indicated, had an excellent draw. On a small table directly across the room, on the other side of the table and chairs, sat a large cake. On another small table next to it sat a mound covered with a sheet.

"Well, come on in the house," Luke said to him.

Andy entered, Elizabeth crowding in beside him, straining to see his face as he entered the house. Tom stood aside to let the children in, then fell in behind the crowd.

Elizabeth was pleased with the look she found on Andy's face. It registered something just short of being overwhelmed, registered it mostly in his wide-open eyes. Andy inched his way forward, his head held far back on his shoulders as if in reaction to something coming at him. The children enjoyed this reaction, as they slipped around to get in front of Andy and look up at him. Rachel jumped up and down, clapping and shouting, "It's a party! It's a party!" Zachariah shifted his feet quickly before the slowly advancing group and turned his head back and forth from the table to Andy, and then just stared up at Andy, his five-year-old eyes wide with the excitement of this special surprise and the joy of being a part of this honor for Andy.

They made their way into the room, Andy needing some coaxing from Elizabeth and Luke until he was seated in the large chair decorated in his honor. He was noticeably uncomfortable being the center of attention, and such attention, but his politeness made him bear up under it for the sake of those who had secretly gone to so much trouble.

Of course, Luke was enjoying Andy's discomfort. Tom sympathized with it. Elizabeth was bustling about to make sure all was in readiness, seemingly able to do so without losing sight of Andy's face, and keeping a close eye to see how he was reacting to all her preparations. Rachel continued to contribute to the proceedings with her clapping, laughing, and repetition of various statements concerning the "party." Zachariah, his smile full, his eyes still wide, continued to stare at Andy, grateful for every little indication that he was enjoying what they had planned and prepared for him.

Soon it was time to begin the meal, and Zachariah received his nod from Elizabeth, which was his signal to get the family Bible and place it before Andy. He took up the Bible from the table that held the cake, as rehearsed, and tried to place the large book in front of Andy, who provided the assistance needed. Then Zachariah returned to his chair, his tongue still pressing against the outside of the corner of his mouth. Luke had watched this, and now he whispered, "Tom." When Tom turned to look at him, Luke pointed at Zachariah, who was still staring at Andy. Tom looked at Zachariah and smiled at the boy's innocent enjoyment and his sense of importance due to his part in the proceedings. Then he looked back at Luke, who pressed his tongue against the outside corner of his mouth, nodding at Zachariah, then opened his mouth into a smile, shaking his head all the while in his own enjoyment of the enjoyment of his son.

Andy sat quietly for a moment, staring at the closed Bible, aware of the honor that had been shown him in this action. Then he nodded slightly and opened the Bible and turned to a page near the front, and he read:

Now the LORD had said unto Abram, Get thee out of
thy country, and from thy kindred, and from thy

father's house, unto a land that I will shew thee:

And I will make of thee a great nation, and I will bless
thee, and make thy name great; and thou shalt be a
blessing:

And I will bless them that bless thee, and curse him that
curseth thee: and in thee shall all families of the
earth be blessed.

So Abram departed, as the LORD had spoken unto
him; and Lot went with him: and Abram was seventy
and five years old when he departed out of Haran.

And Abram took Sarai his wife, and Lot his brother's
son, and all their substance that they had gathered,
and the souls that they had gotten in Haran; and
they went forth to go into the land of Canaan; and
into the land of Canaan they came.

Andy sat silent for a moment when he had finished, and then he
closed the Bible. Zachariah was quickly on his feet, and, holding his
mouth tight as he strained to lift its weight, he took the Bible from
Andy. As he returned the Bible to the side table, Elizabeth nodded to
Luke, who then said, "Andy, would you offer the blessing?"

Andy gave a slight nod, not even considering declining this great
honor. He and Tom made the sign of the cross, to which the others
had grown accustomed, and offered a traditional Catholic blessing
before meals, concluding with the sign of the cross.

This was Elizabeth's cue, and after she sniffed back potential tears
and turned away to dab at her eyes with the end of her sleeve, she
turned back to the table to start the food moving in the right direction.

The food was passed and dished, the wine and milk poured out
and glasses filled. In time, all settled down to feasting, and in time,
Luke finally said what Tom had been waiting for, ever since Andy's
reading of Scripture.

"So, Andy, the Lord goin' to make of you a great nation, goin' to
make your name great?"

Andy, who had just put a fork full of food into his mouth, let his
head fall forward a little and shook it slightly from side to side, trying
to chew his food without laughing. Tom let a short nasal sigh escape in

place of a laugh and shook his own head. Elizabeth wrinkled her brow at this inappropriate comment and tried to send a disapproving look toward Luke, but on seeing the sly smile on the face of her husband, she could not hold the wrinkle in her forehead, and she, too, had to look at her plate and allow the escape of a mirthful sigh of her own. The children, especially Zachariah, watched the expressions of the adults, the children's interest piqued by the start of the bantering they had come to expect and enjoy, as it brought so much enjoyment to the adults.

Andy kept his head down for a while, chewing. Then he sat upright, leaning back to finish the job, and finally managed a swallow. Laughter immediately followed, barely choking up past the swallow on its way down, laughter more liberal due to a bit of wine. "I knew," he all but choked out, "I knew as soon as I read it that you'd have somethin' to say."

"What are you talkin' about?" Luke said, looking about in mock incredulity at whatever Andy might be insinuating.

"I knew it. I knew it," Andy repeated, shaking his head as he reached for the platter of meat.

"What is he talkin' about?" Luke responded, still incredulous, appealing to both Elizabeth and Tom for insight into Andy's cynical reaction.

"I just thought it would be a good Scripture reading, that of Abraham goin' off into the land of Canaan, a land he did not know, goin' off in faith, at the command of the Lord," Andy said, the effect of the wine seen in this uncharacteristic loquaciousness. "That's how I feel about my parting. We started this journey in the same way, leavin' the land of my family, packin' up what we had. Now from here I do the same thing again. I just thought it would be a good reading, the right reading," he concluded in a voice, slightly louder to make his point.

Elizabeth's eyes were moist as she said to Andy for Luke to hear, "It was the perfect passage, Andy, most appropriate."

"I'm not so sure that the Prodigal Son wouldn't've been more appropriate," Luke corrected.

Andy was shaking his head, and Tom was sighing his laughter, before Elizabeth could let lose the expected "Luke!" at her husband. And then all were laughing, nearly to the point of tears, as Andy tried to respond, but unable to think of anything to say, just slumped back against the back of his chair and abandoned his body to laughter, through which he again tried to respond, once, then twice, and then finding himself unable to manage any utterance, had to eventually resort to holding his sides as if they ached, which, as the laughter continued, they eventually did. In this way, laughter broke up the celebration's formality and awkwardness, which had made familiar people feel unfamiliar.

Such was the mood of the feast they shared as it drifted through time into the late afternoon and evening, the shadows of the canyon walls creeping ever nearer the rock house in its inaugural meal. The meal complete, out came the cake, which had hardly been cut and distributed before Zachariah was asking his mother if it were time to bring the presents. Soon, for everyone but Zachariah, it was time for the presents, and bring them he did.

There were two new shirts, along with a fringed deerskin vest and fringed pair of deerskin gloves for his work on the range, all of which represented hours of Elizabeth's handwork. From Luke came his camp cooking set (an indispensable item for the cowboy, which he would have Tom replace on his trip to Dodge City). From Tom came his copy of the *Confessions* of St. Augustine, and Andy well appreciated Tom's giving and parting with this book he so highly valued. Rachel presented a pair of wool socks, and Robert—without leaving his chair and thus with the aid of his older sister—presented another pair.

And then, there was the silent Zachariah, having presented all but the last gift, having watched carefully as Andy had responded, quietly, but truly touched by each gift. There was the silent Zachariah, standing by the table with the sheet over it, the sheet lying flat now except for a long ripple that extended well beyond the length of the table on both ends, the sheet draped out over whatever lay beneath that ripple. There was the silent Zachariah, increasingly conscious of how much his gift was not shirts or gloves or camp cooking sets or valued books or socks. There was the silent Zachariah wondering if silent were not the way to remain.

But his mother would have none of that. As soon as she realized that Zachariah's gift had not been presented, she goaded (in her way that would allow for no alternative) the boy to present it. Then she watched Andy—she, this mother who knew far better than a little boy the value of the gift that Zachariah would present.

So, Zachariah timidly reached beneath the sheet and brought forth a stick, a stick with a line of braided horsehair tied on the end. It was no ordinary stick, as it had been worked some by a knife—by a very dull knife, it appeared—the work resulting in crude renderings of what might have been fish, which ran the length of the stick, and a rough handle grip at the end opposite that on which the line was tied. Zachariah brought forward the stick with his head down and his tongue pressed against the outside of the corner of his mouth. And Andy knew what it was.

Zachariah laid the stick across Andy's lap, where Andy cradled it in his hands and stared at it as he pursed his lips and blinked his eyes, seeing in his mind, through his restrained emotion, a young boy whom he had taken fishing in Schurtz Creek when they had first arrived in the canyon. Thereafter, during that first autumn, they had gone fishing when they had been able to, usually, if not always, on Sundays, as the weather had permitted, the boy searching always for just the right pole. Then, one day, he had found a branch of just the right length, girth, and "bendiness." This pole had then been granted a special priority and, from then on, its own place under his bed, from where he would take it out from time to time and carve on it, as best he could with his dull knife (the only one his mother would allow him to have), the fish he dreamed of catching and the handle that would fit well in his small hand. By spring it was complete. And on their fishing excursions from then on, he would often look over his pole, while it was at work or at rest, and admire its natural qualities and the work of his hands. All this Andy had seen, and now it lay in his hands, a gift.

Andy was silent for a moment, as tears freely rolled down the face of the mother who knew. The other two men at the table looked down. Finally, Andy said, without taking his eyes off the gift, "Thank you, Zack," to the little boy, who had backed away after presenting his gift. Then, still without looking at him, Andy reached out his long arm and tousled the thick, fair hair of the boy and, slipping his hand down around his shoulders, pulled him up against the side of his chair and patted his small back.

"This is a fine gift, Zack," he said, "as fine a gift as ever I have received." Then he patted his back again, and then he let him go. The boy slid back into his chair at the end of the table near Andy and watched that young man intently, gaining, as he did, some notion of the value of his gift in the eyes of the recipient.

A slightly more sober tone characterized what remained of the meal and the rest of the day. A lighter meal followed later in the evening. Then the adults read Shakespeare's *Julius Caesar*, all taking different parts, which was facilitated by Elizabeth's having copied down, over time, the separate parts on paper. Then they played dominoes, with the children joining in, and then they lounged and talked as the children drifted off to sleep near the fire. Eventually all rose to clean up after the party and then to depart for dugout or log house. Elizabeth had made it clear that Andy would not be leaving from that canyon without a hearty breakfast to send him off, so all good-byes had been postponed for the morning. With that reprieve and with an eventful day ahead, they all headed off for sleep.

When Tom and Andy arrived at the log house, they unsaddled their horses and turned them out into the corral. They carried their saddles into the house, where they hung them from their horns on ropes hanging from the rafters, a temporary arrangement until the house would stand complete with the shed attached. This was a precaution against mice and raccoons, which, if the saddles were left outside, might chew away at them for the salt accumulated from perspiration.

Once inside, each man knelt near his bed in separate, silent prayer. Then, when finished, they pulled off their boots and took off their outer clothes and lay on their beds, each on his back with his hands behind his head.

"You remember, Tom," Andy asked, "when you left home?"

"Hmph," Tom emitted into the light blue ambience of the room caused by moonlight flooding in the windows. "Yeah, I guess I do remember," he responded. "That was a long time ago. It's like a different world ago, or a different life ago."

"Yeah," Andy responded, "I know what you mean. This is like a different world from where I grew up. But like you say, it's more than just that, it's like this is a different life. It's like I'm different, too."

"You are," Tom affirmed. "Can't help but be. We're always changin', with every new experience. You can only hope and pray that, with God's help, you're changin' in the right way, growin' into fuller manhood, bein' what God created you to be."

"How'd you feel, Tom, when you first left on your own?"

"Hmph." There was quiet for a moment, as Tom visited another world and life. Then he said, "Well, I was in a bit of the same kind of situation you're in. When I left home at sixteen to work on the railroad, I left with my uncle. So, even though I was leavin' home and settin' out on my own, I was still with my uncle, still had a tie to home. Then came the day that my uncle and I went separate ways, not with any hard feelin's or anything, you understand," Tom clarified, turning his head toward Andy, across the room, to make the point, "just time to go our separate ways, like with you now." He turned his head back to look at the underside of the roof. "On that day, I cannot tell you the feeling: I just remember that it was one of the most, I don't know, exciting, . . . exhilarating, . . . joyful moments of my life. I had what I owned, which wasn't much, tied up in a canvas bag, and I had the money that I had saved workin' on the railroad, and I was headin' to Denver, to a place where nobody knew me and I had never been. There would be so many people to meet, so much to see, my whole life ahead of me to live as best I could. Didn't seem like there was anything I couldn't do."

Tom lay quiet for a moment, then added, "Hmph, that was a long time ago."

"Were you nervous at all, Tom?"

Tom thought for a moment. "Not so much nervous, as I remember it, but more excited. I had the whole world in front of me," Tom responded. Then he turned and saw Andy's face turned toward him in the blue light and added, "I was nervous when I would start a new job, though, sure enough. Always have been, though they almost always work out well, and if they don't, there's always been some place better to work. But, sure enough, was nervous with a new job, you bet. But that goes away as soon as you get workin'." Tom looked again at Andy, who had turned his head back to look at the underside of the roof. What Tom could not see from across the room, was that Andy did so with a calmer expression than that which had molded his features when he had asked the question.

"Do you still feel like you have the whole world in front of you, Tom?" Andy asked, looking up at the roof as if he were looking right through it.

"Hmph, . . . well, that changes in time. You make choices, Andy. And every time you make a choice, it opens a door, or doors. Some doors, it's just as well you never entered. Others open into wonderful opportunities. You ever enter into a door that you shouldn't have, the sooner you back on out and get back on the right trail, the better. Other doors you enter, you wish you could stay inside forever, but for some reason or other, you need to move on. There, just like with the bad experiences, you take whatever you learned with you, and you move back out onto your trail a little wiser. And just as choices open doors, they close others. They might be open again at a later date, or not, but even if they are, never in the same way.

"So, with every choice, there are other options you did not choose, more so, I guess, the more you're capable of doin'. There's a limiting, or a recognition of limitation. I guess the key, Andy, the way I figure it now anyways, is that you've got to fully accept your limitation, that is, accept it in hope and faith, because that is the beginning of freedom, because only then can you live it to its fullness. That sounds paradoxical, and I guess it is one of those paradoxes of the Christian life, and I don't want you to think that I think you should hold back from doin' somethin'. I guess what I'm sayin' is that freedom comes when you accept your vocation, your call, which is a type of limitation that is really freeing. In this way, a man in prison can actually be freer than a man outside, by acceptin' that limitation and then livin' it to its fullness. Acceptin' one's vocation requires discernment, of course, which takes longer for some than for others. In acceptin' that vocation, you accept the limitation that is freeing, because you avoid bein' distracted by other options that may be enticing and maybe you could do but that distract you from what the Maker intended for you.

"It brings to mind a quote from the Bible, from Ecclesiasticus: 'And all men are from the ground, and out of the earth, from whence Adam was created. With much knowledge the Lord hath divided them and diversified their ways.'

"The discernment is important, of course, because in makin' choices you define your life. You choose some things and pass up others. You determine who you are, what sort of man you are."

Tom again looked over at Andy. "So, back to your question, I guess in time you realize that you don't have the whole world in front of you.

Well," he reconsidered, "I guess in a sense you do; it may lie in front of you, but you can't have it all: a mortal person just ain't big enough for that. What you truly got ahead of you is your whole life, and if you live that right, by the grace of God, that could end up bein' bigger than the whole world. Strange thing is, though, it's almost as if it's got to get smaller to get bigger, kind of like the boy Jesus, who wanted to 'be about [his] father's business,' but, instead, went home with his mother and St. Joseph and lived as an obscure carpenter for eighteen years before he began to preach. But as the Scriptures say of that time: 'Jesus advanced in wisdom, and age, and grace with God and men.' We know he didn't preach, or we would have heard about it; it would have changed the world. The greatest human being who ever lived, God's own Son incarnate, and he lived as an obscure carpenter all those years, what the Church calls his 'hidden years.' And you know, just as an aside, I sometimes wonder if those hidden years don't say somethin' about God's respect for the privacy of Jesus' family."

They were both quiet for a moment, pondering the life of their Savior. "Even after the hidden years," Tom eventually said, "he didn't go out and take the world by storm. As a matter of fact, that was one of the temptations of Satan that Christ refused. What he did was to preach and teach and heal for three years in one little country among a conquered people. Then they killed him. Sometimes we forget that. We forget how small he allowed himself to be. We forget the limitations he accepted in becoming human. We forget all that because of the results of his life, death, and resurrection, but it helps to remember the scope of that one man's life, the Lord, that Light which came into the world." Tom paused and pondered, then added, as if an afterthought, "bringing with it judgment, because 'men loved darkness rather than the light.'" With that, he was quiet, as quiet as the blue light invading the darkness.

After a moment, Tom added, "So, I guess it's helpful, Andy, the sooner you learn that you don't have the whole world ahead of you, you've got your whole life, and the better you live that, accordin' to the Lord's commandments, however obscure it may seem, the bigger it will be."

Andy turned his head again to look across the room at the figure of an older friend, who lay in darkness, as if emerging from it, highlighted by the pale blue light. "You been to a lot of places, Tom?"

"I've been around some," Tom said, looking up at the underside of the roof.

"Thanks, Tom."

"Well, thank you for listenin', Andy. I wish you all the best."

"Thanks again, Tom."

"You bet."

Then silence covered the men, lying stretched out on their beds, and in time, sleep.

MORNING ARRIVED EARLY ENOUGH, and Tom awoke to find Andy up and dressed and scrambling around in the low predawn light, gathering his things and laying them out on his bedroll, as noiselessly as possible. Tom rose and dressed, too, and asked Andy if he needed anything.

"No sir," he responded, "I think I've got it all."

"You don't have a rifle, do you?" Tom asked him. "You probably could use my Winchester, don't you reckon?"

"Couldn't take it, Tom."

"Well, you'll need one soon."

"I know," Andy agreed, "I'll be figurin' out a way to purchase one after my first month's wages. Then I'll have enough, while still havin' some laid aside."

"All right, but take some shells for that six-shooter, anyways," Tom said, handing him a couple boxes of shells; "you'll need these."

Andy accepted them graciously, knowing how much Tom needed to give them. Then he tied his bedroll on his saddle, and he and Tom carried their saddles out to the corral. They saddled and bridled their horses, and as they did so, Andy could not help but think of the night on which Luke gave him Stonewall as his first pay, the night on which he had said good-bye to his family. He paused for a moment. Then he finished preparing Stonewall, mounted him, and headed with Tom down for breakfast.

Breakfast at the dugout was as good as any breakfast Elizabeth had ever prepared, though she did so while spending a great deal of energy trying to keep her tears out of it, without always succeeding. Elizabeth remained aloof from the table, busying herself about the stove, fire, and counter, and serving. Her quiet sniffling and sighing made almost any talk seem somehow nearly obscene, though Luke did make an attempt or two at it, but finally abandoned any further attempts due to the solemnity that Elizabeth's obvious sorrow brought to the event.

Zachariah had awakened early, with the quiet sounds of the early breakfast, and was soon dressed and seated at his place at the table. His mother served him, too, without speaking to him, and he ate, distracted by watching Andy across the table.

Finally, it was time for Andy to leave. Elizabeth woke Robert and Rachel, and carried Robert, while she led Rachel by the hand, outside with the men and Zachariah, where they all gathered about the hitching rail to which Andy's horse was tied.

Andy kept his head down, uncomfortable with the act of leaving. A faint idea of how easy it would have been just to ride away earlier that morning was kept down by the reality of how unconscionable such an act would have been.

With all assembled, Luke proffered his hand, which Andy took. Luke said, with a quiet sincerity so different from his common jesting, "Well, Andy, ain't goin' to be the same around here without you. You will be sorely missed. And you are welcome back here at any time. Ol' Colonel Goodnight doesn't treat you to your likin', you mosey on back over here, and there'll always be a place."

"Thank you, Luke."

Next came Tom, who also offered his hand, which Andy took. "I guess we've said most of it. I second what Luke said. You're always welcome." Tom did not care for good-byes either; nor, as one with a strong sense of the eternal, was he ever convinced of their finality.

"Thanks, Tom."

Then Elizabeth stepped forward, her eyes clouded with tears, and handed Robert to Andy. Robert, just awakened from sleep, had little to offer from his repertoire of sounds, but he did smile and hug the familiar Andy. Andy hugged him, too, this little Stuart whom he had known since his birth.

Elizabeth, obviously distracted by the departure, took Robert from Andy and handed him to Tom, who was surprised to find his arm suddenly supporting the child. She then handed Rachel to Andy, saying, "Go on, Rachel, you say good-bye to Andy."

Rachel went easily into Andy's arms and hugged him and kissed his cheek. "Goo' bye, Unca Andy," she said. And she hugged him again.

Luke stepped forward and took the sleepy Rachel from Andy, sensitive to Elizabeth's need to be free of the child to tell Andy good-bye.

Elizabeth now stepped forward, the drying of her eyes and nose, just performed, rendered futile by the appearance of new tears. She buttoned the buttons of Andy's new vest, which he had left unbuttoned, and said, "There now, that was a good fit. I could only guess, using Luke as a model, and him so much broader, but I did get it right," she continued, smoothing the front of the vest with her hand. Then she looked up into his eyes, and her own filled with tears, and she reached out and hugged the tall young man, who did not know what to do, except to awkwardly and lightly hug her back.

"If they don't treat you well over there, or don't feed you well, you come right back here, you hear. You come right back here. We'll feed you." Then she was crying, and she let go of her Andy and stepped back, holding the kerchief to her face and turning to her side.

Andy clamped his jaws together and looked down, and there, in his sight, stood Zachariah. Big tears welled in the big blue eyes of the little face, with glistening trails of tears streaking that face below those eyes.

"Why do you hafta go, Andy? Why can't you stay?" the boy asked through his tears.

Andy reached down and picked up the little boy and held him close in an embrace. "It's just that I've got to go, Zack. You can't understand it now, but some day you will," Andy told him, doing his best to hide the emotion in his voice.

"But why don't you want to stay with us anymore, Andy? Don't you want to go fishin' with me anymore?"

"It's not that I don't want to, Zack. But I've got to go."

"Won't you miss us, Andy?"

"I'll miss you a powerful lot, Zack. I'll think of you, and I'll pray for you, and I'll even come to visit. But, yes, I surely will miss you. I'll never forget you, Zack. You'll see. I'll come and visit."

"Don't go, Andy." Zachariah was clutching the young man, now.

"I've got to go, Zack. But I'll come visit."

Elizabeth stifled her own tears, as much as possible, and stepped forward and took the little boy from Andy and turned him onto her shoulder, though it had been some time since he had been so consoled. There he let his tears flow, as his mother's flowed above him.

Andy turned and whistled for Rita. Then he took his reins and mounted Stonewall, as Rita and three of her puppies came trotting up. The other two puppies were being left for Rachel and Robert, and were tied, with Charlie, in the barn, to keep them from following the other four. The settlers made various hurried good-byes to Rita, the puppies, and Stonewall, as well as they were able. Then Andy looked down on them. "Thank you all, for everything," he said. "I'll never forget, and I will visit."

Then he nodded his head and turned and rode up the trail, finally disappearing through the cleft in the caprock into the life of his choosing.

THE WEEK FOLLOWING ANDY'S DEPARTURE was a sorrowful one for Zachariah. Though Andy's presence was missed by all, as would be expected in a community as small as that of the settlers, his leaving had left a particularly large void in the life of the little boy. Elizabeth watched as Zachariah moped around the yard and ranch, not in self-pity but in true dejection. There was no Andy with whom to ride line, to go hunting, to train Charlie, to skin or butcher, to cut trees, to fish, or to do any of the many things in which the young man had allowed Zachariah to participate, if only as an observer.

The adults did what they could to alleviate his sorrow, especially Elizabeth, who in helping to alleviate Zachariah's sorrow was helping to alleviate her own. She baked molasses cookies and served them up to him and Rachel with milk, cold from the springhouse that Luke and Tom had begun to construct. She tried to keep him busy with various projects and went out of her way to come up with games or other amusements during the day. At night, Luke and Tom took special care to tell Zachariah stories or sit outside and look at the stars, among other things. They also did their best to include Zachariah in their various chores and projects, but they were intent in their work, unlike Andy, who had an easy way about his work, and who had gone out of his way to talk to the boy and explain what he was doing and allow him to participate to the degree that he could. Though Luke and Tom would try as best they could to do the same, in time it would become all work, and it would not be long before Zachariah would tire of watching or of getting underfoot, and he would be taken back to the yard or wander off, more dejected at the loss of Andy than he had been before.

In consideration of all this, the Sunday following Andy's departure, Tom took Zachariah fishing. The timing could not have been better. Besides being good for Zachariah, in light of Andy's leaving, it was an ideal opportunity for Tom. With the roundup complete and his house nearly so, and with his wagon trip to Dodge City to begin the next week, Tom took special relish in what would be, at least for a while, his last Sunday at the ranch.

After the morning's devotions and the Sunday dinner, Tom mounted Ross and watched Zachariah climb aboard a mule from the rails of the corral, which he insisted he could do without help. And with these riders aboard, the two animals sauntered off down the trail.

Tom and Zachariah walked the mounts at a Sunday-afternoon pace along the trail that followed Schurtz Creek. Zachariah led the way to his and Andy's favorite spot. Andy had discovered it earlier that spring, when on a Sunday afternoon, or on another day when the work had allowed for it and the weather had all but demanded it, he and Zachariah had gone hunting for fishing holes. Nearly every Sunday after, they would return to this spot, wet a line, and wait for the catfish to bite. Zachariah had shown an early interest in this pursuit and had proved to be a patient angler for one his age. Tom and Luke had seen that on one occasion when they had accompanied Andy and Zachariah. It was as if Andy's patience had rubbed off on his young apprentice. Luke had not gone along again after that, though Tom had gone once or twice. Luke enjoyed fishing to an extent, but preferred more active pursuits. Besides, Tom knew that when he went fishing, he gave Elizabeth an opportunity to spend time with her husband alone, as much as Rachel and Robert would allow, a rare commodity in this budding ranch community that held so much developmental potential for men to discuss.

Zachariah, for his part, had always reveled in these fishing outings, in his own nondemonstrative way, the camaraderie with Andy being no small part of the reason. As has been seen, Zachariah greatly admired Andy, nearly idolized him: but Andy was gone, and this outing would be with Tom. Zachariah's regard for Tom was very different from his regard for Andy. He held Tom in high esteem, as well, but in a different way, Tom being more fully immersed in that as-yet-elusive and distant world of manhood than the young Andy, who was still only entering it.

Zachariah's regard for Tom was more on the level with his regard for his father, who was also firmly established in that world of manhood, but, of course, it was also very different. The natural intimacy of father and son, between Luke and Zachariah, intermediated between the worlds of boyhood and manhood, bridging the distance and lessening the elusiveness of the latter for the former. Without that intermediation, Tom remained solidly in that distant and elusive world. Luke was a man, but he was Zachariah's father, Zachariah's man, and as such, even with the admiration inherent in that relationship, he could be taken comfortably for granted. Tom was a man, but he did not enjoy that singular intimacy with Zachariah, and as such, he would always hold a certain degree of mystery for the boy and be regarded with a certain degree of awe. Still, Tom was Zachariah's too, but more in the sense of something admired than possessed. Such was the relationship between the boy and man who set out to go fishing that day.

In less than half an hour's time, the horse and mule stepped into a little grove of large cottonwood trees and some hackberry, willows, and wafer-ash. Switchgrass, Indian grass, and big bluestem lined the banks of a widening of the creek into a veritable pool. The scene itself almost cooled the observer in the observation. The man and the boy directed their mounts across the creek, just above the pool, and made their way down the opposite bank, where they pulled up and dismounted.

They scouted around until each had chosen a pole. Then, beneath the shade of a magnificent cottonwood that grew out of the pool itself—the water obviously higher than it had been at other times—they found their spots against certain stones, placed just right to accommodate a posture conducive to this restful pastime. There, each of them whittled at his pole until it suited him, the sun dappling their shade with dancing spots of light that sifted down through the leaves above. Those leaves were not of the cottonwood only, but also of wild grape vines that had wrapped themselves around the trunk of the tree and laced their way in among its branches, mingling their leaves of grape with those of cottonwood. In the active, dappling shade of all those leaves—which flitted and fluttered in the sunlight in response to an intermittent warm, dry breeze—they tied on their lines, baited their hooks, settled those baited hooks in the water, and sat back to wait.

It was not long before Zachariah had caught a fish, then another. Then Tom caught one. Then stillness. The fish did not bite for a while, and a quiet settled over the pond and the fishermen.

After a time, Zachariah spoke up.

"Uncle Tom, have you ever been afraid of heaven?" The boy looked at the man from the side, as if peering around something.

Tom looked at Zachariah in wonder, as a distant, profound memory was stirred. A certain intensity registered across Tom's forehead and eyes, as he said, "What do you mean, Zack?"

Zachariah looked away from him and back out at the water and said, "I mean, were you ever afraid of heaven?" He stared at the water, as if the question were not a very important one.

Tom's stare at the boy deepened. "Do you mean the forever of heaven?"

Zachariah turned quickly on him, his eyes wider than before, as if in making a discovery of wonder. "Yes sir," he said, "the forever part of heaven."

Tom continued to stare in wonder at Zachariah, as his mind took in the boy and his question, while it simultaneously drifted across the years to confirm a unique fellowship. "What about the forever part of heaven, Zack?"

"Well," Zack began, looking back out at the water, "Mama said when my granddad died, he went to heaven, and she said when I die I will go to heaven, and that I will be with God and live there forever."

"Uh huh, and what makes you afraid of that?"

Zachariah was quiet for a moment. Then he turned to look at Tom and said, "Well, forever is forever. Won't I get tired of it, Uncle Tom. Won't it get to be a bore?"

Tom smiled at the earnest face turned on his.

"Well, Zack," Tom said, as he readjusted his position against his rock, "when I was about your age, I had exactly the same reaction."

"You did?" the boy said, his inflection expressing a hopeful surprise.

"I sure did," Tom replied, with a decisive nod.

"What did you do?"

"Well, I was thinkin' about it for a while, and then one night it was frettin' me so much that I got up and went into the kitchen to ask my mother that very question, wasn't she ever scared of heaven, of livin' forever, of just goin' on and on. She seemed a little taken aback." Tom looked at Zachariah, then clarified, "Uh, she looked like she didn't know how to answer me for a minute. Then she looked down and said that no, she was not worried about that, because she trusted in God and knew that he would do what was best for her and he would take care of her."

Tom looked over at Zachariah, who was still looking at him.

"Zack, I've got to tell you that, even though my mother was absolutely right with that answer, I didn't feel much better. In fact, you might say I felt a little worse, because not only was I still afraid of goin' on forever, but I felt a little guilty, felt kind of bad that I did not just trust God the way my mother did. So, I tried to do that, and I prayed that God would show me how not to be afraid of forever. And then one day, an idea came to me that I had not thought of before." He looked over at the expectant young eyes boring into him. "I realized, I just figured, that everything I knew in this life changed and came to an end. My dog got older and would die. I had grown. My brothers and sisters grew. My grandpa died. Our house got older and needed paint. And then I figured that the reason I was afraid of forever was that I had never had any experience of it before: I didn't know what it was like. I could not really get a good idea of what it was like because everything I knew would come to an end. When I figured that, I could realize, could figure, that my fear was just a fear of what I did not know. Then I could look at my mother's answer and do as she did, trust God, who would take care of me. God, who knows forever, would make forever just right for me. I don't know what heaven will be like either, but I do know that God will make it better than anything I've ever known before. I believe that. So I could also believe that forever would be just fine, even better. I was only afraid because I did not ever know anything like forever."

Zack cocked his head a little, looking askew out at the water, but Tom knew his mind's eye was turned inward.

"Does that help any?" Tom asked him.

"I think so."

"Well, look at it this way, Zack. Do you remember when you were small and you were afraid to go into a dark room?" Tom wisely asked about it as something in the past.

"Yes sir," Zachariah answered, considering to himself how that fear could still sneak up on him even as a five-year-old.

"Well, the room was no different than when it was in the light. It's just that you couldn't see what was in it. You weren't really afraid of what was there; you were afraid of what you could not see, what you didn't know about what was in the dark."

Tom looked for a response from Zachariah, who was looking at him, his mind obviously working over this new material.

"Or better yet," Tom continued, "remember when we were goin' to move here to the canyon?"

Zachariah nodded.

"Well, you didn't have any idea what the canyon would be like. You had never seen it before. You were goin' to leave your home to come here. Were you a little sad to leave your old home?"

"Yes sir."

"Were you a little concerned about what the canyon would be like, if you would like it or not?"

"Yes sir."

"Well, now that you live here, you like it, don't you?"

"Yes sir."

"Well, it's the same thing with livin' forever. It's somethin' we've never done, so we're bound to be a little scared of it, but we know that we can trust God."

"Yes sir," Zachariah said, and he nodded. Then he looked back out at the water.

Tom let all this sink in. He looked over at the small person to his left and wondered at all that was going on in the recesses of the brain set within that skull that sat upon that small body, and in the mind set within that soul that animated that body. He smiled and looked back out on the water. In the context of salvation, he thought, Zachariah would have plenty of time to think about it, before forever would become reality and would render time obsolete.

TWO DAYS AFTER FISHING WITH ZACHARIAH, in the heat of the early afternoon, Tom looked up from greasing the axles of the big wagon, which he would be taking to Dodge City, to see a rider enter the canyon and stop at his house and then remount his horse and descend the trail toward the Stuart house. Tom walked away from the wagon toward the yard in front of the Stuarts', wiping his hands as he did so. As the rider rode into the Stuarts' yard, Tom recognized him to be Robert Wilson, a pleasant young man originally from the East (Pennsylvania, Tom thought), of a slight but wiry build, who had worked with the crew of Hill and Colmey on surveying the canyon.

Wilson pulled up and said, "Hello, Tom."

"Robert," Tom said, "how are you?"

Wilson dismounted in front of Tom, and after gathering the reins to hold in his left hand, he advanced toward Tom, his right hand extended.

"I am well, Tom," he said; "I am well.

Tom clasped his hand in his own, and as they shook hands, he said, "Robert, it is good to see you."

"And to see you, too," Wilson responded with a natural sincerity. Slight though he was, and not very tall, he had a good grip in a handshake. He wore a full, dark beard and had the look of a surveyor about him, with his thick, light colored trousers tucked into high boots and a loose, open-collared dark shirt worn over a lighter one that was buttoned all the way to the collar. Above it all sat a flat, round, broad-brimmed hat. Around his waist was fastened a belt and holster that supported his six-shooter, as few needed one more than those surveyors who braved the frontier before most other white men.

Wilson looked around at the buildings in the Stuarts' yard and back up the trail to Tom's place and at the pens. "You've made some progress here, haven't you?"

"We like to think so," Tom agreed with a smile.

"It doesn't seem like it's been long enough for you people to have accomplished so much," Wilson observed, still looking around.

"It's been seven months," Tom responded, "five months since you folks left."

"So it has," Wilson agreed. "Still, you've accomplished a great deal."

"We've worked at it," Tom admitted.

Wilson turned a broad smile on Tom and said, "I imagine you have." Then, as if something had just occurred to him, he turned back toward his horse, and then, glancing between Tom and his horse, he walked sideways to the side of that worthy mount, as he said to Tom, "I suppose I ought to be about the business for which I've come." He unfastened a compartment on his saddlebag and pulled out a leather satchel, which he opened and from which he removed some papers.

He looked over the papers for a moment and thumbed through them, a serious expression now pressed into his face. Then, satisfied that all was in order, he looked up, flashed his broad smile, and stepped toward Tom.

"Here are your patents, Tom," he said, handing the papers to Tom.

Tom took them and thumbed through them, looking at them and seeing far more than the papers revealed.

"Twelve sections of land, all registered with the General Land Office in the name of Stuart and Schurtz," Wilson said, pushing away a momentary wistfulness at the thought of owning such an amount of land. "It's all yours, Tom. You've got to be feeling pretty good about that."

Tom looked up at him, his thoughts returning to the immediate situation. He stared at Wilson for a moment, as he pulled back into the present. "Well," he said, "it's not all mine, or 'ours' I should say, yet. I still owe you a check."

"Well, yes," said Wilson, "but Mr. Colmey said to let you know that his correspondence with the bank in Denver was most satisfactory, and that he has all the confidence in your check for the final half of payment."

Tom responded with a light smile and looked back down at the patents in his hands. Wilson stared at him.

"How does it feel, Tom, to own such a place?" He looked around as he finished the question.

Tom did not raise his eyes from the patents as he answered. "It feels like you've got a home." He raised his eyes to Wilson's and continued, with a certain intensity, "Some place to be, some place to go from and return to, some place to manage and develop, to build upon. It's havin' a home."

Tom looked down at the patents again, and the light smile returned to melt away his intensity. Then he looked up again and said to Wilson, "Robert, why don't you move out here into this country? There's plenty of land, and you're out here ahead of everybody else."

A wistfulness crept over Wilson again, as he looked about the canyon. "A man sure could imagine it," he said. But then he turned back to face Tom and said, "But you know, Tom, I'm married now."

Tom smiled, looking down a bit, remembering how the young man's recent marriage had been the greater part of his contribution to the conversations he and Tom had shared when they had been running the chains for the surveying party the previous fall.

"My wife," Wilson continued, "prefers life in the city and will not hear of moving to the frontier, and I have pledged my life to her, for better or worse, and would prefer to give her as much of the better as I can. She is a wonderful girl, Tom, a fine woman, truly."

Tom smiled again.

"So," Wilson continued further, "as frontier life is so loathsome to her, I have sought my fortune in the city. Mr. Colmey has promised to make me a surveyor after this outing, with his concern putting up the bond. I will be able to make a good living at it, for now, and with so much development occurring in Texas, there will be plenty of opportunities for a man of honest ambition."

Tom smiled once again as he looked at this optimistic man, a man of truly honest ambition, and said, "I think you are right."

"So, Tom, I have resigned myself to the fact that my frontier ambitions must be satisfied by my work as a surveyor," Wilson said, resisting one more urge to look around at the Seven Ox Seven Ranch.

"That's no small resignation," Tom said. "I mean, there are few who've seen more of the frontier than the surveyors."

"That is true, Tom, but it's not the full pioneer experience. It lacks the settling." Wilson could not resist the urge to look around again. "But" he concluded, looking back at Tom, "we each have our lot in life, and mine includes marriage to the finest woman I have ever known, and such a lot as that ought to include some sacrifice."

"That's sound reasoning," Tom agreed, feeling a twinge of wistfulness himself.

"Of course it is, Tom," Wilson said, smiling. "Speaking of pioneers, are the Stuarts and the young man Andy about?"

"The Stuarts are off down the canyon," Tom told him. "Luke is ridin' line, and Elizabeth and the kids took the wagon down to meet him with dinner. Andy has left us."

"He has."

"Yessir, he has gone off to join a trail drive before they become a thing of the past. He is a young man who intends to live his life," Tom said, adding, after looking in appreciation at another young man in front of him, "not unlike yourself, Robert."

"Well, I appreciate that, Tom, but I don't expect to ever join a trail drive," Wilson said, looking off up the canyon, all wistfulness exhausted. "Where did he go?"

"Joined the JA, Charlie Goodnight's concern up in the Palo Duro, north of here."

"I've heard of Mr. Goodnight. He's developed quite a reputation as a cattleman," Wilson said, not without the hint of a question in the saying of it.

"He has," Tom said. "That's why Andy figured he was the man to trail with. Figured the opportunity was right in front of him, and he might never get another one like it. He's probably right. Won't be too many chances to trail with the likes of Charlie Goodnight. Won't be long before there won't be much of a chance to trail with anyone."

A puzzled expression wrinkled young Wilson's brow, as he looked at Tom. "You think people will be losing their taste for beef, Tom?"

"Well, I suppose that's a possibility, too," Tom considered, "but what I was thinkin' about was the progress of the railroads, and of civilization, toward the frontier. Won't be too long before there'll hardly be any distance to trail the beeves, I expect."

Wilson had begun nodding at the start of Tom's explanation, and he now replied, "Of course, of course, I see what you mean. I didn't see your point at first, but of course, at the rate the railroads are moving, it won't be long."

"Not long at all," Tom agreed, not without a sense of loss, as he looked out across the canyon.

Wilson brought him back to the here and now. "Would you mind showing me around the operation, Tom?"

"Not at all, not at all," Tom said, remembering himself. "You'll be stayin' to supper, and overnight. No sense even tryin' to argue it, if you had any intention to. We'll keep our company at least that long, and Elizabeth would never hear of you leavin' any sooner."

"Well, Tom, in truth, I had no intention of arguing it, and was rather looking forward to Mrs. Stuart's cooking."

"Well, good then," Tom said, smiling. "Let's show you around," he added as he began to walk toward the creek, with Wilson falling in beside him.

Suddenly Wilson pulled up short. "Wait a minute," he said, as he headed back to his saddlebags. "There is the matter of some mail, as well." He reached into the saddlebags and pulled out a packet of mail, which he brought to Tom. "Both for the Stuarts and Tom Schurtz and for Andy Grady."

Tom thumbed through the packet and recognized the beautifully flawless script of Molly Banks. He smiled at it (which Wilson noted), then remembering that he was not alone, he looked up from the mail and said, "Let me run these patents and letters inside; then I'll show you around."

Tom did run them inside the dugout, where he singled out those addressed to him and put them in his vest pocket. The other letters and the patents he lay on the table; then he turned away to leave, but, on second thought, he returned and tucked the patents under a book on a shelf until he could present them to the Stuarts that evening. Then he returned outside and led Wilson off toward the creek.

At the creek, he and Wilson crossed on large stones that he and Luke had moved into place after having hewn them flat on top. These were placed far enough apart to allow the creek to flow but still allow a person to cross. This stone crossing would do until they could build the small bridge they had planned. On the other side of the creek, where a cold spring flowed out from under some rocks to empty into the creek, Tom showed Wilson the beginnings of the springhouse they were building, which allowed the spring water to flow into a channel in which crocks or other waterproof containers could be set to keep butter, eggs, meat, and other items from spoiling.

From the springhouse, he showed him the new Stuart home, the original dugout, the barn, the pens, and eventually they rode up to Tom's own house and he showed Wilson around it. There Tom wrote Wilson a check for the remaining money. At that point, Tom also indicated that he and the Stuarts would be interested in purchasing and having located certificates for five or six more sections of land, depending on the price. That they would be paying in gold was something that the partners had agreed to keep to themselves until they could negotiate with Matthew Colmey, as word that people were keeping gold could often find its way to less desirable denizens of the frontier regions.

The interest in purchasing more land and having it surveyed was later confirmed by the Stuarts over supper. Wilson responded that he would let Mr. Colmey know of the offer and that he was sure that Colmey would be able to bring the surveying outfit their way at some time during these three months they were out in the field. Then Elizabeth wanted to know about Dallas, about his wife and their plans, about what ladies were wearing, and about numerous other things. The men, too, had their questions about the settlements, towns, cities, and about the pace of land locating. Hence, they all kept Mr. Wilson busy answering questions long into the night, and again the next morning, over the fortifying breakfast that Elizabeth prepared for him to send him on his way.

It WAS NOT MORE THAN A FEW DAYS LATER, in mid May, that Elizabeth prepared a similar breakfast to send Tom on his way. After breakfast he and Luke hitched up the oxen, which they had rounded up the previous day, to the large wagon, on which Tom had been working for the past several days. They had loaded the wagon the day before with furs and hides, and Elizabeth had prepared provisions to last Tom for camp meals for the next several weeks. Tom had already stowed his gear in the wagon.

With the oxen hitched up and all else in readiness, the group bowed their heads in prayer for a safe and successful trip for Tom, safety and success for those left behind, and a final prayer for the safety and success of their own Andy, now gone. Then, following good-byes to Elizabeth, Rachel, and Robert, Tom cracked the big bullwhip over the heads of the oxen, and they stepped forward, dislodging the wagon from where it sat, and plodded off, with the wagon in tow, up the slow rise toward his house. Tom walked beside the wagon, and Luke walked beside him, and Zachariah, with Charlie at his heels, walked between the two of them. Luke commented several times on the good condition of the wagon and the oxen. Zachariah interjected now and then with questions about Uncle Tom's "journey."

In time they were at the level area near Tom's house, and Tom stopped the oxen to bid Luke and Zachariah farewell.

"Well, sir," Tom said to Luke, "take care of things here while I'm gone."

"I will."

"And you, too, Zachariah. You'll have to help take my place while I'm gone. And I'm askin' you to help keep an eye on my homeplace, here, as your folks see fit."

"Yessir."

Tom then petted the amiable and intelligent Charlie, and crouched down and ruffled his neck fur with both hands and said, "And you take care of all these folks, Charlie, and keep 'em out of trouble." Charlie's smile opened wider with the ruffling.

Tom straightened up from the dog and turned to Luke and shook his hand. "Be careful," he said.

"You be careful, yourself, out there," Luke returned.

"I will," Tom said, as the two men dropped hands and he turned to climb aboard the wagon seat to steer the team through the cleft in the caprock, which he and Luke had widened with pickaxes to accommodate the wagon.

As Tom was taking his seat and picking up the reins, Luke continued, "And I don't just mean to be careful of Indians and renegades and rustlers and gunmen and confidence men, either. I have just as many concerns—and probably graver ones, at that—of the many gals you're likely to meet, every one of 'em clamorin' to be Mrs. Thomas Schurtz."

Tom's head bent as he released a sigh of laughter and shook his head lightly from side to side. He had expected more of this from the beginning, but had just accepted that this serious event of leaving the family alone in the canyon, while he headed out alone across still fairly hostile country, had appropriately sobered Luke. But, perhaps even more appropriately, it had not, so that here, at the latest possible moment of their farewell, that part of Luke that interjected humor into almost any situation had risen to the surface.

Tom looked down past his left shoulder at Luke, who continued, "And write ahead if you need Elizabeth to add the woman's touch to your honeymoon cabin. And I can tell you, too, that it will provide us some kind of relief when we can put a name and a face to this phantom we've all been waitin' on."

Head still bent and lightly shaking from side to side, Tom waved over his shoulder at father and son, and steered the team through the cleft, a narrow enough fit, and out onto the Llano Estacado.

• • •

IT WOULD TAKE AT LEAST THREE, more likely four, days for the lumbering ox team to reach the headquarters of the JA ranch, situated at that time high in the Palo Duro Canyon, near its head. On the afternoon of the second day, Tom crossed paths with a line rider for the JA, who rode with Tom a while and stopped and shared an early supper with him. The young man was grateful for the company, having spent the last few weeks alone in a line dugout at the farthest reaches of the ranch. He told Tom that they had all been informed, down the line, of his offer to broker skins and that he should expect plenty to be waiting for him at headquarters. The rider had already sent his own skins of antelope, deer, wolves, bear, and a panther down the line. He assured Tom that he would also send word along the line that Tom was arriving, so that, if Andy were out on a roundup crew, he could see about coming into headquarters to see Tom before he left for Dodge.

Tom arrived at the headquarters on the afternoon of the fourth day. He met up with Charles Goodnight, who immediately put men to work loading his wagon with furs and skins (bundled and marked according to owner) and handed Tom an inventory of the skins, the types, and from which men they had come. Then he took Tom on a short tour of parts of his ranch before they enjoyed a supper prepared by Goodnight's wife, Mary.

At supper, Tom asked about Andy, and Goodnight, a bit upset with himself for not having thought about it, said, "Of course you'd want to see the young man. He's been doing fine. He probably rode in while we were out. He probably ate with the men. You can catch him as soon as we're done here."

Goodnight was right. Tom did manage to find Andy standing in front of the mess house with a group of hands after supper. These men, at the moment of Tom's approach, were enthralled by the storytelling of one of their number, who spoke in a quiet, low voice, while squatting down on his haunches balanced over the balls of his feet, like many there present, as he rolled a cigarette. Andy caught sight of Tom approaching from the ranch house, and he removed himself from the group, so as not to be forced to introduce Tom to these men he hardly yet knew. He intercepted Tom as he approached.

They met with a handshake and a smile on each face. Tom said to Andy, quiet enough so that the men would not overhear, "Well, you look to be doin' all right."

"I am, Tom, doin' real well," Andy responded in the same volume.

"They're treatin' you well, then?"

"They are, Tom, real well."

"Good," Tom responded. "Why don't you show me around here," he said, so that they could get out of earshot of the others, and so that Andy would have the opportunity to show Tom around his JA ranch.

They moved away, and Andy, with a subdued pride, started Tom on a walking tour of the immediate area. Once out of the others' hearing, he expressed right away how glad he was to see Tom, and he began asking specific questions about all the Stuarts and the way things were at the ranch. Andy might have betrayed a touch of wistfulness when Tom told of the Stuarts and the ranch, and about the recent visit of Robert Wilson and the impending expansion, but Tom could clearly see that Andy had made the right choice, that he was excited about the move, and that he was happy in it. Tom was happy for him.

As Andy showed Tom much of what Tom had already seen, his voice had a new life to it, an excitement and a certain maturity, which Tom had experienced often enough, but which, often enough, had crawled back into its shell while he was still mainly the son of Sean and Maria Grady. Here, no one knew from whence or whom he came, or anything else about him. He was Andy Grady, judged only by his performance and attitude. Tom was not surprised to see that that suited him.

They talked well into the dark, Tom Schurtz and Andy Grady, man to man, and Tom knew that there would never be any going back from that. Andy Grady had stepped off into manhood, and Tom welcomed his entry into that state. Eventually, Andy indicated that he should be getting back to his roundup outfit. Tom remembered again the letters for Andy that Robert Wilson had delivered, which had come to his mind when he had mentioned Wilson's visit, and he pulled these from his vest pocket, where he had put them so as not to forget them, and handed them to Andy. Andy accepted the letters, thanked Tom for them, then stuck them in his own pocket, characteristically saving even a glance at them for when he would be alone.

They shook hands again. "It's good to see this suits you so well, Andy," Tom said.

"Thank you, Tom. I appreciate all the talks we had, your advice and all."

"Well," Tom responded, "I don't know how useful what I have to say is, but if what I know can help you at all, I'm glad to share it."

"It has helped a good deal, Tom. And I've started St. Augustine's *Confessions*."

"Good! You'll have to let me know what you think of it."

"I will."

"You take care of yourself, Andy.

"I will."

Then they shook hands again and bade each other farewell, and Andy returned to his horse and rode off to his outfit, while Tom turned back to the Goodnights' house where he was being put up as a guest.

IN THE MORNING, the Goodnights sent Tom off after a hearty breakfast. Goodnight rode alongside Tom part of the way down the canyon, pointing out his breed cattle, mainly Durham, in the upper reaches of the canyon. Then they bade each other farewell, and Tom headed on toward the mouth of the canyon. He camped three more nights in the canyon before reaching its mouth. The morning after the third night, he cleared the mouth of the canyon and pointed the wagon toward Fort Elliott to the northeast.

In a week, Tom had reached Fort Elliott, where he joined a wagon train for Dodge City, but not before sending a telegraph message to his brother John in Wisconsin, a message that had some connection to the mysterious letter and substantial check he had sent to John the previous August. He had time for little else, as the wagon train left immediately for Dodge City. The train and he reached Dodge before the middle of June 1878.

TOM HAD MANY THINGS TO ATTEND TO when he reached Dodge City in that June of '78. He had to put up his wagon and animals, find a place to stay, and to sum up most of the rest of it, he had a good deal of buying and selling to do. But beyond all these duties lay one other that claimed its own priority in his subconscious and conscious mind and heart, and that was a reacquaintance with the widow Molly Banks.

Tom had been very quietly writing letters to Molly, as she had been to him, ever since he had left Dodge City the previous July. He had sent some from San Antonio, and some more from Fort Griffin, and had received mail from her at both places. Once out in the canyon, he had received letters from her delivered by the Hill and Colmey surveying outfit, which they had picked up for him in Fort Griffin. He had sent letters back by them, informing her in the first of these that all future mail to him should be directed to Fort Elliott. The letters she had sent before she had received that letter—which had taken some time to reach her, as the surveying party had been out in the field for several weeks before returning to Ft Griffin—had been delivered by Robert Wilson, when he had delivered the patents. Those that she had sent after, Tom had picked up at Fort Elliott.

Tom had also corresponded with Nancy Hawkins, the Kentucky beauty he had met at the Higgins-Kendall wedding celebration outside Griffin, as a man had to keep his options open in a land where, and a time when, distances were great, travel slow, and men often outnumbered women ten or more to one. But that young woman had returned to Kentucky, making any relationship less likely, which had encouraged Tom to direct his letter writing more toward the widow Mrs. Banks, relieving him somewhat from the distraction of the other correspondence.

In the letters he had sent last December, Tom had suggested that he might be coming to Dodge in the summer. In retrospect, Tom was somewhat amazed that he had written that to her way back then, as, at that time, it had been nothing more than a passing consideration.

Tom intended to stay at the Krause House, as he had on his last visit to Dodge City, for the first few days, until he could sell all that he had to sell. For the remainder of his time in Dodge, he intended to camp outside town. Of course, with all the cattle outfits in the area, there would be some competition for a good spot, but with his outfit as small as it was, he was sure to squeeze in somewhere.

After he arrived in town, he put up his wagon where he knew it would be safe, at a well-known, reputable livery stable on the south side of town. Then, he did manage to secure a room at the Krause

House and order a bath for some time later. He then went and bought a new set of clothes, head to foot, with boots and hat included. He returned to the Krause for his bath. Then he dressed, and in new clothes, boots, and hat, departed the Krause House.

He stepped out onto the porch, surveyed up and down the street, noting the trees (of which the Dodge of less than ten years before would have been void), then stepped off the porch and headed down into town, to Front Street. Once on Front Street, he stopped in at the Centennial Barber Shop for a haircut and shave, and, when properly trimmed, oiled, and scented, departed that establishment for further wandering on Front Street. He ambled up and down, stopping in various enterprises, looking at various items, but not with the intent to buy, even though he did have a long list of items to purchase, put together by Luke, Elizabeth, and himself. Somehow, at this time, that list was more than his mind could handle. He was just drifting aimlessly through stores and concerns, in a bit of a mental haze, with no direction.

Finally, he admitted to himself that all this browsing was not doing something, it was the avoidance of doing something. That recognized and admitted, he turned away from the Dodge House Billiard Hall, in front of which he had found himself at the time of this admission, and walked west down the boardwalk with determination in his step. Nearly oblivious to the numerous other pedestrians, except for an automatic politeness as he passed, he continued on his way. He passed Mueller's boot shop, where he had purchased his boots. He passed shops and saloons, stopping at the corner in front of the Old House Saloon, where he paused, ruminating, still nearly oblivious to the passing cowhands and citizens and their greetings. Finally, he stepped back in front of the first window that presented itself, removed his hat, smoothed his hair, straightened his clothes, replaced his hat on his head, turned back to the west and continued. He stepped off the boardwalk into the dust of First Avenue, turned to his right, and began to ascend that street.

As he ascended the street, so too did certain emotions make a continued, uncontrollable ascent in him. The emotional ascent was not an overwhelming one, nor was it altogether unpleasant. It was, nonetheless, to some degree, unsettling, disconcerting. It rose somehow simultaneously in his stomach and in his chest, and sent what felt like slight tremors out into his arms and legs; and though he was walking, and had been practicing that form of travel for a good many years, the way his legs moved and his feet hit and lifted from the pavement felt unfamiliar to him. His face and neck were slightly warmer than even the heat of the day could account for, and his hands were moist. In his brain ran a rapid-fire shift of emotions, tempered by reason, confusing reason, reason itself seeming to shift in lightning speed, almost uncontrollably, tossed about upon an ocean of emotions. Expectations, concerns, joys, fears, confidences, insecurities were all bobbing up and down in the rational-emotional mix.

Then, all at once, he had arrived at Walnut Street, and there on the corner sat the schoolhouse. Tom stared at it for a moment, conscious that as long as he had not yet entered it, he could still turn away and be none the worse for the passing, but catching himself in this cowardice, he swallowed hard, straightened his hat, walked forward, climbed the steps onto the porch, and opened the door.

He leaned in with his hand on the knob as if to take a look around, but instead, his vision immediately fell and rested upon a woman sitting at a desk directly opposite the room from him. She raised her eyes from her work, and they almost glowed out to him from across the room, those green eyes out from under the luscious red hair. It was Molly Banks, all right. At the sound of the door opening, she had looked up to see who it was. When her eyes met Tom's, they locked on his, her gaze conveying a certain confusion. Then suddenly, almost involuntarily, she blurted, "Tom," and rose and hurried to him and threw her arms around his middle. At almost the very instant of her embrace, she realized the forwardness of her manner and quickly released him, backing away, apologizing for her forwardness in obvious embarrassment, and reaching up with her hand to wipe a tear or two from her eyes. With a sniffle and a little laugh, she said, "I am sorry." Looking down and laughing lightly, she added, "You just took me so by surprise."

Tom was caught a bit off guard by this reaction to his opening of a door. He knew, of course, that Molly was a schoolteacher, but he did not expect her to be at the school in the summer, as school was not in session. He had supposed, though, that he might start there—unlikely as it was that she would be there—and rather work up to calling on her at home. Yet here she was, preparing things for when school would reconvene.

Tom recovered from his original shock at the embrace and dismissed the forward display of affection, considering that this woman was a widow, after all. He was glad to have valid reason to dismiss the forwardness because he had, in fact, rather enjoyed it. As Molly had backed away from him, Tom had stared at her in surprise, and he continued to stare at her now, the surprise having subsided. Her face drew and held his attention—allowing him to look at little else when she was present—with its attractive combination of colors: the green eyes set in peaches and cream below the red curls, her laugh adding the white teeth framed by full red lips. He saw before him beauty, but it was beauty that went deeper than her appearance. It went right to her very core. She was honest. Tom had recognized this the first time he had seen her talking to Luke. And she was earnest, too. He was at once at ease because of her reaction. She wore her feelings and thoughts right out front, which made it easier for a man to know where he stood.

"Would you like to sit down?" she said, conveniently turning from him and walking toward her desk, drying her eyes and sniffling as she went.

Tom followed behind her, and she absentmindedly walked around to the other side of her desk—still not yet looking at Tom, but more composed—and pulled out her chair and began to sit. Then, suddenly remembering something, she stood bolt upright, pushing back her chair, and said, "I am sorry, you can't very well sit in that desk." She laughed again, only a vestige of a sniffle left in it, as she and Tom both looked down at the child-size desk and chair at his knee.

Still laughing, she said, "Let me get you a chair."

She crossed to the corner of the room, wiping at the bottom of her much drier eyes with the back of her hand. As Tom watched her cross the room, he was involuntarily reminded of what a remarkable figure Molly possessed. Taking a chair from the corner, she began to bring it over to her desk, still avoiding to look at Tom. Tom suddenly came to, as if from some stupor, and intercepted her.

"Let me get that," he said, taking the chair from her.

"All right," she said, her gaze still down, again brushing under her eyes with her knuckle as if to wipe away all trace of the recent tears.

She returned to her desk and seated herself. Tom pulled the chair up next to the desk and sat. Finally, she looked up at him.

Close observation reveals that a person's eyes are really impossible to accurately describe. Their color changes often, depending on setting and backdrop. Indeed, it is not a color at all, but a blending of colors, small numerous bits of colors blending or complementing each other in combination to create a particular hue from a distance, a hue which breaks down into its constituent parts upon closer and closer examination. Oddly enough, even close up, one is not so much aware of those constituents, but rather again aware of the eyes as a whole and, in that awareness, aware of the person. "The eyes are the portals of the soul," wrote that writer who well summed up this observation.

Molly's eyes were open to him now, green lights, deep, not so much with intelligence as with sincerity, though intelligence registered there too, but an intelligence more for learning than for probing. Surrounding those eyes was an ovular face with soft, raised cheekbones; a small, slightly upturned nose; and full cupid-bow lips above a nicely rounded chin. A slight ruddiness darkened what would have otherwise been a peaches and cream complexion. Fine brows arched above her eyes: those eyes, sparkling now from their recent tearing, surrounded by long, moist, glistening lashes. And all was framed by the piled curls of red, not quite auburn, hair, loose strands of which hung down about her ears.

Those strands occupied her now, as she tried to push them up into the rest of her hair. Tom would have had her leave them as they were, but he was well aware that women sometimes missed completely some of the finer elements that made them so attractive to men.

"I really was not prepared to receive any callers today," she said. "I must look a sight."

"You look just fine, Molly."

She smiled and blinked her eyes and looked back at him fully reassured.

Thus commenced the reacquaintance of old friends who were, in many ways, still strangers. They had shared much in their letters but had only conversed, really, on two other occasions. An awkward familiarity existed here. Their intimacies had been shared in the safety of distance. Now they sat in proximity. Tom was aware, down in some place within him, that as pleasurable as was this proximity, he missed, to some degree, that safety of distance.

And pleasurable it was. Molly was like a sponge, wanting to absorb all that she could to fill in around what she had read. She wondered if she had received all his letters and found that, as far as they could determine, she had, except for those that Tom had written since last December. Those he had bundled in a packet, and they lay in his room at the Krause House. Though she looked forward to reading those, she now sought in question after question all the information they contained. She knew them all: Luke, Elizabeth, Andy, Zachariah, Rachel, and little Robert. She loved them all, too. She truly did. She ran the emotional gauntlet as she vicariously experienced all the events that Tom now related.

Still, despite her almost steady questions, Tom managed to get in a few of his own. He had read all her letters, at least once. The last batch from Fort Elliott, he had read on his way to Dodge. Still, he asked questions of what he knew, just to hear Molly share her life with him. In this way, he learned again from Molly that the position at Fringer's Drug Store and Post Office, that Reverend Wright had helped her obtain, had given her enough income to get by until she was hired as a school teacher, on Reverend Wright's recommendation. Her first year had been difficult and demanding, but she had continued to work hard and by the end of the first semester had really found teaching to be rewarding. She had established a classroom with the balance of discipline and freedom necessary for effective study. Students and parents had responded well, with the usual exceptions, and she had been enthusiastically invited back for the following year with an increase in salary. The grateful parents had even provided for a kind, widowed baby sitter for her two children too young to attend school.

She still worked at Fringer's store during the summer, but was able to cut her hours to spend more time with her children, and they, less time with the baby sitter. The four children—Alice, James, John, and Sara—were all healthy, and the older girl and boy, Alice and James, were doing very well in school. She still lived with the children in the upstairs of the large home of the McAllens, a very kind couple beyond the childbearing age, who had been unable to have children of their own. At first, while working at the drug store, Molly had done the cooking and cleaning for both families in exchange for a lower rent, but after she had started teaching and the McAllens had got to know her and her well-behaved children, Mrs. McAllen had agreed to cook for all if Molly and the children would see to certain other chores and pay a slightly higher rent, which was still very reasonable.

As they related what had occurred in their lives since their last meeting, they both reveled in the other's good fortune. Their afternoon drifted away, seemingly free of time's grip, only for them to discover that, though time may have loosened its grip, still it demanded that the afternoon responsibly tread its course into evening. And the lower angle of the sun's rays through the window eventually announced to them that it was late.

Time does its part to remind us of our innate quest for the eternal, and so it now reminded, tweaking a bit the hearts of this man and this woman so wholesomely absorbed. They could have stayed and stayed, but the one responsibility that cannot long be ignored is that of one's children, and Molly knew that she must go. And she gathered her things as she and Tom rose from their seats.

"Where are you staying?" she asked.

"At the Krause House for the present," Tom said. "I will be settin' up camp outside of town in a few days."

"I have friends who would like you to stay with them as a guest, if you would like," Molly said.

Tom registered his hesitance. "Well, I don't know."

"They really would like to have you, Tom. They are older and would appreciate the company. You would be responsible for your own meals, so they say, but I believe Mrs. Murphy, especially once she gets to know you, will prevail upon you to eat with them on occasion. We can just drop by and introduce you, and you can decide."

They did drop by the Murphys'. They were an older couple who had moved the family butcher business from Iowa. Their son's family had moved with them and the business. The business had done quite well, and the older Mr. Murphy now only dropped by the business at very comfortable hours, leaving most of the work to his son and grandchildren. The son's family had moved out of the house two years before, and though the grandchildren visited often, the house seemed all too quiet for the older Murphys, who had left the families of six other children behind in Iowa. Consequently, they strongly prevailed upon Tom to be their guest. Finally, on recognizing the insult they would feel if he did not accept, and the even greater insult they implied when he suggested a monetary arrangement, Tom felt like he could do nothing other than stay with the delightful older couple and accept their hospitality. All agreed. Still, Tom could not help but feel that things were happening a little too fast. In a matter of minutes, he had gone from the Krause House and a trail camp to the Murphys'. He had a certain sense of Molly's world closing in around him. Nevertheless, all seemed pleased with the arrangements, so he shrugged off the feeling for the time being, and with arrangements at the Murphys' settled, Tom walked Molly home.

"Would you like to stay for supper?" she asked him as they stood at the gate outside the McAllen house.

Tom was perceptive enough to note the hesitation in the polite offer and to recognize that the time was lacking that a woman would want to put into a meal for a special guest, and Molly had made enough indication, over the course of the afternoon, that Tom would be a special guest.

"No, I need to settle in and see where I'm at. I'll be tradin' hides tomorrow, and lookin' into some purchases."

"Then, tomorrow night?"

"Well, I can't really say how long I'll be at it tomorrow."

"Sunday, then? The day after tomorrow, Sunday dinner, could you come for that?"

"Now that I could do," Tom said.

"Good," Molly said, a smile indicating her pleasure at this arrangement, and she laid her hand on the gate.

"Molly," Tom said, a different tone in his voice. She turned the bright open eyes upon him, finding the same pleasure in looking into the portals of his soul as he found in looking into hers.

"Molly, may I call on you tomorrow night, later, after supper?"

"Yes, you may," she said with a quiet earnestness.

And he did call. He came for dinner on Sunday, too, and thus began his daily habit of calling on the widow Mrs. Molly Banks.

As this daily habit developed, Mrs. Banks indicated that she wished that Tom could stay longer in Dodge, and so did he wish, and so he did stay. He wrote to the Stuarts—by way of Fort Elliott, hoping that from there the letter would go through the JA to the Stuarts—to let them know that he might be delayed a couple weeks or more.

This extra time would be one of the happiest periods of Tom's life, Molly's too. They spent all their available time together, and people noticed. The McAllens let Molly and Tom each know how highly they thought of the other. The Murphys dropped subtle hints of Molly's suitability for marriage. The women at the Presbyterian Church wondered openly about him, curious about his absence from Sunday services (due to his attendance at Catholic Mass, wherever he could find it, at Union Church or out at Fort Dodge). Still, Tom and Molly attended church socials and other public events, including many of the Fourth of July activities sponsored by the Dodge City Fire Company, which fueled local speculation. Molly and Tom were invited to meals at the Murphys', a great treat for Mr. Murphy if for no other reason than to enjoy his wife's excellent cooking, which he was allowed to do less and less frequently as she got older and her appetite and her desire to cook diminished. Tom was frequently invited to family meals at the McAllens', as well. These events, and others involving the family, did much to assure Molly of Tom's suitability for the role of father of her four children and however many more God would bless them with. And there were the pleasant walks in the evenings, the quiet visits on the porch.

And as this pleasant time passed, Tom grew slowly aware of something. He became aware that he loved Molly, and he loved her family. But most important, despite that love, Tom had begun to realize that he was not in love with her. And he wrestled with this realization. She was kind, a good Christian, a fine mother. She was committed to the things that mattered: God, family, citizenship, . . . She was an excellent cook, a fine housekeeper, a hard worker. She was enthusiastic, energetic, intelligent, . . . and a host of other positive adjectives. She was a true beauty, whose lovely face and voluptuous figure were a constant challenge to Tom's chastity, and it was plain to see that she would be a delight to the eyes for many years to come. He should be blessed to marry her. But something inside nagged at him. Was he just suffering from cold feet? Was he being unrealistic about his standards? But what was it about those standards? What was it that seemed to be missing?

Was it something that did not belong in a relationship until marriage? Was it something that one would discover only in that sacrament, something that one should not expect to have before then? But that sacrament would be for the rest of his life. He would absolutely commit to it. How could he do so without a better sense of surety? He could not definitely identify what he felt was missing in his heart, but it seemed to be a certain complementarity with a corresponding intimacy.

Oh, Tom and Molly had been intimate. They had shared thoughts and feelings. They had embraced. They had even kissed on two occasions. Still, somehow their intimacy seemed constrained, its potential limited. As this became more apparent to Tom, it also crept slowly into his consciousness that he could not go on offering affection to Molly as he had been. Granted, in a later age, four or five weeks might appear to be an unusually short courtship from which to draw much of a conclusion, but this was the American West at a unique period of its development. With trail drives and the arrival of the train, people in this country, who might have otherwise seen only those people who lived within a few miles of their home, were instead meeting and getting to know people from different regions all over the country, for that matter, the world. In Dodge City, Molly might meet, beyond the colorful men of the town itself, Texas cowhands to British lords. People would be here today and gone tomorrow. Courtships often accommodated such conditions. To complicate matters for Tom's consideration, across the West at that time, much less so in towns like Dodge, there were nearly ten men to every woman. His chances of meeting a woman more compatible than Molly did not appear so great.

Still, Tom had realized long before that it was better to be unmarried than badly married. And yet he was strongly attracted to women and just enjoyed the company of a special woman, and he had hopes that the Sacrament of Matrimony, with all its challenges, would eventually grace his life. But this nagging in his soul continued to suggest to him that if marriage was to be a part of his life, this woman and this time were not the right ones. But Molly was as fine a woman as he had met. If not Molly, then would there ever be anyone? How did loneliness weigh against marriage and family, marriage to a fine woman? Could that be worse than being alone? But it should not be a matter of "could it be worse?" It should be a matter of "this I know to do; this I know to be my calling." And that was not there.

Molly needed a man who would take charge of her, who would run the life she envisioned. They would settle in, him to his business, whatever it was, her to her household and social and church obligations. Molly would conform to her man, be his woman. But Tom would need a mate, not a woman who would just conform to him. Besides, he wondered if he were really the kind of man to whom Molly could conform. Molly was comfortable in Dodge City and with her life there. Could she really move out to the Seven Ox Seven and be content? Could she really live, with her four children, the frontier life? And what about the insecurity of such a life? What of failure? Would she be adaptable enough, especially in her state of life, for that? He was not sure.

He was sure, though, that he would need a woman who knew who she was, first, and who was then compatible with him, as herself. Marriage should be intimate, with unlimited potential for deeper intimacy. Tom was a Catholic. He could not somehow exclude that sacramentalism from his conception of marriage. Marriage as a sacrament is an event in which the human meets the divine and, through the divine, re-meets the human. It is a communion, human with human with divine, thus giving the marriage intimacy its profound potential, manifested perhaps best in its potential to cooperate and share with the divine in the creation of human life. Tom knew that, and he knew that marriage for him would demand a mate with whom he could be fully intimate. And he had to wonder, too, whether he could be fully intimate with someone who did not share the Catholic Faith that frees one to plumb the very depths of Truth, of Christianity, with magisterial guidance that originated in Christ himself.

Tom would accept his responsibilities as husband and father, but in fully accepting these, he could not accept a wife as anything other than a full mate. He realized that in marriage both mates should complement each other in their complementary roles. Each should assist the other to grow to his or her full potential: each, together, within the realm of their sacramental bond, questioning, searching, seeking their vocation in the unfolding plan of the Almighty, and together—daily, hourly, momentarily—recommitting and redirecting their lives and life together accordingly. Marriage is not a commitment to working together for the achievement of worldly comfort, however unextravagant that comfort is. Marriage is the commitment to God, spouse, and

the children with whom God graces the union, in which, in communion, a couple seeks God's vocation for them in the world, and, in so
doing, accepts all the responsibilities of that vocation in communion,
toward the goal of eternal life after the world, for all members of the
family. Marriage involves the difficult times, the struggles of separate
personalities struggling separately and (more difficult yet) together to
seek, discern, commit to, and live out vocations within the sacramental bond. That is marriage, and Tom was not sure that Molly fully
appreciated that; and he knew that he would not put any woman who
did not fully appreciate that through a marriage with him who did
appreciate it and would expect it.

Despite the pleasure of Molly's company, Tom's realization of the
limitations of their relationship began to show in a gradual hesitancy,
to which Molly was not insensitive. Molly was in love, as far as she
knew, and as Tom began to grow more distant and to talk more frequently about getting back to the ranch, she knew that she needed to
clear away some confusion. One night after supper and after the children had gone to bed, she and Tom had taken a stroll, as had become
their custom, and had returned to the house and were sitting on the
front-porch swing.

They talked, but a growing distance of noncommitment had begun
to render Tom's participation in conversation slowly more shallow.

After a bit of this increasingly one-sided conversation, Molly
broached the uncomfortable topic of intentions.

"You'll be leaving soon, Tom?" she said to her hands in her lap.

"I reckon I will be," he said, turning to view the profile of her lowered face, something he could not do without the sensation of attraction waving across his inner person.

"Will we continue to write to each other?" she asked, without raising her eyes or her head.

"We can."

Something nearly imperceptible, like a slight wince, wrinkled her
features, and she let out a light sigh that slightly deflated her posture.

"Don't you want to?" she asked, a note of emotion entering her voice.

Tom looked at her, his own discomfort rising at seeing her upset
and not being fully able to resolve the confusion of emotion and reason that sparred within him. Still, he did not answer quickly just to

ease her pain. In his life's experience, he knew that temptation, and he knew what it was to give into that temptation and how doing so solved nothing but rather only exacerbated the problem. He allowed his mind to sift through the fog of feelings and emotions and pull out the truth.

Finally, he said, "I don't know."

Now Molly turned her eyes, burning with tears, on him, which, together with all her features and the slump of her shoulders and her open, upturned hands in her lap, pleaded for some answer. "Is it just going to be good-bye, then?"

That was all her emotions would allow her to get out. Her tearing eyes lay open to Tom, who could not look into them. He lowered his eyes, his brows now furrowed, as the realization of separation finally arrived with companion pangs of the heart.

"Molly, I just don't want to hold you to somethin' I cannot yet promise," he said.

She sniffled and wiped her eyes and nose with one of the kerchiefs she had bought in anticipation of exposing her emotions to Tom at one time or another.

"Would a promise be so bad, some kind of commitment before you go?" She continued to look at him, searching for any communication, though he still could not look up.

"Molly, I just can't promise you anything." He managed to raise his eyes to meet hers as he said it.

"Would it be so bad?" she said through her tears.

"No," he said firmly, slightly shaking his head. "That is not . . ."

"I love you, Tom. The children love you. Our friends love you. But mainly, I love you, Tom."

She had his full attention, and wonder and fear were mixed with the love she read in his wide-open eyes.

"Do you love me, Tom?"

"I do," he said, staring deeply into her eyes. "I truly do." And their eyes held each other's for a moment, Tom loving and being all but overwhelmed by the love he saw in the teary shallows and sensual depths of Molly's eyes. Nevertheless, he could not stay there; he did not belong there; it was not his place, this intimacy; he had no right to it, and he knew it. By a disciplined act of the will, Tom pulled his eyes away to look down and add, "but, I, . . . I just don't know if it's enough."

She sighed at this and turned back to sit forward in the swing, turning her face away from him to wipe her nose and eyes.

"We don't know each other that well, Molly," he nearly pleaded. "We haven't spent that much time together."

"And how can we, Tom?" she asked over her shoulder, and she wiped her nose again.

"I don't think we can," he said.

Still turned away from him, she shook her head and in a feeble voice said, "We poured our hearts out to each other in our letters." She shook her head again, and finally she let the tears flow. Tom fought the desire to put his arm on her shoulder and pull her against him. He did so with the growing commitment to the knowledge that this was not his place and that he must not waver and offer a surface salve to Molly's, and his, gaping feelings, a temporary solution that would only serve to exacerbate those feelings and the confusion that surrounded them.

Besides, what Molly had said made Tom wonder if that were not part of the problem. He did not feel like he had poured out his heart. She obviously believed that he had and that she had to him. There was that different perception of intimacy that would undoubtedly affect the most intimate of human relationships.

She cried, and he fought the desire to hold her. Eventually she began to stop, and eventually they just sat together, the only sound between them being Molly's sniffles and occasional quiet staccato breaths necessary to regulate her breathing after her crying. Tom wanted to say something to soothe her, but something deep and firm within him prevented it. In honesty, there was nothing for him to say or do.

In time, she said, "It's getting late."

"It is."

"Tom," she said, without looking at him and with some embarrassment at needing to resort to this truth, "I've had other callers."

A twinge of jealousy sent a rush of blood to Tom's head, making her even more attractive in her attractiveness to other men, but he fought to push all that away, knowing that justice demanded no less. He looked at her, her face still turned slightly away. She was even more pretty in her sincerity and honesty than she had been in her vulnerability alone. Something inside him ached for her. He fought against his attraction to her, again heeding the demands of justice.

"I'm sure you have," he responded.

"I've turned them away because of you, but I can't wait forever, Tom," she said, turning to face him.

"I know."

"I don't know if you'll be coming back," she said, still seeking even a hint of some commitment.

"That's right."

She took a deep breath and sighed, looking out down the length of the porch and out into the night beyond. "So, I should not hold out any hope, then?"

"It wouldn't be fair for me to ask you to."

She mixed a sigh with a slight, hollow laugh.

That triggered some of the words Tom had been holding back. "Molly, you are one of the finest women I've ever known. You are lovely and gracious, intelligent and kind, but I just don't know yet, and it wouldn't be fair of me to ask you to wait."

Molly cried quietly, and Tom swallowed to keep control of his own emotions.

Finally, Tom said, "There is no reason for me to stay here any longer, Molly. I'll finish up my business tomorrow and leave the day after."

She nodded her head without looking at him or saying anything, her posture indicating her emptiness.

He stood and she stood with him. She wiped her eyes and nose, emitting some sniffles as she walked him to the steps.

Tom said, with sincerity commensurate to the void that would be left in his life, "I'll miss you, Molly."

That sincere sentiment released some of the reserved emotion within them both, and suddenly they found themselves hugging each other tightly.

"I'll miss you too, Tom," Molly said into his chest.

Then they pulled apart, and she reached up and kissed him softly. He embraced her again and kissed her, but she turned her head and pushed away from him and hurried into the house and closed the door.

Tom stood and looked at the closed door for a moment, then turned and walked down the steps and down the walk and out onto the street and into the night.

Molly watched him through her tears from behind a window, then watched the air of the empty night a while. Then she turned from the window and went upstairs to bed.

THE DAY THAT TOM SET OUT TO LEAVE, a Monday early in the last week of July, he had his wagon all lashed down, his supplies all stowed. Among those supplies were milled lumber, window frames and other hardware, a new shotgun, ammunition, clothing and material for sewing, a sewing machine, foodstuffs (including salt, flour, molasses, and various canned goods), and individual purchases for each of the Stuarts and Andy.

Still, not all of Tom's acquisitions were in the wagon. Tied behind the wagon were two large, two-year-old, white-faced bulls. These "thoroughbred" Hereford bulls had been sent by rail by Tom's brother John from Wisconsin. John had been keeping them for Tom since the previous October, having purchased them from T. L. Miller in Beecher, Illinois. In these two bulls was revealed the reason for the letter and substantial check Tom had sent to John from San Antonio the previous August.

Tom had long been interested in the Hereford breed. He had first heard and read about Herefords long before he had come to Texas, and had been intrigued by the claims made of them and by the virulent opposition mounted against them by the advocates of shorthorns. Even though, at that time, ranching had seemed as remote a possibility as many others for Tom's future, and though he had not gone out of his way to seek out information regarding Herefords, still, he had felt drawn to any information he would come across regarding the much-maligned breed. Once Tom had moved to Texas and entered cattle work, the subject had taken on more relevance, and he had enjoyed following, through agricultural and livestock journals, news of the Hereford.

By that time, one voice had stood out among the rest as an advocate for the Hereford breed. That voice belonged to T. L. Miller of Beecher, Illinois, a tireless promoter against a very strong and vocal opposition. The claims then being advanced about Herefords appeared to border on the fantastic. Not only was it claimed that they fattened at an unbelievable rate on grazing alone, but that they would rustle sustenance from even the harshest grazing environments, that they would mature at a much faster rate, and that they would produce more and superior calves, regardless of the breed of the dam.

For Tom, such claims would need to be substantiated before he would believe them; still, he had been inclined, with a certain hopefulness, to believe them, while making allowances for exaggeration. If such claims were true, they certainly were consistent with the aims of the originators of the Hereford. Those men, in Herefordshire, England, in the middle of the eighteenth century, in an attempt to make the most of the growing demand for beef during the Industrial Revolution, had sought to breed into their cattle a trait they had witnessed in certain beeves, which was to fatten well on grazing alone. As they succeeded in their aim, they found that the breed that was developing displayed a marked tendency to mature at a much faster rate. Thus, not only were their beeves fattening without their needing to feed them grain, but they were ready for the market at a much earlier age, rendering impractical the former custom of pressing a beef into service in the yoke for several years before butchering it when its usefulness as a draught animal was ended.

Since the first verifiable importation of Herefords to the United States by the renowned Henry Clay of Kentucky in 1817, American cattle raisers had begun to make their own claims about Herefords, but not without first putting the breed to the test. Experiments by skeptical cattle raisers met with similar surprising results, winning convert after convert. A later example of such results would be found in the experience of Wilbur E. Campbell of Caldwell, Kansas, such a staunch supporter of the shorthorn breed that he was called "Shorthorn" Campbell. Campbell would first bring Herefords to his ranch from G. S. Burleigh in Mechanicsville, Iowa, in 1879. Surprised at how much better his two Hereford bulls wintered than his shorthorns, he purchased twenty-six shorthorns and twenty-five Herefords and put them out to pasture in an experiment. The results he describes as follows:

> When the heat of summer came the Shorthorns could be seen standing along the streams or in the shade while the Herefords were busy grazing. Then, both were allowed to remain on the open range the entire

winter without supplemental feed or shelter of any kind, and compelled to rustle for a living or die. The winter proved to be one of unusual severity and before spring came almost 50 per cent of my beloved Shorthorns had died, and the remainder were but reeling skeletons. With the Herefords the test was perfectly satisfactory as every one of the 25 showed up in good shape.

Later, Campbell would turn out a Hereford bull into "a herd of Shorthorn cows" and, as he described them, "six little $12 southern Texas cows whose colors represented every hue of the rainbow, and none of which exceeded 700 pounds in weight." From those Texas cows came five steers and a heifer. The heifer as a yearling weighed 1,260 pounds. One of the steers weighed 1,680 pounds as a two-year-old, and another, 1,920 pounds as a three-year-old.

D. J. Bernard of Belle Fourche, South Dakota would describe an experiment of his own with an introduction that reads like the beginning of a joke:

Three bulls were turned loose on the range, a Hereford, a Shorthorn and an Aberdeen-Angus. The next spring on the roundup we found the Hereford and the Angus; branded 75 white-faced calves, three blacks and 40 Shorthorns; the Shorthorn bull was dead, the Angus in fair condition, and the Hereford fat enough for beef.

But all that had yet to come. The breed still had much opposition to overcome. It had made a big breakthrough at the Centennial Exposition in Philadelphia in 1876, where Miller and other Hereford breeders had displayed their cattle to great advantage, arousing a good deal of interest from cattle raisers from various states, including those of the West.

That is not to suggest that interest in Herefords had been confined to eastern states and provinces like Maine, Ohio, New York, Illinois, Maryland, Michigan, and Ontario, Canada. Miller had claimed, in 1877, that Herefords had been introduced to the plains ten or twelve years before. He had not been specific about where they had gone on the plains, though Colorado is considered to be the probable destination. It is documented that one Hereford bull from the herd of W.F. Stone, Guelph, Ontario, had been shipped to Las Animas in 1871. Miller himself had sent Hereford bulls to Colorado as early as 1873. By 1875, carloads of Herefords were being shipped to Colorado. It would take Texas a little longer to see the advantages of the breed.

The first Herefords to enter Texas are reputed to have been a bull and heifer sold to J. F. Brady of Houston, Texas, in 1876, by William Powell, an early associate of T. L. Miller. That same year, W. S. Ikard of Henrietta, Texas, was said to have brought in Herefords, as well. Still, it was no overnight conversion that led to the Hereford domination of the Texas plains. In 1878, Powell is said to have brought five head of Herefords to Fort Worth, which, he claimed, he nearly had to give away. By 1880, Lee and Reynolds would bring in seven carloads of Herefords to their ranch near old Tascosa. Others would follow.

By 1883, Charles Goodnight and the JA Ranch would join the movement with the purchase of bulls, cows, and calves from Finch, Lord & Nelson of Burlingame, Kansas, who would be credited with selling ten thousand Hereford bulls to the Panhandle of Texas by 1888. In 1884, Goodnight would purchase from Finch, Lord & Nelson another forty bulls, imported from England, at a price of four hundred dollars apiece, of which he would claim, "Taking them as a whole, they were the best lot of imported cattle I have ever seen." Some of those bulls would serve as foundation stock for Goodnight's purebred JJ herd, which would provide bulls for use in the JA Ranch's commercial herd. This "Hereford top" over the "Texas foundation" and the shorthorn "crosses," (as the cowman John Clay would describe the constituents) managed by a range breeder of Goodnight's ability, would produce what some, including Goodnight himself, would consider to be as fine a beef combination as any that would follow, however highly bred. After observing a herd of these JA cattle over the years, John Clay would write that his "admiration of Goodnight as a cattleman soared skyward."

Still, the Texas conversion to Herefords was yet to follow. In the summer of 1878, as Tom prepared to depart from Dodge City with his two short-legged, full-bodied red and white bulls, support for the breed in Texas still seemed a long way off. Tom remembered how Charles

Goodnight had spoken of Herefords, particularly some of T. L. Miller's Herefords, to Luke and Tom just a couple of months before. What he had said at that time, about Miller's cattle being "no good," had shot a bolt into Tom's stomach, as he had thought of the two bulls, expensive bulls, that he had hired his brother to purchase for him from Miller.

He had made the request of his brother the previous summer by mail, in a letter he had mailed from San Antonio when he and Luke had gone into that city to purchase supplies for their move to the Panhandle. After he had earlier agreed to go into partnership with the Stuarts, he had not been able to get the Herefords out of his mind, and he had decided to take a chance of his own, now that he would have the opportunity. If even half of what he had read about Herefords was true, it would be well worth the investment to breed those qualities into their Texas stock. They would also have the option of starting a pure-bred herd with the purchase of cows and heifers at a later date. Tom had just had a feeling, at that time, that now was the time to strike, before the superior range qualities of these cattle were widely accepted and the demand for bulls and their progeny would quickly rise.

So, he had written his brother John and asked him to travel to Beecher, Illinois, forty miles south of Chicago, and visit T. L. Miller's operation and select two bulls, as much bull as he could purchase for $250 apiece. Tom had included a generous check to cover travel expenses for John and his wife, Anne, shipping expenses for the bulls, boarding expenses for the bulls at the family farm until he could send for them, and $50 for John's trouble, besides the $500 for the bulls.

Unbeknownst to Tom, until he had received a letter delivered by Robert Wilson of the surveying party just before Tom left for Dodge, John had done as he had requested. As it had been after the harvest when he had received Tom's letter, John had put the farm in the charge of their younger brother Michael, who, together with his wife, would also look after John and Anne's children. Then John and Anne had taken the train to Chicago and had enjoyed a relaxing though relatively thorough tour of that city for a few days, then had traveled to Beecher and had purchased two bulls, not yet two years old. John had set his mind on these two bulls, even though Mr. Miller's price exceeded the amount Tom had sent for the purchase. But Mr. Miller—not known much for sentiment, though widely known for his passion for advancing the Hereford cause—had seemed to take a liking to the unassuming John, who knew his cattle, and his kindly wife, Anne, and when he had discovered that the bulls were destined for Texas, a state as yet resistant to his Hereford message, he had agreed to John's price. It had not hurt John's cause that, though the bulls had shown much promise, they were still quite young. In this way, John had fulfilled Tom's request.

John had kept the bulls until Tom had wired a message from Fort Elliott, a few weeks before, to inform John that he would be in Dodge City within two weeks and that John could send the bulls at any time. They had arrived a week before, and Tom had visited them every day at the farm where he had boarded them. He had chosen that particular farm because it had appeared to offer the best chance to keep the bulls as far away from any Texas cattle as possible. He had no intention of watching his new bulls fall victim to Texas fever.

Now, early on a sunny Monday morning, early in the last week of July 1878, those bulls were tied to the back of his wagon, and he was about to set out with them for the ranch. He had prayed a rosary novena for direction in his relationship with Molly. Those prayers had helped clarify his position in regard to Molly. He had already begun another rosary novena for a safe return to the ranch with the bulls. He was sure he would have a safe journey. Still, he intended to do his part in remaining vigilant about keeping the bulls away from Texas cattle.

The wagon, with its oxen in front and bulls in back, now sat on the street in front of the Murphys' house. Tom had finished his packing and stood on the front porch with the Murphys, his bedroll on the floor next to him. He was offering his thanks and saying his good-byes. He was also accepting from Mrs. Murphy a nicely wrapped package of cake and other baked goods, hard-boiled eggs, cold meats, and home-canned foods, which Tom knew, from experience, would be delicious. As he was continuing to offer his thanks, something he saw out of the corner of his eye caught his attention.

It is remarkable how the senses of a young lover are so attuned to the presence of his beloved. A lover can discern from a mix of sounds one slight note of the voice of his beloved, or from a blend of aromas the slightest whiff of her fragrance. In a crowded room or street, a mere glimpse of her—just an arm or her hair or the color of her dress in passing—and he can be surer than he is sure of most things that it is she. And sometimes it is just a movement caught out of the corner of the eye that arouses such surety, clouding out any consideration of whether or not it is she with an immediate emotional response to her who brings a unique pleasure.

Such was Tom's reaction now. As he had been shaking Mr. Murphy's hand, while balancing in his other arm the package from Mrs. Murphy, Tom had caught sight of a movement, or was it the color of a familiar dress? or was it the color of magnificent red hair?— which, upon further examination, would be seen to be pulled up and held by an ornate comb that had taken its wearer much more time to get just right than would seem appropriate for just a short good-bye. It could have been any one of those, or more likely the combination of all of them, but whatever the case, the effect on Tom, of catching sight of whatever it was, was to lose sensibility that he was in the presence of others and to let his words die in midsentence, as he glanced off in the direction of that which had drawn his attention.

What it was, was a stunning Molly Banks, wearing the fetching green and black dress that she had worn when Tom had kissed her for the first time since his return to Dodge and told her that she was as lovely as anything he had ever seen. The black comb accenting the red curls piled delightfully upon her head would be seen, upon closer examination, to be accented itself with green trim. But closer examination was as yet denied, as Molly was still some distance down the street walking toward them.

Molly had experienced much the same reaction to the sight of Tom that he had to the sight of her. She had been walking up the street, her mind a jumble of emotions as she approached the Murphys', and then she had caught a glimpse of him and had immediately colored (she knew, as she could feel the warmth crawl up her neck into her face) and had looked away from the porch to the immediate space before her, missing a step in the process, though continuing up the street, determined to carry out her intention without emotional retreat.

Mr. Murphy had noticed immediately Tom's distraction, as Tom's hand, engaged in a handshake with his own, had suddenly relaxed its grip, and Tom had stopped talking and had looked off beyond him. Mr. Murphy had turned to see where Tom's vision pointed, and, upon seeing Molly there in vision's path, had understood all. He now let go of Tom's hand, which fell like dead weight to Tom's side. Mr. Murphy smiled and took Mrs. Murphy by the elbow and stepped back with her to face the front yard in anticipation of their visitor. They did not know where things stood between the two young people and had been wondering that very thing since learning, just the day before, of Tom's plan to leave. They both felt a certain relief upon seeing Molly, and seeing Tom's reaction to her, because they liked these two young people, and it was plain to see that the two young people liked each other.

All at once, Tom came to his senses and reached down and picked up his bedroll. He turned to thank the Murphys again. Shifting the bedroll into his left hand, below the food package that he had managed to shift to under his left arm, he shook hands with Mr. Murphy again and then tipped his hat to Mrs. Murphy, wished them well, bade them farewell, and stumbled down the steps and out to the front gate, as he juggled the bedroll back to his right hand and the package from under his left arm to his left hand, leaving the Murphys to smile in understanding behind him.

He met Molly at the gate, she on the outside, he still on the inside, a situation that Tom was unsuccessfully trying to remedy, as he fumbled with the sticking gate latch with the thumb and index finger of his right hand, which now held the weighty and cumbersome bedroll.

"Molly," Tom said, as he quickly glanced at her and then looked quickly down to where his hand, still holding the bedroll, fumbled with the latch. A certain urgency exacerbated his fumbling, as he sought to get the gate out from between them, and to close it behind him, as if closing the low picket gate would afford Molly and him some sort of privacy for this their last meeting before his departure, a meeting which, by its nature, would likely involve at least some degree of intimacy.

"Good morning, Tom," she said, and her voice had the effect of immediately drawing his attention, and they looked into each other's eyes as they had become accustomed to doing. In so doing, Tom noticed that, though he found the vision before him just as pleasing (as he could not remember the lovely Molly looking lovelier), and though they had not seen each other for two days (enhancing that desire for the person whom he missed), still, he did not feel the same level of attraction that he had felt, augmented perhaps by hope, in the past. He knew in that instant, as he stood and looked into her eyes, the gate in between them, that he was doing the right thing. Despite the attraction he still felt for Molly, it was not the attraction he had felt for her before, or perhaps it was the same attraction, but, being better informed by longer acquaintance, it had not deepened with that information, that further acquaintance, that exposure, as it should have had it been the level of attraction that draws one deeper into it toward sacramental commitment. Tom knew that now, and Molly, despite an undiminished hope for the opposite, knew it too, as she now saw it in Tom's eyes.

Nevertheless, Tom sought the privacy appropriate for this hello and farewell, and so he looked back down and began to fumble with the latch again. Molly watched his down-turned face, as he did so, and slightly smiled at its intensity, as he struggled with the latch with the hand so weighted by the bedroll. She enjoyed his nervousness and intensity, this lovely Molly, who had taken such pains that morning to assure that she looked her loveliest.

Finally, she looked down at his hand on the latch and said through her light smile, "May I help you with that?"

"That's all right," Tom responded without looking up. "I've almost got it here."

But he did not get it. Just as the latch was about to give, it slipped back shut, and his hand, under the weight of the bedroll, fell away from the latch, stopping in its fall when the bedroll hit his knee.

"All right," he said, his face still down as he slightly shook his head, "go ahead."

Molly, her smile deepening, reached over the gate with her free right hand (she held a large basket in the other), and after a moment of jiggling, opened the latch and pushed the gate in toward him. Slightly embarrassed, Tom thanked her as he made his way through the gate.

As he passed, Molly looked up to see the Murphys on the porch. She had been so absorbed in her own concerns regarding this meeting with Tom that she had failed to offer greetings to the Murphys. She quickly remedied this omission by calling out to them, "Good morning, Mr. and Mrs. Murphy."

"Good morning, Molly," they both answered, Mrs. Murphy adding a "dear." Mrs. Murphy continued, "And how are you, dear?"

"Quite well," Molly responded.

"Are you, dear?" Mrs. Murphy continued, leaning into her question a little, as if trying to discern as much as she could from her place on the porch.

"Yes, quite well," Molly confirmed, looking away a little under Mrs. Murphy's scrutiny.

The scrutiny was not lost on Mr. Murphy either, who felt himself being pulled into it, but he caught himself and said to Mrs. Murphy, "Come along, Mabel, and we'll leave these young people to themselves."

Mrs. Murphy offered some resistance, but with Mr. Murphy gently nudging her along, she returned with him to the house, the two of them exchanging good-byes with Tom, he adding more thank-yous, and the Murphys exchanging it's-good-to-see-yous and we'll-see-you-soons with Molly.

Finally, they were in the house, and Tom and Molly turned to face each other, no gate in between them. They both smiled lightly and looked down.

"They're fine people," Tom finally said, looking up to exchange smiles with Molly, who raised her own eyes at the sound of his voice.

"They are dears," she agreed.

The two stood looking at each other for a moment. Then Tom suddenly realized that he was still holding the package and bedroll. He said, "Let me get rid of these things," and he turned and strode the few steps to the wagon and reached up and stuffed them under the seat. He turned around to find that Molly had followed him and now stood in front of him.

She held the basket out before her and said to him, "I packed you a basket for your trip." She lifted one side of the cover of the basket and began to offer an inventory of some of its contents, distracting the both of them from the good-bye that had to come. "There's cake, and bread, and ham, and muffins," she said as she rummaged a little among the contents. "And there's some cheese, and fresh fruit, and some freshly ground coffee from Wright and Beverly's, ground just this morning, . . . and there are vegetables," she continued, rummaging a little more, "and boiled eggs, . . . and . . ." She rummaged some more, but finally looked up at Tom's chest, not yet at his face, and closing the lid of the basket, said, "Well, there are all manner of goods in here. I think you will enjoy them."

"I'm sure I will, Molly," Tom said, accepting the basket from her.

At his speaking her name, she looked up into his eyes and could not hold back what she said next. "Tom," she began, "I just want you to know how much I have enjoyed your acquaintance and companionship over the last few weeks. I will always hold you in a special place in my heart, and I will not forget you."

"I've enjoyed yours, Molly, and I'll not forget you either."

"Won't you?" she questioned, searching deeply into his eyes.

"No, I won't," he said. Then in an attempt to break the intensity of the moment, he added, "I've got a good memory." He smiled broadly with the comment.

Molly smiled with him and looked down. "Yes, you do," she said, as if in acquiescence to the realization that she was not going to draw any more from Tom than what was there, and, in truth, she really did not want to, though she had made this one last attempt to see if there might be more there than he was admitting. She realized that there was not.

Tom spoke up. "I can put this basket right up by me," he said, as he turned and slid the basket under the wagon seat with his bedroll and the package from Mrs. Murphy, thinking for an instant of all the good food he would have to enjoy on his trip. "These will go a long way," he said over his shoulder, as he rearranged the bedroll and package to allow a good space for the basket.

Then he turned back to face her.

"Are you all ready to go?" she asked.

"I am."

They looked at each other again for an awkward moment that Molly finally broke. "You've got your bulls, I see," she said, stepping toward the back of the wagon to view the magnificent animals.

"Yes ma'am; they're all set."

"Have you named them?"

"Well, they came with names, these bein' thoroughbred Herefords, papers too. Says their names are Emperor and Centennial. Emperor, I call Augustus, shortenin' it to Augie . . ."

She turned and looked at him and laughed.

Tom smiled and continued, "It's a little easier on the tongue." He looked at her still laughing and lightly shaking her head. He said, "The other one, I don't know what I'll call him yet. Centennial is a mouthful, and nothin' has tumbled out of my head yet regardin' a name for him, a manageable one, that is."

They stood and looked at the bulls for a while, the silence eventually becoming uncomfortable. Molly looked from the bulls to the wagon, stepping back and taking in the whole thing from oxen to bulls. "You're all ready to go, then?" she asked him again, still looking over the wagon.

"I am."

"Well, I guess it's good-bye, then," she said, finally looking at him, the tears starting to pool at the bottom of her green eyes.

"I guess it is."

"Good-bye," she said, and she embraced him, her head off to the side.

"Good-bye, Molly," he said, returning her hug.

She reached up and kissed him. Then she stepped away and said, "Here's something else I want you to have." She handed him an envelope. "Now you'd better be on your way. You've seen enough of my tears, and I don't want to make a fool of myself," she said with a sniffle, as she dabbed at her eyes, and then her nose, with a kerchief.

Tom climbed up on the wagon and took the reins.

Molly stepped up to the wagon and looked up at Tom, the green eyes their greenest through the prism of checked tears. In a serious, sensible voice, she said, "Tom, I won't wait. Still, if you are ever back here, would you look me up? I may still be free, and you never know what a little time will do."

Tom looked down, for perhaps the last time, into that face, those eyes, that would long live in the front of his memory, and he said, "I will, Molly."

She smiled slightly with her mouth closed, and nodded. Then she let him go, and Tom Schurtz left Dodge City. Molly Banks was another matter. It would be some time before he would fully leave her and she would fully leave him. She would travel with him, occupying a substantial portion of his thoughts, as he journeyed toward home, and leaving a certain bluntly nagging emptiness inside him. The envelope from her, which he opened at first opportunity, contained a respectful letter expressing succinctly many of the same sentiments she had so far expressed. It also contained a thank-you and a repayment of the money he had given her the summer before.

MID-AUGUST on the Llano Estacado was hot. Tom noted that it was like the heat of Dodge City, in fact, the same kind of heat he had known most of the way back from Dodge City. Except when thunder and lightning storms had added their downpours to temporarily saturate the air, the air remained so dry as to suck up whatever moisture it found into its boundless thirst. It was not the kind of heavy, wet, penetrating heat like down near San Antonio, or even like summers back in Wisconsin. No, it was more like the heat of a dry oven. In fact, one's clothing got about as hot to the touch as they would under the effects of an iron, Tom thought, as he took hold of his sleeve just to verify that thought.

Many of the playa lakes across the northeastern section of the Llano Estacado were dry, he had been correctly informed at the JA, where he had stopped to leave the money for the cowhands whose hides he had brokered. Consequently, Tom had been forced to stay not too far from the escarpment in case he could not find a wet playa and would need to find a spring below the caprock. This had added two days to Tom's trip from the JA to the Seven Ox Seven, though he had been fortunate to find enough water in playas along his way, left from a recent storm, to relieve the thirst of the animals and to render unnecessary the search for a spring.

As Tom had expected, Andy had just recently left on his first drive to Dodge City, so Tom would not be able to give the Stuarts any account of how his first drive had gone. Ah, but what he would bring to the Stuarts: window frames and glass, door frames, hardware, Elizabeth's sewing machine, sewing materials, clothing, boots and shoes, foodstuffs. And how the place might look, how would it have changed? He had been assured of the Stuarts' good health by Charles Goodnight, who had been informed by a surveying party that had passed by the canyon on its way to do some surveying for him. He had said how impressed the surveyors had been with the development of the ranch. Tom imagined it in his mind, as he walked alongside the oxen through the grass of the northeastern Llano Estacado, his mind

as open and broad as the limitless sky that covered the boundless grassland through which he tramped.

Into that broad, open mind came visions of what awaited him. The
Stuart family came to life in his mind, the whole family and each individual member, and the accomplishments of each. How the children
would have grown. Zachariah would have had some time now to adjust
to Andy's going. The family would have had some time now to be alone.
Little Bob would have grown, Tom was sure. And there would be more
calves, and the lambs would have grown and the piglets and the chicks.
There would be the antelope and deer, but not many buffalo; he knew
that. He was near the end of his return trip now and was as eager as he
could ever remember being to bring a trip to an end. He was going
home, to his home, and he was eager to get there.

Hence, he was tramping at a little better pace than he had kept up
most of the trip. He was working the oxen a bit, impatient as he was
to return home. He had camped above the northern of the two smaller
bookend canyons the night before and had known that there was less
than ten miles to go when he had set out that morning. And he had
set out well before first light, as he had not been able to sleep any
longer. Now it was nearly noon, and he could think of nothing better,
as his legs cut through the grass, than to join the Stuarts for dinner. He
was conveying these sentiments to the oxen with a periodic crack of
the whip above their heads, encouraging a quicker pace—which he
justified by thinking how well they and the bulls, hearty as they were,
would recover from the more demanding pace, once they had reached
the canyon and had been turned out into green pastures and spring-
watered draws shaded by towering cottonwoods. They would thank
him for this pace, Tom reasoned, if only they could reason and could
know what awaited them.

Then, there it was, a dark, jagged gash where a draw dropped away
into a canyon carved out over time by occasional floodwater and the
springs that now watered it and flowed out of it, hundreds of feet
below, and combined to form a small creek that flowed into that
greater canyon called Escondido and emptied into that greater creek
called Stuart. Through this gash in the caprock, Tom could see beyond
to the caprock on the far side of the canyon. As he drew nearer, he
could see below the light-colored caprock to the reds and the various

other hues. And then he was at the edge of the canyon itself, and he could see it all.

Below him lay the Escondido, stretching as far to his left as he could see and to his right all the way to a distant head. The grasses were green, being grazed by cattle and antelope and deer. There were sheep out there too, he knew, but they were out of his sight. The buffalo: though he had seen a few small herds on his way, he knew that they were all but gone, had seen it in the hides and bones stacked and awaiting shipment in Dodge City; and in the groups of rotting carcasses and bleached bones that he had seen on his ways to and from; and in the fat wolves, coyotes, and buzzards that had been gorging themselves on the carcasses; and in the blowflies that had bred and fed therein and now swarmed across the plains, high and low, a nuisance and a plague to man and beast alike.

Below, he could see the green of trees and vines crowding the streambeds, of grasses blanketing the pastures, of cedars speckling the canyon sides. He could see the red of the soil showing through.

He returned to the wagon and drove it westward along the canyon's edge. He kept the wagon as far back from the edge as he could so as to travel as directly as possible without needing to skirt the deep draws that opened into the canyon, but as the oxen plodded along, he would periodically leave the wagon to venture nearer the edge to view the canyon below.

In time, from the edge of the canyon, he looked down upon the Stuart home below. There were the stone house, the dugout, the springhouse, the barn, the pens and corrals, and what appeared to be a new chicken coop. There was a very green garden, near the river, watered by irrigation ditches. And there was no one in sight. Tom was late for the noon dinner. A saddled horse and bareback mule, picketed in some grass in the shade of some mesquite not far from the house, assured Tom that Luke was home and the family was at table in the cool dugout. Still, it was not too late to get some leftovers. He turned from the ledge and nearly began to run toward the wagon, when a rattling sound froze him to his spot. Tom looked carefully around and spied a coiled rattlesnake. He stared at it, without moving, until the snake uncoiled and slithered away. With a little more caution after this warning, Tom returned to the wagon, climbed up on the seat, and cracked the whip above the head of the oxen.

•   •   •

WITH THEIR DINNER CONCLUDED, and Robert and Rachel down for their naps, Luke, Elizabeth, and Zachariah emerged from the dugout. Elizabeth had been indoors most of the morning, cooking and baking and working on various projects. She came outside with Luke to see him off to his afternoon of light line riding. It would be light because Zachariah was going along, which he did more frequently since Andy and Tom had left. Zachariah would ride bareback on an old mule, Charlie his dog trotting along beside him. He was quite a good helper, for as much as he could do at his age, and Charlie, with his natural instincts, was making his worth known every day, especially in finding bogged cattle and routing beeves out of deep draws. Besides it being good for the boy to spend the time with his father, and the father with his son, and the boy to learn the value of work, it also provided each with some company, something each of them had lost with Andy's and Tom's departures.

As they sauntered through the heat of the early afternoon sun toward the horse and mule to the east of the house, Luke talked of the area he planned to cover that afternoon. Elizabeth followed with a reminder to be on time for supper, and she was just beginning to remind him of the plum cobbler that she planned to make for after supper, when she stopped in midsentence and then stopped walking. Luke and Zachariah noticed this and stopped and looked at her. Elizabeth first turned her head a little to the right, then a little to the left, a puzzled expression on her face. Then suddenly, she turned around and looked up toward the head of the canyon, and as soon as her eyes landed there, she nearly shouted, "It's Tom!"

Luke and Zachariah both looked toward the head of the canyon to see the wagon pull to a stop near Tom's log house and a figure jump from the seat of the wagon and stride up and enter the house.

"It is Tom!" Luke shouted, and he turned and ran toward his horse. Zachariah ran behind him, yelling, "Daddy, can I come? Daddy, can I come?"

Luke reached his horse, untied him from the stake, and swung into the saddle. He reached down and caught up Zachariah as he approached, sat him in the saddle in front of him, and spurred the horse into a run. Charlie followed in hot pursuit. Zachariah hung onto the horn, his father's right arm wrapped under his arms, around his chest, holding him against him, while Luke's other hand held the reins. The wind blew through the boy's hair and forced him to squint his eyes against it, as the horse continued to pick up speed, galloping along the trail through the mesquite, leaving the determined collie farther and farther in the rear. Zachariah hung on tight and, with his father, fell into the rhythm of the horse's gallop, becoming, with his father, one with the horse, learning the feel and the rhythm of the gallop. As the trail began to incline, the horse's pace slackened a little, though not much, and they were in the yard of Tom's house, alongside the wagon, in little time at all. Luke dismounted and reached up and took Zachariah from the saddle and placed him on the ground. Then, with his son, he approached Tom's house.

Inside the house, Tom had thrown open the shutters on his windows and was going over various features of his home. He was squatting near the fireplace, inspecting the mortar joints he had made just months before, when he heard the horse approaching. He stood up, walked to the door, and stepped out onto the uncovered sleepers of his unfinished porch.

Luke was approaching, with Zachariah right behind him, when Tom emerged from the house. Tom stepped off the porch and met Luke in a handclasp, as Luke enthusiastically inquired, through a broad smile, "How are you, partner?"

Tom smiled too, looking down frequently in the face of the vibrant enthusiasm directed at him. "Pretty good, pretty good," he said as he shook hands with Luke. "And how are you all?" he managed to get in.

"Tolerable," Luke said. "We're all doin' all right."

"How was the trip?" Luke continued, with no less enthusiasm, as he let go of Tom's hand and reached up to rest his hand and forearm against the corner of the house.

"It was a good trip," Tom responded, lightly nodding his head as he looked at the ground. Then, with a mind to directing the enthusiasm away from himself, he nodded toward the wagon and said, "Brought back all kinds of truck."

"So it appears," Luke said, as he turned and made his way toward the wagon, talking over his shoulder as he went. "What all you got here?"

Tom followed, saying, "Well, let's take a look." Then he put his hand on Zachariah's shoulder, and he said more quietly, "How've you been, Zack?"

"Good, Uncle Tom."

"Good to see you lookin' so well. Grown some, haven't you?"

"Yessir," Zachariah responded, after which he massaged the outside corner of his lip with his tongue. Tom smiled, tousled his hair a little, and turned his attention back to Luke. Zachariah, smiling now, accompanied the men to the wagon.

"You sure got a wagon full," Luke said, walking along the side of the wagon, adding, when he came to its rear, in a way that did not conceal his excitement, "and what about these two ornery-lookin' critters?"

"Well," Tom responded, stepping up beside the bulls, "I just hope they make all kinds of ornery-lookin' calves."

"Herefords?"

"Yessir."

"First ones I've ever seen," Luke said as he looked over the animals.

"Thoroughbreds," Tom said. Luke looked up at him. "They got papers," Tom added.

"They are stout-lookin' animals," Luke said, as he ran his hand over the side of the bull nearest him. The bull grunted and eyed him.

"They're two-year-olds," Tom said.

Luke's face swung back toward Tom, its look of incredulity saying quite enough, though he emphasized what it had to say with words. "Two-year-olds?"

"That's right," Tom said. "They're quick to mature, quick to fatten, quick to make calves, plenty of calves, and they'll do it all on grazin' alone, and they'll rustle that up just about anywhere you put 'em." Tom gazed at the bulls. "That's what they say, anyways. The quick-to-mature and -fatten parts speak for themselves. As far as the rest, my brother John wrote me that they do well on grazin'. He fed 'em in the winter, just because he didn't want to subject 'em to a Wisconsin winter without feed, but that's not to say they couldn't have made it on their own. He just didn't want to take a chance on it. If the rustlin' and calvin' parts are half as true as what we can see, we'll be in pretty good shape."

Luke stared at him, then looked at the bulls again, then rested his right hand on his left shoulder as he took hold of the back of his right biceps with his left hand. He massaged the right biceps as he spoke. "Where does your brother John come into this?" Then, looking back over his shoulder and raising his head as if in a sweep of the wagon behind him, he added, "And how could you buy a wagonload of goods and two thoroughbred Hereford bulls?"

"It's all a long story that I'll take pleasure in tellin', but I'd just as soon tell it once. That, and the fact that I am powerful hungry for Mrs. Stuart's cookin', tells me we ought to get this wagon down the canyon here, and I can tell it all to all of you over whatever you left for me from your dinner."

"Won't be much left of that," Luke said, grinning broadly. Tom looked at him, an involuntary look of disappointment weighting his features.

"But there's plenty more to make, and Elizabeth's fixin' to make a big plum cobbler," Luke assured him. Then he hesitated, and he rubbed his stubbled chin with his right hand and said, "You know, there's somethin' funny about that. Elizabeth said that she was goin' to make plum cobbler today, and when I asked her why—as there was nothin' special, no birthday or nothin'—she just said that she had a feelin' that she should make it today. And when you drove in up here, she knew it, didn't even look or anything, just knew it. I didn't even get a chance to ask her about that. She'll just say it's women's intuition. That's what she always says when she does somethin' like that. She does it now and then, too."

Luke pondered this for a while, as Tom responded with a "huh."

As they pondered, Charlie jogged up and rubbed up alongside Zachariah and stuck his head under the boy's hand. Zachariah looked down and subconsciously scratched the top of the dog's head. Tom noted that Charlie had filled out and that there appeared to be a deeper attachment between boy and dog, even just since he had left.

"Charlie followed you all the way up here, Zack?" Tom asked the boy.

"Yessir," Zachariah responded, "Charlie goes everywhere with me." He bent down and rubbed his small hands into the fur around the dog's neck and back of his head, the dog panting a smile through it all.

"He herd as well as it appeared he would?" Tom asked Luke.

"Huh," Luke answered, "let me tell you, Tom, that dog's a natural. You add the trainin' he got from Andy and Rita, and he may well be one of the best."

"He's a handsome dog, too," Tom added, "with that white collar and the breadth of white on his chest."

"Just like these here Herefords," Luke suggested, "which reminds me: you got a lot to tell. So let's head on down, so's Elizabeth can get a look at 'em, and all these goods. She might even want to take a look at you, too." Luke nudged Tom in the arm and laughed. Tom just shook his head, chuckling.

"This calls for a celebration, anyways; I'm done with line ridin' for today," Luke said.

"Done with line ridin'?" Tom questioned incredulously. "It's hardly past noon. I should have expected just such a lackadaisical attitude to take hold here after I left. Here I am trailin' to Dodge, sellin' and buyin' and freightin' back . . ."

". . . and sparkin'," Luke said, interrupting Tom while fixing an inquisitive grin on him.

Tom turned his own inquisitive grin back on Luke. "What are you talkin' about?" he asked him, thinking of no better response.

"I know what you been up to," Luke said through a knowing smile, as he lightly nodded his head and bent to check the wheel of the wagon. "Gone an extra month with nary a word."

"I sent word I'd be longer," Tom protested. "Didn't you get it?"

"Got it all right," Luke confirmed, straightening up as he wiped his hands on his pants. "Came down the line through the riders of the JA. Letter said you'd be held up, but didn't say why."

"No, it didn't," Tom said, holding back his smile, as much as he could, as he defiantly looked Luke in the eye.

"Come on, partner," Luke said, lightly shoving Tom's shoulder as he passed him on the way to his horse, "you think I don't recollect about how Molly was waitin' on the porch of that roomin' house that night, or about that girl at the roomin' house who worked in the dinin' room?" Luke stopped at his horse and took hold of the reins. "Or who knows what other female you might've been sparkin'."

"Zack," Luke said, and Zachariah came over, and Luke lifted him into the saddle and swung in behind him. "And don't think that Elizabeth doesn't know either, and she'll ask you, and you know how good she is at gettin' it out of you."

"Wouldn't you just figure," Tom said, unwilling to surrender yet. "Here I am trailin', and sellin', and buyin', and freightin, and you back here lollygaggin', and you come up with this lame attempt to get off the subject of your lollygaggin'. And now you're goin' to have a celebration, all just because of my return. You think I don't know that it's been one big holiday here ever since I left? You think I don't know better? You're goin' to try to convince me that this party is just for my return, that you all missed me that much?"

Luke sat atop the mount, holding the reins as the horse shifted around beneath him. "No sir," he said, nodding toward the bulls, "party's for your friends there."

Tom glanced at the bulls and then hung his head and shook it, chuckling through his smile. Still not willing to accept complete defeat, he said, as he climbed up on the seat of the wagon and took up the reins, "Christmas every day . . ."

"What's that?" Luke questioned, with a smile.

"Christmas every day," Tom repeated. "That's what it's been here, and you can't make me believe otherwise."

"Well, I suppose you could look at it that way," Luke responded, "it being so much colder here than in Dodge City, with all the sparkin' goin' on there and all."

Tom was defeated. He just hung his head and shook it as he chuckled.

Luke laughed too, silently, through a broad smile. He held the smile a while in sporting hope, giving Tom a chance to come back at him. When no response came from Tom, having already secured Tom's concession of laughter, he continued.

"Hey," he called over to Tom, "Elizabeth'll consider it a holiday too, what with the return of the prodigal son and all. She'll want to slaughter the fatted calf. Besides, tomorrow's Sunday, and we can make a real day of it with a picnic and everything." He paused for a moment and shooed flies away from his face. "Well, maybe with these flies bein' what they are, we can hold off on the picnic. Anyways, after you eat today and we get some word out of you concernin' the gal you left behind—and anything else important, like these two you brought back with you—we can spend the rest of the day unloadin' and sortin' through all you got in that wagon."

"All right," Tom said, still grinning, "let's get started." At that, he cracked the whip over the head of the oxen, and they grudgingly started from where they stood, and the wagon jarred forward.

Luke and Zachariah fell in beside the wagon as it bumped along down the trail.

"How are Elizabeth, Rachel, and Little Bob?" Tom asked.

"They're all real well, Tom. Young'uns growin' like you wouldn't believe."

"How's the herd farin'?"

"Doin' well enough," Luke said. "Still droppin' calves. These blowflies and screwflies've been a real problem. I been doctorin' for screwworms all summer. All those buffalo carcasses rottin' out there on the prairies just breedin' these blowflies. Been all over all summer. Gets so you don't even want to be outside on a calm day. Good thing we branded early, or the sacks on those calves would've really been bad. As it was, I had enough problem with slow healers."

"You doctor with coal oil?"

"Yessir, used coal oil to kill the worms, then would dig 'em out with a stick and then cover the wound with mud. I tried sap from some of the trees and brush, but those just seemed to draw more flies. You pick up any tar in Dodge?"

"Yessir," Tom affirmed with a glance at Luke.

"That'll help," Luke said. "Most of the beeves have done all right, with doctorin', but we've had some loss, and some loss in the sheep, as well."

Tom looked over at Luke, who explained, "Got in under their wool, and I was so busy with the cattle that I didn't see it till it was too late."

Tom shook his head and looked back out over the oxen.

"Had a little pinkeye among the beeves, as well, but pretty much nipped that in the bud," Luke continued, with Tom nodding approval.

"Loafers done their share, too," Luke said of the Lobo wolves. "Shot a number of 'em this summer, but they're thick. Shot some of those pesky coyotes, too. And been shootin' polecats, as Elizabeth would just as soon we get 'em cleared out from around the house. She was just plain gettin' tired of the smell, with the summer heat and all, and she was concerned about hydrophobia with the young'uns. Besides, they're just a plain nuisance. Goin' after the chickens' eggs and all. By the way, I built a chicken coop, a rough affair, but one that'll keep out polecats and coyotes and coons pretty well, covered most of it with chicken wire. Anyways, I'll set out of an evenin' and just pick off polecats as they show up. Had 'em lyin' thick all around the yard. Skinned some. The rest I just dragged away later, or critters carried 'em off.

"Sighted a couple panthers, too, but couldn't get a shot at 'em. They are elusive ones, though. You know they're around with their screamin' at night, but you rarely see 'em, just the work they do, now and then, on the stock. Shot a bear, too."

Tom looked over at Luke and nodded.

"But the herd is increasin' and farin' well all around. It takes more than one loafer to take down a calf of one of these Texas cows. They're nearly as wild as the loafer, and growin' more so every day in this canyon, and they don't take kindly to any loafer tryin' to take off with one of their calves.

"Still, you've got to hand it to those loafers. I saw one runnin'," he looked at Tom and emphasized the point, "runnin', with half a calf in his mouth, up a slope no less. Didn't even bother to fire at him. Just watched him go. Admired him really. Seems a shame sometimes that we have to shoot 'em." Luke looked out over the canyon before him. "But it's either them or us, I guess."

Tom looked out over the canyon, as well, and nodded thoughtfully.

Then Luke turned suddenly back to Tom with a new burst of enthusiasm. "Tom, the bounty of this canyon has been spillin' over all summer. We've been dinin' on bear, turkey, quail, antelope, and deer most of the summer, with wild plums already harvested, and wild grapes offerin' plenty of promise. Elizabeth's garden is producin' all kinds of greens from the seeds she's been collectin' since we were on Herman's place. You ought to see the melons she's growin'.

"And we've had visitors, too. Some Indians called. Comanche and Kiowa, sounded like." Tom looked over at him, his expression betraying his concern. Luke continued, "I was out ridin' line. They came up on Elizabeth, while she was in the yard with the kids and the house and dugout wide open. Elizabeth kept real calm. Gave 'em some fresh bread and milk. They ate and drank and looked the place over and left. Elizabeth said she was scared right through, but she knew she had to not let it show. Sends a shiver right through me to think how that might have turned out on another day or with different Indians. I think of all I've heard about what the Comanche have done to their enemies, even white women and children. But they didn't even touch 'em. There were three of 'em. Elizabeth said the Scripture verse came to her mind about bein' kind to visitors and entertainin' angels unawares. That's what gave her strength and courage and calm."

"That's from prayer," Tom said, as he looked back out over the oxen and considered, himself, how such an encounter might have turned out. He could feel the color drain from his face as a cold wave dropped down his spine.

Luke saw Tom blanch, and he knew what was going through his mind. He was quiet for a while, before he resumed the conversation and filled Tom in on other visitors: some surveyors, including those from Matthew Colmey, and cowboys, few as they were. Zachariah, too, joined the conversation, invited into it by Tom and Luke.

In time they arrived in the Stuart yard, and Elizabeth was there to meet them. She did her best to keep the respectful distance that she and Tom had always maintained, but even in that she could not hide her delight at having him back home. They all talked for a short while in the yard before they started toward the dugout. Then Tom thought again and returned to the wagon to untether the Hereford bulls, who immediately ambled in different directions to graze on the nearest grass available. Luke and Elizabeth and Zachariah returned as well, and Luke took the bridle and saddle off his horse, and let the horse and mule go free to graze. Then he helped Tom finish releasing the oxen from their harnesses, and they watched them seek out green pastures.

Then they went inside the dugout, where Elizabeth served Tom dinner, and all crowded around for the news Tom had to share. Tom told about the Herefords and his time in Dodge, and after the children were dismissed, he told about Molly, too, told much more than he had wanted or intended to tell, but Elizabeth had her quiet, easy way of getting a person to tell more than he wanted to tell, especially if she wanted to know it.

He learned that the Stuarts had purchased and located, in the name of the partnership, five more sections of land: two more sections out onto the rolling plains beyond the mouth of the canyon; one section up on the cap beyond the head of the canyon to the southwest; and two more sections up on the cap, each on opposite sides of the canyon, the next checkerboard squares northeast and southwest of the secion on which their houses sat. They had managed to purchase certificates with locating and registering and delivery of patents, all for twenty-five cents an acre from Hill and Colmey. Now the partnership owned not only the entire canyon, but a comfortable and expanding buffer of land all the way around it. Therefore, especially now that Tom was there to help with the line riding, they could move some of the herd up onto the grass above the canyon, while others drifted out into the grass of the low rolling plains, before the winter months required that all of them be driven back into the canyon.

After a satisfying meal and the beginnings of their celebration, they unloaded the wagon, which was a major part of the celebration for these pioneer ranchers, as item after item, fruits of their hopes and labors, came off the wagon to eventually be put to use to enhance their lives. Their celebration continued with a late supper, which was topped off with the plum cobbler, one of Elizabeth's best.

Their religious observances of the next day, Sunday, took on special significance in light of their reunion and the great gifts they were enjoying from the Lord's bounty. They did start a picnic, as the wind was keeping the blowflies down somewhat, but soon found themselves heading for the dugout to escape the flies, which, even with the wind, nearly covered their food before they could get it into their mouths.

The darkness of the dugout had been alleviated somewhat by old newspaper that had been soaked in hot bear grease and then stretched over the windows, where it had become rigid. This allowed in some light, while keeping out the flies. Still, it made for a dark dwelling amidst the full open sunlight of the incomparable skies of the Texas Panhandle. That was a situation Luke and Tom would remedy that week.

Before that, though, the herd needed tending. On the Monday following, Tom and Luke did not split up, but rode line together, so that Luke could acquaint Tom with the present circumstances of the herd, and so that they could just catch up with each other on news.

Zachariah, on a mule or mare, with Charlie beside him, rode with them sometimes in the days that followed. They worked hard for the next several of those days, Tom getting a good idea of the kind of summer Luke had had. They doctored for screwworms—that putrid, nauseating job that left one with little appetite—and they rescued several beeves that, in their attempts to seek relief from the innumerable flies, had bogged in the wet sand and mud surrounding watering holes that had shrunk in the intense heat of the West Texas summer. One older cow, so well stuck in the mud that she required a good deal of pulling to free her, came through the ordeal very shaky in the legs, and by the next day she was dead.

They could not help themselves from keeping an eye on the Hereford bulls, checking on their whereabouts and doings almost daily, at least at first, with an almost childlike enthusiasm for all that these two bulls represented. Among other things, they represented the raising of their ranch to a new level. No longer were they just herding semiwild Texas cattle; they were starting on the improvement of their herd, on the beginning of a graded herd. These bulls also represented the Seven Ox Seven's participation in the progress of the range-cattle industry into something beyond just herding and letting nature do its work. Here was active husbandry, stewardship of nature toward the end of having it better serve the needs of humanity.

For now they would let these two fine specimens of the results of husbandry be directed by nature, but the introduction of these two bulls had set the stage for a more directed development of their ranch. When they would be ready, they hoped by next season, they would take more control in the breeding of these bulls with selected cows. They also looked forward to bringing in more bulls, possibly some shorthorn, and to consulting Charles Goodnight on his breeding practices. And they were considering that they might eventually bring in Hereford cows and heifers to breed, simultaneously, a purebred herd.

Goodnight had conveyed his plan to them. He kept his blooded shorthorns in the upper canyon, turning out any inferior animals into his main herd in the lower canyon. Inferior cows among this common herd, he spayed and let fatten to be sold for beef. In time he would selectively breed shorthorn bulls with the common stock to grade the JA herd. Not even Goodnight himself knew, at this time, that he would eventually turn to purebred Herefords to top the graded herd. Nor did he know to what extent barbed wire would facilitate his breeding practices, though he had some idea, as he had already used barbed wire on a limited basis.

Tom and Luke would learn more about how barbed wire would allow them more control over breeding and exclusive service of their own bulls, not yet much of a concern for them, as no other herd had been established close enough to cause problems in that regard. In contrast, in areas where one range ran right up against another, a cattleman could never be sure to what degree his bulls were servicing a neighbor's cows rather than his own. With barbed wire, a cattleman could assure exclusive use of his own bulls as he selectively improved his herd. Tom had purchased a limited amount of barbed wire (despite its expense) with which he and Luke could experiment in segregating, as time allowed, for breeding, weaning, or whatever purposes they determined.

At the end of the week, after a good survey of the canyon and the herd, they resumed work on the Stuart rock house. From the milled lumber that Tom had brought back from Dodge City, they selected stout two-by-twelve oak boards. They cut these to fit the dimensions of the window openings and drilled holes in them to match the bolts that they had set into the mortar. Once fitted and drilled, they set the boards back about four inches from the outside edge of the window opening and bolted them onto the bolts they had set into the foot-and-a-half-thick, double-layered stone walls. They countersunk the nuts, so that they could cut off the bolts flush with the face of the boards. They also built solid shutters from the milled boards and fastened them with steel straps and hung them on hinges set into the mortar, so that the shutters fit nicely into the window openings, flush up against the window frame on one side, and flush with the inside wall of the house on the other. This way the shutters, when open, could rest flat against the inside wall of the house, out of the way. When closed, they would provide a solid defense against any party that posed a threat. They also fitted shutters to the outside of the window openings, to help protect even the windows, if necessary. Accordingly, if a threat posed itself, they could shut up the house from the outside and from the inside for a double layer of protection, but if time did not allow, they could do so from the inside alone.

They continued their work at the beginning of the next week, fitting and hanging a heavy oak door that Tom had brought from Dodge. Then they set the windows into the frames and meticulously trimmed around those windows with wood bought for that purpose. Luke had already finished the chimney before Tom had left. Hence, finally, the Stuart home of solid stone walls, floors, hearth, and chimney, with a hardwood second floor, a shingled roof, glass windows, and a sturdy door and shutters, stood complete, including the front porch, which Luke had finished during the summer.

Elizabeth then moved in to clean. She swept and washed, including the windows, using ammonia in the water to make them as clear as the West Texas air. As Elizabeth cleaned, Tom and Luke framed and set windows in Tom's house and replaced the door Tom had made with a solid oak door like the one now on the Stuarts' house. Tom would still need to finish his porch, and he planned to add a lean-to to the back, where he could make use of the door he had just replaced.

At the end of that week, after line riding and moving some of the cattle up onto the high plains beyond the head of the canyon, which they now owned, they moved the Stuart belongings into the new stone house, leaving the dugout, after a new coating of mortar, to be converted to a workshop and storage.

THUS, ON A SATURDAY EVENING in the beginning of September 1878, about three weeks after Tom had returned from Dodge City, with the children already asleep in bed, Luke, Elizabeth, and Tom sat around the table in the Stuart rock house at the end of another week of gratifying hard work and accomplishment. They sat at a comfortable distance from the still-warm hearth, in a warm breeze that blew across the room through the opened windows, and talked of their lives together since the Stuarts had first broached to Tom the idea of a ranch in the Texas Panhandle. They talked of how God had blessed them in the land they had acquired: in the improvements they had made and in the increase in their numbers of cattle and of sheep, pigs, and horses, too. This led the conversation to news of another increase to which Tom had not been privy.

As they sat at the table, visiting, a lull drifted into their conversation during which Luke glanced at Elizabeth, who smiled lightly and nodded, her pretty face golden in the light of the kerosene lamp.

"Tom," Luke began, "we've got some news to share with you."

Tom looked up and raised his eyebrows.

"Elizabeth's expectin'," Luke said, as he glanced again at Elizabeth.

"Is that right?" Tom responded enthusiastically, sitting up straight. "Well, that is good news. Congratulations, folks," he said as he reached out and shook Luke's hand.

"Figure the baby to be comin' early next spring," Luke continued. "We didn't want to be sayin' anything, as we've lost one in the past, until things looked pretty good. Didn't want the young'uns to get their hopes up until it all looked pretty good."

"You know, I believe I've known it," Tom said. "Not known it, well, I guess you'd say, in the front of my mind, but kind of knew it somewhere in the back of my mind. There's been somethin' different about you, Elizabeth, since I been back. Somethin' . . . , well, fuller, I guess. It's in your face, and in your whole person."

"That's right, Tom," Luke agreed, "there is somethin' fuller."

Elizabeth looked down at her belly and said, "You don't suggest I'm showing already, Luke?"

"No, no, Elizabeth," Luke assured her, but then added, "well, maybe a little, but it's like Tom said, there's just somethin' fuller. I've been seein' it develop, from even before you told me. I guess I knew before that, too, just somethin' different, but it's been so gradual, that I lost track of the change." Luke looked at her and she at him, their reciprocated looks penetrating to a greater depth than usual in the day to day. "It is somethin' fuller, . . . a fuller beauty, I guess." With this said to the fuller face, already bathed in the golden red glow from the lamp, and now even fuller in a smile of eyes and cheeks and lips still closed, Tom knew that it was time for him to be leaving.

He made his farewells to the preoccupied couple, and Luke walked him to the door, making short arrangements for worship on the morrow, and they parted. Tom saddled and mounted Ross and let the horse walk him home through the low light of a partial, though unobscured moon, amidst the sounds of the night, those of owl and coyote and wolf.

As the horse sauntered along, so did Tom's thoughts. They sauntered across the time since he had met Luke and, later, Elizabeth and the children and Andy, and learned of the Stuarts' plan, and joined it;

across the preparations, and the drive to the canyon; across their beginnings, and Andy's leaving, and the trip to Dodge, and the dealings with Molly, and his return, and the promise of their canyon, from beginning to present. Now, houses were nearly complete, gardens planted, stock increasing and grading. And now, on top of it, the Stuart family was expanding. Things were looking good. It was true that the time spent with Molly had not brought the beginning of his own family, but now he knew that, and he was free to look elsewhere, and a person never knew what life might bring. There was still Miss Nancy Hawkins from Kentucky. Kentucky was a long way off, but one never knew what providence might do with distance. For that matter, he thought, as he remembered pleasant times with Molly, providence might even bring Molly and him back together, though he doubted it. He wondered, as his mind drifted to the scene of Luke and Elizabeth that he had just left, if he had been crazy to leave Molly and to choose to return to the canyon alone.

Whatever the case, even though alone, life looked good, its potential just lying there before him. And Tom expressed his gratefulness for that soon after he arrived at his home that night. After reading from Sacred Scripture by the light of his kerosene lamp as he knelt by his bed, he extinguished the lamp and began his prayer in thanksgiving, allowing his prayer to drift in thought across the fullness of his experiences of the last year or so. In that thanksgiving was praise for the One who had made it all possible and had made it so full. There was in that praise recognition of his poor capacity to praise the infinite God, and Tom wondered, "Is it in recognition of my poor capacity for praise, of my limitations before You, that I praise You most?" Whether so or not, that recognition prompted examination and then contrition for sins. Then there was petition, petition for blessings, first upon Elizabeth and the new child in her womb, and then for all the Stuarts, and for all of Tom's family, for Molly and hers, for Andy and his, and for countless others. Eventually he wrapped it up in a general petition for all those he had ever met or known and for those most in need.

Then, in that prayer, came an integral moment in Tom's continuing conversion. As a boy, Tom had concentrated his prayer on communication with God the Father, developing, in cooperation with grace, a degree of intimacy with the First Person of the Most Holy Trinity. As a young man, especially after his Confirmation and through the ancient novena to the Holy Spirit, Tom had cooperated with grace in the furthering development of his relationship with the Most Holy Trinity through the development of his relationship with the Third Person, the Holy Spirit. Now, as he knelt within his home, within the canyon God had obviously provided for them, in the world that seemed to be working just right from Tom's perspective, Tom prayed, as a man, to be made more fully aware of Christ. He prayed that Christ, Jesus, the very Son of God made man, the Second Person of the Most Holy Trinity incarnate, be made more real in his life. In that, Tom prayed the necessary prayer for any man seeking real manhood, accessible exclusively through the only real man since Adam compromised the nature of manhood, Jesus Christ.

In that prayer, Tom committed himself to a new level of communion with God, with whom, through the grace of God, he had communed, to some degree, all of his life. He had so communed never more fully than in his participation in the sacred sacraments of the Church, especially the central sacrament, the Eucharist. The sacraments had been instituted by Christ himself as means of grace, true gifts of himself, and Tom had been missing them ever so dearly since he had returned from Dodge, where he had been regularly able to participate in them. And yet, even his communion with God within those sacraments could be deepened further into its limitless potential were Christ to be made more real in Tom's life, were Tom to be made more receptive to that Person truly present in those sacraments, as Tom, in cooperation with the grace of God, committed to deeper participation, fully voluntarily, as a fuller man.

In so doing, Tom committed himself to the necessary and most self-revealing and thus self-threatening and ultimately self-fulfilling segment of the way of one who picks up his cross and follows—in faith, hope, and, most necessarily, in love—the way of the Crucified One, in which one dies to self, so as to live, and learns the sweetness of his yoke and the lightness of his burden. And though Tom could not possibly have foreseen all the consequences of such a prayer and commitment, he did have some sense of the risk they would pose to the self he believed he knew and the life that self now enjoyed, the life for which he had begun his prayer in thanksgiving. But for now, prayers completed, content in the fullness of his present, he retired and he slept.

•   •   •

THE NEXT DAY WAS SUNDAY, which arrived with a stiff breeze that periodically gusted into a wind and then settled back to a breeze sufficient to keep the flies to a minimum, which suited Tom and Zachariah just fine, as, after the morning worship and a light meal, they saddled their respective mounts, climbed aboard them, and, according to previous arrangements, pointed them in the direction of the fishing hole. Zachariah sported a carved pole that he had been whittling with results beyond those to be normally expected of a child his age and advanced beyond those that had graced the pole he had previously given to Andy. These results were achieved with a knife that his father had sharpened a little beyond what his mother would have allowed, wielded by a youth with the developing skills of a craftsman. Tom chose a stick along the way and rigged it out upon their arrival at the spot.

They had agreed that Tom would try a worm and Zachariah a doughball, and they arranged their rigs accordingly and tossed their lines in. It was not long before each had caught a fish and Zachariah, a second. Tom strung each fish through the gills and mouth with a thin line he had brought along for that purpose, and jabbed the stake on the end of the line into the ground, and slid the fish into the water.

As Tom was stringing Zachariah's second fish onto the line, Zachariah scrutinized the fish and said, "Uncle Tom, how do those fish breathe in the water? Why is it that they can live in the water, but if we stay under the water, we'll drownd?"

Tom looked back over his shoulder as he crouched by the edge of the pool. Then he looked back at the work in his hands, finished stringing the fish, and then eased the tethered fish into the water. He rinsed the fish slime off his hands in the water, and drying his hands on his pants and moving himself back into his fishing position, he said, "You know, that's an interestin' question, Zack. A lot of men have been askin' that same question for a long time and tryin' to figure it out.

"Now, if I remember it right, a fellow by the name of Priestley discovered that in the air is this element called *oxygen*. And a fellow by the name of Cavendish discovered that water is made up of this oxygen and another element called *hydrogen*, combined to form what they call a compound. Then there was this other fellow named Lavoisier who pulled a lot of this information together and expanded on it, so much so that he has been called by some, 'the father of modern chemistry.' At least that's how I remember it, though I may be a bit off, as it has been some time since I studied the matter."

He looked at the six-year-old Zachariah, who stared at him.

"Anyways," Tom said, "there's this element oxygen in the air and in the water."

Zachariah continued to stare at him.

"You can't see it. It's invisible," Tom explained.

"Like God?"

"Well, it's different from God, but it is invisible: we cannot see it, in a way like how we cannot see God. But it's not like God, because God is spiritual and oxygen is material (gaseous though it may be), and God made oxygen, and nobody made God." Tom looked at Zachariah, who was looking at him.

"But let's leave God's invisibility out of this for now; we can talk about that another time. Now, this oxygen is in the air, but we can't see it. It's what they call a gas."

"What's a gas?"

"Well, do you know how when your mama boils water, steam rises out of the water?"

"Yessir."

"Well, that steam is a gas. It is water as a gas."

"But I can see it."

"Well, yes you can, at first," Tom conceded, "but as the steam spreads out more, you cannot see it anymore. Anyways, in a way, oxygen is like that steam, except that it is an element and not a compound like steam, but we won't get into that. What we know is that in the air are different elements that you cannot see. When we breathe, we pull in those elements, and our lungs take oxygen out of the air and put it into our blood, so that we can use it, because we need it, like we need food and water, only we need oxygen even more.

"The fish need oxygen in their bodies, too. So, God has given the fish gills." Tom slipped back down to the water's edge and pulled out their catch. He held up one of the catfish and pointed out his gills. "You see, Zack, the water has oxygen in it, just like the air does. These gills on the fish take oxygen out of the water, like our lungs take it out of the air, and the fish can breathe then."

He put the fish back into the water and moved back into his place and said, "Funny thing is, our lungs can't get oxygen out of the water; so if we stay under water, we'll drown, even though there's oxygen in there. And the fish's gills can't get oxygen out of the air, so they will suffocate if they are taken out of the water."

Zachariah looked back out at the water. Then, after a minute or two, he said, "How did those men find out about oxygen if they could not see it, Uncle Tom?"

"Well, Zack, I don't remember all the particulars, but they observed closely the world around them and did a lot of thinkin' about what they saw, and they did what you call experiments."

"What are experiments?"

"Experiments are . . . , well . . . , they are tests, of a sort, where you set somethin' up to try to find somethin' out."

Tom looked over at Zachariah, who sat looking at him.

"Well," Tom said, "it's like what we did when we first got down here. We wanted to see what the fish were bitin', so you put out a doughball, and I put out a worm, and you caught the first fish, and you've caught more than I have. So what have we learned from that experiment?"

"We learned that the fish are bitin' better on doughballs."

"That's right. Today they are. We don't know about tomorrow. You have to be careful not to take more than an experience or an experiment has to teach you. Like Mr. Mark Twain says, once a cat sits down on a hot stove cover, it will never sit down on a hot stove cover again, but it will never sit on a cold one either."

"Who's Mr. Mark Twain?"

"He's the fellow who wrote the *Adventures of Tom Sawyer* that we've been readin' these nights."

"Oh."

A pause followed this remark from Zachariah, during which he looked back out at the water, as did Tom, though Tom continued to glance at Zachariah now and then. He was unsure about what impact any of what he had been saying had had on his young partner. He was also concerned about whether he had confused the boy and about what kind of questions might arise for the boy's mother from what he might have gleaned from what Tom had said.

"Uncle Tom," Zachariah said after a few minutes, "what experiments did those men do to find oxygen?"

"Well, you know, Zack, I can't rightly remember. But they were very clever, as those were clever men. In fact, I believe it was Lavoisier, if it is the same man, who said somethin' about forgiveness once that has stuck with me over the years. I believe he said, 'Forgiveness is the scent of the violet that clings to the heel that has crushed it.'"

"What's that mean, Uncle Tom?"

"Well, I'll tell you, Zack, I think some day you'll figure it out. We all get our share of chances at that. I've had plenty in the past, and I know there are plenty more to come."

Tom could hardly know the chances that awaited him.

Chapter Six

NEW NEIGHBORS, RUSTLERS, INDIANS, AND A LOSS

I have been driven many times to my knees
by the overwhelming conviction that I had nowhere else to go.
—ABRAHAM LINCOLN

IN THE EARLY AUTUMN OF 1878, NEARLY THREE WEEKS after Tom had learned of Luke and Elizabeth's expected baby, one more set of ears arrived in the canyon to learn the news. On that day of arrival, Zachariah was baiting a quail trap not too far from the house—with the help of Charlie, who understood the need to have his wet nose right in on the baiting to assure the success of the venture— when Charlie's black and white head suddenly jerked up to face in the direction of the western entrance to the canyon. His ears stood straight up and he let out a short bark. Zachariah turned to look at his companion, when the dog, whose entire body was tensed and ready for action, barked again, and his muscles jerked forward in a false start in that direction, though he did not move from where he stood. Then Zachariah heard it, an answering bark from up the canyon, and Charlie's next start was not a false one. Like a shot, the dog was off, tearing across the land toward the head of the canyon. Zachariah turned to look in that direction in time to see, through the mesquite cover, flashes of another black and white creature rushing at about the same speed toward Charlie, and, behind that creature, a rider. Something inside the boy recognized the dog and rider before his vision clearly identified them. Then the rider moved into a break in the mesquite.

"Andy," Zachariah heard himself yell, and he was up and running toward the house at a pace that tried to keep up with the pace of his heart. "Mama, Mama," he was yelling as he neared the house. And his mother hurried from the house to see what was the matter, in time to hear him yell, before he reached the yard, "It's Andy!"

Elizabeth looked toward the boy, who was pointing up the trail, then looked up to see Andy riding down the trail on a large sorrel, as Charlie and Rita raced off, chasing each other toward the north, their barking causing Rita's two puppies to bolt from behind the house in their direction. Zachariah saw the expression on his mother's face turn from one of alarm, at the sound of her son's excited call, to one of wonder upon catching sight of Andy. "Oh!" she exclaimed, "it is Andy." Then she stood there expectantly, until she remembered that something was cooking on the stove and that Robert had been left unattended. She ran back into the house and, in a moment, returned holding little Robert, with Rachel following behind her.

She greeted Andy enthusiastically as he entered the yard, and Andy awkwardly responded and then made his way to the hitching rail, where he dismounted and stood, even more awkwardly, to receive Elizabeth's greeting, which, he was thankful to find, did not contain any of the hugging that had attended his departure. Elizabeth, with the children, did crowd him, though, as if to absorb him and the life he had lived since he had left. After a few minutes of greetings and pleasantries, Elizabeth, still holding Robert and with Rachel around her skirts, led him into the house without allowing for any possibility of noncompliance. Zachariah, who had fallen in beside Andy, was staring up at him all the time and pulling at his own fingers as his mind sought a way to make his presence special in the presence of this special visitor. Finally, as he climbed the porch stairs in step with Andy, he blurted, "Andy, Mama's goin' to have a baby."

Andy looked down at Zachariah with an expression that conveyed sufficient surprise to satisfy Zachariah concerning the importance of his communication; then he looked up toward Elizabeth, who was just crossing the threshold into the house. She turned to look back over her shoulder with a full smile and said, "It's true. The children know."

"Congratulations, Elizabeth," he replied exuberantly, as he followed her into the house. Elizabeth motioned him into a chair and told him more about when the baby was expected, as she poured him some coffee. In the conversation that followed, Elizabeth learned that Andy had returned not to stay, but as a sort of "stray hand" to help with the roundup and to brand and herd back to the JA range any JA cattle that might have strayed that way. Goodnight did not expect him to find many that far south, because the JA had kept steady vigilance along its expanding boundaries, and the cattle were less likely to drift south in the summer than they were in the winter.

Andy drank his coffee fairly quickly, trying to avoid the subtle interrogation that he expected from Elizabeth, a type of interrogation, subtle though it might be, that could usually get one to tell more than he wanted to tell. Finishing his first cup of coffee, he suggested that he believed he ought to ride out and find Luke and Tom, who, he had learned from her, were down in the lower canyon constructing pens for the roundup. In light of the surprise visitor, Zachariah had no difficulty securing from his mother permission to ride with Andy down to where the men were working, despite her not allowing him to accompany the men that morning, as she had kept him around the house to do various chores. Even though he had not finished all the chores, as baiting his quail trap had drawn him away from them, she did not even bother to ask him, so glad was she that he would have an opportunity to ride out with Andy again.

As Zachariah and Andy walked toward the corral to catch the mule or older mare, either of which Zachariah usually rode, Zachariah asked Andy if he would help him saddle his mount. Andy looked down at him and asked, "You have a saddle, Zack?"

"Yessir, Daddy and Mama and Uncle Tom gave it to me as a birthday present. Uncle Tom got it in Dodge City," Zachariah responded, revealing a sense of importance with this fact, his face still set straight ahead toward the picket barn they were approaching.

Once in the barn, Zachariah indicated the small, well-worn saddle that Tom had purchased from the saddle and harness shop in Dodge City. Tom had seen it shoved off in a corner when he had visited the shop to purchase bridles and harnesses. He had asked about it and had learned that it had only recently been acquired in partial payment from a local merchant, whose seven sons had all got their fair share of use out of it. The shop owner had not yet had time to give it any attention. It was not a top-rate saddle, but it was good enough and was the right size. Tom had bargained a price with the shop owner, provided the owner would condition the leather and replace or patch the leather in a few places and tighten it up as much as possible. Thus, the saddle still showed its wear but looked a good deal better than when Tom had first seen it. To Zachariah, it might as well have been made of gold.

Zachariah began to wrestle the saddle off the wooden horse. Andy reached down and picked it up for him, saying, "Let me handle that, Zack. You get the bridle."

Zachariah did as he was told and then walked with Andy toward the corral. He pulled some hay out of a bale near the corral and opened the gate and shortly returned leading the old mare munching the hay in his hand. Andy "helped" Zachariah saddle up, and from the hay bale, Zachariah mounted the horse. Andy soon mounted his own, and they were off down the canyon, the dogs joining them on the way.

When they arrived at the pens—which Luke and Tom were constructing against a cliff, out of cedar posts and the barbed wire that Tom had brought back from Dodge City—Andy was well received with warm regards and jocular sentiments, especially from Luke, along the lines of slaughtering the fatted calf. They broke from the work long enough to honor their reunion with conversation over coffee. Luke stoked some coals under the coffeepot and, when the brew was ready, poured some out into each man's cup. He poured out a cup for Zachariah, too, which was a small amount in the bottom of an extra cup that Luke kept with his own, in case Zachariah was along, to which he added water nearly to the top of the cup. It provided enough to warm the boy's water and convey the diluted essence of the drink, without imposing the adult beverage upon the youngster prematurely.

For Zachariah, it made him one of the men. And these men then crouched around the pot nestled in its coals, or sat on a cedar post or a rock, and did a little catching up on what had occurred since last they had spoken.

Among the news was that of the expected baby, which Andy indicated he had already learned, and Zachariah indicated that it was from him that Andy had learned it. Among Andy's news was that he had been hired as a line rider for the JA, so he had continued to stay on there after the drive. Charles Goodnight was expanding the ranch so fast, both in land and cattle, that Andy had no trouble being hired on year-round. For that reason he had returned to the Seven Ox Seven as a stray hand only. Luke, Tom, and Andy accepted Andy's presence for what it was, a gift from Charles Goodnight—justifiable though it may have been, given cattle's general propensity to drift—to help them out with their roundup and to allow Andy and the Stuarts and Tom to get reacquainted after their separation.

Andy told them about how he shared a dugout with another line rider, a clever, loquacious Irishman named Hughes, who was full of good stories and read whatever he could get his hands on, making his conversation not only entertaining but informative. Each morning, the two men would ride their separate lines out from the dugout in opposite directions, looking for signs of straying cattle that might have crossed the line of the range and for bogged cattle and for any in need of doctoring. They would also shoot predators, mainly lobo wolves, wildcats, eagles, coyotes, and panthers.

Andy had admitted to himself that he did not shoot as many of these animals as he could have (and perhaps should have, given his job), but he often felt an admiration for them and appreciated that they were merely doing what came natural to them. Still, the need to kill predators to protect the stock was not something about which he was squeamish. He had learned the practice well enough while tending sheep as a boy, when the sustenance of the family had depended upon it. He had killed predators then; he would kill them now. But there were times when he did not think the killing justified, when his spirit would not permit it, so he would allow the predator to go. And he never killed a bear. Jack Hughes had learned early on that bear meat, despite its plenty and its appealing taste, would be eaten in their dugout by him alone, and that it alone, of all the meats their hunting provided, would be left uneaten by his partner.

Running along the southern wall of Palo Duro Canyon, their line was fairly easily maintained, as the canyon walls did most of the work to contain the beeves, but should any beeves escape the canyon by way of game trails and emerge out onto the plains above, they could drift to the southwest for hundreds of miles. Stopping or just catching up with and following such a drifting herd would be the greatest challenge of Andy's line riding that coming winter.

Andy also informed Luke and Tom of some new neighbors. Brothers by the name of Baker had settled a herd into the Quitaque country between the Seven Ox Seven and the JA. Goodnight's brother-in-law, Leigh Dyer, had moved the herd in for them and then had left to set up his own operation to the west of Goodnight's where the Tierra Blanca Creek emptied into the Palo Duro Creek.

Tom and Luke listened with interest as they pondered that they had early carved out a ranch for themselves in a country to which others were moving to create ranches. They also congratulated Andy on his good fortune and his successes, and began the process of learning about the drive to, and his time in, Dodge City, a process that would continue at its own pace during the next several days of work and rest. In time they returned to the construction of the pens, the work proceeding at an ever better rate with the help of the man and the boy, so that, though they had expected to finally finish the pens that day, they finished earlier than they had expected, and they returned to the Stuart rock house.

Of course, the day of Andy's arrival called for a celebration, and so, supper that night included plum cobbler and grape and currant preserves. It also included talk. Elizabeth questioned Andy about all that had occurred in his life since he had left, in her own way of getting a person, even one as quiet as Andy, to tell more than he intended or sometimes wished to tell. It was not that Andy had anything to hide, but, like many, Andy liked keeping some of his life to himself. Luke and Tom came to his assistance by asking specific, less-personal questions about the trail and his time in Dodge City. The days that would follow would allow them other opportunities to ask more about both trail and Dodge.

The first of those days that would follow, the very next day, and the days that followed it, saw the roundup, branding, and doctoring of the beeves in the upper canyon. Since they had last had a roundup less than six months before, at which time their herd numbered four hundred head, they did not expect to brand many calves. Still, by midafternoon of the final day of this process in the upper canyon, nineteen calves stood branded, earmarked, and the males castrated, but for a couple singular specimens that would grow to be bulls. And some cows and heifers showed signs that more calves would drop in the next few months.

The most recent additions to the herd in the upper canyon, those bawling calves (especially those recently emasculated), stood in need of respite from the trials and tribulations of the domesticated bovine life, as did their bawling mothers still separated from them. Hence, after opening the pens that separated calves from mothers and allowing them to mix about in the pasture adjacent to the pens, so that bawling calves and cows could reunite by call and scent, the men slowly began to drift the herd up the trail toward the plentiful grass of the high plains.

The reunification process continued on this slow drive, as did the bawling: bawling from calves and cows seeking each other, and bawling to express the trauma and pain of the calves and the indignation of the cows. Tom watched some of the castrated calves drift along, and he could not help but feel sorry for them. They drifted along, bleeding from their fresh life-changing wounds and from their ears, their heads hanging, a glazed, worn-out look set in their eyes. These castrated ones, especially some of the smaller ones, did not seem to have quite as much spirit to seek out their cows, though they would bawl now and then as if to Nature itself in brute complaint against the unnatural separation from their mothers and their sex.

In time, cows drifting throughout the ambling herd would discover their lost calves. The mother would nudge up against the calf and check its scent for final assurance, the castrated calf barely noticing now, seeming to concentrate all its effort on moving along with the herd to where and for what purpose it did not know. It moved because the herd moved and because the men on horses and the dogs would not allow it to drift out and stop.

Finally, Luke, at the point, led the herd through the cleft in the caprock up onto the plains. Tom and Andy had been riding drag and flank, while Zachariah and the dogs had been alternating between flank and swing. Now, as the narrowness of the cleft dictated, all but Luke rode drag, following the cattle through the cleft up onto the high plains.

But these men in the rear position had not had all their work before them. Three bulls, one of the Herefords and two Texas bulls, had fallen in behind the herd, one at a time from different places, not long after the herd had left the pens. Tom and Andy had run off the bulls a number of times, and the younger of the Texas bulls had finally dropped off the trail. The other two had not lost interest, but had dropped off to the side of the trail farther along, giving up only for the moment out of annoyance from being run off so many times. And so, each, at his own place, settled in to graze, the Hereford much more intensely, at least for the time being.

Once up on top, the last of the cows and calves were reunited, and the men let them spread out to relax from their recent stress and to graze and get a good start on the healing process. The men would stay out with them the rest of the afternoon, keeping light vigilance over their recuperation and conversing among themselves, a welcome reward for the hard work of the last several days.

As the beeves settled in to grazing, the men noted their preference for the tall, broad-leafed grass growing out of the dry area of a large playa. The men decided to keep the beeves out of the playa and to save that grass for hay, which they could cut and bale after the roundup.

Shooed from the playa, the beeves contented themselves with the short grasses of the high plains, drifting along as they grazed, the men drifting with them as they drifted in and out of the conversation their work allowed.

During one snatch of conversation between Luke and Tom, something drew Luke's attention, and his eyes focused on part of the horizon off to the northwest. Tom noticed the distraction and turned and looked in the direction in which Luke was looking. As Tom did so, Luke nodded toward a large dark object emerging on the edge of the horizon and snaking out from it, and he said, "Look yonder, Tom. That look like a herd to you?"

Without looking back at Luke, Tom replied, "Sure does."

"You reckon that's a Goodnight herd?"

"Don't know why it would be. Andy ought to know if any would be out this way."

"None that I know of," Andy said.

"Looks like we might have company," Tom said.

"Does that," Luke agreed.

The men and boy continued to drift along with the cattle as the autumn sun sank lower in the western sky, glazing with a stunning pink the bottom of a mottled patch of clouds high above and beyond them to the west and a lighter, lower, fluffier patch of clouds to the east. Drifting along, as well, were the two bulls, the Hereford and the Texas, that had followed the cows and calves, and had been run off several times, only to finally emerge from the canyon. The men knew that they were there and left them alone to graze, but they checked any attempts by the bulls to move in among the cows and calves. Now and then, Zachariah, with Charlie's help, would ride back and shoo them back with great authority and enough success that they demanded little attention from the men.

And it was just as well, for the men's attention had been diverted enough by the herd of cattle that continued to move toward them in a long line from the northwestern horizon. By now, they had turned their own herd of cows and calves and had them drifting back in the direction of the canyon so as to have them all back in the canyon before sunset.

Glances to the northwest eventually made them aware of a group of riders heading their way. There were three riders, cast in the orange of the setting sun as if carrying fire, riding directly toward them. As they approached, it was plain to see that the man in the front and middle was an older man—his hair and beard mainly white—with a good-sized, but well-proportioned, solid-looking build. The man on his left-hand side was closer to Luke and Tom in age. He was of about the same size as the older man, but his shoulders were not square like the other's but more sloping and rounded, and his body had a fleshier appearance, in general, with a thick neck on which was perched a round head. The man on the right-hand side of the older man was not nearly the size of the other two, but was a good few inches shorter with a lighter, slighter build.

When the three reached the Seven Ox Seven men, they pulled up to a stop.

"Howdy," Luke and Tom called out to them.

"Lookin' for Cañon Escondido," the older man said, with only a glance at Luke and Tom before he looked back out toward the southeast in a survey of the land in that direction. Closer now, it could be seen that this man was old enough to be Luke's or Tom's father and that there was nothing fat or soft about his broad frame. Tom figured him to be about his own height of six feet. He had probably been a handsome man in his youth, strikingly though ruggedly so, with his dark eyes and brows and well-carved nose, cheeks, and jaw. He might have even been so now, had it not been for a pervasive unpleasantness that seemed to emanate from him, which had not been lost on Tom, Luke, or Andy, even in this the beginning of their acquaintance with him.

"You've found it," Luke said.

The man turned a piercing eye on Luke. Though directed at Luke, the look pierced Tom too, its effect upon him in the present rousing memories of the past. He knew this man. His first sight of him had stirred some vague sense of recognition, but now, in the look the man had turned on Luke, Tom knew him, though he could not place him, displaced as he himself was, in this canyon world, from all but remnants of his past. Instantly and forcefully it struck Tom how much the canyon life in which he was immersed was separated from other times and places of his life. Regardless, the memory had been stirred, and Tom stoked it further, trying to fit the man into various times and places.

"What do you mean I found it?" the man asked Luke.

That voice, too, Tom knew.

"It's right yonder," Luke responded, with a nod toward the canyon.

Paying Luke no further heed, the man, his total attention turned in the direction Luke had indicated, nudged his horse toward the canyon. His two companions fell in behind him. Luke and Tom fell in behind them.

The man let his horse walk through the beeves and beyond them toward the canyon at a slow, almost hesitating, gait. His eyes were focused in the direction of the unseen canyon, and his mouth hung partway open. He appeared to be fully distracted as if in hope, wonder, or fear, or some sort of mix of those emotions and others.

His slow pace brought him gradually up a slight rise. On topping out on that rise, as the orange sun met the horizon behind him and began its descent behind it, the man caught sight of the great gash in the opposite horizon far beyond him, dark now in evening shadow. As he edged closer, the gash in the horizon extended ever so slowly toward him in ever darker depth, stretching toward him as it fell ever farther away in shadowed profundity, until finally it reached him and fell fully away when he arrived at its brink, just as the sun sank out of sight behind him.

"Escondido," he said in nearly a whisper for no other human to hear, as he looked out over the canyon with eyes that sought satiation in the expansive but finite canyon that could never satisfy the hunger set deep in those eyes. "Escondido," he said again, as he slowly nodded his head and looked back and forth across the canyon named.

"This the place, Mr. Edwards?" asked the fleshy man, as he and the smaller man rode up behind their leader and fell in on either side of him at the canyon's edge.

"This is it," said the older man. "This is it."

"Sure is," Luke said, as he and Tom rode up behind the three men, "Cañon Escondido."

"What do you have to do with it?" demanded the older man, as he pulled his horse around to face Luke and Tom, his features less distinct in the fading twilight.

"I own it," Luke shot back, Tom detecting a slight edge in his voice.

"What do you mean you own it?" the older man questioned sharply. "You mean you claim it as range?"

"I mean I own it," Luke replied firmly. "Or we do," he acknowledged with a slight nod in Tom's direction. "All located, surveyed, registered, and paid for."

"What do you mean to own the land?" the man responded, as the twilight retreated further before the approaching night. "This is open-range country, a land for men and cattle, not for nesters," he said, with no attempt to check the contempt in his voice.

And upon hearing the words and the voice and the sentiments expressed, Tom's memory brought to the present another time and place, and he knew who he was, this man who sat before him, between him and his canyon. In the gathering darkness—as a strange sensation ran down his spine, radiating out as it went, finally to settle in his gut—Tom knew this man.

Luke's horse stepped forward, responding to its rider's involuntary nudge, as Luke nearly stuttered out, "We'll show you cattle. We'll show you what kind of men we are, too, if you're anxious to find it out."

The older man dismissed Luke with a contemptuous nasal "huh" and looked off to his left beyond Tom. At the same time, he raised his hand slightly to hold back, with that gesture, the two men with him, who had also turned to face Luke and Tom, just after their leader had, and who had, at Luke's advance, advanced themselves, their hands moving, a little too eagerly for Tom's liking, into closer proximity to the guns on their belts. In the instant Tom noticed this, he realized that his own hand had moved into a like proximity to his own gun, and that tension had pulled his entire body into a tight readiness.

"Cattle," the older man nearly grunted as he surveyed the Seven Ox Seven beeves before him, his eyes adjusting to the deepening darkness. Squinting into that darkness, he said, "What is that? A Hereford? You got one Hereford bull to grade your stock?"

"We don't have just one," Luke responded testily.

"Gradin' stock with that inferior breed," the man continued in the same tone. "They'll never stand up in this country. This country's for Texas cattle. You let your Herefords see one winter, and let 'em have a taste of Texas fever, and we'll see about your cattle."

"We'll see about our cattle," Luke retorted. "They're no business of your'n. And as for Texas fever, those your cattle north of here?"

"They are," the man responded as he turned back to face Luke.

"You better've wintered 'em before bringin' 'em into this country," Luke continued.

The man was not dismissing Luke now. "They've been wintered," he responded with a good deal of the edge off his voice. Texas fever was just the topic to take the edge off a cowman's voice. It was a serious matter that could cause the decimation of an entire herd. Ranchers could be driven to shoot to kill men who might introduce Texas cattle to an area if they had not first been wintered. Luke's sternly delivered question had clearly put on the defensive this man who obviously prided himself on being a seasoned cattleman. "Comin' off high range in Colorado and New Mexico" he added, as if to validate his cowman's credential.

"They better've," Luke responded. "Where you takin' those cattle?"

"To Cañon Escondido. Been makin' the arrangements to start a ranch here for nearly a year."

"Well, you're about a year too late," Luke responded.

"You've been nestin' here for a year?" the man retorted.

"We've been ranchin' here a year," Luke corrected.

"And you claim the whole canyon?"

"I told you we own it."

"How many beeves you runnin'? How many men you . . ."

"Enough." Tom spoke up before Luke could reply.

The man eyed Tom. "Who are you?" he finally asked him.

"His partner." Tom nodded toward Luke.

The man turned a contemptuous sneer on Luke. "And who are you?"

"Stuart, Luke Stuart, and this is Tom Schurtz." He gestured toward Tom. Tom noticed no indication of recognition on the part of the man, and why should there have been? It had been over a year before and had been brief enough, and the man had been drunk.

"And who are you?" Luke asked him.

"I'll tell you who I am when I'm good and ready, boy, but just so's you know who you're dealin' with, name's Edwards, Henry Edwards, and I've been runnin' cattle since before you were even born. I've got fifteen hundred head trailin' this way, with more to come. Got six more men and a wagon, too. Been plannin' and preparin' for near a year, and trailin' for near a month, and you little greenhorn nesters goin' to tell me you claim this whole canyon?"

"I told you we own it," Luke answered.

"There's another canyon a day's drive south of here," Tom interjected before Luke could push his point. "There's no claim on it yet, as far as we know."

Edwards turned his eyes on Tom and scrutinized him, apparently forming no higher regard for him than he had for Luke. "I know about the canyons north and south of the Escondido," he told Tom. "I know that they're smaller, shallower, without near as good water."

"Then you also know that the Escondido was not a sure thing," Tom replied. "You know that it was the stuff of legends, that the two canyons north and south of it and the canyon itself might all have been one small canyon, confused together in various accounts, that even if it did exist, it might only be the size of the smaller canyons. You came here just like we did, takin' a chance on a legend. You gambled: you came here hopin' for the best but prepared for the worst. You were goin' to ranch in this country even if you didn't find the Escondido, otherwise you wouldn't have brought this whole outfit out here without first scoutin' ahead.

"Well, the Escondido is here, but it's taken. There's still plenty of open country to the north and south of here, the south probably likely to be open longer. There are canyons available, though smaller than you had hoped for, but, if you take the larger one to the south, probably better than the worst you were prepared for. Between that canyon and the breaks beyond it, you've got some good protection from northers as well as good grass and water. It's a far sight better'n a lot of other land used for raisin' beeves."

By now Tom's eyes had adjusted to the gathering darkness, lighted only by the fading twilight, as there was no moon. He watched in that darkness the face of Henry Edwards, who now scrutinized him.

"What we got, a philosopher here?" Edwards said. He was smiling at Tom in his scrutiny. It was not a pleasant smile, but more like the smile of a fox, a smile not far removed from a sneer. Finally, he offered a "huh" as a kind of mirthless, contemptuous laugh.

"Philosopher's right, boys," he said over his shoulder to the men with him. "They settled here first. It's their land by rights. We'll move on down to the next canyon and throw these beeves on a range down there." As he said all this, his tone changed dramatically, so that by the time he had finished saying what he had said, his tone better matched the more cultured tone that Tom had used in laying out the matters as they stood. Tom observed that, though Edwards' tone had changed drastically from the one they had heard from him thus far, this new tone was one with which Edwards appeared to be very familiar and very comfortable. The two men with him said nothing to this change in plan, not, Tom got the impression, because they had nothing to say, but more out of deference to their leader.

"Besides," Edwards continued, "we're all going to be neighbors, and it's just as well we all got off on the right foot. We'd hate to be accused of being unneighborly.

"Mr. Stuart," Edwards addressed himself to Luke, "I'm afraid the weeks on the trail, combined with the disappointment of finding this canyon occupied, left me in a bad humor, and I behaved badly. I would appreciate it if you and Mr. . . . uh . . . ," he hesitated and looked over at Tom for some help.

"Schurtz," Tom said.

"Schurtz," Edwards repeated, "you and Mr. Schurtz, here, would accept my apologies and see if we can't forget this unpleasantness and start out on a more congenial footing. I'm Henry Edwards," he said, nudging his horse forward and offering his hand.

"Luke Stuart," Luke said as he accepted the hand and shook it.

"Mr. Schurtz," Edwards said, encroaching on Tom and offering his hand.

"Mr. Edwards," Tom said as he accepted the handshake. Shaking the man's hand and looking into his face as he did so did nothing to reassure Tom against misgivings that gnawed at him.

Edwards turned his horse sideways and indicated with an outstretched hand the two men accompanying him. "This," he said, nodding toward the large, fleshy man, "is John Brown, my foreman." The man nodded his round head—with its round, ruddy face, thinly bewhiskered with a scraggly beard as old as his weeks on the trail—then turned aside and spat a stream of tobacco, as he had done periodically since their arrival, then turned his small dark eyes back on them. Though fleshy, he did not appear soft, but rather fleshy in the way of a bear.

"And this young man of promise," Edwards said, "is Robert Speck."

Perhaps due to Robert Speck's slight build, he appeared to be young, not any older than Andy, and the trail beard that covered his lean, pale, pointed face was scraggly and light. Speck nodded, and he too spat tobacco—in an embarrassingly obvious attempt to emulate his foreman, but with nowhere near the foreman's proficiency—leaving a trail of tobacco juice on his chin, which he quickly wiped off. He eyed Luke and Tom, while in the process of speedily cleaning his face, as if to make sure they found nothing to ridicule in his inadequate expectoration, and with an expression that seemed to suggest that he considered them to blame for it.

Luke and Tom nodded nonetheless, and the young man answered in kind.

"Well," said Edwards, nodding in the direction of the Seven Ox Seven cows, calves, and bulls, which by now were filing through the cleft into the canyon under the direction of Andy, Zachariah, and the dogs, "looks as though you've got your beeves to attend to, and we've got to get back and bed our own; so, we won't trouble you further. I do appreciate your recommendation of the southern canyon. Until we meet again." With this, he nodded, and as Luke and Tom answered with nods, he nudged his mount forward into a walk, his men following, with all three shortly accelerating to a canter.

"What was that all about?" Luke asked Tom, as they watched, as well as they could, the men ride away into the darkness.

"That's a good question," Tom replied, looking out into the darkness in the direction of their departure. After a pause he added, "But whatever it was about, things just changed around here."

"Yeah," Luke said, as much to himself as to anyone else, and he turned and stared at Tom, who was still looking after the departing men, both Luke and Tom pondering in their own minds just what that change portended.

THAT NIGHT, ANDY NOTICED that Tom got up out of his bed several times and listened at the window at the northern end of the house or stepped out onto the porch for minutes at a time. In the morning, he noticed that Tom was slow to leave for breakfast at the Stuarts'. When he finally did saddle and mount Ross, he rode up onto the caprock, just as the orange sun pulled away from the eastern horizon.

Andy saddled his own horse and waited for a while. Then, when Tom did not come back, he finally mounted his horse and rode up through the cleft onto the caprock. Once out on the caprock, he spotted Tom atop Ross at the high point of the low rise to the west of the canyon. Set against the backdrop of the western morning sky as it grew slowly more blue, the team made quite a picture, alone upon the boundless prairie, Tom sitting with his right leg hooked over the horn of his saddle, staring off toward the north, steam puffing periodically from Ross's mouth and nostrils, and escaping now and then from Tom's, as well, into the cool morning air of the Llano Estacado of autumn.

Andy trotted up and pulled in silently alongside Tom. He looked off toward the north, in the direction that Tom was looking. They could see that the Edwards outfit, two miles or so away, was breaking camp. Already the men were on horseback. The cattle were up. The wagon was underway in their direction.

Andy looked off to the east, as the orange sun climbed in behind a low layer of broken clouds (the only clouds in the sky) pushing its light into and through them in its own orange, and in pinks, yellows, purples, reds, and blues. He looked back toward the outfit moving their way in the muted colored light that escaped from the layer of clouds, and felt a chill in the autumn air, but not just in the air: there seemed to be a chill in the light itself, as if the autumn light that warmed the autumn air needed itself to first be warmed.

"I don't know, Andy," Tom finally said without looking away from the outfit to the north, "this ain't good."

"What is it, Tom?"

"I know that man, Andy, that Edwards. I know him."

Andy turned a quizzical expression on Tom. "How do you know him?"

"Met him once before," Tom said. Then he turned toward Andy and, with a smile, said, "Huh, the same day I met Luke, as a matter of fact. Huh." He pondered for a moment. "But anyways," he continued, looking back toward the Edwards outfit, "he's not good. He's a game player."

They both sat silently for a moment, watching the outfit's slow advance.

"What do you mean, Tom?" Andy finally said.

"He's a game player," Tom responded. He looked toward Andy. "He acts like life is one big game of win or lose. Everything's a . . . a competition. I've seen it before, some places more than others. It's not just bein' competitive; it's different from that. I've known competitive people who are not game players. It's a need to turn everything into a competition so that they can win. It's a need to believe that everyone else is a game player, that everyone else is competin' with them the way they are competin' with everyone else, so that they can justify their behavior and attitudes."

Tom looked back out ahead. "For some it's just a mark of immaturity. They may have grown up in settings that foster that mentality, and with maturity, if they have integrity, they can move away from game playin', and grow up from it. Some never move away from it, because they never grow up."

Tom looked back at Andy. "But then there are others," he said with a certain gravity, "and these can be dangerous. They sell their souls to this mentality." Tom looked back to the north as he continued. "They have built themselves up through the lie of their game, and as they mature, they continue to build up this false god of self by committin' ever deeper to that lie. The false self created by their pride must be maintained. As they mature and the truth about their game becomes more apparent, they have to work harder to refuse that truth and the necessary humbling that attends that truth and hollows out their game, leavin' it empty. The harder they work to refuse the truth, the deeper they work into the lie. As they work into the lie, the immaturity and ignorance that may have at one time maintained the lie give way to evil, really, because down inside, in their souls, they know it's a lie, and the more they commit to it, the more they know it, and the more they have to lie to themselves. And in committin' to this evil, they make themselves vulnerable to all the other vices that seek to pull them further into the evil, and one of the most insidious is fear. They fear the destruction of their false selves, which, in the lie of the game, they have come to regard as their real selves, their only selves. So, in their confusion, in the lie, they come to fear the self-annihilation that is truly their liberation to be their true selves. They can mask this fear with meanness and bravado, which are really based in a disregard for their own lives, which they have come to hate. But it's fear, real fear, however subtly it works into their souls. The deeper they go into the lie, the deeper they go into fear, and the more courage will be required to break free from it."

Tom turned his head a little to the right and looked sideways at Andy, who wondered at this Tom beside him, this Tom who continued to speak as he looked at him. "It takes real courage to accept the truth and the humility that goes with it after long committin' to the lie of the game, because that truth empties out and breaks down the game player, leavin' just the man, or what's left of him. Then he's free to see himself as he really is, in light of the truth, through conversion, by the grace of God."

A distinct tension sank into Tom's brow, and he looked back toward the outfit to the north. "The dangerous thing about them is that they cannot stand good in others. They cannot allow themselves to believe that some men try to live by values, by virtues, that some men actually achieve some level of integrity. So they reduce virtues and values and integrity to tactics. They pretend that good men are not really good, that their virtues and values and integrity are just tactics they use to get ahead in the game. They have to believe that all men are playin' the game, or they would have to accept the truth. And those men who most challenge their lie, not necessarily the men who are most virtuous, because they can often be dismissed as extreme, but maybe more the men who have committed to struggle against the vices that most beset them: those men the game players must themselves beset, and, if it comes to it, try to destroy."

By now Andy was staring at Tom—in the rising, deepening, warming light of morning—who still looked out ahead, the tension having drained from his face, along with some of his color, as he concluded his discourse with the expression of these last sentiments. Andy's stare intensified, seeking a depth beyond the surface available to him. He had seen this side of Tom before. Finally he spoke. "Where all've you been, Tom?"

It seemed to take a moment for the question to reach Tom, but when it finally did, Tom shook off his concentration on the scene to the north and turned his head a little toward Andy. "Huh," he let escape through a smile, "I've been around a bit, I guess."

"How do you know all this about Edwards?" Andy asked, unable to completely mask the concern built up in him during Tom's discourse.

"I know it in my gut," Tom responded, looking back to the north. "I've seen it before, and I had one short run-in with Edwards—well, it really wasn't much of a run-in—anyways, I saw it in him. A person might not think I had much to go on, but I've seen it before, and I saw it with Edwards. I saw it then, and I saw it last night with him. Maybe I ought to say I felt it. Anyways, it's there, and I know it's real. Whenever I don't listen to my gut, these gut feelings, make myself believe I'm not givin' the fellow a fair chance, I always find out I was right in the first place and regret that I didn't listen to myself. I just know we need to beware of this one. And," he glanced back toward Andy, "I'll be honest with you, Andy, I'm not sure bein' aware of him will be enough."

Andy's own eyebrows were knit together, as he looked at Tom. "Did he know you, Tom, I mean, recognize you?"

"Huh," Tom answered through a light smile as he looked back to the north, "I don't know, Andy. He didn't appear to last night, and there's no reason why he should, but I don't know."

Tom turned his head and looked at Andy and watched him turn his own eyes back to the north. Tom saw the serious concern registered in the young man's face, and he regretted having burdened him with all that he had said. Tom appreciated that this concern in the young man was for his friends, as he was no longer a part of their ranch, with his position now set with the JA. A slight, closed-mouth smile worked its way into Tom's features in admiration of the good in Andy.

"Come on," he said to Andy as he pulled his horse around, "I'm probably makin' too much of the whole thing. Probably just a little nervous about havin' other folks movin' into our country here.

"Anyways," he continued, as Andy turned his horse and pulled in alongside him and they headed back toward the canyon, "we've got a roundup to finish up, and Mr. Stuart will be wonderin' what's keepin' us."

With that they nudged their horses into a canter and returned to the canyon and rode down to breakfast at the Stuarts'.

AFTER BREAKFAST THAT MORNING, which was preceded by a jocular chastisement from Luke about Tom and Andy's late arrival, for which no explanation was given, the three men, Zachariah, and the dogs began to round up the lower canyon. They began some distance below the house and gathered as they swept east down the canyon. They continued this operation for the next several days. They made a very thorough survey of the widening canyon as they continued east, checking the draws not only for beeves, but for signs of dead beeves, so that they could get some idea of their losses, which, despite their best efforts, were still considerable, given the predators, rattlesnakes, parasites, and disease. In one of the draws, Luke's horse suffered a rattlesnake bite and threw Luke, who landed on his side on some loose rock with his hands out to break his fall. His gloves kept the damage to his hands down to bruises and a few cuts, but his right hip suffered quite a blow, and it bothered him for several days after. (The horse's leg was treated with coal oil, the horse left to graze, and the animal recovered with little bad effect.)

Luke killed the snake with a rock and brought the six-footer back to noon camp, where Zachariah, who was out with the men that day, twisted off its tail, and cut off its head and placed it on an anthill to be cleaned of flesh by the ants. He would add the head and tail to his growing collection. Tom skinned the snake after dinner and laid the fresh skin on the back of his saddle, with the outside up. The skin dried to his saddle as if glued there.

Each day the men would set up a noon camp and cook a hot meal that Elizabeth had prepared for them. Then, at the end of each day, they would take the beeves that they had rounded up to the draw that they had fenced off the year before, near where they had built the new pens, and release the beeves into that draw, where a spring provided plenty of water and the grass provided plenty of grazing for the time required. Though only six years old, Zachariah often, though not always, accompanied the men and helped with the work as he was able.

In the evening the men and Zachariah, when he was out with them, would ride back to the ranch house and enjoy a hearty late supper prepared by Elizabeth. Elizabeth and the two younger children did not accompany the roundup in the wagon and make camps, as they had the year before. She had been ill with the pregnancy for weeks now, and though she missed being part of the roundup, she knew that it was for the best that she stay near home and rest whenever she felt the need, to which Luke forcefully agreed.

She kept a Winchester at the house and knew to give three quick shots if there were an emergency, whether of health or mishap or unwelcome visitors. She felt safe in her rock house with its stout doors and shutters. One could argue that the dugout had been more defensible against attack from Indians, but the rock house was plenty defensible, and yet it offered the luxuries of light through the windows and views in every direction.

After the men had rounded up the cattle down to where they had built the pens, they branded and doctored those they had rounded up. This was short work, as there were only twelve calves through this section of the canyon. Once finished with the doctoring and branding, they herded the calves and their "mawmaws," as Luke would pronounce it, to a level pasture to allow reunification and healing. This they did on their way home in the evening, as the pasture was on the way back toward the house.

When they started out on the next day to round up the rest of the lower canyon, that which lay below the lower pens, they had not yet seen any sign of the second Hereford bull. Luke and Tom had noted this to each other without any real concern, as there were still the bottom of the canyon, the mouth, and the rolling plains beyond that they would need to round up. They worked the bottom of the canyon that day, down to the mouth.

They had decided to camp out that night to get an early start in the morning, and had not brought Zachariah along for that reason. In the morning they started out in the cool before sunrise to round up out onto the plains. They did not expect to find many beeves out there, because Luke had ridden line faithfully up until the roundup, because there was plenty of grass in the canyon, and because the outliers offered a natural boundary. Still, on occasion, they had herded the cattle out beyond the mouth of the canyon onto the rolling plains to graze. Consequently, the beeves knew the way and knew that between the two rivers there was plenty of water and grass.

The breaks around and beyond the outliers did not make the roundup any easier, and the dogs were a great help at routing some of the beeves from well-hidden spots. Beyond the breaks, the roundup required less work, as the land rounded off, making for fewer places where cattle could disappear from view. After a full day of working through the breaks and just starting on the rolling plains, they believed that they had routed out most of the beeves below the lower pens, one hundred and fifty or so, and they headed these back to the corral in the draw. They would camp there one more night and in the morning make a quick run through the breaks and sweep across the rolling plains beyond and figure they had brought in all the beeves. What they did not yet know was that, when finished with this last batch of beeves, they would have branded another sixteen calves, bringing the total number of calves for this roundup to forty-seven, out of a total of about four hundred and forty head (including Andy's ten and taking into account the loss since spring), up from four hundred in the spring, with most cows and heifers expecting to drop calves by next spring.

Beyond making one last sweep for beeves, the men were seeking the other Hereford bull. There had been no sign of him. As they had worked their way down the canyon without seeing him, their level of concern had risen. When they had not found him in the breaks, even though they still had the proximate rolling plains to investigate, they had already begun to speculate about what had happened to him. In sweeping across the rolling plains the next day, they would cut for sign to determine if he had drifted off or been driven off, a distinct possibility in a land in which rustlers were never far behind ranchers.

In the morning they rose before the sun and breakfasted around the fire. Still before sunrise, they headed out through the breaks onto the low rolling plains beyond the canyon. The three men, with the dogs, made a sweep across the rolling plains and saw no sign of cattle. At the far eastern extent of their range, they split up to ride line and cut for sign. Tom would ride the eastern line, Andy the north, and Luke the south.

Just before noon, two shots rang out from near the mouth of the canyon, signaling that one of the men had found something. Tom was nearly finished riding his line, but he left where he was and urged his mount into a full gallop. As he drew near the canyon, he saw Andy riding at as much of a gallop as the land would allow through the breaks before the outliers. Andy rounded the southern outlier out of Tom's sight, and shortly thereafter, Tom rounded it to see Luke and Andy high up on the slope at the base of the vertical wall of the escarpment on the south side of the mouth of the canyon.

Luke was off his horse, his horse picketed not far away, and he was crouched before a fire in which he had already set a coffee pot and a kettle. He had found a fairly level area on the slope on which to build his fire. Andy was still on his horse, having just arrived, and was talking with Luke. Andy then dismounted, hobbled his horse, and let him loose.

As Tom rode up, Luke glanced up from a bowl in which he was mixing sour dough and said, as he looked back down, "Found sign of ol' Seventy-six." That was the nickname that had eventually "tumbled out" of Tom's head for the bull named Centennial. "He's headed south, and it's been a couple of days, so I figured we'd better have our noon meal before we head out."

"He didn't just drift off on his own?" Tom questioned.

Without looking up, Luke replied, "No, he had some help. Two riders, white men." Looking up and pointing a fork back over his shoulder toward where Andy was now squatting and examining the ground, he added, "Sign's just up yonder, if you want to take a look."

Tom dismounted, hobbled his horse, and climbed the short distance to where Andy had been examining the beginning of the sign Luke had discovered. Andy was now up and following alongside the sign as it continued off toward the southwest. Tom also squatted and examined the sign, distinct tracks of the Hereford bull along with those of two shod horses. Tom rose and followed along beside the tracks until he came to where Andy had stopped at a cedar bush.

"Brought him as far up along the side as they could," Andy said.

"Yessir," Tom concurred, as he looked back and forth and noted the degree to which he had to lean to remain standing vertically, "it's amazin' that that stout ol' Seventy-six didn't roll right on down this hill."

"He came close a couple of times," Andy said, nodding back to places where the bull had had to catch his footing.

"Yeah," Tom noted, looking back, as well, and nodding. "They sure were interested in keepin' his tracks as far out of sight as possible, and went to some trouble about it."

Andy nodded, as they both looked up and down the trail. Then they turned and made their way down to where Luke was preparing the noon meal. Luke was just taking the bacon off the fire when they arrived. He poured off some of the grease and was putting the dough, rolled into balls for biscuits, into the pan, when Tom spoke up. "Save me a little of that dough?"

Luke looked at him and then looked down and shook his head a little. "All right," he said.

Tom got up and scouted around a little until he found a good stick with a fork at the end. He took the dough that Luke had saved him and fixed it around the fork on the stick and stuck it over the fire to roast it.

Luke shook his head and said, "I can understand that when it's out of necessity, when you're on the trail without a skillet or some such, but how you can take good dough and stick it in the fire on some stick when real biscuits are cookin' right in front of you, I cannot understand."

"Somethin' about it," Tom said. "I'll eat my share of biscuits, too. Don't you worry about that. But there's somethin' about how this gets so crisp."

Luke looked at Andy, who just smiled and looked down as Luke shook his head.

In time the beans were ready, and they enjoyed them with the bacon, biscuits, and coffee. As they ate, they speculated about the whereabouts of the bull. They were not overly surprised that the bull had been rustled. As they had worked their way down the canyon without a sign of him day after day, the possibility of rustling had become increasingly probable. (So had other possibilities, like predation or snake bite.) If Indians had rustled him, they might have butchered him on the spot. But since the bull had left the canyon alive, driven by white men, there was still a chance of recovery.

AFTER THE NOON MEAL, they followed the trail of bull and rustlers as it continued along the base of the escarpment to the southwest. The trail worked in and out of the breaks and then entered a creek, which they followed until the trail emerged on the other side, two hundred yards or so from where it had entered the water. Then it angled to the south beyond the breaks, and then turned southwest, at which point the rustlers had increased their speed, getting some run out of the stout Seventy-six.

As they rode southwest, Luke, Tom, and Andy began to hear the low and bawl of cattle, which sharpened to let penetrate more deeply a suspicion that had been growing inside Tom right along with the growing suspicion and eventual realization that the bull was missing. That suspicion was that Henry Edwards had something to do with it. For Tom there had never been a separation between the two suspicions, that of the bull missing and that of Henry Edwards having something to do with it. They had both been born in the same inkling, and both had waxed and waned as the roundup had progressed, to finally reach realization in the discovery of the rustlers' sign. They were two different aspects of the same thing.

As the men crested the top of a rise and saw cattle in the distance, scattered throughout the breaks and across the plains beyond the mouth of the canyon they had recommended to Henry Edwards, Tom realized, in retrospect, that when they had learned for certain that the bull had been rustled, at the discovery of the sign, he had accepted, just as certainly, that Henry Edwards was behind the rustling. There had no longer been any suspicion about it.

And yet, Tom had not said anything about it. Why had he not? As they rode on, he pondered that very question. He realized that he had probably said nothing about his suspicion because it would have sounded so groundless: the Seven Ox Seven could not find their bull, so the conclusion would naturally be that the outfit that had just moved into the range ten miles to the south, just a couple days before, had sent someone back around to the eastern entrance to their canyon to rustle a single bull? It sounded crazy, but down inside, Tom believed that this was the kind of mentality they were dealing with in Henry Edwards.

Beyond that, by stating his suspicions out loud, he would have been admitting that his suspicions were real, that things had changed that much in their canyon home from the serenity of just a few days before, that Henry Edwards was as bad as Tom had suspected. There was a part of Tom that did not want to accept that.

But accepting it was becoming increasingly difficult to avoid. On the rise, Tom got off his horse and checked the trail. It pointed directly toward the Edwards outfit. He nodded an affirmative to Luke and Andy, then remounted his horse, and the three cantered off toward the Edwards herd.

Finally, Tom spoke up. "That trail is days old. He had to send someone around first thing they got in that canyon, just to get that bull."

The conjecture hung heavily among the three men. Then Luke, still looking straight ahead, posed this question, as if to the air, although he intended it for Tom, though he was not of a mind to acknowledge it: "How did they know there was another bull?"

"You told him," Tom said.

"I did?"

"Yessir, he got it out of you when he said we were goin' to grade our stock with one bull. He probably had an idea for somethin' like this in the askin'," Tom said, a little bit aware that he might be speculating out loud more than the others could accept to be true, though Tom had no doubt of its possibility.

They rode on in a grave silence, their sights set on the canyon. As they neared the canyon and began to get a closer look at the cattle, Tom noticed that many of these "Texas cattle" that Henry Edwards had extolled showed definite signs of grading with shorthorn blood.

Eventually, they passed over the breaks at the mouth of the canyon and did not have far to ride before they spotted Seventy-six from a high mound inside the mouth of the canyon. The bull was being close herded with a herd of heifers, cows, and calves, by two men, in a pasture beyond another lower rise.

"Dagnabit," Luke said, staring straight at the sight, his mouth hanging open.

"Son of a gun," Tom said, at the confirmation.

"'Gradin' with an inferior breed,' he said. Look who's gradin' with the breed now," Luke sneered. He paused for a moment, drinking in the scene, his anger rising with each second, until he finally said, "I'll show them to mess with my property."

With that he spurred his horse, which jumped forward into a dead run. Tom and Andy were right behind him and soon right even with him. They flew down the mound and up and over the low rise and were nearly on top of the two herders before the herders knew what was happening. When they did know, they fell back a little, with one of them pulling out his six-shooter and shooting in their direction. That was Robert Speck.

Luke charged right into Speck as he was pulling out of his gallop, knocking Speck from his horse. The other herder had begun to run, but Tom was quickly upon him. Grabbing the reins of his horse, Tom pulled to a stop with him. Andy had reined in his horse behind Luke so that, when Luke knocked Speck from his horse, Andy was able to dismount on the run to reach Speck just as he was rising from the ground. Andy pushed him back to the ground and then searched around until he found his gun and picked it up.

By then Luke had turned around and was riding back. Dismounting on the run, as Robert Speck got to his feet again, Luke slammed into Speck, laying his right shoulder into the smaller man's chest, knocking him off his feet and landing on top of him with all his weight, driving his back into the ground. Speck had all the wind knocked out of him as well as having his head slammed against the ground.

"What do you mean to shoot at me?" Luke exploded into Speck's face, as he slapped once back and forth across it. Then looking into that face, he could see that Speck was dazed and was trying to get his breath, so he climbed off him and let him roll over onto his side and choke and gasp for air.

At about that time, Tom rode up with the other herder, a man younger than Speck, younger than Andy, not really a man but a boy of about sixteen years, red-haired, freckled, with a pug nose. Tom had him dismount; then he dismounted. He already held the boy's gun.

Tom tossed the boy's gun to Andy and said, "Keep an eye on him, Andy," to which Andy nodded.

Tom stepped up next to Luke, who stood looking down at the figure catching his breath on the ground.

"It's that fellow from the other day, Speck, isn't it?" Tom asked, looking down at Speck still lying on his side, facing away from them, gulping air.

"It's him."

Still looking at the man on the ground, Tom said, "You think he was tryin' to hit us?"

"I think he was."

"You hit anywhere?" Tom asked as he looked his friend up and down.

Luke came out of his concentration on the man on the ground for a moment, and looked himself over. "Nah, I don't think so," he said.

"Andy," Tom said over his shoulder, "you all right? Were you hit at all?"

Andy gave himself a look over, without too much concern about the young cowboy, who showed little inclination to try to get away. If anything, the redheaded boy looked scared. "No, I think I'm all right," Andy said.

"Ahright," Tom said, as he turned his attention back to Speck on the ground, who had begun to catch his breath. Finally, Speck rolled over onto his hands and knees and gulped a few more breaths. Luke stepped over, pulled up the man's shoulder with one hand and grabbed the front of his shirt with the other and lifted him to his feet.

"Why you shootin' at us?" he said as he shook the man by his shirt.

"I thought you was Indians or rustlers," Speck said, still breathing hard. With his hat off, his straight hair (which was a blond-brown) hung down nearly to his eyes. Up close, he did not look quite so young as his small frame implied.

"We look like Indians to you?"

Speck looked down without answering. Luke shook him and shouted, "We look like Indians to you?"

"No," Speck nearly shouted back without looking up.

"What are you doin' with our bull?" Luke asked with such intensity that he lifted the man so that his feet barely touched the ground. Speck continued to look down, away from Luke's eyes. Luke lifted him higher, his feet clearing the ground, and shook him again and shouted at him, "Answer me!"

"They drifted in here," Speck finally responded as if it pained him. "So we were holdin' 'em from driftin' farther 'til we could get 'em back to you."

"Yeah," Luke said with derision, "holdin' him with cows and heifers."

Luke pushed the man away with disgust, and Speck backpedalled until he regained his balance. He looked around and reached for his hat.

As he picked up his hat, Tom, whose brows had knit together at an earlier answer from Speck, said, "What do you mean, 'they'?"

Speck froze for a second, then picked up his hat and, straightening up, returned it to his head. Luke, who had turned away from the man in anger and disgust to look out instead over that part of the Edwards herd in his view, turned back to face Speck as Tom's question struck home. "Yeah," he said.

"I don't catch your meanin'," Speck replied.

"You said, '*they* drifted in here,'" Tom replied. "What do you mean by 'they'?"

Speck looked at Tom, a cold lack of emotion washing over Speck's face, his eyes seeming to empty of life, and he said in a voice that transmitted in its flat tone a derision of his own, "I meant 'he.' I said 'he.'"

"No, you didn't," Tom said, dismissing this man he did not trust in looking away from him and out over the cattle in this lower part of the canyon. "Maybe, we need to look around a little for more Seven Ox cattle that might have 'drifted in'."

"That's right," Luke said, again looking away from Speck, still unable to hide his disdain for the man. As he looked away, Luke spotted his horse. His brows tensed, and he walked past Tom and Andy and the boy and headed toward him.

Meanwhile, as Tom came around to face the other Edwards herder, whom Andy was holding at gunpoint off to the side, he said, "What do you know?"

"I don't know nothin'," the boy said, betraying the fear he was trying to hide.

Tom did not push the point, considering the boy's youth and his fear. Instead, he said, "You the wrangler?"

"Yessir."

"You know," Tom said, "you ought to pull out of this rustlers' outfit and hitch up with a legitimate concern. Charlie Goodnight's just north in the Palo Duro. There're others: Bugbee, Bakers, Dyer. Other outfits'll be movin' into this country all the time. You're young, got a lot ahead of you. You're better off gettin' a better start than this. You're too young to be lookin' at a career as an outlaw." Tom realized that to some extent he was speaking to Henry Edwards through this boy and, even more, through Speck.

The boy said nothing, just stared at Tom, periodically letting his eyes dart to Speck and then back to Tom. Concern and fear were mixed in his eyes, as he stood with his hands up before Andy, who was holding his own gun on him. At the same time, Speck, who had sufficiently recovered his poise since his run-in with Luke, said not a word at all. He stood—with that same nearly lifeless look in his eyes, a cold smile touching his thin lips—and watched Tom talk to the boy.

Then something distracted Tom, and his vision focused beyond the boy to where Luke had met up with his horse. The horse was down on the ground, and Luke had just drawn his gun and pointed it at the animal's head. As Tom watched, Luke fired. The boy jumped at the sound and whirled toward it. Andy, too, had been startled and looked over, but kept the gun pointed at the boy. Neither Tom nor Speck had moved, as both had seen it happen. Tom walked past Andy and the boy, heading toward where Luke stood. "Keep an eye on both of 'em," he said to Andy as he passed. Andy nodded, motioning with the gun to Speck to get him to move over by the boy so that he could follow Tom's order and still see what was going on with Tom and Luke off to his left.

As Tom reached Luke, Luke, who was on bended knee in front of the dead horse, a bay, looked up at Tom, his eyes expressing the gravity of the situation. Touching a wound in the animal's chest, he said, "He's shot in the lung."

"He meant to hit us," Tom said.

"He sure did. His first two shots must've gone into the ground as he was pullin' up."

"Huh," Tom responded, nodding his head. "Didn't hurt any that we were comin' down that rise. A little lower ground and that shot would've been just right. Good thing he only shot three times."

"He didn't," Luke said as he stood up.

"He didn't?"

"No," Luke said, still looking down at the dead horse, "I had my eyes on him all the way down. He shot at least five times, but the last few didn't fire."

"Huh," Tom again responded. He looked at the dead horse for a moment, then turned and walked back to Andy and said to him, "Give me Speck's gun." Andy looked at Tom, and Tom nodded toward Speck. "The little one," he said, and Speck turned his cold stare onto Tom.

Andy handed Tom the gun, and Tom checked the cylinders. "All fired," he said under his breath. He turned back and walked over to Luke. "I guess you're right," he said as he handed Luke the gun, "must have had three spent shells." Tom looked over his shoulder at the emotionless Speck and quietly said, "He would've killed us."

"Yessir," Luke said as he finished examining the gun.

"As far as thinkin' we were rustlers," Tom said, "if he was expectin' anybody, he was expectin' us comin' after that bull."

"Hmh," Luke responded, nodding as he did so.

"Tells us a little somethin' about Mr. Speck," Tom said.

"Might say somethin' about his boss, too," Luke added.

"Expect so," Tom said. "But we don't know that yet."

"You just called 'em a rustlers' outfit," Luke reminded Tom.

"Well, that's from my gut. Maybe I just don't want to believe it yet," Tom said. "But we better find out. If Edwards doesn't know about it, he's got to be told."

"You think he doesn't know about it?" Luke asked, reaching for that last ray of hope.

"I think it's doubtful he doesn't know," Tom admitted, as Luke nodded his acceptance of that probability, "but I guess it's only fair to give him the benefit of the doubt."

"Fair could get us killed," Luke replied, looking down at the horse. "What would Elizabeth and the young'uns do if we didn't come home?"

"That's a good point," Tom said, "and how would they even know we weren't comin' home?"

A profound seriousness tensed its way into Luke's features.

"I'll go alone, Luke. I know this Edwards," Tom said. "You and Andy take the bull back." It sounded ridiculous to Tom as soon as he finished saying it, but he sincerely meant it.

"You know Edwards?" Luke questioned, keying in on that one point.

"I had a run-in with him once before."

"You did?"

"It was nothin', just an argument . . . , well, it wasn't really an argument, because I wasn't arguin'. He was arguin' both sides. Anyways, I saw enough of his character to have my concerns."

"I saw enough the other night," Luke said. "How long ago was that?"

"Same day I met you, in Dodge City."

"Same day?" Luke responded, as he turned a look of near incredulity on Tom.

"Yessir," Tom replied, raising his eyebrows and nodding his head lightly.

"He didn't recognize you the other night?"

"Didn't appear to."

"Huh," Luke responded, as he considered their situation.

"I can't let you go alone, Tom," he finally said. "Wouldn't even think of it. But if we go, we could get killed, leavin' Elizabeth and the young'uns, and if we don't . . ."

"If we don't, we leave here after gettin' shot at, havin' a horse killed, and havin' our bull rustled. And we'll leave this Speck hombre without any repercussions to his actions," Tom completed the thought. "That'll just say we're rollin' over for more of the same."

"That's right," Luke said, chewing his lip.

"I can just go alone," Tom assured him.

"I can't let you go alone, Tom."

"But you got a family."

"And you're my partner," Luke quickly retorted. "Besides, this is for my family."

Tom knew that if he went, Luke would have to go too. He would insist on the same thing if the situation were reversed. He also knew that

Luke's main concern was his family. Finally, Tom said, "We'll send Andy back with the bull. It's not his fight, and he's too young to get mixed up in this anyways. We'll have him go on to the house to watch out for the family and, if we don't come back, to ride to the JA for help."

Luke pondered it and said, "I was thinkin' along those lines. Yessir, let's do that."

They returned to where Andy was holding the two men, and Tom went to the wrangler's horse and took his rope from the saddle. He tied the two men's hands together behind their backs, and then, pushing them together, back to back, tied the rope around their waists. Then he made them lie down on their sides, and he tied their feet together.

Tom and Luke told Andy their plan. Andy resisted the idea that he should go back alone, but after the concerns about the family had been laid before him, he reluctantly agreed that he would return with the bull and proceed on to the house and wait for them. If they did not return by morning, he was to secure the family in the house and ride for the JA.

Luke returned to his dead horse and took off the saddle. He carried it over to the horse of the young wrangler, a mustang bay, and, after removing the wrangler's saddle, put his own saddle on the bay. He had chosen the horse because, though Speck's horse was, at a glance, a more attractive animal, it would never stand up to the mustang in stamina. After cinching up his saddle on the mustang, he took the boy's saddle over to Speck's horse, a blue roan with socks and a blaze. He removed Speck's well-tooled saddle from the horse and threw it on the ground. Then he put the boy's inferior saddle on Speck's horse.

As he was cinching up the boy's saddle, he said over the back of the horse to Tom and Andy, "Figure the one that shot at us can take the time to hunt up his saddle."

He heard no arguments from Andy or Tom. When he finished with the saddle, he hobbled the horse. Then Tom checked the knots of the ropes binding the men on the ground, and finding them secure, he mounted his horse. Andy and Luke mounted up, too, and then they all rode out to make a survey of what cattle they could see for any signs of Seven Ox Seven stock. After looking for about an hour without finding any of their cattle, they returned to where the men lay on the ground.

They all dismounted. Andy covered the men with his gun as Tom began to untie them. Meanwhile, Luke took the rope from Speck's saddle, where it lay on the ground, and then fetched Speck's horse, without yet taking off the hobble. As he approached Tom, he tossed Speck's rope to him. Tom untied the men, all except the hands of the wrangler, which he left tied behind his back. He led the wrangler to the roan and helped him into the saddle, as Luke held the horse's reins. Then he told Speck to climb into the saddle behind the boy, which he did, ever with that cold near-smile. Then Tom mounted his own horse, the black Othello, and rode up against the roan and took the rest of the rope that hung from the boy's tied hands and wrapped it twice around Speck's waist, pulling it tight. Then he pulled the rope back around behind Speck's back and tied his hands tightly with it.

"There," he said as he completed the knot. "Either of you gets to movin' too much, it's goin' to pull on your hands, Speck. So, it's to your advantage to help us finish our business as quick as possible."

Speck could not hide his discomfort, especially as a creature who avoided discomfort at all costs. The cold, calculated near-smile gave way a little to the winces that betrayed the discomfort he was experiencing.

"Andy," Tom said, as Andy put his gun away, "tie this boy's foot into his stirrup, and Mr. Speck's foot to his." He tossed Speck's rope to Andy. "Then pull that rope under the horse's belly to the other side and do the same thing."

Andy tied them as Tom had instructed. With the Edwards men thus secured, Luke unhobbled the roan and took its reins and tied them to the back of his saddle. Then he and Andy mounted their horses.

"Be careful, Andy," Tom said.

"You all be careful, yourselves," Andy responded.

"We'll see you tonight," Luke added.

"We'll see you," Andy replied. Then he pulled his horse around and rounded up the bull Centennial, ol' Seventy-six, and moved him off toward the mouth of the canyon. Tom and Luke, with the Edwards men trailing behind, rode in the other direction.

By now it was late afternoon, and Luke and Tom figured that it would be to their advantage to conduct the impending interview and make their way away from it in the light of day. So they sought the cooperation of the two men on the roan to help them get to the Edwards headquarters as quickly as possible. Directions to the headquarters were difficult to come by from the two men, but as Luke and Tom meandered about the lower canyon, now and then checking for signs of their cattle, riding up and down through draws, and as the ropes which held the men began to pull and chafe, the men, more Speck than the boy, became increasingly helpful in finding the headquarters.

At last they arrived in the vicinity of the headquarters. Speck indicated that the headquarters were beyond a mound up ahead. They rode to the base of that mound and stopped. They gagged Speck and the boy with their own neckerchiefs, and hobbled the roan and tied it, along with their own horses, to a mesquite tree. Then they climbed to the top of the mound and lay down, so as to stay out of sight, and peered over the top of the mound. The headquarters lay beyond them to the south, in the canyon's bottom, surrounded by verdant pastures. Men were busy at work. Having completed a cottonwood-log half-dugout in a bank above the creek that cut through the canyon's floor, some of the men were building a cedar log house to the north of the half-dugout, up from the creek in Tom and Luke's direction. Tom noticed, even from that distance, that the house was being constructed of unhewn logs, apparently with single-saddle-notched corners. Tom caught himself thinking that he would have expected nothing better from the outfit than this low level of craftsmanship. Beyond the house to the west, other men were constructing pens.

Edwards was there, directing the construction of the pens. While they watched, he climbed aboard a saddled horse nearby and rode back to the house, dismounted, and began to supervise its construction. His horse stood by, off to the side, tied loosely to a tree, much as it had been down by the pens, giving the impression that Edwards had been traveling between the two projects as supervisor.

While Luke and Tom had been searching for the headquarters and their cattle, they had arrived at two conclusions. The first conclusion was that the Edwards outfit had rustled no more of their cattle when they had taken the bull. Speck, after a particularly rough descent into one of the draws to check for Seven Ox Seven cattle, had finally let out that there were no other Seven Ox Seven cattle in the canyon. He would say no more than that, but it was clear that, tied up as he was, this ride was an experience Mr. Speck would just as soon bring to an

end. Despite that his statement could well have been a lie to bring his
ordeal to a quicker end, Tom and Luke believed him, because they had
seen no trace of Seven Ox Seven cattle, and just because there was
something about Speck's confession that rang true.

The boy had said little. Though some of that may have been attributable to a strong character or constitution, it was also true that Tom
and Luke did not put much pressure on him, due to his youth, and
that Speck was taking a good deal more of the brunt of the suffering
of the ride, as every move pulled or tugged at the rope around his
hands. In fact, Tom did not want to seem to soften with regards to
Speck, but as he would drop back now and then and check on the two
men, he had been concerned about Speck's hands and the tightness of
the ropes around them, and he was looking forward to getting the men
to a place where they could be untied as soon as possible.

The second conclusion (after concluding that there were no more
Seven Ox Seven cattle in the canyon) was in regard to a plan of action,
and now that they had arrived at their destination, they put that plan
into effect. They made their way back down to the base of the mound,
where Tom unhobbled the roan, with the men still aboard, untied it
from the tree, and tied it with a slipknot to the back of his saddle. He
then untied his own horse and swung into the saddle. Luke untied his
horse and mounted up as well. Then Luke and Tom nodded to each
other, and Luke rode farther up the canyon behind the mound, while
Tom turned to ride the other way. After a short distance, Tom stopped
and pulled his Winchester from its scabbard and laid it across the saddle in front of him. He tied his reins together in a knot, down a bit
from where he normally held them, switched the reins to his right
hand, and reached around and untied the reins of the horse behind
him and held them in his left hand. And he waited. After several minutes, he said a silent prayer, gave his horse a nudge, and with the roan
carrying the Edwards men trailing a little behind him off to the left,
he rode around the base of the mound and out into the open on his
way down into the Edwards camp.

Well, it was not completely out into the open, as there were still
bushes and some trees to obscure his advance. But as he rode ahead,
those that stood between him and the Edwards camp grew fewer and
fewer, until just some scattered mesquite stood between him and the

open pasture where the Edwards outfit was constructing the house.

He was still one hundred yards from the house when he was spotted by a man who had climbed one of the skids to put the final touches on a corner notch. With the wind doing its typical job of overwhelming and blotting out sound, Tom could hear little of what he could see, which was that the man called to Edwards, who stepped away from the house in Tom's direction. At the same time, another man turned from his work and saw Tom and then hurried to a gun belt that lay not far away and withdrew the gun and fired three times into the air, sounding what amounted to a general alarm, in response to which all hands came running or riding up to the house.

The knot that had been slowly forming in Tom's belly grew far larger very quickly and wrung itself tight as he looked at the other six men assembling in various places behind Edwards, three with rifles in hand. Still, he rode forward at a slow, deliberate pace. When he got to within twenty feet of Edwards, he stopped, pulled the roan forward by its reins, tossed the reins over the horse's neck, and gave the horse a swat on its behind, after which it trotted, with the two men still tied to it, into the Edwards camp.

Edwards watched the roan trot by to where it was caught by one of the men, who then began to study how to untie those men upon it. Edwards turned back on Tom with a sneer that conveyed such deep malevolence, especially pouring out from his eyes, that Tom could not at that moment remember any time when he had seen anything quite like it. An almost paralyzing sensation ran down Tom's spine, as the knot in his stomach twisted tighter. He steeled himself against them both, and fought off thoughts that, even if successful, this would be but a battle in what he imagined would be a war with this hate-filled foe.

"What do you mean to bring my men in here like that?" Edwards snarled.

"They're rustlers," Tom said, "and we brought 'em in to let you know they're rustlers and to find out if you're a rustler, too."

"You callin' me a rustler?" Edwards said as if he wished Tom were.

"We're askin'."

"Who's 'we'?"

"Me and my partner, whose got a fifty-caliber Sharps trained right on your belly. He's not as good a shot as I am, but I've rarely known

him to miss at under five hundred yards." This was a bit of an exaggeration. Tom was the better shot, which had been a cause of some discussion between Luke and him about which one of them would take
the men in and which would cover. They had agreed that Tom would
probably be the one who would be more likely to take the men in and
not lose his temper in a way that might get him killed, and that he was
more likely to remember exactly what was said for future reference. In
truth, Luke was a good shot, but to say that he had rarely missed at
under five hundred yards left a lot of room for success at far less than
five hundred yards. And since Luke had not often used the Sharps in
Tom's presence, even if he had missed every time, which he had not, it
would have been rare. Beyond all that, the consideration that outweighed all others was that he had a family.

Tom continued, "And my partner and I want those men behind
you to put down their guns, take off their holsters if they're wearin' 'em,
and throw 'em all far enough away, then lie face down where they are."

Edwards was calculating. Tom could see it in his eyes. Finally he
said, more in challenge than from doubting Tom's word, "What if
you're bluffin'?"

Obviously prepared for just such a challenge, Tom raised his hand,
and shortly thereafter a clattering bang was heard, followed immediately by the report of a rifle, as a bullet passed through a large metal
wash pan that was leaning against the wheel of the chuck wagon
parked over to the right of the house, and the pan tumbled atop the
rocks and rolled down the bank.

All of Edwards' men crouched down at the sound of the noise, and
at least three pointed guns at Tom. Tom realized that this dramatic
aspect of their plan might well get him killed. He realized that this was
a critical moment. They might react to Luke's shot and immediately
kill him. The smoke from the black powder would let them know
where Luke was, and they would have a fair chance of getting to cover.
Tom realized that the position that Edwards had taken as Tom had ridden up now proved providential, because he stood a good distance out
from protection of any kind. Still, it was at this point that Tom played
his trump card. In the heat of the moment, he knew he had to get to
the words that would have the greatest impact right from the start.

"Charlie Goodnight," Tom shot out, "will be headin' this way by mornin', with his men, if we don't come home."

He caught Edwards' attention with this bit of information, as he had expected. Tom remembered how Edwards had considered himself a cattleman when he had met him in Dodge City, and among cattlemen, few men were better known than Goodnight. Not only would Edwards not want to be visited by Goodnight and his men, as Goodnight's reputation included plenty of lore about his fearlessness and his fight, but Edwards would not want to have his own reputation sullied before a cattleman of Goodnight's standing.

Tom continued, "A hand from the JA went back with our bull. He was with us when we found the bull with these rustlers." Tom nodded toward Speck and the boy, whose release had stalled upon the sound of Luke's shot. "No word has to get to the JA, at all, if we come back with a reasonable explanation."

Tom could see in Edwards' eyes that his mind was working through it all. Tom knew that among all the information he was considering was the part about the "reasonable explanation." Edwards would understand that this caveat would allow him to talk his way out of the situation, whatever the circumstances, so that all could just forget that the whole thing had occurred and understand that there would be no such incidences in the future. They would go their way; he would stay and ranch from where he was; and that would be the end of it. But Tom's life hung in the balance with every second Edwards delayed.

"Make your call," Tom said.

Edwards looked at Tom and, with an expression that admitted some resignation, yelled back over his shoulder, "Throw your guns away."

The men hesitated, and Brown, the foreman, called out, "You sure you wanna do that, Mr. Edwards?"

"I said throw 'em away," Edwards shouted back.

The men lowered their guns and looked around, but there were still no sounds of guns hitting the ground.

"Throw 'em away!" Edwards bellowed over his shoulder.

The men threw the guns away.

"Now, lie down on your bellies," Edwards shouted back. He could feel their hesitation, so he shouted louder, "Do it. Lie down on your bellies!"

The men slowly complied so that all were lying face down, their guns a safe distance away from each.

"That fellow over there," Tom said, nodding off to his left, "can keep untyin' those two, so we can get to the bottom of this."

Edwards glanced over to where the two hands still sat tied to the horse, though on one side the knot around their feet was loose. "Henderson," he called out. The man lying on the ground near the horse raised his head. "Keep untyin' those two," Edwards said, and the man slowly rose and went back to work on the knots.

Before long Henderson had untied the two men's feet. As soon as their feet were untied, Speck pulled his legs back and tried to stretch them out as much as possible. The wrangler pulled his feet from the stirrups and did the same. Meanwhile, after examining the rope around their waists and hands, Henderson settled on the knots around Speck's wrists as the key to untying them. As soon as Speck's hands were untied, his arms shot out to the sides as if from a coiled spring that had been released. He opened and closed his fingers, outstretched at the end of his outstretched hands and arms, and turned his wrists several times. Then he reached up and pulled the gag down from around his mouth and then helped Henderson uncoil the rope from around him and the wrangler. As soon as he was free of the rope, he leaned back and held his hands in front of him and examined them. Tom felt a pang of guilt as he watched this, but, in the present circumstances, found it better not to dwell on this; so he said a silent prayer of repentance and concentrated again on the wariness that his present circumstances required.

After examining his hands, Speck slid gingerly down off the horse. Once on the ground, he stomped life into his feet and legs, and limped around in a small area, letting all his muscles get back to normal. The wrangler was soon free and reacted in a similar manner.

As soon as the wrangler had done a little stomping of his own, Edwards ordered Henderson back to the ground, and Henderson complied. Then he yelled to the other two men, "Speck, Billy, come over here."

Speck and the wrangler walked over a little more slowly and stiffly than they normally would. When they got to where Edwards stood, he asked them, "You two been rustlin' cattle as this man says?"

"No sir," said the boy, his wide eyes still betraying a serious fear.

"No," said Speck, who turned his emotionless eyes on Tom as he said so. Tom noticed that Speck's wrists, especially the one he was rubbing with his other hand, were red, chafed, swollen, and bleeding a little, worse than the boy's.

"Billy," Edwards barked at the youth.

"Yes sir."

"Was this man's bull down in our canyon?"

The boy's eyes glanced quickly back and forth between Edwards and Speck, and finally, finding no help from either of them, he took a chance and answered the truth. "Yes sir."

"How did he get there?"

"I don't know, sir," the boy said. Tom did not doubt this and, for that reason, also accepted Speck's claim that he and the boy had not rustled the bull. Tom still suspected Speck, but he also suspected the involvement of some other hand. With that in his mind, Tom managed to glance now and then at the foreman, Brown, lying not too far away, who seemed to be straining to hear as much as he could.

"Speck?" Edwards said.

"Probably drifted down," Speck replied.

"He was driven down," Tom corrected.

"Probably Indians," Speck tried again.

"They were white men," Tom corrected again.

"Probably rustlers," Speck tried one more time.

"Now we agree," Tom said. Speck turned his eyes back on him.

Speck then turned back to Edwards and said, "Rustlers probably drove 'im this far, and got spooked or somethin'. Maybe they were figurin' to come back for 'im. Anyways, that's what I was thinkin', so I decided to hold 'im until we could get 'im back or 'til they could come get 'im."

"Hold him with a herd of cows and heifers," Tom said.

"Seems to me," Speck said, turning back to face Tom, "a greenhorn who can't keep his cattle on his own range shouldn't be too particular about how others keep 'em for 'im."

Tom caught the full range of meaning in Speck's comment and look. His mind filled with clever and pointed rejoinders, but he passed on them, remembering that a solution that would stop any conflict between the two ranches right at the beginning was the goal. Besides, he was dealing with Edwards, the owner of the outfit, and he was better off not to get pulled down to Speck's level, in more ways than one.

Instead, he asked Edwards, "Is it your policy to have your men shoot at your neighbors?"

Edwards turned on Speck as if shocked, "You shoot at them?"

"Thought they were Indians or rustlers."

"Shot awful quick and often for somebody who expected us to come after our bull," Tom said to Edwards.

"I couldn't've known who they was," Speck said to Edwards, though he turned his expressionless look on Tom. "There're renegades all over this country."

"Lately," Tom replied, staring back at Speck.

"What do you mean by that, Schurtz?" Edwards demanded.

"Just what we been talkin' about here," Tom replied. "But look here, Edwards, your man shot my partner's horse. Would've shot my partner, too, except he ran out of bullets. We're takin' the boy's unbranded mustang in payment. If the horse is the boy's, I expect you to make it up to him. If it's the concern's, that's your business."

"That'll come out of your pay, Speck," Edwards said to the icy Speck. Tom had his doubts.

"We'll figure, then, if we need to chase down any strays headin' this way, your men'll look first before they shoot," Tom stated.

"We'll figure," Edwards responded, "you'll keep your cattle on your own range, like a cattleman ought." Tom knew that Edwards knew that even the best cattlemen had to deal with drifting herds, especially in hard winters when they drifted toward the south. Tom tempered his response, hoping that as long as Edwards did not lose face, even though Tom believed that he knew about the bull, that would be the end of it, and the two ranches could go on as they were, even if there weren't friendly feelings between them.

"And we'll figure," Tom said, a little self-conscious about the one "we'll figure" too many, "that as a cattleman, you'll respect and abide by the customs of the range and recognize our right to collect and return our cattle."

"I know the customs of the range," Edwards sneered back.

"We'll count on it," Tom replied. "Now my partner is goin' to keep that Sharps trained right on your belly until I'm up and over that hill.

If anyone tries anything, he'll be aimin' at you first." Tom noticed Billy and Speck both step back from Edwards when he said this.

"We'll talk again, Schurtz," Edwards seemed to threaten.

"I hope on better terms."

"We'll see."

Tom nodded, turned his horse around, and cantered off in the direction from which he had come. A whole mix of emotions washed through his head and chest and settled in his belly. In that mix was the relief of having the interview concluded as well as the anxiety of having his back turned to a group of men he considered to be little more than cutthroats. Beyond that was the larger background anxiety of where things really stood with the Edwards outfit. Tom had a sick feeling in his gut that this would not be the end. Edwards' final comment had done nothing to alleviate that feeling.

Still, it was some distance yet to the mound from which he had come, and as much as he wanted to gallop straight to it, he kept his canter as leisurely as he could, trying not to transmit his anxiety to Ross, so as not to let the Edwards outfit have any idea that there was even a trace of fear on the Seven Ox Seven side. Eventually, as he neared the mound, he picked up the pace a little and finally pulled in around behind it.

Once behind the mound, he rode as fast as the terrain would allow up to where Luke had been hiding behind a higher ridge. Luke was already down from the ridge and mounting his horse when Tom caught sight of him.

"How'd it go?" Luke asked him, as he rode up.

"I'll tell you," Tom said. "What did they do after I turned around?"

"They stayed where they were until you got pretty close to that hill down there. Then they got up, but it looked like Edwards stopped 'em from goin' for their guns or horses, so I let 'em be. Figured they were just bein' defiant."

"Let's get out of here," Tom said.

With that the two men rode toward the head of the canyon to the northwest. Tom was glad to have concluded the interview with Edwards when he had, as the shadows of the canyon walls were growing plenty long, and sunset was less than an hour away. They passed through the shadows with little concern about being seen from the

Edwards camp, as, from that point until they rode up the trail out of the canyon, they would be out of sight due to hills, mounds, and ridges. They knew the canyon, Tom and Luke, as they had scouted it on a few occasions in the past, and they were soon climbing the gradually ascending trail out of it. They stopped for a moment to look back at the camp, and could see no sign of anyone trying to follow them. It looked as if all hands were back at work to accomplish as much as possible in the waning light. Tom and Luke hoped it was a sign of things to come.

They rode up out of the canyon, relieved to have the whole thing behind them, and began to make their way through the Edwards cattle grazing up on top, when suddenly they both stopped. There, off to their left, in a herd of cows, calves, and heifers, was Augie, the other Hereford bull.

THE TWO MEN STARED IN NEAR DISBELIEF at the bull for a moment, and then, almost simultaneously, they wheeled their horses around and started back in the opposite direction, until Tom suddenly shouted, "Hold it," as he began to pull up to a stop. Luke continued on, so Tom shouted louder, "Hold it, Luke! Hold it!"

Luke pulled up, turned, and galloped back to where Tom had stopped.

"We don't want to go back down there," Tom said.

"Why not?" Luke demanded, the anger apparent in his eyes.

"Because . . . ," Tom began, but seeing that Luke was barely keeping himself from bolting away back down into the canyon, he shouted, "now listen," and he continued, talking loud and fast, as if to hold Luke physically with the force of his words, "last time we went down on our terms. This time we'd be goin' in on his terms. It's just what he wants, and he'd be ready for us. As it is, we settled the matter of the bull and the horse. We can count this bull in with that deal. If we go back down there, it opens things up again for the same deal, and we could come out a lot worse than we just did."

Luke was ruminating. "All right," he said, at last, "maybe you're right."

"Well, I hope so," Tom said, thinking it through out loud. "We just rode out of there with our bull back, our horse recompensed, Edwards' men rebuked, even if it was a sham, and we rode out alive.

And he knows we have some connection with Goodnight's outfit, which will probably make him less likely to bother us much in the future. We ride back in there now, and it's for the same problem, and he's suckered us in, and we could come out a lot worse off. He knew this bull was up here. He's probably hopin' we'll come back about it. He can just say it drifted, and he can go on again about how to be real cattlemen. It puts the whole thing back in his hands."

Luke was nodding his head. "You're right," he said.

Tom pulled around and said, as they started to ride toward the bull, "Let's get ol' Augie back to those superior Seven Ox cows and heifers, like he deserves."

Some time after they had cut out the bull and had him headed toward the Escondido, after they had covered some distance, after the sun had set, Tom said, "You know, I'll bet they took him that mornin' after we met their drive. I'll bet they took him when they trailed by the head of the canyon."

"I reckon so."

"I was sittin' out there watchin' 'em that mornin', knowin' they were goin' to pull somethin'. I told Andy. I knew it."

Then they were quiet, silhouette horsemen driving a silhouette bull against the orange western sky of twilight on the Llano Estacado of west Texas.

THE NEXT DAY, Luke, Tom, and Andy finished branding and doctoring in the lower canyon. They counted their blessings as they added the last batch of sixteen calves to those already branded and arrived at a total of forty-seven, raising the entire herd (with losses taken into account) to four hundred and forty, with most cows and heifers expected to drop calves by spring.

With the roundup complete, the men drove the beeves out onto the rolling plains to let cows and calves reunite and heal. In the evening, they drove the beeves back into the canyon, as a norther could blow down at any time and the beeves might need the protection of the canyon walls.

The day after that, it was time for Andy to leave for the JA. By now, Zachariah was more accustomed to not having Andy around and to spending more time with his father, Tom, and his mother and siblings.

Thus, when he said his good-bye to Andy, he was more composed, almost to the point of distraction, because he wanted to finish with the good-byes so that he could get back to his breakfast. Elizabeth was more composed, too, as she had adjusted more to her canyon life and to the maturing company of her children. And, of course, there was always Luke, the unfailing husband, and Tom, a true friend. Beyond that, she saw that Andy was growing into his manhood. It was right that he had gone out on his own. She could say good-bye to him now knowing that it was right, despite how much she would miss him. The tears came, nonetheless.

Andy made his good-byes and noticed, not without a slight pang in his heart, that he no longer held the same place in Zachariah's heart, but he accepted that as the natural result of age and growth. He noticed, too, that there was no hug from Elizabeth this time, just the tears. He knew she now saw him as a man. The younger children were still in bed when Andy left, and that was as it had often been.

Once outside, the men hitched up the smaller wagon and loaded up scythes, rakes, and pitchforks and started up the trail to the Staked Plains. Luke drove the wagon, while Tom and Andy rode alongside. Luke and Tom intended to cut the hay on the playa, which they would later bale for use in the winter. Andy was in no hurry to break from the camaraderie of his two friends. The men spoke of the migrating waterfowl that flew overhead in search of various playa lakes. They spoke of the winter that would come and of the increase of the herd, both at the Seven Ox Seven and at the JA.

In time, they passed through the cleft and out onto the plains. They drove on until they reached the playa and stopped short. The tall, broad-leafed grass that they had saved for hay was gone. Luke looked over at Tom, who looked back at him. They drove closer and stopped in the midst of where their grass had been.

"What's this?" Luke said. He sat looking at it for a moment, then jumped down from the wagon seat.

Tom was already off his horse, kicking through the nubs of grass. "Edwards," he said, nodding his head as a look of disgust soured his features. "He grazed that entire herd here."

"Must've," Luke concurred, with no sunnier disposition.

"This had to be deliberate. He did it to spite us," Tom said.

"Maybe, or they might've just seen it was good grass for grazin'," Luke said.

"No, they had plenty to graze all the way. This would have taken some time. They saw us with the beeves up here. They'd know what kind of hay that grass makes. It's deliberate," Tom countered.

"Well, that may be," Luke said. "But, in any case, it looks like we won't be doin' any hayin' up here."

Andy was kicking at some of the stubs of grass stalks near Tom. He turned and looked sideways at Tom and saw the anger in his face. He had never seen a look like that on Tom's face. He was seeing Tom in a light in which he had not seen him before. A few days before, not far from where they now stood, he had seen the beginnings of fear and now this anger. Andy felt a real concern for these friends of his, concern of a larger magnitude than the situation would seem to warrant.

There was no point in staying up on the plains, as the hay was all gone, so the men finally parted from Andy, sad to see him go. After he had ridden a little distance, Andy turned and watched his friends descend into their canyon, and a dark wave of an anxious sadness went through him. It went right through him and was gone, leaving the earlier concern behind. He sat and pondered a while, wondering if he should leave. He thought of his obligations at the JA and tried to put together the reasons he would stay. The night before, Tom and Luke had seemed to think this problem with Edwards was finished. And what had Edwards done? Well, it appeared that his outfit had borrowed a bull—well, two bulls—or that some of his men had. And they had let their herd graze on some hay. Tom seemed to be more concerned about it than Luke, and Luke did not seem to make much of the hay part. Both things had been done before Edwards had been confronted and had learned of their connection to the JA. That information itself may have put an end to the whole matter. And Andy was just up at the JA if they needed him or needed any help from the JA. Thus, after considering for a while, Andy turned around and rode off in the direction of the Palo Duro Canyon and the JA Ranch.

TWO WEEKS WENT BY in the Escondido and it was late October. There had been no more signs of trouble from the Edwards outfit, which was running the HE brand. The brand, like that of the JA, was intended to be read by pronouncing the letters, hence "H" "E", but Tom and Luke immediately took to calling the HE brand "HE" as the word "he," in some way like how the Irish might refer to someone as "himself." Thus, in pronunciation, the HE hands were the "he-hands," or "he-men," the HE cattle, the "he-beeves," etc.

Besides having no more trouble from the HE outfit, the grass in the canyon was good, and Tom and Luke had managed to lay up some hay from above and below the canyon, even if it was not from one particular playa. The herd was still increasing, even just after the roundup. All in all, things appeared to be going quite well.

Then a norther hit, and the canyon was blanketed in four inches of snow. Tom had seen no sign of cattle above the caprock the day before. The next day, he and Luke had been riding line outside the mouth of the canyon, getting the beeves off the prairie beyond and tucked well into the canyon, when, in the afternoon, they had seen the norther on the horizon. As there had been few cattle out on the prairie, their work had soon been done. So they had ridden for the ranch to attend to chores there, closing up all that needed to be closed up before the weather changed. That night the norther came upon them, and by morning, its four inches of snow lay fresh on the ground.

Tom and Luke rode out in the morning despite the cold and the wind and the biting snow that continued to fall, though nowhere near as heavily as earlier. They rode up on top of the caprock to cut for sign, getting hit by the full force of the wind of the high plains as soon as they emerged from the protection of the canyon. Absence of tracks in the cleft out of the canyon, the only way out of the head of the canyon, suggested there would be none up above, but they had ridden up, nevertheless, in case any cattle had left the canyon before the snow or while they had been in the lower end the day before. Cattle out on top of the caprock could drift all the way to the Pecos River, especially during such a storm, and they would need to catch up with them early and drift with them, if necessary, or possibly lose them altogether. The men rode the southern line of their range above the caprock, and even scouted out beyond it, and found no cattle; so they headed back toward the canyon.

They were relieved to escape from the unchecked wind of the high plains and return to those of the canyon, which, though they had plenty of force, especially in gusts, were nothing like those up above. The men made their way down to the eastern end of the canyon and scouted for sign along their southern line, checking beyond it, as well, for sign, though they did not expect to find much, as it had only been hours since they had herded most of the cattle well into the canyon.

In the days that followed they rode line faithfully, on some occasions needing to chase down cattle when sign was detected. They knew, though neither said it, that their diligence was due in part to the presence of the HE outfit to the south.

Elizabeth knew it too. She had heard, with concern, the men speak of the Edwards outfit on the evening of their first encounter. Then they had said nothing on the evening of their late arrival, after recovering the bulls. She could sense their anger though, and she would catch pieces of the quiet animated talk that they would exchange when they thought she was out of earshot, but when she would ask of the events of that day, they would say nothing about the incident involving the bulls. They were different, these men, whom she knew so well. Her husband, her intimate, had brooded the night of the incident of the bulls and for a few days after. Tom's personality was darker too, and edgy, like she had not seen him before. She noticed that after that day they were much more diligent, and just plain serious, about riding line. She also knew that the main reason they kept whatever it was to themselves was that they did not want to upset her, especially in her condition. And she wondered of what magnitude was this matter that weighed upon them that they took such pains not to let her know of it.

On one of the nights during the norther, after Tom had left and Luke and Elizabeth had retired to their room, Elizabeth finally broached the subject. She had seen that the darkness had, to some degree, loosened its hold on Luke and Tom in the several days previous, though they still rode line as diligently, and she believed that she must finally know what was her husband's concern.

"Luke," she began, as she combed out her hair before her mirror in a chair near her side of the bed, "why don't you stay in tomorrow instead of riding line? You and Tom have both nearly frozen your fingers and toes, and your ears. Can't you just leave those cattle alone for a day and then check for drifting, as before?"

Luke was sitting on his side of the bed with his back to Elizabeth. He had been pulling off his boots when Elizabeth had begun to speak.

He had stopped for a moment to listen to the question. Now, he lowered his head and said, "Uh, can't do that, Elizabeth. Herds increasin', and some of those ol' steers and cows, they got that Texas blood in 'em, and they want to get back south."

"But doesn't the canyon hold them back?"

"Mostly it does, except for the ends, and those few game trails. But see, with the increase, there's more cattle in the same area, and they just need to move."

Elizabeth turned around in her chair and said to her husband, "Luke."

Luke had just finished pulling off his boots when he heard her. He turned around at the slight change of tone in his wife's voice.

"Tell me, Luke," she said. "Tell me your concerns. I'm your wife, Luke. You cannot hide this from me. I know you don't want to upset me, but you don't know how upsetting it is to know that there is something of such concern to you that you do not tell me in order to protect me, and then not know what it is. When you leave, I worry all day long, and I have noticed that you and Tom take extra care about your guns."

Luke looked at her across their bed. He saw his lovely wife, her hair down and framing the face that manifested the beauty of a soul he had come to know, more beautiful now in her motherly condition. He looked at her from under lowered brows and then lowered his eyes beneath them, in embarrassment at having been discovered in his deception and in thought as he sought to know how to best serve her.

"Luke," his wife said again, and again he looked up into her face. "I'm your wife, Luke. Talk to me."

Luke kept his eyes lowered, considering for a moment, and then, without raising his eyes and in a voice halting due to uncertainty about whether or not he was doing the right thing, he said, "It's that outfit to the south, Elizabeth. They rustled our bulls . . ."

"Rustled our bulls!"

"Yes ma'am, those Herefords. The day after we had that first run-in with that Edwards, they took Augie. Must've been the next day or so, they took ol' Seventy-six."

"But, . . . how? . . . what?" Elizabeth said, as she looked around trying to grapple with the notion that people—neighbors, in fact—could and would just come into their canyon and steal their prized bulls.

"Augie, they just gathered and drove into their herd as they were trailin' by, as we were roundin' up down the canyon. Ol' Seventy-six, they had to be pretty sneaky about, as he was rustled from the far end not long after, during the time we were workin' that end."

"So this is very deliberate?" Elizabeth queried.

"It's deliberate, all right."

"Well, what happened to the bulls?"

"Tom and Andy and I fetched 'em."

"How did you fetch them? Wasn't it dangerous?"

"No, it wasn't dangerous, much," Luke understated, but Elizabeth was not satisfied with that answer. She questioned and cajoled him until he finally gave up the story to his wife, to whom he could not lie, leaving out as much of the more dangerous parts, including the shooting of his horse, as was possible.

"So," Luke concluded, "our neighbors to the south are not real neighborly, and we've been ridin' line lately just to avoid havin' the beeves drift their way, to save us some trouble."

Elizabeth had listened intently to the story. She knew that her husband had softened the story so as not to scare her. Still, what she had heard frightened her enough.

"But I don't think it's goin' to be a problem, Elizabeth," Luke said, when he noted the contraction of her features as her eyes studied intently the side of the bed. "They're miles to the south, and their stock'll tend to drift south, as well. We're just takin' extra care is all."

Elizabeth continued to study the side of the bed for a while, asking questions now and then, which she continued to do periodically even after they had got into bed. Finally, she asked no more. Luke lay thinking. He remembered what Tom had said after their first encounter with Edwards on that first day. He had said that things had just changed around there. Elizabeth, Luke thought, had just learned the same.

TWO DAYS LATER the norther departed, and not long after, so did its snow. The following day, Luke and Tom split up to ride line, with Tom taking his customary western end, and Luke taking the eastern. That night, after supper, Tom and Luke wandered off to the dugout (now a storage shed and workshop) to get some leather to mend bridles.

On the way there, out of earshot from the house, Tom asked Luke, "You see Seventy-six?"

"No," he said. "You?" He looked over at Tom and, clarifying, added, "See Augie?"

"Nope," said Tom. After a few more steps, he added, "Seems like a little more than coincidence."

"Yessir, it does," Luke assented, nodding his head with a look of concern.

They arrived at the dugout, opened the door, and entered. Luke dug around in the dark until he found the leather and tools. Then they stepped back out into the midautumn night, slightly chilly even without the norther. They stood outside the door and looked up at the sky.

"This time of year seems to bring out the stars, doesn't it?" Tom said.

"Yessir."

"No more of 'em than summer, but it seems the cooler air makes 'em sharper, or somethin'," Tom said. Then he considered for awhile and said, "Course, if it were summer, I'd probably be sayin' it was the warm air that brought out the stars."

"Eh, heh, heh, heh," Luke responded with his chuckle laugh, a welcome sound to both of them, considering the seriousness of the past several days. Tom was laughing, too, as his head nodded slightly up and down. After a little while, Tom changed the subject back to the earlier topic.

"You want to do a thorough scout of the rest of the canyon tomorrow and then go lookin'?" he said.

"Reckon we should," Luke agreed.

"With that snow on the ground, we wouldn't've missed their sign," Tom said. "Means they been missin' since before the snow, but we saw 'ol Seventy-six the day we tucked those beeves into the canyon, down below, and I saw ol' Augie the day before that. The only thing I can figure—and my mind's been figurin' on it all day—is that they took Augie while we were workin' down below, because if it would've been at night, I would've heard 'em. And they took ol' Seventy-six after we finished down below, but before the snow came that night. Makes me almost think they're watchin' us."

"You think they'd be watchin' us, Tom?" Luke turned a look on Tom that mixed incredulity with real concern.

"Well, how else can they snatch that bull in the few hours between when we finish workin' down there and the time the snow flies?"

"But to be watchin' us. They'd need all their men to set up camps before the cold and snow. Besides, watchin' us . . . That just seems mighty . . ."

"Obsessive," Tom finished the sentence for him.

"Right," Luke said, not really sure that that was the word he intended, but he had grown accustomed to Tom doing this now and then, with just the right word, and he trusted him now.

"Yeah, I know, Luke, it's not normal. It's more than just the bulls, Luke, and that's what bothers me. There's somethin' more sinister here than rustlin', bad as that is."

"You think so?"

"Yes sir, but the first thing we need to do is to get those bulls back."

"If they're gone," Luke qualified.

"That's right," Tom said, dropping some of the intensity from his voice. "And we can find that out tomorrow. If they're gone, and I expect they are, they been gone about a week. That's another little spot of time to have 'em in with cows and heifers."

They changed the subject again, and there, out under the stars, they again talked of plans as they had not done for some time, but this time that talk was tainted by an unstated foreboding that had never tainted it before.

In time, it was darker, the stars brighter, and it was time to return to the house. They did, and some time later Tom rode home, and all settled down, as best they could, to their rest.

THE NEXT DAY, Tom hurriedly rode line up on the plains and then began a thorough search of the canyon, starting just above where he had left off the day before, so as not to miss anything. Luke did the same from the other end of the canyon. By evening, they had concluded that the bulls were gone.

Outside again, after supper, leaning against the hitching post in front of the dugout, they both admitted that there was little possibility that either bull was in the canyon, an occurrence too coincidental for chance alone. They knew they would need to go after the bulls, but they also knew that this time there was no Andy.

"I'm goin' to have to go alone, Luke," Tom said.

"Can't let you do that, Tom."

"We don't have a choice, Luke," Tom responded. "Andy's gone. He's not here to ride to the JA. If we go to the JA to get him, we'd have to let Goodnight know why we're takin' his hand, and with Edwards' word against ours, we've got nothin' really to stand on. There're rustlers in this country. Goodnight himself has had trouble with 'em. Andy even said so. Indians could show up at any time. Edwards' story is plausible, and we'd end up lookin' like we're overreactin' to some driftin' bulls."

Luke considered this. He shook his head. "I don't like it, Tom. I don't like the idea of you facin' that outfit alone."

"They won't do anything, especially now that they know we're connected to the JA. Edwards won't do anything up front like that. It'll be more of this petty stuff, drivin' off the bulls when we're not lookin', stuff like that. That's what he'll be doin'. He's tryin' to get us to react in a way that he can react to."

Luke was not so sure, but eventually Tom convinced him that the only way was for Tom to go alone. Tom would leave the next morning. Luke would stay near the house for the protection of the family, doing some work around the house so as not to arouse Elizabeth's suspicions. They would not let Elizabeth know at this point. As it was, Luke did not like the way she had been affected by the news of the bulls that she had got out of him a few nights before. He sensed a subtle worry in her, especially in the way she watched him and Tom if they went out of her presence together, like she suspected there was trouble. He regretted that he had told her anything. He would not let her know this time. If Tom did not come back by the following morning, Luke would lock up the family in the house and ride to the JA for help.

In the morning Tom left. Elizabeth had sensed a tension in the men as she had served them breakfast, though she had said nothing to them. She had pushed Luke to tell her before. She knew that the news had affected her. She knew that Luke knew it too. If he was not telling her something now, she could not force herself to push him to tell her; and beyond that, there was a part of her that did not want to know, a part of the expectant mother that wanted to live in the peace they had so enjoyed in their canyon until the drastic change of the last couple weeks. Still, she knew something was wrong. Her quiet anxiety was edging toward quiet fear.

Tom and Luke had gone out of the house, and Elizabeth had watched the two men from the window. She had read some significance in that they had shaken hands before Tom had mounted up and departed. Luke had not returned to the house, and she knew that he was avoiding her.

TOM RODE UP AND OUT OF THE CANYON. Once out on the high plains, he headed south at a comfortable pace. In time, he topped out on a low rise and could see, at some distance before him, the Edwards herd. He could also see, very shortly after spotting the herd, that they were being tended by two HE hands. This he was able to see so soon after spotting the herd, because one of the hands, on spotting Tom, rode at a gallop toward the small canyon that held their ranch, the canyon that would be called Edwards Canyon.

Tom's immediate reaction to the herder's sudden and speedy departure was to realize that these herders had been waiting for him and to realize that this did not surprise him at all: in fact, it too well fit his expectations. He could see, when his eyes settled on the spot from where the herder had left, that the other herder remained. So it was not out of fear that the first had fled. The second was remaining to meet Tom. The first had left to inform Edwards, Tom was sure.

Tom was furthermore not surprised, as he approached, to eventually make out the form of Augie very near the herder. Nor was he surprised to find, upon approaching closer, that Augie was in among cows and heifers. He envisioned the same scenario at the eastern end of the canyon, with Seventy-six also guarded by two herders, even with so much work to be done.

Tom had opened and tucked back the cover of his rifle scabbard before he had left the Escondido. Though he did not think that he would need the Winchester, he wanted it to be ready to the hand in case he did. The six-gun in his holster was also ready.

As he drew closer to the herder who remained, he recognized him as Henderson, the man who had untied the other two HE men the last time Tom had visited the outfit. He was a good-sized man, about Tom's height, lean like Tom but more filled out. His skin had been tanned by the elements to a degree that set off well the light blue eyes that awaited Tom's arrival.

"Howdy," Tom said as he pulled up in front of Henderson.

"Howdy," the man replied, displaying some of his straight white teeth. Those teeth almost appeared to want to show off some more, as lines around the man's mouth and eyes suggested that humor was a close companion.

"You've got my bull," Tom said.

"Just watchin' 'im for ya," Henderson responded, without any sign of animosity.

Tom's tension was lessening some in this man's presence. He almost felt friendly toward him and almost felt that the feeling would be reciprocated.

"You know how he came to be here?" Tom asked him.

"Drifted with the norther," Henderson replied, adding with a subtle show of teeth and wrinkling of lines around his eyes, "so I'm told."

Tom had been looking at Augie. With Henderson's comment, he turned to face the man and saw the smile in his eyes and felt his calmness. Maybe things did not have to be so bad with the Edwards outfit after all.

"Drifted all by himself, without leavin' any sign in the snow, just after I'd seen him securely in the upper reaches of the Escondido? Drifted right in here with just cows and heifers?" Tom said.

"So I'm told."

Tom nodded a light smile at this reply. Henderson held his own smile, careful not to let it deepen any.

"Well," Tom said, "any objection to me driftin' him back to where he belongs?"

Tom's choice of verb was not lost on Henderson, and his smile deepened a little bit despite his best efforts.

"He's your bull."

"I'm glad to hear someone remembers that," Tom said. Then he remembered the other herder who had ridden for the canyon. "Where'd your partner go?"

"To get Edwards."

"What's your job?"

"To keep you here."

"How'd you intend to do that?"

"Didn't really. Reckoned you'd wait for 'im. Yonder he comes," Henderson said, nodding to his right in the direction of the canyon.

Edwards was on his way with his foreman, Brown, and the herder who had gone to get him. He was working his horse pretty hard and arrived with the force of the animal's speed behind him, pulling up right in front of Tom, with Tom's horse stepping back in reaction. He was talking before his horse had completely stopped.

"What kind of trouble you tryin' to make this time, Schurtz?" he demanded.

"No trouble," Tom said, as a bit of anger mixed with the nervousness he had felt in anticipation of this confrontation. Brown and the other man pulled up alongside on either side of Edwards. The other man was a small-framed, bony sort of a man with a large, long nose and shaggy blond hair that stuck out from under his hat. He was a number of years older than Tom and had the appearance of an old boy. "Just lookin' for our bulls," Tom concluded.

"You better not be intendin' to accuse my men of rustlin' again, Schurtz."

"Then maybe you can explain to me how our bull got here and, for that matter, where our other bull is."

"Seems plain enough that your bull drifted with the norther. As for your other bull, if you can't keep track of your own stock, don't be expectin' us to do it for you," Edwards responded as if offering a challenge.

"Drifted with the norther, without leavin' any sign, without any other stock driftin' with him, except, I expect, the other Hereford bull at the other end of the canyon? Drifted right in here with your cows and heifers?"

"That's right, Schurtz," Edwards sneered, "and I don't appreciate your pollutin' my stock with that inferior breed. This keeps up, we're goin' to have to take some action."

Tom looked at the hulking Brown on Edwards' right-hand side and saw his little brown eyes seem to grow smaller in regarding Tom. The slight, shaggy man on the other side of Edwards appeared to make up in eagerness what he may have lacked in ability. Tom glanced over at Henderson, who had remained off to the side of the other three (and who appeared to be somewhat off to the side in his sentiments, as no animosity appeared to register with him, but rather a low-level concern and preparedness).

"What do you mean by 'action'?" Tom asked Edwards.

"I mean some means to keep your bulls from pollutin' my stock. Somethin'll have to be done."

"Like what?"

"That'll take some deliberation," Edwards replied. "But it's got to be somethin' that'll preserve my stock." He stared at Tom for a moment with a hint of his sneer. "But," he finally said, "I'm sure it won't happen again, will it, Schurtz?"

Tom kept a calm exterior, though his emotions were roiling inside. Anger flared up in him so hot that a part of him wanted to grab the older though much larger Edwards off that horse and throw him to the ground and stomp on him. Edwards and the two on either side of him saw hints of that heat in Tom's eyes and were enjoying it.

But anger did not reside as the sole emotion inside Tom. Down beneath it, a dark lick of fear also made its presence known inside him. Edwards had not only stolen, if only temporarily, their two blooded bulls, but he showed every indication that he would do so again, and he was offering a thinly veiled threat of some further course of action should he and his men continue to be successful in stealing the Seven Ox Seven bulls. It was a very neat little scheme that Edwards had concocted, and in that instant, Tom could think of no way to foil it. If a third party were brought in—and the most likely one, given their remote location, was the JA—it would be one party's word against the other's over whether or not one party's bulls had a tendency to drift. And that would be the case only if the Edwards party would even admit that the bulls had been found on their land in the first place. It was the kind of a dispute that a third party could tire of in a short amount of time. On their own, Luke and Tom could spend the rest of their time guarding the bulls, or they could corral them, which would defeat their purpose. They did eventually intend to contain them for more control in breeding, but until then, they wanted to get as much out of the bulls as they could reasonably expect.

Those considerations in mind, Tom had to take an immediate course of action. At least three armed men, possibly four (he wasn't sure about Henderson) sat in opposition to him. He could not prove that they had rustled his bull, though he and they both knew that they had. There was not much he could say to discourage future thefts of the bulls or whatever further action Edwards intended to take.

"Well," he finally said, "I'll be driftin' this bull back to where he was taken." Tom purposely used the same verb he had used for Henderson's benefit.

Edwards ignored the first verb and settled on the second. "What do you mean, 'taken'?"

Tom had already turned and started to cut out the bull from the herd. "Stands as I said it," he said, taking away at least one small victory from what appeared to be a major defeat with the potential to grow into an even worse defeat.

Edwards could not let that small victory conclude the meeting. "With that attitude," he yelled through his sneer to the departing Tom, "don't you even consider cuttin' through my canyon to go huntin' your other bull."

Tom had no further response. He gathered Augie, pointed him toward the Escondido, and was on his way, with frustration, anger, and that little imp, fear, growing within him as he rode.

When he arrived at the Escondido, he drove Augie farther down the canyon than was the custom, well below the Stuart home, staying far to the north to avoid being seen from the Stuart house. He left Augie among a herd of heifers, cows, and calves, and then headed back to the Stuarts'. It was afternoon when he arrived at the house. The family had already eaten, but Luke was nursing a cup of coffee and Elizabeth was still cleaning up. She quickly served Tom a plate of turkey, potatoes, and beans.

Luke sat with Tom at the table, and the two men awkwardly tried to make conversation, as they had learned to do, without mentioning the one topic they truly wanted to talk about, the retrieval of the bulls. Elizabeth continued to clean up the dishes at the counter, pretending not to be aware of the men's uncharacteristic awkwardness. Thus, deception continued to creep its way into the family and friendships that made up the Seven Ox Seven community. Tom ate hurriedly and nervously, and shortly had his plate cleaned up. He carried it over to where Elizabeth was washing and gave it to her, thanked her, and turned down her offer of more food, offering further thanks as he did so. Then he and Luke left the house, Zachariah following them out. Elizabeth had turned to watch them go, a new and subtle listlessness betrayed in her features.

Once outside, Tom and Luke walked toward the pens beyond the house to the north, Zachariah tagging along and asking questions about what they were going to do. The men answered distractedly until they arrived at the pens, where Luke picked up Zachariah and set him on a fence rail.

"What is it you want to know, Zack?" Luke asked him.

"What are you and Uncle Tom goin' to do, Daddy?"

"Well, we're not sure yet, but more'n likely I'm goin' to finish up the roof on the springhouse," Luke replied, referring to that outbuilding near Schurtz Creek that had slowly gone up, as time had allowed, and was finally, due to circumstances, nearing completion. "You're intendin' to keep helpin' me, aren't you?"

"Yessir," came the reply from the young open face.

"Then why don't you go on over there and see if you can't pick out the straightest logs from those we gathered for the rafters."

"Can I talk with you and Uncle Tom first, Daddy?"

"Well, I need you to take care of those logs right now, son. So, you git." Luke lifted the boy down and gave him a light shove on the behind.

"Yessir," Zachariah said as he ran off with a smile.

Luke and Tom watched him, Luke with his elbow resting on a fence rail. "Wouldn't it be nice to have that boy's concerns, Tom?"

"Hmh," Tom offered in return, as he watched the boy depart and let his head nod lightly to accommodate the wistful sentiments. Then he turned from those sentiments to face Luke and to relate what had occurred that morning.

Luke listened thoughtfully with his head down, his eyes studying the ground while Tom spoke. When Tom had finished relating the encounter with Edwards, the expression on Luke's face, still bent toward the ground, indicated that he had grasped the seriousness of the position in which Edwards had placed them.

"So," he said, "he's rustlin' our bulls and tellin' us if we keep lettin' him rustle 'em, he's goin' to do somethin' worse."

"That's about it," Tom replied.

"What a son of a gun."

"He's that."

"So what are we goin' to do?" Luke said, turning to face Tom.

"That's what we're goin' to have to figure out," Tom said. "For now, I've got to go back and get Seventy-six off the eastern end of their range. But we're goin' to have to come up with some kind of a plan, because this ain't goin' to go away, and it's goin' to get worse."

Luke nodded his head, looking down again, as the various ramifications of their present circumstances continued to accrue in his mind. He thought of Elizabeth and wondered how he could keep from telling her, and whether or not he should, and what if he did not.

"Anyways, I've got to get after that other bull," Tom said as he leaned away from the fence against which he had been leaning. He and Luke started walking back toward the house, where he had tied his horse at the rail. "We can think on this some and figure what we're goin' to do. For the time bein', I've got Augie east of here a ways, by Buzzard's Draw. I'll tuck Seventy-six farther in, as well. But we do have some figurin' to do."

Luke agreed, with more quiet nodding. They parted with a handshake, as they had that morning, and Tom rode off down the canyon. Luke turned and headed toward the springhouse, where his young son was doing his part to build up their ranch.

TOM RODE TOWARD THE END OF THE CANYON and, once out on the prairie beyond, headed toward Edwards Canyon, eventually making his way through Edwards cattle. When he did finally see Seventy-six, he could see that the bull was herded with a group of cows and heifers and was guarded by a herder, but when that hand spotted Tom, he rode as fast as he could away from the bull and into the canyon toward the ranch headquarters.

Tom did not know what to make of this change in behavior. Was the hand going to fetch help? And, if so, for what? Was he going to report to Edwards for some other reason? Was he just afraid, after having seen what had happened to Speck and Billy? Tom's mind worked these possibilities through. Regardless, retrieving Seventy-six turned out to be a relatively simple operation, despite its nuisance. By the end of the day, ol' Seventy-six was settled farther into the canyon, and Tom and Luke were working on possible ways to stop the Edwards rustling.

As time passed, Tom and Luke did devise different means to keep track of the bulls. At first, they decided to keep both bulls closer to the house, but not so close that Elizabeth would be suspicious. They would daily check the bulls, despite their other chores. Among those other chores was the increased line riding that they had begun so as to avoid any other mischief from the Edwards outfit. Hence, the threat of the Edwards outfit was having a significant impact on how they were allotting their time. Despite the daily check of the bulls and the increased line riding, as soon as the first Saturday night arrived, the bulls were rustled, this time both of them being taken through the eastern or lower end of the canyon.

The theft was not discovered until Monday, because Luke and Tom had determined that, with all the precautions they had taken, they could still observe the Lord's day by abstaining from work. Upon discovery of the theft, Tom and Luke left on angry impulse for Edwards Canyon without even thinking of plans for the family's safety, in contrast to the priority they had given to the family's safety in the past. They located the bulls not far from where Tom had recovered Seventy-six the time before. Once again, the herder—who this time happened to be the blond, bony man Tom had seen with Edwards the last time he had retrieved Augie— rode away from the bulls as soon as he spotted Tom and Luke, and he rode toward the HE headquarters as fast as he could. Tom and Luke collected the two bulls, as Tom had with Seventy-six not long before, and returned with them to the Escondido without any sign of repercussions following the herder's departure.

This behavior would become a pattern to which Tom and Luke would grow accustomed over the course of the next several months. The bulls or a bull would disappear; they would go to retrieve the bull; and, just as the herder would see them, the herder would depart at full gallop, so that there was not a chance of catching him unless they chased him to the ranch. In fact, such was the case with every Edwards hand, whether guarding the bulls or just riding line. As soon as an HE hand would see Tom or Luke, he would ride as fast as he could toward the ranch headquarters.

Tom and Luke had determined not to give in. After the Saturday night rustling, they had decided that they would check the bulls even on Sunday, though this added a further deception to their dealing with

Elizabeth, as they did not tell her the real reason they were working on Sunday. When a few weeks passed without incident, and they once again observed a Sunday without work, the bulls were rustled again on the following Saturday night.

Over the course of the next several months, Luke and Tom tried one means after another to curtail the rustling. They would corral the bulls at night, but the men would weary of that regime because of its nuisance and because it restricted the bulls' availability for servicing cows and heifers. They would corral them around the clock, but that drastically limited their servicing of cows and heifers, requiring Tom and Luke to gather and drive estrous cows and heifers to them. It also required the men to feed hay to these bulls of a breed that had as one of its primary positive traits a marked capacity to fatten on grazing alone in even some of the most inhospitable lands and climates. They took turns guarding them on the range, but that was monotonous and wasted a man's entire labor for that day. One thing after another they tried, often returning to a previous method when a new one failed, but every time they abandoned a method, sooner or later, the bulls or a bull would disappear, and they would execute their recovery routine.

And routine it did become. Sometimes the period between thefts would be longer, as if the Edwards outfit might be temporarily occupied with something else, but eventually the thefts would resume, and again, Tom, sometimes with Luke, would ride to Edwards Canyon to fetch the animal and watch the cowhand guarding the bull ride at full gallop toward headquarters. Despite the different lapses of time between thefts or between when they would be less diligent in protecting the bulls and a theft, or perhaps because of the differences in those lapses, eventually, as a certain uneasy feeling settled into him, Luke became convinced that Tom had been right, that they were being watched. The timing of the thefts and their failure to catch the rustlers in the act, even though they had followed their sign soon after the rustling, made coincidence just too unlikely. He realized too, as Tom had, that their setting in a deep canyon, where a person could watch from a variety of places and avoid detection, made them especially vulnerable to observation. And, like Tom, he wondered exactly what kind of man, what kind of outfit they were up against that would sacrifice the labor of at least one of its men, and maybe more, to watch them so as to steal their bulls, apparently for spite with the added benefit of breeding, when there was so much work to be done.

As the rustling and recovery cycle did take on the characteristics of a routine, that routine began to have its effects on the Seven Ox Seven Ranch community. Slowly, subtly, life at the Seven Ox Seven began to revolve around the bulls. Luke and Tom had become reactors in the Henry Edwards game. Soon they were working far more and accomplishing far less because so much of that work was going toward their part in the rustling game. When they were not working on that game, they were trying to devise new ways to counter their opposition, or they worried about what would be the next step. They grew less communicative at meals, and they seemed to be devoted to their own little pact, slipping out right after meals, away from the family, to discuss their latest plan or the results of the latest one before that.

The men had less time for the children, as they were often in bed by the time Luke returned to the house and Tom departed for his own. The children no longer easily slid into their father's lap or hung on his hand, as they had in the past, sensing from his demeanor and from recent rebuffs that his availability to them was not as it had been.

Most significant, though, due to the sacramental nature of the bond, was the effect the Edwards rustling game was having on the relationship between Luke and Elizabeth, husband and wife. Elizabeth suspected that the bulls were being rustled. She had been informed by Luke of the first occurrence. Since then, she had observed the men's behavior and had heard bits and pieces of conversation, enough to feel confident in her suspicion. Still, now excluded from the men's talk about the ranch, she was left alone in her suspicion without benefit of the truth, and her suspicion was thus free to expand to the limit of her imagination, allowing therein an expansion of that great debilitant, fear. Nevertheless, she did not ask Luke any more about it. She realized that he was avoiding talking to her, even after she had coaxed him into telling her about the rustling at the beginning of the whole game. She knew that he had not wanted to tell her then, to protect her and the baby, and that she had encouraged him anyway. She knew that a certain lethargy had been growing in her ever since, and that Luke could see it as well. She was sure that he regretted having told her in the first place, and because of that and because of her fear of losing the life they had had before the Edwards outfit had moved in, she did not ask. And yet, she knew, and Luke knew that she knew, but they did not speak of it. They no longer went to bed at the same time, avoiding that easy talk that had long been such an integral part of their life together.

Thus, by his game did Henry Edwards subtly manipulate the community of the Seven Ox Seven. Their work now centered around guarding and retrieving their bulls, to such a degree that they hardly questioned any more the necessity of that priority. Their social life, too, fell victim to this priority, so that even the marriage at the center of the Stuart family was assailed by it, with secrecy, avoidance, distrust, fear, and loneliness filling in where once their opposites had dwelled. Life at the Seven Ox Seven carried on in this way, sliding slowly, subtly, ever more deeply into the dark mood of this new priority.

Advent and Christmas provided somewhat of a break from this routine. Preparations for the holy day, especially with the children involved and Elizabeth's pregnancy showing more every day, helped make the adults more open to the theological virtues of faith, hope, and love that defied the fear, despair, and anger that had been generated in their reaction to the Edwards game. Still, even the grand spirit of that sacred observance only managed to lift the settlers slightly and temporarily out of their gloomy grind. This was particularly true for Elizabeth, for whom the shortening days prior to Christmas (more often overcast at that time of the year) and the cold had only served to exacerbate the cold darkness that had been subtly replacing the warmth and light that had characterized their canyon settlement— even during the earliest days of adjustment—before the arrival of their neighbors to the south.

Nevertheless, it was the arrival of persons other than the neighbors to the south that provided for the most dramatic break from the routine, if not from its darkness. This arrival occurred two days after Christmas. Snow covered the region, and bitter cold had descended from the north. Luke and Tom had left early that morning to ride line. They had been riding line every day, even on Christmas, not only to monitor the bulls but to keep any member of the herd from drifting to the south to escape the cold. Though such drifting was a common occurrence that was eventually rectified in the spring roundup if not before, Luke and Tom were not placing any faith in a later rectification with the Edwards outfit. Consequently, they rode line diligently and kept the Seven Ox Seven cattle well within the safety of the canyon during the cold.

On this particular day, Elizabeth waited until midafternoon and then bundled up Zachariah and Rachel. Then she sent them out into the yard in front of the house, despite the low temperature, to play and exhaust some of the pent-up energy accumulated in their little persons during several days of being housebound in the cold. Elizabeth did not intend to leave the children outside very long, and she intended to watch them from the windows for signs that they were getting cold. Still, these intentions were not so easily fulfilled, as young Robert, now nearly eighteen months, had plenty of his own energy to relieve. Elizabeth, therefore, had her hands full playing with her baby son, which served, as it usually did, to push the melancholy from her mind in favor of the immediate joy and laughter of the playful toddler.

All at once the joy and laughter were shattered by a cry unlike anything she had ever heard from her oldest son, and in that cry was uttered a word that drove fear, like a stake, into her heart.

"Indians! Mamma! Indians!"

For an instant Elizabeth froze. Then suddenly she was on her feet and at the door in time to open it and have her son and daughter rush in. With a presence of mind she could not later explain, she barred the door as soon as it was shut and then turned to her son, who was still shouting, "Indians, Mamma!" and firmly grabbed him by both shoulders and said to him, "Where?"

"There!" he shouted, pointing toward the easternmost window on the north side of the house. Elizabeth turned and hurried to the window. What she saw pushed the fear, now nearly terror, deeper into her heart, from where it radiated out to every part of her body in something like a shivering weakness that raced out to the ends of every extremity. A band of roughly fifty Indians was riding westward up the canyon. They had not yet reached the pens and barn north of the house. They appeared not to have heard Zachariah—which was no surprise, as the strong winds carried away or blotted out most sounds beyond one's immediate vicinity. Elizabeth was right in assuming that they were Comanche, and as she watched them, memories rose in her mind of tales she had heard of various killings, kidnappings, and tortures at the hands of that people.

It was true that Elizabeth had fed three Indians on another occasion, when, on a warm day, they had come upon the children and her in the yard. That time all had gone well, but there had only been three Indians, and it had been apparent that white men were not far away. She knew, from talk of surveyors and Goodnight and Andy, that, even since they had been on the reservation, some Comanche had tried to force their way into settlers' houses. Besides, watching this group of Indians as they entered the yard, Elizabeth felt in her heart that they were of a different purpose than had been that earlier group of three.

And, suddenly, Elizabeth knew that she must act. She flew into action, running from one window to the next securing the solid oak shutters. Then she returned to the first window and watched the Indians through the gun hole in the shutter. As the Comanche neared the pens and barn, they stopped to look at those structures, and then they looked toward the house.

Elizabeth watched them, hoping that they would think the house abandoned and then ride away, but to her dismay, they began to ride in the direction of the house, spreading out as they did so. All at once, she thought of the stove and the fireplace and of smoke coming from the chimney. Though there was no fire in the fireplace, a hot fire burned in the stove. She hurried toward the stove to put out the fire, but realized, as she did so, that the smoke had surely already been seen and that dowsing the fire would only make the smoke worse and the house cold. She had to accept that the Indians knew that someone was in the house.

By the time she returned to the window, it seemed like the Comanche were everywhere. One group within her view had stopped at the picket horse corral, and one man was already standing on the ground examining the padlock. The rest of the Comanche rode around the grounds.

Elizabeth ran to where she had left little Robert, at the sound of Zachariah's alarm, and scooped up the child, whose face still held the wide-eyed expression that had set into his features from the moment he had witnessed his mother's reaction to Zachariah's cry. She gathered Zachariah and Rachel, as well, and hurried all three children into the bedroom, where she made them lie under the bed so as not to be seen by anyone looking in one of the gun holes. In the bedroom, she immediately thought of the windows on both ends of the upstairs and rushed up the stairs to close and bar the shutters over those windows. Those secured, she knew that the only way to gain entrance to the home of stone, lime mortar, and oak was to burn the door, shutters, or roof, and she would have plenty of time to shoot perpetrators before they could gain access in that manner.

Shoot. Yes, she might need to shoot other human beings, and she would shoot, she knew in that instant, if it meant the protection of those children God had given her to protect. To shoot, she would need a gun. She rushed back downstairs, and she admonished the children to remain silent as she flew through the bedroom into the main room of the house. There, she pulled down the Winchester from above the fireplace. This she nearly dropped, as at that moment, someone pounded on the stout oak door, the sound resonating as poorly as would be expected from so thick a door of solid oak set in solid stone. She froze for a moment, and then, as if wondering what she was waiting for, she took down a box of shells from the mantel and quickly loaded the rifle. Then, carrying the gun and shells, she hurried to the window next to the door to look out. Even before she reached the window, pounding again fell upon the door.

Once at the window, she looked through the gun hole to see three or four Comanche men standing on the porch in front of the door. Many more were mounted behind them. Most of the men wore buckskin tunics and breechcloths of various colors and leggings. Moccasins or buffalo-hide boots covered their feet. Over their shoulders they wore buffalo robes or blankets. One man wore a white man's suit of clothes, including vest and suit coat. On his feet he wore moccasins, and over his shoulders, a buffalo robe. A few of the others wore one or more articles of white man's dress.

Looking beyond the men on the porch and those in the yard, she saw a group of men taking food items, like butter and meats, from the springhouse. Watching this pillaging, Elizabeth was struck by the irony of keeping food in the springhouse when all of it, due to the weather, would be frozen at this time anyway. Still, one never knew what to expect of the weather in the Panhandle of Texas, so the springhouse proved useful even in winter. She could not help but wish that the Comanche would leave her ceramics and crockery behind, as they made such suitable containers, especially those with the lids. This hope was dashed as she saw the men take containers and all, and mount their horses with the spoils.

The men on the porch were talking to each other and to the man wearing the suit of clothes, who was still sitting on his horse. Elizabeth noticed, as she watched this man, that Zachariah's and Rachel's small footprints were still clearly visible in the snow.

Pounding fell again upon the door, registering this time the impatience of the pounder. Elizabeth's heart jumped again, and she heard herself suck in her breath with a quiet "huh" as she turned away from the window and fortified herself against the stone wall between the window and door. Then there was more impatient pounding. She turned back to the gun hole at the window and, this time, let out a small cry and pulled herself away, when she found herself looking right into the face of one of the men, barely six inches away, on the other side of the glass. The grim expression on that face and the fact that he had seen her and had looked into her eye brought again to her mind, in a rush, thoughts of the worst she had heard about the Comanche.

She was nearly paralyzed with fear as she sat against that wall, all the strength in her body feeling as if it were retracting into her center, leaving the shivering fear in its place. She felt the gun in her hand, but, though she still held it firmly, she felt her inner self recoil from it and all that it meant, all that would be required of her in the present situation. It was then that she heard herself praying, in her heart, whispering with her lips, "Lord, show me what to do. Give me the courage and strength to do it. Watch over my children and me. Let us not come to harm. And please, Lord, bless these people outside, bring out the best in them, and let them not harm us."

This prayer in her heart was barely finished when she was aroused from her spot by the sound of pounding, but a different kind of pounding, farther away and sharper, coming from the north of the house. She hurried to the gun hole of the window from which she had first seen the Comanche. Through that hole, she saw one of the men striking at the padlock on the picket horse corral with the ax that Luke had left in the stump where he split firewood.

Elizabeth felt her grip on her gun tighten, as she considered whether she should fire a warning shot through her glass window to scare off the Comanche from stealing their horses. Instantly, she knew that she should not fire, as if she had been told not to do so, though she had heard nothing. She also realized that her fear had left her. She realized that she was prepared to do what was required of her, and that she would know what that was, and that, at that present moment, it was to not fire the rifle.

With new confidence and calmness, Elizabeth looked back out at the men at the corral. As she watched them, she heard shouts from another of the men, from the direction of the yard in front of the dugout to the west of the house. The man with the ax dropped it and swung back onto his horse and rode around to the front of the house. The rest of those on horseback followed him. Some of them, Elizabeth was seeing for the first time, were women, some with children, and one in particular, huddling over a small child in front of her, was coughing in a way that brought out feelings of sympathy in the expectant mother ensconced inside the warm house.

Nevertheless, Elizabeth needed to keep in mind the potential danger of her present situation. She returned to the gun hole in the window next to the door. She looked quickly out of it, and seeing no Comanche face peering into her eye, she did not retreat from the hole. The Comanche were off the porch and standing in the yard and, together with those on horseback, were looking up the trail to the west. She saw that some had raised their guns. All at once she thought of Luke, and she gasped. She thought of Tom, as well, but of Tom as if he were wrapped up in the thought of Luke. With that thought, she immediately prepared to fire a warning shot. She lifted the gun to shove it through the gun hole and through the window, but, as before, something stopped her.

She pulled the gun down and looked back out the gun hole. Suddenly, two men rode into the yard, from the trail to the west, one of them shouting, "How, how." Though these men were bundled against the cold, Elizabeth recognized her husband as the man who was shouting.

The two men rode in with their hands up. As soon as they stopped in the yard, Luke yelled over the wind toward the house, "Elizabeth, everything's fine. Do not open the door, no matter what." Then he turned back toward the Indians on the horses.

Elizabeth felt a wave of relief pass through her with these words from her husband, despite the fact that Luke and . . . Luke and who?

Who was that other man with Luke? Though he was bundled, all of a sudden it was clear to Elizabeth that he was not Tom. This other man was speaking to the Comanche. She watched this man and tried to hear what he was saying, and finally realized that the second man was Andy.

What Elizabeth could not hear all that well she could not have understood, as Andy was speaking to the Comanche in broken Apache (which one of the men did understand), at first, and then in Spanish, when it was discovered that one of the women was a Mexican captive, who had obviously been with the Comanche for some time but still spoke Spanish exceptionally well.

Andy was telling the Mexican woman that another band of Comanche, under Quanah Parker, had treated with Charles Goodnight in the Palo Duro Canyon and had reached an agreement for the provision of beef, until they could locate some buffalo to hunt. He told her that the United States cavalry was on its way, and that it would be in their best interest to make their way to the Palo Duro and to take up Goodnight on his offer while it stood and before the cavalry arrived.

The Comanche listened to what Andy had to say, asking questions and making statements of their own, all through the Spanish-speaking interpreter. They wanted him to know that the land on which they all stood was theirs. Andy answered this point, and others that followed, based on coaching he had received from Charles Goodnight. He understood that they believed that the land was theirs, but that the governor ("great Captain") of Texas made the same claim. The people who now lived there had bought the land from the State of Texas and had paid for it. So the Comanche had to settle the matter with the State of Texas, and the settlers in those parts would be willing to deal with whoever was the proven owner.

They asked him if he and Luke were Texans. Andy had been warned by Goodnight about the Indians' hatred of the *Tejanos*, so he informed them that he was from Mexico (which really was the place of his birth) and that Luke was from Tennessee and that another person there was from Wisconsin. The Indians were dubious about this answer, but after Andy answered several questions about these other places, with Luke's help, they let the matter lie.

Then the Comanche asked if these white people had settled there to kill buffalo. Andy assured them that they were there to raise cattle.

As he did so, he could not help but feel a pang of sadness for these Indian people who had left the reservation at Fort Sill in Indian Territory because they were not being given sufficient rations, these people who only a few years before had lived freely off the plenty provided by that great beef of the prairie, the buffalo. He thought of the tons of meat that had lain rotting on the prairies in the wake of white men who had shot millions of the great beasts for hides alone. He thought of the great migratory herds, millions and millions, that had been reduced, in a few years of greed and waste, to small, scattered herds. The red man had committed his crimes, as had the white, Andy knew, but as he looked at this remnant of a humbled people, he could not help but think of how unnecessary was the great waste of the buffalo slaughter and these people's present hunger.

The Comanche questioned further about whether the settlers were there to kill buffalo, until they finally accepted that they were not. Then they complained about how they did not have enough to eat from the Indian agencies, and about how they sought to hunt buffalo but could find none. What they found instead were bones innumerable, making the ground white in some places, even where there was no snow. They could hardly believe that the white man had wiped out the buffalo.

The conference continued until the chief of the band, the man in the white-man's suit, said that they would not go on to Palo Duro Canyon and await the arrival of the cavalry. He said that they would return to the Indian Territory, as there were no buffalo to hunt and his people were hungry, and that they would have to rely on what the agency provided or starve. He indicated, though, that they would need meat to eat on their way.

Luke let them know, through Andy, that they could slaughter as many as five steers to take with them. The man in the suit said that they would take this offer and take no more than five steers. Finally, the conference concluded, and the Comanche turned and rode slowly out of the yard and back down the canyon, except for a few, including the woman with the cough, who stopped at the springhouse to fill their skins with water from the spring.

When most of the Comanche were well out of the yard, Luke dismounted and bounded toward the house, yelling as he reached the door, "Open the door, Elizabeth."

He could hear the bar being raised on the other side of the door. Then the door flew open and Elizabeth rushed into his arms, and he hugged her into his thick clothing in a desperate thankfulness unlike any he had ever known before. In that embrace, Elizabeth let her tears flow in her own thankfulness and release of emotion. Luke, not letting go of the embrace, worked himself, still holding Elizabeth, into the house, as Andy came up behind him. He closed the door after Andy was in, and Andy lowered the bar. Luke continued to hold Elizabeth, while Andy strode toward the stove, opened it, and fed it with wood.

"How're the kids?" Luke asked Elizabeth.

"Oh," she replied, tearing herself away from him and hurrying toward the bedroom. She found the children safe, though frightened. She would later recount, as part of the answer to her prayer, that, though afraid, the children did not utter one cry, not even Robert, during the whole period of their concealment under the bed.

With the children recovered, Elizabeth turned on Luke suddenly and asked, the concern apparent in her voice, "What about Tom?"

"He's all right," Luke assured her. "He was coverin' us from above, the whole time, with the Sharps."

Elizabeth had looked out the gun hole as she had asked about Tom. As Luke assured her that Tom would arrive before long, her eye fell upon the sight of the woman with the cough and two other women, the Spanish-speaking woman included, just finishing filling their skins with water at the spring. They loaded the skins on their horses and were climbing back onto those mounts, when the woman with the cough stopped to lean against her horse as she was racked by yet another bout of coughing. Without even thinking, Elizabeth grabbed her coat from a peg by the door and threw it on as she hurried to the stove—past Luke, Andy, and the children—and poured out a cup of coffee from the pot on the stove. With cup of steaming coffee in hand, she rushed to the door, where she grabbed her woolen shawl from a peg and threw it over her arm. Then, with coffee in left hand and shawl over left arm, she unbarred and opened the door and was outside before a stunned Luke dashed after her.

By the time Luke was out the door, he could see that Elizabeth was at the end of the porch, intercepting the woman with the cough as she road past the house on her way to join the group that had just left.

Elizabeth gave the woman the coffee and encouraged her to drink it as, from the platform of the porch, she threw the shawl around her shoulders. She then turned back and ordered Luke to get the wool blanket from off the bench inside the door and also a fresh loaf of bread and a venison sausage from the kitchen. Luke obeyed without question, and Elizabeth handed the bread and sausage to the woman, and took the blanket and wrapped it around the child, a young girl close to Rachel's age, huddled in front of her mother on the horse. The look of deprivation, and of shock at Elizabeth's act, in that child's dark eyes, set in a dirty face that was much too old for its age, would forever haunt Elizabeth, especially when she would contrast it to the look of satisfaction and expectation of kindness that she was accustomed to seeing in the eyes of her Rachel.

The encounter was really a very simple one, and one that was soon over, soon enough that the woman with the cough was but a short distance behind the other two women with whom she had stopped for water. Yet, before it was over, the woman from a different culture, and indeed a different world from that of Elizabeth, looked at Elizabeth and reached down and took her hand in her own and spoke her appreciation in her own language. Then she let go of Elizabeth's hand, gulped down the rest of the coffee, returned the cup to Elizabeth with another look of appreciation, then started her horse after her people.

Elizabeth then turned from where she had encountered the woman and drifted back toward Luke and the door, wiping a tear from her eye and a sniffle from her nose. She would not accept the futility of her act, a drop of kindness in an ocean of misery. It was not enough; it could never be enough, but it had been done to one of the least of her sisters, and so had been done to Him. In the universality of that reality even the smallest seed could become the greatest tree.

Luke caught her, as she returned to the door, and embraced her, as quiet tears rolled from her eyes. Then he hurried her inside, out of the cold, and closed and barred the door.

Once inside, warmed up and settled down, the Stuarts and Andy waited for Tom, as Luke related to Elizabeth how he had seen the Comanche near the mouth of the canyon, though he was still not sure whether they had seen him or not. Regardless, he had made his way, behind hills and through draws, out of the mouth of the canyon and into the breaks, where he had headed to the southwest until he had reached the old game trail up onto the caprock. He had climbed it to the top, and from there he had ridden as fast as he could to the head of the canyon, with the intention of getting Tom and getting back to the house before the Indians could reach it. On reaching Tom, he had found Andy there, as well, having been sent by Goodnight to let them know of the state of affairs with the Indians. After Luke had told Tom and Andy about the Comanche he had seen, the three men had devised the plan that would place Tom with the Sharps up on the caprock, in case anything went wrong.

In time, Tom arrived, and various tellings and retellings of pieces of the incident from its several perspectives ensued, stimulated by the hot coffee that flowed freely in the wake of the encounter. Eventually, the men left to round up the Hereford bulls, so as to make sure that the Comanche did not choose one or both of them as a more fitting recompense than a Texas steer for their lost buffalo. Given the commotion with the Indians, Luke and Tom did not want to leave the bulls open for any opportune foul play on the part of the Edwards outfit. Thus, with Andy's help, they located and gathered the two bulls and penned them for the night and for several nights thereafter. They kept them closer to home, even after they stopped penning them, for weeks following the incident.

It took that much time for the Indian matter to be settled anyway. Goodnight had sent one of the JA hands, young Frank Mitchell, to Fort Elliott to report the outbreak of the Indians from the reservation. All told, besides the bands of Comanche, there were bands of Apache, Kiowa, and Pawnee in the region. In early January 1879, Lieutenant A. M. Patch and a detachment of cavalry arrived from Fort Elliott. Captain Nicholas Nolan also arrived from Fort Sill with a detachment of the 10th Cavalry (a troop of black soldiers called buffalo soldiers, which included the first African-American officer in the military of the United States, Lieutenant Henry Ossian Flipper). Nolan and his troopers had been sent after the Indians by General J. W. Davidson, the commanding officer of Fort Sill, after he had learned that the Indian agent had given the Indians permission to go hunting without first notifying him. It was the responsibility of Davidson and his soldiers at the post to protect the Indians and the settlers, and, therefore, they usually provided an escort for such hunting trips to prevent the Indians from crossing into Texas to steal horses and cattle. The escorts were also to keep the Indians from bringing harm to settlers or incurring harm themselves. After arriving on the scene, Nolan negotiated with the Indians, and by the end of January 1879, the Indians agreed to return to the reservation.

Nevertheless, throughout this period of negotiations, the various bands of Indians in the region searched for buffalo and were occasionally seen in Escondido Canyon. Not all of these groups were as compliant as the Comanche band that Luke and Andy had confronted. The Kiowa, in particular, were not beyond making mischief of their own, and the five steers Luke had promised to the Comanche were not the total tally of Seven Ox Seven loss attributable to the Indian presence in the region during that period.

This Indian presence pushed Elizabeth to the brink of her endurance. She had been edging ever closer well before the Comanche had visited. Knowing that Luke was in daily danger from the Edwards outfit and that he had, due to the Edwards game, withdrawn with Tom into a world of secrecy regarding the operation of the ranch had taken its toll on Elizabeth. Before the Edwards outfit had occupied the southern canyon, she had dealt well with the absence of the company of women, with the challenging land, with the daily dangers from a variety of potential sources, and with being pregnant in those circumstances. But since the Edwards harassment had begun, the burden of those circumstances had grown heavier. Now there was this Indian business, with its potential danger of horrific proportions. All of it was straining her nearly to the breaking point. In addition to it all, shortly after the day of the Comanche visit, she had developed sniffles, a runny nose, sneezing, and a cough.

When Andy arrived one day to inform the Seven Ox Seven community that the Indians had agreed to return to the reservation, it was as if something finally let go in Elizabeth. All the tension that had risen within her (and, to some degree, had kept her going) just gave way, and all her defenses came down. The next day, Andy returned to the JA. That night, Luke awoke to find his wife burning with fever. By morning she was incoherent and would not respond to anything anyone said to her. Luke bathed her head in cold compresses, and he and

Tom tried to nurse her as best they knew how, but there was little if any response.

Elizabeth languished in this condition for several days, during which Luke continued to nurse her and to take care of the children, while Tom took care of the work around the ranch. Tom would help with Elizabeth and the children, with the meals and cleaning up, and in any way he could. From the day that Elizabeth first became ill, he moved in and stayed at the Stuarts', sleeping in the main room of the house, to be available to help as much as possible.

Still, most of the care of Elizabeth fell to Luke. He kept the compresses on her, and kept the liquids going into her. He tried, with limited success, to feed her. And he kept her clean. Still, the concern showed in Luke's face. In just those few days, he seemed to age years, as lines seemed to set more deeply into his face. Could he lose his beloved Elizabeth? Had he been wrong to bring her out to this place? How were the children faring? What about the baby?

These questions and doubts took their toll, as did the ongoing care of his ailing wife. Luke knelt praying, in great distress, next to the bedside of his wife on the night of the fifth day. It was late. The children had long ago gone to bed. Tom had retired about an hour before, though, unbeknownst to Luke, he lay awake in the next room, in case they might have need of him and because questions and doubts of his own, along the lines of those entertained by Luke, plagued his mind.

And those entertained by Luke poured out in his quiet prayer. Though not as sentimental as Tom, Luke could not keep his eyes from filling with tears, as he laid his case before God. He loved Elizabeth with all his heart. She was more important to him than anything in the world. He could not imagine going on in life without her. How would he raise the children? Who could ever replace her companionship? Had he been wrong to bring her out to this strange land? Everything had seemed so good, until the Edwards outfit had moved in and turned everything the other way around. It had all seemed so right before. Had he been wrong in moving her from Medina County? Had his motivations been wrong? Had he been greedy? But Elizabeth had wanted to move, too. They had wanted to build something for family. They had envisioned having other families in the region, as well. They had envisioned a church and a school, a real community centered on

God. Had they been wrong? He found it hard to believe so, when he thought back to their life before Edwards. Besides, it was Edwards who was wrong, bad, not what they were trying to do. Finally, he prayed, "But this is where we are; this is all I know to do. Please, bless it, God."

Then he came back to the immediate matter of Elizabeth. He begged God to heal her. He accepted that God might well take the baby, and Luke gave the baby up to God. But, he begged God, let him keep his beloved Elizabeth. He prayed and begged this, until he finally realized that he would also have to give Elizabeth to God. Through the tears and the desperate pleading, he gradually accepted that Elizabeth was God's, as she had always wanted to be, and that he had to give her to God, that, in love, he could not hold her. She was God's: he had to relinquish her, himself, his children, all that he knew to God's providence, as, in the end, God's will would be done. Like God's own Son, in his own distress, he had to pray, "Not my will, but thine, be done." God's will would be done, and peace lay in accepting that will in faith, hope, and, ultimately, in love. Luke's tears stopped in that realization, and he gave his beloved to him to whom she truly belonged, and he let her go. In that instant, a peace born of faith, hope, and love settled into him. It was not a soft, easy peace, but the hard peace of acceptance, of submission, of ultimate freedom.

Luke looked at the fevered face of the lovely woman whom God had given him and whom he had given back to God. He gently stroked her face and hair with his hand. He kissed her and said quietly to her, "I love you, Elizabeth, and I give you back to God." He watched her thus, in timelessness, and when time returned, he kissed her again, and then rose and went into the main room. There he added wood to the fire in the fireplace and sat down in a chair before it and looked into its flames.

From where he lay on some wolf skins not too far from the fire, Tom had watched Luke take his place before the fire. "Luke," he finally said, after allowing Luke some quiet time before the fire, "how's Elizabeth?"

"She's restin'."

"Want me to watch over her for a while?"

"No, she's just restin' now. It's in God's hands."

Tom noted the matter-of-fact way in which Luke had made this answer. He looked at Luke and studied him as he sat with the flickering orange light of the fire painting his face and form. Tom saw the traces of emotional anguish on his face and, yet, saw in his expression and heard in his words and tone of voice that a calm, a strong calm, had taken hold of him. He left Luke alone in this calm.

After a long pause, during which both men looked into the fire, letting their thoughts rest in observation of its lively restlessness, Luke's voice invaded the silence that had lain complete but for the fire's crackling and the periodic whistle of the wind or the sound of its rush against the window panes.

"I gave her back to God, Tom," he said with a very slight quiver in his voice. "I've been holdin' onto her, Tom," he added with a sniff, as his eyes moistened. "I've been holdin' her back from God. I didn't know I was, but I was." Tom felt his own eyes moisten, as he sniffed and checked his own tears. Luke continued, "God loves her even more than I do. He loves her more than I can even imagine. I can't hold her back from God. I have to let her go and trust in God's will."

Tom stared back into the fire, still checking the tears that sought to well in his eyes. He was overwhelmed by the actualization of this profound theological truth and reality. He felt, only to the degree that he could feel in empathy, the depth of the love between Luke and Elizabeth, the depth of the love between that couple and God; and he felt the deep love he himself had for this friend and for Elizabeth, for the two of them and their family; and he felt, beyond all that, the great love for God who created them and brought them into his life and brought him into theirs. He felt the great love for God, who would give so much and teach so deeply that Luke, in his life, could realize the great love of giving over all, even that which he loved above all other creatures, to the providence of the One whom all must love above everything else in order to truly love at all. Tom could now witness a tiny reflection of God's perfect love in the selfless witness of his humble, salt-of-the-earth friend, who could realize, in his life, what theologians could discuss and preach about and explain but never realize in discussion, in preaching, or in explanation. "'For God so loved the world,'" Tom thought, "'as to give his only begotten Son.'"

"God'll take care of us. The Lord'll show us the way. It won't be easy, but he'll show us," Luke said into the flames.

Into those flames the men looked and sometimes spoke, though not often, until the deepest point of night gave over to the birth of morning, and then they retired, Luke to his bed beside his sick wife, and Tom to his wolf skins. And peace descended on the home.

"LUKE."

His spoken name came to him through a heavy sleep that would not be put off.

"Luke."

It came again. His name, cutting through the thick sleep.

"Luke."

Cutting through again, in that voice he so missed, that voice he might never hear again.

"Luke."

Her voice. Elizabeth's voice. Where was her voice? Where was she? He rolled over in unconsciousness.

The voice came again and again. He tried, in his sleep, to find its source. Where was she in his unconsciousness? Where was she? He sought and sought, until consciousness slowly invaded unconsciousness to let him know that she was not to be found there. With the invasion of consciousness, and the slow realization that she was not to be found in unconsciousness, his eyes slowly cast off the weight of sleep. Slowly he turned toward consciousness to seek her there, and slowly, slowly, his eyes opened.

There, in consciousness, he found her. In eyes that had always been the most beautiful he had ever seen, those into which he could look to the greatest depth, he found her. He lay looking into those eyes that looked into his, unable yet to move, so newly reintroduced to consciousness. Those eyes in that face that brought to him such a deepening peace, that he did not yet understand. Then the lips of the face moved, and he heard again:

"Luke."

And he knew. Elizabeth was back. He knew now. She had been gone, so sick. He had given her to God. She was back. God would continue to share her. In that instant of realization, his heart swelled to a capacity he had not known before, and moisture welled in his eyes, and he reached out and pulled his wife to him.

"I've missed you terrible," he said.

"Where have I been?"

"You don't even know, Elizabeth. You don't even know."

And so the husband held his wife, and she held him, and, in time, he told her of her ordeal of the last several days. She was immediately concerned about her baby, and so was Luke, though having already given both up to God, he would revel in the return of at least one, his intimate, for the present. The fever had completely left Elizabeth, and she was very hungry. Tom and Luke immediately went to work, waiting hand and foot on Elizabeth, making whatever food she had a taste for, or broth, or tea, whatever she wanted, to the point of going out and hunting for it, if none was at hand.

And she ate, easy foods at first: broth, tea, bread. But by the second day, she began to take more solid food.

Still, it was her baby about which she was most concerned. All through her first day of recovery she felt no movement from the child. Nor did she feel movement on the second. On the third, her worst fears were confirmed when she went into labor and eventually delivered a son, stillborn. He was a perfect baby, even in death, two months or so premature, but all intact and beautiful. At his delivery, Tom, who was assisting Luke (off to the side in deference to Elizabeth's privacy) reached over with water and baptized the dead infant in the name of the Father and of the Son and of the Holy Spirit, even though the child was already dead and the child's parents were Baptists. Neither of the Baptist parents, recognizing in Tom's action a sincere and profound witness of faith, even considered objecting. Tom knew that one could not baptize the dead, but he did what he did in good intention and desire; he would leave it to God to determine its efficacy.

Luke carefully and solemnly bathed the tiny body and dressed it in a linen dress, which Elizabeth had directed him to take from a trunk. He then handed it to Elizabeth, who looked it over, in tears. Tom had said something quietly to Luke and had then gone out to the dugout to construct a coffin. He made a marker, too, a cross that would bear the name Luke Thomas Stuart, though he did not yet know this. He then chose a picturesque spot on the hill to the northwest of the house, behind the dugout, and began to dig a grave into the cold earth.

Two days later, as soon as Elizabeth was able to stand for any period of time, they lowered the little coffin, with the small corpse inside, down into the earth. They all stood present, even little Robert, in the sunlit cold, and read Scripture, sang hymns, prayed. Tom also read what he believed were the appropriate parts from his missal. Then Luke helped Elizabeth back to the house, while Tom picked up a shovel and filled in the grave.

Chapter Seven

A LIAR
FROM THE BEGINNING

Beware of entrance to a quarrel; but being in,
Bear't that th' opposed may beware of thee.
—WILLIAM SHAKESPEARE

WHEN ELIZABETH HAD AWAKENED FROM THE delirium of her fever, she had been conscious of a nearly overwhelming sense of one thing: Life! She was alive, so very much alive. Luke was alive. The children were alive. Tom was alive. Before she had even been made aware of the state of delirium through which her own life had passed, this sensibility had forcefully impressed itself upon her. Life, life in itself, was now, was so full, and was of inestimable value.

Enter Death. With the death of her baby, a death that she had carried within her, life was hollowed out. Though Elizabeth believed that her baby was with God, she could not detach herself from the darkness of mortality, the darkness of the evil in it, the darkness of plodding along in the drudgery of the day to day under the shadow of that evil.

From her profound experience of life upon her recovery, she had fallen into concern for her baby, then the reality of his death, his burial. She sank into a postpartum depression severely aggravated by the loss of her child. Then entered the drudgery of the day-to-day existence in an isolated canyon, in the winter, in the cold, in the dark. Upon that was heaped the realization of the continued Edwards harassment, such pettiness that held such potential for real harm to the life and lives she loved.

And the Edwards harassment did continue. As soon as Tom and Luke allowed the bulls any freedom, after the Indians were several weeks removed from the area, the bulls disappeared. Luke and Tom sought them out and rounded them up from the HE range, in the vicinity of an HE herd of cows and heifers and a fleeing HE hand, as they would continue to do, time after time.

The Edwards game and its routine again ordered their lives. The Indian scare, despite its potential danger, had at least given some respite from the Edwards game. Now the routine was back, and Luke and Tom fell into their reactive roles, growing so accustomed to the situation and their lack of control in it, that they no longer questioned its necessity. It was part of their life, their lives, part of the drudgery that their lives were becoming because of it.

Secrecy continued as part of that drudgery, secrecy from Elizabeth, secrecy about the Edwards game, ever-more-guarded secrecy, as Luke grew ever more concerned about Elizabeth's state of mind. He saw in her behavior a growing emptiness of indifference. But what he saw in her eyes concerned him far more. There he saw something he had never seen there before, not even during the Edwards game before the illness. There he saw the growing emptiness of despair.

He had watched her, had noticed that she no longer took much care about her appearance or about the appearance of the house. The children she would feed and clothe and entertain as best she could. Luke and Tom she would feed and care for, as from a sense of duty, but there was no life about it. There was duty, but no life. She slept much, ate little, and was tired all the time. The dark circles under her eyes that had developed from the sickness and the loss of the child had never left. She appeared to drag herself through every day. When Luke would try to arouse interest in her, in a book, or an excursion on a temperate day, she would often not respond at all, or listlessly decline the offer, or sometimes snap at him with a suddenness that never failed to surprise him.

And Elizabeth knew. She knew that she had lost all interest. She knew that she was merely dragging. She knew that she had lost a sense of life. And she knew that Luke knew. She would catch him watching her: see him out of the corner of her eye, or turn on him quickly before he could avert his eyes. At such times she would see in his eyes his fear, and she knew that it was fear about what was happening to her. It was in that look in Luke's eyes that Elizabeth really knew, more than in any other way, the depths of her own despair, and in that knowledge, she despaired deeper still.

In such a manner did the life of the Stuart family plod on through the winter. Tom Schurtz's life plodded along with theirs.

And winter itself plodded on, plodded on from its beginning in darkness and cold, plodded on in its progression into light and warmth. From the extremity of solstice, winter plodded, eventually surrendering to the evenness of equinox. And it was spring.

A few weeks into this spring, and the grass began to green, trees began to bud, flowers began to blossom. Warmth entered the canyon again, teasingly, making one day as hot as summer, then another, just a few days later, cold as winter. Hot or cold, each day was longer in light, as the sun rose ever higher in the southern sky toward its peak of summer.

And with the days, Elizabeth, too, began to brighten. The lengthening light began, ever so gradually, to fill the emptiness in her eyes. The growing warmth began, ever so gradually, to melt the chill that surrounded her. As the browns, blonds, and grays of the canyon gradually gave over to greens, and as those greens grew speckled with whites and yellows and purples of primroses and feather dahlias and other blooming flowers, Elizabeth herself began to give over the untidiness that had come to characterize her life. Like the canyon around her, Elizabeth was breaking free from winter in life's perennial drive to blossom.

Luke saw this gradual change in Elizabeth and encouraged it, gently, so as not to overwhelm its natural pace. After dinner, if it were a nice day, he might stay a little longer, rather than return immediately to work, and take a walk in the warmth and light with Elizabeth. At the end of the day, on his ride home, he might stop and pick fresh blossoms to present to his wife. These she would demurely receive in a way that reminded him of how she had first received gifts from him, when he had first begun to give them, many years before.

Thus, love blossomed, too: between husband and wife, and between parents and children, and among friends. A friend to the Stuarts, Tom Schurtz, had shared Luke's concern over the melancholy of his wife and over the well-being of his family, and had added to that concern his own concern for his friend Luke. Hence were another's concerns alleviated by the blossoming taking place in the Stuart household. And when the friend Andy Grady rode into the canyon to help with the roundup, and Elizabeth had one more man to care for—and a young, handsome one at that, who had been like a little brother to her—she needed more and more of the time and energy that hungry melancholy had been appropriating, and hungry melancholy began to waste.

Melancholy suffered further want when the rustling of the bulls discontinued for a while, even though Tom and Luke had let the bulls roam the canyon. Tom and Luke were under no delusions concerning the matter. They knew that it was time for the roundup and that the HE outfit would be plenty busy with the work that was integral to the whole ranching business. Furthermore, neither Tom nor Luke ruled out the possibility that the rustling had ended for the time being due to the presence of Andy, a JA hand, in the canyon. They had come to accept that they were being watched, and they had come to expect anything from that outfit to the south. But for now, the bulls (more mature at three years old) were free amidst the Seven Ox Seven cows and heifers, free within that fecund time of spring.

Fecundity characterized the roundup, as well, though the concern had suffered its share of loss to the elements and predators, mainly lobo wolves. Tom and Luke regretted that their preoccupation with the bulls had caused them to neglect the task of killing lobos. Still, the roundup showed nearly two hundred new calves. They spoke with anticipation of the roundup in the fall, when they would be able to judge the value of the Hereford bulls by the number of white-faced calves.

With the roundup over, Andy stayed as long as he could justify, and then headed back to the JA. He would have a report for Goodnight regarding the Seven Ox Seven four-year-old beeves, which the Seven Ox Seven would let fatten over the summer and cut out in the fall roundup to join Goodnight's late drive of fattened cattle.

To fatten, those beeves would need to graze, and for that purpose, Tom and Luke drove the beeves out onto the high plains above the canyon and the low rolling plains below, after the grasses had greened nicely. Because their portion of the high plains was contiguous, right along the escarpment, they were fortunate to have a good mix of medium and short grasses on the plains both above and below the canyon. Blue grama, little bluestem, buffalo grass, sideoats grama, hairy grama, curly mesquite, and sand bluestem were among the grasses on which the cattle could graze.

They rode line faithfully, both above and below, during those days, but were less inclined to hold the cattle in the canyon for protection from the HE outfit. There was rebellion in the way they allowed the Herefords to graze with the other cattle on the plains outside the canyon. The grasses were good both above and below. It was their range. For better or worse, the remaining buffalo had been largely wiped out in the winter of 1877–78, leaving only small, scattered herds, which were being further reduced by those hunters who had bothered to continue to hunt the dwindling numbers through the winter of 1878–79 that had just passed. The range was open but for antelope and deer. They wanted to get the cattle out of the canyon, to allow its grasses to recover from the winter grazing and to take advantage of the undergrazed pastures on the plains, both above and below, and they were not going to be intimidated out of it. Sure, there were just the two of them now, but they had come through the winter and were ready for the challenge. And, as far as there being only two of them, they were considering making Andy an offer of a position with ownership options after the fall roundup and the JA's late drive to Dodge. But for now, they were fresh and hardened after the winter, and they were tired of the nonsense. If there was going to be a showdown, let it come.

It did not come at first. Tom and Luke rode their respective lines daily and doctored as needed, and things went well. The calves had recovered well from the ordeal of the roundup, and the entire herd was fattening nicely. Tom and Luke took the time to be more diligent in their war on the lobo wolves, toward the end of cutting their depredation of the Seven Ox Seven stock.

Then one day in mid spring the Hereford bulls were not to be found. When the men tracked them down, they were met with the same routine they had come to know: the sight of their bulls among HE cows and heifers and an HE cowhand riding away toward HE headquarters as fast as possible. Tom and Luke returned the bulls to their own range and awaited the next theft, hoping to catch the rustlers in the act. They did not catch them, though they rustled again and again and again. These rustlers had grown so careless so as not to even bother to try to hide their tracks anymore. They were obviously flaunting their rustling in Tom's and Luke's faces, which made Tom and Luke wonder even more about what exactly their object was in this rustling game, besides improving their herd at Seven Ox Seven expense (despite Edwards' disingenuous critique of the Hereford breed).

And Tom and Luke were tired of it. They had put up with this behavior through the winter. They had allowed it to become routine. But it was spring now. They had a sense of new life, new vitality, new beginnings, and they did not intend to get caught up in the trap of that routine again.

But what could they do? That was what was so maddening about the HE rustling pattern. When they followed up the bulls, any HE hand that would come into sight would ride for headquarters. They had never yet been close enough to catch one of these hands, and even if they had been close enough to take the chance of giving chase, there was always the chance of an ambush, either at the headquarters or before. And what if they did catch the individual, what would they do? Neither was prepared to hang the man. And regardless of any evidence, which was scant and fleeting, they were sure that no Edwards hand would admit to the rustling anyway.

Tom and Luke entertained no delusions concerning the men who made up the HE outfit. Their suspicions had been confirmed one Sunday when Andy had ridden over from the JA. Andy had discreetly asked around at the JA roundup to find out if any of the hands knew of John Brown or any of the men who made up the HE outfit. He had learned that Brown was one of the man's names and that he was the leader of a band of outlaws and cutthroats that had preyed on settlements in northeastern New Mexico and southern Colorado some years before, until vigilance committees had raised the stakes on their crimes, after which they had gone quiet. Various reports had since placed him in several locations throughout the West. Some indicated that he had hunted buffalo for a time, and others that he had gone into cattle. Some of the descriptions of members of Brown's outlaw band matched those of HE hands.

Speck was another matter. He did not seem to fit the description of any of Brown's known associates, though one of the JA hands said that he sounded like a young hombre he had run across in Denver, who fancied himself a fast hand with a gun, though the cowhand did not know that he had ever made a name for himself as such. In fact, the hand could not remember the would-be gunman's name. It could have been Speck, but he was not sure.

This information regarding the character of the HE outfit confirmed Tom and Luke's concerns about possible ambush. Nevertheless, they were still inclined to risk it, except for the possibility of leaving Elizabeth and the children behind, should they disappear. And, beyond that, Tom had another reason not to risk it. In truth, Tom did not believe that Edwards would allow an ambush, at least not one that would immediately threaten their lives. Still, Tom was not sure enough of this belief, or of Edwards' control of his men, to disregard the possibility completely. Tom based this belief upon another, which was that, though he considered Edwards' character to be little above that of his men, he *did* believe it to be above that of his men. Whatever Edwards had become, Tom believed that there was some trace of something better, more cultured, behind it. That trace of something more cultured might also have been the basis for Tom's belief that, because Edwards regarded himself as a cattleman, he would avoid, as much as possible, any action that might sully his reputation as such, even, and perhaps especially, if that reputation resided solely with himself.

That being the case, Tom's other reason for not following up a fleeing HE hand rested in the belief that the pattern of the fleeing cowhand was a play in the Edwards' game, a play designed to draw them further into that game. Tom was not exactly sure what Edwards' game was, but he was sure of one thing, that its goal was the acquisition of Cañon Escondido.

Tom had known this from the beginning. He had seen the lust for the canyon in the man's eyes from that first evening. Edwards had said that he had been planning for his ranch in the Escondido for an entire year. A man like Edwards, especially at his age, did not plan that long for something and then just change his mind about it, just let it go, as he had that day when Luke and Tom had first let him know that they owned it.

And that was something that had always bothered Tom about Edwards. Tom had noted, on that day, the abrupt change in Edwards' manner when Tom had offered a reasoned argument for Edwards to move on from the Escondido to one of the smaller canyons. Even though the men with Edwards had obviously not expected a change in his demeanor or purpose—as they had apparently been quite ready and willing to draw their weapons to back up his spurious claim on the canyon—still, Edwards had abruptly shifted from an attitude of bullying to one of acceptance and neighborliness. The shift had never registered with Tom as even the least bit sincere. It was as if Edwards had deferred the immediate gratification of a confrontational approach to secure the canyon for one that would be far less direct, longer lasting, more effective, and one from which Edwards could derive the greatest degree of pleasure in victory, this final criterion being not the least important to Edwards, Tom was sure.

So, what was left to Tom and Luke? Obstinacy for now, if for no better reason than that they had no better plan and were just tired of being manipulated by the HE outfit. They would keep their bulls where they pleased on their range, and if they disappeared, they would go get them. In time, if Edwards escalated the level of his game, they might have the kind of evidence that would speak clearly to a third party. In the meantime, they would do their best to make sure that that evidence would not be one of their corpses.

Spring drifted toward summer, and the men kept up their end of the bull game without letting it govern them as much as they had in the past. Elizabeth pulled, little by little, farther out of her gloom, and the children's dispositions reflected her rising spirits. Days were warm or hot now, with pleasant evenings of cooler, breezy air. Days were longer, too, with plenty of time for outings after supper or even for supper. And so, the settlers enjoyed picnics, fishing, plum gathering, gardening, hunting, and even family attempts at baseball.

One thing that had changed about the men's approach to the HE game, which allowed for the more relaxed attitude around the family, was that Luke and Tom were far less secretive about it. It was true that Luke did not keep Elizabeth informed about the rustling, but neither did he and Tom talk about it much. Luke and Tom put into practice a valuable lesson that Luke had learned, at a considerable price, the previous winter. He had learned to let go. He had given Elizabeth, his intimate, to God. If he could let go of Elizabeth, he could let go of the bulls, or even the ranch, for that matter. And so he did.

Tom had not learned the lesson that Luke had learned. He had witnessed it and could appreciate and intellectualize it, but he had not experienced it, had not had it actualized within him. Still, he participated in the same attitude of letting go. So what if they lost the bulls? They would go on. As it was, they still had the bulls, and after they would be rustled, they could still go get them. Whatever service those bulls provided their cows and heifers was better than no service at all, and as it was, they expected at least one bull out of the calves these bulls would sire. So, it would not be a total loss.

And this belief, that it would not be a total loss, was realized one day in late May, when Tom rode into the yard of the Stuart home with a white-faced calf across the saddle in front of him. He was followed by the Texas cow that was the mother of the calf, and she made sure that Elizabeth's and the children's petting and admiring of the young calf was kept to a minimum. Tom drove the cow and calf into one of the pens behind the house, so that Luke could see them upon his return from the lower canyon. Luke rode in with a calf of his own, followed, as well, by a cow that disputed that ownership, and he claimed to have seen another. These sightings of white-faced calves following along behind Texas cows grew slowly, day to day, more frequent, giving credence to the policy of accepting and letting go and recognizing that, no matter what, it was not a total loss anyway.

Of course, with such an attitude, there was less diligence in hunting down the Hereford bulls after they were rustled. This declining diligence did not go unnoticed among those men who did the rustling and herding of the bulls among estrous HE cows and heifers. As the interest in the game on the part of the Seven Ox Seven men waned, those on the other side of the game realized that they were losing their manipulative control of the situation. If Tom was correct, and the acquisition of Escondido Canyon was Henry Edwards' goal, and if his means of bringing about that eventual end had begun to grow less effective, it would be reasonable to expect, especially if Edwards lusted after the canyon to the degree that Tom suspected, that the HE outfit, now placed in the role of reactor, might change tactics.

It was within this atmosphere of potential change that Luke, one day in late spring, rode down to the eastern end of the canyon to ride his line. He passed through the mouth of the canyon and rode to the southwest along the base of the escarpment. When he reached the southern line of the range claimed by the Seven Ox Seven, he began to ride to the east. He rode up and down through the breaks, as was his custom, and eventually, in a dry creek bed, cut the sign, still fresh, of a number of cows and calves trailed to the south by two riders.

This was new.

Luke checked his gun for bullets and tucked back the flap on the scabbard holding his Winchester. He hated riding with a scabbard on his saddle. It was just such a nuisance to a cowboy. Still, given the circumstances, both Tom and he had grown accustomed to it. With his weapons in order, he followed the trail.

The trail led him through the breaks at the base of the escarpment, winding through dry streambeds as much as possible. Luke guessed that this was to keep the rustlers out of sight and to make the trail that much more difficult to follow, though it certainly did not make the sign very difficult to read. He found himself looking up along the edge of the caprock as he went. This was in reaction to that strange feeling, which had developed over several months, that the Seven Ox Seven was being watched. He followed the trail for over an hour, eventually spotting and passing HE cattle along the way, before the trail turned up one dry creek bed into a deep draw, a small box canyon really, cut into the escarpment.

Luke checked his weapons again and then slowly proceeded. He kept to the arroyo, allowing its sand bottom to absorb any noise from his horse's shod hooves. Before long, he could hear bawling of herded cattle and soon saw smoke rising just ahead of him. He dismounted from his horse and led him up a narrow, dry tributary and tied him to an exposed mesquite root sticking out of its wall.

He pulled the Winchester from the scabbard and, on foot, made his way back into the main channel of the arroyo. There he stopped and looked in the direction of the smoke. He listened and could hear the sounds of the cattle, but sound was strange in these arroyos carved out of sand and clay. Sound was absorbed and muffled, and far away as it seemed to be, he knew the bawling of the herded cattle was coming from where that smoke came, and the smoke was coming from around the bend in front of him.

Luke quickly considered his options for getting a look at what was going on around the bend without being seen. He could climb out of the arroyo onto the ground above on either side, which was about ten feet above the creek bed on which he stood. The problem with that option was that the land was so carved and tortured in these breaks that he might climb right into the rustlers' view and not realize it until it was too late. Even if the land above him were flat, if he tried to get close enough to see the rustlers in the creek bed ahead of him, he might stick out very plainly against the sky on their horizon.

Another option was to proceed ahead and try to peer around the bend of the arroyo. But that, too, could expose him, as he had no idea how the arroyo bent and, hence, no idea at what angle and, for that matter, how close the rustlers were around the bend.

There was one other option, and that one appealed to Luke. That option lay with an island that sat in the middle of the arroyo, where flows of water had carved through the land on either side of it, leaving it at least as high as the arroyo's ten-foot-high walls. The island was situated just ahead, right in the arroyo's bend, and its length extended from a point just ahead of where Luke was standing to its beginning in the bend itself. Its top was rounded and rough, where soil had fallen away due to erosion, and vegetation grew out of it; and it would provide a better opportunity for Luke to get a look beyond without exposing himself to the rustlers' view.

Luke proceeded toward the island and, with Winchester in hand, managed to climb its clay side to its top and then crawl to its other end, where a mesquite tree still clung to life and the soil, creating a little mound around its base. He crawled in behind the mesquite and its mound.

Before he even looked, Luke knew that branding was part of whatever was going on in the arroyo below him. Of course, rustling cows and calves with the aim of branding the calves in their own brand had registered with him as a possibility from when he had first begun to follow the rustlers' trail. Still, his mind had not readily accepted it as a very likely possibility, because it would indicate quite an elevation of the level of harassment on the part of the HE outfit. Branding another's calves in your own brand was pure rustling, cut and dry, far more blatant than the temporary theft of bulls that could be said to be drifting. But now, as he lay crouched behind the mesquite tree, the wind wafted in that distinct mixture of smells, dry and slightly sweet, of dust, beeves, blood, and burning flesh. Wafting with the mix of smell was the mix of sounds, those of the bawling cows and calves separated from each other. Luke raised his head and peered over.

What he saw indicated that this was not a spur-of-the-moment action. The spot had been well chosen. The arroyo widened out here with plenty of room to hold the calves. The HE had obviously been cutting cedar in the area, as stumps, which Luke could see from his vantage point, dotted the surrounding land. A wagon road, probably cut to accommodate wagons for hauling the cedar, ran down into the arroyo from the south and then followed its course to the west, for a ways, before climbing back out up ahead where the bank was lower. To the north, another branch of the arroyo cut into the earth, but, like the one in which Luke had tied his horse, it was a dead end. Across the face of this dead end was a barbed wire fence. Behind the fence stood the bawling cows.

As Luke looked at the operation, he thought how quickly a flash flood, caused by water rushing off the high plains from a thunderstorm, could turn the arroyo into a raging river and put an end to this whole thing. He guessed, though, that these men believed that they could get away fast enough. Besides, a good deal of the loss would be his and Tom's, not theirs. Whatever the case, this was not set up for just this handful of Seven Ox Seven calves. A few here, a few there, and pretty soon most of the Seven Ox Seven calves, especially the white-faced ones, would be wearing the HE brand.

Three men were running the operation. Brown, the foreman, stood off to Luke's left over a fire with a stamp iron sticking out of it. Out in front of the fire was the blond man with the large nose who had ridden up with Brown and Edwards the time Tom had retrieved Augie from Henderson. Luke had never seen this blond man up close before, though he had seen him flee when he had come for the bulls on a few occasions. The third man, seated on his horse, was an average-sized man, about Luke's height but not as stout. He was light complected with brown hair and a rather nondescript sort of face and general appearance. Brown's and the blond man's horses were tied to mesquite roots in the side of the arroyo, off to the side.

They were branding, all right. There were more cows behind the fence, and more calves bunched up against it, than would account for those trailed from the Seven Ox Seven range. Luke correctly assumed that, as long as these men were going to brand calves, they had pulled in a few of the HE brand to make it worth their trouble.

Luke watched as the nondescript man threw a rope around the two hind feet of a young white-faced calf, which Luke figured would have to belong to the Seven Ox Seven. It would be another few weeks before the Edwards cows started to drop white-faced calves, compliments of the Seven Ox Seven bulls. Regardless, the nondescript man was pulling the calf over to where the blond man waited. The blond man came up to meet the small calf, flanked him, tied his feet and held him down. Brown then approached with the iron and the knife. Brown put his foot on the calf's rump and was about to apply the HE brand.

"Hold it!" Luke shouted.

At the sound of these words, the two men doing the branding froze, as did the man on the horse.

"Don't even think of movin'," Luke added. "I've got a Winchester and a six-gun pointed at you, and I ain't particular about which rustler gets it.

"Now," he continued, "you on the horse, there, you pull that gun out of your belt and throw it up over the bank there. Then follow it up with your rifle."

The man, whose back was turned to Luke, complied, throwing his weapons up onto the bank, above where the cows were being held.

"Knife, too," Luke said, and a bowie knife followed the guns.

"All right now, Brown, you can return that iron to the fire and throw your guns up, includin' that Winchester over there by your fire. Throw your knife up, too. Just throw up that whole belt with those two six-shooters in it."

Brown did return to the fire, as the blond man started to let the calf up.

"You just hold that calf right where you got him," Luke said. "Keeps you busy. I'll get back to you in a minute."

Brown took the occasion of Luke's distraction to deposit the branding iron in the fire and pick up his Winchester. When Luke looked back at Brown, he was not able to see his face, as the back of Brown's left shoulder was pointed toward Luke. Still, Luke read hesitation in his manner. Luke was angry enough about what was going on in front of him; he did not need Brown's help to encourage that anger. He shot at a prickly pear on the edge of the bank above Brown's head.

"The next one's goin' right through you, and nobody'll blame me for defendin' myself against a rustler," Luke yelled at Brown.

Brown froze, his arms going limp as if from the weight of the Winchester in his hands.

"Throw that gun away," Luke called, "up over the bank." Brown hesitated a moment, and Luke shouted, "Do it!" Brown then complied.

Luke called out, "Now the gun belt and the six-shooters."

Brown slowly unfastened his gun belt and removed it and threw it up over the bank.

"Knife," Luke called out.

Brown complied by throwing his knife up over the bank. Then, on Luke's command, the blond man who had been holding down the calf did the same with his rifle (which he first removed from the scabbard on his saddle), his six-gun, and his knife, leaving the calf to struggle against the rope around his feet. Then Luke told the three men to turn around and look up at him. They did so.

Luke stayed where he was behind the base of the mesquite. He had a clear view of the area below, and, with the deep roots of the mesquite, a reasonable assurance that this soil under him, near the edge of the island, would not give way under his weight. Furthermore, he was going to keep as much of himself as possible behind cover for as long as possible, because he did not trust these men, and he did not think it beyond the realm of possibility that Brown, in particular, the two-gun man, might have another weapon.

"How many of those calves you got branded?" Luke called down.

He received no answer. Luke pointed the rifle toward Brown. "Brown?"

"Why don't you come on down and look?" Brown replied.

"I'm real comfortable right where I am, especially with rustlers all about. You tell me how many of those calves you got branded."

Brown played the tough and said nothing. So Luke turned the rifle on the nondescript man on the horse and pointed the barrel right between his eyes—which Luke noticed, upon this closer inspection, to be a light hazel color—and took aim. "How about you?" he said to the man. "How about you tellin' me how many calves you've branded?"

The man stared into the rifle, and Luke could see a kind of conversion take place within him, right in Luke's sights. "How many?" Luke said to him in a voice deadly serious.

"Two," the man answered.

"Smith!" Brown bellowed, "don't you . . ."

Luke turned his rifle on Brown and yelled at him, "That's all I want to hear out of you, Brown! Remember, shootin' a rustler, people'd think I was doin' 'em a favor. And from what I know about you, I might even have a reward comin'."

These last sentiments appeared to have the effect of drawing the seemingly insensitive Mr. Brown into a state of reflection. He immediately grew quiet, pensive, and Luke turned his sights back on the nondescript Mr. Smith.

"How many calves you got total here, twelve?" Luke demanded to know.

"Twelve," Smith confirmed.

"How many from the Seven Ox?"

"Six."

"You say you branded two, that include the one you were just startin' on, or is that number three?"

"Two besides that one. That was number three."

"All right now," Luke said to Smith, "I want you to go in there and cut out a Seven Ox cow from those you got there."

Brown began to respond, as if by instinct, but Luke cut him off.

"Don't even think about tellin' me there ain't no Seven Ox cows over there, Brown. You just go ahead and get one, Mr. Smith."

Smith did as he was told and opened the makeshift gate of the makeshift pen and soon returned with an agitated Texas cow with a clear Seven Ox Seven brand on her hip. Bawling and nudging about among the calves, while Smith closed the gate, the mother was soon reunited with her bawling calf, which wore the HE brand.

"Well, look what we got here," Luke said, "a Seven Ox cow with an HE calf, a white-faced calf at that, when the HE didn't even start rustlin' our bulls until October. Seems there's been some kind of mistake."

Turning back to Smith, who was now back on his horse, Luke said, "You say there's a dozen cows and calves?"

"Yessir."

"And you say six of those dozen are Seven Ox pairs, and you've already branded two of those six calves with the HE brand?"

"Yessir."

"Then," Luke continued, "that leaves ten unbranded calves. Four of 'em Seven Ox calves, six of 'em HE. That right?"

Smith nodded.

"All right, now," Luke said, "I want all three of you to take a good look at that Seven Ox Seven brand on that cow. I want you to study it, and then you're goin' to practice puttin' it on the rest of those calves with that runnin' iron. Since you were about ready to brand half a dozen of my calves with your brand, seems only right you practice on some of the HE stock, as well, especially seein' how you've already stolen two of my calves by brandin' 'em with the HE, and I'm goin' to end up carin' for 'em and grazin' 'em and everything else, seein's how they'll be stayin' with their mamas, and then old Mr. Edwards'll claim 'em by brand when roundup comes. And tryin' to fix those brands'll just make the Seven Ox look like rustlers, instead of the the other way around, which is the truth of it. Besides, considerin' how superior these Seven Ox calves are to these pitiful HE ones, three to one is a bargain on your end. And I want every one of you to take a turn at those irons, so to make sure you got the brand down real well. Make sure you get that earmark right, too, but leave the doctorin' to me. I won't trust you all with that. And you, Brown, I want you to flank a couple of those calves and not leave all the fun to your amigos."

And so the branding went, under Luke's supervision. Before long, the calves were branded and mixing with the cows in the makeshift pen, as bawling and sniffing cows and calves sought their own.

The beeves were mixing in the pen, because, as the branding had been going on, Luke had been thinking about how he was going to leave the situation. He did not trust these men to allow him to just ride away. These breaks provided plenty of opportunity for an ambush from disgruntled rustlers doubling back to get even. On the other hand, if Luke made them ride with him until he was safely back to Seven Ox Seven range, he would first have to find a way to get back to his horse without allowing these men an opportunity to escape or ambush him or both. With all this in mind, Luke had decided to have the men pen the calves with the cows. Then he had the men lie face down on the ground below him, where he could clearly see them, with their feet pointed toward him and their heads pointed away.

Now that Luke had the men lying face down, he began to climb down from the top of the island to the bottom of the arroyo. He slid down a good bit of the way. And though Brown raised his head and peered around, against the orders given him, with hopes that Luke might have fallen or at least lost the gun, Luke had done neither, and he answered Brown's violation with a sharp rebuke. Once on the ground, Luke walked around to beyond where their heads lay and ordered the men to get up, which they did. He then had them walk in front of him the short distance to where his horse was tied. There he had them lie face down again. He was not about to take chances with this outfit.

Luke pulled out his revolver and returned the Winchester to its scabbard. Then he mounted his horse and had the men get up and, in front of his gun, walk back to where their own horses were tied. There he had them mount up, except for the blond man, whom the others called Whitey. He had this Whitey open wide the gate of the pen and then mount up. He then had the men gather the Seven Ox Seven cows with their calves, even the two branded HE, and drive them down the arroyo back toward the Seven Ox Seven range. The HE cows, with their Seven Ox Seven calves, he left on the HE range. He would leave the dilemma of how to deal with them up to Henry Edwards, either to change the brand (which would look suspicious), to kill them and take that loss, to raise them as Seven Ox Seven beeves, or to come up with some other solution.

Luke had the HE men drive the beeves toward the east, out of the worst of the breaks and out onto more level ground, so that there would be less chance for them to try something on him. He had made them leave their weapons where they had thrown them. He thought of them trying to find those weapons later. It served them right, he thought.

Luke upbraided the men whenever one of them drew near enough to another to allow for any talk. Brown, in particular, chafed under Luke's stern supervision, but he rode along, driving the beeves, in front of Luke and the six-shooter he held in his hand. Eventually the men entered Seven Ox Seven range, and they began encountering Seven Ox Seven cattle, truly superior—even the Texas beeves—to those of the HE outfit.

"All right," Luke shouted, once they were well onto the Seven Ox Seven range, "hold up." The men stopped in front of him, leaving the beeves to drift on beyond them.

"Turn around," Luke said.

The men turned their horses around to face him.

"I've been easy on you all this time," Luke said. "As rustlers I could've treated you plenty worse. But I'm tellin' you all, we're gettin' plenty tired of playin' with you rustlers. I'm just warnin' you, that if this keeps up, somebody's goin' to pay, and it won't be Edwards. It'll be one of you all. You notice Edwards ain't out here. He's got you all doin' his dirty work. But I'm just warnin' you."

"That a threat?" Brown asked him in a surly tone.

"You take it any way you want it," Luke replied. "We'd like to get along neighborly with you all, but we're not about to let neighborliness overlook flat out rustlin'. This country's gettin' more settled, with other ranchers movin' in, and the Rangers aren't out of the question any-more. So you all think about your ways, and just be warned that we're not goin' to put up with any more of this. I don't want to make a habit of bringin' rustlers onto my own range, so I want you all to git."

Whitey and Smith, especially Whitey, had been glancing now and then at Brown throughout Luke's little talk. Brown all the time looked at Luke with such a look of malevolence that it was understandable that the other two would be interested in his reaction. Luke had, for the most part, ignored Brown's look and the sentiments he intended to convey by it, though he could not help but see it.

With Luke's talk concluded and with his order to "git" given, Whitey and Smith turned their heads and looked at Brown, who continued to stare menacingly at Luke. Finally, as if to indicate that he would leave on his own decision in his own sweet time, Brown exhaled a haughty "hmph" and slowly turned his horse to the southwest at a walk, the two other men falling in behind him. Luke watched their slow retreat, with Brown's hauteur obvious even in his posture in the saddle, and he could not resist the urge to fire his pistol into the air. Then he watched, with no small satisfaction, as the HE men, Brown first, spurred their horses into a gallop toward the southwest.

TOM PRESSED AND ROLLED HIS BOTTOM LIP between his thumb and forefinger, as he leaned against the rail of the corral listening to Luke's account of that day's incident with the rustlers. He watched, through the rails, a young mustang colt that he had caught in the spring and had given to Zachariah to raise. Zachariah had taken right to the task, feeding the colt daily with milk from a pail, developing quite a mutually affectionate relationship with the animal. Mutually beneficial, too, as Zachariah intended to ride the colt as soon as it was old enough to carry him, and the colt had continued to grow strong and fleet under Zachariah's devoted care. Now, in the corral before him, that fleet, strong brown colt pranced and bucked in the soft fading sunlight of a spring evening, an apt metaphor—Tom had immediately thought when they had walked up to the corral—of the wildness of this land they had entered and sought to settle, its wildness and freedom corralled in the fading light of the setting sun. Now Tom's eyes followed the colt, watching him though not really seeing him, as his mind's eye clouded out the sight in front of him with its own vision of Luke's confrontation with the rustlers that day.

Luke, leaning on the rail to Tom's right and looking into the side of Tom's face, was finishing up his account of the incident, almost pushing his story into Tom in his desire to know his partner's response to it.

"And I watched that hombre, Brown, ridin' away all high and mighty, and I pulled up that ol' six-gun and fired it into the air, and you should've seen those boys run, Brown right out in front," Luke concluded, without any clearer sense of Tom's reaction to the incident, except that it seemed to have stimulated in him the need for a good lip massage.

Finally, Tom, conscious of Luke's desire for a response from him, turned away from the rail he had been leaning against, his head down as he turned past Luke. He nodded his head slowly and deliberately as he turned around to lean his back against the same rail. Now he pushed under his chin with his thumb, and his forefinger alone pressed against his bottom lip, which he chewed now as he continued to nod slowly and deliberately.

"I didn't know what else to do, Tom," Luke admitted, with less of the assurance he had conveyed when delivering the story. "They were brandin' our calves."

Tom continued the slow nod, though he dropped his hand from his mouth and clasped it with his other hand over his abdomen, as he leaned more comfortably back against his elbows, which supported him against the rail.

"I don't know what else you could've done, Luke," he finally said. "How else you deal with this kind?" he added, as much to Luke as to himself and to God. Then he was quiet for a moment, as Luke offered reasons to justify his actions of that day.

"I know, Luke," Tom finally said, responding to Luke's justifications. "I don't know if I, or anyone else, could have responded any better or as well. The problem is they're outlaws and we're not, and they, at least some of 'em, are willin' to go farther than we are. You know?" he added, turning toward Luke.

Luke looked at Tom and then looked down, his knit brows registering his frustration with their predicament as well as his disappointment at finding his conduct of that day, of which he had been somewhat proud, increasingly flawed under further scrutiny. "Well, we can't just sit by and let 'em rustle and brand our cattle. We'll be out of business in no time."

"I know," Tom said. "The problem is—I'm tryin' to figure this out—brandin' our calves is a big step from runnin' off our bulls. It's of the same order, but it's one more stage into the sin of commission. You know what I mean?" Tom said, looking toward Luke.

Luke did not, without thinking about it, but he nodded anyway, having got the gist of what Tom was saying.

"This is an elevation of tactics. This is plenty more serious, less able to deny if caught. It's not fleeting like rustlin' up a bull for a few days. This is deliberate theft, leavin' hard evidence in a brand. If the Texas Rangers happened by, there would be no contest, with those HE calves with our cows, especially if they could see where it was done and could hear your tale, but . . ."

"But what?" Luke asked him, his mind already working to fill in the answer to his own question.

"Well, uh," Tom began, not wanting to say what he meant, "you know, um, . . ."

"What, Tom?" Luke said.

"Well, uh," Tom began again, and then just said straight out, "those rangers would have to wonder why HE cows had Seven Ox calves, as well. And those HE rustlers could tell 'em all kinds of tales, which they wouldn't be able to lightly dismiss, with the hard evidence of the calves, no matter what kind of outlaws those HE hands are."

Tom had not wanted to say it, and the truth, finally spoken, hit Luke hard. What Tom was saying he had known. He had known it down inside himself, in a slight gnawing sensation, when he had decided on the action, but that sensation had been easily overridden by the satisfaction of the action and the apparent justice of it. It was when he had first thought of telling Tom about what had happened that the gnawing sensation had begun to grow, until it was about ready to gnaw right through out into the open, as he had related the events to Tom. And then Tom had said it, what he and Luke both knew: Luke had played into their game. He had crossed the line. He had put the ball in their court, as Tom would say. He had given Henry Edwards cause to react.

LUKE DID NOT FEEL MUCH BETTER about the possible repercussions of his actions the next day, either. In fact, after a night of wrestling with them, he felt worse. It did not help matters any that he knew that Elizabeth had sensed that something was wrong. She had been doing better all the time, actually to the point that, at this time in late spring, she had some of the old color back in her cheeks, and her blue eyes had most of their old life back, with the dark circles gone from below them. Part of her recovery had been due to her letting go of concern over the ranch. She had just let that go, left it to Luke and Tom. Luke's and Tom's own ways of letting things go, not worrying as much about the bulls, had helped. The morning after the rustling and branding incident, however, witnessed some of her old nervous behavior: watching Luke; asking him—with that searching look in her eyes, that faraway fear—how things had gone the day before; asking him what he and Tom would do that day.

Luke had had to tell her, keeping as much detail out of the telling as was possible. He had had to tell her mainly out of concern for her own safety and that of the children. He was going to have her lock up the house, to shutter and bar the windows and doors, all day, for the next few days. He and Tom both hated to make her do so, to give her reason to fear, to make her lock herself up and lock out the light, but this was a serious matter and they truly were concerned about the family's safety. Luke and Tom had decided that they would ride line together, for at least the next few days. They were not sure what they would do after that. They considered taking turns riding line and having the other man work around the house, to be there for the protection of the family. This was a bad element to the south of them, and Tom and Luke had both heard their shares of stories of depredations committed by white renegades that were later blamed on Indians. Indians were coming and going from the reservation enough to make it plausible. Still, neither man was happy about the situation, and at breakfast that morning, both men responded vaguely to Elizabeth's questions, and both avoided looking into her eyes.

They had decided on their immediate plan of action the night before while standing at the corral. As soon as breakfast was over, they set out to do it. First, they would ride up on top of the caprock to make sure that nothing like what had happened below had yet occurred up above. They would make sure that whatever cattle they had up above were securely on their range, which extended about a mile in every direction from the land they owned outright. They considered that, if things continued to escalate, they would move the cattle back into the canyon.

They rode line up above that day and had to doctor some for screwworms, which did little for their appetite. Elizabeth noted this lack of appetite at noon dinner and was about to attribute it to the seriousness of their circumstances, but Luke indicated that it was because of the screwworms, which helped Elizabeth identify the hint of a putrid smell that had accompanied the men into the house. The smell would accompany them into the house in the evening, as well, since they had found screwworms in some of the sheep that afternoon. They had their work cut out for them with the sheep, because they had been neglecting them in favor of the cattle for some time.

The next day, the men had Elizabeth secure the house on their departure, as they had the day before. Then they started down the canyon to finish riding line from where they had left off the day before. They pulled out a few bogged cattle from around a water tank they had created next to a creek that served as a tributary to Stuart Creek. Two of the cattle were mere standing skeletons, having been stripped to the bone of their meat by wolves, which did nothing for the equanimity of those cattle that had bogged since. Rains had been few and far between for some time, and the tank had nearly dried up, leaving the cattle little access to its water without wading through the thick mud to get to it.

Around midday, they stopped, made a fire, put on a pot of coffee, and fixed dinner, which consisted mainly of venison, biscuits, and vegetables that Elizabeth had packed for them. Over dinner they decided that, because the day was wearing on (the bogged cattle having taken longer than they had expected), they would continue to split up, one on the north and one on the south, as they had done all the way down the canyon, using a single shot of a rifle to let the other know when help was needed. Thus, at the mouth of the canyon, Luke would exit the canyon where Schurtz Creek flowed out and continue riding the southern line, and Tom would exit the canyon to the north, where Stuart Creek flowed out, and ride the northern line. They intended to meet on the far eastern line.

As they rode off to cover their respective lines, Tom had misgivings about the plan for that afternoon. He did not like that they were splitting up. It was true that they had been split up for most of that day, except when they had worked together to pull out the bogged cattle, but as he reflected upon it, it gnawed at him that they had strayed from their original plan. He realized that they had been lulled into a sense of security due to the uneventfulness of the day before, a sense of security that was easy to accept because they had a lot of work to do and could get more done split up and were somewhat resentful of, and rebellious toward, anything that might force them to depart from their habitual work patterns. Perhaps that was why Luke had been quietly persistent about them staying split up to ride line beyond the mouth of the canyon, even though that was where they might be most likely to run into trouble from the HE outfit.

Nevertheless, the plan for the day had been that the two of them would ride together to avoid any foul play on the part of the HE hands. And here they were split up, Tom thought, as he entered the narrow pass between the escarpment and the northernmost outlier, the pass that made up the northern exit from the canyon onto the plains beyond. As Tom rode on and thought more about it, he liked less and less that they had split up, and he had a growing feeling that he should ride south and meet up with Luke. The feeling grew and nagged at him, as he worked through the breaks, and he was sorely tempted to follow it through, but he knew that Luke had been adamant about them splitting up. And then, the more Tom thought about it, the more he realized that Luke had been wrong. They had agreed, after the incident of the other day, that they would ride together. They had both agreed to it for very good reasons. All of a sudden, Luke had abandoned the agreement at the very time when it would be most crucial. Tom finally recognized Luke's reaction for what it was. He had been stubbornly refusing to rely on another's help to face up to an unspoken threat from some underhanded rustlers. Tom understood it, and considered that he would probably have felt the same way, but there was that fine line between courage and foolhardiness, and Tom was afraid that Luke had crossed it. In that instant, Tom knew, without any doubts, that he had to get to Luke, and he turned Ross to the south and gave him full rein, letting him run as fast as the rugged terrain of the breaks would allow.

Ross was equal to the task, as he flew across creek beds and up over hills and down the other side, jumping a drop of several feet, in one instance, where the ground fell away abruptly on the other side of a hill. Through trees, brush, and grass, over sand, rock, and soil, they flew, sending the native fauna fleeing before them. Tom realized that he was steering Ross recklessly, but an almost desperate urgency rising within him demanded no less.

As he drew nearer the southern line, Tom noticed, in the few seconds that it took to cross the top of a mound along the way, something strange across the land, a ways up ahead, that he could not quite make out. Finally, after topping out on a few succeeding mounds and seeing the same thing in the distance each time, Tom recognized the strange thing for what it was, a fence, or at least the posts for a fence. Edwards was fencing them in.

He continued to ride recklessly through the breaks, seeing more and more of the fence as he approached. It snaked its way up and down through the breaks, in what would have been a straight line on a map, right along where the boundary of their purchased land was marked by the surveyors' corners.

Tom estimated, as he rode toward the fence, that they already had nearly a mile of fence up, at least the posts; and the wire was not running far behind. They were stretching wire right behind the posts. "They must've started workin' on it yesterday, the day after that run-in with Luke, if not before," he thought to himself. "They must've had this planned. Just waitin' for the opportunity," he thought. "They're stretchin' barbed wire. Where'd they get all that wire?" he wondered, as he quickly calculated that, for the cost of the wire and the cost of having it hauled out to the area, it would easily run over one hundred dollars a mile. "How'd Edwards pay for all that?"

Tom had begun riding toward the southeast after he had seen the fence. He was instinctively heading toward where those building it would be working, its present terminus, which appeared to be on the other side of a low hill behind which the fence disappeared and did not yet emerge on the top of the hill beyond it. He rode hard and, in time, was at the base of his side of the low hill.

He did not slow up, but circled around the base of the hill to the east. Rounding the hill, he came in sight of the last fence post standing. Beyond it to the east lay two others, spaced, as the set posts were, about forty feet apart (though later experience would favor a span of sixty feet, with three stays in each span). These last two, however, lay on the ground next to newly dug holes. Shovels and posthole diggers lay on the ground, too. But there were no men. Where were the men?

Tom looked for these men and for the next fence post toward the west, as he came around the hill, but he saw neither. To the west of the last standing fence post, the land sloped down behind a hillock that was now directly in front of Tom to the south. Tom steered Ross toward it. As he rode up the hillock, he pulled his Winchester from its scabbard. Upon reaching the top of the rise, he saw below and beyond him the men who had been constructing the fence. They stood gathered near where the last of the wire had been stretched. In the midst of them was Luke. He was surrounded by four men who would move in to strike or kick at him. He seemed to be concentrating on one man, the large foreman, Brown. Two other men stood off to the side.

Tom fired the Winchester into the air, as he cleared the top of the rise, and then leveled it in the direction of Brown, the biggest and most likely target. The men all stopped with the sound of the gun, except for Luke, who took the occasion to land a good right-hand punch into Brown's face, which sent Brown stumbling backward until he fell on the seat of his pants. Speck, who was one of the men surrounding Luke, pulled his six-gun from its holster. The other two men surrounding Luke (Whitey and another dark-complected man whom Tom remembered from his one encounter at the HE headquarters) did the same.

Tom sent a bullet into the ground near Speck. Speck began firing at him, and Tom shot him in the leg, which caused Speck to drop his gun and grab at his leg. Meanwhile, Luke turned and stepped into Whitey, who had his gun drawn and pointed in Tom's direction. Luke grabbed Whitey's gun with his left hand and hit him hard in the side of the face with his right fist, to send Whitey crumpling to the ground. Tom was riding fast toward the scene and was now close enough to be heard. He shouted at the dark man with the gun, "Drop it!"

The man hesitated a moment, as Tom bore down on him, and then, after quickly glancing back and forth between Speck and Brown lying on the ground to either side of him, he turned his head to see, behind him, the fate of Whitey. At that moment, Luke, who was still behind him, hit him full in the face with his large fist, and he staggered off balance a step or two, and went down.

Immediately after the man hit the ground, Tom pulled Ross to a hard stop near where he fell. He threw the rifle to Luke and pulled his six-gun from its holster. He covered the men on the ground with his gun, as Luke, covering them as well with the rifle, backed his way out of the circle the four men had created around him, finally backing away from that circle toward Tom.

"You all right?" Tom asked without taking his eyes off the men, as Luke backed up next to Ross.

"Yeah," Luke said shortly.

Tom glanced down at Luke, whose face he could not see from where he sat his horse above him. What he could see was that his hat was off, his shirt torn, and his hands, which now held the Winchester, were bloody, and they were shaking.

Tom surveyed the men before him. Brown was getting up from the ground. Whitey was still down and out. Speck was writhing, moaning, and sighing on the ground, his right leg pulled up into his abdomen and held there by his hands, which were wrapped around his shin. His hands were red with blood. The fourth man, whom Tom did not know, was staggering to his feet, holding his hand over his nose as blood flowed from it.

Then Tom glanced over at the two other men who were standing off to the side to the left of him. One he recognized as Henderson. The other he did not know, though he had seen him at HE headquarters the day he had brought in Speck and the wrangler. It was Smith, one of the three men that Luke had caught branding Seven Ox Seven calves. Neither of the two men had made a move of any kind. They so well played the parts of spectators that Tom had inadvertently overlooked them. They both wore their gun belts, as did all the other men but Brown. Tom saw two gun belts over near a fence post (the last one to which wire had been attached) to his right and behind the men. Tom gathered that Luke and Brown had removed their gun belts to make it a fair fight. Since Luke knew the character of this outfit, Tom took for granted that he had been compelled to remove his gun belt.

As the HE men began to get up from the ground, Tom (still mounted on Ross) and Luke instinctively backed up to have a better command of the scene before them. As they backed up, Tom called out, "Get rid of those guns, belts, knives, everything. Take 'em off and throw 'em out in front of you." The men complied, except for Speck and Whitey, still on the ground.

"You, with the nose," Tom called to the swarthy man he did not know. The man turned a pair of dark, deep-set eyes under black eyebrows on Tom. "Take Speck's gun, knife, and whatever else he has and throw them out there in front." The man did as he was told.

"Now, the other one, over there," Tom said, pointing with his gun toward Whitey. The man with the bloody nose went over and relieved Whitey of his weapons, which brought Whitey around. Whitey rolled around a bit, then sat up.

"Now," Tom said loudly enough for all to hear, "you all gather round your man, Speck, there, and lie down on the ground. Lie with your heads pointin' toward me."

The men slowly made their ways toward Speck, with Brown taking his time, and Whitey having a hard time standing up and, once on his feet, walking straight. Tom noticed that Brown had a bloody nose, too, though not as bad as that of the dark man. His face had a number of cuts and bruises on it, as well. Regardless, he was moving toward Speck far too slowly for Tom's satisfaction, and Tom let him know it.

"Brown, so help me, if you're not on the ground in two seconds, I'll shoot both your legs." Brown stabbed a menacing look at Tom, and Tom, growing angrier as the scene became ever clearer to him, shot a bullet into the sand near Brown's feet. Brown picked up his pace just enough to say he did, though he kept the look on Tom. Finally, all men were lying on the ground, Speck still on his back, holding his leg and sighing.

Tom climbed down from Ross and stood next to Luke. Still watching the men on the ground, he said quietly, so that the HE hands could not hear him over the wind, "What went on here?" He glanced over at Luke and saw blood trickling from his mouth and nose, and cuts and bruises on his face. "How long this been goin' on?"

"Not too long," Luke replied, not taking his eyes off the men on the ground. "Came across this fence, and I was so mad I started cuttin' it. Then, after cuttin' a few spans, I figured they couldn't be too far gone, so I started followin' it. Came up on these hombres putting' up the fence. I had my rifle out and had the drop on 'em, but I never saw Speck. He was off somewhere and came up behind me and got the drop on me. Then Brown and I were goin' to have a fair fight. Started out that way, until I got a few good licks in on him. Well, you saw what was becomin' of it. Appreciate your gettin' here when you did."

"What's this all about?" Tom said, nodding toward the fence.

"They're claimin' the range all the way up to the land we own," Luke said. "Brown made some wisecrack about them bein' open-rangers and us bein' nesters. Said if we can't keep our cattle on our own land, they're goin' to have to fence off their range."

Tom could see Edwards behind this. That was it: Edwards was saying that because the Seven Ox Seven had bought the land—something that the open-range, free-grass ranchers considered to be nearly sacrilege—they could not make any claim to range beyond their purchased land. Of course, Tom and Luke had always assumed the opposite: because they had purchased the land, they had a stronger claim to the range beyond it.

"What do you think?" Tom said. "With all this manpower here, you think we ought to put 'em to work takin' down this nuisance fence?"

"Yeah," Luke said dryly, without taking his eyes off the men on the ground, "after we finish the fair fight."

"You want to finish it?" Tom looked over his wounded partner.

"Yessir."

"You sure you want to do that? You already gave 'em more than they could handle."

"Yessir," Luke said with finality.

"All right," Tom said, still looking at Luke. Then turning toward the men on the ground, he added, "We better see about Speck's leg first, though.

"Henderson," Tom called out.

Henderson raised his head.

"Can you doctor Mr. Speck's leg?"

"I can try," Henderson replied.

"Go ahead, then."

Henderson got up and took a look at the leg. The bullet had missed the bone, but had caught the fleshy part of the calf and had cut right through it. Henderson fetched a canteen from near where Luke's and Brown's gun belts lay, without even looking at the gun belts, and, with the water and his neckerchief, cleaned the wound. Then, using his and Speck's neckerchiefs, he bandaged the wound.

When he was finished, Tom asked him, "How is he?"

"Missed the bone," Henderson said. "I packed it. It oughtta be all right. Just take a while to heal, is all."

"What about the fellow with the nose?" Tom asked, nodding toward the man with the bleeding nose.

Henderson looked at the nose and said, "Broken." Then he took the man's neckerchief, soaked it with water, and had the man sit up, tilt his head back, and hold the kerchief on it. "He'll be all right," he called out to Tom.

"All right," Tom said, "now gather up those weapons and pile 'em over by those gun belts over by the fence." Henderson did so.

"Now," Tom said, when Henderson had finished, "back on the ground."

Henderson looked at Tom with a slight smile, as if to say, "Is that necessary?"

"The price you pay for the company you keep," Tom responded.

Henderson grinned and nodded, as if to say that it was worth a try, and lay back down.

"Brown," Tom called out. Brown looked up. "Get up. You've got some unfinished business."

Brown rose slowly to his feet, and Tom saw a nervousness come over the big man. He had started a fight with Luke, and Luke had been beating him, which had caused Brown's men to enter the fray. Brown now knew what he was up against. He could only hope that the extra beating that Luke had taken, due to the other three men entering the fight, had been enough to take the fight out of him.

Luke handed the Winchester to Tom and advanced toward Brown. Though Brown looked as though he would just as soon head in the other direction, he did move toward Luke, though more slowly and, apparently, with less confidence. As Tom watched the two men approach the fight, the words "Beware the fury of a patient man" came to mind from somewhere out of his past. Though not necessarily the most patient man Tom had ever met, Luke was one of the less violent, but these men had stirred something in him that Brown was now being forced to face.

The other HE men all raised their heads to watch the fight, except for the man with the broken nose, who was sitting off to the side with his head back. Luke looked at the HE men on the ground and realized that the fight should be out of Tom's line of fire, so he moved off to his right a number of paces. Brown moved toward where Luke stopped.

Luke and Brown met, and they stepped around in a circle for a while, taking each other's measure. Luke let his fists down a little and opened up, inviting Brown to take a swing. They circled for a while, squaring off at each other and looking into each other's eyes: Brown seeing a determined anger in Luke's; Luke seeing, down beneath everything else in Brown's, fear.

Finally, as they stepped around—Luke patiently measuring his opponent, Brown anxiously trying to draw in and intimidate his with ineffective feints—Brown gave in to the anxiety rising within him, and he swung his big right fist at Luke. Luke ducked it and hit Brown—first with the right fist, then the left, both to the body—and then stepped deftly back. Brown doubled over, still remaining on his feet. He had taken one blow in his ample belly, the other in his rib cage. He had the wind partly knocked out of him. He stood aside, bent over, gulping air, his hands resting the weight of his upper body on his knees. Luke circled him patiently.

In time, Brown rose back to his full height. Again he and Luke faced off, circling. Again Brown gave in to emotions, anxiety and frustration, and swung at Luke. This time he grazed the top of Luke's head, as Luke ducked out of the way. Again Luke hit him with two punches to the body. These did not land as squarely as had his last two. Still, the punches had their effects on Brown, even if they were not as noticeable as those that followed the first two. Brown staggered off a bit, then caught his balance and put up his fists again, and again began to circle with Luke.

And so the fight proceeded. Tom watched, trying to make sure he did not become so engrossed in the fight as to forget the men that he was covering. As he glanced over at these men, he realized he had little to be concerned about. They were as engrossed in the fight as he was.

There was something about the fight that drew and held one's interest, attention. Tom watched and wondered about that. Brown would swing with varying degrees of success or failure; Luke would strike hard and fast, and then step off again and circle. Perhaps it was that methodical approach of Luke's, his patience, his dogged persistence in the role of reactive defender, not attacker, compared to which Brown's undisciplined attack, his wild swings, stood out in sharp contrast.

In watching the fight, Tom was impressed by Luke's physique in a way he had never been before. Luke was a stout man, solid, but stout.

His good-sized head, which was not at all out of proportion to his body, sat atop a solid neck, that neck upon a set of broad, square shoulders. Below that was a lot of muscle, muscle in his arms, chest, legs. And all that muscle moved solidly, powerfully, though with surprising lightness and quickness when necessary. And solidly it received its blows. Luke could take a punch, and another, and another. Luke had already taken his share from the four men surrounding him by the time Tom had arrived. Though Brown was an undisciplined fighter, still, he was a large man, who did, however much he might try to avoid it, do some of the work that would be expected of a foreman on a ranch, and thus he had some muscle of his own. Despite his lack of discipline, this large man did manage to land a punch now and then, and Tom was amazed to see Luke take a punch to the face with little more of a reaction than a slight recoil from the blow and sometimes a short step back. Blows to his body had little effect.

Another thing that was immediately striking was Luke's persistent position of defense. He would not take the role of aggressor. The manner in which he conducted his end of the fight adamantly maintained his role of defender. He was defending himself (and, in a larger sense, his family, friend, and property) against attack. And, as such, he almost never struck at Brown's face or head, despite Brown's unwavering commitment to try to hit his. Tom understood this. He had been in his share of scrapes, and—if it were necessary, or if he were forced to react without time for sufficient reflection after having received a blow himself—he could hit a man in the face, but, for the most part, something inside (his conscience, he believed) impressed upon him that aiming a blow at a man's face was striking out at the man's life, something to which he had a fundamental aversion, as he was sure Luke did, as well. Hitting a man in the body could do its damage, but it was more likely to wear a man down or mortify him some. Striking a man in the face could knock the life out of him in one blow, either temporarily or permanently, and a man should only resort to such a measure in the most threatening of circumstances.

As the fight continued, and continued to hold Tom's attention, he wondered at that, too, in the light of his conscience. Should he allow it to hold his attention as it did? Should he, for lack of a better word, "enjoy," or perhaps better, "appreciate" it as much as he did (which he only did because Luke was getting the better of Brown)? Was it a sense of justice that made the fight attractive? Or was it a motive of revenge or of something even more base or primitive? If he believed it was justice, was he being honest with himself? Besides, was it their place to mete out justice?

This thought fell within the context of a considerable amount of thinking Tom had done since the beginning of the appearance of Henry Edwards in the region of Cañon Escondido. Tom knew Sacred Scripture fairly well, and he had a working knowledge of Holy Tradition. He considered that Christ had said: "Blessed are the meek. . . . Blessed are the peacemakers . . ." "Put up again thy sword into its place; for all that take the sword shall perish with the sword." "But I say to you, that whosoever is angry with his brother, shall be in danger of the judgment. And whosoever shall say to his brother, Raca, shall be in danger of the council. And whoever shall say, Thou fool, shall be in danger of hell fire." "But I say to you not to resist evil: but if one strike thee on thy right cheek, turn to him also the other: And if a man will contend with thee in judgment, and take away thy coat, let go thy cloak also unto him. And whosoever will force thee one mile, go with him other two." "But I say to you, Love your enemies: do good to them that hate you: and pray for them that persecute and calumniate you: That you may be the children of your Father who is in heaven, who maketh his sun to rise upon the good, and bad, and raineth upon the just and the unjust. For if you love them that love you, what reward shall you have? do not even the publicans this? And if you salute your brethren only, what do you more? do not also the heathens do this? Be you therefore perfect, as also your heavenly Father is perfect?" So Christ said. And how did he act? He was interrogated, struck, spat upon, humiliated, publicly scourged, crowned with thorns, forced to carry his own Cross, nailed to that Cross, publicly rebuked and renounced, abandoned by all but a very few of his followers and his Mother, and he accepted all this unto death. "Father, forgive them, for they know not what they do."

Tom continued to ponder, as he watched the fight before him: But the Old Testament tells of God guiding his people in their destruction of other peoples under holy leaders like Moses, Joshua, Levi, Elijah, David, and others. And Jesus himself called the scribes and Pharisees

"hypocrites," "blind guides," "foolish," "whited sepulchres, which out-
wardly appear to men beautiful, but within are full of dead men's
bones, and of all filthiness," "serpents," "generation of vipers." He also
cleared the temple, using his belt as a whip to defend his Father's
house. And he said he had "not found so great faith, not even in Israel"
as he found in the witness of a Roman centurion, a soldier, who recognized the nature of authority and Christ's own authority to heal his
servant. And did not St. Paul write of legitimate authorities, "But if
thou do that which is evil, fear: for he beareth not the sword in vain.
For he is God's minister; an avenger to execute wrath upon him that
doth evil."

And, as for authority, Christ established the Magisterium of the
Church, giving to Peter and the apostles the power to loose and to
bind, and to Peter exclusively the power of the keys: powers which
have been handed on to their successors, the pope and the other bish-
ops, to this present day. This he did to assure authentic interpretation
of the Word of God, whether transmitted in Sacred Scripture or Holy
Tradition, to which the Magisterium is servant. The Church has canonized warriors like St. Louis IX, King of France, a Crusader. Even
Joan of Arc, who at age seventeen led the armies of France against
those of the English, was rehabilitated by the Church within thirty
years or so of her death, and she could well be beatified and canonized
one day. The Church also teaches that there is such a thing as a just
war, and gives the conditions for it. And the *Roman Catechism* states
that a soldier who, fighting in a just war, in service to his country,
without ambition or cruelty, takes the life of an enemy is without guilt.
The *Roman Catechism* further states that if a man kills another man in
self-defense, he does not break the fifth commandment. Of course,
this statement is qualified by requiring that the defender has used
"every means consistent with his own safety to avoid the infliction of
death." This accords with St. Thomas Aquinas' requirement of "moderation," that a man use no more force than is necessary, but that, if in
using necessary force in self-defense he kills the other, it is not unlaw-
ful. And here Tom remembered that he had read in a quotation from
St. Thomas' *Summa Theologiae*, on this very matter of self-defense,
that "one is bound to take more care of one's own life than of another's." He had always intended to look up that quotation to read it in

its full context, but he had yet to do it, and he could only guess, in his present setting, to what distance and in which direction he would be required to travel to find a complete set of the *Summa Theologiae*. Regardless, Tom remembered reading elsewhere that one could, in charity, choose not to defend oneself so as to preserve the life of the unjust aggressor, but that, in some cases, one's duty may require that one defend oneself to the utmost. As far as duty was concerned, Tom knew that the Church also taught that an individual not only has a right but, in some cases, a duty to defend the lives of others—as in the case of a man toward his wife and children, or in cases of others in positions of legitimate authority.

These were matters to which Tom had devoted some thought and reading (of the books he had, which did include the *Roman Catechism*) during this period of harassment from the Edwards outfit. And he had wondered, and he wondered still, about what constituted moderation in their present circumstances. He wondered to what extent they could defend themselves against ongoing rustling, when the rustlers fled from capture and, in many cases, from certain identification. To what extent did their legitimate defense allow them to take preemptive action in their circumstances. Yes, the Church gave moral guidelines (based in authentic interpretation of the Word of God) to make such decisions, but in the end, the individual or the community had to make decisions based on his or its best application of those guidelines and the guidance of the Holy Spirit, to whom one was obligated to pray and subject himself, knowing full well that the effects of original sin compromised his receptiveness to what the Holy Spirit was communicating to him. In the end, one must do one's best to discern and follow God's will in all circumstances, doing his best to choose a plan of action in accordance with that will. And this was all very important, because the consequences of these decisions could be of the gravest kind. Tom and the Stuarts were now in the position of making the kinds of decisions that could result in consequences of the gravest kind. They must make those decisions: their circumstances demanded no less. They must choose, and were already in the process of choosing, courses of action in reaction to aggression. In their present case, the provocation or aggression may have begun in serious theft, that of Hereford bulls, but serious theft carried out in such a way as to make it almost petty. This only continued to more deeply confirm for Tom what he had suspected from Edwards at the beginning, that he was capable of twisted games, so twisted as to confuse any who attempted to order their lives according to any kind of moral code, such as did Tom Schurtz and the Stuarts.

In fact, it was Luke Stuart's moral code that was ordering the fight that continued to play itself out in front of Tom as he pondered. Slowly it had continued, with Brown striking out at the life in Luke, and Luke punishing him in his body for it. And that, too, had its place, Tom thought, as he watched. Among the secular humanists of his time, the value of legitimate punishment was already being undermined. By the latter half of the next century, they would have achieved considerable success in disparaging the term and the practice, while often practicing, themselves, a most primitive and vindictive form of illegitimate punishment on those who, far from failing to adhere to established objective norms, would refuse to adopt their subjective, relativistic perspectives and conclusions. The universal Church, though, would not be swayed by this latest flight from rationality. It would maintain:

> Legitimate public authority has the right and the duty to inflict punishment proportionate to the gravity of the offense. Punishment has the primary aim of redressing the disorder introduced by the offense. When it is willingly accepted by the guilty party, it assumes the value of expiation. Punishment then, in addition to defending public order and protecting people's safety, has a medicinal purpose: as far as possible, it must contribute to the correction of the guilty party.

Tom was of this same mind, as he watched the progress of the fight between Luke and Brown. There was something right in Luke's punishment of Brown, though one did need to guard against the tendency toward revenge. Still, as for the "value of expiation" in this punishment of Brown, one familiar with the man would have had good reason to doubt a "[willing acceptance] by the guilty party." Certainly, Brown showed no indication of a willing acceptance as the fight slowly,

slowly circled and slowly, slowly progressed. An unwilling acceptance did seem to overtake him, though, as he took more time to recover from each blow, while Luke maintained a steady, disciplined defense, showing only a little weakening. Once again Brown fell to his knees after a set of body blows. He returned to his feet, after a little while, but looked more and more like he wished this ordeal to end, betraying even less discipline in ever wilder swings, for which, each time, he paid dearly. The next time down, he stayed on his knees longer. Then, finally, he did not get up at all, but remained on the ground holding his ribcage, breathing heavily and wheezing. Watching him, Tom rightly suspected that he had cracked, or even broken, some ribs.

Luke, as determined as he had been from the beginning, circled the fallen man. Brown raised his head for a moment, from his position of kneeling in the dust in the increasing heat and light of the bright, warm day. He raised his head and then his eyes, and saw Luke still circling, his determination unabated. Brown looked back down, closed his eyes as he held his ribs in pain, then looked up again at the circling Luke. Looking down again, he said in an exhalation of breath, "You won."

Luke stopped circling. "What did you say, Brown?" he called out.

Brown knelt, holding his side, panting.

"Say it again, Brown," Luke demanded, "and say it loud."

Brown knelt in the dust panting. He raised his head into the sun, which washed out the color from his face, save for the red of blood.

"Say it again, Brown," Luke repeated.

"You won."

"Louder!"

"You won!" Brown shouted. Then, still panting, he slipped down into a sitting position in the dust.

Luke turned and walked away from the fight, as a wave of relaxation passed through him, taking, as it passed, the solid posture he had maintained throughout and leaving him looking as if he had been in a fight. He dragged himself over to where he and Brown had left their guns, knives, and hats, and he picked his up and returned them to their respective places on his person. Then he picked up Brown's hat, carried it over to Brown, and tossed it toward him, so that it landed within that man's reach. Then he picked up as many of the weapons of the HE men as he could, and he carried them to his horse, where he began to stow them in his own saddlebags.

Next, Luke mounted his horse and rode around to the HE horses, tethered here and there, and to the wagon, and removed rifles and shotguns from three of the five saddles and one from the wagon. Neither Henderson nor the man with the broken nose had a rifle or shotgun, though Henderson had an empty scabbard on his saddle.

With these guns across the front of his saddle, he rode over to where Tom still covered the HE men with his gun.

"I'll cover 'em a while, if you want to bind up these guns and tie 'em up on your saddle," Luke said to Tom. "My hands aren't set for any delicate work."

Tom looked at the swollen hands and, nodding his head, said, "Will do," as he took the guns from Luke. He unloaded each gun. Then he pulled a couple leather thongs from one of his saddlebags and bound them up. Then he tied them across the back of his saddle.

That complete, he turned to Luke and said, "Let's put these outlaws to work."

They had Speck placed in the back of the wagon, joined by the man with the broken nose. The rest of the men, including Brown, they kept on foot. They had Henderson and Smith remove the wire. Luke stayed with them, guarding them. At every post he had them cut the wire, so that the entire fence would be reduced to spans of wire roughly forty feet long. These he had them leave lying on the ground. They would pick them up on their return. Brown and Whitey were to remove posts. They were to use saws, taken from the back of the wagon, and were to cut off the posts right at the ground, to render them too short for future use as fence posts.

Before long, Henderson and Smith had cut all the wire and were already working their way back toward the wagon, under Luke's careful watch, gathering the lengths of cut wire as they went. When each man had collected an armload of wire, they would make one pile of their armloads on the ground, so that they could come back later and pick up the piles of wire with the wagon. Eventually, they walked up to where Brown and Whitey, under the barrel of Tom's six-gun, were sawing off a post. Just behind where the men were working was the wagon, with the man with the broken nose, whom they called Coe, sitting on the seat. Henderson and Smith carried their latest armloads of wire over and deposited them in the wagon. Already in the wagon were a number of fence posts that had been sawed off at the ground. Speck lay off to the side, finding it more and more difficult to save some room for himself among the posts and wire. To the back of the wagon were tied the HE hands' horses.

There were three axes in the back of the wagon, as well. Tom had not trusted Brown and Whitey with the axes, but Luke was not as concerned about Henderson and Smith. He had each take an ax, and moving to the next posts beyond Tom's workers, he had them cut down the posts with axes. These they would leave lying until the wagon came by, and whichever group was in the rear would pick up the posts and put them in the wagon. So they continued, one group leapfrogging the one ahead whenever the rear group finished before the one ahead did.

It was a little after suppertime when the men cut down the last of the posts and piled them all in the full wagon. White clouds from the southeast had been bunching up for some time and were beginning now to turn gray. Some lightning even flickered through them, as the wind from that direction picked up. Speck had long before been displaced by posts and wire in the back of the wagon and had had to join Coe up on the seat, despite the obvious pain in his leg. Periodically, Tom or Luke would have Henderson check on Speck's leg and Coe's nose. Coe, for the most part, took care of himself, washing out the neckerchief and reapplying it. The bleeding from his nose was slowing down. The bleeding from Speck's leg Henderson continued to check by changing the dressing and keeping the wound packed. Speck would be out of circulation for a little while, but he would be all right.

With the work all done—the fence completely down and its short posts and wires loaded in the wagon—it was time for Tom and Luke to dismiss their appropriated crew, and so they did.

"Coe," Tom called out to the man with the broken nose. That man, seated next to Speck (though Speck nearly lay on the seat of the wagon), turned to look out at Tom over the kerchief that his left hand held pressed to his face. "You see that red rock sticking out of that hill yonder?" Tom said, pointing off toward a point about two miles to the south. Coe looked off toward the south for a moment, then turned back toward Tom and nodded. "I want you to drive this wagon," Tom continued, "with those horses tied to it, down to that rock and wait there for these hombres."

Coe continued to look at Tom, as if awaiting further instructions. "That's it," Tom said. "Go on."

Coe set the bloody kerchief in his lap and picked up the reins and slapped them against the backs of the mules. "Giddap," he called to the animals, in a way that sounded as though he had a bad head cold. The mules responded and the wagon lurched forward, as Speck gasped and straightened up on the seat and held on. Coe quickly grabbed at the kerchief in his lap, just as it was about to fall off, and held it in his right hand as he held the reins in his left. He would periodically press the kerchief against his face, as his attention to the reins would allow. Thus rolled the wagon out of the vicinity of Tom and Luke, seated on their horses, and the other four HE hands, all afoot.

"Well," Tom said to the HE hands, "you can all lie down on your bellies and wait. It's goin' to take him a while to get there."

The HE hands, tired from their exertions of the last two days (those of erecting a fence and those of tearing one down), gave Tom no trouble when it came to carrying out this order. They almost gave the impression that they welcomed it. These were still the days of the open range, when a cowboy had little appreciation for work that could not be done from the saddle. The introduction of barbed-wire fencing and the work that went with it, of which their recent exertions were but a sample, would lead eventually to the fencing of the range, which would considerably alter the day to day work of a cowboy.

Tom and Luke backed their horses up a little and settled back in their saddles. They talked a little, but, for the most part, just sat and kept an eye on the men on the ground and watched for Coe and the wagon to appear to the south. After about half an hour, they saw the wagon climb up and over a hill still on their side of the hill that was his destination, but he was close enough as far as they were concerned.

"All right," Tom said, "you all get up and start walkin' south. Your man Coe will be waitin' for you with the wagon and your horses down at that red rock yonder. We'll keep these weapons to bolster our own defenses and to disarm those we most need to defend against. And that's a pretty sorry comment on your character. Problem is, with character such as yours, you probably don't care much about that. Anyways, you got a ways to walk, so get walkin'."

The men had stood in front of him as he had addressed them. Brown, despite the fatigue that resulted from his beating and subsequent labors, had stared defiantly at Tom with a sneer worthy of his employer. Whitey had looked down and around, without ever looking Tom in the eye. Smith had looked at Tom with eyes that conveyed some anger, but he had kept looking in a way that made Tom unsure about whether that anger was directed at him or elsewhere. Henderson had not looked at Tom much, but had shifted uncomfortably a time or two as Tom had spoken. When Tom had finished, Henderson had looked up at him, and, pressing his lips together, had given Tom a nod. Now, with the other men, he turned and started to walk.

Luke and Tom turned their horses and rode for home.

LUKE AND TOM rode up the canyon at a walk. There was a hesitation within each of them and between them. They would have to face Elizabeth with Luke's battered condition. As it was, he could have looked a good deal worse. Still, his face was cut, bruised, and swollen, the bruises and swelling setting in more as time passed. They stopped along the way to wash up his wounds in a cold spring, so that he would look as good as possible when Elizabeth would see him. And Elizabeth would have to see him. He and Tom talked about that as they rode up the canyon. They, especially Luke, were going to have to tell Elizabeth about what was going on. There were decisions to be made.

At that conclusion, Luke and Tom slowly, somberly, and regretfully arrived, as they rode up the canyon. Recent events had made it clear that the behavior of the Edwards outfit had suddenly taken on a more confrontational and even more criminal character. As Tom had pointed out before, they were outlaws, at least some of them, and they would be willing to go farther in their aggression toward the Seven Ox Seven than he and Luke would be willing to answer in kind. And, if their behavior was not answered, then they would continue it until they had run the Seven Ox Seven out of the canyon.

Accordingly, the partners considered the real possibility of leaving the canyon. If it were just the two of them, they could fight it out, but there were Elizabeth and the children to be concerned about. Elizabeth had already suffered considerably due to this conflict. The Stuarts had lost their baby. What might come next? So far the effects on Elizabeth had been secondary, her suffering based in knowledge of the primary effects the HE's behavior was having on Luke and Tom and the ranch. What if the effects on Elizabeth became primary? What if these men hurt Luke and Tom where they were most vulnerable, in Luke's family?

And yet, this was their canyon, their ranch, their home. They had built so much. There was yet so much promise. Law and order were not far behind. More ranchers were moving into the area. The Texas Rangers were making their presence felt more in west Texas. Things could only get better, if they could just hold out. But for how long? They were still essentially isolated. What the HE had done—rustling bulls in a way that left little evidence that could not be blamed on drifting—would be difficult to fight legally. The evidence of the calves they had rustled could easily be offset by the HE calves that Luke had forced them to brand with the Seven Ox Seven. The Seven Ox Seven could not rely on the fact that their calves were white-faced, because the HE cows would soon start dropping white-faced calves, courtesy of Seven Ox Seven bulls. The issue of the fence and whose land was whose could go either way, and could actually work in Edwards' favor, depending upon which court it wound up in and that judge's senti-ments regarding open range, free grass, especially as that issue would grow increasingly volatile in the succeeding years.

Darkness appeared to loom on the horizon for the future of their canyon ranch. For Luke, the most recent events concerning the HE outfit raised serious concerns about the safety of his family. As these concerns played out more and more in his mind, he entertained more and more doubts about the possibility of continuing the ranch. But what was there beyond the ranch? Where would they go? What would become of all that they had put into the ranch? What about their com-mitment to Tom?

Tom shared Luke's concerns about his family. He too had a sense of the darkness on the horizon. But Tom, despite this darkness, was less inclined to seriously consider moving on just yet. Like Luke, he could not see beyond their canyon ranch. He could not see leaving it all behind. He accepted that possibility for the protection of Luke's family, but the reality of it, the reality of giving up the canyon, of letting go of all that it meant—family, vocation, home, the place where they would live out the rest of their lives—that he had not yet accepted. He did not hold on so much from hope as from a refusal to accept that they could lose it all. There was also in his tenacity a sort of wistfulness, an idea of what had been and could have been. And there was a resentment toward those who would dare take it all away for their own depraved greed and spitefulness.

In time, they arrived at the house. It was late enough that the children would probably be in bed, though it was still light out, being late spring. Luke rode to the dugout to unsaddle his horse and put away the saddle, and then he led the horse by the reins to the corral. Tom rode up to the house. He dismounted, loosened the cinch of his saddle, and picketed Ross in a nice bit of grass to the side of the house. He climbed the steps of the porch and knocked at the door. Elizabeth looked out through the gun hole in the closed shutters of the window nearest the door and, after seeing Tom on the porch, opened the door.

"Where's Luke?" she immediately asked.

"He's puttin' his horse away," Tom said, as he closed the door behind him. "Are the kids in bed?" he asked Elizabeth, as he looked around and saw not a trace of them.

"They are," she said, looking at him as if searching for something. "Why?"

"Just wonderin'," Tom replied. "Luke wants you to meet him around at the corral. Got somethin' he wants to show you. I'll walk out with you. The kids'll be fine."

Tom took Elizabeth gently by the elbow and guided her out of the house. She was staring at him as they went, and though he would not look at her, he could feel it. "What's wrong, Tom?" she asked him, as they were stepping down the front porch stairs.

"Well, Elizabeth," Tom began, drawing that introduction out as far as he could as they turned the corner toward the back of the house. He was trying to get her as far away from the house and the hearing of the children as was possible. He continued in a loud voice, so as to be heard above the gathering wind, "We had a little trouble today." She sucked in her breath in a short gasp, as she raised a hand to her mouth. He did not look at her, but he could feel the fear rising in her, and he quickly said, "Luke's all right. We're both just fine. It's just that Luke got in a tussle with some of the HE men, and I'm just here to prepare you, because he's got a few scrapes and cuts, but he's just . . ."

Elizabeth continued to stare at Tom—though much more intently, with near terror in her eyes—as he began this explanation of what was wrong. At the mention of scrapes and cuts, she pulled away from him and ran to the corral, where she met Luke just closing and locking the gate.

When she reached Luke, Elizabeth pulled him around by the shoulder so that she could look into his face. Luke turned around to face her. In the low light of evening, and in its shadow, Luke saw the intensity of concern in her eyes, as those eyes surveyed his entire face. He saw the tears welling in them, as she noted his wounds: the cuts, bruises, swellings, and deformities beaten into his face by other men's fists. She moved in closer and inspected the wounds in the fading light, gently touching here and there to check their severity. And, as she surveyed this evidence of violence visited upon his face, the tears began to run over and spill out of her eyes. Then she looked into the eyes of that face so brutalized and saw, therein, her husband, and finally she was crying, and she dropped her vision from his and lay her head upon his shoulder and embraced him, saying through her tears as she did so, "Oh, Luke."

Luke dropped the bridle from his hand and raised both bruised and swollen hands up to gently hold his wife. He looked up to see Tom motion toward the house and then turn and head back around toward the front door.

Tom walked toward the front of the house, into the wind, which shoved against him from the southeast. The gusts had grown stronger just since he and Luke had got home. He turned at the corner and felt one forceful gust slam into his back, just as he turned away from it, and push him forward. He made the steps, climbed them, and entered the house.

Once inside, Tom washed up and then helped himself to some of the venison stew that Elizabeth had warming on the stove. He also started a fire in the fireplace, and he fed it with a few logs in anticipation of the chill he believed the recent gusts portended. He poured out some coffee and sat down on the north side of the table, facing toward the door, to eat and wait for Elizabeth and Luke.

By the time Elizabeth and Luke came in, it was completely dark outside. The twilight had abruptly given over to darkness, intensified by the heavy cloud cover moving in from the southeast. Flashes from distant lightning could be seen through the gun holes in the shutters covering the windows, followed, some time later, by rumbling thunder. Little by little, the time between lightning and thunder was shortening.

The shutters remained closed over the windows, as Elizabeth had been instructed to keep them. Tom had not bothered to open any, because he had been hungry and had gone straight for the food. Now that it was completely dark, there was no reason for anyone to open them.

Elizabeth had already lighted the lamp on the table before the men had arrived, due to the darkness in the house with the shutters closed. The fire added its dancing orange light, and companion dancing shadows, to that of the whiter glow of the lamp.

Into that light moved Elizabeth and Luke. Elizabeth went right to the counter, where she poured water from a bucket into a pan and placed it on the hot stove, and then dished up some stew and poured coffee for Luke. That done, she went into their bedroom and shortly returned with some rags, and then she stood at the stove waiting for the water to heat.

Luke had come directly to the table and taken a place across from Tom. When Tom looked at his partner in the low light of the lamp and the dancing light and shadow of the fire, his wounds appeared more pronounced. Tom was sure that Luke's bruises had swollen considerably from when he had last seen him in the light. He was also aware of how the lamp and fire served to accentuate the bruising and swelling, casting shadow with their light to distort even the lightest bruise— now raising it, now flattening it, now lighting it, now darkening it— so that Tom found himself staring at his friend to study just how bad the wounds really were.

Soon Elizabeth was seated next to Luke, a pan of hot water in front of her on a hot pad on the table. She had laid some clean rags and a block of soap on the table next to the pan. She took one of the rags and dipped it into the hot water and rubbed it on the soap. With it she began to wash Luke's wounds.

Luke pulled slightly away from the first touch of the hot, soapy rag to one of his cuts, somewhat annoyed that this operation, if it had to take place at all, would need to be performed while he was eating. But he knew that Elizabeth needed to do this, so he accepted it and tried to eat, as well as he could, as she cleaned his wounds. (She had already washed his hands, amidst her tears, at the stand on the porch before they had come in.) Eventually she moved around to the other side of him to work on that side of his face.

As Luke ate, Tom and Luke made light talk about certain work they would need to get done in the following days. Elizabeth paid little attention to their talk, concentrating instead on the task before her. In time, Luke finished eating and Elizabeth finished doctoring, and all sat for a little while, avoiding the serious matters they needed to discuss, resting instead in a stillness that allowed for a thoughtful study of the complementary sounds of wind and thunder announcing the advancing storm, muffled as these sounds were within the home of stone with oak door and shutters fastened snugly.

Finally, Tom spoke up. "I guess we got some things to talk about," he said.

The Stuarts agreed that they had, and so they began. They outlined their present situation, noting that until the previous fall they had had no complaints, that though their venture had offered its share of challenges, they had been encouraged to meet those challenges and overcome them, or at least to try. In any event, no challenge had been more than they were willing to take on or accept. But since the arrival of the Edwards outfit, that had begun to change.

The several problems associated with Edwards' arrival were itemized: the stolen bulls, which deprived them of their own breeding bulls and caused them the trouble of chasing down their own property; the rustled calves, which showed that Edwards was willing to move into clearly criminal behavior that could be documented; the fencing, which showed that Edwards was willing to use his superiority of manpower (and questionable manpower at that) to bully them out of land they had every right to claim as range; the attack on Luke, which showed that these men were willing to use excessive force to cause physical injury or perhaps worse; and there was, in that, Speck's apparent eagerness to shoot at both Luke, early in the rustling game, and Tom, just that very day.

As they extracted these points from their experiences of the last several months, the winds continued to make their presence known, even with more force now, as they rushed against the windows outside the shutters, pressing and rattling the panes in their frames. The winds whistled and moaned, too, in various pitches and tones, through any tight spot through which they might pass, near or far. And from far to near rolled the thunder, louder now and closer in occurrence to its causal lightning, which still flashed and flickered through the gun holes in the shutters. Now, into the mix of the sounds of wind and thunder, Charlie added his barking, bold and urgent, though often drowned out by wind and thunder, and to his, the puppies added their own.

Shortly came a sound from inside the house, as little Robert's cry could be heard above that of the storm. Elizabeth hurried up the stairs to get him before he woke the others. She arrived too late. And thus she descended the stairs with Robert in her arms, and she was followed by Rachel (also afraid of the storm) and Zachariah (who preferred not to be left alone upstairs). Elizabeth let them, all three, crawl into their parents' bed. Robert was comforted there, happy to be in the company of his brother and sister, where he could hear the quiet voices of his parents and Uncle Tom in the next room.

Elizabeth returned and the discussion continued. Before they began to discuss the possible solutions to the Edwards outfit, they looked at the positive aspects of the canyon ranch: the herd was increasing; they had bought more land, and could buy even more; other ranchers were moving into the region, though still far apart; they were beginning to grade their stock, and as they progressed, they could do so in a more controlled manner; the railroad was pushing ever deeper into the West, which would eventually mean more settlers, settlements, towns, and law and order. These were just a few of the reasons for them to be encouraged about the future that had looked so promising just a year before, and which would still look promising if it were not for one modification in their circumstances.

That one modification, of course, was the arrival of the Edwards outfit. As they approached the matter of Edwards, the winds pushed ever harder, the thunder grew ever closer and louder, the barking of Charlie and the puppies sounded ever more furious. With the change of subject to the Edwards outfit, and the break in the train of thought, Tom looked at Luke in response to the dogs' barking. They had all heard the dogs bark excitedly on other nights, caused perhaps by a rattlesnake, skunk, wildcat, coyote, wolf, or puma. Still, the barking did sound particularly aggressive.

"What's with Charlie and the puppies?" Tom said.

Luke shrugged his shoulders and wished he hadn't, as he winced a little from where one of Brown's errant punches had hit the side of his neck. "Polecat?" he said through his wince.

They dismissed the dogs' barking and returned their attention, as the storm raged without, to the storm that was raging within, concerning the Edwards outfit. As for the bulls, after this general breeding with the Texas stock, they could corral them, as they had planned to do eventually, to gain more control in breeding. The branded calves . . .

"You hear that?" Tom said, in the wake of an especially loud crash of thunder, as he turned his left ear back toward the window behind him, and his brows knit in a look of concern.

"You mean the thunder?" Luke replied, piqued by the look on Tom's face.

"No, I mean a shot."

"I heard the thunder," Luke said.

"Listen," Tom said, his ear still cocked toward the window behind him.

Luke did listen. Elizabeth did, too, concentrating, as she stared at the shutter right in front of her. Drops of rain could now be heard being driven by the wind against the window pane. Elizabeth listened with the men, as intently as Tom's command warranted. She listened as she stared at the gun hole in the shutter, listening more than looking, her mind concentrating on sound over sight, though her vision rested on the gun hole and the orange glow that was slowly rising within it.

"There," Tom said, and Elizabeth and Luke trained their hearing ever more intently. In a lull in the wind and thunder and rain, there came a distressed cry, a yelping, where Charlie's barking had been, along with frantic cries from the colt and the puppies, and in the instant they heard all this, Tom and Luke were on their feet. In that same instant, Elizabeth's vision pushed past her hearing in its message to her brain, and as she rose with the men, she did so in great agitation and cried out the reality that now rushed upon her, the reality of what the orange glow in the gun hole signified.

"FIRE!"

Tom and Luke, already on their feet and flying to their guns, froze and swung around to stare at Elizabeth as her cry made its cold and rapid descent down their backbones.

"FIRE!" she cried again, and she rushed for the window. She hurriedly unbarred the shutter and flung it open. Luke and Tom moved with her, so that Luke was right behind her by the time she opened the shutter and Tom was at her side. Fire lighted up the vision before them, fire framed by the structure of their barn, fire not content to remain within its frame, fire thrusting formlessly into the black sky of the dark night through any weakness in the structure that it could exploit. Then across that living picture of fire rode the dark silhouettes of at least two men, in the direction of the head of the canyon.

Luke grabbed Elizabeth by the shoulders and pulled her to the side, as Tom flung the shutter back over the window and lowered the bar across it.

"How many you see?" Luke shot at Tom.

"At least two."

"That's what I saw."

"But that's just what we saw," Tom cautioned.

"Where's the fire, Mama?" said Zachariah, who had just entered the scene from the bedroom to stand behind his parents, with Rachel and Robert right behind him.

"Oh," Elizabeth said, turning around and out of Luke's hold of her. She crouched down and said, "It's just outside. There's nothing to worry about."

"Is it in the barn?" Zachariah demanded excitedly. He read the silent answer in his mother's eyes.

"Brownie's in the barn, and the puppies!" he cried, and he ran for the door.

Luke caught him at the door and said, "We'll take care of Brownie, Zack. You stay with your mother, in the house."

Zachariah cried, "But Brownie's in the fire, Daddy! Brownie's in the fire!"

As Luke held his son and tried to reassure him, Tom was loading the Winchesters to make sure each had a full complement. With each loaded, he went to the door, just as Luke turned from leaving Zachariah in the hold of his mother. Tom unbarred the door and turned to hand Luke his rifle.

"I'll go around the west side," Tom said. "You go around the east."

"All right," Luke said, his set features evincing a stark determination as he took the gun. "Elizabeth," Luke called back, "you bar this door behind us and don't open it for anyone, until you see for sure it's one of us. Zack," he added, looking into the face of his son with an authority that would not be denied, "you stay with your mother. Now, Elizabeth!" he called to her again, as he disappeared out the door behind Tom. And as he was closing the door, he added, "Bar this door behind me!"

Elizabeth rushed to the door and caught the handle, as Luke pulled it behind him. Luke waited on the other side until he heard the bar slide into place. Then he tried the door to be sure, then made his way to the far eastern end of the porch, where he stopped to let his eyes adjust to the surrounding darkness, though he squinted against the moisture-laden wind. Then he stepped off the porch into the rain.

He crept along the side of the house, scouring the darkness for anyone who might be lurking there. When he arrived at the northern end of the house and looked straight ahead to the north, he could see the entire scene of the burning barn. From off to the left, a figure ran into the scene. He recognized it to be Tom. Then he himself started running. As he ran, he saw Tom, who had stopped running and was standing as near the opening of the barn as possible, aiming his rifle into the fire and shooting repeatedly. After six shots, Tom stopped firing. He turned his ear toward the flame for a moment and then lowered his gun and turned and walked back from the heat of the fire.

Luke met him in the light, heat, and noise of the blaze. "You get Brownie and the puppies?" Luke shouted.

"Yeah," Tom answered, "their cries were pitiful. I fired till I didn't hear 'em anymore, then fired a couple more."

"Hmh," Luke responded.

The two men stood in the rain, wind, lightning, and thunder and watched the fire—fed, teased, and twisted by the wind—quickly consume the cottonwood-picket barn. The structure and the hay, which made up most of what was in it, burned as only wood and hay cured in the dry air of that region could. The rain had little effect, as the fire burned under the protection of the roof until it finally fell in, signaling the demise of the structure.

But before that dramatic event, something in Tom's mind suddenly distracted him from the mesmerizing sight of the blaze. His features tensed up, and his eyes seemed to bore into something only he could see. He turned suddenly and looked to the west toward the head of the canyon.

"My house!" he yelled, and he took off at a run toward Ross picketed under a tree to the southeast of the Stuart house. Luke turned toward the head of the canyon in time to see the flickering of flames, though nothing like those that had just consumed their barn, coming from Tom's house. He stared at the sight for a moment, then turned and ran after Tom.

Luke caught up with Tom as he was swinging into the saddle, after having tightened its cinch and untethered Ross from the picket. The rain was pouring down ever harder now, the lightning and thunder surrounding them.

"Tom!" Luke shouted into the rain and thunder, as lightning made him visible to the mounted Tom.

Tom wheeled his horse around.

"I'll be right behind you!" Luke shouted.

"No!" Tom yelled. "You've got to stay here. Take care of the family."

Tom did not wait for further reply, but, wheeling Ross around in a flash of lightning, a frozen scene of magnificence, spurred him into full gallop.

The land flew away beneath Ross, as he charged through the night of darkness and lightning, rain, wind, and thunder and across familiar land made unfamiliar by all those elements. Lightning periodically lighted the way, its thunder simultaneous. The rain, torrential now, poured as if the heavens could not be rid of it fast enough, pounding its cold into both man and horse.

Tom rode on, coaxing all the speed he could get out of Ross, with his eyes fixed on the fire that flickered inside the frames of his windows and door. As he neared the house, he could see smoke still misting into the downpour from charred patches of the roof, smoldering still, despite the dousing from the rain. Ignoring the dying fire on the roof, he swung from his saddle as he was reining Ross to a stop. Hitting the ground on the run, he raced to his rain barrel at the northeast corner of the house. The barrel—which stood beneath a log pipe that channeled water from the gutter Tom had built along the front of the roof—was nearly overflowing, though it had been less than a quarter full when he had left that day.

Tom grabbed the bucket that hung on a peg on the side of his house and scooped it full of water from the barrel. He dashed into the open door to find that the flames had died down, from when he had first seen them while standing in front of the barn, because most of the fuel was spent. His table and chairs and second bed had been removed to the southwest corner occupied by his bed: the table angled over the corner of his bed, the second bed thrown on top of the bed and table, and the chairs thrown on top of it. Firewood had been piled under the table and dumped on the beds, table, and chairs. All of it had been doused with kerosene and set ablaze.

Licks of fire still played among what was left of this fuel, which was still enough for one to recognize that it had been the beds, table, chairs, and firewood, though portions of these were completely burned away, and what remained was charred black. The corner of the walls, too, was black, in a Christmas-tree pattern that reached for the roof, where flames from below had met flames from above to burn through the roof, those from above finally extinguished by the rain, which then ran into the house to extinguish those from below. Licks of fire also danced along the floor and up the walls in places where the kerosene had not been fully consumed. These licks advanced and retreated at the whim of the wind, which blew in, in gusts, through windows that had been broken, obviously to feed air to the fire. Instead, the air rushing in from outside had somewhat hindered the blaze, as the violent rain of that west Texas storm had so suddenly saturated the air with moisture.

Of course, Tom did not stop to analyze all of this at the time; instead, he threw the water onto the greatest concentration of flames, where the fuel had been most concentrated. He then ran back out for another bucket full, and another, and another, and before long, by this process, he had put out what remained of the fire.

Then Tom could examine and analyze. His examination revealed what has already been described. It further revealed that, though the northern part of the house had also been burned, the damage there had been confined to where kerosene had been splashed on the floor and walls. His books had miraculously survived, all pressed tightly together on the shelves he had built for them and attached to the north wall, to the side of the window under which the table had sat. Had flames even reached the books, and it did not appear that any had, being pressed so tightly together might well have preserved them from total loss. For that same reason, the walls and, to a lesser extent, the floor had sustained far less damage than they might have otherwise. Because the walls were made of logs, there was a low proportion of surface area to mass, so that the core of the log was less likely to heat up, especially since the charred surface also insulated the core against the heat. Add to that the lime-mortar chinking, and the fire had been given little chance to do its worst. The puncheon floor, of course, had offered far more surface area, but the puncheons were at least two inches thick, of dense solid oak, with the surface smoothed, all of which had contributed to its resistance to the fire. In fact, most of the damage to the floor had occurred where kerosene had been splashed, and even there, the charring from the initial burning had provided the core of the puncheons insulation against the heat of the fire.

Like the furniture, floor, and walls, the roof had sustained damage. In addition to the hole over the southwest corner—through which the rain now poured in, saturating the charred walls and floor below—other leaks were apparent. Rain seeped in at various places where Tom suspected that fire, started on the roof with kerosene, had damaged the shingles and possibly the laths underneath. This damage Tom could mainly hear, feel, and remember, after he had put out the fire, because the night, except for the lightning, was so dark.

Tom wanted to take a better inventory of the damage, but his kerosene lamp, which he had kept on the table, had been dumped out on the pile, thrown into it, and burned. Lightning still offered flashes and flickers of light through the windows and doors, but it was once again anticipating its accompanying thunder as it moved on toward the northwest. He did find some matches on the shelf on the far side of the window of the north wall, where he kept his food and cookware. One light of the match showed little more than what he expected from what he had seen in the fire. Though the house had been saved, there was considerable damage. Several of the puncheons, which he had so meticulously cut, fit, and smoothed, would need to be replaced. It was also possible that, where the fire had done its worst, some might have burned through into a sleeper or two. Some of the logs, or portions thereof, might also need to be replaced.

The match burned out. He did not light another. Already his mind was figuring how he might replace parts of the southwest corner without replacing entire logs. In so thinking, he realized how difficult it would be, and that reminded him of how masterfully he had cut and fit those joints, of how well he had mortared the chinks, of what a fine piece of craftsmanship his house had been. And as Tom thought, a deep, quiet, bitter, and resentful anger, which had been developing and smoldering inside him throughout the period of the HE's petty harassment, slowly flared up with this new dose of fuel. At its root was righteous indignation in response to clearly evil activity, but beyond that root had been developing more than what was righteous. His house, his home. They, that Edwards outfit, had been picking at the home he had developed with the Stuarts all along: at their livelihood, with the bulls; at their tranquility, with its effects on all of them, particularly Elizabeth; at their very persons, with their attack on Luke; and now at his house, his home, built with his own hands, in their own canyon, his own monument to some sense of permanence, rootedness, . . . home. He could fix it, but it would not be that same fine piece of work, that integral creation. It would be patched. Besides, this destruction was so unnecessary. It was plain mean, in the lowest sense of meanness. And Tom decided there and then, not in a thought as much as in a new orientation of his inner person, that this would not stand.

There was no point in lighting more matches. He had seen enough and would not be able to do much until the light of day, when the rain would have stopped. Regardless, he was eager to get back to the Stuarts and see how matters stood down below.

As Tom turned to leave, he grew suddenly very cold: cold in his wet clothing, cold in his charred house, cold in his anger and in a suddenly very impressive fear that he would lose all of this, his home, all that it meant; he would lose it all. He stood there and shivered involuntarily in this cold, shivered all through his body, as he stood looking out his doorway, watching the distancing lightning periodically light up, in a spectral glow, the canyon he had made his home. He could not move from the spot where he stood, shivering, frozen in the cold that had settled upon him. Finally, he thought of his slicker, which hung on a peg behind the door, and he pulled the door away from the wall to find that the fire had spared it, though, as he put it on, he found that the smoke had not.

Still, despite its heavy smell of smoke, he kept the slicker on and fastened it up, desperate to keep out the cold. Against the rain, the slicker was largely effective (he gratefully acknowledged on his ride down to the Stuarts'), because the rain came from outside the man; but against the cold, the slicker was largely ineffective (he regretfully accepted), because so much of the cold came from within.

WHEN TOM ARRIVED AT THE STUARTS', steamy smoke still rose from the charred remains of the barn, as wet wood still sizzled in the smoldering fire beneath the collapsed roof. The rain fell with less force now, and the wind gusted less severely, though the rain still fell in a constant shower, and the wind still pushed that shower around as it draped from the sky.

There was no sign of anyone outside, so Tom rode around to the front of the house and dismounted. He had begun to ride to the front of the dugout to unsaddle Ross, but some inner urging had inclined him to check on the Stuarts first.

He climbed the steps onto the porch, and as he stepped under the roof and approached the door, he saw, in the low flickering light from the distancing lightning, blood: large drops of it, close together, leading to the door. Tom followed the drops with his eyes, stunned at what he was seeing. On the door handle, blood was smeared by what had been a bloody hand.

Tom lunged at the door and pounded at it. No one answered immediately, and he pounded again. He saw an eye look through the gun hole, and then the door opened. Tom pushed open the door and stepped into the house.

No one was there to meet him when he entered. Instead, Luke was rushing back to the hearthstones before the fireplace. Once there, Luke crouched to hold down Charlie, as Elizabeth tried to apply bandages to his upper front leg and chest, and Zachariah, sobbing, petted the side of his ailing companion. Rachel stood behind those gathered over the dog, watching it all in the glow of the warm fire. (Robert, returned to his parents' bed by his mother, had fallen back to sleep there.)

After viewing the scene for a moment, Tom stepped back outside and took off his slicker and shook some of the rain off it, then reentered the house and hung the slicker on a peg near the door. He shivered as his cold, wet form stepped into the warmth of the house, and the shiver stayed with him as he moved toward the hearth. At the table he grabbed a chair and pulled it around to face the fire and then sat down on it, just behind Zachariah.

Elizabeth was trying desperately to stop the bleeding from the dog's wounds, caused by bullets. Every time she was just about to arrange a bandage that would keep pressure on the wound, Charlie would struggle to get up, and she would slip with the bandage. Now, however, Charlie lay ever more still, and as Luke held the dog, Elizabeth was at last applying a bandage which might stay. Meanwhile, Charlie's eyes were slowly closing, opening, then closing again, while Zachariah cried and petted his side. Finally, Charlie's eyes closed and did not reopen.

"Is he dead?" Zachariah cried out through his tears.

"No, no, dear," Elizabeth said. "He's resting. He's lost a lot of blood and he'll need plenty of rest."

"He's not dead?"

"No, no," Elizabeth said, as she washed the blood from her hands in a basin of water next to her on the hearth. After drying them, she reached out and petted her son's head and said to him, "Charlie's not dead, Zachariah. But we must keep this bandage on him and try to keep him still. And we must pray. Now he needs to rest."

Zachariah lay down across the animal, hugging the dog with wide-open arms, as he had so often done when the animal was more responsive.

Luke, next to Zachariah, patted his son's back and turned to the side and said quietly to Tom, "He knows about Brownie and the pups. Watched the roof cave in from the gun hole, while Elizabeth was tendin' to little Bob, puttin' him back to bed."

Tom looked down upon the little boy lying across his constant companion, his small arms spread out and trying to surround the dog's black and white chest, which rose and fell in labored breath. He watched the child's back shake from quiet sobs. He tried to imagine the impression the sight had made on the little boy, to see the barn where he had secured his colt and the puppies ablaze and to watch the roof cave in upon them. It was a cruel death for the puppies, and all regretted it, but for the colt, it was almost unimaginable. Zachariah had doted on the colt for several months now. Brownie had been almost as dear to him as Charlie, who was trained well enough that he did not need to be tied in the barn. As Tom imagined the impression all this had had on Zachariah, the compound anger that had broken from constraint upon viewing his own burned house now rose up again. Then he rose up from his chair and turned and headed for the door.

"Where you goin'?" Luke said after Tom, as he watched him walk away. Tom did not answer but continued to the door, stopped in front of the pegs where his slicker hung, and took down a box of shells from the shelf above it. Seeing this, Luke turned and looked at Zachariah and Charlie, and at Elizabeth, petting the boy's hair with her right hand while her left rested softly on the dog's neck. He rubbed his son's back for a moment, then stood up and strode to the door as Tom, holding the shells and his slicker, was stepping out.

Luke caught the door as Tom was pulling it shut behind him. "Where you goin'?" he asked Tom again, as he pulled the door open and looked out through the doorway at his partner, who stood highlighted by the escaping light from the house against the fluid backdrop of the rainy darkness.

Tom's eyes rose and met Luke's. "I'm goin' to see Edwards," he said.

Luke saw an anger and determination in Tom's eyes that sent a strange sensation into his spine and belly. He had seen Tom angry before, especially through this whole ordeal, and he had expressed plenty of anger to Tom about the same, but what he now saw in Tom was different. It was dangerous.

Tom stepped back farther away from the door, and he swung his slicker out and around to slip his arms into it. He began fastening it up, as Luke stepped out onto the porch, closing the door behind him.

"Tom, you can't go up there alone," Luke said. "They'll kill you. They're probably waitin' for us right now."

"Well, you can't go," Tom said, as he buttoned up his slicker. "Seems you've got to stay around here just to protect your family."

"But you can't go alone, Tom."

"What else we goin' to do?" Tom said, as he finished buttoning his slicker.

Luke looked down and his eyebrows knit together. "Maybe we shouldn't do anything," he said without raising his eyes.

Tom froze. "What do you mean?" he asked, as his eyes bored into Luke.

"Maybe this isn't goin' to work, Tom," Luke said, his eyes still down.

"What do you mean?"

Luke shifted around so that his left shoulder pointed toward Tom. "I mean," he began, raising his eyes to look sideways across his shoulder at Tom, "they burned our barn, Tom. They burned my boy's horse and shot his dog. They burned the puppies. They burned your house. They might've beat me to death today, and that Speck shot at you. That's what I mean," he concluded and looked back down, this time off into a puddle off the side of the porch, into which water dripped from the edge of the roof, far slower now than it had, as the shower had dwindled to a light rain.

"Maybe . . . ," Luke began again, after a pause. "Maybe we need to consider movin' on, Tom," he said as he watched the water drip into the puddle.

"Movin' on, Luke? Movin' on?" Tom said with near incredulity. "After all we've built here, just leave it all?"

"Well, I don't know, Tom," Luke responded, as he looked at the puddle as if speaking to it, the frustration apparent in his knit brows and tone of voice. "Sure we've built a lot, but my wife's nearly fallen apart. We lost a baby. I've nearly been killed by that outfit twice. What good is all we built," he concluded, turning his head to look at Tom across his shoulder, "if my family has to go without their husband and daddy? What good is it, if they have to stay shut up in their house all day? And what if they don't stay shut up inside and somebody gets hurt? What good is any of it then?"

Luke turned his head back to look at the puddle, as he raised his right hand and rubbed it across his stubbled chin. Tom had bowed his head, during these last expressions of Luke's, so that he stared at the porch floor near Luke's feet. Luke was right about all of that, and Tom accepted that with a certain humility. But there was frustration with that humility, and anger with that frustration, and thus the lowered head held a lowered brow, pushed down and furrowed in a menacing look unnatural to the face that formed it. Luke was right, all right, and he was right for one reason: because Henry Edwards had decided to locate his ranch in the same country as they had.

"We could get some help, from the JA, or call in the Texas Rangers," Luke continued, having turned and leaned his back against the wall next to the door to face Tom, "but those HE boys'll behave themselves as long as they need to, and neither the Rangers nor the JA is goin' to stay out here forever, and just as soon as they're gone, it'll just go back to more of the same. We're out here on our own, up against outlaws and cutthroats, and we got a family and they just got outlaws and cutthroats. We're more . . . uh . . . , more, uh . . ."

"Vulnerable," Tom said from where he now stood, turned to face west, his shoulder turned toward Luke.

"Yessir, that's it, 'vulnerable.'"

Luke was right again, and Tom knew it. As he stood looking out into the muddy yard cloaked in the darkness of night and peppered with a light drizzle, hazy reflections of points of light began to appear in the shiny mud as stars peeked out high above them, if only momentarily, from behind thinning clouds drifting by fast, overhead, toward the northwest.

Tom stared into the mud, speckled as it was by stellar reflections, shimmering here and there as drops of water, from the roof or a tree or the sky, splashed down into it. Could it all just be over? He could not believe that. It was not over; he knew it. It was not over, could not be; he would not accept it. It was that Henry Edwards. That was where the problem lay. Tom stared into the mud and ruminated. Finally, after his brows had sunk lower, the furrows above them deeper, he turned and stepped off the porch into the mud and mounted Ross.

"Where you goin', Tom?" Luke said as he pushed himself away from the wall against which he had been leaning.

"For a ride," Tom said as he pulled Ross around to point him toward the west.

"I'll follow you."

"You can't, you've got a family to take care of."

"Then you're puttin' me in a real fix, aren't you?" Luke said, looking up at Tom with an expression that conveyed his annoyance.

The truth about what Luke was saying broke through to Tom. He had tried to avoid admitting to himself that truth. He was putting his partner in a fix by going off alone. Luke would be torn between going with his partner to protect him from certain danger or staying with his family to protect them from possible danger. For all they knew, HE men could be watching them at that very moment.

Tom sat atop his horse and looked up the trail, up and out of the canyon, as if, in thought, he were already on his way along it. He appeared for a moment to be suspended at that point closest to when a rider coaxes his mount forward without yet having done so. Thus suspended he remained, staring intently off up the trail, and then, suddenly, he relaxed, and his head and shoulders slumped. He dismounted Ross and stepped back up onto the porch.

"All right," Luke was saying, as he backed up toward the door, the tension draining out of him with Tom's decision to stay, "let's . . ."

He never finished the statement. As soon as Tom was on the porch, on the same level as Luke, he quickly raised his arms up and brought down his forearms with great force at an angle on either side of Luke's neck. Luke's eyes opened wide for a moment, and he fell to his knees. Then his eyes closed, and Tom caught him—trying to avoid adding any more injuries to his beaten body—and lowered him to the floor of the porch. After checking his pulse and breathing, he leaned Luke against the door, then opened the door and dragged him just inside it.

"Elizabeth," Tom called as quietly as he could call across the room.

Elizabeth looked up from Zachariah and his dog—and little Rachel, now also kneeling and petting the dog—and saw Tom with Luke and let out a muffled cry, muffled instantly so as not to upset the children. She rose and hurried to Luke and Tom.

Tom was crouched over his friend when Elizabeth fell to her knees beside him.

"He's all right," Tom said before she could voice a word. "He'll be fine in just a minute, but," he continued, looking intently into her eyes to indicate his seriousness, "he must not leave this house. Do you understand that, Elizabeth?" he said, staring intently into eyes that stared intently back into his, eyes that had seen enough violence visited upon her family. "Do not let him go. Lock up this house and keep your husband here. He must stay here. You need him here."

Elizabeth stared at Tom and nodded her head, then looked at her unconscious husband and back at Tom, and again dumbly nodded her head.

"Bar the door behind me," Tom said, and he slipped out the door. Upon hearing the bar slide into its place on the other side, he turned and left the porch. He mounted Ross and spurred him on his way up and out of the canyon.

OUT ON THE GREAT LLANO ESTACADO, Tom, small and seemingly insignificant upon the apparently endless prairie plateau, rode through its wet grass under the now clear, moonless sky. Though bounded on every side by scarp that fell away to the land below, the plateau appeared to stretch off into infinity in every direction, whereas the nearly unbounded heavens appeared to have contracted into a sort of celestial roof, which pressed itself down far closer to earth than was comfortable for the angry cowboy, as the stars—as bright and numerous as he had ever seen them, set in a night as conversely dark—cluttered the blackness of the sky with their innumerable points of light, pushing that sky ever nearer the earth.

Pressed down, too, was Tom's spirit, pressed down under the weight of emotion, a cacophony of emotions, loud and discordant, in his head and heart. The heaviest of these emotions was anger. Anger, anger, pressing anger. Anger at all that had been done, at all that might be lost, anger at the cruelty of the HE outfit, anger at learning that human beings could be so successful at such cruelty. Somewhere beneath the anger was fear. Fear at what could be lost, at what awaited him, at what was going on inside his head and heart.

What was going on inside Tom's head and heart? Besides the dominant anger and its companion fear, and the host of other negative dispositions that now insinuated themselves, there were also positive dispositions of love, hope, faith, courage, honesty, kindness, goodness, and their companions. Hence, inside Tom's head and heart, did virtues wrestle against opposing vices.

Hamlet's words ran through Tom's brain:

Thus conscience does make cowards of us all,
And thus the native hue of resolution

Is sicklied o'er with the pale cast of thought,
And enterprises of great pitch and moment
With this regard their currents turn awry
And lose the name of action.

Fine words, Tom thought as he rode along, well expressed, as only Shakespeare could do, but they were wrong, Tom contended, if by *conscience* Hamlet meant that law divinely inscribed in the heart of man, what Tom's contemporary, Cardinal Newman, would call "the aboriginal Vicar of Christ." For, in conscience, it is courage, not fear, that "makes us rather bear those ills we have than fly to others we know not of," or resolve to undertake "enterprises of great pitch and moment."

But where did conscience direct Tom now? He did not know: he could not hear his conscience under all the noise in his head and heart, all the confusion in each and between the two. He could not hear it, and he could not stop to listen, to take the time to push out the noise in meditation: he must act, now, lest all be lost. He counted on the conscience that he had been long forming to be acting in him at a subconscious level, what he might call a "gut level." But was that conscience or instinct? And could instinct be informed by conscience?

And act how? What action was he about to take? What was his plan in going to see Henry Edwards? Was he intending violence? No. Still his heart and head conjured visions of violent retribution. But that was wrong! "Blessed are the peacemakers: for they shall be called the children of God. . . . Blessed are ye when they shall revile you, and persecute you, and speak all that is evil against you, untruly, for my sake: Be glad and rejoice for your reward is very great in heaven." Turn the other cheek. "Lord, make me an instrument of thy peace. Where there is hatred, let me sow love; where there is injury, pardon . . ."

"Yes, Lord," Tom prayed in mind and, somewhat, in voice, "but self-defense is justifiable, but to what point, how preemptive may it be? You died on the Cross for us, Lord. You accepted the torture before the Cross and the torture of the Cross, but you also cleared the temple, your Father's house. We're not building a temple, but we are trying to build something decent, where we can worship you in our daily work, rest, and prayer. We are not saints, but we try. The Stuarts are good people. To what extent do we protect all that?

"Lord," Tom continued, his head slumping over the neck of Ross as he cantered along to the south, "I don't know what to do. Should I turn back? I am afraid of this anger in me. I can hardly pray to you. It's pulling me away from you, tempting me to follow my passions. I don't want violence, Lord. I do not want to desire violence. I want to desire peace. I intend to talk to him, Lord, to see if there is any good in him, to try to find a peace through reason. I can be humble: I can reject this anger for humility, especially in the face of another human being who has even a hint of decency, but what if he has none? Please, stay with me, God. Let your Spirit descend upon me and rule my anger and let me act according to your counsel. Rule me, Lord: I need your help. Did you bring us here to have us leave all this? I cannot believe you did, God. In that faith, I ride into the "midst of the shadow of death," and "I will fear no evils, for thou art with me."

Such was the nature of Tom's prayer, which vied with angry considerations of his present circumstances for his head's and heart's attention, as Ross carried him across the eastern edge of the high plains.

In time, Tom reached Edwards Canyon and began the descent into it. He did not notice that, once he had entered the canyon and had proceeded down the trail a ways, a fire flared to life behind him, high up on a rocky outcrop. It flared to life when a match, lighted by an HE cowhand, touched off a pile of fuel consisting of mesquite firewood specifically preserved from the rain and soaked with kerosene for just this purpose. And it was immediately seen at the Edwards headquarters below.

Tom rode on, oblivious to the fire signal behind him. He rode on as his inner emotional and spiritual struggle vied with perceptions of his immediate surroundings for control of his mind. Down the gradual trail he rode, mainly on sand not long eroded, compared to that of the Escondido, from the canyon walls enclosing him. This canyon, considerably shallower than the Escondido, was also less rugged, and its presentation had a calming effect on the rider who ventured into it.

Such an effect it had on Tom, so that, ironically, as he neared the source of his anxiety, he actually grew, slowly, a little more calm. Still, this calm was more the product of a sort of meditation to which Tom had resorted, as he rode toward the HE with such a conflicted mind and heart—a conflicted soul, really. He decided, as he rode, that he must push past the confusion in his soul and trust himself to God. Hence, as he rode along, he continued to recite in his head various appropriate passages from Sacred Scripture.

In this manner, Tom neared the HE headquarters. Committed as he now was to "Blessed are the peacemakers," he withdrew himself from his meditation so as to concentrate more on his surroundings and not to be caught unawares. He had made up his mind that, in the interest of his mission as peacemaker, he would ride right into the Edwards ranch and not sneak in. The Edwards outfit had proved shifty enough; he intended to remain above their tactics.

He was passing through a mesquite thicket, not far from the headquarters, watching out ahead of him for possible ambush, when, suddenly, three men on horses emerged from behind a large rock off to the left behind him. They quickly surrounded him with guns drawn, a Winchesters, a shotgun, and a six-gun.

Tom reined Ross to a stop. Other than the initial start from these men rushing out of the darkness to surround him, he was not afraid of them. He had no fear of being shot. Though he could see no reason for any feeling of security, still, he had no concern that they might shoot him. It was as if he was certain, somehow, that they would not.

"Where you headin', Schurtz?" It was Brown who asked the question. Tom could see him clearly, even in the faint light from the stars, as his eyes had fully adjusted to the darkness. Brown looked especially mean tonight. Even though Luke had rarely hit the big man in the face, when he had, he had landed his punches squarely, and Brown showed the effects. His face was swollen—not least his nose—and cuts and bruises could be seen even in the low light. Besides that, the man sat pretty gingerly in the saddle, and his breathing was labored. Tom was right in guessing that Brown's chest was wrapped up due to bruised, cracked, or broken ribs.

"Goin' to see your boss," Tom answered, and he started to ride on again, not with any serious consideration that these men would allow it, but with the intention of letting them know that he was not there to deal with them.

Brown nudged his horse into Tom's path and, still pointing a six-shooter at him, said, "What for?"

"That's between him and me," Tom said. He was concentrating so as not to let his nervousness come through in his voice or in any tremble of the hand in which he held his horse's reins.

"Anything you have to say to Mr. Edwards you can say to me," Brown said.

Tom looked around. Brown was in front of him, off to his left. Whitey was to his right. Coe was to his left.

"How about I tell him and he tells you?" Tom responded.

"How 'bout you disappearin' and no one ever hearin' from you again?" Brown rejoined.

"Texas Rangers probably wouldn't like it."

"You trying' to tell me you sent for the Texas Rangers?"

"Maybe."

"How long you expect it'll take 'em to get here?"

"No tellin'."

"They wouldn't even find you once they got here," Brown said. "We'd tell 'em we ran you out, 'cause you was rustlin' HE cattle, like those Seven Ox calves with our HE cows."

"What about those HE calves with our Seven Ox cows?" Tom responded, immediately regretting that he had let himself, in a momentary loss of self-control, get pulled into this pettiness with this underling, regardless of its implications.

"What're you talkin' about?" Brown queried.

"You know what I'm talkin' about," Tom said and then turned his head straight ahead, toward the headquarters.

"I don't think I do, Schurtz. Could be you don't either," Brown said. "Maybe you need to take stock of your beeves, Schurtz. You know how dangerous it is for calves out in these canyons and breaks, what with the lobos and panthers and coyotes. You know how they like veal. Some even like it cooked."

Tom slowly looked over at Brown, whose beaten face now held a sinister grin, and Tom realized that, along with building the fence, they had slaughtered the falsely branded calves, or at least Brown was wanting him to think they had, or would.

"Besides," Brown continued, "gonna be mighty hard for those Rangers to separate Seven Ox beeves from HE, when these HE cows start droppin' white-faced."

"Well," Tom said, "they might be interested in arson."

"Lightnin'."

"With kerosene?"

"Carelessness."

Tom had had enough. He nudged Ross along, and Brown shook his gun at Tom.

"I ain't finished with you, Schurtz," he said.

Tom rode on past the gun pointed at the side of his head, as his stomach churned.

"I said I ain't finished with you . . ."

"Yessir, you are," a voice said from out of the darkness. "Drop it, Brown."

Brown hesitated. He heard the lever action of a Winchester, from where the voice had come, and heard again, "Drop it."

Brown tossed down his Colt .45.

"You two do the same," another voice said from behind the other men. They dropped their weapons.

"That you, Henderson?" Brown demanded, as Henderson emerged on foot from the cover of the mesquite behind him.

"That's right," Henderson said, as he picked up the Colt. "Y'all got any other weapons?" They indicated that they did not, and Henderson believed them because he had been there that afternoon when Tom and Luke had kept most of their weapons. Smith emerged from the shadows behind the other two men and picked up their guns.

"Smith, too?" Brown said.

"Yessir," said Henderson.

"I always figured you for a traitor, Henderson," Brown said.

"Traitor," Whitey nearly spat at Smith. Coe just looked at Smith and Henderson over his swollen nose and appeared to accept his fate.

"And I always figured you for a cutthroat, Brown. Now do that horse a favor and get your fat body off 'im," Henderson said. "You other two do the same; climb down." The three men did as they were told.

"Mr. Schurtz," Henderson called out to Tom, and as he did so, he took Brown's rope off his saddle, "you wanna show us how you tied Speck up that day? I sure did have a time gettin' him and Billy untied . . .

"S'pose we're gonna hafta tie this rope a little tighter around Mr. Brown's ribs, so's they mend all the faster," Henderson said to Tom, as

Tom approached after dismounting from Ross. "Your man Stuart did quite a job on 'im."

"He did," Tom said, taking the rope from Henderson. "Lie down, Brown," Tom commanded. Brown was slow to comply, but with his own six-shooter touched to the back of his neck by Henderson, he did lie down. Tom then knelt down and started tying Brown's hands behind his back, being as sensitive as he could to the fact that the man did have injured ribs.

Meanwhile, Henderson and Smith tied up the other two men. Then Tom, Henderson, and Smith looked over their location and decided to lay the men, all tied up, over near the rock, where they could be easily watched. They thus moved the men. Then they moved the men's horses off to the side of the trail and tied them to some mesquite. Then Henderson and Smith went into the darkness and retrieved their own horses and a third, all of which were loaded with gear.

"Looks like you're ready to travel," Tom said.

"We are," Henderson said. "Shakin' the dust of this place from our feet, so to speak."

"As a testimony against the place?" Tom asked, picking up the biblical allusion.

"That's right," Henderson said, through his infectious smile, not missing a beat. "This is one sorry outfit." He shook his head as he looked back at the three men tied near the rock. Then, as if remembering something, he turned back to Tom. "What kind of havoc these three wreak on your place tonight?"

"Burned the barn, and my house . . ."

"Oooh," Henderson exclaimed, lowering his face and wincing as if truly pained by what he had heard. "You don't mean that log house at the head of the canyon?"

"I do."

"Ooh," Henderson exclaimed again. "That was one beautiful log house. You build it?"

Tom nodded. "When did you see it?"

"A few of us boys saw it that first day, when we first arrived in this country, when we drove the beeves by the Escondido," Henderson said. "Edwards had us close herd the beeves on that dry playa, so they could graze on your hay, just one of the things early on that seemed to be a little more than bad judgment. Anyways, we took turns ridin' over to look into the Escondido, and I looked that log house up and down and was mightily impressed."

"Appreciate the compliment," Tom said.

"You remember that, Joe?" Henderson said to Smith.

Smith was nodding his head. "'Twas a mighty purty house," Smith said, and Tom realized it was the first time the man had spoken to him.

"Thank you," Tom said. Smith nodded.

"They burn it bad?" Henderson asked Tom.

"Damaged, but it can be repaired," Tom answered. "The barn's a total loss, and they burned up a mustang colt the boy was raisin' and keepin' in the barn, and some puppies, and they shot his dog."

Henderson turned and looked back at Brown, Whitey, and Coe and shook his head. Smith pursed his lips and nodded his head solemnly.

"Real mean hombres, these," Henderson said. He turned back toward Tom. "You see Billy when you came into the canyon? He's the wrangler you had tied up with Speck that day."

"No sir."

"Well, he was up there. He lit that fire," Henderson said, stepping around and pointing toward the west. "Well," he said, "you can't hardly see it over here." He took a few more steps to the south and then pointed again and said, "There it is."

Tom and Smith followed and saw the fire where Henderson pointed.

"Billy told Joe and me he had to go up there and sit in the rain and keep a pile of wood dry and then light it with kerosene when he saw you Seven Ox men enter the canyon," Henderson said. "We'd seen those other three ride out earlier and knew they was up to no good. That fencin' and gangin' up on your partner pretty much made up our minds for us. And I want you to know, Schurtz, that me and Joe had just arrived before you had. We were just gettin' ready to go against our own outfit and help 'im out. I mean, there's loyalty to the brand and all, but I ain't no outlaw, and I knew they was keepin' me in the dark on some of these operations, but I didn't know how much, and I was curious to find out, but this is too far. Joe here's been with this outfit since before the drive here, but he's had a sort of . . . conversion, I guess is the word. Has seen the light, anyway. He's decided to ride out with me."

Smith nodded his head, and Tom wondered how much of his conversion was due to the good influence of Mr. Henderson.

"And young Billy up yonder," Henderson continued, "he's too young to fall in with company such as this. So we're takin' 'im with us, even though he don't know it yet. Packed up all his things and took his own horse. We can let the HE horse he's ridin' graze where it is."

"Where you headin'?" Tom asked him.

"Don't know yet, but we heard tell of other outfits movin' into these parts, before we ever left Colorado. There's plenty up on the Canadian. So we'll head that way. Maybe even ol' Charlie Goodnight might be lookin' to hire."

"Tell him I sent you."

"That do us any good?"

"Might," Tom said. "He knows us, and we've always been friendly. Besides our friend Andy Grady's workin' for the JA. You might look him up."

"Might do that," Henderson said. "Just for that recommendation, old Joe and I'll sit right here and keep an eye on these hombres while you go on down and speak your piece with Edwards."

"Appreciate that," Tom said.

"Watch out for that Speck, cause he's around and he's nursin' it bad for you, in his quiet, snakelike way," Henderson warned. "Of course, he's a bit out of action with that gunshot in his calf, but don't rule 'im out on any account. Still, I don't think Edwards would want 'im to shoot you or anything, but I never really knew just how much Edwards was behind any of this, so, there's no tellin'."

"What about that?" Tom said. "How much *is* Edwards behind any of this?"

"Like I was sayin', I can't really say," Henderson replied. "He meets with Brown real regular, and Brown and Speck are . . . Well, there's old Ike, too, the Negro cook, but he don't count, as he don't do much more than work around the headquarters. He's a fine hand, though. Some of us saw some of his handiwork on the drive, when Edwards let him trail a time or two. He's a wizened old hand, but like I say, Edwards keeps him around the headquarters.

"Anyways, like I was sayin'," Henderson continued, "if Edwards is behind the funny stuff, then he's mighty careful not to be seen to be.

Brown's been behind it all, as far as a body can see, but he's always meetin' with Edwards, and Speck is right in there often enough, so it's hard to tell. My gut tells me Edwards is in it up to his scalp, but if he is, makes me wonder a little bit about a man who takes so much care not to look like he is."

Tom nodded, concurring wholeheartedly with Henderson's assessment. Tom realized, after a moment, that he was still nodding, longer than was necessary, and that none of them was talking any more. He knew it was time to leave this refreshing neighborliness and carry on with his mission. Henderson and Smith knew it too: he could see it in their faces and hear it in their silence.

"Well," Tom said, "I appreciate your help. I better be moseyin' on about my business."

Tom caught up with Ross and mounted him. He swung him around and said to Henderson and Smith, "Thanks again."

"You bet," Henderson said, "We'll wait for you."

Tom nodded, turned Ross around, and headed toward the headquarters of the HE Ranch.

Once out of the mesquite thicket, Tom, looking all around, absorbed through his vision a darkened panorama of a pleasant valley with which he was not unfamiliar. The land sloped gently down from soft hills off to the left (to the north) behind which Tom and Luke had taken cover the only other time Tom had visited HE headquarters. Before him, a little off to the right, in this pleasant valley, along the major stream that watered the canyon—which now rushed, gurgled, and babbled, swollen from the recent rains—lay the buildings of the HE.

As he approached the buildings, he made out a large, double-pen, dogtrot-style log house: the pens were each about fifteen feet square, separated by a breezeway about ten feet wide, with a single roof connecting them and covering, as well, the breezeway. This was the log building the HE outfit had been constructing the last time Tom and Luke had visited. To the east beyond the house sat a rectangular log structure, which Tom took to be the bunkhouse. Below the log house, built into the bank, was the half-dugout he had seen on his last visit. Not far from this dugout stood a small smokehouse. Off to Tom's right, west of the log house, stood a large picket barn and a number of pens.

As Tom rode up, he scrutinized the buildings and found them wanting. Edwards' house, like the bunkhouse, sat in the dirt, apparently without foundations, with nothing but a dirt floor, not uncommon in log-house construction, (and not as dirty as one might think, as a well-packed dirt floor was easily maintained with sweeping). The logs that made up the structure had been left unhewn. They were chinked with mud and joined at the corners with simple saddle notches. Beyond the notches, the logs stuck out unevenly, not having been trimmed. At the outside gable end of each pen stood a rough stone chimney, which Tom correctly suspected to be mortared with mud. The roof was of a very low pitch, of the Anglo western type that consisted merely of an unhewn ridgepole laid across the entire pen to rest in the middle of the top logs of the pen. Between this ridgepole and the plates rested the rafters. Tom rightly suspected that the ridgepole consisted of two or more cottonwood logs. This roofing structure was covered with boards rather than shakes or shingles.

The low level of skill required to build the HE structures, especially Edwards' house (really a cabin), was evident even in the distant perusal of them in the dark, and it provided further evidence, as far as Tom was concerned, of the low level of character of the man who had built them or had had them built. This observation was not attributable to bare hauteur on Tom's part. In his travels, Tom had known many fine people who lived in more primitive dwellings. Indeed, he himself had lived in the most primitive dugouts at times. But now, as he rode toward these buildings, having come from the scene of the burning of his own house, he could not help but see, in his mind, that house— the blackened, scarred, hand-cut and hand-fit puncheon floors; the blackened southwest corner, with its precise double-notched and trimmed corners; the burned-through shingled roof—and hold a certain contempt for the brutes who could build such mean structures as these and then burn his.

So taken with this perusal and mental comparison was Tom, that his mind had accepted the figure of a black man sitting in a chair in the covered breezeway as merely part of the scene of which the house was a part. With the comparison complete and his mental verdict rendered, Tom turned his attention to that human element of the scene.

The man was older, perhaps in his fifties, and was lean but powerfully built, which was evident when he stood up at Tom's approach. He was a little taller than Tom, with broad, square shoulders and a wide chest. He had picked up a rifle when he had stood up. He held it in both hands before him in a casual sort of way that seemed more from obligation or custom than from any intention to use it. Still, Tom had the distinct feeling that, despite his casual manner, if this man wanted to put that weapon to use, he could do so and do so with serious effect.

Tom reined Ross's slow walk to a stop in front of the man, whose broad facial features he could now make out. "I'm lookin' for Henry Edwards. He around?" Tom said.

"In deah," the man said, motioning with his rifle and a nod of his head toward the room to his left, Tom's right.

Tom dismounted and wrapped Ross's reins around the hitching post in front of the structure.

"Pleasant evenin'," Tom said to old Ike (he assumed) as he passed him on his way into Edwards.

"Yehsuh."

As Tom passed beyond this man Ike, he noticed, out of the corner of his eye, that Ike turned his chair to an angle that made it possible for him to see in the direction he had been looking and, at the same time, to see the entrance to the western room of the dogtrot log house.

Tom now approached that entrance, stepping into the light that poured out of it before arriving at the doorway. Then he was standing in the doorway, and what he saw inside the room surprised him. Off to his left, at a table with a lighted lantern on it, sat Henry Edwards reading a book. In fact, lining a rough shelf behind Edwards were a number of books, well-bound books, above the quality often found on the range. That is not to say that cowboys and cattlemen were not readers. On the contrary, in many long hours in line shacks, dugouts, and ranch headquarters, a great many works of every grade and level were read by a wide variety of individuals. Still, it was not often on the range that a cowboy was privileged enough to come across the quality, at least as it appeared from their covers, of books that now rested on the shelf behind Henry Edwards.

Tom's mind did not linger long on the sight of the books, as Edwards' voice brought him back to his purpose. "Schurtz?" Edwards called out as if surprised. Tom's gaze returned from the books to Edwards, who, seated with his back to the southern wall, was looking off to his right at Tom.

"A bit late for a social call, isn't it?" Edwards said.

Tom would have preferred to enter the conversation in a genial tone and manner. Seeing Edwards as he now saw him and considering that he had never seen Edwards directly involved in any of the misdeeds that had been committed combined to give Tom all the more reason to give Edwards the benefit of the doubt that he was inclined to give people out of a sense of fairness. But Tom brought to mind the serious reasons for his making this extraordinary visit, and he resolved to push away any attempt on Edwards' part to distract him with easy pleasantries. He had to remember that it had been just a short time before that he had left Luke unconscious at the Stuart home, after Luke had suggested that it might be for the best that they completely abandon the very home they had worked so hard to create, and that the only reason for such a drastic change in attitude was the presence of this man and his outfit in the region.

"Not here to be sociable," Tom responded as he stepped uninvited into the room.

"Well, pull up a chair there, anyway," Edwards said, rising from the table, the embodiment of graciousness, as he nodded toward two chairs set facing him, pulled out from the opposite side of the table. Tom looked at the crude chairs and at another one pulled against the northern wall on the opposite side of the room from Edwards. He noticed that red embers still crackled in the fireplace set into the western wall, directly across the room from the doorway through which he had entered. In the northeast corner adjacent the fireplace, the kitchen supplies and utensils were set up in a construction of a crude counter and shelves that extended out from the corner along the perpendicular walls. The shelves were well stocked with provisions.

Tom stepped a little farther into the room and nearer the table. "I'll stand," he said, looking into Edwards' eyes.

"Well, suit yourself," Edwards said, as he sat back down. He moved the lantern—which was off to his right, directly between Tom and him—to another spot on the table beyond where his left hand rested.

"Need the light to read," he said. "Got so's I could hardly read at all in the dark. So I made sure we brought a healthy supply of kerosene along on this venture. Never hurts to have extra coal oil." And then he looked up at Tom and added, "You never know when it might come in handy."

Tom thought he detected a certain glint in Edwards' eyes when he made this last comment, and his intuition told him that Edwards intended to allude to the burning of his house and the barn with these seemingly innocuous statements. Still, Tom almost dismissed that this statement could possibly refer to what had happened to their buildings, as he could hardly allow himself to believe that Edwards, who had done so well to keep himself distanced from such crimes, would offer such an obvious allusion to those crimes in such a casual manner. Whatever the case, he was somewhat taken aback by the allusion, especially in light of Edwards' cordial behavior and Tom's inability to objectively connect Edwards to any of the crimes.

"So, if you're not here to be sociable," Edwards said, "what is the nature of your visit?"

"I want to know," Tom said, looking down at the seated man, "what you know about our buildin's being burned."

"What buildings?"

"Our barn and . . ." Tom hesitated for a moment, not wanting to mention the burning of his house, as if, in doing so, he would open himself to a certain vulnerability before a foe. Nevertheless, he finally said, ". . . and my house," accepting the vulnerability that went with the honesty.

"Your house?" Edwards exclaimed, and as he did so, Tom saw the faintest hint of a smile in his dark eyes and in the weathered lines around them. "You mean the log house at the head of the canyon?"

"How do you know where it is?"

"Saw it that first day," Edwards said, "when I brought my herd by. 'Twas a fine house. You mean to say it's burned?"

That smile around Edwards' eyes had deepened a little, and Tom's smoldering anger slowly rose. "It's burned enough, and I want to know what you had to do with it," Tom said, Edwards' attitude having erased any patience he might have had with dancing around the issue.

"What I had to do with it?" Edwards said, sitting back in his chair, the smile around his eyes deepening further as he offered a little laugh to indicate the absurdity of such a suggestion.

"Yeah, what did you have to do with it?"

Edwards eyed Tom a bit, his smile giving way a little to an anger of his own that could be seen to rise up a little in his dark eyes. But he pushed down that anger, and the smile could be seen again in the lines around those eyes and in his exposed teeth. He laughed out again.

Tom did not laugh with Edwards but stood staring unwaveringly at the older man, as though he had expectations of that man and would see those expectations met. Something in Tom's attitude seemed to have an effect on Henry Edwards, and after trying to draw out his laugh and smile as long as he could, he sat back silently and regarded Tom, who continued to stare at him without even a trace of humor in his manner. Edwards' smile slowly took on an increasingly sinister form, until it was not a smile at all, but rather the sneer which Tom had seen before.

"What do you mean to be comin' in here askin' me to make some sort of account to you, Schurtz?" Edwards said over his curled lip. "Just who do you think you are?"

"An honest man tired of bein' patient with outlaws."

"Who you callin' outlaws?" Edwards demanded from where he leaned back in his chair.

"The men who burned our buildin's."

"Probably lightning."

Tom was not surprised to hear the same explanation that Brown had proffered. "Lightnin' doesn't ride horses and shoot at dogs," he replied.

Edwards appeared to be a little surprised to hear this mention of evidence of human involvement in the fires. Tom noted this and continued. "No, it was outlaws, all right," he said, "outlaws with extra coal oil."

Edwards caught Tom's allusion, and he squinted his eyes as he continued to regard him.

"Same sort of outlaws that would rustle another man's bulls, brand another man's calves, and fence another man's range. Those are the kind of outlaws I'm here to talk to you about," Tom said, as he stared down at Edwards with a face so devoid of any sign of humor that it made Edwards' earlier attempts at humor seem grossly inappropriate. "And I'm here to tell you that you'd better take care, from now on, what you and these outlaws you got workin' for you venture into. I'm here to warn you to leave us alone."

"Or what?" Edwards challenged, finally casting aside all pretense. And out from behind the pretense, unmasked, the man's countenance took on an ugliness that welled up from some place far deeper than his superficially handsome features.

Edwards fell forward, from where he had been leaning back in his chair, and leaned out upon the table toward Tom. "What're you gonna do about it, Schurtz?" You gonna rustle my cattle? You gonna brand my calves? You gonna burn my house? Go ahead, Schurtz, burn it. You see it. I'll just build another one, unhewn, unfloored, saddle-notched. Throw up another one before you'd know the first was gone. This ain't the work of no craftsman; is it, Schurtz? You wouldn't even think of buildin' somethin' like this; would you, Schurtz? Somethin' that had almost no value, even to the man who built it. Now, if it had value, say, was the work of a craftsman, now then it would be somethin' worth protectin', somethin' to worry about, somethin' that would be a real loss if it were ever . . . , say, . . . burned."

Tom stared at the old man in his ugliness, in the ugliness of his honesty. He saw, materialized before him, the attitude he had spoken about to Luke, the reality that these outlaws would always be willing to go farther than they would. He saw the attitude of one who valued nothing of beauty, nothing of goodness, of one so selfish that he would rather destroy the beauty and goodness in other peoples' lives than allow them to enjoy what he could not. He saw this man's commitment to that: he saw its frightening potential.

Edwards saw things, too. He saw them in Tom's eyes. He saw the stark seriousness of committed justice, with its justifiable anger, give way, just a bit, to the fear of the reality of the picture he had just painted for Tom.

"Naw, you couldn't do any of those things; could you, Schurtz? Except maybe the fencin'. In fact, Schurtz, I'm surprised you didn't beat me to the fencin'. And then, after you fence your place, you could put up a windmill, like a real homesteader. Ain't that your idea, Schurtz?"

A cold chill ran down Tom's spine as he heard the words come out of Edwards to manifest the depths of the man's cold and calculating spirit, a part of which Tom could glimpse as he looked into the man's dark eyes.

"That's right; I remember you," Edwards said, pleased with the reaction he saw in Tom's face. "I recognized you that first day, there at the Escondido, when you expressed so intelligently the reasons why I should just forget all about the Escondido and leave it all to you nesters, and I recollected the name. The rest came back to me that night. I've known it was you all along, Schurtz, the man who was goin' to settle the West with windmills and white niggers."

Tom stared at the man, no longer caring to hide the concern that had taken over his features as Edwards had made his motivations and intentions increasingly clear. This man was evil. To keep in one's memory, as at least part of the motivation for the destruction of peoples' lives, an opinion that the one opining had not even been allowed to completely express, in the only conversation the two of them had had before Edwards' move to the region, indicated to Tom the kind of man with whom he was now dealing.

Edwards read the incredulity in Tom's eyes, and he read the deepening fear there, too. "So, Schurtz," he said, leaning back in his chair again, "I don't see what good your warnin' is. Fact is, Schurtz, I'm gonna run you out of that canyon, you and that nice Stuart family. In fact, you might help those nice folks realize that before somebody gets hurt."

"People have already been hurt," Tom said, staring into the man, trying to wrap his mind around all that was being revealed to him.

"Hurt worse," Edwards rejoined. Then he nonchalantly moved the lantern back to his right, between Tom and him, and picked up the book that he had left on the table before him when Tom had entered, as if to indicate that his conversation with Tom was over.

Tom stared at him, realizing that he would allow it, allow for people to be hurt worse, and it did not appear that he cared who it might be. Anger welled up inside of Tom, as he realized all that Edwards was willing to ruin for his own selfish gain and to prove him, Tom, wrong. Anger welled higher, as he thought of all the good that their ranch had meant to them, and possibly to others later, all the good that this man was willing to sacrifice for his evil self. Anger welled still higher, as Edwards appeared to dismiss Tom with the casual action of picking up his book and moving his lantern back to where it accommodated his reading.

And anger spilled over when Edwards, without even bothering to look up from his book at Tom, whom he had already dismissed, said, "I hope they didn't burn that house too bad, as I was not decided whether to make that one or that nice rock house my headquarters when I move over to the Escondido."

In what seemed like a single action, Tom pulled his gun from its holster and stepped toward Edwards. With his right hand, which held the gun, he swept the lamp between him and Edwards to the dirt floor, where it broke, and fire flared up from the spilled kerosene. With his left hand, he reached out and grabbed Edwards by the front of his shirt and pulled the big man up to his feet to lean out over the table, where Tom held his gun to Edwards' head.

Edwards' wide eyes and mouth betrayed his surprise and momentary fear resulting from Tom's rash actions, but he soon recovered himself and recovered his features, which fluctuated very subtly between a sneer and a smile. Though held as he was by Tom, he glanced off to his right.

"It's all right, Ike," he said to the man standing in the doorway with his Winchester pointed at Tom's back. Tom knew he was there behind him, though he could not see him. Still, at that point he had no intention of letting go of Edwards.

Ike did not move at Edwards' assurance.

"I said it's all right, Ike," Edwards said a little louder, conveying his annoyance at the man's failure to relax his protective posture at his command.

"But deh man's goin' to kill you, Mr. Edwards," Ike said, his rifle still aimed at Tom.

"No, he's not, Ike," Edwards said as he looked into Tom's eyes and met the goodness he saw there with his own evil. "Mr. Schurtz ain't gonna kill me," he continued, adding in a quieter voice, "Are you Schurtz? You can't kill me; can you, Schurtz? Even though that'd solve all your problems. You could go back to the way things used to be, you and those nice folks buildin' up your little ranch with your little herd, gradin' it with those Herefords. Nobody to bother you. You could stay in your nice house, no one to burn it, maybe next time to the ground. No, nothin' like that to worry about. That pretty Mrs. Stuart would always be safe."

The reaction in Tom's eyes, to this reference to Elizabeth, was exactly what Edwards wanted to see. "That's right, Schurtz. Some of the hands here have taken a fancy to her. They know what day she does her wash, where she gathers her plums and grapes. They know all about her. But with me gone, there'd be no concern. These cowhands'd drift on, and you could even expand your concern down to this canyon. All that, Schurtz, all that just for pullin' that trigger."

Tom held Edwards' shirt ever tighter, as that man spoke forth his litany of solutions, and Tom pressed the gun ever harder against his head. And he looked ever deeper into Edwards' eyes, and he did so by invitation. Edwards' litany was an invitation into the evil to which he had given himself over. As Tom's anger flared, with the progress of the litany, he saw deeper into the man's dark eyes, until what he saw there finally chilled him, quashing completely the heat of his anger. What he saw there was the end of Edwards' invitation, which was integrally tied up with his litany: what he saw there was Edwards' desire for Tom to kill him, unarmed, without any real proof of his guilt, with old Ike as a witness.

Tom saw, in the depth of Edwards' invitation to evil, Edwards' desire to sacrifice his life, which had become so empty in selfishness, to sacrifice that life for Tom's corruption and, thus, for the further propagation of evil. In the instant that he saw it, Tom's own gaze instantly retracted, and he shoved Edwards away from him with such force that Edwards stumbled back over his chair and would have fallen over if he had not fallen against the wall behind him.

Tom stepped back from the table as if he had been stunned, and he stared at Edwards sprawled against the wall, a much smaller man than he had been minutes before. Tom stared at the reduced man and realized how far into a dangerous journey he had just ventured. He stared at the man; then he recovered himself, holstered his gun, turned away from the man and the table and the book and the kerosene fire burning itself out on the dirt floor, turned away from all of it, and walked out past old Ike, who lowered his gun and stepped out of the doorway to allow Tom to pass.

Tom walked directly to his horse, and as he stopped to untie the reins from the hitching post, that same cold that had struck through him as he had stood in the doorway of his burned house struck him again. He stood frozen for a moment and let the shiver pass through him. When it had mainly passed, leaving behind a sort of weakness, Tom stepped around to the side of Ross and mounted up. As he did, his eyes fell upon old Ike, still standing in the doorway watching him. Tom's eyes met Ike's. Ike had seen, had seen the shiver, the cold. He knew. The two men stared at each other for a moment; then Tom turned Ross around and rode away toward the head of the canyon.

ON HIS WAY OUT OF THE CANYON, Tom stopped where Henderson and Smith awaited him. He said nothing to them about his confrontation with Edwards, and they did not ask. They sensed a distraction about Tom, and they left him alone in it.

Henderson and Smith had already unsaddled and unbridled the horses of Brown, Whitey, and Coe; turned them loose; and chased them off. After Tom arrived, they made sure that the three men had no hidden weapons and decided, for the safety of the region, that they would keep the weapons that they had already taken from them. Then they untied Coe and made him walk alongside their horses, as they (Henderson, Smith, and Tom) began their slow ride out of the canyon. Eventually, they arrived at the head of the canyon, where Billy was still waiting, warming himself on this wet, chill night, by the fire he had started to signal Tom's arrival. Billy offered no resistance to Henderson and Smith's directive that he leave the HE with them. With Billy they continued up the trail and rode out of Edwards Canyon. One of their party still belonged in Edwards Canyon, so, after riding about half an hour out onto the Llano Estacado, they released a tired and footsore Coe to return, afoot, and untie his comrades.

Now, shed of Coe, the three men and the boy wrangler rode toward the north across the great plateau, under a west Texas sky that was now clear and lighted with about half a moon and stars innumerable. They said little and felt no inclination to speak, feeling, to a man, as if something had been wrung out of them. What little talk they dragged up seemed to go around Tom or bounce off him, so distracted was he. At the head of Escondido Canyon, Henderson, Smith, and Billy resisted Tom's offer for them to stay at the Stuarts' or in what was left of his place. Noting Tom's distraction and having fairly well comprehended the nature of it, Henderson answered for all of them that they would ride on, despite the lateness of the hour. Tom did not press them, which Henderson accepted as vindication of his refusal of the offer.

They parted cordially. Henderson, Smith, and Billy headed north, and Tom turned and rode down into the Escondido. Tom rode right past his log house, as he made his way down the trail to the Stuarts'.

At the Stuarts', he saw through the gun hole in the shutter that a lamp still burned, so he knocked at the door. Luke opened the door, after looking out, and ushered Tom in. Elizabeth was behind the door with Luke, and she uncharacteristically hugged Tom when he entered the house. She hugged him with a desperate relief that Tom was sorry to have brought upon her.

"Thank God, you've come back alive, Tom. Praise God. Praise God," she said in a hushed tone as she hugged him. Then she let go, stepped back from him, and wiped tears from her eyes.

"What do you mean to be knockin' me out like that?" Luke said to Tom, also in a hushed tone, as he took his hand in a handshake and did not let go.

"It was the only way I could see . . ." Tom began to respond, in the same low level of voice that they often used at night when the children were asleep and which they would all maintain during their talk that night.

"I know. I know," Luke said, as he let go of Tom's hand and put his arm around Tom's shoulder and guided him, with Elizabeth, toward the table.

As they crossed the room and approached the table, Tom saw that Zachariah and Charlie lay asleep on a quilt on the hearth with a blanket over them. He nodded toward them and asked, "How they doin'?"

"Time'll tell," Luke said. "Elizabeth packed the wounds pretty well, and it appeared that the bleedin' had let up quite a lot, but he lost a lot of blood. Zachariah lost as much in tears, I reckon. I'll tell you, Tom, it's mighty fortunate for them that did this that I did not go with you. As it is, the only thing that keeps me from losin' my head about it is that the dog looks like he might make it, or I'd be on my way over there right now, and might be yet when it all sinks in."

Tom nodded, as the two men sat down at the table while Elizabeth placed cups and poured coffee. She then joined them.

"But you're back safe and sound, Tom, and lookin' none the worse for wear," Luke said. "How's that?"

"Well," Tom began, "I'll tell you what. That Edwards is an evil man. He's everything I thought he was and worse. He's behind all of this, just as I thought he was. Henderson, Smith, and Billy just rode out on him this very night. But the worst of the lot has stayed, with no Hendersons and Smiths to balance them out."

"So what all happened, I mean from the time you left here?" Luke asked him.

Tired as he was and just wrung out from all that he had experienced that night—and that day, too, for that matter—and from realizing all that it meant, Tom found it difficult to get down to the details of what had happened, tending more toward the general. Nevertheless, guided by Luke's, and sometimes Elizabeth's, specific questions, he managed to give them a fairly full account of what had happened after he had ridden down into Edwards Canyon. He told it all. He told of his own rage, of meeting Edwards' hands in the ambush, of Henderson and Smith's ambush of the ambushers. He told of Ike and his rifle. And he told of Edwards. He told them everything, having seen in Edwards what they had a right to know about. He told them that, at the instant when he had pushed Edwards away, he had known that no matter how much all they had built meant to them, it was not worth what it would cost to hold onto it: not in light of what the evil he had seen in Edwards' eyes portended. He told them that, though he would stay and fight for what they had as long as they would wish to, he was willing to abide by what they decided. What Tom was telling them, without exactly saying it, was that he had finally let go, that he had finally accepted that the canyon—their home and all that they had built in it—was only salvageable at a cost beyond what they, as decent people, could afford to pay.

They sat and somberly discussed the grave matter for a while longer. Tom took his part in the discussion, but for all his participation, Tom had already made up his mind. It was over. He knew it was. He knew it was for him, and for the Stuarts. He knew it, and he knew that they knew it, too.

After a little while, Tom pushed back his bench from the table and stood to leave. Luke, and especially Elizabeth, entreated him to stay, but he said that his house was still fit for him to spend the night in, and he intended to do so. Luke understood and did not try to dissuade him. Elizabeth finally accepted Tom's wish and let him go. Hence, Tom made his way to the door, where he restated his position: that the

Stuarts could take as long about deciding as they wanted, and that whatever they decided, by that he would abide. Then Tom left, certain that within a week's time the Stuarts and he would be departing for places yet unknown, having been forced from their own Escondido Canyon, their ranch, their home.

END PART ONE

ACKNOWLEDGMENTS

THIS STORY WAS BEGUN IN 1992. After it had expanded to two parts, then three, while I was well through the final draft of part one, I shelved it in August of 1999. Rescued from the shelf in 2001 and attended to on vacations and early Saturday mornings, part one's completion was intended to be a Christmas gift for my wife, which was accomplished belatedly on January 5, 2002. Back to the shelf it went. Within a few months, I began to approach the daunting world of publishing and eventually slogged my way into and through it, with this product as the result.

To attempt to mention those who may have contributed in some way, over the course of fifteen years, to the creation and publication of this novel is to risk insufficient acknowledgment or none at all, but attempt I must.

MARY F. RITZER DEVOTED COUNTLESS HOURS to the unsung task of copyediting. No thanks or praise sufficiently compensates that work.

I would like to thank the following people who read, in whole or in part, and commented on my manuscript: Linda Doyle, associate publisher of Westcliffe Publishers; Jamie Harrison, novelist; Sandy Whelchel, executive director of the National Writers Association; Most Reverend Leroy Theodore Matthiesen, retired bishop of Amarillo; Bud Gardner, author.

Among those who offered their time and advice regarding the publishing process I would especially like to mention: Michael Medved, author, film critic, radio host, Seattle, WA; Dan Poynter, author, publisher, Para Publishing, Santa Barbara, CA; Judith Briles, author, publisher, president emeritus, Colorado Independent Publishers Association (CIPA), Denver, CO; and all the members of CIPA.

Rebecca Finkel's design and Kenneth Wyatt's painting speak for themselves. I thank these talented artists for the look of the book.

In her quiet work at the Panhandle-Plains Historical Museum (PPHM) Archives in Canyon, Texas, Betty Bustos helped create the best work experience of those I enjoyed at the fine institutions at which I worked during this project. Mrs. Bustos provided me with a carrel, made me aware of any items that might be relevant to my work, and introduced me to people who she thought would be helpful. She even directed me to dormitory housing the day after I looked at the office in the back seat of my car and spontaneously prayed, "Lord, this is no longer workable." Lisa Shippee Lambert, the Archivist at PPHM, was also most accommodating and friendly, as were the students who worked there: Elisa, CZ, and Cessa.

There are several other people I would like to thank for assisting or informing my work in some way: Noel Ary, director, and Dave Webb, Kansas Heritage Center, Dodge City, KS; Professor Gary Nall, West Texas A & M University (WTAMU), Canyon, TX; Professor Frederick Rathjen (emeritus WTAMU), editor, Panhandle-Plains Historical Review, Canyon, TX; Dr. Bill Green, curator of history, PPHM, Canyon, TX; Lester W. Galbreath, park manager and longhorn herd manager, Fort Griffin State Historical Park, Albany, TX; Jack, Zoe, K.W., Cliff, Will, Joel, Drew Kirkpatrick, and foreman Tom Taylor, Kirkpatrick Ranch, Post, TX; Michael Moore, archivist, and Bobby Santiesteban, Texas General Land Office Archives and Records, Austin, TX; Dr. Ramon Powers, director, Kansas State Historical Society, Topeka, KS; Scott Burgan, photographer and researcher, Amarillo, TX; Bill Harrison, WTAMU staff and presenter at Caprock Canyons State Park, Quitaque, TX; Verna Anne Wheeler, curator, and Linda Jones, Crosby County Pioneer Memorial Museum, Crosbyton, TX; Robert C. Haywood, author, Topeka, KS; Bill Bennett, retired teacher, Crosbyton, TX; Daniel Vinzant, former Baptist minister, Waco, TX; Joe and Virginia Taylor, guides for the railroad trail, Quitaque, TX; Gene Barksdale, Amarillo, TX; Don Douglas, Douglas Surveying Company, Lubbock, TX; John Cieszinski, Abacus Engineering Surveying, Lubbock, TX; John Wilson, Wilson Surveying, Lubbock, TX; Carl Williams, surveyor, Plainview, TX; Ben Thompson, Texas Society of Professional Land Surveyors; Ed Logan, district conservationist, Natural Resources Conservation Service, Crosbyton, TX; Jimmy Myers and Matthew Kast, Natural Resources Conservation Service, Silverton, TX; Dora Ross, Floyd County Soil and Water Conservation District, #104, Floyd County, TX; Dr. Randy Lewis, veterinarian, Lubbock, TX; John Alexander, woodworker and author, Baltimore, MD; Brian Collins, archivist, Dallas Public Library, Dallas, TX.

The State Historical Society of Wisconsin Library, Madison, WI, made possible extensive research into the setting for this story while I was still a long distance from the location of that setting. Its resources, staff, atmosphere, and the building itself not only inspired me to delve deeper into my research, but also served to rank it among the great libraries I have visited. A director of another state's historical society told me that not only was his state's modeled on Wisconsin's, but that Wisconsin's was what other states' societies aspired to be.

In addition to the individuals noted above, I thank the entire staffs and volunteers of all the institutions and organizations mentioned. And I add to that list the following, which served my research and writing so well: Texas Tech University Library, the Southwest Collection, and the Law Library, Texas Tech, Lubbock, TX; WTAMU Library, Canyon, TX; San Antonio Public Library, San Antonio, TX; Institute of Texan Cultures Archives, San Antonio, TX; Palo Duro Canyon State Park and Museum, Canyon, TX; National Ranching Heritage Center, Lubbock, TX; Old Cowtown Museum, Wichita, KS; Homestead National Monument, Beatrice, NE; American Quarter Horse Heritage Center & Museum, Amarillo, TX; Cattleman's Museum, Fort Worth, TX; Fort Sill Museum and Old Post, Fort Sill, OK; Wichita Mountains Wildlife Refuge, Indiahoma, OK; Aurora Public Library (Central), Aurora, CO; Amarillo Public Library (Central), including the Bush-Fitzsimmons Collection, Amarillo, TX; Denver Public Library (Central and Ross-University Hills), especially the Western History Collection, Denver, CO; Crosbyton Public Library, Crosbyton, TX; Madison Public Library (Central), Madison, WI; Fort Larned National Historic Site, Larned, KS; Boot Hill Museum, Dodge City, KS; Buffalo Lake National Wildlife Refuge, Umbarger, TX; Dodge City Convention and Visitors Bureau, Dodge City, KS; Official Texas Historical Marker program, Texas Historical

Commission, Austin, TX; Bureau of Indian Affairs, Washington, DC; Forest Products Laboratory, Madison, WI.

THE PURSUIT OF THIS BOOK brought me providentially into marriage with my wife, Hiep. If nothing else were to come from this project, that singular grace alone would suffice. Her quiet confidence in me and this work (not to mention her hours of editing and proofreading) has sustained my long-suffering attendance to it. Our children, too, have borne this attendance and have offered incomparable distraction from it and incentive to bring it to fulfillment.

I thank my parents, Jim and Margaret Ritzer, for more than I could write in all the pages of this book. They impressed upon me the values that preclude convention in our modern culture and which contribute to an approach to life that allowed this book project to germinate, take root, and flower. Beyond that, I here specifically acknowledge their support and encouragement throughout this project, including their reading of and commenting on the manuscript.

Upon determining that I should drive off into the West to finish this novel, I shared this nebulous plan with three trusted friends: my brother Mark, Ruth Larenas, and Rev. James J. Uppena. Their support and encouragement, along with that of Mark's wife, Janet, and Ruth's husband, Jorge, manifested in innumerable ways throughout the venture, proved them worthy of that trust and of my special thanks. Cathy Hubka, along with her husband, Tim, and their children—who opened their home, their lives, and their hearts to me—falls into the same category as the three above, that of individuals whose support throughout (which, in her case, includes the reading of the manuscript) would be impossible to quantify and to aptly thank. My godmother, Rosemary Luckey, along with her husband, Jim, must also be included in this good company.

An introduction to Ron Graves on a tour of a cotton gin and denim factory led to the meeting of his wife, Melinda, and their children, the use of their printer, later to work, lodging, and a friendship that survives the separation of time and distance. I thank them for all of that and for Ron's reading and commenting on the manuscript. I am grateful to the Most Rev. George O. Wirz for blessing my car for this book-writing odyssey, which no doubt contributed to the Aries pushing on to 177,000 total miles before succumbing to electrical problems. Brian Meyer, my brother-in-law, deserves special mention for first suggesting to me the idea of making a Western movie.

I thank Mrs. Koeppe, my eighth-grade English teacher at Sacred Hearts School, for seeing and encouraging in me, and thereby making me aware of, a talent for writing.

I would furthermore like to acknowledge the hospitality of: my sister Mary; Toby, Brent, and Mo of Stafford Hall, WTAMU; Georgia Mae Ericson, granddaughter of Hank and Elizabeth Smith; Professors Charles and Ingrid (Fry) Grair (Texas Tech); Patty, Keith, and Leyna Hutchinson; Bob and Deb Silvis (to Bob I attribute the "young enough to fail" philosophy); Rob and Renee Porter; and Janice Paxton.

Others I would like to thank include: the Lions Club, Crosbyton, TX; Skip Watson, Channel 11, Lubbock, TX; Chris Albracht, Pete Valdez, Clyde and Nancy Goff, all of Amarillo, TX; John R. Dunlap, Floydada, TX.

I would further like to thank all others whose friendship and hospitality I enjoyed throughout this venture.

I THANK GOD FOR THIS BOOK. I thank Him for all that it took from me and all that it has meant in my life. I thank Him for what I believe was the inspiration for it. "Necessity is the mother of taking chances," according to Mark Twain. Well, I thank God for allowing me to find myself in sufficient necessity, for giving me sufficient courage and faith to truly strike out into the unknown with little or none of the delusory safety nets in which our culture has placed so much of its faith. I thank Him for keeping me in His providence, this human speck, creeping along antlike in my little gray car under that expansive share of the firmament which stretches over the American Midwest and West. I thank Him for what I learned, whom I met, what I experienced, suffered, enjoyed. I thank Him for all of it. And I thank His angels and saints, especially His Blessed Daughter, Mother, Spouse, Mary, whose intercession I regularly sought, with a hope in its efficacy validated by the effects at an ancient wedding feast at Cana and by the Tradition of the Church from its very inception.

AUTHOR'S NOTE

THIS BOOK IS A WORK OF FICTION. Still, great pains were taken to make it an accurate depiction of the times and places in which this story is set, and to provide accurate background for those times and places. The characters are fictional, including the characterizations of historical figures. Nevertheless, those characterizations, of Mr. and Mrs. Henry Clay Smith and Charles Goodnight, were respectfully formed to portray those public figures in their best light consistent with the historical record. May the reader forgive me for denying the Charles Goodnight character the historical cowman's excellence in the use of profanity, which J. Evetts Haley recognized in his celebrated biography for its superlative variety, eloquence, and beauty. I call on that biography and the historical Goodnight in my defense, and rest on Goodnight's observation of a single "serious fault" in an otherwise good man whom he knew, that of cursing "too damned much."

NOTES

BIBLE QUOTATIONS ARE TAKEN FROM THREE SOURCES. The Stuart family Bible is the King James Version: readings from their Bible and quotations from the Bible by the Stuarts are also from this version. Tom's Bible is the Douay–Rheims (Challoner): quotations from the Bible by Tom are also from this translation. Excerpts from the Bible in the narrative are taken, with little if any exception, from The Catholic Edition of the Revised Standard Version of the Bible (Division of Christian Education of the National Council of Churches of Christ in the United States of America, 1965, 1966).

CHAPTER ONE
The definition of *civilize* comes from *The Living Webster Encyclopedic Dictionary of the English Language* (Chicago: The English Language Institute of America, 1972). The Dodge City *Times* and excerpts from it are historical. The first comments on homesteading from Thomas Jefferson and Galusha Grow are quoted from displays at the Homestead National Monument, Nebraska, U.S. Department of the Interior. Biblical quotations in the section about man and the land come for the most part from Chapters 1, 2, and 3 of Genesis, mainly from the Douay-Rheims and King James, with the Catholic RSV's "living being" in place of "living soul." Psalm 89:29 from the Catholic RSV is also quoted, as are a few short phrases from throughout Scripture drawn from memory. Ulysses S. Grant is quoted from his *Personal Memoirs of U. S. Grant* (New York: Charles L. Webster, 1886) 2:509. For the matter of the income tax, see Article 1, Sections 2 and 9 of the *Constitution*. Quotations from Abraham Lincoln, Jefferson Davis, John Brown, and Justin Morrill are in the public record and taken from various of the sources listed below. The quotations of

Thomas Jefferson and Abraham Lincoln about parcels of land are taken from displays at the Homestead National Monument. The quotation on the conscience is from John Henry Cardinal Newman's "Letter to the Duke of Norfolk," V, in *Certain Difficulties felt by Anglicans in Catholic Teaching* II (London: Longmans Green, 1885), 248, as quoted in the English translation of the *Catechism of the Catholic Church: Modifications from the Editio Typica* (United States Catholic Conference, 1997) #1778 (note 50), p. 439. Robert Wright is quoted from his *The Cowboy Capital and the Great Southwest in the Days of the Wild Indian, the Buffalo, the Cowboy, Dance Halls, Gambling Halls and Bad Men* (copy at West Texas A&M University library, no date, place, or publisher given).

CHAPTER THREE

The Hank Smith character's quoted comments about Lord Jamison as well as his story about the captain trying to ride the buffalo, paraphrased and quoted here, are derived from the historical Hank Smith's article "Along Down the Reminiscent Line," in the *Crosbyton Review*, February 29, 1912. The story of the Chief of Red Mud in Griffin is derived from Edgar Rye's *The Quirt and the Spur: Vanishing Shadows of the Texas Frontier* (Chicago: W. B. Conkley Company, 1909). Tom recounts a buffalo hunting story, paraphrased and quoted from Robert Wright's *The Cowboy Capital and the Great Southwest in the Days of the Wild Indian, the Buffalo, the Cowboy, Dance Halls, Gambling Halls and Bad Men*. Captain R. B. Marcy's description of the Llano Estacado comes from his *Route From Fort Smith to Santa Fe*, 31st Congress, 1st Session, 1850, House Ex. Doc. 45, 42.

CHAPTER FOUR

The Mark Twain quotation is from *Roughing It*, as quoted in the brochure "Homestead: Official Map and Guide," (Homestead National Monument of America, National Park Service, U.S. Department of the Interior). The quotation about a season for everything is from Ecclesiastes 3:1. The quotation about participation in the "divine eternity" is from the *Catechism of the Catholic Church*, #1085, p. 282.

Josiah Gregg is quoted from his *Commerce of the Prairies* (New York: Henry G. Langley, 1844), 2:213. The W.B. Parker quotation comes from his *Notes Taken during the Expedition Commanded by Capt. R. B. Marcy* (Philadelphia: Hayes and Zell, 1856), 101. The Charles Goodnight quotation about the size of the southern herd of buffalo comes from *Charles Goodnight: Cowman and Plainsman* by J. Evetts Haley (Norman: University of Oklahoma Press, 1949), 437. The William T. Hornaday quotations come from his *The Extermination of the American Bison* (Washington: Government Printing Office, 1889), 387, 435. For the estimate of 500,000 buffalo killed annually by the Plains Indians, see Carl Coke Rister's *Fort Griffin on the Texas Frontier* (Norman: University of Oklahoma Press, 1956), 164. Charles Goodnight's encounter with Dutch Henry, including the quoted material, is adapted from Haley's *Charles Goodnight*, pp. 287–88, 335–36.

Among the various sources I consulted for the section on the Comanche, I am especially indebted to two works: Ernest Wallace and E. Adamson Hoebel's *The Comanches: Lords of the South Plains* (Norman: University of Oklahoma Press, 1952) and Rupert Norval Richardson's *The Comanche Barrier to South Plains Settlement* (Austin, Texas: Eakin Press, 1996). The Kicking Bird quotation is taken from *The Comanche Barrier*, p. 192. The General Philip H. Sheridan quotation is taken from John R. Cook's *The Border and the Buffalo* (Topeka, Kansas, 1907), 113. The derivation "anyone who wants to fight me all the time" can be found in Wallace and Hoebel's *The Comanches*, pp. 4–5. The first of the quotations from the *Telegraph and Texas Register* is from May 30, 1838; the second is from a correspondent called X.Y., June 16, 1838. The George Catlin quotation comes from his *Letters and Notes on the Condition of the North American Indians*, vol. 2 (Philadelphia: Willis P. Hazard, 1857), 437. The Colonel Dodge quotations come from his *The Plains of the Great West and Their Inhabitants* (New York: G.P. Putnam's Sons, 1877), xxv. Captain Marcy's quotations are from his and George McClellan's report to the U. S. Senate, *Exploration of the Red River of Louisiana in the Year 1852* (Washington, 1853), 95, 98. The George F. Ruxton quotations come from his *Adventures in Mexico and the Rocky Mountains* (New York: Harper and Brothers, 1855) 111–12.

Rousseau's quotation is taken from Hoxie Neal Fairchild's *The Noble Savage: A Study in Romantic Naturalism* (New York: Russell and Russell, 1961), 134. The Maximus the Confessor quotation is from the

Catechism of the Catholic Church, #398, p. 100 (*Ambigua*: PG 91, 1156C). For the section on original holiness and justice see the *Catechism*, #374–76, p. 95. The quotations about deprivation of original holiness and justice, corruption, and concupiscence are from the *Catechism*, #404, 405, p. 102. The quotation from St. Thomas Aquinas is from the *Catechism*, #412, p. 104 (*Summa theologiae* III, 1,3 ad 3); St. Leo the Great's is from the *Catechism*, #412, p. 104 (*Sermo* 73, 4: PL 54, 396). The quotation from St. Irenaeus is from the *Catechism*, #460, p. 116 (*Adversus haereses* 3, 19, 1: PG 7/1, 939); St. Thomas Aquinas' is from the *Catechism*, #460, p. 116 (*Opusculum* 57: 1–4); St. Athanasius' is from the *Catechism*, #460, p. 116 (*De incarnatione* 54, 3: PG 25, 192B). The G. K. Chesterton quotations are from his *St. Thomas Aquinas* (New York: Image/Doubleday, 1956), 144, 145–46.

For the knowledge of log-house construction I turned to and wish to especially acknowledge Terry G. Jordan's *Texas Log Buildings: A Folk Architecture* (Austin: University of Texas Press, 1982).

For the terminology "pray the Gospel" for the rosary, I thank Fr. John Corapi. "The sacred deposit of the Word of God" is from the *Catechism*, #97, p. 29 (*Dei Verbum* 10); "instrument for the salvation of all" from the *Catechism*, #776, p.205 (*Lumen Gentium* 9, 2); sacrament of the missions from the *Catechism*, #738, p. 195; "the sacrament of the Holy Trinity's communion with men" from the *Catechism*, #747, p. 196; "participates in the divine eternity, . . ." from the *Catechism*, #1085, p. 282; "poured our for many" from Mt 26:28, Mk 14:24, Lk 22:20; "instituted his apostles as priests" from the *Catechism*, #611, p. 158; "according to the flesh, but in the Spirit" from *Lumen Gentium* 9, 1.

CHAPTER FIVE

The Charles Goodnight character's contribution to the discussion on grading cattle, including his comments on Durhams, Aberdeen-Angus, and Herefords; his comments on the New Zealand dogs; the story about trailing cattle with the dog Shep, much of which is word for word; the story of the Casner dog; and his grading plan and its results are all derived from Haley's *Charles Goodnight*, pp. 318, 320; 340, 341; 219–22; 285–86; 316.

Andy reads Gen 12:1–5. Tom quotes from Sir (Ecclesiasticus) 33:10–11; Lk 2:52; and Jn 3:19.

For the section on the Herefords, I am especially indebted to Donald R. Ornduff's *The Hereford in America: A Compilation of Historic Facts About the Breed's Background and Bloodlines* (Kansas City, Missouri: By the Author, 1960). W. E. Campbell's quotation about his experiment with Herefords and shorthorns comes from the September 4, 1884 edition of *The Breeder's Gazette* of Chicago. The D.J. Bernard quotation is from Ornduff's *The Hereford*, p. 147 (the original source is not cited). The Charles Goodnight quotation about the best imported Hereford bulls is taken from a letter from Goodnight to Alvin H. Sanders and appears in Sanders' *The Story of the Herefords* (Chicago: *The Breeder's Gazette*, 1914), 712. John Clay's quotation is from his *My Life on the Range* (Chicago, 1924), 187.

For the account of a loafer running up a rise with half a calf in his mouth, I am indebted to Dr. Andy Gray, Lubbock, Texas.

CHAPTER SIX

The return of the Comanche, along with members of several other peoples, to the canyon region to hunt buffalo in the winter of 1878–79 leans upon that recorded in Haley's *Charles Goodnight*, pp. 306–12. It is further supported by the witness of Henry O. Flipper in *Negro Frontiersman The Western Memoirs of Henry O. Flipper*, ed. Theodore D. Harris (El Paso: Texas Western College Press, 1963), p. 5.

CHAPTER SEVEN

Tom's meditation during the Luke–Brown fight includes: Mt 5:4,9; Mt 26:52; Mt 5:22; Mt 5:39–41; Mt 5:44–48; Lk 23:34; Mt 23:13–39; Lk 7:9; Rom 13:4. The qualification for self-defense is taken from the *Catechism of the Council of Trent*, trans. John A. McHugh and Charles J. Callan (New York: Joseph F. Wagner: 1934), 422. The Thomas Aquinas quotation is taken from the *Catechism*, #2264, p.545 (*Summa theologiae* II-II, 64,7, corp. art.). The quotation on proportionate punishment is from the *Catechism*, #2266, p. 546.

As Tom rides toward HE headquarters he meditates on: *Hamlet* III, i, 84–88; the John Henry Newman quotation cited above, found in the *Catechism*, #1778 (note 50), p. 439; *Hamlet* III, i, 81–82, 86; Mt 5:9; Mt 5:11–12; Mt 5:39; the Prayer of St. Francis; Ps 23 (22 in Douay–Rheims):4; Mt 5:9.

SOURCES

I read or consulted the following in the research behind this work of fiction.

Adams, Andy. *The Log of a Cowboy*. London: Senate, 1994.

Aldridge, Reginald. *Life on a Ranch: Ranch Notes in Kansas, Colorado, The Indian Territory and Northern Texas*. New York: Argonaut Press, 1966.

Alexander, Drury Blakeley. *Texas Homes of the Nineteenth Century*. Austin, Texas: University of Texas Press, 1966.

Anderson, Bernhard W. *Understanding the Old Testament*. Englewood Cliffs, New Jersey: Prentice Hall, 1975.

Aquinas, Thomas. *Light of Faith: The Compendium of Theology*. Translated by Cyril Vollert. Manchester, New Hampshire: Sophia Institute Press, 1993.

Bailey, Thomas A., and Kennedy, David M. *The American Pageant*. Vol. 2, *A History of the Republic*. Lexington, Massachusetts: D. C. Heath, 1979.

Ball, Eve; Henn, Nora; Sanchez, Lynda. *An Apache Odyssey: Indeh*. Provo, Utah: Brigham Young University Press, 1980.

Bennett, William J., ed. *The Book of Virtues: A Treasury of Moral Stories*. New York: Simon and Schuster, 1993.

The Bible. Douay Rheims Version.

The Bible. King James Version.

The Bible. Revised Standard Version.

The Bible. Revised Standard Version. Catholic Edition.

Biggers, Don Hampton. *Buffalo Guns and Barbed Wire*. Lubbock, Texas: Texas Tech University Press, 1991.

Bishop, Curtis, and Giles, Bascom. *Lots of Land: (From Material Compiled under the Direction of the Commissioner of the General Land Office of Texas, Bascom Giles)*. Austin, Texas: The Steck Company, 1949.

Boley, Tommy J., ed. *An Autobiography of a West Texas Pioneer: Ella Elgar Bird Dumont*. Austin, Texas: University of Texas Press, 1988.

Bowser, David. *City of Mystery and Romance: Fifteen True Stories from San Antonio's Past*. 1993.

Boyer, L. Bryce. *Childhood and Folklore: A Psychoanalytical Study of Apache Personality*. New York: The Library of Psychological Anthropology, 1979.

Bradfield, Nancy. *Costume Design in Detail: Women's Dress 1730–1930*. Boston: Plays, 1968.

Branda, Eldon Stephen. *The Handbook of Texas: A Supplement*. Austin, Texas: Texas State Historical Association, 1976.

Brown, Raymond E.; Fitzmyer, Joseph A.; and Murphy, Roland E., eds. *The New Jerome Biblical Commentary*. Englewood Cliffs, New Jersey: Prentice Hall, 1990.

Campbell, Harry H. *The Early History of Motley County*. Wichita Falls, Texas: Nortex Offset Publications, 1971.

Carroll, John M., ed. *The Black Military Experience in the American West*. New York: Liveright, 1973.

Carson, Gerald. *The Golden Egg: The Personal Income Tax: Where it Came From, How it Grew*. Boston: Houghton Mifflin, 1977.

Carter, Samuel, III. *Cowboy Capital of the World: The Saga of Dodge City*. New York: Doubleday, 1973.

Castro Colonies Heritage Association. *The History of Medina County, Texas*. Castro Colonies Heritage Association.

Catechism of the Catholic Church. Morristown, New Jersey: Silver Burdett Ginn, 1994.

Catechism of the Catholic Church: Modifications from the Editio Typica. Washington: United States Catholic Conference, Inc. — Libreria Editrice Vaticana, 1997.

Catechism of the Council of Trent for Parish Priests. Translated by John A. McHugh and Charles J. Callan. New York: Joseph F. Wagner: 1934.

Catlin, George. *Letters and Notes on the Condition of the North American Indians*. Vol. 2. Philadelphia: Willis P. Hazard, 1857.

Chesterton, G. K. *Saint Thomas Aquinas: "The Dumb Ox."* New York: Doubleday: Image Books, 1956.

Chodorov, Frank. *The Income Tax: Root of All Evil*. New York: Devin-Adair, 1959.

Chrisman, Harry E. *Lost Trails of the Cimarron*. Denver: Sage Books, 1961.

Chudacoff, Howard P.; Escott, Paul D.; Katzman, David M.; Norton, Mary Beth; Patterson, Thomas G.; and Tuttle, William M., Jr. *A People and a Nation: A History of the United States*. Vol. 1, *To 1877*. Boston: Houghton Mifflin, 1982.

Clay, John. *My Life on the Range*. Chicago, 1924.

Cook, John R. *The Border and the Buffalo: An Untold Story of the Southwest Plains*. Topeka, Kansas, 1907.

Cro, Stelio. *The Noble Savage: Allegory of Freedom*. Waterloo, Ontario: Wilfrid Laurier University Press, 1990.

Curry, W. Hubert. *Sun Rising on the West: The Saga of Henry Clay and Elizabeth Smith*. Crosbyton, Texas, 1979.

Dale, Edward Everett. *The Range Cattle Industry*. Norman, Oklahoma: University of Oklahoma Press, 1930.

Dary, David. *Cowboy Culture: A Saga of Five Centuries*. New York: Alfred A. Knopf, 1981.

Davis, John L. *San Antonio: A Historical Portrait*. Austin, Texas: Encino Press, 1978.

Dobie, Frank J. *The Flavor of Texas*. Austin, Texas: Jenkins Publishing, 1975.

Dodge, Richard Irving. *The Plains of the Great West and Their Inhabitants*. New York: G.P. Putnam's Sons, 1877.

Drago, Harry Sinclair. *The Great Range Wars: Violence on the Grasslands*. New York: Dodd, Mead, 1970.

Dumont, Ella Elgar Bird. *Autobiography*. (see Boley, Tommy J. above)

Dykstra, Robert R. *The Cattle Towns*. New York: Alfred A. Knopf, 1968.

Elliot, W. J. *The Spurs*. The Texas Spur, 1939, Reprinted Kerrville, Texas, 1967.

Fairchild, Hoxie Neal. *The Noble Savage: A Study in Romantic Naturalism*. New York: Russell and Russell, 1961.

Fehrenbach, T. R. *Lone Star: A History of Texas and the Texans*. New York: MacMillan, 1968.

Flipper, Henry Ossian. *The Colored Cadet at West Point: Autobiography of Lieut. Henry Ossian Flipper, U.S.A.: First Graduate of Color from the U.S. Military Academy*. New York: Homer Lee, 1878.

———. *The Colored Cadet at West Point*. New York: Arno Press and the New York Times, 1969.

———. *Negro Frontiersman: The Western Memoirs of Henry O. Flipper*. Edited by Theodore D. Harris. El Paso, Texas: Texas Western College Press, 1963.

Flores, Dan. *Caprock Canyonlands*. Austin, Texas: University of Texas Press, 1990.

Foote, Shelby. *The Civil War: A Narrative: Fort Sumter to Perryville*. New York: Vintage Books, 1986.

Forbis, William H., and the editors of Time-Life Books. *The Old West: The Cowboys.* Alexandria, Virginia: Time-Life Books, 1980.

Franks, Lan(pseud.), and Connor, Seymour V. *A Biggers Chronicle: Consisting of a Reprint of the Extremely Rare "History That Will Never be Repeated" and a Biography of its Author Don Hampton Biggers.* Lubbock: Texas Technological College (Southwest Collection), 1961.

Galbreath, Lester W. *Fort Griffin and the Clear Fork Country: Locations of Historic Sites and Buildings with Notes and Interesting Facts on Each.* Albany, Texas: By the Author, 1995.

Grant, Ulysses S. *Personal Memoirs of U. S. Grant.* 2 vols. New York: Charles L. Webster, 1885.

_____. *Personal Memoirs of U. S. Grant,* edited by E. B. Long. New York: World Publishing, 1952.

Green, John Duff. *Recollections.* (Part I and Part II.) Edited by Joan Green Lawrence. (Received from Ron Graves, Crosbyton, Texas.)

Gregg, Josiah. *Commerce of the Prairies: Or the Journal of a Santa Fe Trader during Eight Expeditions across the Great Western Prairies, and a Residence of Nearly Nine Years in Northern Mexico.* Vol. 2. New York: Henry G. Langley, 1844.

Guerra, Mary Ann Noona. *The History of San Antonio's Market Square.* San Antonio: Alamo Press, 1988.

———. *The History of the San Antonio River.* San Antonio: Alamo Press, 1987.

Guy, Duane F., ed. *The Story of Palo Duro Canyon.* Canyon, Texas: Panhandle Plains Historical Society, 1979.

Haley, J. Evetts. *Charles Goodnight: Cowman and Plainsman.* Norman, Oklahoma: University of Oklahoma Press, 1949.

———. *Charles Goodnight: Cowman and Plainsman.* Norman, Oklahoma: University of Oklahoma Press, 1983.

Haley, James L. *Texas: An Album of History.* Garden City, New York: Doubleday, 1985.

Hamilton, Charles Granville. *Lincoln and the Know Nothing Movement.* Washington, D. C.: Public Affairs Press, 1954.

Hansen, Harry, ed. *Texas: A Guide to the Lone Star State.* New York: Hastings House, 1969.

Hardon, John A. *Pocket Catholic Dictionary.* New York: Image Books/ Doubleday, 1985.

Hazelton, Jno. M. *History and Handbook of Hereford Cattle and Hereford Bull Index.* Kansas City: Hereford Journal, 1929.

Hill, J. L. *The End of the Cattle Trail*. Long Beach, California: Geo. W. Moyle, 192?.

Holden, Frances Mayhugh. *Lambshead before Interwoven: A Texas Range Chronicle 1848–1878*. College Station, Texas: Texas A&M University Press, 1982.

Holden, W. C. *Rollie Burns or An Account of the Ranching Industry on the South Plains*. College Station, Texas: Texas A&M University Press, 1986.

Holmes, Jon. *Texas: A Self-Portrait*. New York: Harry N. Abrams, 1983.

Hornaday, William T. *The Extermination of the American Bison*. Washington: Government Printing Office, 1889.

House, Boyce. *San Antonio: City of Flaming Adventure*. San Antonio: Naylor, 1968.

Hunter, J. Marvin. *The Trail Drivers of Texas*. Austin, Texas: University of Texas Press, 1996.

Jenkins, John Cooper, et al. *Estacado: Cradle of Culture and Civilization on the Staked Plains of Texas*. Crosbyton, Texas: Crosby County Memorial Library, 1986.

Johnson, Barry C. *Flipper's Dismissal. The Ruin of Lt. Henry O. Flipper, U. S. A., First Coloured Graduate of West Point*. London: (private printing), 1980.

Jordan, Terry, G. *Texas Log Buildings: A Folk Architecture*. Austin, Texas: University of Texas Press, 1978.

Lehmann, V. W. *Forgotten Legions: Sheep in the Rio Grande Plain of Texas*. El Paso, Texas: Texas Western Press, 1969.

Matthews, Sallie Reynolds. *Interwoven: A Pioneer Chronicle*. College Station, Texas: Texas A&M University Press, 1982.

McGinnis, Ralph Y., and Smith, Calvin N., eds. *Abraham Lincoln and the Western Territories*. Chicago: Nelson-Hall Publishers, 1994.

McGregor, Gaile. *The Noble Savage in the New World Garden: Notes toward a Syntactics of Place*. Toronto: University of Toronto Press, 1988.

Miller, Thomas Lloyd. *The Public Lands of Texas: 1519–1970*. Norman, Oklahoma: University of Oklahoma Press, 1972.

Myres, S. D., ed. *Pioneer Surveyor/Frontier Lawyer: The Personal Narrative of O. W. Williams: 1877–1902*. El Paso, Texas: Texas Western Press, 1968.

Oldham County Centennial Book. (1881–1981) p. 40.

Ornduff, Donald R. *The Hereford in America: A Compilation of Historic Facts About the Breed's Background and Bloodlines*. Kansas City, Missouri: By the Author, 1960.

Parker, W.B. *Notes Taken During the Expedition Commanded by Capt. R. B. Marcy, U.S.A., through Unexplored Texas in the Summer and Fall of 1854*. Philadelphia: Hayes and Zell, 1856.

Price, Byron, and Rathjen, Frederick W. *The Golden Spread: An Illustrated History of Amarillo and the Texas Panhandle.* Northridge, California: Windsor Publications, 1986.

Ramsdell, Charles, and Perry, Carmen. *San Antonio: A Historical and Pictorial Guide.* Austin, Texas: University of Texas Press, 1976.

Rathgen, Frederick W. *The Texas Panhandle Frontier.* Austin, Texas: University of Texas Press, 1973.

Richardson, Rupert Norval. *The Comanche Barrier to South Plains Settlement.* Austin, Texas: Eakin Press, 1996.

Rister, Carl Coke. *Fort Griffin on the Texas Frontier.* Norman, Oklahoma: University of Oklahoma Press, 1956.

Robinson, Charles M., III. *The Frontier World of Fort Griffin: The Life and Death of a Western Town.* Spokane, Washington: Arthur Clark, 1992.

Rooney, Nellie, O.S.F. *A History of the Catholic Church in the Panhandle Plains Area of Texas from 1875 to 1916.* Amarillo, Texas: By the Author, 1996.

Rouse, John E. *World Cattle III: Cattle of North America.* Norman, Oklahoma: University of Oklahoma Press, 1973.

Ruxton, George F. *Adventures in Mexico and the Rocky Mountains.* New York: Harper and Brothers, 1855.

Rye, Edgar. *The Quirt and the Spur: Vanishing Shadows of the Texas Frontier.* Chicago: W. B. Conkley, 1909.

Sadler, Jerry. *History of Texas Land.* Austin, Texas: General Land Office of the State of Texas.

Sandburg, Carl. *Abraham Lincoln: The War Years.* Vol. 1. New York: Harcourt, Brace & World, 1939.

Sanders, Alvin H. *The Story of the Herefords.* Chicago: *The Breeder's Gazette*, 1914.

Seagraves, Anne. *Soiled Doves: Prostitution in the Early West.* Hayden, Idaho: Wesanne Publications, 1994.

Shirley, Glenn. *Temple Houston: Lawyer with a Gun.* Norman, Oklahoma: University of Oklahoma Press, 1980.

Siringo, Charles A. *A Texas Cowboy: or Fifteen Years on the Hurricane Deck of a Spanish Pony.* Lincoln, Nebraska: University of Nebraska Press, 1979.

Spearing, Darwin. *Roadside Geology of Texas.* Missoula, Montana: Mountain Press, 1994.

Stanley, Robert. *Dimensions of Law in the Service of Order: Origins of the Federal Income Tax, 1861–1913.* New York: Oxford University Press, 1993.

Stephens, A. Ray, and Holmes, William (McCaffree, Phyllis M., consultant). *Historical Atlas of Texas*. Norman, Oklahoma: University of Oklahoma Press, 1989.

Tanner, Karen Holliday. *Doc Holliday: A Family Portrait*. Norman, Oklahoma: University of Oklahoma Press, 1998.

Tanner, Ogden, and the editors of Time-Life Books. *The Old West: The Ranchers*. Alexandria, Virginia: Time-Life Books, 1977.

Texas General Land Office. *Land: A History of the Texas General Land Office*. Austin, Texas: Texas General Land Office, 1992.

Townshend, S. Nugent. *Our Indian Summer in the Far West: An Autumn Tour of Fifteen Thousand Miles in Kansas, Texas, New Mexico, Colorado, and the Indian Territory*. London: Charles Whittingham, 1880.

Vestal, Stanley. *Queen of Cowtowns: Dodge City*. Lincoln, Nebraska: University of Nebraska Press, 1952.

Wallace, Ernest, and Hoebel, E. Adamson. *The Comanches: Lords of the South Plains*. Norman, Oklahoma: University of Oklahoma Press, 1952.

Watkins, Sue, ed. *One League to Each Wind: Accounts of Early Surveying in Texas*. Compiled by Historical Committee, Texas Surveyors Association. Austin, Texas, 1968.

Webb, Walter Prescott, ed. in chief. *The Handbook of Texas*. Vol. I. Austin, Texas: The Texas State Historical Association, 1952.

————, ed. in chief. *The Handbook of Texas*. Vol. II. Austin, Texas: The Texas State Historical Association, 1952.

Wenzl, Timothy. *The Centennial of Sacred Heart Parish: Mission to Cathedral*. Dodge City, Kansas: Sacred Heart Cathedral Parish, 1982.

Whitlock, V. H. *Cowboy Life on the Llano Estacado*. Norman, Oklahoma: University of Oklahoma Press, 1970.

Williams, O. W. *Pioneer Surveyor/Frontier Lawyer*. (see Myres, S. D. above).

Wolff, Robert Paul, ed. *Ten Great Works of Philosophy*. New York: Mentor/New American Library, 1969.

Wright, Robert M. *Dodge City: The Cowboy Capital and the Great Southwest in the Days of the Wild Indian, the Buffalo, the Cowboy, Dance Halls, Gambling Halls and Bad Men*. (copy at West Texas A&M University library, no date, place or publisher given)

————. *Dodge City: The Cowboy Capital and the Great Southwest*. New York: Arno Press, 1975.

Young, Frederic R. *Dodge City: Up Through A Century in Story and Pictures*. Dodge City, Kansas: Boot Hill Museum, 1985.

PUBLIC DOCUMENTS

Abstract of Land Titles of Texas Comprising the Titled, Patented and Located Lands in the State. Galveston, Texas: Shaw and Blaylock, 1878.

Hamman, Philip J., and Neeb, Charles W. "Cicadas." Texas Agricultural Extension Service, The Texas A&M University System. College Station, Texas. (West Texas State University Library Documents)

Marcy, Randolph B., and George B. McClellan. *Exploration of the Red River of Louisiana.* 30th Cong., 2nd sess., 1853. S. Doc. 54.

————. *Route From Fort Smith to Santa Fe.* House Ex. Doc. 45, 31st Congress, 1st Session. Washington, D.C., 1850.

Texas Agricultural Extension Service. *Know Your Grasses.* (B-182). Cooperative Extension Work in Agriculture and Home Economics, Texas A&M University and the United States Department of Agriculture cooperating. College Station, Texas: Texas Agricultural Extension Service, 1978 or later.

Texas General Land Office Website. www.glo.state.tx.us. "Historical Documents and Other Information." Last updated 26 October 1997.

Texas General Land Office Website. www.glo.state.tx.us. " Categories of Texas Land Grants." Last updated 1 April 1997.

Texas General Land Office Website Archives. www.glo.state.tx.us/central/arc/. "Historical Programs: Overview." April 1997.

Texas General Land Office Website Archives. www.glo.state.tx.us/central/arc/process. html. "Information for Researchers: The Land Grant Process in Texas after 1836." 2 April 1997.

Texas Historical Markers.

U.S. Department of Agriculture, Soil Conservation Service, in Cooperation with the Texas Agricultural Experiment Station. *Soil Survey of Briscoe County, Texas.* By Luther C. Geiger and Wayburn D. Mitchell. Washington, D.C.: U.S. Government Printing Office, 1977.

U.S. Department of Agriculture, Soil Conservation Service, in Cooperation with the Texas Agricultural Experiment Station. *Soil Survey of Crosby County, Texas.* By William M. Koos, Lee A. Putnam, and Wayburn D. Mitchell. Washington, D.C.: U.S. Government Printing Office, 1966.

U.S. Department of Agriculture, Soil Conservation Service, in Cooperation with the Texas Agricultural Experiment Station. *Soil Survey of Floyd County, Texas.* By Conrad L. Neitsch and Don A. Blackstock. Washington, D.C.: U.S. Government Printing Office, 1978.

U.S. Department of Agriculture, Soil Conservation Service, in Cooperation with the Texas Agricultural Experiment Station. *Soil Survey of Motley County, Texas*. By Wayne E. Richardson, Johnny Hajek, and Conrad Neitsch. Washington, D.C.: U.S. Government Printing Office, 1977.

BOOKS RECORDED ONTO AUDIO TAPE

Billings, John D. *Hard Tack and Coffee: Or the Unwritten Story of Army Life*. Read by Jim Roberts. Jimcin Records, 1992.

Grant, Ulysses S. *The Personal Memoirs of U. S. Grant.—One: The Early Years, West Point, Mexico*. Narrated by Peter Johnson. Charlotte Hall, Maryland: Recorded Books, Inc., 1988.

NEWSPAPERS

Dodge City Times. 31 March 1877.

Dodge City Times. 28 April 1877.

Dodge City Times. 23 June 1877.

Dodge City Times. 30 June 1877.

Dodge City Times. 7 July 1877.

Dodge City Times. 14 July 1877.

Dodge City Times. 4 August 1877.

Frontier Echo. Jacksboro, Texas, 15 September 1876.

UNPUBLISHED WORKS

Baker, Ruth E. "Memoirs of John R. Snider." Amarillo, Texas, from interviews with Mr. Snider: John R. Snider to Ruth E. Baker: May 16, 1936; July 18, 1936; July 26, 1936. For History 411 at West Texas A&M, Instructor L. F. Sheffy, August 18, 1936, Location not on card, probably Panhandle Plains Historical Museum Archives, Canyon, Texas or Southwest Collection, Texas Tech., Lubbock, Texas.

Barksdale, Eugene Frank, ed. Collection of papers of Woods and Simpsons. "The following information was gathered from various sources, especially from Georgia Simpson Elliott, by Gene Barksdale, December, 1991." Includes: interview with Georgia Simpson Elliott; manuscript of Sylvania Wood Simpson; affidavit by Isaac Simpson; manuscript of Jonathan Berry Wood to L. F. Sheffy, Dec. 28, 1929; manuscript at Panhandle Plains Museum Archives in Canyon, TX; story from Iva (Wood); Hez Wood's story excerpted from *Cowmen and their Ladies* by Sallie Harris; and a letter from Georgia Simpson to granddaughter, Bonnie Thomas, Feb. 28, 1931; and memoirs of George A. Simpson by L. F. Sheffy, Nov. 30, 1929.

Brown, Robert William. A Historical Account of Col. Charles Goodnight and the Quitaque / Lazy F Ranch. (Location not on card but probably Panhandle Plains Historical Archives, Canyon, Texas; Southwest Collection, Texas Tech., Lubbock Texas: or Wisconsin State Historical Society Library, Madison Wisconsin.) Unpublished, 1986.

Cator, J. H. Recollections. Unpublished, untitled, undated. In possession of Charles Broadhurst (352-7250). (Do not remember this source, but, because it is in pencil, probably from Panhandle Plains Historical Museum Archives, or connected with it, or Southwest Collection, Texas Tech., Lubbock, Texas.)

Cobea, C. May. "Pioneer Women." Prepared by the Personnel: Work Projects Administration, O.P. No. 665-66-3-299. Panhandle Plains Historical Museum Archives, Canyon, Texas, (no date).

Collinson, Frank. "The First Cattle Ranch on Tongue River Motley County, Texas: (two parts) Ranch Romances." Panhandle Plains Historical Museum Archives, Canyon, Texas, July, 1936 (date approximate).

———. "Tongue River's First Ranch." Panhandle Plains Historical Museum Archives, Canyon, Texas, (no date).

Cox, Mrs. Bob. "Biography of Martha Lou Wesley." History 412, West Texas A&M University, Panhandle Plains Historical Museum Archives, Canyon, Texas, (no date).

Dobie, J. Frank. "Charles Goodnight Observer and Man." Panhandle Plains Historical Museum Archives, Canyon, Texas, (no date).

Doshier, Carroll. "The Camp Life of a Cowpuncher." Panhandle Plains Historical Museum Archives, Canyon, Texas, (no date).

———. "The Outside Man." Panhandle Plains Historical Museum Archives, Canyon, Texas, (no date).

Gerdes, Bruce. "Transformation of the Buffalo Range." Tulia Texas. Panhandle Plains Historical Museum Archives, Canyon, Texas, (no date).

Greer, Betty Joe. "Interview with Mr. and Mrs. E. A. Upfold, Canyon, Texas, Feb. 24, 1945." Panhandle Plains Historical Museum Archives, Canyon, Texas, 24 February 1945.

Harris, Theodore Delano. "Henry Ossian Flipper: The First Negro Graduate of West Point: A Thesis Submitted to the Faculty of the Graduate School of the University of Minnesota." (Do not remember location of this manuscript; possibly Wisconsin State Historical Society Library or Panhandle Plains Historical Museum Archives), 1971.

Hatfield, Col. Chas. A. "The Comanche, Kiowa and Cheyenne Campaign in Northwest Texas and MacKenzie's Fight in the Palo Duro Canyon." (Do not recall location, possibly Panhandle Plains Historical Museum Archives, Canyon, Texas, or Southwest Collection, Texas Tech, Lubbock, Texas), 26 September 1874.

Hood, Evelyn. "Viewing a Half Century of Progress on the Plains." An interview with H. Frank Mitchell. Panhandle Plains Historical Museum Archives, Canyon, Texas, 28 March 1933 and 24 January 1934.

Jennings, Corinne Jowell. "One Key to the Past—Food." Vandale Essay Contest. Panhandle Plains Historical Museum Archives, Canyon, Texas, (date? probably after 1947).

Jones, Stella G. "Memoirs of Mr. and Mrs. J. A. White of 1923 Pierce Street, Amarillo, Texas, December 27, 1945." Panhandle Plains Historical Museum Archives, Canyon, Texas, 27 December 1945.

"History of the Montgomery Family: From 1825 to the Present Time." (no author given) Panhandle Plains Historical Museum Archives, Canyon, Texas, 1937.

Patterson, Bessie Chambers. "Palo Duro State Park: The Grand Canyon of Texas." Prepared for 1953 contest of Panhandle Plains Historical Society. Panhandle Plains Historical Museum Archives, 1953.

Stark, Madeleine Whiteley. "The James Clark Whiteley Family." Panhandle Plains Historical Museum Archives, Canyon, Texas, (no date given).

Webb, J. R. "Recollections and Experiences of the Frontier Life of Phin W. Reynolds as told to J. R. Webb by Phin Reynolds at Albany, Texas, during the months of May 1936, and during April 1938." Southwest Collection, Texas Tech University, Lubbock, Texas, C14.3B, 1936, 1938. (See *West Texas Historical Association Yearbook*. Vol. XXI (October 1945): 110–143.

Young, Jessica M. "Pioneer Days in the Panhandle." (Third prize, Amarillo Tri-State Fair, Sept. 26, Oct. 1, 1925) Panhandle Plains Historical Museum Archives, Canyon, Texas, 1925.

ARTICLES

Alexander, John. "Riving Wood for 17th Century Joint Furniture." www.green-woodworking.com.

Archambeau, Ernest R. "The First Federal Census in the Panhandle: 1880" (Bound in binder at Panhandle Plains Historical Museum Archives). Article appeared in *Panhandle Plains Historical Review*, 23 (1950) 22–132.

Branch, Douglas. "The Long Drive North." In *The Western Story: Fact, Fiction, and Myth*, edited by Philip Durham and Everett L. Jones. New York: Harcourt Brace Jovanovich, 1975.

Burns, Joseph E. "A Catholic American Asks, 'Are All Wars Evil?'" *Denver Catholic Register*. November 14, 2001: 6.

Connellee, C.U. "Some Experiences of a Pioneer Surveyor." *West Texas Yearbook*. VI (June 1930): 80–93.

Eide, Clyde. "Free As the Wind." *Nebraska History* (Nebraska State Historical Society) (Spring 1970): 25–47.

Giles, Bascom. "History and Disposition of Texas Public Domain." In *Introduction to Texas Land Surveying* (5th Edition), edited by M.E. Spry, C.E. Odessa, Texas: 1980?.

Haley, J. Evetts. "The Comanchero Trade." *Southwestern Historical Quarterly* 38 (January 1935).

———. "Hank Smith: Frontier Settler." (Have article, but no setting or reference.)

———. "John Bouldin's First Christmas on the Plains." *The Shamrock*, Winter 1958.

Harger, Charles Moreau. "Cattle-Trails of the Prairies." Originally appeared in *Scribner's Magazine*, 1892, A Highlands Historical Press Facsimile. Dallas: Highlands Historical Press, 1961.

Haywood, Robert C. "'No Less a Man': Blacks in Cow Town Dodge City, 1876–1886." *The Western Historical Quarterly* 19 (May 1988): 161–182.

"Hispanic Patriarch of the Panhandle: Casimero Romero Founder of Old Tascosa." *Amarillo Globe*, 13 October 1993.

Hood, Charles H., and Underwood, James R., Jr. "Geology of Palo Duro Canyon." In *The Story of Palo Duro Canyon*, edited by Duane F. Guy. Canyon, Texas: Panhandle-Plains Historical Society, 1979.

Hughes, Jack T. "Archeology of Palo Duro Canyon." In *The Story of Palo Duro Canyon*, edited by Duane F. Guy. Canyon, Texas: Panhandle-Plains Historical Society, 1979.

Hutto, John R. "Mrs. Elizabeth (Aunt Hank) Smith." *West Texas Historical Association Yearbook*. vol. XV, Abilene, TX, 1938, p. 40–47.

Lang, Aldon Socrates. "Financial History of the Public Lands of Texas." *The Baylor Bulletin*. 35 (July 1932).

Mabry, W. S. "Early West Texas and Panhandle Surveys." *Panhandle Plains Historical Review*. 2 (1929): 22–42.

McCampbell, C.W. "W.E. Campbell, Pioneer Kansas Livestockman." *Kansas Historical Quarterly* 16, 3 (August 1948): 245–273.

McKitrick, Reuben. "The Public Land System of Texas, 1823–1910." *Bulletin of the University of Wisconsin*. No. 905. *Economics and Political Science Series*. Vol. 9, No. 1 (1918): 1–172.

Oswald, James M. "History of Fort Elliott." *Panhandle-Plains Historical Review* 32 (1959): 1–59.

Pattie, Jane. "Monte Ritchie: The Man and His Legacy—The JA Ranch." *The Cattleman* (March 1993): ?–47.

Rister, Carl Coke. "Fort Griffin." (Adapted from an article by Carl Coke Rister in West Texas Historical Association Yearbook, 1925.) *The Cyclone* (Journal of the West Texas Historical Association.) 5 (15 August 1998): 3–4.

Roosevelt, Theodore. "The Cattle Country of the Far West." *The Western Story: Fact, Fiction, and Myth*, edited by Philip Durham and Everett L. Jones. New York: Harcourt Brace Jovanovich, 1975.

Schultz, Gerald E. "The Paleontology of Palo Duro Canyon." In *The Story of Palo Duro Canyon*, edited by Duane F. Guy. Canyon, Texas: Panhandle-Plains Historical Society, 1979.

Shine, Darrell D. "The Story of Texas Lands." In *TSPS: Basic Surveying Technicians Short Course Manual*.

Smith, Uncle Hank. "Along Down the Reminiscent Line." *Crosbyton Review*. 29 February 1912.

Wright, Robert A. "The Vegetation of Palo Duro Canyon." In *The Story of Palo Duro Canyon*, edited by Duane F. Guy. Canyon, Texas: Panhandle-Plains Historical Society, 1979.

ENCYCLOPEDIA ARTICLES

Academic American Encyclopedia. 1995 ed., s.v. "Apache." By Fred W. Voget.

Academic American Encyclopedia. 1995 ed., s.v. "Income Tax."

Academic American Encyclopedia. 1998 ed., s.v. "Comanche." By Fred W. Voget.

Academic American Encyclopedia. 1998 ed., s.v. "Noble Savage."

Catholic Encyclopedia. 1913 ed., 1996 electronic version, s.v. "John Calvin." By William Barry. Transcribed by Tomas Hancil.

Catholic Encyclopedia. 1913 ed., 1996 electronic version, s.v. "Calvinism." By William Barry. Transcribed by Tomas Hancil.

Catholic Encyclopedia. 1913 ed., 1997 electronic version, s.v. "Gnosticism." By J.P. Arendzen. Transcribed by Christine J. Murray.

Catholic Encyclopedia. 1913 ed., 1996 electronic version, s.v. "Hegelianism." By William Turner. Transcribed by Geoffrey K. Mondello.

Catholic Encyclopedia. 1913 ed., 1996 electronic version, s.v. "Manichaeism." By J. P. Arendzen. Transcribed by Tom Crossett.

Catholic Encyclopedia. 1913 ed., 1998 electronic version, s.v. "Masonry (Freemasonry)." By Hermann Gruber. Transcribed by Bobie Jo M. Bilz.

Catholic Encyclopedia. 1913 ed., 1996 electronic version, s.v. "Philosophy of Immanuel Kant." By William Turner. Transcribed by Rick McCarty.

Catholic Encyclopedia. 1913 ed., 1997 electronic version, s.v. "Rationalism." By Francis Aveling. Transcribed by Douglas J. Potter.

Catholic Encyclopedia. 1913 ed., 1998 electronic version, s.v. "University of Tubingen." By Johannes Baptist Sagmuller. Transcribed by Vivek Gilbert and John Fernandez.

Collier's Encyclopedia. 1995 ed., s.v. "Apaches." By Nahum Waxman.

Collier's Encyclopedia. 1996 ed., s.v. "Comanches." By Caleb E. Crowell.

Encyclopedia Americana (International Edition). 1995 ed., s.v. "Apaches." By Oliver LaFarge.

Encyclopedia Americana (International Edition). 1997 ed., s.v. "Comanche Indians." By Omer C. Stewart.

Encyclopedia Americana (International Edition). 1997 ed., s.v. "Hegel, Georg Wilhelm Friedrich." By Carl Joachim Friedrich.

Encyclopedia Americana (International Edition). 1997 ed., s.v. "Homestead Movement." By Paul W. Gates.

Encyclopedia Americana (International Edition). 1997 ed., s.v. "Income Tax." By Harold M. Groves.

Encyclopedia Americana (International Edition). 1997 ed., s.v. "Know-Nothing Movement." By Joel H. Sibley.

New Encyclopaedia Britannica (Micropedia, Ready Reference). 1997 ed., s.v. "Comanche."

New Encyclopaedia Britannica (Macropaedia). 1997 ed., s.v. "Hegel and Hegelianism."

New Encyclopaedia Britannica (Macropaedia). 1997 ed., s.v. "Marx and Marxism."

New Encyclopedia Britannica. (Macropaedia). 1997 ed., s.v. "Nietzsche."

New Encyclopaedia Britannica (Micropaedia). 1997 ed., s.v. "Noble Savage."

New Encyclopaedia Britannica (Macropaedia). 1997 ed., s.v. "Jean-Jacques Rousseau."

World Book Encyclopedia. 1997 ed., s.v. "Homestead Act." By Jerome O. Steffen.

World Book Encyclopedia. 1996 ed., s.v. "Income Tax." By Vito Tanzi.

PAMPHLETS

Carver, George Washington. "1897 or Thereabouts - George Washington Carver's Own Brief History of His Life." ca. 1897.

"Christmas in the Panhandle." *Gazette: Christmas Edition.* Pioneertown, Texas: December, 1994.

Lane, Eloise. "The Log House on White Deer Creek." (Received from Eugene Frank Barksdale, 25 October 1995.)

Texas Parks and Wildlife Department. "A Walk Through Fort Griffin: 1867–1881." Fort Griffin State Historical Park. Austin, Texas: Texas Parks and Wildlife Department.

Texas Parks and Wildlife Department. "Fort Griffin: State Historical Park." Fort Griffin State Historical Park. Texas Parks and Wildlife Department, November 1996.

U.S. Department of the Interior: National Park Service. "Homestead: Official Map and Guide." Homestead National Monument of America, Nebraska. Government Printing Office, 1995.

U.S. Department of the Interior: National Park Service. "Trail Map and Guide." Homestead National Monument, Nebraska. 1990.

FILMS

Burns, Ken. *The Civil War: A Film by Ken Burns.* Florentine Films and WETA-TV, 1990.

ATLASES AND MAPS

State Farm Road Atlas. Rand McNally, 1995.

Texas Atlas and Gazetteer (First Edition, Second Printing). Freeport, Maine: DeLorme Mapping, 1995.

"1852 Map of the State of Texas." Facsimile of the Original. (Panhandle Plains Historical Museum Archives.) Dallas, Texas: Highlands Historical Press, 1961.

"General Highway Map: Motley County Texas." Texas State Department of Highways and Public Transportation and U.S. Department of Transportation, 1982.

"Map of the Parts of Kansas, Indian Ter, Texas and New Mexico." (Panhandle Plains Historical Museum Archives.), 1875.

"Texas." Washington, D. C.: National Geographic Magazine, 1986.

"Texas Official Travel Map." Texas Department of Transportation, 1994.

"The Texas Panhandle – 1885." (Panhandle Plains Historical Museum Archives.)
    Canyon, Texas: Panhandle-Plains Historical Review, 1965.

"Trails Made and Routes Used by the Fourth U.S. Cavalry Under Command of
    General R.S. Mackenzie in its Operations Against Hostile Indians in Texas,
    Indian-Territory (now Oklahoma), New Mexico and Old Mexico during the
    Period of 1871–2–3–4 and 5." Compiled from military and other sources.
    (Panhandle Plains Historical Museum Archives.) Freeport, Texas: E.D.
    Dorchester, 1927.

PHOTOGRAPH COLLECTIONS

Institute of Texan Cultures Archives. San Antonio, Texas.

Panhandle Plains Historical Museum Archives. Canyon, Texas.